Dawn, Adulthood Rites, and *Imago*
The classic trilogy complete in one volume —

LILITH'S BROOD

Praise for **LILITH'S BROOD** and Octavia E. Butler

• • •

"This is vintage Butler . . . a perfect introduction to her work for the unfamiliar. Butler sets the imagination free, blending the real and the possible."

—**United Press International**

"Impeccably crafted . . . satisfying . . . Butler's literary crafts-manship is superb."

—*Washington Post Book World*

"Butler in top form . . . spare, vivid prose . . . intriguing, well-developed ideas, solid characters, and crisp narrative."

—*Kirkus Reviews*

"[She creates] some of the most fascinating female characters in the genre . . . real women caught in impossible situations."

—*Village Voice*

"Butler brings Toni Morrison to mind."

—*Publishers Weekly*

"She is one of those rare authors who pay serious attention to the way human beings actually work together and against each other, and she does so with extraordinary plausibility."

—*Locus*

BOOKS BY OCTAVIA E. BUTLER

*Fledgling**

*Parable of the Talents**

*Parable of the Sower**

*Lilith's Brood**
Dawn
Adulthood Rites
Imago

*Seed to Harvest**
Wild Seed
Mind of My Mind
Clay's Ark
Patternmaster

Kindred

Survivor

Bloodchild and Other Stories

*available from Hachette Book Group

OCTAVIA E. BUTLER

LILITH'S BROOD

GRAND CENTRAL
PUBLISHING

NEW YORK   BOSTON

Compilation copyright © 1989 by Octavia E. Butler
Dawn copyright © 1987 by Octavia E. Butler
Adulthood Rites copyright © 1988 by Octavia E Butler
Imago copyright © 1989 by Octavia E. Butler

Grand Central Publishing
Hachette Book Group
1290 Avenue of the Americas
New York, NY 10104

www.HachetteBookGroup.com

Printed in the United States of America

Individual novels originally published in hardcover by Warner Books.
Originally published as *The Xenogenesis Trilogy*

First Trade Edition: June 2000
Reissued: January 2007
20 19 18 17 16

Grand Central Publishing is a division of Hachette Book Group, Inc.
The Grand Central Publishing name and logo is a trademark of Hachette Book Group, Inc.

Library of Congress Cataloging-in-Publication Data

Butler, Octavia E.
   Lilith's Brood / Octavia E. Butler
      p. cm.
   Contents: Dawn—Adulthood Rites—Imago.
   ISBN 978-0-446-67610-6
   1. Science fiction. American.   I. Title.
PS3552.U827 L55 2000
813'.54—dc21   00-025057

Book design by L&G McRee
Cover design by Don Puckey
Cover illustration by Marc Yancus

CONTENTS

DAWN

*In memory of Mike Hodel who,
through his READ/SF campaign
for literacy, sought to share
with everyone the pleasure and
usefulness of the written word.*

I

WOMB

1

Alive!

Still alive.

Alive. . . again.

Awakening was hard, as always. The ultimate disappointment. It was a struggle to take in enough air to drive off nightmare sensations of asphyxiation. Lilith Iyapo lay gasping, shaking with the force of her effort. Her heart beat too fast, too loud. She curled around it, fetal, helpless. Circulation began to return to her arms and legs in flurries of minute, exquisite pains.

When her body calmed and became reconciled to reanimation, she looked around. The room seemed dimly lit, though she had never Awakened to dimness before. She corrected her thinking. The room did not only seem dim, it *was* dim. At an earlier Awakening, she had decided that reality was whatever happened, whatever she perceived. It had occurred to her—how many times?—that she might be insane or drugged, physically ill or injured. None of that mattered. It could not matter while she was confined this way, kept helpless, alone, and ignorant.

She sat up, swayed dizzily, then turned to look at the rest of the room.

The walls were light-colored—white or gray, perhaps. The bed was what it had always been: a solid platform that gave slightly to the touch and that seemed to grow from the floor. There was, across the room, a doorway that probably led to a bathroom. She was usually given a bathroom. Twice she had not been, and in her windowless, doorless cubicle, she had been forced simply to choose a corner.

She went to the doorway, peered through the uniform dimness, and satisfied herself that she did, indeed, have a bathroom. This one had not only a toilet and a sink, but a shower. Luxury.

What else did she have?

Very little. There was another platform perhaps a foot higher than the bed. It could have been used as a table, though there was no chair. And there were things on it. She saw the food first. It was the usual lumpy cereal or stew, of no recognizable flavor, contained in an edible bowl that would disintegrate if she emptied it and did not eat it.

And there was something beside the bowl. Unable to see it clearly, she touched it.

Cloth! A folded mound of clothing. She snatched it up, dropped it in her eagerness, picked it up again and began putting it on. A light-colored, thigh-length jacket and a pair of long, loose pants both made of some cool, exquisitely soft material that made her think of silk, though for no reason she could have stated, she did not think this was silk. The jacket adhered to itself and stayed closed when she closed it, but opened readily enough when she pulled the two front panels apart. The way they came apart reminded her of Velcro, though there was none to be seen. The pants closed in the same way. She had not been allowed clothing from her first Awakening until now. She had pleaded for it, but her captors had ignored her. Dressed now, she felt more secure than she had at any other time in her captivity. It was a false security she knew, but she had learned to savor any pleasure, any supplement to her self-esteem that she could glean.

Opening and closing her jacket, her hand touched the long scar across her abdomen. She had acquired it somehow between her second and third Awakenings, had examined it fearfully, wondering what had been done to her. What had she lost or gained, and why? And what else might be done? She did not own herself any longer. Even her flesh could be cut and stitched without her consent or knowledge.

It enraged her during later Awakenings that there had been moments when she actually felt grateful to her mutilators for letting her sleep through whatever they had done to her—and for doing it well enough to spare her pain or disability later.

She rubbed the scar, tracing its outline. Finally she sat on the bed and ate her bland meal, finishing the bowl as well, more for a change of texture than to satisfy any residual hunger. Then she began the oldest and most futile of her activities: a search for some crack, some sound of hollowness, some indication of a way out of her prison.

She had done this at every Awakening. At her first Awakening, she had called out during her search. Receiving no answer, she had shouted, then cried, then cursed until her voice was gone. She had pounded the walls until her hands bled and became grotesquely swollen.

There had not been a whisper of response. Her captors spoke when they were ready and not before. They did not show themselves at all. She remained sealed in her cubicle and their voices came to her from above like the light. There were no visible speakers of any kind, just as there was no single spot from which light originated. The entire ceiling seemed to be a speaker and a light—and perhaps a ventilator since the air remained fresh. She imagined herself to be in a large box, like a rat in a cage. Perhaps people stood above her looking down through one-way glass or through some video arrangement.

Why?

There was no answer. She had asked her captors when they began, finally, to talk to her. They had refused to tell her. They had asked her questions. Simple ones at first.

How old was she?

Twenty-six, she thought silently. Was she still only twenty-six? How long had they held her captive? They would not say.

Had she been married?

Yes, but he was gone, long gone, beyond their reach, beyond their prison.

Had she had children?

Oh god. One child, long gone with his father. One son. Gone. If there were an afterworld, what a crowded place it must be now.

Had she had siblings? That was the word they used. *Siblings.*

Two brothers and a sister, probably dead along with the rest of her family. A mother, long dead, a father, probably dead, various aunts, uncles, cousins, nieces, and nephews . . . probably dead.

What work had she done?

None. Her son and her husband had been her work for a few brief years. After the auto accident that killed them, she had gone back to college, there to decide what else she might do with her life.

Did she remember the war?

Insane question. Could anyone who had lived through the war forget it? A handful of people tried to commit humanicide. They had nearly succeeded. She had, through sheer luck, managed to survive—only to be captured by heaven knew who and imprisoned. She had offered to answer their questions if they let her out of her cubicle. They refused.

She offered to trade her answers for theirs: Who were they? Why did they hold her? Where was she? Answer for answer. Again, they refused.

So she refused them, gave them no answers, ignored the tests, physical and mental, that they tried to put her through. She did not know what they would do to her. She was terrified that she would be hurt, punished. But she felt she had to risk bargaining, try to gain *something,* and her only currency was cooperation.

They neither punished her nor bargained. They simply ceased to talk to her.

Food continued to appear mysteriously when she napped. Water still flowed from the bathroom faucets. The light still shone. But beyond that, there was nothing, no one, no sound unless she made it, no object with which to amuse herself. There were only her bed and table platforms. These would not come up from the floor, no matter how she abused them. Stains quickly faded and vanished from their surfaces. She spent hours vainly trying to solve the problem of how she might destroy them. This was one of the activities that helped keep her relatively sane. Another was trying to reach the ceiling. Nothing she could stand on put her within leaping distance of it. Experimentally, she threw a bowl of food—her best available weapon—at it. The food spattered against it, telling her it was solid, not some kind of projection or mirror trick. But it might not be as thick as the walls. It might even be glass or thin plastic.

She never found out.

She worked out a whole series of physical exercises and would have done them daily if she had had any way of distinguishing one day from the next or day from night. As it was, she did them after each of her longer naps.

She slept a lot and was grateful to her body for responding to her alternating moods of fear and boredom by dozing frequently. The small, painless awakenings from these naps eventually began to disappoint her as much as had the greater Awakening.

The greater Awakening from what? Drugged sleep? What else could it be? She had not been injured in the war; had not requested or needed medical care. Yet here she was.

She sang songs and remembered books she had read, movies and television shows she had seen, family stories she had heard, bits of her own life that had seemed so ordinary while she was free to live it. She made up stories and argued both sides of questions she had once been passionate about, *anything*!

More time passed. She held out, did not speak directly to her captors except to curse them. She offered no cooperation. There were moments when she did not know why she resisted. What would she be giving up if she answered her captors' questions? What did she have to lose beyond misery, isolation, and silence? Yet she held out.

There came a time when she could not stop talking to herself, when it seemed that every thought that occurred to her must be spoken aloud. She would make desperate efforts to be quiet but somehow the words began to spill from her again. She thought she would lose her sanity; had already begun to lose it. She began to cry.

Eventually, as she sat on the floor rocking, thinking about losing her mind, and perhaps talking about it too, something was introduced into the room—some gas, perhaps. She fell backward and drifted into what she had come to think of as her second long sleep.

At her next Awakening, whether it came hours, days, or years later, her captors began talking to her again, asking her the same questions as though they had not asked them before. This time she answered. She lied when she wanted to but she always responded. There had been healing in the long sleep. She Awoke with no particular inclination to speak her thoughts aloud or cry or sit on the floor and rock backward and forward, but her memory was unimpaired. She remembered all too well the long period of silence and isolation. Even an unseen inquisitor was preferable.

The questions became more complex, actually became conversations during later Awakenings. Once, they put a child in with her—a small boy with long, straight black hair and smoky-brown skin, paler than her own. He did not speak English and he was terrified of her. He was only about five years old—a little older than Ayre, her own son. Awakening beside her in this strange place was probably the most frightening thing the little boy had ever experienced.

He spent many of his first hours with her either hiding in the bathroom or pressed into the corner farthest from her. It took her a long time to convince him that she was not dangerous. Then she began teaching him English—and he began teaching her whatever language he spoke. Sharad was his name. She sang songs to him and he learned them instantly. He sang them back to her in almost accentless English. He did not understand why she did not do the same when he sang her his songs.

She did eventually learn the songs. She enjoyed the exercise. Anything new was treasure.

Sharad was a blessing even when he wet the bed they shared or became impatient because she failed to understand him quickly enough. He was not much like Ayre in appearance or temperament, but she could touch him. She could not remember when she had last touched someone. She had not realized how much she had missed it. She worried about him and wondered how to protect him. Who knew what their captors had done to him—or what they would do? But she had no more power than he did. At her next Awakening, he was gone. Experiment completed.

She begged them to let him come back, but they refused. They said he was with his mother. She did not believe them. She imagined Sharad locked alone in his own small cubicle, his sharp, retentive mind dulling as time passed.

Unconcerned, her captors began a complex new series of questions and exercises.

2

What would they do this time? Ask more questions? Give her another companion? She barely cared.

She sat on the bed, dressed, waiting, tired in a deep, emptied way that had nothing to do with physical weariness. Sooner or later, someone would speak to her.

She had a long wait. She had lain down and was almost asleep when a voice spoke her name.

"Lilith?" The usual, quiet, androgynous voice.

She drew a deep, weary breath. "What?" she asked. But as she spoke, she realized the voice had not come from above as it always had before. She sat up quickly and looked around. In one corner she found the shadowy figure of a man, thin and long-haired.

Was he the reason for the clothing, then? He seemed to be wearing a similar outfit. Something to take off when the two of them got to know each other better? Good god.

"I think," she said softly, "that you might be the last straw."

"I'm not here to hurt you," he said.

"No. Of course you're not."

"I'm here to take you outside."

Now she stood up, staring hard at him, wishing for more light. Was he making a joke? Laughing at her?

"Outside to what?"

"Education. Work. The beginning of a new life."

She took a step closer to him, then stopped. He scared her somehow. She could not make herself approach him. "Something is wrong," she said. "Who are you?"

He moved slightly. "And what am I?"

She jumped because that was what she had almost said.

"I'm not a man," he said. "I'm not a human being."

She moved back against the bed, but did not sit down. "Tell me what you are."

"I'm here to tell you . . . and show you. Will you look at me now?"

Since she was looking at him—it—she frowned. "The light—"

"It will change when you're ready."

"You're . . . what? From some other world?"

"From a number of other worlds. You're one of the few English speakers who never considered that she might be in the hands of extraterrestrials."

"I did consider it," Lilith whispered. "Along with the possibility that I might be in prison, in an insane asylum, in the hands of the FBI, the CIA, or the KGB. The other possibilities seemed marginally less ridiculous."

The creature said nothing. It stood utterly still in its corner, and she knew from her many Awakenings that it would not speak to her again until she did what it wished—until she said she was ready to look at it, then, in brighter light, took the obligatory look. These things, whatever they were, were incredibly good at waiting. She made this one wait for several minutes, and not only was it silent, it never moved a muscle. Discipline or physiology?

She was not afraid. She had gotten over being frightened by "ugly" faces long before her capture. The unknown frightened her. The cage she was in frightened her. She preferred becoming accustomed to any number of ugly faces to remaining in her cage.

"All right," she said. "Show me."

The lights brightened as she had supposed they would, and what had seemed to be a tall, slender man was still humanoid, but it had no nose—no bulge, no nostrils—just flat, gray skin. It was gray all over—pale gray skin, darker gray hair on its head. The hair grew down around its eyes and ears and at its throat. There was so much hair across the eyes that she wondered how the creature could see. The long, profuse ear hair seemed to grow out of the ears as well as around them. Above, it joined the eye hair, and below and behind, it joined the head hair. The island of throat hair seemed to move slightly, and it occurred to her that that might be where the creature breathed—a kind of natural tracheostomy.

Lilith glanced at the humanoid body, wondering how humanlike it really was. "I don't mean any offense," she said, "but are you male or female?"

"It's wrong to assume that I must be a sex you're familiar with," it said, "but as it happens, I'm male."

Good. "It" could become "he" again. Less awkward.

"You should notice," he said, "that what you probably see as hair isn't hair at all. I have no hair. The reality seems to bother humans."

"What?"

"Come closer and look."

She did not want to be any closer to him. She had not known what held her back before. Now she was certain it was his alienness, his difference, his literal unearthliness. She found herself still unable to take even one more step toward him.

"Oh god," she whispered. And the hair—the whatever-it-was—moved. Some of it seemed to blow toward her as though in a wind—though there was no stirring of air in the room.

She frowned, strained to see, to understand. Then, abruptly, she did understand. She backed away, scrambled around the bed and to the far wall. When she could go no farther, she stood against the wall, staring at him.

Medusa.

Some of the "hair" writhed independently, a nest of snakes startled, driven in all directions.

Revolted, she turned her face to the wall.

"They're not separate animals," he said. "They're sensory organs. They're no more dangerous than your nose or eyes. It's natural for them to move in response to my wishes or emotions or to outside stimuli. We have them on our bodies as well. We need them in the same way you need your ears, nose, and eyes."

"But . . ." She faced him again, disbelieving. Why should he need such things—tentacles—to supplement his senses?

"When you can," he said, "come closer and look at me. I've had humans believe they saw human sensory organs on my head—and then get angry with me when they realized they were wrong."

"I can't," she whispered, though now she wanted to. Could she have been so wrong, so deceived by her own eyes?

"You will," he said. "My sensory organs aren't dangerous to you. You'll have to get used to them."

"No!"

The tentacles were elastic. At her shout, some of them lengthened, stretching toward her. She imagined big, slowly writhing, dying night crawlers stretched along the sidewalk after a rain. She imagined small, tentacled sea slugs—nudibranchs—grown impossibly to human size and shape, and, obscenely, sounding more like a human being than some humans. Yet she needed to hear him speak. Silent, he was utterly alien.

She swallowed. "Listen, don't go quiet on me. Talk!"

"Yes?"

"Why do you speak English so well, anyway? You should at least have an unusual accent."

"People like you taught me. I speak several human languages. I began learning very young."

"How many other humans do you have here? And where's here?"

"This is my home. You could call it a ship—a vast one compared to the ones your people have built. What it truly is doesn't translate. You'll be understood if you call it a ship. It's in orbit around your Earth, somewhat beyond the orbit of Earth's moon. As for how many humans are here: all of you who survived your war. We collected as many as we could. The ones we didn't find in time died of injury, disease, hunger, radiation, cold. . . . We found them later."

She believed him. Humanity in its attempt to destroy itself had made the world unlivable. She had been certain she would die even though she had survived the bombing without a scratch. She had considered her survival a misfortune—a promise of a more lingering death. And now. . . ?

"Is there anything left on Earth?" she whispered. "Anything alive, I mean."

"Oh, yes. Time and our efforts have been restoring it."

That stopped her. She managed to look at him for a moment without being distracted by the slowly writhing tentacles. "Restoring it? Why?"

"For use. You'll go back there eventually."

"You'll send me back? And the other humans?"

"Yes."

"Why?"

"That you will come to understand little by little."

She frowned. "All right. I'll start now. Tell me."

His head tentacles wavered. Individually, they did look more like big worms than small snakes. Long and slender or short and thick as. . . . As what? As his mood changed? As his attention shifted? She looked away.

"No!" he said sharply. "I'll only talk to you, Lilith, if you look at me."

She made a fist of one hand and deliberately dug her nails into her palm until they all but broke the skin. With the pain of that to distract her, she faced him. "What's your name?" she asked.

"Kaaltediinjdahya lel Kahguyaht aj Dinso."

She stared at him, then sighed, and shook her head.

"Jdahya," he said. "That part is me. The rest is my family and other things."

She repeated the shorter name, trying to pronounce it exactly as he had, to get the unfamiliar ghost *j* sound just right. "Jdahya," she said, "I want to know the price of your people's help. What do you want of us?"

"Not more than you can give—but more than you can understand here, now. More than words will be able to help you understand at first. There are things you must see and hear outside."

"Tell me *something* now, whether I understand it or not."

His tentacles rippled. "I can only say that your people have something we value. You may begin to know how much we value it when I tell you that by your way of measuring time, it has been several million years since we dared to interfere in another people's act of self-destruction. Many of us disputed the wisdom of doing it this time. We thought . . . that there had been a consensus among you, that you had agreed to die."

"No species would do that!"

"Yes. Some have. And a few of those who have have taken whole ships of our people with them. We've learned. Mass suicide is one of the few things we usually let alone."

"Do you understand now what happened to us?"

"I'm aware of what happened. It's . . . alien to me. Frighteningly alien."

"Yes. I sort of feel that way myself, even though they're my people. It was . . . beyond insanity."

"Some of the people we picked up had been hiding deep underground. They had created much of the destruction."

"And they're still alive?"

"Some of them are."

"And you plan to send *them* back to Earth?"

"No."

"What?"

"The ones still alive are very old now. We've used them slowly, learned biology, language, culture from them. We Awakened them a few at a time and let them live their lives here in different parts of the ship while you slept."

"Slept . . . Jdahya, how long have I slept?"

He walked across the room to the table platform, put one many-fingered hand on it, and boosted himself up. Legs drawn against his body, he walked easily on his hands to the center of the platform. The whole series of movements was so fluid and natural, yet so alien that it fascinated her.

Abruptly she realized he was several feet closer to her. She leaped away. Then, feeling utterly foolish, she tried to come back. He had folded himself compactly into an uncomfortable-looking seated position. He ignored her sudden move—except for his head tentacles which all swept toward her as though in a wind. He seemed to watch as she inched back to the bed. Could a being with sensory tentacles instead of eyes watch?

When she had come as close to him as she could, she stopped and sat on the floor. It was all she could do to stay where she was. She drew her knees up against her chest and hugged them to her tightly.

"I don't understand why I'm so . . . afraid of you," she whispered. "Of the way you look, I mean. You're not that different. There are—or were—life forms on Earth that looked a little like you."

He said nothing.

She looked at him sharply, fearing he had fallen into one of his long silences. "Is it something you're doing?" she demanded, "something I don't know about?"

"I'm here to teach you to be comfortable with us," he said. "You're doing very well."

She did not feel she was doing well at all. "What have others done?"

"Several have tried to kill me."

She swallowed. It amazed her that they had been able to bring themselves to touch him. "What did you do to them?"

"For trying to kill me?"

"No, before—to incite them."

"No more than I'm doing to you now."

"I don't understand." She made herself stare at him. "Can you really see?"

"Very well."

"Colors? Depth?"

"Yes."

Yet it was true that he had no eyes. She could see now that

there were only dark patches where tentacles grew thickly. The same with the sides of his head where ears should have been. And there were openings at his throat. And the tentacles around them didn't look as dark as the others. Murkily translucent, pale gray worms.

"In fact," he said, "you should be aware that I can see wherever I have tentacles—and I can see whether I seem to notice or not. I can't not see."

That sounded like a horrible existence—not to be able to close one's eyes, sink into the private darkness behind one's own eyelids. "Don't you sleep?"

"Yes. But not the way you do."

She shifted suddenly from the subject of his sleeping to her own. "You never told me how long you kept me asleep."

"About . . . two hundred and fifty of your years."

This was more than she could assimilate at once. She said nothing for so long that he broke the silence.

"Something went wrong when you were first Awakened. I heard about it from several people. Someone handled you badly—underestimated you. You are like us in some ways, but you were thought to be like your military people hidden underground. They refused to talk to us too. At first. You were left asleep for about fifty years after that first mistake."

She crept to the bed, worms or no worms, and leaned against the end of it. "I'd always thought my Awakenings might be years apart, but I didn't really believe it."

"You were like your world. You needed time to heal. And we needed time to learn more about your kind." He paused. "We didn't know what to think when some of your people killed themselves. Some of us believed it was because they had been left out of the mass suicide—that they simply wanted to finish the dying. Others said it was because we kept them isolated. We began putting two or more together, and many injured or killed one another. Isolation cost fewer lives."

These last words touched a memory in her. "Jdahya?" she said.

The tentacles down the sides of his face wavered, looked for a moment like dark, muttonchop whiskers.

"At one point a little boy was put in with me. His name was Sharad. What happened to him?"

He said nothing for a moment, then all his tentacles stretched themselves upward. Someone spoke to him from above in the usual way and in a voice much like his own, but this time in a foreign language, choppy and fast.

"My relative will find out," he told her. "Sharad is almost certainly well, though he may not be a child any longer."

"You've let children grow up and grow old?"

"A few, yes. But they've lived among us. We haven't isolated them."

"You shouldn't have isolated any of us unless your purpose was to drive us insane. You almost succeeded with me more than once. Humans need one another."

His tentacles writhed repulsively. "We know. I wouldn't have cared to endure as much solitude as you have. But we had no skill at grouping humans in ways that suited them."

"But Sharad and I—"

"He may have had parents, Lilith."

Someone spoke from above, in English this time. "The boy has parents and a sister. He's asleep with them, and he's still very young." There was a pause. "Lilith, what language did he speak?"

"I don't know," Lilith said. "Either he was too young to tell me or he tried and I didn't understand. I think he must have been East Indian, though—if that means anything to you."

"Others know. I was only curious."

"You're sure he's all right?"

"He's well."

She felt assured at that and immediately questioned the emotion. Why should one more anonymous voice telling her everything was fine reassure her?

"Can I see him?" she asked.

"Jdahya?" the voice said.

Jdahya turned toward her. "You'll be able to see him when

you can walk among us without panic. This is your last isolation room. When you're ready, I'll take you outside."

3

Jdahya would not leave her. As much as she had hated her solitary confinement, she longed to be rid of him. He fell silent for a while and she wondered whether he might be sleeping—to the degree that he did sleep. She lay down herself, wondering whether she could relax enough to sleep with him there. It would be like going to sleep knowing there was a rattlesnake in the room, knowing she could wake up and find it in her bed.

She could not fall asleep facing him. Yet she could not keep her back to him long. Each time she dozed, she would jolt awake and look to see if he had come closer. This exhausted her, but she could not stop doing it. Worse, each time she moved, his tentacles moved, straightening lazily in her direction as though he were sleeping with his eyes open—as he no doubt was.

Painfully tired, head aching, stomach queasy, she climbed down from her bed and lay alongside it on the floor. She could not see him now, no matter how she turned. She could see only the platform beside her and the walls. He was no longer part of her world.

"No, Lilith," he said as she closed her eyes.

She pretended not to hear him.

"Lie on the bed," he said, "or on the floor over here. Not over there."

She lay rigid, silent.

"If you stay where you are, I'll take the bed."

That would put him just above her—too close, looming over her, Medusa leering down.

She got up and all but fell across the bed, damning him, and, to her humiliation, crying a little. Eventually she slept. Her body had simply had enough.

She awoke abruptly, twisting around to look at him. He was still on the platform, his position hardly altered. When his head tentacles swept in her direction she got up and ran into the bathroom. He let her hide there for a while, let her wash and be alone and wallow in self-pity and self-contempt. She could not remember ever having been so continually afraid, so out of control of her emotions. Jdahya had done nothing, yet she cowered.

When he called her, she took a deep breath and stepped out of the bathroom. "This isn't working," she said miserably. "Just put me down on Earth with other humans. I can't do this."

He ignored her.

After a time she spoke again on a different subject. "I have a scar," she said, touching her abdomen. "I didn't have it when I was on Earth. What did your people do to me?"

"You had a growth," he said. "A cancer. We got rid of it. Otherwise, it would have killed you."

She went cold. Her mother had died of cancer. Two of her aunts had had it and her grandmother had been operated on three times for it. They were all dead now, killed by someone else's insanity. But the family "tradition" was apparently continuing.

"What did I lose along with the cancer?" she asked softly.

"Nothing."

"Not a few feet of intestine? My ovaries? My uterus?"

"Nothing. My relative tended you. You lost nothing you would want to keep."

"Your relative is the one who . . . performed surgery on me?"

"Yes. With interest and care. There was a human physician with us, but by then she was old, dying. She only watched and commented on what my relative did."

"How would he know enough to do anything for me? Human anatomy must be totally different from yours."

"My relative is not male—or female. The name for its sex is ooloi. It understood your body because it is ooloi. On your world there were vast numbers of dead and dying humans to study. Our ooloi came to understand what could be normal or abnormal, possible or impossible for the human body. The ooloi who went to the planet taught those who stayed here. My relative has studied your people for much of its life."

"How do ooloi study?" She imagined dying humans caged and every groan and contortion closely observed. She imagined dissections of living subjects as well as dead ones. She imagined treatable diseases being allowed to run their grisly courses in order for ooloi to learn.

"They observe. They have special organs for their kind of observation. My relative examined you, observed a few of your normal body cells, compared them with what it had learned from other humans most like you, and said you had not only a cancer, but a talent for cancer."

"I wouldn't call it a talent. A curse, maybe. But how could your relative know about that from just . . . observing."

"Maybe *perceiving* would be a better word," he said. "There's much more involved than sight. It knows everything that can be learned about you from your genes. And by now, it knows your medical history and a great deal about the way you think. It has taken part in testing you."

"Has it? I may not be able to forgive it for that. But listen, I don't understand how it could cut out a cancer without . . . well, without doing damage to whichever organ it was growing on."

"My relative didn't cut out your cancer. It wouldn't have cut you at all, but it wanted to examine the cancer directly with all its senses. It had never personally examined one before. When it had finished, it induced your body to reabsorb the cancer."

"It . . . induced my body to reabsorb . . . cancer?"

"Yes. My relative gave your body a kind of chemical command."

"Is that how you cure cancer among yourselves?"

"We don't get them."

Lilith sighed. "I wish we didn't. They've created enough hell in my family."

"They won't be harming you anymore. My relative says they're beautiful, but simple to prevent."

"Beautiful?"

"It perceives things differently sometimes. Here's food, Lilith. Are you hungry?"

She stepped toward him, reaching out to take the bowl, then realized what she was doing. She froze, but managed not to scramble backward. After a few seconds, she inched toward him. She could not do it quickly—snatch and run. She could hardly do it at all. She forced herself forward slowly, slowly.

Teeth clenched, she managed to take the bowl. Her hand shook so badly that she spilled half the stew. She withdrew to the bed. After a while she was able to eat what was left, then finish the bowl. It was not enough. She was still hungry, but she did not complain. She was not up to taking another bowl from his hand. Daisy hand. Palm in the center, many fingers all the way around. The fingers had bones in them, at least; they weren't tentacles. And there were only two hands, two feet. He could have been so much uglier than he was, so much less . . . human. Why couldn't she just accept him? All he seemed to be asking was that she not panic at the sight of him or others like him. Why couldn't she do that?

She tried to imagine herself surrounded by beings like him and was almost overwhelmed by panic. As though she had suddenly developed a phobia—something she had never before experienced. But what she felt was like what she had heard others describe. A true xenophobia—and apparently she was not alone in it.

She sighed, realized she was still tired as well as still hungry. She rubbed a hand over her face. If this were what a phobia was like, it was something to be gotten rid of as quickly as possible. She looked at Jdahya. "What do your people call themselves?" she asked. "Tell me about them."

"We are Oankali."

"Oankali. Sounds like a word in some Earth language."

"It may be, but with different meaning."

"What does it mean in your language?"

"Several things. Traders for one."

"You are traders?"

"Yes."

"What do you trade?"

"Ourselves."

"You mean . . . each other? Slaves?"

"No. We've never done that."

"What, then?"

"Ourselves."

"I don't understand."

He said nothing, seemed to wrap silence around himself and settle into it. She knew he would not answer.

She sighed. "You seem too human sometimes. If I weren't looking at you, I'd assume you were a man."

"You have assumed that. My family gave me to the human doctor so that I could learn to do this work. She came to us too old to bear children of her own, but she could teach."

"I thought you said she was dying."

"She did die eventually. She was a hundred and thirteen years old and had been awake among us off and on for fifty years. She was like a fourth parent to my siblings and me. It was hard to watch her age and die. Your people contain incredible potential, but they die without using much of it."

"I've heard humans say that." She frowned. "Couldn't your ooloi have helped her live longer—if she wanted to live longer than a hundred and thirteen years, that is."

"They did help her. They gave her forty years she would not have had, and when they could no longer help her heal, they took away her pain. If she had been younger when we found her, we could have given her much more time."

Lilith followed that thought to its obvious conclusion. "I'm twenty-six," she said.

"Older," he told her. "You've aged whenever we've kept you awake. About two years altogether."

She had no sense of being two years older, of being, suddenly, twenty-eight because he said she was. Two years of solitary confinement. What could they possibly give her in return for that? She stared at him.

His tentacles seemed to solidify into a second skin—dark

patches on his face and neck, a dark, smooth-looking mass on his head. "Barring accident," he said, "you'll live much longer than a hundred and thirteen years. And for most of your life, you'll be biologically quite young. Your children will live longer still."

He looked remarkably human now. Was it only the tentacles that gave him that sea-slug appearance? His coloring hadn't changed. The fact that he had no eyes, nose, or ears still disturbed her, but not as much.

"Jdahya, stay that way," she told him. "Let me come close and look at you . . . if I can."

The tentacles moved like weirdly rippling skin, then resolidified. "Come," he said.

She was able to approach him hesitantly. Even viewed from only a couple of feet away, the tentacles looked like a smooth second skin. "Do you mind if . . ." She stopped and began again. "I mean . . . may I touch you?"

"Yes."

It was easier to do than she had expected. His skin was cool and almost too smooth to be real flesh—smooth the way her fingernails were and perhaps as tough as a fingernail.

"Is it hard for you to stay like this?" she asked.

"Not hard. Unnatural. A muffling of the senses."

"Why did you do it—before I asked you to, I mean."

"It's an expression of pleasure or amusement."

"You were pleased a minute ago?"

"With you. You wanted your time back—the time we've taken from you. You didn't want to die."

She stared at him, shocked that he had read her so clearly. And he must have known of humans who did want to die even after hearing promises of long life, health, and lasting youth. Why? Maybe they'd heard the part she hadn't been told about yet; the reason for all this. The price.

"So far," she said, "only boredom and isolation have driven me to want to die."

"Those are past. And you've never tried to kill yourself, even then."

". . . no."

"Your desire to live is stronger than you realize."

She sighed. "You're going to test that, aren't you? That's why you haven't told me yet what your people want of us."

"Yes," he admitted, alarming her.

"Tell me!"

Silence.

"If you knew anything at all about the human imagination, you'd know you were doing exactly the wrong thing," she said.

"Once you're able to leave this room with me, I'll answer your questions," he told her.

She stared at him for several seconds. "Let's work on that, then," she said grimly. "Relax from your unnatural position and let's see what happens."

He hesitated, then let his tentacles flow free. The grotesque sea-slug appearance resumed and she could not stop herself from stumbling away from him in panic and revulsion. She caught herself before she had gone far.

"God, I'm so tired of this," she muttered. "Why can't I stop it?"

"When the doctor first came to our household," he said, "some of my family found her so disturbing that they left home for a while. That's unheard-of behavior among us."

"Did you leave?"

He went smooth briefly. "I had not yet been born. By the time I was born, all my relatives had come home. And I think their fear was stronger than yours is now. They had never before seen so much life and so much death in one being. It hurt some of them to touch her."

"You mean . . . because she was sick?"

"Even when she was well. It was her genetic structure that disturbed them. I can't explain that to you. You'll never sense it as we do." He stepped toward her and reached for her hand. She gave it to him almost reflexively with only an instant's hesitation when his tentacles all flowed forward toward her. She looked away and stood stiffly where she was, her hand held loosely in his many fingers.

"Good," he said, releasing her. "This room will be nothing more than a memory for you soon."

4

Eleven meals later he took her outside.

She had no idea how long she was in wanting, then consuming, those eleven meals. Jdahya would not tell her, and he would not be hurried. He showed no impatience or annoyance when she urged him to take her out. He simply fell silent. He seemed almost to turn himself off when she made demands or asked questions he did not intend to answer. Her family had called her stubborn during her life before the war, but he was beyond stubborn.

Eventually he began to move around the room. He had been still for so long—had seemed almost part of the furniture—that she was startled when he suddenly got up and went into the bathroom. She stayed where she was on the bed, wondering whether he used a bathroom for the same purposes she did. She made no effort to find out. Sometime later when he came back into the room, she found herself much less disturbed by him. He brought her something that so surprised and delighted her that she took it from his hand without thought or hesitation: A banana, fully ripe, large, yellow, firm, very sweet.

She ate it slowly, wanting to gulp it, not daring to. It was literally the best food she had tasted in two hundred and fifty years. Who knew when there would be another—if there would be another. She ate even the white, inner skin.

He would not tell her where it had come from or how he had gotten it. He would not get her another. He did evict her from the bed for a while. He stretched out flat on it and lay utterly still, looked dead. She did a series of exercises on the floor, deliberately

tired herself as much as she could, then took his place on the platform until he got up and let her have the bed.

When she awoke, he took his jacket off and let her see the tufts
of sensory tentacles scattered over his body. To her surprise, she
got used to these quickly. They were merely ugly. And they made
him look even more like a misplaced sea creature.

"Can you breathe underwater?" she asked him.

"Yes."

"I thought your throat orifices looked as though they could
double as gills. Are you more comfortable underwater?"

"I enjoy it, but no more than I enjoy air."

"Air . . . oxygen?"

"I need oxygen, yes, though not as much of it as you do."

Her mind drifted back to his tentacles and another possible
similarity to some sea slugs. "Can you sting with any of your
tentacles?"

"With all of them."

She drew back, though she was not close to him. "Why
didn't you tell me?"

"I wouldn't have stung you."

Unless she had attacked him. "So that's what happened to
the humans who tried to kill you."

"No, Lilith. I'm not interested in killing your people. I've
been trained all my life to keep them alive."

"What did you do to them, then?"

"Stopped them. I'm stronger than you probably think."

"But . . . if you had stung them?"

"They would have died. Only the ooloi can sting without
killing. One group of my ancestors subdued prey by stinging
it. Their sting began the digestive process even before they
began to eat. And they stung enemies who tried to eat them.
Not a comfortable existence."

"It doesn't sound that bad."

"They didn't live long, those ancestors. Some things were
immune to their poison."

"Maybe humans are."

He answered her softly. "No, Lilith, you're not."

Sometime later he brought her an orange. Out of curiosity, she broke the fruit and offered to share it with him. He accepted a piece of it from her hand and sat down beside her to eat it. When they were both finished, he turned to face her—a courtesy, she realized, since he had so little face—and seemed to examine her closely. Some of his tentacles actually touched her. When they did, she jumped. Then she realized she was not being hurt and kept still. She did not like his nearness, but it no longer terrified her. After . . . however many days it had been, she felt none of the old panic; only relief at somehow having finally shed it.

"We'll go out now," he said. "My family will be relieved to see us. And you—you have a great deal to learn."

5

She made him wait until she had washed the orange juice from her hands. Then he walked over to one of the walls and touched it with some of his longer head tentacles.

A dark spot appeared on the wall where he made contact. It became a deepening, widening indentation, then a hole through which Lilith could see color and light—green, red, orange, yellow. . . .

There had been little color in her world since her capture. Her own skin, her blood—within the pale walls of her prison, that was all. Everything else was some shade of white or gray. Even her food had been colorless until the banana. Now, here was color and what appeared to be sunlight. There was space. Vast space.

The hole in the wall widened as though it were flesh rippling aside, slowly writhing. She was both fascinated and repelled.

"Is it alive?" she asked.

"Yes," he said.

She had beaten it, kicked it, clawed it, tried to bite it. It had been smooth, tough, impenetrable, but slightly giving like the bed and table. It had felt like plastic, cool beneath her hands.

"What is it?" she asked.

"Flesh. More like mine than like yours. Different from mine, too, though. It's . . . the ship."

"You're kidding. Your ship is alive?"

"Yes. Come out." The hole in the wall had grown large enough for them to step through. He ducked his head and took the necessary step. She started to follow him, then stopped. There was so much space out there. The colors she had seen were thin, hairlike leaves and round, coconut-sized fruit, apparently in different stages of development. All hung from great branches that overshadowed the new exit. Beyond them was a broad, open field with scattered trees—impossibly huge trees—distant hills, and a bright, sunless ivory sky. There was enough strangeness to the trees and the sky to stop her from imagining that she was on Earth. There were people moving around in the distance, and there were black, German shepherd–sized animals that were too far away for her to see them clearly—though even in the distance the animals seemed to have too many legs. Six? Ten? The creatures seemed to be grazing.

"Lilith, come out," Jdahya said.

She took a step backward, away from all the alien vastness. The isolation room that she had hated for so long suddenly seemed safe and comforting.

"Back into your cage, Lilith?" Jdahya asked softly.

She stared at him through the hole, realized at once that he was trying to provoke her, make her overcome her fear. It would not have worked if he had not been so right. She was retreating into her cage—like a zoo animal that had been shut up for so long that the cage had become home.

She made herself step up to the opening, and then, teeth clenched, step through.

Outside, she stood beside him and drew a long, shuddering breath. She turned her head, looked at the room, then turned away quickly, resisting an impulse to flee back to it. He took her hand and led her away.

When she looked back a second time, the hole was closing and she could see that what she had come out of was actually a huge tree. Her room could not have taken more than a tiny fraction of its interior. The tree had grown from what appeared to be ordinary, pale-brown, sandy soil. Its lower limbs were heavily laden with fruit. The rest of it looked almost ordinary except for its size. The trunk was bigger around than some office buildings she remembered. And it seemed to touch the ivory sky. How tall was it? How much of it served as a building?

"Was everything inside that room alive?" she asked.

"Everything except some of the visible plumbing fixtures," Jdahya said. "Even the food you ate was produced from the fruit of one of the branches growing outside. It was designed to meet your nutritional needs."

"And to taste like cotton and paste," she muttered. "I hope I won't have to eat any more of that stuff."

"You won't. But it's kept you very healthy. Your diet in particular encouraged your body not to grow cancers while your genetic inclination to grow them was corrected."

"It has been corrected, then?"

"Yes. Correcting genes have been inserted into your cells, and your cells have accepted and replicated them. Now you won't grow cancers by accident."

That, she thought, was an odd qualification, but she let it pass for the moment. "When will you send me back to Earth?"

"You couldn't survive there now—especially not alone."

"You haven't sent any of us back yet?"

"Your group will be the first."

"Oh." This had not occurred to her—that she and others like her would be guinea pigs trying to survive on an Earth that must have greatly changed. "How is it there now?"

"Wild. Forests, mountains, deserts, plains, great oceans. It's a rich world, clean of dangerous radiation in most places. The greatest diversity of animal life is in the seas, but there are a number of small animals thriving on land: insects, worms, amphibians, reptiles, small mammals. There's no doubt your people can live there."

"When?"

"That will not be hurried. You have a very long life ahead of you, Lilith. And you have work to do here."

"You said something about that once before. What work?"

"You'll live with my family for a while—live as one of us as much as possible. We'll teach you your work."

"But *what* work?"

"You'll Awaken a small group of humans, all English-speaking, and help them learn to deal with us. You'll teach them the survival skills we teach you. Your people will all be from what you would call civilized societies. Now they'll have to learn to live in forests, build their own shelters, and raise their own food all without machines or outside help."

"Will you forbid us machines?" she asked uncertainly.

"Of course not. But we won't give them to you either. We'll give you hand tools, simple equipment, and food until you begin to make the things you need and grow your own crops. We've already armed you against the deadlier microorganisms. Beyond that, you'll have to fend for yourself—avoiding poisonous plants and animals and creating what you need."

"How can you teach us to survive on our own world? How can you know enough about it or about us?"

"How can we not? We've helped your world restore itself. We've studied your bodies, your thinking, your literature, your historical records, your many cultures. . . . We know more of what you're capable of than you do."

Or they thought they did. If they really had had two hundred and fifty years to study, maybe they were right. "You've inoculated us against diseases?" she asked to be sure she had understood.

"No."

"But you said—"

"We've strengthened your immune system, increased your resistance to disease in general."

"How? Something else done to our genes?"

He said nothing. She let the silence lengthen until she was certain he would not answer. This was one more thing they had done to her body without her consent and supposedly for her own good. "We used to treat animals that way," she muttered bitterly.

"What?" he said.

"We did things to them—inoculations, surgery, isolation—all for their own good. We wanted them healthy and protected—sometimes so we could eat them later."

His tentacles did not flatten to his body, but she got the impression he was laughing at her. "Doesn't it frighten you to say things like that to me?" he asked.

"No," she said. "It scares me to have people doing things to me that I don't understand."

"You've been given health. The ooloi have seen to it that you'll have a chance to live on your Earth—not just to die on it."

He would not say any more on the subject. She looked around at the huge trees, some with great branching multiple trunks and foliage like long, green hair. Some of the hair seemed to move, though there was no wind. She sighed. The trees, too, then—tentacled like the people. Long, slender, green tentacles.

"Jdahya?"

His own tentacles swept toward her in a way she still found disconcerting, though it was only his way of giving her his attention or signaling her that she had it.

"I'm willing to learn what you have to teach me," she said, "but I don't think I'm the right teacher for others. There were so many humans who already knew how to live in the wilderness—so many who could probably teach you a little more. Those are the ones you ought to be talking to."

"We have talked to them. They will have to be especially careful because some of the things they 'know' aren't true anymore. There are new plants—mutations of old ones and additions we've made. Some things that used to be edible are lethal now. Some things are deadly only if they aren't prepared properly. Some of the animal life isn't as harmless as it apparently once was. Your Earth is still your Earth, but between the efforts of your people to destroy it and ours to restore it, it has changed."

She nodded, wondering why she could absorb his words so easily. Perhaps because she had known even before her capture that the world she had known was dead. She had already absorbed that loss to the degree that she could.

"There must be ruins," she said softly.

"There were. We've destroyed many of them."

She seized his arm without thinking. "You destroyed them? There were things left and you destroyed them?"

"You'll begin again. We'll put you in areas that are clean of radioactivity and history. You will become something other than you were."

"And you think destroying what was left of our cultures will make us better?"

"No. Only different." She realized suddenly that she was facing him, grasping his arm in a grip that should have been painful to him. It was painful to her. She let go of him and his arm swung to his side in the oddly dead way in which his limbs seemed to move when he was not using them for a specific purpose.

"You were wrong," she said. She could not sustain her anger. She could not look at his tentacled, alien face and sustain anger—but she had to say the words. "You destroyed what wasn't yours," she said. "You completed an insane act."

"You are still alive," he said.

She walked beside him, silently ungrateful. Knee-high tufts of thick, fleshy leaves or tentacles grew from the soil. He stepped carefully to avoid them—which made her want to kick them. Only the fact that her feet were bare stopped her. Then she saw, to her disgust, that the leaves twisted or contracted out of the way if she stepped near one—like plants made up of snake-sized night crawlers. They seemed to be rooted to the ground. Did that make them plants?

"What are those things?" she asked, gesturing toward one with a foot.

"Part of the ship. They can be induced to produce a liquid we and our animals enjoy. It wouldn't be good for you."

"Are they plant or animal?"

"They aren't separate from the ship."

"Well, is the ship plant or animal?"

"Both, and more."

Whatever that meant. "Is it intelligent?"

"It can be. That part of it is dormant now. But even so, the ship can be chemically induced to perform more functions than you would have the patience to listen to. It does a great deal on its own without monitoring. And it . . ." He fell silent for a moment, his tentacles smooth against his body. Then he continued, "The human doctor used to say it loved us. There is an affinity, but it's biological—a strong, symbiotic relationship. We serve the ship's needs and it serves ours. It would die without us and we would be planetbound without it. For us, that would eventually mean death."

"Where did you get it?"

"We grew it."

"You . . . or your ancestors?"

"My ancestors grew this one. I'm helping to grow another."

"Now? Why?"

"We'll divide here. We're like mature asexual animals in that way, but we divide into three: Dinso to stay on Earth until it is ready to leave generations from now; Toaht to leave in this ship; and Akjai to leave in the new ship."

Lilith looked at him. "Some of you will go to Earth with us?"

"I will, and my family and others. All Dinso."

"Why?"

"This is how we grow—how we've always grown. We'll take the knowledge of shipgrowing with us so that our descendants will be able to leave when the time comes. We couldn't survive as a people if we were always confined to one ship or one world."

"Will you take . . . seeds or something?"

"We'll take the necessary materials."

"And those who leave—Toaht and Akjai—you'll never see them again?"

"I won't. At some time in the distant future, a group of my

descendants might meet a group of theirs. I hope that will happen. Both will have divided many times. They'll have acquired
much to give one another."

"They probably won't even know one another. They'll remember this division as mythology if they remember it at all."

"No, they'll recognize one another. Memory of a division is
passed on biologically. I remember every one that has taken
place in my family since we left the homeworld."

"Do you remember your homeworld itself? I mean, could
you get back to it if you wanted to?"

"Go back?" His tentacles smoothed again. "No, Lilith,
that's the one direction that's closed to us. This is our homeworld now." He gestured around them from what seemed to
be a glowing ivory sky to what seemed to be brown soil.

There were many more of the huge trees around them now,
and she could see people going in and out of the trunks—
naked, gray Oankali, tentacled all over, some with two arms,
some, alarmingly, with four, but none with anything she recognized as sexual organs. Perhaps some of the tentacles and
extra arms served a sexual function.

She examined every cluster of Oankali for humans, but
saw none. At least none of the Oankali came near her or
seemed to pay any attention to her. Some of them, she noticed with a shudder, had tentacles covering every inch of
their heads all around. Others had tentacles in odd, irregular
patches. None had quite Jdahya's humanlike arrangement—
tentacles placed to resemble eyes, ears, hair. Had Jdahya's
work with humans been suggested by the chance arrangement of his head tentacles or had he been altered surgically
or in some other way to make him seem more human?

"This is the way I have always looked," he said when she
asked, and he would not say any more on the subject.

Minutes later they passed near a tree and she reached out to
touch its smooth, slightly giving bark—like the walls of her
isolation room, but darker-colored. "These trees are all buildings, aren't they?" she asked.

"These structures are not trees," he told her. "They're part

of the ship. They support its shape, provide necessities for us—
food, oxygen, waste disposal, transport conduits, storage and
living space, work areas, many things."

They passed very near a pair of Oankali who stood so close
together their head tentacles writhed and tangled together. She
could see their bodies in clear detail. Like the others she had
seen, these were naked. Jdahya had probably worn clothing
only as a courtesy to her. For that she was grateful.

The growing number of people they passed near began to
disturb her, and she caught herself drawing closer to Jdahya as
though for protection. Surprised and embarrassed, she made
herself move away from him. He apparently noticed.

"Lilith?" he said very quietly.

"What?"

Silence.

"I'm all right," she said. "It's just . . . so many people, and
so strange to me."

"Normally, we don't wear anything."

"I'd guessed that."

"You'll be free to wear clothing or not as you like."

"I'll wear it!" She hesitated. "Are there any other humans
Awake where you're taking me?"

"None."

She hugged herself tightly, arms across her chest. More isolation.

To her surprise, he extended his hand. To her greater surprise, she took it and was grateful.

"Why can't you go back to your homeworld?" she asked.
"It . . . still exists, doesn't it?"

He seemed to think for a moment. "We left it so long
ago . . . I doubt that it does still exist."

"Why did you leave?"

"It was a womb. The time had come for us to be born."

She smiled sadly. "There were humans who thought that
way—right up to the moment the missiles were fired. People
who believed space was our destiny. I believed it myself."

"I know—though from what the ooloi have told me, your

people could not have fulfilled that destiny. Their own bodies handicapped them."

"Their . . . our bodies? What do you mean? We've been into space. There's nothing about our bodies that prevented—"

"Your bodies are fatally flawed. The ooloi perceived this at once. At first it was very hard for them to touch you. Then you became an obsession with them. Now it's hard for them to let you alone."

"What are you talking about?"

"You have a mismatched pair of genetic characteristics. Either alone would have been useful, would have aided the survival of your species. But the two together are lethal. It was only a matter of time before they destroyed you."

She shook her head. "If you're saying we were genetically programmed to do what we did, blow ourselves up—"

"No. Your people's situation was more like your own with the cancer my relative cured. The cancer was small. The human doctor said you would probably have recovered and been well even if humans had discovered it and removed it at that stage. You might have lived the rest of your life free of it, though she said she would have wanted you checked regularly."

"With my family history, she wouldn't have had to tell me that last."

"Yes. But what if you hadn't recognized the significance of your family history? What if we or the humans hadn't discovered the cancer?"

"It *was* malignant, I assume."

"Of course."

"Then I suppose it would eventually have killed me."

"Yes, it would have. And your people were in a similar position. If they had been able to perceive and solve their problem, they might have been able to avoid destruction. Of course, they too would have to remember to reexamine themselves periodically."

"But what was the problem? You said we had two incompatible characteristics. What were they?"

Jdahya made a rustling noise that could have been a sigh,

but that did not seem to come from his mouth or throat. "You are intelligent," he said. "That's the newer of the two characteristics, and the one you might have put to work to save yourselves. You are potentially one of the most intelligent species we've found, though your focus is different from ours. Still, you had a good start in the life sciences, and even in genetics."

"What's the second characteristic?"

"You are hierarchical. That's the older and more entrenched characteristic. We saw it in your closest animal relatives and in your most distant ones. It's a terrestrial characteristic. When human intelligence served it instead of guiding it, when human intelligence did not even acknowledge it as a problem, but took pride in it or did not notice it at all . . ." The rattling sounded again. "That was like ignoring cancer. I think your people did not realize what a dangerous thing they were doing."

"I don't think most of us thought of it as a genetic problem. I didn't. I'm not sure I do now." Her feet had begun to hurt from walking so long on the uneven ground. She wanted to end both the walk and the conversation. The conversation made her uncomfortable. Jdahya sounded . . . almost plausible.

"Yes," he said, "intelligence does enable you to deny facts you dislike. But your denial doesn't matter. A cancer growing in someone's body will go on growing in spite of denial. And a complex combination of genes that work together to make you intelligent as well as hierarchical will still handicap you whether you acknowledge it or not."

"I just don't believe it's that simple. Just a bad gene or two."

"It isn't simple, and it isn't a gene or two. It's many—the result of a tangled combination of factors that only begins with genes." He stopped, let his head tentacles drift toward a rough circle of huge trees. The tentacles seemed to point. "My family lives there," he said.

She stood still, now truly frightened.

"No one will touch you without your consent," he said. "And I'll stay with you for as long as you like."

She was comforted by his words and ashamed of needing comfort. How had she become so dependent on him? She shook her head. The answer was obvious. He wanted her dependent. That was the reason for her continued isolation from her own kind. She was to be dependent on an Oankali—dependent and trusting. To hell with that!

"Tell me what you want of me," she demanded abruptly, "and what you want of my people."

His tentacles swung to examine her. "I've told you a great deal."

"Tell me the price, Jdahya. What do you want? What will your people take from us in return for having saved us?"

All his tentacles seemed to hang limp, giving him an almost comical droop. Lilith found no humor in it. "You'll live," he said. "Your people will live. You'll have your world again. We already have much of what we want of you. Your cancer in particular."

"What?"

"The ooloi are intensely interested in it. It suggests abilities we have never been able to trade for successfully before."

"Abilities? From cancer?"

"Yes. The ooloi see great potential in it. So the trade has already been useful."

"You're welcome to it. But before when I asked, you said you trade . . . yourselves."

"Yes. We trade the essence of ourselves. Our genetic material for yours."

Lilith frowned, then shook her head. "How? I mean, you couldn't be talking about interbreeding."

"Of course not." His tentacles smoothed. "We do what you would call genetic engineering. We know you had begun to do it yourselves a little, but it's foreign to you. We do it naturally. We *must* do it. It renews us, enables us to survive as an evolving species instead of specializing ourselves into extinction or stagnation."

"We all do it naturally to some degree," she said warily. "Sexual reproduction—"

"The ooloi do it for us. They have special organs for it. They can do it for you too—make sure of a good, viable gene mix.

It is part of our reproduction, but it's much more deliberate than what any mated pair of humans have managed so far.

"We're not hierarchical, you see. We never were. But we are powerfully acquisitive. We acquire new life—seek it, investigate it, manipulate it, sort it, use it. We carry the drive to do this in a minuscule cell within a cell—a tiny organelle within every cell of our bodies. Do you understand me?"

"I understand your words. Your meaning, though . . . it's as alien to me as you are."

"That's the way we perceived your hierarchical drives at first." He paused. "One of the meanings of Oankali is gene trader. Another is that organelle—the essence of ourselves, the origin of ourselves. Because of that organelle, the ooloi can perceive DNA and manipulate it precisely."

"And they do this . . . inside their bodies?"

"Yes."

"And now they're doing something with cancer cells inside their bodies?"

"Experimenting, yes."

"That sounds . . . a long way from safe."

"They're like children now, talking and talking about possibilities."

"What possibilities?"

"Regeneration of lost limbs. Controlled malleability. Future Oankali may be much less frightening to potential trade partners if they're able to reshape themselves and look more like the partners before the trade. Even increased longevity, though compared to what you're used to, we're very long-lived now."

"All that from cancer."

"Perhaps. We listen to the ooloi when they stop talking so much. That's when we find out what our next generations will be like."

"You leave all that to them? They decide?"

"They show us the tested possibilities. We all decide."

He tried to lead her into his family's woods, but she held back. "There's something I need to understand now," she said. "You call it a trade. You've taken something you value from us and you're giving us back our world. Is that it? Do you have all you want from us?"

"You know it isn't," he said softly. "You've guessed that much."

She waited, staring at him.

"Your people will change. Your young will be more like us and ours more like you. Your hierarchical tendencies will be modified and if we learn to regenerate limbs and reshape our bodies, we'll share those abilities with you. That's part of the trade. We're overdue for it."

"It is crossbreeding, then, no matter what you call it."

"It's what I said it was. A trade. The ooloi will make changes in your reproductive cells before conception and they'll control conception."

"How?"

"The ooloi will explain that when the time comes."

She spoke quickly, trying to blot out thoughts of more surgery or some sort of sex with the damned ooloi. "What will you make of us? What will our children be?"

"Different, as I said. Not quite like you. A little like us."

She thought of her son—how like her he had been, how like his father. Then she thought of grotesque, Medusa children. "No!" she said. "No. I don't care what you do with what you've already learned—how you apply it to yourselves—but leave us out of it. Just let us go. If we have the problem you think we do, let us work it out as human beings."

"We are committed to the trade," he said, softly implacable.

"No! You'll finish what the war began. In a few generations—"

"One generation."

"No!"

He wrapped the many fingers of one hand around her arm. "Can you hold your breath, Lilith? Can you hold it by an act of will until you die?"

"Hold my—?"

"We are as committed to the trade as your body is to breathing. We were overdue for it when we found you. Now it will be done—to the rebirth of your people and mine."

"No!" she shouted. "A rebirth for us can only happen if you let us alone! Let us begin again on our own."

Silence.

She pulled at her arm, and after a moment he let her go. She got the impression he was watching her very closely.

"I think I wish your people had left me on Earth," she whispered. "If this is what they found me for, I wish they'd left me." Medusa children. Snakes for hair. Nests of night crawlers for eyes and ears.

He sat down on the bare ground, and after a minute of surprise, she sat opposite him, not knowing why, simply following his movement.

"I can't *unfind* you," he said. "You're here. But there is . . . a thing I *can* do. It is . . . deeply wrong of me to offer it. I will never offer it again."

"What?" she asked barely caring. She was tired from the walk, overwhelmed by what he had told her. It made no sense. Good god, no wonder he couldn't go home—even if his home still existed. Whatever his people had been like when they left it, they must be very different by now—as the children of the last surviving human beings would be different.

"Lilith?" he said.

She raised her head, stared at him.

"Touch me here now," he said, gesturing toward his head tentacles, "and I'll sting you. You'll die—very quickly and without pain."

She swallowed.

"If you want it," he said.

It was a gift he was offering. Not a threat.

"Why?" she whispered.

He would not answer.

She stared at his head tentacles. She raised her hand, let it reach toward him almost as though it had its own will, its own intent. No more Awakenings. No more questions. No more impossible answers. Nothing.

Nothing.

He never moved. Even his tentacles were utterly still. Her hand hovered, wanting to fall amid the tough, flexible, lethal organs. It hovered, almost brushing one by accident.

She jerked her hand away, clutched it to her. "Oh god," she whispered. "Why didn't I do it? Why can't I do it?"

He stood up and waited uncomplaining for several minutes until she dragged herself to her feet.

"You'll meet my mates and one of my children now," he said. "Then rest and food, Lilith."

She looked at him, longing for a human expression. "Would you have done it?" she asked.

"Yes," he said.

"Why?"

"For you."

II
FAMILY

1

Sleep.

She barely remembered being presented to three of Jdahya's relatives, then guided off and given a bed. Sleep. Then a small, confused awakening.

Now food and forgetting.

Food and pleasure so sharp and sweet it cleared everything else from her mind. There were whole bananas, dishes of sliced pineapple, whole figs, shelled nuts of several kinds, bread and honey, a vegetable stew filled with corn, peppers, tomatoes, potatoes, onions, mushrooms, herbs, and spices.

Where had all this been, Lilith wondered. Surely they could have given her a little of this instead of keeping her for so long on a diet that made eating a chore. Could it all have been for her health? Or had there been some other purpose—something to do with their damned gene trade?

When she had eaten some of everything, savored each new taste lovingly, she began to pay attention to the four Oankali who were with her in the small, bare room. They were Jdahya and his wife Tediin—Kaaljdahyatediin lel Kahguyaht aj Dinso. And there was Jdahya's ooloi mate Kahguyaht—Ahtrekahguyahtkaal lel Jdayhatediin aj Dinso. Finally there was the family's ooloi child Nikanj—Kaalnikanj oo Jdahyatediinkahguyaht aj Dinso.

The four sat atop familiar, featureless platforms eating Earth foods from their several small dishes as though they had been born to such a diet.

There was a central platform with more of everything on it, and the Oankali took turns filling one another's dishes. One of them could not, it seemed, get up and fill only one dish. Others were immediately handed forward, even to Lilith. She filled Jdahya's with hot stew and returned it to him, wondering when he had eaten last—apart from the orange they had shared.

"Did you eat while we were in that isolation room?" she asked him.

"I had eaten before I went in," he said. "I used very little energy while I was there so I didn't need any more food."

"How long were you there?"

"Six days, your time."

She sat down on her platform and stared at him. "That long?"

"Six days," he repeated.

"Your body has drifted away from your world's twenty-four-hour day," the ooloi Kahguyaht said. "That happens to all your people. Your day lengthens slightly and you lose track of how much time has passed."

"But—"

"How long did it seem to you?"

"A few days . . . I don't know. Fewer than six."

"You see?" the ooloi asked softly.

She frowned at it. It was naked as were the others except for Jdahya. This did not bother her even at close quarters as much as she had feared it might. But she did not like the ooloi. It was smug and it tended to treat her condescendingly. It was also one of the creatures scheduled to bring about the destruction of what was left of humanity. And in spite of Jdahya's claim that the Oankali were not hierarchical, the ooloi seemed to be the head of the house. Everyone deferred to it.

It was almost exactly Lilith's size—slightly larger than Jdahya and considerably smaller than the female Tediin. And it had four arms. Or two arms and two arm-sized tentacles. The big tentacles, gray and rough, reminded her of elephants' trunks—except that she could not recall ever being disgusted by the trunk of an elephant. At least the child did not have them yet—though Jdahya had assured her that it was an ooloi child. Looking at Kahguyaht, she took pleasure in the knowledge that the Oankali themselves used the neuter pronoun in referring to the ooloi. Some things deserved to be called "it."

She turned her attention back to the food. "How can you eat all this?" she asked. "I couldn't eat your foods, could I?"

"What do you think you've eaten each time we've Awakened you?" the ooloi asked.

"I don't know," she said coldly. "No one would tell me what it was."

Kahguyaht missed or ignored the anger in her voice. "It was one of our foods—slightly altered to meet your special needs," it said.

Thought of her "special needs" made her realize that this might be Jdahya's "relative" who had cured her cancer. She had somehow not thought of this until now. She got up and filled one of her small bowls with nuts—roasted, but not salted—and wondered wearily whether she had to be grateful to Kahguyaht. Automatically she filled with the same nuts, the bowl Tediin had thrust forward to her.

"Is any of our food poison to you?" she asked flatly.

"No," Kahguyaht answered. "We have adjusted to the foods of your world."

"Are any of yours poison to me?"

"Yes. A great many of them. You shouldn't eat anything unfamiliar that you find here."

"That doesn't make sense. Why should you be able to come from so far away—another world, another star system—and eat our food?"

"Haven't we had time to learn to eat your food?" the ooloi asked.

"What?"

It did not repeat the question.

"Look," she said, "how can you learn to eat something that's poison to you?"

"By studying teachers to whom it isn't poison. By studying your people, Lilith. Your bodies."

"I don't understand."

"Then accept the evidence of your eyes. We can eat anything you can. It's enough for you to understand that."

Patronizing bastard, she thought. But she said only, "Does that mean that you can learn to eat anything at all? That you can't be poisoned?"

"No. I didn't mean that."

She waited, chewing nuts, thinking. When the ooloi did not continue, she looked at it.

It was focused on her, head tentacles pointing. "The very old can be poisoned," it said. "Their reactions are slowed. They might not be able to recognize an unexpected deadly substance and remember how to neutralize it in time. The seriously injured can be poisoned. Their bodies are distracted, busy with self-repair. And the children can be poisoned if they have not yet learned to protect themselves."

"You mean . . . just about anything might poison you if you weren't somehow prepared for it, ready to protect yourselves against it?"

"Not just anything. Very few things, really. Things we were especially vulnerable to before we left our original homeworld."

"Like what?"

"Why do you ask, Lilith? What would you do if I told you? Poison a child?"

She chewed and swallowed several peanuts, all the while staring at the ooloi, making no effort to conceal her dislike. "You invited me to ask," she said.

"No. That isn't what I was doing."

"Do you really imagine I'd hurt a child?"

"No. You just haven't learned yet not to ask dangerous questions."

"Why did you tell me as much as you did?"

The ooloi relaxed its tentacles. "Because we know you, Lilith. And, within reason, we want you to know us."

2

The ooloi took her to see Sharad. She would have preferred to have Jdahya take her, but when Kahguyaht volunteered, Jdahya leaned toward her and asked very softly, "Shall I go?"

She did not imagine that she was intended to miss the unspoken message of the gesture—that Jdahya was indulging a child. Lilith was tempted to accept the child's role and ask him to come along. But he deserved a vacation from her—and she from him. Maybe he wanted to spend some time with the big, silent Tediin. How, she wondered, did these people manage their sex lives, anyway? How did the ooloi fit in? Were its two arm-sized tentacles sexual organs? Kahguyaht had not used them in eating—had kept them either coiled against its body, under its true arms or draped over its shoulders.

She was not afraid of it, ugly as it was. So far it had inspired only disgust, anger, and dislike in her. How had Jdahya connected himself with such a creature?

Kahguyaht led her through three walls, opening all of them by touching them with one of its large tentacles. Finally they emerged into a wide, downward-sloping, well-lighted corridor. Large numbers of Oankali walked or rode flat, slow, wheelless conveyances that apparently floated a fraction of an inch above the floor. There were no collisions, no near-misses, yet Lilith saw no order to the traffic. People walked or drove wherever they could find an opening and apparently depended on others not to hit them. Some of the vehicles were loaded with unrecognizable freight—transparent beachball-sized blue spheres filled with some liquid, two-foot-long centipede-like animals stacked in rectangular cages, great trays of oblong, green shapes about six feet long and three feet thick. These last writhed slowly, blindly.

"What are those?" she asked the ooloi.

It ignored her except to take her arm and guide her where

traffic was heavy. She realized abruptly that it was guiding her with the tip of one of its large tentacles.

"What do you call these?" she asked, touching the one wrapped around her arm. Like the smaller ones it was cool and as hard as her fingernails, but clearly very flexible.

"You can call them sensory arms," it told her.

"What are they for?"

Silence.

"Look, I thought I was supposed to be learning. I can't learn without asking questions and getting answers."

"You'll get them eventually—as you need them."

In anger she pulled loose from the ooloi's grip. It was surprisingly easy to do. The ooloi did not touch her again, did not seem to notice that twice it almost lost her, made no effort to help her when they passed through a crowd and she realized she could not tell one adult ooloi from another.

"Kahguyaht!" she said sharply.

"Here." It was beside her, no doubt watching, probably laughing at her confusion. Feeling manipulated, she grasped one of its true arms and stayed close to it until they had come into a corridor that was almost empty. From there they entered a corridor that was empty. Kahguyaht ran one sensory arm along the wall for several feet, then stopped, and flatted the tip of the arm against the wall.

An opening appeared where the arm had touched and Lilith expected to be led into one more corridor or room. Instead the wall seemed to form a sphincter and pass something. There was even a sour smell to enhance the image. One of the big semitransparent green oblongs slid into view, wet and sleek.

"It's a plant," the ooloi volunteered. "We store it where it can be given the kind of light it thrives best under."

Why couldn't it have said that before, she wondered.

The green oblong writhed very slowly as the others had while the ooloi probed it with both sensory arms. After a time, the ooloi paid attention only to one end. That end, it massaged with its sensory arms.

Lilith saw that the plant was beginning to open, and suddenly she knew what was happening.

"Sharad is in that thing, isn't he?"

"Come here."

She went over to where it had sat on the floor at the now-open end of the oblong. Sharad's head was just becoming visible. The hair that she recalled as dull black now glistened, wet and plastered to his head. The eyes were closed and the look on the face peaceful—as though the boy were in a normal sleep. Kahguyaht had stopped the opening of the plant at the base of the boy's throat, but she could see enough to know Sharad was only a little older than he had been when they had shared an isolation room. He looked healthy and well.

"Will you wake him?" she asked.

"No." Kahguyaht touched the brown face with a sensory arm. "We won't be Awakening these people for a while. The human who will be guiding and training them has not yet begun his own training."

She would have pleaded with it if she had not had two years of dealing with the Oankali to tell her just how little good pleading did. Here was the one human being she had seen in those two years, in two hundred and fifty years. And she could not talk to him, could not make him know she was with him.

She touched his cheek, found it wet, slimy, cool. "Are you sure he's all right?"

"He's fine." The ooloi touched the plant where it had drawn aside and it began slowly to close around Sharad again. She watched the face until it was completely covered. The plant closed seamlessly around the small head.

"Before we found these plants," Kahguyaht said, "they used to capture living animals and keep them alive for a long while, using their carbon dioxide and supplying them with oxygen while slowly digesting nonessential parts of their bodies: limbs, skin, sensory organs. The plants even passed some of their own substance through their prey to nourish the prey and keep it alive as long as possible. And the plants were enriched by the prey's waste products. They gave a very, very long death.

Lilith swallowed. "Did the prey feel what was being done to it?"

"No. That would have hastened death. The prey . . . slept."

Lilith stared at the green oblong, writhing slowly like an obscenely fat caterpillar. "How does Sharad breathe?"

"The plant supplies him with an ideal mix of gasses."

"Not just oxygen?"

"No. It suits its care to his needs. It still benefits from the carbon dioxide he exhales and from his rare waste products. It floats in a bath of nutrients and water. These and the light supply the rest of its needs."

Lilith touched the plant, found it firm and cool. It yielded slightly under her fingers. Its surface was lightly coated with slime. She watched with amazement as her fingers sank more deeply into it and it began to engulf them. She was not frightened until she tried to pull away and discovered it would not let go—and pulling back hurt sharply.

"Wait," Kahguyaht said. With a sensory arm, it touched the plant near her hand. At once, she felt the plant begin to let go. When she was able to raise her hand, she found it numb, but otherwise unharmed. Feeling returned to the hand slowly. The print of it was still clear on the surface of the plant when Kahguyaht first rubbed its own hands with its sensory arms, then opened the wall and pushed the plant back through it.

"Sharad is very small," it said when the plant was gone. "The plant could have taken you in as well."

She shuddered. "I was in one . . . wasn't I?"

Kahguyaht ignored the question. But of course she had been in one of the plants—had spent most of the last two and a half centuries within what was basically a carnivorous plant. And the thing had taken good care of her, kept her young and well.

"How did you make them stop eating people?" she asked.

"We altered them genetically—changed some of their requirements, enabled them to respond to certain chemical stimuli from us."

She looked at the ooloi. "It's one thing to do that to a plant. It's another to do it to intelligent, self-aware beings."

"We do what we do, Lilith."

"You could kill us. You could make mules of our children—sterile monsters."

"No," it said. "There was no life at all on your Earth when our ancestors left our original homeworld, and in all that time we've never done such a thing."

"You wouldn't tell me if you had," she said bitterly.

It took her back through the crowded corridors to what she had come to think of as Jdahya's apartment. There it turned her over to the child, Nikanj.

"It will answer your questions and take you through the walls when necessary," Kahguyaht said. "It is half again your age and very knowledgeable about things other than humans. You will teach it about your people and it will teach you about the Oankali."

Half again her age, three-quarters her size, and still growing. She wished it were not an ooloi child. She wished it were not a child at all. How could Kahguyaht first accuse her of wanting to poison children, then leave her in the care of its own child?

At least Nikanj did not look like an ooloi yet.

"You do speak English, don't you?" she asked when Kahguyaht had opened a wall and left the room. The room was the one they had eaten in, empty now except for Lilith and the child. The leftover food and the dishes had been removed and she had not seen Jdahya or Tediin since her return.

"Yes," the child said. "But . . . not much. You teach."

Lilith sighed. Neither the child nor Tediin had said a word to her beyond greeting, though both had occasionally spoken in fast, choppy Oankali to Jdahya or Kahguyaht. She had wondered why. Now she knew.

"I'll teach what I can," she said.

"I teach. You teach."

"Yes."

"Good. Outside?"

"You want me to go outside with you?"

It seemed to think for a moment. "Yes," it said finally.

"Why?"

The child opened its mouth, then closed it again, head tentacles writhing. Confusion? Vocabulary problem?

"It's all right," Lilith said. "We can go outside if you like."

Its tentacles smoothed flat against its body briefly, then it took her hand and would have opened the wall and led her out but she stopped it.

"Can you show me how to make it open?" she asked.

The child hesitated, then took one of her hands and brushed it over the forest of its long head tentacles, leaving the hand slightly wet. Then it touched her fingers to the wall, and the wall began to open.

More programmed reaction to chemical stimuli. No special areas to press, no special series of pressures. Just a chemical the Oankali manufactured within their bodies. She would go on being a prisoner, forced to stay wherever they chose to leave her. She would not be permitted even the illusion of freedom.

The child stopped her once they were outside. It struggled through a few more words. "Others," it said, then hesitated. "Others see you? Others not see human . . . never."

Lilith frowned, certain she was being asked a question. The child's rising inflection seemed to indicate questioning if she could depend on such clues from an Oankali. "Are you asking me whether you can show me off to your friends?" she asked.

The child turned its face to her. "Show you . . . off?"

"It means . . . to put me on display—take me out to be seen."

"Ah. Yes. I show you off?"

"All right," she said smiling.

"I talk . . . more human soon. You say . . . if I speak bad."

"Badly," she corrected.

"If I speak badly?"

"Yes."

There was a long silence. "Also, goodly?" it asked.

"No, not goodly. Well."

"Well." The child seemed to taste the word. "I speak well soon," it said.

3

Nikanj's friends poked and prodded her exposed flesh and tried to persuade her through Nikanj to take off her clothing. None of them spoke English. None seemed in the least child-like, though Nikanj said all were children. She got the feeling some would have enjoyed dissecting her. They spoke aloud very little, but there was much touching of tentacles to flesh or tentacles to other tentacles. When they saw that she would not strip, no more questions were addressed to her. She was first amused, then annoyed, then angered by their attitude. She was nothing more than an unusual animal to them. Nikanj's new pet.

Abruptly she turned away from them. She had had enough of being shown off. She moved away from a pair of children who were reaching to investigate her hair, and spoke Nikanj's name sharply.

Nikanj disentangled its long head tentacles from those of another child and came back to her. If it had not responded to its name, she would not have known it. She was going to have to learn to tell people apart. Memorize the various head-tentacle patterns, perhaps.

"I want to go back," she said.

"Why?" it asked.

She sighed, decided to tell as much of the truth as she thought it could understand. Best to find out now just how far the truth would get her. "I don't like this," she said. "I don't want to be shown off anymore to people I can't even talk to."

It touched her arm tentatively. "You . . . anger?"

"I'm angry, yes. I need to be by myself for a while."

It thought about that. "We go back," it said finally.

Some of the children were apparently unhappy about her leaving. They clustered around her and spoke aloud to Nikanj, but Nikanj said a few words and they let her pass.

She discovered she was trembling and took deep breaths to relax herself. How was a pet supposed to feel? How did zoo animals feel?

If the child would just take her somewhere and leave her for a while. If it would give her a little more of what she had thought she would never want again: Solitude.

Nikanj touched her forehead with a few head tentacles, as though sampling her sweat. She jerked her head away, not wanting to be sampled anymore by anyone.

Nikanj opened a wall into the family apartment and led her into a room that was a twin of the isolation room she thought she had left behind. "Rest here," it told her. "Sleep."

There was even a bathroom, and on the familiar table platform, there was a clean set of clothing. And replacing Jdahya was Nikanj. She could not get rid of it. It had been told to stay with her, and it meant to stay. Its tentacles settled into ugly irregular lumps when she shouted at it, but it stayed.

Defeated, she hid for a while in the bathroom. She rinsed her old clothing, though no foreign matter stuck to it—not dirt, not sweat, not grease or water. It never stayed wet for more than a few minutes. Some Oankali synthetic.

Then she wanted to sleep again. She was used to sleeping whenever she felt tired, and not used to walking long distances or meeting new people. Surprising how quickly the Oankali had become people to her. But then, who else was there?

She crawled into the bed and turned her back to Nikanj, who had taken Jdahya's place on the table platform. Who else would there be for her if the Oankali had their way—and no doubt they were used to having their way. Modifying carnivorous plants . . . What had they modified to get their ship? And what useful tools would they modify human beings into? Did they know yet, or were they planning more experiments? Did they care? How would they make their changes? Or had they made them already—done a little extra tampering with her while they took care of her tumor? Had she ever had a tumor? Her family history led her to believe she had. They probably had not lied about that. Maybe they had not lied about anything. Why should they bother to lie? They owned the Earth and all that was left of the human species.

How was it that she had not been able to take what Jdahya offered?

She slept, finally. The light never changed, but she was used to that. She awoke once to find that Nikanj had come onto the bed with her and lay down. Her first impulse was to push the child away in revulsion or get up herself. Her second, which she followed, wearily indifferent, was to go back to sleep.

4

talk to another human

It became irrationally important to her to do two things: First, to talk to another human being. Any human would do, but she hoped for one who had been Awake longer than she had, one who knew more than she had managed to learn.

Second, she wanted to catch an Oankali in a lie. Any Oankali. Any lie.

But she saw no sign of other humans. And the closest she came to catching the Oankali lying was to catch them in half-truths—though they were honest even about this. They freely admitted that they would tell her only part of what she wanted to know. Beyond this, the Oankali seemed to tell the truth as they perceived it, always. This left her with an almost intolerable sense of hopelessness and helplessness—as though catching them in lies would make them vulnerable. As though it would make the thing they intended to do less real, easier to deny.

Only Nikanj gave her any pleasure, any forgetfulness. The ooloi child seemed to have been given to her as much as she had been given to it. It rarely left her, seemed to like her—though what "liking" a human might mean to an Oankali, she did not know. She had not even figured out Oankali emotional ties to one another. But Jdahya had cared enough for her to offer to do something he believed was utterly wrong. What might Nikanj do for her eventually?

In a very real sense, she was an experimental animal. Not a pet. What could Nikanj do for an experimental animal? Protest tearfully (?) when she was sacrificed at the end of the experiment?

But, no, it was not that kind of experiment. She was intended to live and reproduce, not to die. Experimental animal, parent to domestic animals? Or . . . nearly extinct animal, part of a captive breeding program? Human biologists had done that before the war—used a few captive members of an endangered animal species to breed more for the wild population. Was that what she was headed for? Forced artificial insemination. Surrogate motherhood? Fertility drugs and forced "donations" of eggs? Implantation of unrelated fertilized eggs. Removal of children from mothers at birth . . . Humans had done these things to captive breeders—all for a higher good, of course.

reproduction

This was what she needed to talk to another human about. Only a human could reassure her—or at least understand her fear. But there was only Nikanj. She spent all her time teaching it and learning what she could from it. It kept her as busy as she would permit. It needed less sleep than she did, and when she was not asleep, it expected her to be learning or teaching. It wanted not only language, but culture, biology, history, her own life story. . . . Whatever she knew, it expected to learn.

This was a little like having Sharad with her again. But Nikanj was much more demanding—more like an adult in its persistence. No doubt she and Sharad had been given their time together so that the Oankali could see how she behaved with a foreign child of her own species—a child she had to share quarters with and teach.

Like Sharad, Nikanj had an eidetic memory. Perhaps all Oankali did. Anything Nikanj saw or heard once, it remembered, whether it understood or not. And it was bright and surprisingly quick to understand. She became ashamed of her own plodding slowness and haphazard memory.

She had always found it easier to learn when she could write things down. In all her time with the Oankali, though, she had never seen any of them read or write anything.

"Do you keep any records outside your own memories?" she asked Nikanj when she had worked with it long enough to become frustrated and angry. "Do you ever read or write?"

"You have not taught me those words," it said.

"Communication by symbolic marks . . ." She looked around for something she could mark, but they were in their bedroom and there was nothing that would retain a mark long enough for her to write words—even if she had had something to write with. "Let's go outside," she said. "I'll show you."

It opened a wall and led her out. Outside, beneath the branches of the pseudotree that contained their living quarters, she knelt on the ground and began to write with her finger in what seemed to be loose, sandy soil. She wrote her name, then experimented with different possible spellings of Nikanj's name. *Necange* didn't look right—nor did *Nekahnge. Nickahnge* was closer. She listened in her mind to Nikanj saying its name, then wrote *Nikanj*. That felt right, and she liked the way it looked.

"That's about what your name would look like written down," she said. "I can write the words you teach me and study them until I know them. That way I wouldn't have to ask you things over and over. But I need something to write with—and on. Thin sheets of paper would be best." She was not sure it knew what paper was, but it did not ask. "If you don't have paper, I could use thin sheets of plastic or even cloth if you can make something that will mark them. Some ink or dye—something that will make a clear mark. Do you understand?"

"You can do what you're doing with your fingers," it told her.

"That's not enough. I need to be able to keep my writing . . .
to study it. I need—"

"No."

She stopped in midsentence, blinked at it. "This isn't anything dangerous," she said. "Some of your people must have
seen our books, tapes, disks, films—our records of history,
medicine, language, science, all kinds of things. I just want to
make my own records of your language."

"I know about the . . . records your people kept. I didn't
know what they were called in English, but I've seen them.
We've saved many of them and learned to use them to know
humans better. I don't understand them, but others do."

"May I see them?"

"No. None of your people are permitted to see them."

"Why?"

It did not answer.

"Nikanj?"

Silence.

"Then . . . at least let me make my own records to help me
learn your language. We humans need to do such things to
help us remember."

"No."

She frowned. "But . . . what do you mean, 'no'? We do."

"I cannot give you such things. Not to write or to read."

"Why!"

"It is not allowed. The people have decided that it should
not be allowed."

"That doesn't answer anything. What was their reason?"

Silence again. It let its sensory tentacles droop. This made it
look smaller—like a furry animal that had gotten wet.

"It can't be that you don't have—or can't make—writing
materials," she said.

"We can make anything your people could," it said.
"Though we would not want to make most of their things."

"This is such a simple thing . . ." She shook her head. "Have
you been told not to tell me why?"

It refused to answer. Did that mean not telling her was its

own idea, its own childish exercise of power? Why shouldn't the Oankali do such things as readily as humans did?

After a time, it said, "Come back in. I'll teach you more of our history." It knew she liked stories of the long, multispecies Oankali history, and the stories helped her Oankali vocabulary. But she was in no mood to be cooperative now. She sat down on the ground and leaned back against the pseudotree. After a moment, Nikanj sat down opposite her and began to speak.

"Six divisions ago, on a white-sun water world, we lived in great shallow oceans," it said. "We were many-bodied and spoke with body lights and color patterns among ourself and among ourselves. . . ."

She let it go on, not questioning when she did not understand, not wanting to care. The idea of Oankali blending with a species of intelligent, schooling, fishlike creatures was fascinating, but she was too angry to give it her full attention. Writing materials. Such small things, and yet they were denied to her. Such *small* things!

When Nikanj went into the apartment to get food for them both, she got up and walked away. She wandered, freer than she ever had before through the parklike area outside the living quarters—the pseudotrees. Oankali saw her, but seemed to pay no more than momentary attention to her. She had become absorbed in looking around when abruptly Nikanj was beside her.

"You must stay with me," it said in a tone that reminded her of a human mother speaking to her five-year-old. That, she thought, was about right for her rank in its family.

After that incident she slipped away whenever she could. Either she would be stopped, punished, and/or confined, or she would not be.

She was not. Nikanj seemed to get used to her wandering. Abruptly, it ceased to show up at her elbow minutes after she had escaped it. It seemed willing to give her an occasional hour or two out of its sight. She began to take food with her, saving easily portable items from her meals—a highly seasoned rice dish wrapped in an edible, high-protein envelope, nuts, fruit or quatasayasha, a sharp, cheeselike Oankali food that Kahguyaht had said was safe. Nikanj had acknowledged its acceptance of her wandering by advising her to bury any uneaten food she did not want. "Feed it to the ship," was the way it put the suggestion.

She would fashion her extra jacket into a bag and put her lunch into it, then wander alone, eating and thinking. There was no real comfort in being alone with her thoughts, her memories, but somehow the illusion of freedom lessened her despair.

Other Oankali tried to talk with her sometimes, but she could not understand enough of their language to hold a conversation. Sometimes even when they spoke slowly, she would not recognize words she should have known and did know moments after the encounter had ended. Most of the time she wound up resorting to gestures—which did not work very well—and feeling impenetrably stupid. The only certain communication she managed was in enlisting help from strangers when she was lost.

Nikanj had told her that if she could not find her way "home" she was to go to the nearest adult and say her name with new Oankali additions: Dhokaaltediinjdahyalilith eka Kahguyaht aj Dinso. The *Dho* used as prefix indicated an adopted non-Oankali. *Kaal* was a kinship group name. Then Tediin's and Jdahya's names with Jdahya's last because he had brought her into the family. *Eka* meant child. A child so young it literally had no sex—as very young Oankali did not. Lilith had accepted this designation hopefully. Surely sexless children were not used in breeding experiments. Then there was Kahguyaht's name. It was her third "parent," after all. Finally there was the trade status name. The Dinso group was staying on Earth, changing itself by taking part of humanity's genetic heritage, spreading its own genes like a disease among unwilling humans . . . Dinso. It wasn't a surname. It was a terrible promise, a threat.

Yet if she said this long name—all of it—people immediately

understood not only who she was but where she should be, and they pointed her toward "home." She was not particularly grateful to them.

On one of these solitary walks, she heard two Oankali use one of their words for humans—kaizidi—and she slowed down to listen. She assumed the two were talking about her. She often supposed people she walked among were discussing her as though she were an unusual animal. These two confirmed her fears when they fell silent at her approach and continued their conversation silently with mutual touching of head tentacles. She had all but forgotten this incident when, several walks later, she heard another group of people in the same area speaking again of a kaizidi—a male they called Fukumoto.

Again everyone fell silent at her approach. She had tried to freeze and listen, just hidden by the trunk of one of the great pseudotrees, but the moment she stopped there, conversation went silent among the Oankali. Their hearing, when they chose to focus their attention on it, was acute. Nikanj had complained early on in her stay about the loudness of her heartbeat.

She walked on, ashamed in spite of herself of having been caught eavesdropping. There was no sense to such a feeling. She was a captive. What courtesy did a captive owe beyond what was necessary for self-preservation?

And where was Fukumoto?

She replayed in her mind what she remembered of the fragments she had heard. Fukumoto had something to do with the Tiej kinship group—also a Dinso people. She knew vaguely where their area was, though she had never been there.

Why had people in Kaal been discussing a human in Tiej? What had Fukumoto done? And how could she reach him?

She would go to Tiej. She would do her wandering there if she could—if Nikanj did not appear to stop her. It still did that occasionally, letting her know that it could follow her anywhere, approach her anywhere, and seem to appear from nowhere. Maybe it liked to see her jump.

She began to walk toward Tiej. She might manage to see the
man today if he happened to be outside—addicted to wandering as she was. And if she saw him, he might speak English. If
he spoke English, his Oankali jailers might not prevent him
from speaking to her. If the two of them spoke together, he
might prove as ignorant as she was. And if he were not ignorant, if they met and spoke and all went well, the Oankali
might decide to punish her. Solitary confinement again? Suspended animation? Or just closer confinement with Nikanj
and its family? If they did either of the first two she would simply be relieved of a responsibility she did not want and could
not possibly handle. If they did the third, what difference
would it really make? What difference balanced against the
chance to see and speak with one of her own kind again, finally?

None at all.

She never considered going back to Nikanj and asking it or
its family to let her meet Fukumoto. They had made it clear to
her that she was not to have contact with humans or human
artifacts.

The walk to Tiej was longer than she had expected. She had
not yet learned to judge distances aboard the ship. The horizon, when it was not obscured by pseudotrees and hill-like en-
trances to other levels, seemed startlingly close. But how close,
she could not have said.

At least no one stopped her. Oankali she passed seemed to
assume that she belonged wherever she happened to be. Unless
Nikanj appeared, she would be able to wander in Tiej for as
long as she liked.

She reached Tiej and began her search. The pseudotrees in
Tiej were yellow-brown rather than the gray-brown of Kaal,
and their bark looked rougher—more like what she expected
of tree bark. Yet people opened them in the way to come and
go. She peered through the openings they made when she got
the chance. This trip, she felt, would be worthwhile if she
could just catch a glimpse of Fukumoto—of any human
Awake and aware. Anyone at all.

She had not realized until she actually began looking how important it was for her to find someone. The Oankali had removed her so completely from her own people—only to tell her they planned to use her as a Judas goat. And they had done it all so softly, without brutality, and with patience and gentleness so corrosive of any resolve on her part.

She walked and looked until she was too tired to continue. Finally, discouraged and more disappointed than even she thought reasonable, she sat down against a pseudotree and ate the two oranges she had saved from the lunch she had eaten earlier in Kaal.

Her search, she admitted finally, had been ridiculous. She could have stayed in Kaal, daydreamed about meeting another human, and gotten more satisfaction from it. She could not even be certain how much of Tiej she had covered. There were no signs that she could read. Oankali did not use such things. Their kinship group areas were clearly scent-marked. Each time they opened a wall, they enhanced the local scent markers—or they identified themselves as visitors, members of a different kinship group. Ooloi could change their scent, and did when they left home to mate. Males and females kept the scents they were born with and never lived outside their kinship area. Lilith could not read scent signs. As far as she was concerned Oankali had no odor at all.

That was better, she supposed, than their having a foul odor and forcing her to endure it. But it left her bereft of signposts.

She sighed and decided to go back to Kaal—if she could find her way back. She looked around, confirmed her suspicions that she was already disoriented, lost. She would have to ask someone to aim her toward Kaal.

She got up, moved away from the pseudotree she had been leaning against, and scratched a shallow hole in the soil—it actually was soil, Nikanj had told her. She buried her orange peelings, knowing they would be gone within a day, broken down by tendrils of the ship's own living matter.

Or that was what was supposed to happen.

As she shook out her extra jacket and brushed herself off,

the ground around the buried peelings began to darken. The color change recaptured her attention and she watched as the soil slowly became mud and turned the same orange that the peelings had been. This was an effect she had never seen before.

The soil began to smell, to stink in a way she found hard to connect with oranges. It was probably the smell that drew the Oankali. She looked up and found two of them standing near her, their head tentacles swept toward her in a point.

One of them spoke to her, and she tried hard to understand the words—did understand some of them, but not fast enough or completely enough to catch the sense of what was being said.

The orange spot on the ground began to bubble and grow. Lilith stepped away from it. "What's happening?" she asked. "Do either of you speak English?"

The larger of the two Oankali—Lilith thought this one was female—spoke in a language neither Oankali nor English. They confused her at first. Then she realized the language sounded like Japanese.

"Fukumoto-san?" she asked hopefully.

There was another burst of what must have been Japanese, and she shook her head. "I don't understand," she said in Oankali. Those words she had learned quickly through repetition. The only Japanese words that came quickly to mind were stock phrases from a trip she had made years before to Japan: *Konichiwa, arigato gozaimaso, sayonara. . . .*

Other Oankali had gathered to watch the bubbling ground. The orange mass had grown to be about three feet across and almost perfectly circular. It had touched one of the fleshy, tentacled pseudoplants and the pseudoplant darkened and lashed about as though in agony. Seeing its violent twisting Lilith forgot that it was not an individual organism. She focused on the fact that it was alive and she had probably caused it pain. She had not merely caused an interesting effect, she had caused harm.

She made herself speak in slow, careful Oankali. "I can't

change this," she said, wanting to say that she couldn't repair the damage. "Will you help?"

An ooloi stepped up, touched the orange mud with one of its sensory arms, held the arm still in the mud for several seconds. The bubbling slowed, then stopped. By the time the ooloi withdrew, the bright orange coloring was also beginning to fade to normal.

The ooloi said something to a big female and she answered, gesturing toward Lilith with her head tentacles.

Lilith frowned suspiciously at the ooloi. "Kahguyaht?" she asked, feeling foolish. But the pattern of this ooloi's head tentacles was the same as Kahguyaht's.

The ooloi pointed its head tentacles toward her. "How have you managed," it asked her, "to remain so promising and yet so ignorant?"

Kahguyaht.

"What are you doing here?" she demanded.

Silence. It shifted its attention to the healing ground, seemed to examine it once more, then said something loudly to the gathered people. Most of them went smooth and began to disperse. She suspected it had made a joke at her expense.

"So you finally found something to poison," it said to her.

She shook her head. "I just buried a few orange peelings. Nikanj told me to bury my leavings."

"Bury anything you like in Kaal. When you leave Kaal, and you want to throw something away, give it to an ooloi. And don't leave Kaal again until you're able to speak to people. Why are you here?"

Now she refused to answer.

"Fukumoto-san died recently" it said. "No doubt that's why you heard talk of him. You did hear people talking about him, didn't you?"

After a moment she nodded.

"He was one hundred and twenty years old. He spoke no English."

"He was human," she whispered.

"He lived here awake for almost sixty years. I don't think he saw another human more than twice."

She stepped closer to Kahguyaht, studying it. "And it doesn't occur to you that that was a cruelty?"

"He adjusted very well."

"But still—"

"Can you find your way home, Lilith?"

"We're an adaptable species," she said, refusing to be stopped, "but it's wrong to inflict suffering just because your victim can endure it."

"Learn our language. When you have, one of us will introduce you to someone who, like Fukumoto, has chosen to live and die among us instead of returning to Earth."

"You mean Fukumoto chose—"

"You know almost nothing," it said. "Come on. I'll take you home—and speak to Nikanj about you."

That made her speak up quickly. "Nikanj didn't know where I was going. It might be tracking me right now."

"No, it isn't. I was. Come on."

5

Kahguyaht took her beneath a hill onto a lower level. There it ordered her onto a small, slow-moving flat vehicle. The transport never moved faster than she could have run, but it got them home surprisingly quickly, no doubt taking a more direct route than she had.

Kahguyaht would not speak to her during the trip. She got the impression it was angry, but she didn't really care. She only hoped it wasn't too angry with Nikanj. She had accepted the possibility that she might be punished somehow for her Tiej trip, but she had not intended to make trouble for Nikanj.

Once they were home, Kahguyaht took Nikanj into the room she and Nikanj shared, leaving her in what she had come to think of as the dining room. Jdahya and Tediin were there, eating Oankali food this time, the products of plants that would have been deadly to her.

She sat down silently and after a while, Jdahya brought her nuts, fruit, and some Oankali food that had a vaguely meaty taste and texture, though it was actually a plant product.

"Just how much trouble am I in?" she asked as he handed her her dishes.

He smoothed his tentacles. "Not so much, Lilith."

She frowned. "I got the impression Kahguyaht was angry."

Now the smooth tentacles became irregular, raised knots. "That was not exactly anger. It is concerned about Nikanj."

"Because I went to Tiej?"

"No." His lumps became larger, uglier. "Because this is a hard time for it—and for you. Nikanj has left you for it to stumble over."

"What?"

Tediin said something in rapid, incomprehensible Oankali, and Jdahya answered her. The two of them spoke together for a few minutes. Then Tediin spoke in English to Lilith.

"Kahguyaht must teach . . . same-sex child. You see?"

"And I'm part of the lesson," Lilith answered bitterly.

"Nikanj or Kahguyaht," Tediin said softly.

Lilith frowned, looked to Jdahya for an explanation.

"She means if you and Nikanj weren't supposed to be teaching each other, you would be learning from Kahguyaht."

Lilith shuddered. "Good god," she whispered. And seconds later, "Why couldn't it be you?"

"Ooloi generally handle the teaching of new species."

"Why? If I have to be taught, I'd rather you did it."

His head tentacles smoothed.

"You like him or Kahguyaht?" Tediin asked. Her unpracticed English, acquired just from hearing others speak was much better than Lilith's Oankali.

"No offense," Lilith said, "but I prefer Jdahya."

"Good," Tediin said, her own head smooth, though Lilith did not understand why. "You like him or Nikanj?"

Lilith opened her mouth, then hesitated. Jdahya had left her completely to Nikanj for so long—deliberately, no doubt. And Nikanj . . . Nikanj was appealing—probably because it was a child. It was no more responsible for the thing that was to happen to the remnants of humanity than she was. It was simply doing—or trying to do—what the adults around it said should be done. Fellow victim?

No, not a victim. Just a child, appealing in spite of itself. And she liked it in spite of herself.

"You see?" Tediin asked, smooth all over now.

"I see." She took a deep breath. "I see that everyone including Nikanj wants me to prefer Nikanj. Well you win. I do." She turned to Jdahya. "You people are manipulative as hell, aren't you?"

Jdahya concentrated on eating.

"Was I that much of a burden?" she asked him.

He did not answer.

"Will you help me to be less of a burden in one way, at least?"

He aimed some of his tentacles at her. "What do you want?"

"Writing materials. Paper. Pencils or pens—whatever you've got."

"No."

There was no give behind the refusal. He was part of the family conspiracy to keep her ignorant—while trying as hard as they could to educate her. Insane.

She spread both hands before her, shaking her head. "*Why?*"

"Ask Nikanj."

"I have! It won't tell me."

"Perhaps it will now. Have you finished eating?"

"I've had enough—in more ways than one."

"Come on. I'll open the wall for you."

She unfolded herself from her platform and followed him to the wall.

"Nikanj can help you remember without writing," he told her as he touched the wall with several head tentacles.

"How?"

"Ask it."

She stepped through the hole as soon as it was large enough, and found herself intruding on the two ooloi who refused to notice her beyond the automatic sweep of some of their head tentacles. They were talking—arguing—in very fast Oankali. She was, no doubt, the reason for their dispute.

She looked back, hoping to step back through the wall and leave them. Let one of them tell her later what had been decided. She didn't imagine it would be anything she would be eager to hear. But the wall had sealed itself—abnormally quickly.

Nikanj seemed to be holding its own, at least. At one point, it beckoned to her with a sharp movement of head tentacles. She moved to stand beside it, willing to offer whatever moral support she could against Kahguyaht.

Kahguyaht stopped whatever it had been saying and faced her. "You haven't understood us at all, have you?" it asked in English.

"No," she admitted.

"Do you understand me now?" it asked in slow Oankali.

"Yes."

Kahguyaht turned its attention back to Nikanj and spoke rapidly. Straining to understand, Lilith thought it said something close to, "Well, at least we know she's capable of learning."

"I'm capable of learning even faster with paper and pencil," she said. "But with or without them, I'm capable of telling you what I think of you in any one of three human languages!"

Kahguyaht said nothing for several seconds. Finally it turned, opened a wall, and left the room.

When the wall had closed, Nikanj lay down on the bed and crossed its arms over its chest, hugging itself.

"Are you all right?" she asked.

"What are the other two languages?" it asked softly.

She managed a smile. "Spanish and German. I used to speak a little German. I still know a few obscenities."

"You are . . . not fluent?"

"I am in Spanish."

"But why not in German?"

"Because it's been years since I've studied it or spoken it—years before the war, I mean. We humans . . . if we don't use a language, we forget it."

"No. You don't."

She looked at its tightly contracted body tentacles and decided it did not look happy. It really was concerned over her failure to learn quickly and retain everything. "Are you going to let me have writing materials?" she asked.

"No. It will be done our way. Not yours."

"It ought to be done the way that works. But what the hell. You want to spend two or three times as long teaching me, you go right ahead."

"I don't."

She shrugged, not caring whether it missed the gesture or failed to understand it.

"Ooan was upset with me, Lilith, not with you."

"But because of me. Because I'm not learning fast enough."

"No. Because . . . because I'm not teaching you as it thinks I should. It fears for me."

"Fears . . . ? Why?"

"Come here. Sit here. I will tell you."

After a time, she shrugged again and went to sit beside it.

"I'm growing up," it told her. "Ooan wants me to hurry with you so that you can be given your work and I can mate."

"You mean . . . the faster I learn, the sooner you mate?"

"Yes. Until I have taught you, shown that I can teach you, I won't be considered ready to mate."

There it was. She was not just its experimental animal. She was, in some way she did not fully understand, its final exam. She sighed and shook her head. "Did you ask for me Nikanj, or did we just get dumped on one another?"

It said nothing. It doubled one of its arms backward in a

way natural to it, but still startling to Lilith, and rubbed its
armpit. She tilted her head to one side to examine the place it
was rubbing.

"Do you grow the sensory arms after you've mated or before?" she asked.

"They will come soon whether I mate or not."

"*Should* they grow in after you're mated?"

"Mates like them to come in afterward. Males and females
mature more quickly than ooloi. They like to feel that they
have . . . how do you say? Helped their ooloi out of childhood."

"Helped raise them," Lilith said, "or helped rear them."

". . . rear?"

"The word has multiple meanings."

"Oh. There's no logic to such things."

"There probably is, but you'd need an etymologist to explain it. Is there going to be trouble between you and your
mates?"

"I don't know. I hope not. I'll go to them when I can. I've
told them that." It paused. "Now I must tell you something."

"What?"

"Ooan wanted me to act and say nothing . . . to . . . surprise
you. I won't do that."

"*What!*"

"I must make small changes—a few small changes. I must
help you reach your memories as you need them."

"What do you mean? What is it you want to change?"

"Very small things. In the end, there will be a tiny alteration
in your brain chemistry."

She touched her forehead in an unconsciously protective
gesture. "Brain chemistry?" she whispered.

"I would like to wait, do it when I'm mature. I could make
it pleasurable for you then. It should be pleasurable. But
Ooan . . . I understand what it feels. It says I have to change
you now."

"I don't want to be changed!"

"You would sleep through it the way you did when Ooan Jdahya corrected your tumor."

"Ooan Jdahya? Jdahya's ooloi parent did that? Not Kahguyaht?"

"Yes. It was done before my parents were mated."

"Good." No reason at all to be grateful to Kahguyaht.

"Lilith?" Nikanj laid a many-fingered hand—a sixteen-fingered hand—on her arm. "It will be like this. A touch. Then a . . . a small puncture. That's all you'll feel. When you wake up the change will be made."

"*I don't want to be changed!*"

There was a long silence. Finally it said, "Are you afraid?"

"I don't have a disease! Forgetting things is normal for most humans! I don't need anything done to my brain!"

"Would it be so bad to remember better? To remember the way Sharad did—the way I do?"

"What's frightening is the idea of being tampered with." She drew a deep breath. "Listen, no part of me is more definitive of who I am than my brain. I don't want—"

"Who you are won't be changed. I'm not old enough to make the experience pleasant for you, but I'm old enough to function as an ooloi in this way. If I were unfit, others would have noticed by now."

"If everyone's so sure you're fit, why do you have to test yourself with me?"

It refused to answer, remained silent for several minutes. When it tried to pull her down beside it, she broke away and got up, paced around the room. Its head tentacles followed her with more than their usual lazy sweep. They kept sharply pointed at her and eventually she fled to the bathroom to end the staring.

There, she sat on the floor, arms folded, hands clutching her forearms.

What would happen now? Would Nikanj follow orders and surprise her sometime when she was asleep? Would it turn her over to Kahguyaht? Or would they both—please heaven—*let her alone!*

6

She had no idea how much time passed. She found herself thinking of Sam and Ayre, her husband and son, both taken from her before the Oankali, before the war, before she realized how easily her life—any human life—could be destroyed.

There had been a carnival—a cheap little vacant-lot carnival with rides and noise and scabby ponies. Sam had decided to take Ayre to see it while Lilith spent time with her pregnant sister. It had been an ordinary Saturday on a broad, dry street in bright sunshine. A young girl, just learning to drive, had rammed head-on into Sam's car. She had swerved to the wrong side of the road, had perhaps somehow lost control of the car she was driving. She'd had only a learner's permit and was not supposed to drive alone. She died for her mistake. Ayre died—was dead when the ambulance arrived, though paramedics tried to revive him.

Sam only half died.

He had head injuries—brain damage. It took him three months to finish what the accident had begun. Three months to die.

He was conscious some of the time—more or less—but he did not know anyone. His parents came from New York to be with him. They were Nigerians who had lived in the United States long enough for their son to be born and grow up there. Still, they had not been pleased at his marriage to Lilith. They had let Sam grow up as an American, but had sent him to visit their families in Lagos when they could. They had hoped he would marry a Yoruban girl. They had never seen their grandchild. Now they never would.

And Sam did not know them.

He was their only son, but he stared through them as he stared through Lilith, his eyes empty of recognition, empty of him. Sometimes Lilith sat alone with him, touched him, gained the empty attention of those eyes briefly. But the man himself had already gone. Perhaps he was with Ayre, or caught between her and Ayre—between this world and the next.

Or was he aware, but isolated in some part of his mind that could not make contact with anyone outside—trapped in the narrowest, most absolute solitary confinement—until, mercifully, his heart stopped.

That was brain damage—one form of brain damage. There were other forms, many worse. She saw them in the hospital over the months of Sam's dying.

He was lucky to have died so quickly.

She had never dared speak that thought aloud. It had come to her even as she wept for him. It came to her again now. He was lucky to have died so quickly.

Would she be equally lucky?

If the Oankali damaged her brain, would they have the decency to let her die—or would they keep her alive, a prisoner, permanently locked away in that ultimate solitary confinement?

She became aware abruptly that Nikanj had come into the bathroom silently and sat down opposite her. It had never intruded on her this way before. She stared at it, outraged.

"It isn't my ability to cope with your physiology that anyone questions," it said softly. "If I couldn't do that, my defects would have been noticed long ago."

"Get out of here!" she shouted. "Get away from me!"

It did not move. It continued to speak in the same soft voice. "Ooan says humans won't be worth talking to for at least a generation." Its tentacles writhed. "I don't know how to be with someone I can't talk to."

"Brain damage isn't going to improve my conversation," she said bitterly.

"I would rather damage my own brain than yours. I won't damage either." It hesitated. "You know you must accept me or Ooan."

She said nothing.

"Ooan is an adult. It can give you pleasure. And it is not as . . . as angry as it seems."

"I'm not looking for pleasure. I don't even know what you're talking about. I just want to be let alone."

"Yes. But you must trust me or let Ooan surprise you when it's tired of waiting."

"You won't do that yourself—won't just spring it on me?"

"No."

"Why not?"

"There's something wrong with doing it that way—surprising people. It's . . . treating them as though they aren't people, as though they aren't intelligent."

Lilith laughed bitterly. "Why should you suddenly start to worry about that?"

"Do you want me to surprise you?"

"Of course not!"

Silence.

After a while, she got up and went to the bed platform. She lay down and eventually managed to fall asleep.

She dreamed of Sam and awoke in a cold sweat. Empty, empty eyes. Her head ached. Nikanj had stretched out beside her as usual. It looked limp and dead. How would it be to awaken with Kahguyaht there instead, lying beside her like a grotesque lover instead of an unhappy child? She shuddered, fear and disgust almost overwhelming her. She lay still for several minutes, calming herself, forcing herself to make a decision, then to act on it before fear could silence her.

"Wake up!" she said harshly to Nikanj. The raw sound of her own voice startled her. "Wake up and do whatever it is you claim you have to do. Get it over with."

Nikanj sat up instantly, rolled her over onto her side and pulled away the jacket she had been sleeping in to expose her back and neck. Before she could complain or change her mind, it began.

On the back of her neck, she felt the promised touch, a harder pressure, then the puncture. It hurt more than she had expected, but the pain ended quickly. For a few seconds she drifted in painless semiconsciousness.

Then there were confused memories, dreams, finally nothing.

7

When she awoke, at ease and only mildly confused, she found herself fully clothed and alone. She lay still, wondering what Nikanj had done to her. Was she changed? How? Had it finished with her? She could not move at first, but by the time this penetrated her confusion, she found the paralysis wearing off. She was able to use her muscles again. She sat up carefully just in time to see Nikanj coming through a wall.

Its gray skin was as smooth as polished marble as it climbed onto the bed beside her. "You're so complex," it said, taking both her hands. It did not point its head tentacles at her in the usual way, but placed its head close to hers and touched her with them. Then it sat back, pointing at her. It occurred to her distantly that this behavior was unusual and should have alarmed her. She frowned and tried to feel alarmed.

"You're filled with so much life and death and potential for change," Nikanj continued. "I understand now why some people took so long to get over their fear of your kind."

She focused on it. "Maybe it's because I'm still drugged out of my mind, but I don't know what you're talking about."

"Yes. You'll never really know. But when I'm mature, I'll try to show you a little." It brought its head close to hers again and touched her face and burrowed into her hair with its tentacles.

"What are you *doing*?" she asked, still not really disturbed.

"Making sure you're all right. I don't like what I had to do to you."

"What did you do? I don't feel any different—except a little high."

"You understand me."

It dawned on her slowly that Nikanj had come to her speaking Oankali and she had responded in kind—had responded without really thinking. The language seemed natural to her, as easy to understand as English. She remembered all that she had been taught, all that she had picked up on her own. It was even easy for her to spot the gaps in her knowledge—words and expressions she knew in English, but could not translate into Oankali; bits of Oankali grammar that she had not really understood; certain Oankali words that had no English translation, but whose meaning she had grasped.

Now she was alarmed, pleased, and frightened. . . . She stood slowly, testing her legs, finding them unsteady, but functional. She tried to clear the fog from her mind so that she could examine herself and trust her findings.

"I'm glad the family decided to put the two of us together," Nikanj was saying. "I didn't want to work with you. I tried to get out of it. I was afraid. All I could think of was how easy it would be for me to fail and perhaps damage you."

"You mean . . . you mean you weren't sure of what you were doing just now?"

"That? Of course I was sure. And your 'just now' took a long time. Much longer than you usually sleep."

"But what did you mean about failing—"

"I was afraid I could never convince you to trust me enough to let me show you what I could do—show you that I wouldn't hurt you. I was afraid I would make you hate me. For an ooloi to do that . . . it would be very bad. Worse than I can tell you."

"But Kahguyaht doesn't think so."

"Ooan says humans—any new trade partner species—can't be treated the way we must treat each other. It's right up to a point. I just think it goes too far. We were bred to work with

you. We're Dinso. We should be able to find ways through
most of our differences."

"Coercion," she said bitterly. "That's the way you've
found."

"No. Ooan would have done that. I couldn't have. I would
have gone to Ahajas and Dichaan and refused to mate with
them. I would have looked for mates among the Akjai since
they'll have no direct contact with humans."

It smoothed its tentacles again. "But now when I go to Ahajas and Dichaan, it will be to mate—and you'll go with me.
We'll send you to your work when you're ready. And you'll be
able to help me through my final metamorphosis." It rubbed
its armpit. "Will you help?"

She looked away from it. "What do you want me to do?"

"Just stay with me. There will be times when having Ahajas
and Dichaan near me would be tormenting. I would be . . .
sexually stimulated, and unable to do anything about it. Very
stimulated. You can't do that to me. Your scent, your touch is
different, neutral."

Thank god, she thought.

"It would be bad for me to be alone while I change. We need
others close to us, more at that time than at any other."

She wondered what it would look like with its second pair
of arms, what it would be like as a mature being. More like
Kahguyaht? Or maybe more like Jdahya and Tediin. How
much did sex determine personality among the Oankali? She
shook her head. Stupid question. She did not know how much
sex determined personality even among human beings.

"The arms," she said, "they're sexual organs, aren't they?"

"No," Nikanj told her. "They protect sexual organs: the
sensory hands."

"But . . ." She frowned. "Kahguyaht doesn't have anything
like a hand at the end of its sensory arms." In fact, it had nothing at all at the end of its sensory arms. There was only a blunt
cap of hard, cool skin—like a large callus.

"The hand is inside. Ooan will show you if you ask."

"Never mind."

It smoothed. "I'll show you myself—when I have something to show. Will you stay with me while they grow?"

Where else was she going? "Yes. Just make sure I know anything I might need to know about you and them before they start."

"Yes. I'll sleep most of the time, but still, I'll need someone there. If you're there, I'll know and I'll be all right. You . . . you might have to feed me."

"That's all right." There was nothing unusual about the way Oankali ate. Not on the surface, anyway. Several of their front teeth were pointed, but their size was well within the human range. She had, twice, on her walks, seen Oankali females extend their tongues all the way down to their throat orifices, but normally, the long gray tongues were kept inside the mouths and used as humans used tongues.

Nikanj made a sound of relief—a rubbing together of body tentacles in a way that sounded like stiff paper being crumpled. "Good," it said. "Mates know what we feel when they stay near us, they know the frustration. Sometimes they think it's funny."

Lilith was surprised to find herself smiling. "It is, sort of."

"Only for the tormentors. With you there, they'll torment me less. But before all that . . ." It stopped, aimed a loose point at her. "Before that, I'll try to find an English-speaking human for you. One as much like you as possible. Ooan will not stand in the way of your meeting one now."

8

A day, Lilith had decided long ago, was what her body said it was. Now it became what her newly improved memory said it was as well. A day was long activity, then long sleep. And now, she remembered every day that she had been awake. And she counted the days as Nikanj searched for an English-speaking human for her. It went alone to interview several. Nothing she said could induce it to take her along or at least tell her about the people it had talked to.

Finally Kahguyaht found someone. Nikanj had a look, then accepted its parent's judgment. "It will be one of the humans who has chosen to stay here," Nikanj told her.

She had expected that from what Kahguyaht had said earlier. It was still hard to believe, though. "Is it a man or a woman?" she asked.

"Male. A man."

"How . . . how could he not want to go home?"

"He's been here among us for a long time. He's only a little older than you are, but he was Awakened young and kept Awake. A Toaht family wanted him and he was willing to stay with them."

Willing? What kind of choice had they given him? Probably the same kind they had given her, and he had been years younger. Only a boy, perhaps. What was he now? What had they created from their human raw material? "Take me to him," she said.

For the second time, Lilith rode one of the flat transports through the crowded corridors. This transport moved no faster than the first one she had ridden. Nikanj did not steer it except occasionally to touch one side or the other with head tentacles to make it turn. They rode for perhaps a half hour before she and Nikanj dismounted. Nikanj touched the transport with several head tentacles to send it away.

"Won't we need it to go back?" she asked.

"We'll get another," Nikanj said. "Maybe you'll want to stay here awhile."

She looked at it sharply. What was this? Step two of the captive breeding program? She glanced around at the retreating transport. Maybe she had been too quick to agree to see this man. If he were thoroughly enough divorced from his humanity to want to stay here, who knew what else he might be willing to do.

"It's an animal," Nikanj said.

"What?"

"The thing we rode. It's an animal. A tilio. Did you know?"

"No, but I'm not surprised. How does it move?"

"On a thin film of a very slippery substance."

"Slime?"

Nikanj hesitated. "I know that word. It's . . . inadequate, but it will serve. I've seen Earth animals who use slime to move. They are inefficient compared to the tilio, but I can see similarities. We shaped the tilio from larger, more efficient creatures."

"It doesn't leave a slime trail."

"No. The tilio has an organ at its rear that collects most of what it spreads. The ship takes in the rest."

"Nikanj, do you ever build machinery? Tamper with metal and plastic instead of living things?"

"We do that when we have to. We . . . don't like it. There's no trade."

She sighed. "Where is the man? What's his name, by the way?"

"Paul Titus."

Well, that didn't tell her anything. Nikanj took her to a nearby wall and stroked it with three long head tentacles. The wall changed from off-white to dull red, but it did not open.

"What's wrong?" Lilith asked.

"Nothing. Someone will open it soon. It's better not to go in if you don't know the quarters well. Better to let the people who live there know you are waiting to go in."

"So what you did is like knocking," she said, and was about to demonstrate knocking for it when the wall began to open. There was a man on the other side, dressed only in a pair of ragged shorts.

She stared at him. A human being—tall, stocky, as dark as she was, clean shaved. He looked wrong to her at first—alien and strange, yet familiar, compelling. He was beautiful. Even if he had been bent and old, he would have been beautiful.

She glanced at Nikanj, saw that it had become statue-still. It apparently had no intention of moving or speaking soon.

"Paul Titus?" she asked.

The man opened his mouth, closed it, swallowed, nodded. "Yes," he said finally.

The sound of his voice—deep, definitely human, definitely male—fed a hunger in her. "I'm Lilith Iyapo," she said. "Did you know we were coming or is this a surprise to you?"

"Come in," he said, touching the wall opening. "I knew. And you don't know how welcome you are." He glanced at Nikanj. "Kaalnikanj oo Jdahyatediinkahguyaht aj Dinso, come in. Thank you for bringing her."

Nikanj made a complex gesture of greeting with its head tentacles and stepped into the room—the usual bare room. Nikanj went to a platform in a corner and folded itself into a sitting position on it. Lilith chose a platform that allowed her to sit almost with her back to Nikanj. She wanted to forget it was there, observing, since it clearly did not intend to do anything but observe. She wanted to give all her attention to the man. He was a miracle—a human being, an adult who spoke English and looked more than a little like one of her dead brothers.

His accent was as American as her own and her mind overflowed with questions. Where had he lived before the war? How had he survived? Who was he beyond a name? Had he seen any other humans? Had he—

"Have you really decided to stay here?" she demanded abruptly. It was not the first question she had intended to ask.

The man sat cross-legged in the middle of a platform large enough to be a serving table or a bed.

"I was fourteen when they woke me up," he said. "Everyone I knew was dead. The Oankali said they'd send me back to Earth eventually if I wanted to go. But once I had been here for a while, I knew this was where I wanted to be. There's nothing that I care about left on Earth."

"Everyone lost relatives and friends," she said. "As far as I know, I'm the only member of my family still alive."

"I saw my father, my brother—their bodies. I don't know what happened to my mother. I was dying myself when the Oankali found me. They tell me I was. I don't remember, but I believe them."

"I don't remember their finding me either." She twisted around. "Nikanj, did your people do something to us to keep us from remembering?"

Nikanj seemed to rouse itself slowly. "They had to," it said. "Humans who were allowed to remember their rescue became uncontrollable. Some died in spite of our care."

Not surprising. She tried to imagine what she had done when in the middle of the shock of realizing that her home, her family, her friends, her world were all destroyed. She was confronted with a collecting party of Oankali. She must have believed she had lost her mind. Or perhaps she did lose it for a while. It was a miracle that she had not killed herself trying to escape them.

"Have you eaten?" the man asked.

"Yes," she said, suddenly shy.

There was a long silence. "What were you before?" he asked. "I mean, did you work?"

"I had gone back to school," she said. "I was majoring in anthropology." She laughed bitterly. "I suppose I could think of this as fieldwork—but how the hell do I get out of the field?"

"Anthropology?" he said, frowning. "Oh yeah, I remember reading some stuff by Margaret Mead before the war. So you wanted to study what? People in tribes?"

"Different people anyway. People who didn't do things the way we did them."

"Where were you from?" he asked.

"Los Angeles."

"Oh, yeah. Hollywood, Beverly Hills, movie stars. . . . I always wanted to go there."

One trip would have shattered his illusions. "And you were from . . . ?"

"Denver."

"Where were you when the war started?"

"Grand Canyon—shooting the rapids. That was the first time we'd ever really done anything, gone anywhere really good. We froze afterward. And my father used to say nuclear winter was nothing but politics."

"I was in the Andes in Peru," she said, "hiking toward Machu Picchu. I hadn't been anywhere either, really. At least not since my husband—"

"You were married?"

"Yes. But he and my son . . . were killed—before the war, I mean. I had gone on a study tour of Peru. Part of going back to college. A friend talked me into taking that trip. She went too . . . and died."

"Yeah." He shrugged uncomfortably. "I was sort of looking forward to going to college myself. But I had just gotten through the tenth grade when everything blew up."

"The Oankali must have taken a lot of people out of the southern hemisphere," she said, thinking. "I mean we froze too, but I heard the southern freeze was spotty. A lot of people must have survived."

He drifted into his own thoughts. "It's funny," he said. "You started out years older than me, but I've been Awake for so long . . . I guess I'm older than you are now."

"I wonder how many people they were able to get out of the northern hemisphere—other than the soldiers and politicians whose shelters hadn't been bombed open." She turned to ask Nikanj and saw that it was gone.

"He left a couple of minutes ago," the man said. "They can move really quietly and fast when they want to."

"But—"

"Hey, don't worry. He'll come back. And if he doesn't, I can open the walls or get food for you if you want anything."

"You can?"

"Sure. They changed my body chemistry a little when I decided to stay. Now the walls open for me just like they do for them."

"Oh." She wasn't sure she liked being left with the man this way—especially if he was telling the truth. If he could open walls and she could not, she was his prisoner.

"They're probably watching us," she said. And she spoke in Oankali, imitating Nikanj's voice: "Now let's see what they'll do if they think they're alone."

The man laughed. "They probably are. Not that it matters."

"It matters to me. I'd rather have watchers where I can keep an eye on them, too."

The laughter again. "Maybe he thought we might be kind of inhibited if he stayed around."

She deliberately ignored the implications of this. "Nikanj isn't male," she said. "It's ooloi."

"Yeah, I know. But doesn't yours seem male to you?"

She thought about that. "No. I guess I've taken their word for what they are."

"When they woke me up, I thought the ooloi acted like men and women while the males and females acted like eunuchs. I never really lost the habit of thinking of ooloi as male or female."

That, Lilith thought, was a foolish way for someone who had decided to spend his life among the Oankali to think—a kind of deliberate, persistent ignorance.

"You wait until yours is mature," he said. "You'll see what I mean. They change when they've grown those two extra things." He lifted an eyebrow. "You know what those things are?"

"Yes," she said. He probably knew more, but she realized that she did not want to encourage him to talk abo~~ even Oankali sex.

"Then you know they're not arms, no matte us to call them. When those things grow in, oo know who's in charge. The Oankali need a littl men's lib up here."

She wet her lips. "It wants me to help it through its meta-morphosis."

"Help it. What did you tell it?"

"I said I would. It didn't sound like much."

He laughed. "It isn't hard. Puts them in debt to you, though. Not a bad idea to have someone powerful in debt to you. It proves you can be trusted, too. They'll be grateful and you'll be a lot freer. Maybe they'll fix things so you can open your own walls."

"Is that what happened with you?"

He moved restlessly. "Sort of." He got up from his platform, touched all ten fingers to the wall behind him, and waited as the wall opened. Behind the wall was a food storage cabinet of the kind she had often seen at home. Home? Well, what else was it? She lived there.

He took out sandwiches, something that looked like a small pie—that was a pie—and something that looked like French fries.

Lilith stared at the food in surprise. She had been content with the foods the Oankali had given her—good variety and flavor once she began staying with Nikanj's family. She had missed meat occasionally, but once the Oankali made it clear they would neither kill animals for her nor allow her to kill them while she lived with them, she had not minded much. She had never been a particular eater, had never thought of asking the Oankali to make the food they prepared look more like what she was used to.

"Sometimes," he said, "I want a hamburger so bad I dream about them. You know the kind with cheese and bacon and dill pickles and—"

"What's in your sandwich?" she asked.

"Fake meat. Mostly soybean, I guess. And quat."

Quatasayasha, the cheeselike Oankali vegetable. "I eat a lot of quat myself," she said.

"Then have some. You don't really want to sit there and watch me eat, do you?"

She smiled and took the sandwich he offered. She was not

hungry at all, but eating with him was companionable and safe. She took a few of his French fries, too.

"Cassava," he told her. "Tastes like potatoes, though. I'd never heard of cassava before I got it here. Some tropical plant the Oankali are raising."

"I know. They mean for those of us who go back to Earth to raise it and use it. You can make flour from it and use it like wheat flour."

He stared at her until she frowned. "What's the matter?" she asked.

His gaze slid away from her and he stared downward at nothing. "Have you really thought about what it will be like?" he asked softly. "I mean . . . Stone Age! Digging in the ground with a stick for roots, maybe eating bugs, rats. Rats survived, I hear. Cattle and horses didn't. Dogs didn't. But rats did."

"I know."

"You said you had a baby."

"My son. Dead."

"Yeah. Well, I'll bet when he was born, you were in a hospital with doctors and nurses all around helping you and giving you shots for the pain. How would you like to do it in a jungle with nothing around but bugs and rats and people who feel sorry for you but can't do shit to help you?"

"I had natural childbirth," she said. "It wasn't any fun, but it went okay."

"What do you mean? No painkiller?"

"None. No hospital either. Just something called a birthing center—a place for pregnant women who don't like the idea of being treated as though they were sick."

He shook his head, smiled crookedly. "I wonder how many women they had to go through before they came up with you. A lot, I'll bet. You're probably just what they want in ways I haven't even thought of."

His words bit more deeply into her than she let him see. With all the questioning and testing she had gone through, the two and a half years of round-the-clock observation—the Oankali must know her in some ways better than any human being ever had. They knew how she would react to just about everything they put her through. And they knew how to manipulate her, maneuver her into doing whatever they wanted. Of course they knew she had had certain practical experiences they considered important. If she had had an especially difficult time giving birth—if she had had to be taken to the hospital in spite of her wishes, if she had needed a caesarean—they would probably have passed over her to someone else.

"Why are you going back?" Titus asked. "Why do you want to spend your life living like a cavewoman?"

"I don't."

His eyes widened. "Then why don't you—"

"We don't have to forget what we know," she said. She smiled to herself. "I couldn't forget if I wanted to. We don't have to go back to the Stone Age. We'll have a lot of hard work, sure, but with what the Oankali will teach us and what we already know, we'll at least have a chance."

"They don't teach for free! They didn't save us out of kindness! It's all trade with them. You know what you'll have to pay down there!"

"What have you paid to stay up here?"

Silence.

He ate several more bites of food. "The price," he said softly, "is just the same. When they're finished with us there won't be any real human beings left. Not here. Not on the ground. What the bombs started, they'll finish."

"I don't believe it has to be like that."

"Yeah. But then, you haven't been Awake long."

"Earth is a big place. Even if parts of it are uninhabitable, it's still a damn big place."

He looked at her with such open, undisguised pity that she drew back angrily. "Do you think they don't know what a big place it is?" he asked.

"If I thought that, I wouldn't have said anything to you and whoever's listening. They know how I feel."

"And they know how to make you change your mind."

"Not about that. Never about that."

"Like I said, you haven't been Awake long."

What had they done to him, she wondered. Was it just that they had kept him Awake so long—Awake and for the most part without human companions? Awake and aware that everything he had ever known was dead, that nothing he could have on Earth now could measure up to his former life. How had that gone down with a fourteen-year-old?

"If you wanted it," he said, "they'd let you stay here . . . with me."

"What, permanently?"

"Yeah."

"No."

He put down the small pie that he had not offered to share with her and came over to her. "You know they expect you to say no," he said. "They brought you here so you could say it and they could be sure all over again that they were right about you." He stood tall and broad, too close to her, too intense. She realized unhappily that she was afraid of him. "Surprise them," he continued softly. "Don't do what they expect—just for once. Don't let them play you like a puppet."

He had put his hands on her shoulders. When she drew back reflexively, he held on to her in a grip that was almost painful.

She sat still and stared at him. Her mother had looked at her the way she was looking at him now. She had caught herself giving her son the same look when she thought he was doing something he knew was wrong. How much of Titus was still fourteen, still the boy the Oankali had awakened and impressed and enticed and inducted into their own ranks?

He let her go. "You could be safe here," he said softly. "Down on Earth . . . how long will you live? How long will you want to live? Even if you don't forget what you know, other people will forget. Some of them will want to be cavemen—drag you around, put you in a harem, beat the shit out of you." He shook his head. "Tell me I'm wrong. Sit there and tell me I'm wrong."

She looked away from him, realizing that he was probably

right. What was waiting for her on Earth? Misery? Subjuga-
tion? Death? Of course there were people who would toss
aside civilized restraint. Not at first, perhaps, but eventually—
as soon as they realized they could get away with it.

He took her by the shoulders again and this time tried awkwardly to kiss her. It was like what she could recall of being
kissed by an eager boy. That didn't bother her. And she caught
herself responding to him in spite of her fear. But there was
more to this than grabbing a few minutes of pleasure.

"Look," she said when he drew back. "I'm not interested in
putting on a show for the Oankali."

"What difference do they make? It's not like human beings
were watching us."

"It is to me."

"Lilith," he said, shaking his head, "they will *always* be
watching."

"The other thing I'm not interested in doing is giving them
a human child to tamper with."

"You probably already have."

Surprise and sudden fear kept her silent, but her hand
moved to her abdomen where her jacket concealed her scar.

"They didn't have enough of us for what they call a normal
trade," he said. "Most of the ones they have will be Dinso—
people who want to go back to Earth. They didn't have
enough for the Toaht. They had to make more."

"While we slept? Somehow they—"

"Somehow!" he hissed. "*Anyhow!* They took stuff from
men and women who didn't even know each other and put it
together and made babies in women who never knew the
mother or the father of their kid—and who maybe never got
to know the kid. Or maybe they grew the baby in another kind
of animal. They have animals they can adjust to—to incubate
human fetuses, as they say. Or maybe they don't even worry
about men and women. Maybe they just scrape some skin
from one person and make babies out of it—cloning, you
know. Or maybe they use one of their prints—and don't ask
me what a print is. But if they've got one of you, they can use

it to make another you even if you've been dead for a hundred years and they haven't got anything at all left of your body. And that's just the start. They can make people in ways I don't even know how to talk about. Only thing they can't do, it seems, is let us alone. Let us do it our own way."

His hands were almost gentle on her. "At least they haven't until now." He shook her abruptly. "You know how many kids I got? They say, 'Your genetic material has been used in over seventy children.' And I've never even seen a woman in all the time I've been here."

He stared at her for several seconds and she feared him and pitied him and longed to be away from him. The first human being she had seen in years and all she could do was long to be away from him.

Yet it would do no good to fight him physically. She was tall, had always thought of herself as strong, but he was much bigger—six-four, six-five, and stocky.

"They've had two hundred and fifty years to fool around with us," she said. "Maybe we can't stop them, but we don't have to help them."

"The hell with them." He tried to unfasten her jacket.

"*No!*" she shouted, deliberately startling him. "Animals get treated like this. Put a stallion and a mare together until they mate, then send them back to their owners. What do they care? They're just animals!"

He tore her jacket off then fumbled with her pants.

She threw her weight against him suddenly and managed to shove him away.

He stumbled backward for several steps, caught himself, came at her again.

Screaming at him, she swung her legs over the platform she had been sitting on and came down standing on the opposite side of it. Now it was between them. He strode around it.

She sat on it again and swung her legs over, keeping it between them.

"Don't make yourself their dog!" she pleaded. "Don't do this!"

He kept coming, too far gone to care what she said. He actually seemed to be enjoying himself. He cut her off from the bed by coming over it himself. He cornered her against a wall.

"How many times have they made you do this before?" she asked desperately. "Did you have a sister back on Earth? Would you know her now? Maybe they've made you do it with your sister."

He caught her arm, jerked her to him.

"Maybe they've made you do it with your mother!" she shouted.

He froze and she prayed she had hit a nerve.

"Your mother," she repeated. "You haven't seen her since you were fourteen. How would you know if they brought her to you and you—"

He hit her.

Staggered by shock and pain, she collapsed against him and he half pushed and half threw her away as though he had found himself clutching something loathsome.

She fell hard, but was not quite unconscious when he came to stand over her.

"I never got to do it before," he whispered. "Never once with a woman. But who knows who they mixed the stuff with." He paused, stared at her where she had fallen. "They said I could do it with you. They said you could stay here if you wanted to. And you had to go and mess it up!" He kicked her hard. The last sound she heard before she lost consciousness was his ragged, shouted curse.

9

She awoke to voices—Oankali near her, not touching her. Nikanj and one other.

"Go away now," Nikanj was saying. "She is regaining consciousness."

"Perhaps I should stay," the other said softly. Kahguyaht. She had thought once that all Oankali sounded alike with their quiet androgynous voices, but now she couldn't mistake Kahguyaht's deceptively gentle tones. "You may need help with her," it said.

Nikanj said nothing.

After a while Kahguyaht rustled its tentacles and said, "I'll leave. You're growing up faster than I thought. Perhaps she's good for you after all."

She was able to see it step through a wall and leave. Not until it was gone did she become aware of the aching of her own body—her jaw, her side, her head, and in particular, her left arm. There was no sharp pain, nothing startling. Only dull, throbbing pain, especially noticeable when she moved.

"Be still," Nikanj told her. "Your body is still healing. The pain will be gone soon."

She turned her face away from it, ignoring the pain.

There was a long silence. Finally it said, "We didn't know." It stopped, corrected itself. "I didn't know how the male would behave. He has never lost control so completely before. He hasn't lost control at all for several years."

"You cut him off from his own kind," she said through swollen lips. "You kept him away from women for how long? Fifteen years? More? In some ways you kept him fourteen for all those years."

"He was content with his Oankali family until he met you."

"What did he know? You never let him see anybody else!"

"It wasn't necessary. His family took care of him."

She stared at it, feeling more strongly than ever, the difference between them—the unbridgeable alienness of Nikanj. She could spend hours talking to it in its own language and fail to communicate. It could do the same with her, although it could force her to obey whether she understood or not. Or it could turn her over to others who would use force against her.

"His family thought you should have mated with him," it

said. "They knew you wouldn't stay with him permanently, but they believed you would share sex with him at least once."

Share sex, she thought sadly. Where had it picked up that expression? She had never said it. She liked it, though. Should she have shared sex with Paul Titus? "And maybe gotten pregnant," she said aloud.

"You would not have gotten pregnant," Nikanj said.

And it had her full attention. "Why not?" she demanded.

"It isn't time for you to have children yet."

"Have you done something to me? Am I sterile?"

"Your people called it birth control. You are slightly changed. It was done while you slept, as it was done to all humans at first. It will be undone eventually."

"When?" she asked bitterly. "When you're ready to breed me?"

"No. When you're ready. Only then."

"Who decides? You?"

"You, Lilith. You."

have a decision "agency"

Its sincerity confused her. She felt that she had learned to read its emotions through posture, sensory tentacle position, tone of voice. . . . It seemed not only to be telling the truth—as usual—but to be telling a truth it considered important. Yet Paul Titus, too, had seemed to be telling the truth. "Does Paul really have over seventy children?" she asked.

"Yes. And he's told you why. The Toaht desperately need more of your kind to make a true trade. Most humans taken from Earth must be returned to it. But Toaht must have at least an equal number stay here. It seemed best that the ones born here be the ones to stay." Nikanj hesitated. "They should not have told Paul what they were doing. But that's always a difficult thing to realize—and sometimes we realize it too late."

"He had a right to know!"

"Knowing frightened him and made him miserable. You discovered one of his fears—that perhaps one of his female relatives had survived and been impregnated with his sperm. He's been told that this did not happen. Sometimes he believes; sometimes he doesn't."

"He still had a right to know. I would want to know."

Silence.

"Has it been done to me, Nikanj?"

"No."

"And . . . will it be?"

It hesitated, then spoke softly. "The Toaht have a print of you—of every human we brought aboard. They need the genetic diversity. We're keeping prints of the humans they take away, too. Millenia after your death, your body might be reborn aboard the ship. It won't be you. It will develop an identity of its own."

"A clone," she said tonelessly. Her left arm throbbed, and she rubbed it without actually focusing on the pain.

"No," Nikanj said. "What we've preserved of you isn't living tissue. It's memory. A gene map, your people might call it—though they couldn't have made one like those we remember and use. It's more like what they would call a mental blueprint. A plan for the assembly of one specific human being: You. A tool for reconstruction."

It let her digest this, said nothing more to her for several minutes. So few humans could do that—just let someone have a few minutes to think.

"Will you destroy my print if I ask you to?" she asked.

"It's a memory, Lilith, a complete memory carried by several people. How would I destroy such a thing?"

A literal memory, then, not some kind of mechanical recording or written record. Of course.

After a while, Nikanj said, "Your print may never be used. And if it is, the reconstruction will be as much at home aboard the ship as you were on Earth. She'll grow up here and the people she grows up among will be her people. You know they won't harm her."

She sighed. "I don't know any such thing. I suspect they'll do what they think is best for her. Heaven help her."

It sat beside her and touched her aching left arm with several head tentacles. "Did you really need to know that?" it asked. "Should I have told you?"

It had never asked such a question before. Her arm hurt more than ever for a moment, then felt warm and pain-free. She managed not to jerk away, though Nikanj had not paralyzed her.

"What are you doing?" she asked.

"You were having pain in that arm. There's no need for you to suffer."

"I hurt all over."

"I know. I'll take care of it. I just wanted to talk to you before you slept again."

She lay still for a moment, glad that the arm was no longer throbbing. She had barely been aware of this individual pain before Nikanj stopped it. Now she realized it had been among the worst of the many. The hand, the wrist, the lower arm.

"You had a bone broken in your wrist," Nikanj told her. "It will be completely healed by the time you awaken again." And it repeated its question. "Did you really need to know, Lilith?"

"Yes," she said. "It concerned me. I needed to know."

It said nothing for a while and she did not disturb its thoughts. "I will remember that," it said softly, finally.

And she felt as though she had communicated something important. Finally.

"How did you know my arm was bothering me?"

"I could see you rubbing it. I knew it was broken and that I had done very little to it. Can you move your fingers?"

She obeyed, amazed to see the fingers move easily, painlessly.

"Good. I'll have to make you sleep again now."

"Nikanj, what happened to Paul?"

It shifted the focus of some of its head tentacles from her arm to her face. "He's asleep."

She frowned. "Why? I didn't hurt him. I couldn't have."

"He was . . . enraged. Out of control. He attacked members of his family. They say he would have killed them if he could have. When they restrained him, he wept and spoke incoherently. He refused to speak Oankali at all. In English, he cursed his family, you, everyone. He had to be put to sleep—perhaps for a year or more. The long sleeps are healing to nonphysical wounds."

"A year . . . ?"

"He'll be all right. He won't age. And his family will be waiting for him when he Awakes. He is very attached to them—and they to him. Toaht family bonds are . . . beautiful, and very strong."

She rested her right arm across her forehead. "His family," she said bitterly. "You keep saying that. His *family* is dead! Like mine. Like Fukumoto's. Like just about everyone's. That's half our problem. We haven't got any real family bonds."

"He has."

"He has *nothing!* He has no one to teach him to be a man, and he damn sure can't be an Oankali, so don't talk to me about his family!"

"Yet they are his family," Nikanj insisted softly. "They have accepted him and he has accepted them. He has no other family, but he has them."

She made a sound of disgust and turned her face away. What did Nikanj tell others about her? Did it talk about her family? According to her new name, she had been adopted, after all. She shook her head, confused and disturbed.

"He beat you, Lilith," Nikanj said. "He broke your bones. If you had gone untreated, you might have died of what he did."

"He did what you and his so-called family set him up to do!"

It rustled its tentacles. "That's truer than I would like. It's hard for me to influence people now. They think I'm too young to understand. I did warn them, though, that you wouldn't mate with him. Since I'm not yet mature, they didn't believe me. His family and my parents overruled me. That won't happen again."

It touched the back of her neck, pricking the skin with several sensory tentacles. She realized what it was doing as she felt herself beginning to lose consciousness.

"Put me back, too," she demanded while she could still talk.

"Let me sleep again. Put me where they've put him. I'm no more what your people think than he was. Put me back. Find someone else!"

10

But the ease of her awakening, when it came, told her that her sleep had been ordinary and relatively brief, returning her all too quickly to what passed for reality. At least she was not in pain.

She sat up, found Nikanj lying stone-still next to her. As usual, some of its head tentacles followed her movements lazily as she got up and went to the bathroom.

Trying not to think, she bathed, worked to scrub off an odd, sour smell that her body had acquired—some residual effect of Nikanj's healing, she supposed. But the smell would not wash away. Eventually she gave up. She dressed and went back out to Nikanj. It was sitting up on the bed, waiting for her.

"You won't notice the smell in a few days," it said. "It isn't as strong as you think."

She shrugged, not caring.

"You can open walls now."

Startled, she stared at it, then went to a wall and touched it with the fingertips of one hand. The wall reddened as Paul Titus' wall had under Nikanj's touch.

"Use all your fingers," it told her.

She obeyed, touching the fingers of both hands to the wall. The wall indented, then began to open.

"If you're hungry," Nikanj said, "you can get food for yourself now. Within these quarters, everything will open for you."

"And beyond these quarters?" she asked.

"The walls will let you out and back in again. I've changed them a little too. But no other walls will open for you."

So she could walk the corridors or walk among the trees, but she couldn't get into anything Nikanj didn't want her in. Still, that was more freedom than she had had before it put her to sleep.

"Why did you do this?" she asked, staring at it.

"To give you what I could. Not another long sleep or solitude. Only this. You know the layout of the quarters now, and you know Kaal. And the people nearby know you."

So she could be trusted out alone again, she thought bitterly. And within the quarters, she could be depended on not to do the local equivalent of spilling the drain-cleaner or starting a fire. She could even be trusted not to annoy the neighbors. Now she could keep herself occupied until someone decided it was time to send her off to the work she did not want and could not do—the work that would probably get her killed. How many more Paul Tituses could she survive, after all?

Nikanj lay down again and seemed to tremble. It was trembling. Its body tentacles exaggerated the movement and made its whole body seem to vibrate. She neither knew nor cared what was wrong with it. She left it where it was and went out to get food.

In one compartment in the seemingly empty little living-room-dining-room-kitchen, she found fresh fruit: oranges, bananas, mangoes, papayas, and melons of different kinds. In other compartments she found nuts, bread, and honey.

Picking and choosing, she made herself a meal. She had intended to take it outside, to eat—the first meal she had not had to ask for or wait for. The first meal she would eat under the pseudotrees without first having to be let out like a pet animal.

She opened a wall to go out, then stopped. The wall began to close after a moment. She sighed and turned away from it.

Angrily, she reopened the food compartments, took out extra food and went back in to Nikanj. It was still lying down, still trembling. She put a few pieces of fruit down next to it.

"Your sensory arms have already begun, haven't they?" she asked.

"Yes."

"Do you want anything to eat?"

"Yes." It took an orange and bit into it, eating skin and all. It hadn't done that before.

"We generally peel them," she said.

"I know. Wasteful."

"Look, do you need anything? Want me to find one of your parents?"

"No. This is normal. I'm glad I changed you when I did. I wouldn't trust myself to do it now. I knew this was coming."

"Why didn't you tell me it was so close?"

"You were too angry."

She sighed, tried to understand her own feelings. She was still angry—angry, bitter, frightened . . .

And yet she had come back. She had not been able to leave Nikanj trembling in its bed while she enjoyed her greater freedom.

Nikanj finished the orange and began on a banana. It did not peel this either.

"Can I see?" she asked.

It raised one arm, displaying ugly, lumpy, mottled flesh perhaps six inches beneath the arm.

"Does it hurt?"

"No. There isn't a word in English for the way it makes me feel. The closest would be . . . sexually aroused."

She stepped away from it, alarmed.

"Thank you for coming back."

She nodded. "You're not supposed to feel aroused with just me here."

"I'm becoming sexually mature. I'll feel this way from time to time as my body changes even though I don't yet have the organs I would use in sex. It's a little like feeling an amputated limb as though it were still there. I've heard humans do that."

"I've heard that we do, too, but—"

"I would feel aroused if I were alone. You don't make me feel it any more than I would if I were alone. Yet your presence helps me." It drew its head and body tentacles into knots. "Give me something else to eat."

She gave it a papaya and all the nuts she had brought in. It ate them quickly.

"Better," it said. "Eating dulls the feeling sometimes."

She sat down on the bed and asked, "What happens now?"

"When my parents realize what's happening to me, they'll send for Ahajas and Dichaan."

"Do you want me to look for them—your parents, I mean?"

"No." It rubbed the bed platform beneath its body. "The walls will alert them. Probably they already have. Wall tissues respond to beginning metamorphosis very quickly."

"You mean the walls will feel different or smell different or something?"

"Yes."

"Yes, what? Which one?"

"All that you said, and more." It changed the subject abruptly. "Lilith, sleep during metamorphosis can be very deep. Don't be afraid if sometimes I don't seem to see or hear."

"All right."

"You'll stay with me?"

"I said I would."

"I was afraid . . . good. Lie here with me until Ahajas and Dichaan come."

She was tired of lying down, but she stretched out beside it.

"When they come to carry me to Lo, you help them. That will tell them the first thing they need to know about you."

11

Leavetaking.

There was no real ceremony. Ahajas and Dichaan arrived and Nikanj immediately retreated into a deep sleep. Even its head tentacles hung limp and still.

Ahajas alone could have carried it. She was big like most Oankali females—slightly larger than Tediin. She and Dichaan were brother and sister as usual in Oankali matings. Males and females were closely related and ooloi were outsiders. One translation of the world *ooloi* was "treasured strangers." According to Nikanj, this combination of relatives and strangers served best when people were bred for specific work—like opening a trade with an alien species. The male and female concentrated desirable characteristics and the ooloi prevented the wrong kind of concentrations. Tediin and Jdahya were cousins. They had both not particularly liked their siblings. Unusual.

Now Ahajas lifted Nikanj as though it were a young child and held it easily until Dichaan and Lilith took its shoulders. Neither Ahajas nor Dichaan showed surprise at Lilith's participation.

"It has told us about you," Ahajas said as they carried Nikanj down to the lower corridors. Kahguyaht preceded them, opening walls. Jdahya and Tediin followed.

"It's told me a little about you, too," Lilith replied uncertainly. Things were moving too fast for her. She had not gotten up that day with the idea that she would be leaving Kaal—leaving Jdahya and Tediin who had become comfortable and familiar to her. She did not mind leaving Kahguyaht, but it had told her when it brought Ahajas and Dichaan to Nikanj that it would be seeing her again soon. Custom and biology dictated that as same-sex parent, Kahguyaht was permitted to visit Nikanj during its metamorphosis. Kahguyaht, like Lilith, smelled neutral and could not increase Nikanj's discomfort or stir inappropriate desires in it.

Lilith helped to arrange Nikanj on the flat tilio that sat waiting for them in a public corridor. Then she stood alone, watching as the five conscious Oankali came together, touching and entangling head and body tentacles. Kahguyaht stood between Tediin and Jdahya. Ahajas and Dichaan stood together and made their contacts with Tediin and Jdahya. It was almost as though they were avoiding Kahguyaht too. The Oankali could

communicate this way, could pass messages from one to another almost at the speed of thought—or so Nikanj had said.
Controlled multisensory stimulation. Lilith suspected it was
the closest thing to telepathy she would ever see practiced.
Nikanj had said it might be able to help her perceive this way
when it was mature. But its maturity was months away. Now
she was alone again—the alien, the uncomprehending outsider.
That was what she would be again in the home of Ahajas and
Dichaan.

When the group broke up, Tediin came over to Lilith, took
both Lilith's arms. "It has been good having you with us," she
said in Oankali. "I've learned from you. It's been a good
trade."

"I've learned too," Lilith said honestly. "I wish I could stay
here." Rather than go with strangers. Rather than be sent to
teach a lot of frightened, suspicious humans.

"No," Tediin said. "Nikanj must go. You would not like to
be separated from it."

She had nothing to say to that. It was true. Everyone, even
Paul Titus inadvertently, had pushed her toward Nikanj. They
had succeeded.

Tediin let her go and Jdahya came to speak to her in English.
"Are you afraid?" he asked.

"Yes," she said.

"Ahajas and Dichaan will welcome you. You're rare—a
human who can live among us, learn about us, and teach us.
Everyone is curious about you."

"I thought I would be spending most of my time with
Nikanj."

"You will be, for a while. And when Nikanj is mature, you'll
be taken for training. But there'll be time for you to get to
know Ahajas and Dichaan and others."

She shrugged. Nothing he said settled her nervousness now.

"Dichaan has said he would adjust the walls of their home
to you so that you can open them. He and Ahajas can't change
you in any way, but they can adjust your new surroundings."

So at least she wouldn't have to go back to the house pet

stage, asking every time she wanted to enter or leave a room or eat a snack. "I'm grateful for that, at least," she said.

"It's trade," Jdahya said. "Stay close to Nikanj. Do what it has trusted you to do."

12

Kahguyaht came to see her a few days later. She had been installed in the usual bare room, this one with one bed and two table platforms, a bathroom, and Nikanj who slept so much and so deeply that it too seemed part of the room rather than a living being.

Kahguyaht was almost welcome. It relieved her boredom, and, to her surprise, it brought gifts: a block of tough, thin, white paper—more than a ream—and a handful of pens that said Paper Mate, Parker, and Bic. The pens, Kahguyaht said, had been duplicated from prints taken of centuries-gone originals. This was the first time she had seen anything she knew to be a print re-creation. And it was the first time she had realized that the Oankali re-created nonliving things from prints. She could find no difference between the print copies and the remembered originals.

And Kahguyaht gave her a few brittle, yellowed books—treasures she had not imagined: A spy novel, a Civil War novel, an ethnology textbook, a study of religion, a book about cancer and one about human genetics, a book about an ape being taught sign language and one about the space race of the 1960s.

Lilith accepted them all without comment.

Now that it knew she was serious about looking after Nikanj, it was easier to get along with, more likely to answer if she asked it a question, less ready with its own sarcastic rhetorical questions. It returned several times to sit with her as she attended Nikanj and, in fact, became her teacher, using its body and Nikanj's to help her understand more of Oankali biology. Nikanj slept through most of this. Most often it slept so deeply that its head tentacles did not follow movement.

"It will remember all that happens around it," Kahguyaht said. "It still perceives in all the ways that it would if it were awake. But it cannot respond now. It is not aware now. It is . . . recording." Kahguyaht lifted one of Nikanj's limp arms to observe the development of the sensory arms. There was nothing to be seen yet but a large, dark, lumpy swelling—a frightening-looking growth.

"Is that the arm itself," she asked, "or will the arm come out of that?"

"That is the arm," Kahguyaht said. "While it's growing, don't touch it unless Nikanj asks you to."

It did not look like anything Lilith would want to touch. She looked at Kahguyaht and decided to take a chance on its new civility. "What about the sensory hand?" she asked. "Nikanj mentioned that there was such a thing."

Kahguyaht said nothing for several seconds. Finally, in a tone she could not interpret, it said, "Yes. There is such a thing."

"If I've asked something that I shouldn't, just tell me," she said. Something about that odd tone of voice made her want to move away from it, but she kept still.

"You haven't," Kahguyaht said, its voice neutral now. "In fact, it's important that you know about the . . . sensory hand." It extended one of its sensory arms, long and gray and rough-skinned, still reminding her of a blunt, closed elephant's trunk. "All the strength and resistance to harm of this outer covering is to protect the hand and its related organs," it said. "The arm is closed, you see?" It showed her the rounded tip of the arm, capped by a semitransparent material that she knew was smooth and hard.

"When it's like this, it's merely another limb." Kahguyaht coiled the end of the arm, wormlike, reached out, touched

Lilith's head, then held before her eyes a single strand of hair, pulled straight in a twist of the arm. "It is very flexible, very versatile, but only another limb." The arm drew back from Lilith, releasing the hair. The semitransparent material at the end began to change, to move in circular waves away to the sides of the tip and something slender and pale emerged from the center of the tip. As she watched, the slender thing seemed to thicken and divide. There were eight fingers—or rather, eight slender tentacles arranged around a circular palm that looked wet and deeply lined. It was like a starfish—one of the brittle stars with long, slender, snakelike arms.

"How does it seem to you?" Kahguyaht asked.

"On Earth, we had animals that looked like that," she replied. "They lived in the seas. We called them starfish."

Kahguyaht smoothed its tentacles. "I've seen them. There is a similarity." It turned the hand so that she could see it from different angles. The palm, she realized, was covered with tiny projections very like the tube feet of a starfish. They were almost transparent. And the lines she had seen on the palm were actually orifices—openings to a dark interior.

There was a faint odor to the hand—oddly flowery. Lilith did not like it and drew back from it after a moment of looking.

Kahguyaht retracted the hand so quickly that it seemed to vanish. It lowered the sensory arm. "Humans and Oankali tend to bond to one ooloi," it told her. "The bond is chemical and not strong in you now because of Nikanj's immaturity. That's why my scent makes you uncomfortable."

"Nikanj didn't mention anything like that," she said suspiciously.

"It healed your injuries. It improved your memory. It couldn't do those things without leaving its mark. It should have told you."

"Yes. It should have. What is this mark? What will it do to me?"

"No harm. You'll want to avoid deep contact—contact that involves penetration of the flesh—with other ooloi, you un-

derstand? Perhaps for a while after Nikanj matures, you'll
want to avoid all contact with most people. Follow your feelings. People will understand."

"But . . . how long will it last?"

"It's different with humans. Some linger in the avoidance
stage much longer than we would. The longest I've known it
to last is forty days."

"And during that time, Ahajas and Dichaan—"

"You won't avoid them, Lilith. They're part of the household. You'll be comfortable with them."

"What happens if I don't avoid people, if I ignore my feelings?"

"If you managed to do that, you'd make yourself sick, at
least. You might manage to kill yourself."

". . . that bad."

"Your body will tell you what to do. Don't worry." It shifted
its attention to Nikanj. "Nikanj will be most vulnerable when
the sensory hands begin to grow. It will need a special food
then. I'll show you."

"All right."

"You'll actually have to put the food into its mouth."

"I've already done that with the few things it's wanted to
eat."

"Good." Kahguyaht rustled its tentacles. "I didn't want to
accept you, Lilith. Not for Nikanj or for the work you'll do. I
believed that because of the way human genetics were expressed in culture, a human male should be chosen to parent
the first group. I think now that I was wrong."

"Parent?"

"That's the way we think of it. To teach, to give comfort, to
feed and clothe, to guide them through and interpret what will
be, for them, a new and frightening world. To parent."

"You're going to set me up as their *mother*?"

"Define the relationship in any way that's comfortable to
you. We have always called it parenting." It turned toward a
wall as though to open it, then stopped, faced Lilith again. "It's
a good thing that you'll be doing. You'll be in a position to

help your own people in much the same way you're helping Nikanj now."

"They won't trust me or my help. They'll probably kill me."

"They won't."

"You don't understand us as well as you think you do."

"And you don't understand us at all. You never will, really, though you'll be given much more information about us."

"Then put me back to sleep, dammit, and choose someone you think is brighter! I never wanted this job!"

It was silent for several seconds. Finally, it said, "Do you really believe I was disparaging your intelligence?"

She glared at it, refusing to answer.

"I thought not. Your children will know us, Lilith. You never will."

III

NURSERY

1

The room was slightly larger than a football field. Its ceiling was a vault of soft, yellow light. Lilith had caused two walls to grow at a corner of it so that she had a room, enclosed except for a doorway where the walls would have met. There were times when she brought the walls together, sealing herself away from the empty vastness outside—away from the decisions she must make. The walls and floor of the great room were hers to reshape as she pleased. They would do anything she was able to ask of them except let her out.

She had erected her cubicle enclosing the doorway of a bathroom. There were eleven more bathrooms unused along one long wall. Except for the narrow, open doorways of these facilities, the great room was featureless. Its walls were pale green and its floors pale brown. Lilith had asked for color and Nikanj had found someone who could teach it how to induce the ship to produce color. Stores of food and clothing were encapsulated within the walls in various unmarked cabinets within Lilith's room and at both ends of the great room.

The food, she had been told, would be replaced as it was used—replaced by the ship itself which drew on its own substance to make print reconstructions of whatever each cabinet had been taught to produce.

The long wall opposite the bathrooms concealed eighty sleeping human beings—healthy, under fifty, English-speaking, and frighteningly ignorant of what was in store for them.

Lilith was to choose and Awaken no fewer than forty. No wall would open to let her or those she Awakened out until at least forty human beings were ready to meet the Oankali.

The great room was darkening slightly. Evening. Lilith found surprising comfort and relief in having time divided visibly into days and nights again. She had not realized how she had missed the slow change of light, how welcome the darkness would be.

"It's time for you to get used to having planetary night again," Nikanj had told her.

On impulse, she had asked if there were anywhere in the ship where she could look at the stars.

Nikanj had taken her, on the day before it put her into this huge, empty room, down several corridors and ramps, then by way of something very like an elevator. Nikanj said it corresponded closer to a gas bubble moving harmlessly through a living body. Her destination turned out to be a kind of observation bubble through which she could see not only stars, but the disk of the Earth, gleaming like a full moon in the black sky.

"We're still beyond the orbit of your world's satellite," it told her as she searched hungrily for familiar continental outlines. She believed she had found a few of them—part of Africa and the Arabian peninsula. Or that was what it looked like, hanging there in the middle of a sky that was both above and beneath her feet. There were more stars out there than she had ever seen, but it was Earth that drew her gaze. Nikanj let her look at it until her own tears blinded her. Then it wrapped a sensory arm around her and led her to the great room.

She had been in the great room alone for three days now, thinking, reading, writing her thoughts. All her books, papers, and pens had been left for her. With them were eighty dossiers—short biographies made up of transcribed conversations, brief histories, Oankali observations and conclusions, and pictures. The human subjects of the dossiers had no living relatives. They were all strangers to one another and to Lilith.

She had read just over half the dossiers, searching not only for likely people to Awaken, but for a few potential allies—people she could Awaken first and perhaps come to trust. She needed to share the burden of what she knew, what she must do. She needed thoughtful people who would hear what she had to say and not do anything violent or stupid. She needed people who could give her ideas, push her mind in directions she might otherwise miss. She needed people who could tell her when they thought she was being a fool—people whose arguments she could respect.

On another level, she did not want to Awaken anyone. She was afraid of these people, and afraid for them. There were so many unknowns, in spite of the information in the dossiers. Her job was to weave them into a cohesive unit and prepare them for the Oankali—prepare them to be the Oankali's new trade partners. That was impossible.

How could she Awaken people and tell them they were to be part of the genetic engineering scheme of a species so alien that the humans would not be able to look at it comfortably for a while? How would she Awaken these people, these survivors of war, and tell them that unless they could escape the Oankali, their children would not be human?

Better to tell them little or none of that for a while. Better not to Awaken them at all until she had some idea how to help them, how not to betray them, how to get them to accept their captivity, accept the Oankali, accept anything until they were sent to Earth. Then to run like hell at the first opportunity.

Her mind slipped into the familiar track: There was no escape from the ship. None at all. The Oankali controlled the ship with their own body chemistry. There were no controls that could be memorized or subverted. Even the shuttles that traveled between Earth and the ship were like extensions of Oankali bodies.

No human could do anything aboard the ship except make trouble and be put back into suspended animation—or be killed. Therefore, the only hope was Earth. Once they were on Earth—somewhere in the Amazon basin, she had been told—they would at least have a chance.

That meant they must control themselves, learn all she could teach them, all the Oankali could teach them, then use what they had learned to escape and keep themselves alive.

What if she could make them understand that? And what if
it turned out that that was exactly what the Oankali wanted
her to do? Of course, they knew it was what she *would* do.
They knew her. Did that mean they were planning their own
betrayal: No trip to Earth. No chance to run. Then why had
they made her spend a year being taught to live in a tropical
forest? Perhaps the Oankali were simply very certain of their
ability to keep humans corralled even on Earth.

What could she do? What could she tell the humans but
"Learn and Run!" What other possibility for escape was
there?

None at all. Her only other personal possibility was to
refuse to Awaken anyone—hold out until the Oankali gave up
on her and went looking for a more cooperative subject. Another Paul Titus, perhaps—someone who had truly given up
on humanity and cast his lot with the Oankali. A man like that
could make Titus' predictions self-fulfilling. He could under-
mine what little civilization might be left in the minds of those
he Awoke. He could make them a gang. Or a herd.

What would she make them?

She lay on her bed platform, staring at a picture of a man.
Five-seven, his statistics said. One hundred and forty pounds,
thirty-two years old, missing the third, fourth, and fifth fingers
of his left hand. He had lost the fingers in a childhood accident
with a lawn mower, and he was self-conscious about the incomplete hand. His name was Victor Dominic—Vidor
Domonkos, really. His parents had come to the United States
from Hungary just before he was born. He had been a lawyer.
The Oankali suspected he had been a good one. They had
found him intelligent, talkative, understandably suspicious of
unseen questioners, and very creative at lying to them. He had
probed constantly for their identity, but was, like Lilith, one of
the few native English-speakers who had never expressed the
suspicion that they might be extraterrestrials.

He had been married three times already, but had fathered
no children due to a biological problem the Oankali believed
they had corrected. Not fathering children had bothered him

intensely, and he had blamed his wives, all the while refusing to see a doctor himself.

Apart from this, the Oankali had found him reasonable and formidable. He had never broken down in his unexplained solitary confinement, had never wept or attempted suicide. He had, however, promised to kill his captors if he ever got the chance. He had said this only once, calmly, more as though he were making a casual remark than as though he were seriously threatening murder.

Yet his Oankali interrogator had been disturbed by the words, and had put Victor Dominic back to sleep at once.

Lilith liked the man. He had brains and, except for the foolishness with his wives, self-control—exactly what she needed. But she also feared him.

What if he decided she was one of his captors? She was bigger, and now certainly stronger than he was, but that did not have to matter. He would have too many chances to attack when she was off guard.

Better to Awaken him later when she had allies. She put his dossier to one side on the smaller of two piles—people she definitely wanted, but did not dare to Awaken first. She sighed and picked up a new dossier.

Leah Bede. Quiet, religious, slow—slow-moving, not slow-witted, though the Oankali had not been particularly impressed by her intelligence. It was her patience and self-sufficiency that had impressed them. They had not been able to make her obey. She had outwaited them in stolid silence. Outwaited Oankali! She had starved herself almost to death when they stopped feeding her to coerce her cooperation. Finally, they had drugged her, gotten the information they wanted, and, after a period of letting her regain weight and strength, they had put her back to sleep. Why, Lilith wondered. Why hadn't the Oankali not simply drugged her as soon as they realized she was stubborn? Why had they not drugged Lilith herself? Perhaps because they wanted to see how far human beings had to be pushed before they broke. Perhaps they even wanted to see *how* each individual broke. Or per-

haps the Oankali version of stubbornness was so extreme from
a human point of view that very few humans tried their patience. Lilith had not. Leah had.

The photo of Leah was a pale, lean, tired-looking woman,
though an ooloi had noted that she had a physiological tendency to be heavy.

Lilith hesitated, then put Leah's folder atop Victor's. Leah,
too, sounded like a good potential ally, but not a good one to
Awaken first. She sounded as though she could be an intensely
loyal friend—unless she got the idea Lilith was one of her captors.

Anyone Lilith Awakened might get that idea—almost certainly would get it the moment Lilith opened a wall or caused
new walls to grow, thus proving she had abilities they did not.
The Oankali had given her information, increased physical
strength, enhanced memory, and an ability to control the walls
and the suspended animation plants. These were her tools.
And every one of them would make her seem less human.

"What else shall we give you?" Ahajas had asked her when
Lilith saw her last. Ahajas had worried about her, found her
too small to be impressive. She had discovered that humans
were impressed by size. The fact that Lilith was taller and
heavier than most women seemed not enough. She was not
taller and heavier than most men. But there was nothing to be
done about it.

"Nothing you could give me would be enough," Lilith had
answered.

Dichaan had heard this and come over to take Lilith's hands.
"You want to live," he told her. "You won't squander your
life."

They were squandering her life.

She picked up the next folder and opened it.

Joseph Li-Chin Shing. A widower whose wife had died before the war. The Oankali had found him quietly grateful for
that. After his own period of stubborn silence, he had discovered that he didn't mind talking to them. He seemed to accept
the reality that his life was, as he said, "on hold" until he

found out what had happened in the world and who was running things now. He constantly probed for answers to these questions. He admitted that he remembered deciding, not long after the war, that it was time for him to die. He believed that he had been captured before he could attempt suicide. Now, he said, he had reason to live—to see who had caged him and why and how he might want to repay them.

He was forty years old, a small man, once an engineer, a citizen of Canada, born in Hong Kong. The Oankali had considered making him a parent of one of the human groups they meant to establish. But they had been put off by his threat. It was, the Oankali questioner thought, soft, but potentially quite deadly. Yet the Oankali recommended him to her—to any first parent. He was intelligent, they said, and steady. Someone who could be depended on.

Nothing special about his looks, Lilith thought. He was a small, ordinary man, yet the Oankali had been very interested in him. And the threat he had made was surprisingly conservative—deadly only if Joseph did not like what he found out. He would not like it, Lilith thought. But he would also be bright enough to realize that the time to do something about it would be when they were all on the ground, not while they were caged in the ship.

Lilith's first impulse was to Awaken Joseph Shing—Awaken him at once and end her solitude. The impulse was so strong that she sat still for several moments, hugging herself, holding herself rigid against it. She had promised herself that she would not Awaken anyone until she had read all the dossiers, until she had had time to think. Following the wrong impulse now could kill her.

She went through several more dossiers without finding anyone she thought compared with Joseph, though some of the people she found would definitely be Awakened.

There was a woman named Celene Ivers who had spent much of her short interrogation period crying over the death of her husband and her twin daughters, or crying over her own unexplained captivity and her uncertain future. She had wished herself dead over and over, but had never made any attempt at suicide. The Oankali had found her very pliable, eager to please—or rather, fearful of displeasing. Weak, the Oankali had said. Weak and sorrowing, not stupid, but so easily frightened that she could be induced to behave stupidly.

Harmless, Lilith thought. One person who would not be a threat, no matter how strongly she suspected Lilith of being her jailer.

There was Gabriel Rinaldi, an actor, who had confused the Oankali utterly for a while because he played roles for them instead of letting them see him as he was. He was another they had finally stopped feeding on the theory that sooner or later hunger would bring out the true man. They were not entirely sure that it had. Gabriel must have been good. He was also very good-looking. He had never tried to harm himself or threatened to harm the Oankali. And for some reason, they had never drugged him. He was, the Oankali said, twenty-seven, thin, physically stronger than he looked, stubborn and not as bright as he liked to think.

That last, Lilith thought, could be said of most people. Gabriel, like the others who had defeated or come near defeating the Oankali, was potentially valuable. She did wonder whether she would ever be able to trust Gabriel, but his dossier remained with those she meant to Awaken.

There was Beatrice Dwyer who had been completely unreachable while she was naked, but whom clothing had transformed into a bright, likable person who seemed actually to have made a friend of her interrogator. That interrogator, an experienced ooloi, had attempted to have Beatrice accepted as a first parent. Other interrogators had observed her and disagreed for no stated reason. Maybe it was just the woman's extreme physical modesty. Nevertheless, one ooloi had been completely won over.

There was Hilary Ballard, poet, artist, playwright, actress, singer, frequent collector of unemployment compensation. She really was bright; she had memorized poetry, plays, songs—her own and those of more established writers. She had something that would help future human children remember who they were. The Oankali thought she was unstable, but not dangerously so. They had had to drug her because she injured herself trying to break free of what she called her cage. She had broken both her arms.

And that was not dangerously unstable?

No, it probably was not. Lilith herself had panicked at being caged. So had a great many other people. Hilary's panic had simply been more extreme than most. She probably should not be given crucial work to do. The survival of the group should never depend on her—but then it should not depend on any one person. The fact that it did was not the fault of human beings.

There was Conrad Loehr—called Curt—who had been a cop in New York, and who had survived only because his wife had finally dragged him off to Colombia where her family lived. They had not gone anywhere for years before that. The wife had been killed in one of the riots that began shortly after the last missile exchange. Thousands had been killed even before it began to get cold. Thousands had simply trampled one another or torn one another apart in panic. Curt had been picked up with seven children, none of them his own, whom he had been guarding. His own four children, left back in the States with his relatives, were all dead. Curt Loehr, the Oankali said, needed people to look after. People stabilized him, gave him purpose. Without them, he might have been a criminal—or dead. He had, alone in his isolation room, done his best to tear out his own throat with his fingernails.

Derick Wolski had been working in Australia. He was single, twenty-three, had no strong idea what he wanted to do with his life, had done nothing so far except go to school and work at temporary or part-time jobs. He'd fried hamburgers, driven a delivery truck, done construction work, sold household products door to door—badly—bagged groceries, helped clean office buildings, and on his own, done some nature photography. He'd quit everything except the photography. He liked the outdoors, liked animals. His father thought that sort of thing was nonsense, and he had been afraid his father might be right. Yet, he had been photographing Australian wildlife when the war began.

Tate Marah had just quit another job. She had some genetic problem that the Oankali had controlled, but not cured. But her real problem seemed to be that she did things so well that she quickly became bored. Or she did them so badly that she abandoned them before anyone noticed her incompetence. People had to see her as a formidable presence, bright, dominant, well off.

Her family had had money—had owned a very successful real estate business. Part of her problem, the Oankali believed, was that she did not *have* to do anything. She had great energy, but needed some external pressure, some challenge to force her to focus it.

How about the preservation of the human species?

She had attempted suicide twice before the war. After the war, she fought to live. She had been alone, vacationing in Rio de Janeiro when war came. It had not been a good time to be a North American, she felt, but she had survived and managed to help others. She had that in common with Curt Loehr. Under Oankali interrogation, she had engaged in verbal fencing and game playing that eventually exasperated the ooloi questioner. But in the end, the ooloi had admired her. It thought she was more like an ooloi than like a female. She was good at manipulating people—could do it in ways they did not seem to mind. That had bored her too in the past. But boredom had not driven her to do harm to anyone except herself. There had been times when she withdrew from people to protect them from the possible consequences of her own frustration. She had withdrawn from several men this way, occasionally pairing them off with female friends. Couples she brought together tended to marry.

Lilith put Tate Marah's dossier down slowly, left it by itself on the bed. The only other one that was by itself was Joseph Shing's. Tate's dossier fell open, once again displaying the woman's small, pale, deceptively childlike face. The face was smiling slightly, not as though posing for a picture, but as though sizing up the photographer. In fact, Tate had not known the picture was being made. And the pictures were not photographs. They were paintings, impressions of the inner person as well as the outer physical reality. Each contained print memories of their subjects. Oankali interrogators had painted these pictures with sensory tentacles or sensory arms, using deliberately produced bodily fluids. Lilith knew this, but the pictures looked like, even felt like photos. They had been done on some kind of plastic, not on paper. The pictures looked alive enough to speak. In each one, there was nothing except the head and shoulders of the subject against a gray background. None of them had that blank, wanted-poster look that snapshots could have produced. These pictures had a lot to say even to non-Oankali observers about who their subjects were—or who the Oankali thought they were.

Tate Marah, they thought, was bright, somewhat flexible, and not dangerous except perhaps to the ego.

Lilith left the dossiers, left her private cubicle, and began building another near it.

The walls that would not open to let her out responded to her touch now by growing inward along a line of her sweat or saliva drawn along the floor. Thus the old walls extruded new ones, and the new ones would open or close, advance or retreat as she directed. Nikanj had made very sure she knew how to direct them. And when it finished instructing her, its mates, Dichaan and Ahajas, told her to seal herself in if her people attacked her. They had both spent time interrogating isolated humans and they seemed more worried about her than Nikanj did. They would get her out, they promised. They would not leave her to die for someone else's miscalculation.

Which was fine if she could spot the trouble and seal herself in in time.

Better to choose the right people, bring them along slowly, and Awaken new ones only when she was sure of the ones already Awake.

She drew two walls to within about eighteen inches of each

other. That left a narrow doorway—one that would preserve as much privacy as possible without a door. She also turned one wall inward, forming a tiny entrance hall that concealed the room itself from casual glances. There would be nothing among the people she Awoke to borrow or steal, and anyone who thought now was a good time to play Peeping Tom would have to be disciplined by the group. Lilith might be strong enough now to handle troublemakers herself, but she did not want to do that unless she had to. It would not help the people become a community, and if they could not unite, nothing else they did would matter.

Within the new room, Lilith raised a bed platform, a table platform, and three chair platforms around the table. The table and chairs would be at least a small change from what they were all used to in the Oankali isolation rooms. A more human arrangement.

Creating the room took some time. Afterward Lilith gathered all but eleven of the dossiers and sealed them inside her own table platform. Some of these eleven would be her core group, first Awake, and first to show her just how much of a chance she had to survive and do what was necessary.

Tate Marah first. Another woman. No sexual tension.

Lilith took the picture, went to the long, featureless stretch of wall opposite the rest rooms and stood for a moment, staring at the face.

Once people were Awake, she would have no choice but to live with them. She could not put them to sleep again. And in some ways, Tate Marah would probably be hard to live with.

Lilith rubbed her hand across the surface of the picture, then placed the picture flat against the wall. She began at one end of the wall and walked slowly toward the other, far away, keeping the face of the picture against the wall. She closed her eyes as she moved, remembering that it had been easier when she practiced this with Nikanj if she ignored her other senses as much as possible. All her attention should be focused on the hand that held the picture flat against the wall. Male and female Oankali did this with head tentacles. Oankali did it with their sensory arms. Both did it from memory, without pictures impregnated with prints. Once they read someone's print or examined someone and took a print, they remembered it, could duplicate it. Lilith would never be able to read prints or duplicate them. That required Oankali organs of perception. Her children would have them, Kahguyaht had said.

She stopped now and then to rub one sweaty hand over the picture, renewing her own chemical signature.

More than halfway down the hall, she began to feel a response, a slight bulging of the surface against the picture, against her hand.

She stopped at once, not certain at first that she had felt anything at all. Then the bulge was unmistakable. She pressed against it lightly, maintaining the contact until the wall began to open beneath the picture. Then she drew back to let the wall disgorge its long, green plant. She went to a space at one end of the great room, opened a wall, and took out a jacket and a pair of pants. These people would probably welcome clothing as eagerly as she had.

The plant lay, writhing slowly, still surrounded by the foul odor that had followed it through the wall. She could not see well enough through its thick, fleshy body to know which end concealed Tate Marah's head, but that did not matter. She drew her hands along the length of the plant as though unzipping it, and it began to come apart.

There was no possibility this time of the plant trying to swallow her. She would be no more palatable to it now than Nikanj would.

Slowly, the face and body of Tate Marah became visible. Small breasts. Figure like that of a girl who had barely reached puberty. Pale, translucent skin and hair. Child's face. Yet Tate was twenty-seven.

She would not awaken until she was lifted completely clear of the suspended animation plant. Her body was wet and slippery, but not heavy. Sighing, Lilith lifted her clear.

2

Get away from me!" Tate said the moment she opened her eyes. "Who are you? What are you doing?"

"Trying to get you dressed," Lilith said. "You can do it yourself now—if you're strong enough."

Tate was beginning to tremble, beginning to react to being awakened from suspended animation. It was surprising that she had been able to speak her few coherent words before succumbing to the reaction.

Tate made a tight, shuddering fetal knot of her body and lay moaning. She gasped several times, gulping air as she might have gulped water.

"Shit!" she whispered minutes later when the reaction began to wane. "Oh shit. It wasn't a dream, I see."

"Finish dressing," Lilith told her. "You knew it wasn't a dream."

Tate looked up at Lilith, then down at her own half naked body. Lilith had managed to get pants on her, but had only gotten one of her arms into the jacket. She had managed to work that arm free as she suffered through the reaction. She picked up the jacket, put it on, and in a moment, had discovered how to close it. Then she turned to watch silently as Lilith closed the plant, opened the wall nearest to it, and pushed the plant through. In seconds the only sign left of it was a rapidly drying spot on the floor.

"And in spite of all that," Lilith said, facing Tate, "I'm a prisoner just as you are."

"More like a trustee," Tate said quietly.

"More like. I have to Awaken at least thirty-nine more people before any of us are allowed out of this room. I chose to start with you."

"Why?" She was incredibly self-possessed—or seemed to be. She had only been Awakened twice before—average among people not chosen to parent a group—but she behaved almost as though nothing unusual were happening. That was a relief to Lilith, a vindication of her choice of Tate.

"Why did I begin with you?" Lilith said. "You seemed least likely to try to kill me, least likely to fall apart, and most likely to be able to help with the others as they Awaken."

Tate seemed to think about that. She fiddled with her jacket, reexamining the way the front panels adhered to one another, the way they pulled apart. She felt the material itself, frowning.

"Where the hell are we?" she asked.

"Some distance beyond the orbit of the moon."

Silence. Then finally, "What was that big green slug-thing you pushed into the wall?"

"A . . . a plant. Our captors—our rescuers—use them for keeping people in suspended animation. You were in the one you saw. I took you out of it."

"Suspended animation?"

"For over two hundred and fifty years. The Earth is just about ready to have us back now."

"We're going back!"

"Yes."

Tate looked around at the vast, empty room. "Back to what?"

"Tropical forest. Somewhere in the Amazon basin. There are no more cities."

"No. I didn't think there would be." She drew a deep breath. "When are we fed?"

"I put some food in your room before I Awoke you. Come on."

Tate followed. "I'm hungry enough to eat even that plaster of Paris garbage they served me when I was Awake before."

"No more plaster. Fruit, nuts, a kind of stew, bread, something like cheese, coconut milk . . ."

"Meat? A steak?"

"You can't have everything."

Tate was too good to be true. Lilith worried for a moment

that at some point she would break—begin to cry or be sick or scream or beat her head against the wall—lose that seemingly easy control. But whatever happened to her, Lilith would try to help. Just these few minutes of apparent normality were worth a great deal of trouble. She was actually speaking with and being understood by another human being—*after so long.*

Tate dove into the food, eating until she was satisfied, not wasting time talking. She had not, Lilith thought, asked one very important question. Of course there was a great deal she had not asked, but one thing in particular made Lilith wonder.

"What's your name, by the way?" Tate asked, finally resting from her eating. She sipped coconut milk tentatively, then drank it all.

"Lilith Iyapo."

"Lilith. Lil?"

"Lilith, I've never had a nickname. Never wanted one. Is there anything apart from your name that you'd like to be called?"

"No. Tate will do. Tate Marah. They told you my name, didn't they?"

"Yes."

"I thought so. All those damn questions. They kept me Awake and in solitary for . . . it must have been two or three months. Did they tell you that? Or were you watching?"

"I was either asleep or in solitary myself, but yes, I knew about your confinement. It was three months in all. Mine was just over two years."

"It took them that long to make a trustee of you, did it?"

Lilith frowned, took a few nuts and ate them. "What do you mean by that?" she asked.

For an instant, Tate looked uncomfortable, uncertain. The expression appeared and vanished so quickly that Lilith could have missed it through just a moment's inattention.

"Well, why should they keep you awake and alone for so long?" Tate demanded.

"I wouldn't talk to them at first. Then later when I began to talk, apparently a number of them were interested in me. They weren't trying to make a trustee of me at that point. They were trying to decide whether I was fit to be one. If I had had a vote, I'd still be asleep."

"Why wouldn't you talk to them? Were you military?"

"God, no. I just didn't like the idea of being locked up, questioned, and ordered around by I-didn't-know-who. And Tate, it's time you knew who—even though you've been careful not to ask."

She drew a deep breath, rested her forehead on her hand and stared down at the table. "I asked them. They wouldn't tell me. After a while I got scared and stopped asking."

"Yeah. I did that too."

"Are they . . . Russians?"

"They're not human."

Tate did not move, did not say anything for so long that Lilith continued.

"They call themselves Oankali, and they look like sea creatures, though they are bipedal. They . . . are you taking any of this in?"

"I'm listening."

Lilith hesitated. "Are you believing?"

Tate looked up at her, seemed to smile a little. "How can I?"

Lilith nodded. "Yeah. But you'll have to sooner or later, of course, and I'm supposed to do what I can to prepare you. The Oankali are ugly. Grotesque. But we can get used to them, and they won't hurt us. Remember that. Maybe it will help when the time comes."

3

For three days, Tate slept a great deal, ate a great deal, and asked questions that Lilith answered completely honestly. Tate also talked about her life before the war. Lilith saw that it seemed to relax her, ease that shell of emotional control she usually wore. That made it worthwhile. It meant Lilith felt obligated to talk a little about herself—her past before the war—something she would not normally have been inclined to do. She had learned to keep her sanity by accepting things as she found them, adapting herself to new circumstances by putting aside the old ones whose memories might overwhelm her. She had tried to talk to Nikanj about humans in general, only occasionally bringing in personal anecdotes. Her father, her brothers, her sister, her husband and son. . . . She chose now to talk about her return to college.

"Anthropology," Tate said disparagingly. "Why did you want to snoop through other people's cultures? Couldn't you find what you wanted in your own?"

Lilith smiled and noticed that Tate frowned as though this were the beginning of a wrong answer. "I started out wanting to do exactly that," Lilith said. "Snoop. Seek. It seemed to me that my culture—ours—was running headlong over a cliff. And, of course, as it turned out, it was. I thought there must be saner ways of life."

"Find any?"

"Didn't have much of a chance. It wouldn't have mattered much anyway. It was the cultures of the U.S. and the U.S.S.R. that counted."

"I wonder."

"What?"

"Human beings are more alike than different—damn sure more alike than we like to admit. I wonder if the same thing wouldn't have happened eventually, no matter which two cultures gained the ability to wipe one another out along with the rest of the world."

Lilith gave a bitter laugh. "You might like it here. The Oankali think a lot like you do."

Tate turned away, suddenly disturbed. She wandered over to look at the new third and fourth rooms Lilith had grown on either side of the second restroom. One of them was back to back with her own room, and in part, an extension of one of her walls. She had watched the walls growing—watched first with disbelief, then anger, refusing to believe she was not being tricked somehow. Then she began to keep her distance from Lilith, to watch Lilith suspiciously, to be jumpy and silent.

That had not lasted long. Tate was adaptable if nothing else. "I don't understand," she had said softly, though by then, Lilith had explained why she could control the walls, how she could find and Awaken specific individuals.

Now, Tate wandered back and said again, "I don't understand. None of this makes sense!"

"I had an easier time believing," Lilith said. "An Oankali sealed himself in my isolation room and refused to leave until I got used to him. You can't look at them and doubt that they're alien."

"Maybe *you* can't."

"I won't argue with you about it. I've been Awake a lot longer than you have. I've lived among the Oankali and I accept them as what they are."

"What they say they are."

Lilith shrugged. "I want to start Awakening more people. Two new ones today. Will you help me?"

"Who are you Awakening?"

"Leah Bede and Celene Iver."

"Two more women? Why don't you wake up a man?"

"I will eventually."

"You're still thinking about your Paul Titus, aren't you?"

"He wasn't mine." She wished she had not told Tate about him.

"Awaken a man next, Lilith. Awaken the guy who was found protecting the kids."

Lilith turned to look at her. "On the theory that if you fall off a horse, you should immediately get back on?"

"Yes."

"Tate, once he's Awake, he stays Awake. He's six-three, he weighs two-twenty, he's been a cop for seven years, and he's used to ordering people around. He can't save us or protect us

here, but he can damn sure screw us up. All he has to do to
hurt us is refuse to believe we're on a ship. After that, everything he does will be wrong and potentially deadly."

"So what? You're going to wait until you can Awaken him
to a kind of harem?"

"No. Once we've got Leah and Celene awake and reason-
ably stable, I'm going to Awaken Curt Loehr and Joseph
Shing."

"Why wait?"

"I'm going to get Celene out first. You take care of her while
I get Leah out. I think Celene might be someone for Curt to
take care of."

She went to her room, brought back pictures of both
women, and was about to begin hunting for Celene when Tate
caught her arm.

"We're being watched, aren't we?" she asked.

"Yes. I don't know that we're watched every minute, but
now, when we're both Awake, yes, I'm sure they're watching."

"If there's trouble, will they help?"

"If they decide it's bad enough. I think there were some who
would have let Titus rape me. I don't think they would have let
him kill me. They might have been too slow to prevent it,
though."

"Wonderful," Tate muttered bitterly. "We're on our own."

"Exactly."

Tate shook her head. "I don't know whether I should be
shedding the constraints of civilization and getting ready to
fight for my life or keeping and enhancing them for the sake of
our future."

"We'll do what's necessary," Lilith said. "Sooner or later,
that will probably mean fighting for our lives."

"I hope you're wrong," Tate said. "What have we learned if
all we can do now is go on fighting among ourselves?" She
paused. "You didn't have kids, did you Lilith?"

Lilith began to walk slowly along the wall, eyes closed, Celene's picture flat between the wall and her hand. Tate walked
along beside her, distracting her.

"Wait until I call you," Lilith told her. "Searching like this takes all my attention."

"It's really hard for you to talk about your life before, isn't it?" Tate said, with sympathy Lilith did not begin to trust.

"Pointless," Lilith said. "Not hard. I lived in those memories for my two years of solitary. By the time the Oankali showed up in my room, I was ready to move into the present and stay there. My life before was a lot of groping around, looking for I-didn't-know-what. And, as for kids, I had a son. He was killed in an auto accident before the war." Lilith took a deep breath. "Let me alone now. I'll call you when I've found Celene."

Tate moved away, settled against the opposite wall near one of the rest rooms. Lilith closed her eyes and began inching along again. She let herself lose track of time and distance, felt as though she were almost flowing along the wall. The illusion was familiar—as physically pleasing and emotionally satisfying as a drug—a needed drug at this moment.

"If you have to do something, it might as well feel good," Nikanj had told her. It had become very interested in her physical pleasures and pains once its sensory arms were fully grown. Happily, it had paid more attention to pleasure than to pain. It had studied her as she might have studied a book—and it had done a certain amount of rewriting.

The bulge in the wall felt large and distinct when her fingers found it. But when she opened her eyes and looked, she could not see any irregularity.

"There's nothing there!" Tate said over her right shoulder.

Lilith jumped, dropped the picture, refused to turn and glare at Tate as she bent to pick it up. "Get away from me!" she said quietly.

Grudgingly, Tate moved back several steps. Lilith could have found the spot again without any particular concentration, without having Tate move away, but Tate had to learn to accept Lilith's authority in anything to do with controlling the walls or dealing with the Oankali and their ship. What the hell

did she think she was doing, coming back, creeping along behind Lilith? What was she looking for? Some trick?

Lilith rubbed one hand on the face of the picture and placed
it against the wall. She found the bulge at once, though it was
still too slight to be seen. It had ceased to grow with the removal of the picture, but had not yet vanished. Now Lilith
rubbed it gently with the picture, encouraging it to grow.
When she could see the protrusion, she stepped away and
waited, gesturing for Tate to come.

Standing together, they watched the wall disgorge the long,
translucent green plant. Tate made a sound of disgust and
stepped back as the smell drifted to her.

"You want to look at it before I open it?" Lilith asked.

Tate came closer and stared at the plant. "Why is it moving?"

"So that every part of it is exposed to the light for a while.
If you could mark it, you would see that it's very slowly turning over. The movement is supposed to be good for the people
inside, too. It exercises their muscles and changes their position."

"It doesn't really look like a slug," Tate said. "Not when
someone's in it." She went to it, stroked it with several fingers,
then looked at her fingers.

"Be careful," Lilith told her. "Celene isn't very big. The
plant probably wouldn't mind taking someone else in."

"Would you be able to get me out?"

"Yes." She smiled. "The first Oankali to show these to me
didn't warn me. I put my hand on the plant and almost panicked when I realized the plant was holding me and growing
around my hand."

Tate tried this, and the plant obligingly began to swallow
her hand. She tugged at her hand, then looked at Lilith, obviously afraid. "Make it let go!"

Lilith touched the plant around her captive hand and the
plant released her. "Now," Lilith said, moving to one end of
the plant. She drew her hands along the length of the plant. It

opened in its usual slow way, and she lifted Celene out and put her on the floor where Tate could look after her.

"Get some clothes on her before she wakes up if you can," she told Tate.

But by the time Celene was fully awake, Lilith had Leah Bede out of the wall and out of her plant. She dressed Leah quickly. Not until both women were fully awake and looking around did Lilith push the two plants back through the wall. When that was done, she turned, meaning to sit down with Leah and Celene and answer their questions.

Instead, she was suddenly staggered by Leah's weight as the woman leaped onto her back and began strangling her. Lilith began to fall. Time seemed to slow down for her.

If she fell on Leah, the woman would probably injure her back or her head. The injury might be only superficial, but could be serious. It would be wrong to let a potentially useful person be lost for one act of stupidity.

Lilith managed to fall on her side so that only Leah's arm and shoulder struck the floor. Lilith reached up and took Leah's hands from her throat. It was not difficult. Lilith was even able to go on taking care not to cause injury. She also took care not to let Leah see how easy it was for Lilith to defeat her. She gasped as she tore Leah's hands from her throat, though she was nowhere near desperate for air yet. And she allowed Leah's hands to move in her own as Leah struggled.

"Will you stop it!" she shouted. "I'm a prisoner here just like you. I can't let you out. I can't get out myself. Do you understand?"

Leah stopped struggling. Now she glared up at Lilith. "Get off me." Her voice was naturally deep and throaty. Now it was almost a growl.

"I intend to," Lilith said. "But don't jump me again. I'm not your enemy."

Leah made a wordless sound.

"Save your strength," Lilith said. "We've got a lot of rebuilding to do."

"Rebuilding?" Leah growled.

"The war," Lilith said. "Remember?"

"I wish I could forget." The growl had softened.

"You kill me here and you'll prove you haven't had enough war. You'll prove you're not fit to take part in the rebuilding."

Leah said nothing. After a moment, Lilith released her.

Both women stood up warily.

"Who decides whether or not I'm fit?" Leah asked. "You?"

"Our jailers."

Unexpectedly, Celene whispered, "Who are they?" Her face was already streaked with tears. She and Tate had come up silently to join the discussion—or watch the fight.

Lilith glanced at Tate, and Tate shook her head. "And you were afraid Awakening a man would cause violence," she said.

"I still am," Lilith told her. She looked at Celene, then Leah. "Let's get something to eat. I'll answer any questions I can."

She took them to the room that would be Celene's and watched their eyes widen when they saw, not the expected bowls of god-knew-what, but recognizable food.

It was easier to talk to them when they'd eaten their fill, when they were relatively relaxed and comfortable. They refused to believe they were on a ship beyond the moon's orbit. Leah laughed aloud when she heard that they were being held by extraterrestrials.

"Either you're a liar or you're crazy," she said.

"It's true," Lilith said softly.

"It's crap."

"The Oankali modified me," Lilith told her, "so that I can control the walls and the suspended animation plants. I can't do it as well as they can, but I can Awaken people, feed them, clothe them, and give them a certain amount of privacy. You shouldn't get so wrapped up in doubting me that you ignore the things you see me do. And remember two things in particular that I've told you. We are on a ship. Act as though you believe that even if you don't. There is no place to run on a ship. Even if you could get out of this room, there would be nowhere to go, nowhere to hide, nowhere to be free. On the other hand, if we endure our time here, we'll get our world back. We'll be put down on Earth as the first of the returning human colonists."

"Just do as we're told and wait, huh?" Leah said.

"Unless you like it here well enough to stay."

"I don't believe a word you say."

"Believe what you want! I'm telling you how to act if you ever want to feel the ground under your feet again!"

Celene began to cry quietly and Lilith frowned at her. "What's the matter with you?"

Celene shook her head. "I don't know what to believe. I don't even know why I'm still alive."

Tate sighed and shook her head in disgust.

"You are alive," Lilith said coldly. "We have no medical supplies here. If you want to commit suicide, you might succeed. If you want to hang around and help get things started back on Earth . . . well, that seems a lot more worth succeeding at."

"Did you have any children?" Celene asked, clearly expecting the answer to be no.

"Yes," Lilith made herself reach out, take the woman's hand, though already she disliked her. "All the people I have to Awaken are here without their families. We're all alone. We've got each other, and nobody else. We'll become a community—friends, neighbors, husbands, wives—or we won't."

"When will there be men?" Celene demanded.

"In a day or two. I'll Awaken two men next."

"Why not now?"

"No. I'll get rooms ready for them, get food and clothing out for them—the way I have for you and Leah."

"You mean you build the rooms?"

"It's more accurate to say I grow them. You'll see."

"You grow the food, too?" Leah asked, one eyebrow raised.

"Food and clothing is stored along the walls at each end of the big room. They're replaced as we use them. I can open the storage cabinets, but I can't open the wall behind them. Only the Oankali can do that."

There was silence for a moment. Lilith began gathering her

own fruit peelings and seeds. "Any garbage goes into one of the toilets," she said. "You don't have to worry about stopping them up. They're more than they appear to be. They'll digest anything that isn't alive."

"Digest!" Celene said, horrified. "They . . . they're alive themselves?"

"Yes. The ship is alive and so is almost everything in it. The Oankali use living matter the way we used machinery." She started away toward the nearest bathroom, then stopped. "The other thing I meant to tell you," she said focusing on Leah and Celene, "is that we're being watched—just as we were all watched in our isolation rooms. I don't think the Oankali will bother us this time—not until forty or more of us are Awake and getting along fairly well together. They will come in, though, if we start to murder each other. And the would-be murderers—or actual murderers—will be kept here on the ship for the rest of their lives."

"So you're protected from us," Leah said. "Convenient."

"We're protected from one another," Lilith said. "We're an endangered species—almost extinct. If we're going to survive, we need protection."

4

Lilith did not release Curt Loehr from his suspended animation plant until Joseph Shing's plant lay beside it. Then, quickly, she opened both plants, lifted Joseph out and dragged Loehr out. She set Leah and Tate to work dressing Curt and worked alone to dress Joseph since Celene would not touch him while he was naked. Both men were fully clothed by the time they struggled to full consciousness.

After the initial misery of Awakening, they sat up and

looked around. "Where are we?" Curt demanded. "Who's in charge here?"

Lilith winced. "I am," she said. "I Awoke you. We're all prisoners here, but it's my job to Awaken people."

"And who are you working for?" Joseph demanded. He had a slight accent and Curt, hearing it, turned to stare, then to glare at him.

Lilith introduced them quickly. "Conrad Loehr of New York, this is Joseph Shing of Vancouver." Then she introduced each of the women.

Celene had already settled close to Curt, and once she was introduced, she added: "Back when things were normal, everyone called me Cele."

Tate rolled her eyes and Leah frowned. Lilith managed not to smile. She had been right about Celene. Celene would put herself under Curt's protection if he let her. That would keep Curt occupied. Lilith caught a faint smile on Joseph's face.

"We have food if you two are hungry," Lilith said, slipping into what was becoming a standard speech. "While we eat, I'll answer your questions."

"One answer now," Curt said. His question: "Who are you working for? Which side?"

He had not seen her push his suspended animation plant back into the wall. She had not turned her back on him since he had been fully Awake.

"Down on Earth," she said carefully, "there are no people left to draw lines on maps and say which sides of those lines are the right sides. There is no government left. No human government, anyway."

He frowned, then glared at her as he had earlier at Joseph. "You're saying we've been captured by . . . something that isn't human?"

"Or rescued," Lilith said.

Joseph stepped up to her. "You've seen them?"

Lilith nodded.

"You believed they are extraterrestrials?"

"Yes."

"And you believe we are on some kind of . . . what? Space ship?"

"A very, very large one, almost like a small world."

"What proof can you show us?"

"Nothing that you couldn't perceive as a trick if you wanted to."

"Please show us anyway."

She nodded, not minding. Each pair or group of new people would have to be handled slightly differently. She explained what she could of the changes that had been made in her body chemistry, then, with both men watching, she grew another room. Twice she stopped to allow them to inspect the walls. She said nothing when they attempted to control the walls as she did, and then attempted to break them. The living tissue of the walls resisted them, ignored them. Their strength was meaningless. Finally they watched silently as Lilith completed the room.

"It's like the stuff my cell was made of when I was Awake before," Curt said. "What the hell is it? Some kind of plastic?"

"Living matter," Lilith said. "More plant than animal." She let their surprised silence last for a moment, then led them into the room where she and Leah had left the food. Tate was already there, eating a hot rice and bean dish.

Celene handed Curt one of the large edible bowls of food and Lilith offered one to Joseph. But Joseph kept focused on the subject of the living ship. He refused to eat himself or let Lilith eat in peace until he knew everything she did about the way the ship worked. He seemed annoyed that she knew so little.

"Do you believe what she says?" Leah asked him when he finally gave up the interrogation and tasted his cold food.

"I believe that Lilith believes," he said. "I haven't decided yet what I believe." He paused. "It does seem important, though, for us to behave as though we are in a ship—unless we find out for certain that we aren't. A ship in space could be an excellent prison even if we could get out of this room."

Lilith nodded gratefully. "That's it," she said. "That's what's important. If we endure this place, behave as though it's a ship no matter what anyone thinks individually, we can survive here until we're sent to Earth."

And she went on to tell them about the Oankali, about the plan to reseed Earth with human communities. Then she told them about the gene trade because she had decided they must know. If she waited too long to tell them, they might feel betrayed by her silence. But telling them now gave them plenty of time to reject the idea, then slowly begin to think about it and realize what it could mean.

Tate and Leah laughed at her, refused absolutely to believe that any manipulation of DNA could mix humans with extraterrestrial aliens.

"As far as I know," Lilith told them, "I haven't seen any human-Oankali combinations. But because of the things I *have* seen, because of the changes the Oankali have made in *me*, I believe they can tamper with us genetically, and I believe they intend to. Whether they'll blend with us or destroy us . . . that I don't know."

"Well, I haven't seen *anything*," Curt said. He had been quiet for a long time, listening, slipping his arm around Celene when she sat near him and looked frightened. "Until I do see something—and I don't mean more moving walls—this is all bullshit."

"I'm not sure I'd believe no matter what I saw," Tate said.

"It isn't hard to believe our captors intend to do some kind of genetic tampering," Joseph said. "They could do that whether they were human or extraterrestrial. There was a lot of work being done in genetics before the war. That may have devolved into some kind of eugenics program afterward. Hitler might have done something like that after World War Two if he had had the technology and if he had survived." He took a deep breath. "I think our best bet now is to learn all we can. Get facts. Keep our eyes open. Then later we can make the best possible use of any opportunities we might have to escape."

Learn and run, Lilith thought almost gleefully. She could have hugged Joseph. Instead, she took a bite of her cold food.

5

Two days later when Lilith saw that Curt was not likely to cause trouble—at least, not soon—she Awakened Gabriel Rinaldi and Beatrice Dwyer. She asked Joseph to help her with Gabriel and turned Beatrice over to Leah and Curt. Celene was still useless when it came to getting people dressed and oriented. Tate was apparently becoming bored with the process of Awakening people.

"I think we ought to double our numbers every time," she told Lilith. "That way we go through less repetition, get things done faster, get down to Earth faster."

At least now she was beginning to accept the idea that she was not already on Earth, Lilith thought. That was something.

"I'm probably already Awakening people too fast," Lilith told her. "We've got to be able to work together before we reach Earth. It isn't enough for us just to refrain from killing one another. Down in the forest, we'll probably be more interdependent than most of us have ever been. We might be a little better at that if we give each new set of people time to fit in and a growing structure to fit into."

"What structure?" Tate began to smile. "You mean like a family . . . with you as Mama?"

Lilith only looked at her.

After a time, Tate shrugged. "Just wake up a group of them, sit them down, tell them what's going on—they won't believe you, of course—take questions, feed them, and the next day, start on the next batch. Quick and easy. They can't learn to work together if they aren't Awake."

"I've always heard that small classes worked better than large ones," Lilith said. "This is too important to rush."

The argument ended as Lilith's arguments with Tate usually ended. No resolution. Lilith continued to Awaken people slowly and Tate continued to disapprove.

After three days, Beatrice Dwyer and Gabriel Rinaldi seemed to be settling in. Gabriel paired with Tate. Beatrice avoided the men sexually, but joined in the endless discussions of their situation, first refusing to believe it, then finally accepting it along with the group's learn-and-run philosophy.

Now, Lilith decided, was the time to Awaken two more people. She Awoke two every two or three days, no longer worrying about Awakening men since there had been no real trouble. She did deliberately Awaken a few more women than men in the hope of minimizing violence.

But as the number of people grew, so did the potential for disagreement. There were several short, vicious fist-fights. Lilith tried to keep out of them, allowing people to sort things out for themselves. Her only concern was that the fights do no serous harm. Curt helped with this in spite of his cynicism. Once as they pulled two struggling, bleeding men apart, he told her she might have made a pretty good cop.

There was one fight that Lilith could not keep out of—one begun for a foolish reason as usual. A large, angry, not particularly bright woman named Jean Pelerin demanded an end to the meatless diet. She wanted meat, she wanted it *now*, and Lilith had better produce it if she knew what was good for her.

Everyone else had accepted, however grudgingly, the absence of meat. "The Oankali don't eat it," Lilith had told them. "And because we can get along without it, they won't give it to us. They say once we're back on Earth, we'll be free to keep and kill animals again—though the ones we're used to are mostly extinct."

Nobody liked the idea. So far she had not Awakened a single voluntary vegetarian. But until Jean Pelerin, no one had tried to do anything about it.

Jean lunged at Lilith, punching, kicking, obviously intending to overwhelm at once.

Surprised, but far from overwhelmed, Lilith struck back. Two short, quick jabs.

Jean collapsed, unconscious, bleeding from her mouth.

Frightened, still angry, Lilith checked to see that the woman was breathing and not badly hurt. She stayed with her until Jean had regained consciousness enough to glare at Lilith. Then, without a word, Lilith left her.

Lilith went to her room, sat thinking for a few moments about the strength Nikanj had given her. She had pulled her punches, not intending to knock Jean unconscious. She was no longer concerned about Jean now, but it bothered her that she no longer knew her own strength. She could kill someone by accident. She could maim someone. Jean did not know how lucky she was with her headache and her split lip.

Lilith slipped to the floor, took off her jacket, and began doing exercises to burn off excess energy and emotion. Everyone knew she exercised. Several other people had begun doing it as well. For Lilith, it was a comfortable, mindless activity that gave her something to do when there was nothing she could do about her situation.

Some people would attack her. She had probably not yet experienced the worst of them. She might have to kill. They might kill her. People who accepted her now might turn away from her if she seriously injured or killed someone.

On the other hand, what could she do? She had to defend herself. What would people say if she had beaten a man as easily as she beat Jean? Nikanj had said she could do it. How long would it be before someone forced her to find out for sure?

"May I come in?"

Lilith stopped her exercising, put her jacket on, and said, "Come."

She was still seated on the floor, breathing deeply, perversely enjoying the slight ache in her muscles when Joseph Shing came around her new curving entrance-hall partition and into the room. She leaned against the bed platform and looked up at him. Because it was him, she smiled.

"You aren't hurt at all?" he asked.

She shook her head. "A couple of bruises."

He sat down next to her. "She's telling people you're a man. She says only a man can fight that way."

To her own surprise, Lilith laughed aloud.

"Some people aren't laughing," he said. "That new man, Van Weerden said he didn't think you were human at all."

She stared at him, then got up to go out, but he caught her hand and held it.

"It's all right. They're not standing out there muttering to themselves and believing fantasy. In fact, I don't think Van Weerden really believes it. They only want someone to focus their frustration on."

"I don't want to be that someone," she muttered.

"What choice have you?"

"I know." She sighed. She let him pull her down beside him again. She found it impossible to delude herself when he was around. This caused her enough pain sometimes to make her wonder why she encouraged him to stay around. Tate, with typical malice, had said, "He's old, he's short, and he's ugly. Haven't you got any discrimination at all?"

"He's forty," Lilith had said. "He doesn't seem ugly to me, and if he can deal with my size, I can deal with his."

"You could do better."

"I'm content." She never told Tate that she had almost made Joseph the first person she Awakened. She shook her head over Tate's halfhearted attempts to lure Joseph away. It wasn't as though Tate wanted him. She just wanted to prove she could have him—and in the process, try him out. Joseph seemed to find the whole sequence funny. Other people were less relaxed about similar situations. That caused some of the most savage fights. An increasing number of bored, caged humans could not help finding destructive things to do.

"You know," she told him, "you could become a target

yourself. Some people could decide to take their anger at me out on you."

"I know kung fu," he said examining her bruised knuckles.

"Do you really?"

He smiled. "No, just a little tai chi for exercise. Not so much sweating."

She decided he was telling her she smelled—which she did. She started to get up to go wash, but he would not let her go.

"Can you talk to them?" he asked.

She looked at him. He was growing a thin black beard. All the men were growing beards since no razors had been provided. Nothing hard or sharp had been provided.

"You mean talk to the Oankali?" she asked.

"Yes."

"They hear us all the time."

"But if you ask for something, will they provide it?"

"Probably not. I think it was a major concession for them just to give us all clothing."

"Yes. I thought you might say that. Then you should do what Tate wants you to do. Awaken a large number of people at once. There's too little to do here. Get people busy helping one another, teaching one another. There are fourteen of us now. Awaken ten more tomorrow."

Lilith shook her head. "Ten? But—"

"It will take some of the negative attention off you. Busy people have less time for fantasizing and fighting."

She moved away from his side to sit facing him. "What is it, Joe? What's wrong?"

"People being people, that's all. You're probably not in any danger now, but you will be soon. You must know that."

She nodded.

"When there are forty of us, will the Oankali take us out of here or—"

"When there are forty of us, and the Oankali decide we're ready, they'll come in. Eventually, they'll take us to be taught to live on Earth. They have a . . . an area of the ship that they've made over into a fragment of Earth. They've grown a small tropical forest there—like the forest we'll be sent to on Earth. We'll be trained there."

"You've seen this place?"

"I spent a year there."

"Why?"

"First learning, then proving I'd learned. Knowing and using the knowledge aren't the same thing."

"No." He thought for a moment. "The presence of the Oankali will bring them together, but it might turn them even more strongly against you. Especially if the Oankali really scare them."

"The Oankali will scare them."

"That bad?"

"That alien. That ugly. That powerful."

"Then . . . don't come into the forest with us. Try to get out of it."

She smiled sadly. "I speak their language, Joe, but I've never yet been able to convince them to change one of their decisions."

"Try, Lilith!"

His intensity surprised her. Had he really seen something she had missed—something he wouldn't tell her? Or was he simply understanding her position for the first time? She had known for a long time that she might be doomed. She had had time to get used to the idea and to understand that she must struggle not against nonhuman aliens, but against her own kind.

"Will you talk to them?" Joseph asked.

She had to think for a moment to realize he meant the Oankali. She nodded. "I'll do what I can," she said. "You and Tate may be right about Awakening people faster, too. I think I'm ready to try that."

"Good. You have a fair core group around you. The new ones you Awaken can work things out in the forest. There they should have more to do."

"Oh, they'll have plenty to do. The tedium of some of it, though . . . wait until I teach you to weave a basket or a hammock or to make your own garden tools and use them to grow your food."

"We'll do what's necessary," he said. "If we can't, then we won't survive." He paused, looked away from her. "I've been a city man all my life. I might not survive."

"If I do, you will," she said grimly.

He broke the mood by laughing quietly. "That's foolishness—but it's a lovely foolishness. I feel the same way about you. You see what comes of being shut up together and having so little to do. Good things as well as bad. How many people will you Awaken tomorrow?"

She had bent her body almost in thirds, arms clasped around doubled knees, head resting on knees. Her body shook with humorless laughter. He had awakened her one night, seemingly out of the blue and asked her if he might come to bed with her. She had had all she could do to stop herself from grabbing him and pulling him in.

But they had not talked about their feelings until now. Everyone knew. Everyone knew everything. She knew, for instance, that people said he slept with her to get special privileges or to escape their prison. Certainly, he was not someone she would have noticed on prewar Earth. And he would not have noticed her. But here, there had been a pull between them from the moment he Awoke, intense, inescapable, acted upon, and now, spoken.

"I'll Awaken ten people as you said," she told him finally. "It seems a good number. It will occupy everyone I would dare to trust to look after a newly Awakened person. As for the others . . . I don't want them free to wander around and cause trouble or get together and cause trouble. I'll double them with you, Tate, Leah, and me."

"Leah?" he said.

"Leah's all right. Surly, moody, stubborn. And hardworking, loyal, and hard to scare. I like her."

"I think she likes you," he said. "That surprises me. I would have expected her to resent you."

Behind him, the wall began to open.

Lilith froze, then sighed and deliberately stared at the floor. When she looked up again, seemingly to look at Joseph, she could see Nikanj coming through the opening.

6

She moved over beside Joseph who, leaning against the bed platform, had noticed nothing. She took his hand, held it for a moment between her own, wondering if she were about to lose him. Would he stay with her after tonight? Would he speak to her tomorrow beyond absolute necessity? Would he join her enemies, confirming to them things they only suspected now? What the hell did Nikanj want anyway? Why couldn't it stay out as it had said it would. There: She had finally caught it in a lie. She would not forgive it if that lie destroyed Joseph's feelings for her.

"What is it?" Joseph was saying as Nikanj strode across the room in utter silence and sealed the doorway.

"For God knows what reason, the Oankali have decided to give you a preview," she said softly, bitterly. "You aren't in any physical danger. You won't be hurt." Let Nikanj make a lie of that and she would force it to put her back into suspended animation.

Joseph looked around sharply, froze when he saw Nikanj. After a moment of what Lilith suspected was absolute terror, he jerked himself to his feet and stumbled back against the wall, cornering himself between the wall and the bed platform.

"What is it!" Lilith demanded in Oankali. She stood to face Nikanj. "Why are you here?"

Nikanj spoke in English. "So that he could endure his fear now, privately, and be of help to you later."

A moment after hearing the quiet androgynous, human-sounding voice speak in English, Joseph came out of his corner. He moved to Lilith's side, stood staring at Nikanj. He was trembling visibly. He said something in Chinese—the first time Lilith had heard him speak the language—then somehow, stilled his trembling. He looked at her.

"You know this one?"

"Kaalnikanjl oo Jdahyatediinkahguyaht aj Dinso," she said, staring at Nikanj's sensory arms, remembering how much more human it had looked without them. "Nikanj," she said when she saw Joseph frowning.

"I didn't believe," he said softly. "I couldn't, even though you said it."

She did not know what to say. He was handling the situation better than she had. Of course he had been warned and he was not being kept isolated from other humans. Still, he was doing well. He was as adaptable as she had suspected.

Moving slowly, Nikanj reached the bed and boosted itself up with one hand, folding its legs under it as it settled. Its head tentacles focused sharply on Joseph. "There's no hurry," it said. "We'll talk for a while. If you're hungry, I'll get you something."

"I'm not hungry," Joseph said. "Others may be, though."

"They must wait. They should spend a little time waiting for Lilith, understanding that they're helpless without her."

"They're just as helpless with me," Lilith said softly. "You've made them dependent on me. They may not be able to forgive me for that."

"Become their leader, and there'll be nothing to forgive."

Joseph looked at her as though Nikanj had finally said something to distract him from the strangeness of its body."

"Joe," she said, "it doesn't mean leader. It means Judas goat."

"You can make their lives easier," Nikanj said. "You can help them accept what is to happen to them. But whether you lead them or not, you can't prevent it. It would happen even if you died. If you lead them, more of them will survive. If you don't, you may not survive yourself."

She stared at it, remembered lying next to it when it was weak and helpless, remembered breaking bits of food into small pieces and slowly, carefully feeding it those pieces.

After a time its head and body tentacles drew themselves into knotted lumps and it hugged itself with its sensory arms. It spoke to her in Oankali: "I want you to live! Your mate is right! Some of these people are already plotting against you!"

"I told you they would plot against me," she said in English. "I told you they would probably kill me."

"You didn't tell me you would help them!"

She leaned against her table platform, head down. "I'm trying to live," she whispered. "You know I am."

"You could clone us," Joseph said. "Is that right?"

"Yes."

"You could take reproductive cells from us and grow human embryos in artificial wombs?"

"Yes."

"You can even re-create us from some kind of gene map or print."

"We can do that too. We have already done these things. We must do them to understand a new species better. We must compare them to normal human conception and birth. We must compare the children we have made to those we took from Earth. We're very careful to avoid damaging new partner-species."

"Is that what you call it?" Joseph muttered in bitter revulsion.

Nikanj spoke very softly. "We revere life. We had to be certain we had found ways for you to live with the partnership, not simply to die of it."

"You don't need us!" Joseph said. "You've created your own human beings. Poor bastards. Make them your partners."

"We . . . do need you." Nikanj spoke so softly that Joseph leaned forward to hear. "A partner must be biologically interesting, attractive to us, and you are fascinating. You are horror and beauty in rare combination. In a very real way, you've captured us, and we can't escape. But you're more than only the composition and the workings of your bodies. You are your personalities, your cultures. We're interested in those too. That's why we saved as many of you as we could."

Joseph shuddered. "We've seen how you saved us—your prison cells and your suspended animation plants, and now this."

"Those are the simplest things we do. And they leave you relatively untouched. You are what you were on Earth—minus any disease or injury. With a little training, you can go back to Earth and sustain yourselves comfortably."

"Those of us who survive this room and the training room."

"Those of you who survive."

"You could have done this another way!"

"We've tried other ways. This way is best. There is incentive not to do harm. No one who has killed or severely injured another will set foot on Earth again."

"They'll be kept here?"

"For the rest of their lives."

"Even . . ." Joseph glanced at Lilith, then faced Nikanj again. "Even if the killing is in self-defense?"

"She is exempt," Nikanj said.

"What?"

"She knows. We've given her abilities that at least one of you must have. They make her different, and therefore they make her a target. It would be self-defeating for us to forbid her to defend herself."

"Nikanj," Lilith said, and when she saw that she had its attention she spoke in Oankali. "Exempt him."

"No."

Flat refusal. That was that, and she knew it. But she could not help trying. "He's a target because of me," she said. "He could be killed because of me."

Nikanj spoke in Oankali. "And I want him to live because of you. But I didn't make the decision to keep humans who kill away from Earth—and I didn't exempt you. It was a consensus. I can't exempt him."

"Then . . . strengthen him the way you did me."

"He would be more likely to kill then."

"And less likely to die. I mean give him more resistance to injury. Help him heal faster if he is injured. Give him a chance!"

"What are you talking about?" Joseph said to her angrily. "Speak English!"

She opened her mouth, but Nikanj spoke first. "She's speaking for you. She wants you protected."

He looked at Lilith for confirmation. She nodded. "I'm afraid for you. I wanted you exempted too. It says it can't do that. So I've asked it to . . ." She stopped, looked from Nikanj to Joseph. "I've asked it to strengthen you, give you at least a chance."

He frowned at her. "Lilith, I'm not large, but I'm stronger than you think. I can take care of myself."

"I didn't speak in English because I didn't want to hear you say that. Of course you can't take care of yourself. No one person could against what might happen out there. I only wanted to give you more of a chance than you have now."

"Show him your hand," Nikanj said.

She hesitated, fearing that he would begin to see her as alien or too close to aliens—too much changed by them. But now that Nikanj had drawn attention to her hand, she could not conceal it. She raised her no-longer-bruised knuckles and showed them to Joseph.

He examined her hand minutely, then looked at the other one just to be certain he had not made a mistake. "They did this?" he asked. "Enabled you to heal so quickly?"

"Yes."

"What else?"

"Made me stronger than I was—and I was strong before—and enabled me to control interior walls and suspended animation plants. That's all."

He faced Nikanj. "How did you do this?"

Nikanj rustled its tentacles. "For the walls, I altered her body chemistry slightly. For the strength, I gave her more efficient use of what she already has. She should have been stronger. Her ancestors were stronger—her nonhuman ancestors in particular. I helped her fulfill her potential."

"How?"

"How do you move and coordinate the fingers of your hands? I'm an ooloi bred to work with humans. I can help them do anything their bodies are capable of doing. I made biochemical changes that caused her regular exercises to be much more effective than they would have been otherwise. There is also a slight genetic change. I haven't added or subtracted anything, but I have brought out latent ability. She is as strong and as fast as her nearest animal ancestors were." Nikanj paused, perhaps noticing the way Joseph was looking at Lilith. "The changes I've made are not hereditary," it said.

"You said you changed her genes!" Joseph charged.

"Body cells only. Not reproductive cells."

"But if you cloned her . . ."

"I will not clone her."

There was a long silence. Joseph looked at Nikanj, then stared long at Lilith. She spoke when she thought she had endured his stare long enough.

"If you want to go out and join the others, I'll open the wall," she said.

"Is that what you think?" he asked.

"That's what I fear," she whispered.

"Could you have prevented what was done to you?"

"I didn't try to prevent it." She swallowed. "They were going to give me this job no matter what I said. I told them they might as well kill me themselves. Even that didn't stop them. So when Nikanj and its mates offered me as much as they could offer, I didn't even have to think about it. I welcomed it."

After a time, he nodded.

"I'll give you some of what I gave her," Nikanj said. "I won't increase your strength, but I will enable you to heal faster, recover from injuries that might otherwise kill you. Do you want me to do this?"

"You're giving me a choice?"

"Yes."

"The change is permanent?"

"Unless you ask to be changed back."

"Side effects?"

"Psychological."

Joseph frowned. "What do you mean, psycho . . . Oh. So that's why you won't give me the strength."

"Yes."

"But you trust . . . Lilith."

"She has been Awake and living with my families for years. We know her. And, of course, we're always watching."

After a time, Joseph took Lilith's hands. "Do you see?" he asked gently. "Do you understand why they chose you—someone who desperately doesn't want the responsibility, who doesn't want to lead, who is a woman?"

The condescension in his voice first startled, then angered her. "Do *I* see, Joe? Oh, yes. I've had plenty of time to see."

He seemed to realize how he had sounded. "You have, yes—not that it helps to know."

Nikanj had shifted its attention from one of them to the other. Now it focused on Joseph. "Shall I make the change in you?" it asked.

Joseph released Lilith's hands. "What is it? Surgery? Something to do with blood or bone marrow?"

"You will be made to sleep. When you awake, the change will have been made. There won't be any pain or illness, no surgery in the usual sense of the word."

"How will you do it?"

"These are my tools." It extended both sensory arms. "Through them, I'll study you, then make the necessary adjustments. My body and yours will produce any substances I need."

Joseph shuddered visibly. "I . . . I don't think I could let you touch me."

Lilith looked at him until he turned to face her. "I was shut up for days with one of them before I could touch him," she said. "There were times . . . I'd rather take a beating than go through anything like that again."

Joseph moved closer to her, his manner protective. It was easier for him to give comfort than to ask for it. Now he managed to do both at once.

"How long are you going to stay here now?" he demanded of Nikanj.

"Not much longer. I'll come back. You'll probably feel less afraid when you see me again." It paused. "Eventually you must touch me. You must show at least that much control before I change you."

"I don't know. Maybe I don't want you to change me. I don't really understand what it is you do with those . . . those tentacles."

"Sensory arms, we call them in English. They're more than arms—much more—but the term is convenient." It focused its attention on Lilith and spoke in Oankali. "Do you think it would help if he saw a demonstration?"

"I'm afraid he would be repelled," she said.

"He's an unusual male. I think he might surprise you."

"No."

"You should trust me. I know a great deal about him."

"No! Leave him to me."

It stood up, unfolding itself dramatically. When she saw that it was about to leave, she almost relaxed. Then in a single swift sweep of motion, it stepped to her and looped a sensory arm around her neck forming an oddly comfortable noose. She was not afraid. She had been through this often enough to be used to it. Her first thoughts were concern for Joseph and anger at Nikanj.

Joseph had not moved. She stood between the two of them.

"It's all right," she told him. "It wanted you to see. This is all the contact it would need."

Joseph stared at the coil of sensory arm, looked from the arm to Nikanj and back to the arm again where it rested against Lilith's flesh. After a moment, he raised his hand toward it. He stopped. His hand twitched, drew back, then slowly reached out again. With only a moment's hesitation, he touched the cool, hard flesh of the sensory arm. His fingers rested on its hornlike tip and that tip twisted to grasp his wrist.

Now Lilith was no longer their intermediary. Joseph stood rigid and silent, sweating, but not trembling, his hand upright, fingers clawlike, a noose of sensory tentacles settled in a painless, unbreakable grip around the wrist.

With a sound that could have been the beginning of a scream, Joseph collapsed.

Lilith stepped to him quickly, but Nikanj caught him. He was unconscious. She said nothing until she had helped Nikanj put him on the bed. Then she caught it by the shoulders and turned it to face her.

"Why couldn't you let him alone!" she demanded. "I'm supposed to be in charge of them. Why didn't you just leave him to me?"

"Do you know," it said, "that no undrugged human has ever done that before? Some have touched us by accident this soon after meeting us, but no one has done it deliberately. I told you he was unusual."

"Why couldn't you let him alone!"

It unfastened Joseph's jacket and began to remove it. "Because there are already two human males speaking against him, trying to turn others against him. One has decided he's something called a faggot and the other dislikes the shape of his eyes. Actually, both are angry about the way he's allied himself with you. They would prefer to have you without allies. Your mate needs any extra protection I can give him now."

She listened, appalled. Joseph had talked about the danger to her. Had he known how immediate his own danger was?

Nikanj threw the jacket aside and lay down beside Joseph. It wrapped one sensory tentacle around Joseph's neck and the other around his waist, drawing Joseph's body close against its own.

"Did you drug him, or did he faint?" she asked—then wondered why she cared.

"I drugged him as soon as I grasped his arm. He had reached his breaking point, though. He might have fainted on his own. This way, he can be angry with me for drugging him, not for making him look weak in front of you."

She nodded. "Thank you."

"What is a faggot?" it asked.

She told it.

"But they know he's not that. They know he's mated with you."

"Yes. Well, there's been some doubt about me, too, I hear."

"None of them really believe it."

"Yet."

"Serve them by leading them, Lilith. Help us send as many of them home as we can."

She stared at it for a long time, feeling frightened and empty. It sounded so sincere—not that that mattered. How could she become the leader of people who saw her as their jailer? On some level, a leader had to be trusted. Yet every act she performed that proved the truth of what she said also made her loyalties, and even her humanity suspect.

She sat down on the floor, cross-legged and at first stared at nothing. Eventually, her eyes were drawn to Nikanj holding Joseph on the bed. The pair did not move, though once she heard Joseph sigh. Was he no longer completely unconscious, then? Was he already learning the lesson all adult ooloi eventually taught? So much in only one day.

"Lilith?"

She jumped. Both Joseph and Nikanj had spoken her name, though clearly, only Nikanj was enough awake to know what it was saying. Joseph, drugged and under the influence of multiple neural links, would shadow everything Nikanj said or did unless Nikanj split its attention enough to stop him. Nikanj did not bother.

"I have adjusted him, even strengthened him a little, though he'll have to exercise to be able to use that to his best advantage. He will be more difficult to injure, faster to heal, and able to survive and recover from injuries that would have killed him before." Joseph, unknowing, spoke every word exactly in unison with Nikanj.

"Stop that!" Lilith said sharply.

Nikanj altered its connection without missing a beat. "Lie here with us," it said, speaking alone. "Why should you be down there by yourself?"

She thought there could be nothing more seductive than an ooloi speaking in that particular tone, making that particular suggestion. She realized she had stood up without meaning to and taken a step toward the bed. She stopped, stared at the two of them. Joseph's breathing now became a gentle snore and he seemed to sleep comfortably against Nikanj as she had awakened to find him sleeping comfortably against her many times. She did not pretend outwardly or to herself that she would resist Nikanj's invitation—or that she wanted to resist it. Nikanj could give her an intimacy with Joseph that was beyond ordinary human experience. And what it gave, it also experienced. This was what had captured Paul Titus, she thought. This, not sorrow over his losses or fear of a primitive Earth.

She clenched her fists, holding back. "This won't help me," she said. "It will just make it harder for me when you're not around."

Nikanj freed one sensory arm from Joseph's waist and extended it toward her.

She stayed where she was for a moment longer, proving to herself that she was still in control of her behavior. Then she tore off her jacket and seized the ugly, ugly elephant's trunk of an organ, letting it coil around her as she climbed onto the bed. She sandwiched Nikanj's body between her own and Joseph's, placing it for the first time in the ooloi position between two humans. For an instant, this frightened her. This was the way she might someday be made pregnant with an other-than-human child. Not now while Nikanj wanted other work from her, but someday. Once it plugged into her central nervous system it could control her and do whatever it wanted.

She felt it tremble against her, and knew it was in.

7

She did not lose consciousness. Nikanj did not want to cheat itself of sensation. Even Joseph was conscious, though utterly controlled, unafraid because Nikanj kept him tranquil. Lilith was not controlled. She could lift a free hand across Nikanj to take Joseph's cool, seemingly lifeless hand.

"No," Nikanj said softly into her ear—or perhaps it stimulated the auditory nerve directly. It could do that—stimulate her senses individually or in any combination to make perfect hallucinations. "Only through me," its voice insisted.

Lilith's hand tingled. She released Joseph's hand and immediately received Joseph as a blanket of warmth and security, a compelling, steadying presence.

She never knew whether she was receiving Nikanj's approximation of Joseph, a true transmission of what Joseph was feeling, some combination of truth and approximation, or just a pleasant fiction.

What was Joseph feeling from her?

It seemed to her that she had always been with him. She had no sensation of shifting gears, no "time alone" to contrast with the present "time together." He had always been there, part of her, essential.

Nikanj focused on the intensity of their attraction, their union. It left Lilith no other sensation. It seemed, itself, to vanish. She sensed only Joseph, felt that he was aware only of her.

Now their delight in one another ignited and burned. They moved together, sustaining an impossible intensity, both of them tireless, perfectly matched, ablaze in sensation, lost in one another. They seemed to rush upward. A long time later, they seemed to drift down slowly, gradually, savoring a few more moments wholly together.

Noon, evening, dusk, darkness.

Her throat hurt. Her first solitary sensation was pain—as

though she had been shouting, screaming. She swallowed painfully and raised her hand to her throat, but Nikanj's sensory arm was there ahead of her and brushed her hand away. It laid its exposed sensory hand across her throat. She felt it anchor itself, sensory fingers stretching, clasping. She did not feel the tendrils of its substance penetrate her flesh, but in a moment the pain in her throat was gone.

"All that and you only screamed once," it told her.

"How'd you let me do even that?" she asked.

"You surprised me. I've never made you scream before."

She let it withdraw from her throat, then moved languidly to stroke it. "How much of that experience was Joseph's and mine?" she asked. "How much did you make up?"

"I've never made up an experience for you," it said. "I won't have to for him either. You both have memories filled with experiences."

"That was a new one."

"A combination. You had your own experiences and his. He had his and yours. You both had me to keep it going much longer than it would have otherwise. The whole was . . . overwhelming."

She looked around. "Joseph?"

"Asleep. Very deeply asleep. I didn't induce it. He's tired. He's all right, though."

"He . . . felt everything I felt?"

"On a sensory level. Intellectually, he made his interpretations and you made yours."

"I wouldn't call them intellectual."

"You understand me."

"Yes." She moved her hand over its chest, taking a perverse pleasure in feeling its tentacles squirm, then flatten under her hand.

"Why do you do that?" it asked.

"Does it bother you?" she asked stilling her hand.

"No."

"Let me do it, then. I didn't used to be able to."

"I have to go. You should wash, then feed your people. Seal

your mate in. Be certain you're the first to talk to him when he wakes."

She watched it climb over her, joints bending all wrong, and lower itself to the floor. She caught its hand before it could head for a wall. Its head tentacles pointed at her loosely in unspoken question.

"Do you like him?" she asked.

The point focused briefly on Joseph. "Ahajas and Dichaan are mystified," it said. "They thought you would choose one of the big dark ones because they're like you. I said you would choose this one—because he's like you."

"What?"

"During his testing, his responses were closer to yours than anyone else I'm aware of. He doesn't look like you but he's like you."

"He might . . ." She forced herself to voice the thought. "He might not want anything more to do with me when he realizes what I helped you do with him."

"He'll be angry—and frightened and eager for the next time and determined to see that there won't be a next time. I've told you, I know this one."

"How do you know him so well? What have you had to do with him before?"

Its head and body smoothed so that even with its sensory arms, it resembled a slender, hairless, sexless human.

"He was the subject of one of my first acts of adult responsibility," it said. "I knew you by then, and I set out to find someone for you. Not another Paul Titus, but someone you would want. Someone who would want you. I examined memory records of thousands of males. This one might have been taught to parent a group himself, but when I showed other ooloi the match, they agreed that the two of you should be together."

"You . . . You chose him for me?"

"I offered you to one another. The two of you did your own choosing." It opened a wall and left her.

8

People gathered around silently, radiating hostility when Lilith called them out to eat. Most were already out, waiting for her sullenly, impatiently, hungrily. Lilith ignored their annoyance.

"It's about time," Peter Van Weerden muttered as she opened the various wall cabinets and people began to come forward and take food. This was the man who claimed she was not human, she recalled.

"If you're through screwing, that is," Jean Pelerin added.

Lilith turned to look at Jean and managed to examine the woman's bruised, swollen face before Jean turned away.

Troublemakers. Only two of them out in the open so far. How long would that last?

"I'll be Awakening ten more people tomorrow," she said before anyone could leave. "You'll all be helping with them singly or in pairs." She paced alongside the food wall, automatically drawing her fingers around the circular cabinet openings, keeping them from closing while people chose what they wanted. Even the newest people were used to this, but Gabriel Rinaldi complained mildly.

"It's ridiculous for you to have to do that, Lilith. Make them stay open."

"That's the idea," she said. "They stay open for two or three minutes, then they close unless I touch them again." She stopped, took the last bowl of hot, spicy beans from one cabinet, and let it close. The cabinet would not begin to refill itself until the wall was sealed. She put the beans on the floor to one side for her own meal later. People sat around on the floor, eating from edible dishes. There was comfort in eating together—one of their few comforts. Groups formed and people talked quietly among themselves. Lilith was taking fruit for herself when Peter spoke from his group nearby. His group of Jean, Curt Loehr, and Celene Ivers.

"If you ask me, the walls are fixed that way to keep us from thinking about what we ought to do to our jailor," Peter said.

Lilith waited, wondering whether anyone would defend her. No one did, though silence spread to other groups.

She drew a deep breath, walked over to Peter's group. "Things can change," she said quietly. "Maybe you can turn everybody here against me. That would make me a failure." She raised her voice slightly, though even her quiet words had carried. "That would mean all of you put back into suspended animation so that you can be separated and put through all this again with other people." She paused. "If that's what you want—to be split up, to begin again alone, to go through this however many times it takes for you to let yourself get all the way through it, keep trying. You might succeed."

She left him, took her food and joined Tate, Gabriel, and Leah.

"Not bad," Tate said when people had resumed their own conversations. "Clear warning to everyone. It's overdue."

"It won't work," Leah said. "These people don't know each other. What do they care if they have to start again?"

"They care," Gabriel told her. Even with his blue-black beard, he was one of the best looking men Lilith had ever seen. And he was still sleeping exclusively with Tate. Lilith liked him, but she was aware that he did not quite trust her. She could see that in his expression when she caught him watching her sometimes. Yet he was careful to keep her goodwill—keep his options open.

"They've made personal ties here," he said to Leah. "Think what they had before: War, chaos, family and friends dead. Then solitary. A jail cell and shit to eat. They care very much. So do you."

She turned to face him angrily, mouth already open, but the handsome face seemed to disarm her. She sighed and nodded sadly. For a moment she seemed close to tears.

"How many times can you have everyone taken from you and still have the will to start again?" Tate muttered.

As many times as it took, Lilith thought wearily. As many times as human fear, suspicion, and stubbornness made necessary. The Oankali were as patient as the waiting Earth.

She realized that Gabriel was staring at her.

"You're still worried about them, aren't you?" he asked.

She nodded.

"I think they believed you. All of them, not just Van Weerden and Jean."

"I know. They'll believe me for a little while. Then some of them will decide I'm lying to them or that I've been lied to."

"Are you sure you haven't?" Tate asked.

"I'm sure I have," Lilith said bitterly. "By omission, at least."

"But then—"

"This is what I *know*," Lilith said. "Our rescuers, our captors are extraterrestrials. We are aboard their ship. I've seen and felt enough—including weightlessness—to be convinced that it is a ship. We're in space. And we're in the hands of people who manipulate DNA as naturally as we manipulate pencils and paintbrushes. That's what I know. That's what I've told you all. And if any of you decide to behave as though it isn't true, we'll all be lucky if we're just put to sleep and split up."

She looked at the three faces and forced a weary smile. "End of speech," she said. "I'd better get something for Joseph."

"You should have gotten him out here," Tate said.

"Don't worry about it," Lilith told her.

"You could bring me a meal now and then," Gabriel said to her as Lilith left them.

"See what you've done!" Tate called after her.

Lilith found herself smiling an unforced smile as she took more food from the cabinets. It was inevitable that some of the people she Awakened would disbelieve her, dislike her, distrust her. At least there were others she could talk to, relax with.

There was hope if she could only keep the skeptics from self-destructing.

9

For a time, Joseph would not speak or take food from her hands. Once she understood this, she sat with him to wait. She had not Awakened him when she came back to the room, had sealed the room and slept beside him until his movements woke her. Now she sat with him, worried but feeling no real hostility from him. He did not seem to resent her presence.

He was sorting out his feelings, she thought. He was trying to understand what had happened.

She had put a few pieces of fruit on the bed between them. She had said, knowing he would not answer, "It was a neurosensory illusion. Nikanj stimulates nerves directly, and we remember or create experiences to suit the sensations. On a physical level, Nikanj feels what we feel. It can't read our thoughts. It can't get away with hurting us—unless it's willing to suffer the same pain." She hesitated. "It said it strengthened you a little. You'll have to be careful at first, and exercise. You won't get hurt easily. If something does happen to you you'll heal the way I do."

He had not spoken, had not looked at her, but she knew he had heard. There was nothing vacant about him.

She sat with him, waited, oddly comfortable, nibbling at the fruit now and then. After a time, she lay back, feet on the floor, body stretched across the bed. The movement attracted him.

He turned, stared at her as though he had forgotten she was there. "You should get up," he said. "The light's coming back. Morning."

"Talk to me," she said.

He rubbed his head. "It wasn't real? Not any of it?"

"We didn't touch each other."

He grabbed her hand and held it. "That thing . . . did it all."

"Neural stimulation."

"How?"

"They hook into our nervous systems somehow. They're more sensitive than we are. Anything we feel a little, they feel a lot—and they feel it almost before we're conscious of it. That helps them stop doing anything painful before we notice that they've begun."

"They've done it to you before?"

She nodded.

"With . . . other men?"

"Alone or with Nikanj's mates."

Abruptly, he got up and began to pace.

"They aren't human," she said.

"Then how can they . . . ? Their nervous systems can't be like ours. How can they make us feel . . . what I felt?"

"By pushing the right electrochemical buttons. I don't claim to understand it. It's like a language that they have a special gift for. They know our bodies better than we do."

"Why do you let them . . . touch you?"

"To have changes made. The strength, the fast healing—"

He stopped in front of her, faced her. "Is that all?" he demanded.

She stared at him, seeing the accusation in his eyes, refusing to defend herself. "I liked it," she said softly. "Didn't you?"

"That thing will never touch me again if I have anything to say about it."

She did not challenge this.

"I've never felt anything like that in my *life*," he shouted.

She jumped, but said nothing.

"If a thing like that could be bottled, it would have outsold any illegal drug on the market."

"I'm going to Awaken ten people this morning," she said. "Will you help?"

"You're still going to do that?"

"Yes."

He breathed deeply. "Let's go then." But he did not move. He still stood watching her. "Is it . . . like a drug?" he asked.

"You mean am I addicted?"

"Yes."

"I don't think so. I was happy with you. I didn't want Nikanj here."

"I don't want him here again."

"Nikanj isn't male—and I doubt whether it really cares what either of us wants."

"Don't let him touch you! If you have a choice, keep away from him!"

The refusal to accept Nikanj's sex frightened her because it reminded her of Paul Titus. She did not want to see Paul Titus in Joseph.

"It isn't male, Joseph."

"What difference does that make!"

"What difference does any self-deception make? We need to know them for what they are, even if there are no human parallels—and believe me, there are none for the ooloi." She got up, knowing that she had not given him the promise he wanted, knowing that he would remember her silence. She unsealed the doorway and left the room.

10

Ten new people.

Everyone was kept busy trying to keep them out of trouble and give them some idea of their situation. The woman Peter was helping laughed in his face and told him he was crazy when he mentioned, as he said, "the possibility that our captors might somehow be extraterrestrials . . ."

Leah's charge, a small blond man, grabbed her, hung on, and might have raped her if he had been bigger or she smaller. She stopped him from doing any harm, but Gabriel had to help her get him off. She was surprisingly tolerant of the man's efforts. She seemed more amused than angry.

Nothing the new people did for the first few minutes was taken seriously or held against them. Leah's attacker was simply held until he stopped trying to get to her, until he grew quiet and began to look around at the many human faces, until he began to cry.

The man's name was Wray Ordway and a few days after his Awakening, he was sleeping with Leah with her full consent.

Two days after that, Peter Van Weerden and six followers seized Lilith and held her while a seventh follower, Derrick Wolski, swept a dozen or so leftover biscuits out of one of the food cabinets and climbed into it before it could close.

When Lilith realized what Derrick was doing she stopped struggling. There was no need to hurt anyone. The Oankali would take care of Derrick.

"What does he think he's going to do?" she asked Curt. He had taken part in holding her, though, of course Celene had not. He still held one of her arms.

Watching him, she shook the others off. Now that Derrick was gone from sight, they did not try hard to hold her. She knew now that if she had been willing to hurt or kill them, they could not have held her. She was not stronger than all six combined, but she was stronger than any two. And faster than any of them. The knowledge was not as comforting as it should have been.

"What's he supposed to be doing?" she repeated.

Curt released the arm she had left in his hands. "Finding out what's really going on," he said. "There are people refilling those cabinets and we intend to find out who they are. We want to get a look at them before they're ready to be seen—before they're ready to convince us they're Martians."

She sighed. He had been told that the cabinets refilled automatically. Just one more thing he had decided not to believe. "They're not Martians," she said.

He crooked his mouth in something less than a smile. "I knew that. I never believed your fairy tales."

"They're from another solar system," she said. "I don't know which one. It doesn't matter. They left it so long ago, they don't even know whether it still exists."

He cursed her and turned away.

"What's going to happen?" another voice asked.

Lilith looked around, saw Celene, and sighed. Wherever Curt was, Celene was trembling nearby. Lilith had matched them as well as Nikanj had matched her with Joseph. "I don't know," she said. "The Oankali won't let him get hurt, but I don't know whether they'll put him back in here."

Joseph strode up to her, obviously concerned. Someone had apparently gone to his room and told him what was going on.

"It's all right," she said. "Derrick has gone out to look at the Oankali." She shrugged at his look of alarm. "I hope they send him back—or bring him back. These people are going to have to see for themselves."

"That could start a panic!" he whispered.

"I don't care. They'll recover. But if they keep doing stupid things like this, they'll eventually manage to hurt themselves."

Derrick was not sent back.

Eventually even Peter and Jean did not object when Lilith went to the wall and opened the cabinet to prove that Derrick had not asphyxiated inside. She had to open every cabinet in the general area of the one he had used because most of the others could not locate the individual cabinet on the broad, unmarked expanse of wall. Lilith had at first been surprised at her own ability to locate each one easily and exactly. Once she found them the first time she remembered their distance from floor and ceiling, from right and left walls. Some people, since they could not do this themselves, found the ability suspicious.

Some people found everything about her suspicious.

"What happened to Derrick!" Jean Pelerin demanded.

"He did something stupid," Lilith told her. "And while he was doing it, you helped hold me so that I couldn't stop him."

Jean drew back a little, spoke louder. "What happened to him?"

"I don't know."

"Liar!" The volume increased again. "What did your friends do to him? Kill him?"

"What ever happened to him, you're partly to blame," Lilith said. "Handle your own guilt." She looked around at other equally guilty, equally accusing faces. Jean never made her complaints privately. She needed an audience.

Lilith turned and went to her room. She was about to seal herself in when Tate and Joseph joined her. A moment later, Gabriel followed them in. He sat on the corner of Lilith's table and faced her.

"You're losing," he said flatly.

"You're losing," she countered. "If I lose, everyone loses."

"That's why we're here."

"If you have an idea, I'll listen."

"Give them a better show. Get your friends to help you impress them."

"My friends?"

"Look, I don't care. You say they're extraterrestrials. Okay. They're extraterrestrials. What the hell are they going to gain if those assholes out there kill you?"

"I agreed. I was hoping they would send or bring Derrick back. They might still. But their timing is terrible."

"Joe says you can talk to them."

She turned to stare at Joseph in betrayal and surprise.

"Your enemies are gathering allies," he said. "Why should you be alone?"

She looked at Tate and the woman shrugged. "Those people out there are assholes," she said. "If they had a brain between them they'd shut up and open their eyes and ears until they had some idea what was really going on."

"That's all I hoped for," Lilith said. "I didn't expect it, but I hoped for it."

"Those are frightened people looking for someone to save them," Gabriel said. "They don't want reason or logic or your hopes or expectations. They want Moses or somebody to come and lead them into lives they can understand."

"Van Weerden can't do that," Lilith said.

"Of course he can't. But right now they think he can, and they're following. Next, he'll tell them the only way to get out of here is to knock you around until you tell all your secrets. He'll say you know the way out. And by the time it's clear that you don't, you'll be dead."

Would she? He had no idea how long it would take to torture her to death. Her and Joseph. She looked at him bleakly.

"Victor Dominic," Joseph said. "And Leah and that guy she's picked up and Beatrice Dwyer and—"

"Potential allies?" Lilith asked.

"Yes, and we'd better hurry. I saw Beatrice with one of the guys from the other side this morning."

"Loyalties can change according to who people are sleeping with," Lilith said.

"So what!" demanded Gabriel. "So you don't trust anybody? So you wind up in pieces on the floor?"

Lilith shook her head. "I know it has to be done. So stupid, isn't it. It's like 'Let's play Americans against the Russians. Again.'"

"Talk to your friends," Gabriel said. "Maybe that's not the show they had in mind. Maybe they'll help you rewrite the script."

She stared at him, frowning. "Do you really talk like that?"

"Whatever works," he said.

11

The Oankali did not choose to play the part of Lilith's friends. When she sealed herself into her room and spoke to them, they neither appeared nor answered her calls. And they continued to hold Derrick. Lilith thought he had probably been made to sleep again.

None of this surprised her. She would organize the humans into a coherent unit or she would serve as a scapegoat for whoever else organized them. Nikanj and its mates would save her life if they could—if it seemed her life was in immediate danger. But beyond that, she was on her own.

But she did have *powers*. Or that was the way people thought of the things she could do with the walls and the suspended animation plants. Peter Van Weerden had nothing. Some people believed he had caused Derrick's disappearance, perhaps his death. Fortunately Peter was not eloquent enough, not charismatic enough to shift blame for this to Lilith— though he tried.

What he did manage to do was portray Derrick as a hero, a martyr who had acted for the group, who had at least *tried* to do something. What the hell was Lilith doing, he would demand. What was her group doing? Sitting on their hands, talking and talking, waiting for their captors to tell them what to do next.

People who favored action sided with Peter. People like Leah and Wray, Tate and Gabriel who were biding their time, waiting for more information or a real chance to escape sided with Lilith.

There were also people like Beatrice Dwyer who were afraid of any kind of action, but who had lost hope of ever controlling their own destinies. These sided with Lilith in the hope of peace and continued life. They wanted, Lilith thought, only to be let alone. That was all many people had wanted before the war. It was the one thing they could not have, then or now.

Nevertheless, Lilith recruited these, too, and when she Awakened ten more people, she used only her recruits to help them. Peter's people were reduced to heckling and jeering. The new people saw them first as troublemakers.

Perhaps that was why Peter decided to impress his followers by helping one of them get a woman.

The woman, Allison Zeigler, had not yet found a man she liked, but she had chosen Lilith's side over Peter's. She screamed Lilith's name when Peter and the new man, Gregory Sebastes, stopped arguing with her and decided to drag her off to Gregory's room.

Lilith, alone in her own room, frowned, not certain what she had heard. Another fight?

Wearily, she put down the stack of dossiers that she had been going through in search of a few more allies. She went out and saw the trouble at once.

Two men holding a struggling woman between them. The trio was prevented from reaching any of the bedrooms by Lilith's people who stood blocking the way. And Lilith's people were prevented from reaching the trio by several of Peter's people.

A standoff—potentially deadly.

"What the hell is she saving herself for?" Jean was demanding. "It's her duty to get together with someone. There aren't that many of us left."

"It's my duty to find out where I am and how to get free," Allison shouted. "Maybe you want to give whoever's holding us prisoner a human baby to fool around with, but I don't!"

"We pair off!" Curt bellowed, drowning her out. "One man, one woman. Nobody has the right to hold you. It just causes trouble."

"Trouble for who!" someone demanded.

"Who the shit are you to tell us our rights!" called someone else.

"What is she to you!" Gregory used his free hand to knock someone away from Allison. "Get your own damn woman!"

At that moment, Allison hit him. He cursed and hit her. She screamed, twisted her body violently. Blood streamed from her nose.

Lilith reached the crowd. "Stop," she called. "Let her go!" But her voice was lost in the many.

"*Goddammit, stop!*" She shouted in a voice that surprised even her.

People near her froze, staring at her, but the group around Allison was too involved to notice her until she reached it.

This was too familiar, too much like what Paul Titus had said and done.

She stepped up to the knot of people surrounding Allison, too furious to worry about their blocking her. Two of them caught her arms. She threw them aside without ever seeing their faces. For once she did not care what happened to them. Cavemen. *Fools!*

She grabbed Peter's free arm as he tried to hit her. She held the arm, squeezed it, twisted it.

Peter screamed and fell to his knees, his grip on Allison released, forgotten. For a moment, Lilith stared at him. He was garbage. Human garbage. How had she made the mistake of Awakening him? And what could she do with him now?

She threw him aside, not caring that he hit a nearby wall.

The other man, Gregory Sebastes, held his ground. Curt stood beside him, challenging Lilith. They had seen what she had done to Peter, but they did not seem to believe it. They let her walk up to them.

She hit Curt hard in the stomach, doubling him, toppling him.

Gregory let go of Allison and lunged at Lilith.

She hit him, catching him in midair, snapping his head back, collapsing him to the floor unconscious.

Abruptly, all was still except for Curt's gasping and Peter's groaning—"My arm! Oh, god, my arm!"

Lilith looked at each of Peter's people, daring them to attack, almost wanting them to attack. But now five of them were injured, and Lilith was untouched. Even her own people stood back from her.

"There'll be no rape here," she said evenly. She raised her voice. "Nobody here is property. Nobody here has the right to the use of anybody else's body. There'll be no back-to-the-Stone-Age, caveman bullshit!" She let her voice drop to normal. "We stay human. We treat each other like people, and we get through this like people. Anyone who wants to be something less will have his chance in the forest. There'll be plenty of room for him to run away and play at being an ape."

She turned and walked back toward her room. Her body trembled with residual anger and frustration. She did not want the others to see her tremble. She had never come closer to losing control, killing people.

Joseph spoke her name softly. She swung around, ready to fight, then made herself relax as she recognized his voice. She stood looking at him, longing to go to him, but restraining herself. What did he think of what she had done?

"I know those guys don't deserve it," he said, "but some of them need help. Peter's arm is broken. The others . . . Can you get the Oankali to help them?"

Alarmed, she looked back at the carnage she had created. She drew a deep breath, managed to still her trembling. Then she spoke quietly in Oankali.

"Whoever is on watch, come in and check these people. Some of them may be badly hurt."

"Not so badly," a disembodied voice answered in Oankali. "The ones on the floor will heal without help. I'm in contact with them through the floor."

"What about the one with the broken arm?"

"We'll take care of him. Shall we keep him?"

"I'd love to have you keep him. But no, leave him with us. You're already suspected of being murderers."

"Derrick is asleep again."

"I thought so. What shall we do with Peter?"

"Nothing. Let him think for a while about his behavior."

"Ahajas?"

"Yes?"

Lilith drew another deep breath. "I'm surprised to realize how good it is to hear your voice."

There was no answer. Nothing more to be said.

"What did he say?" Joseph wanted to know.

"She. She said no one was seriously hurt. She said the Oankali would take care of Peter after he's had time to think about his behavior."

"What do we do with him until then?"

"Nothing."

"I thought they wouldn't talk to you," Gabriel said, his voice filled with unconcealed suspicion. He and Tate and a few others had come over to her. They stood back cautiously.

"They talk when they want to," she said. "This is an emergency so they decided to talk."

"You knew that one, didn't you?"

She looked at Gabriel. "Yes, I knew her."

"I thought so. Your tone and the way you looked when you talked to her . . . You relaxed more, seemed almost wistful."

"She knows I never wanted this job."

"Was she a friend?"

"As much as it's possible to be friends with someone of a totally different species." She gave a humorless laugh. "It's hard enough for human beings to be friends with each other."

Yet she did think of Ahajas as a friend—Ahajas, Dichaan, Nikanj . . . But what was she to them? A tool? A pleasurable perversion? An accepted member of the household? Accepted as what? Round and round. It would have been easier not to care. Down on Earth, it would not matter. The Oankali used her relentlessly for their own purposes, and she worried about what they thought of her.

"How can you be this strong?" Tate demanded. "How can you do all this?"

Lilith rubbed a hand over her face wearily. "The same way I can open walls," she said. "The Oankali changed me a little.

I'm strong. I move fast. I heal fast. And all that is supposed to help me get as many of you as possible through this experience and back on Earth." She looked around. "Where's Allison?"

"Here." The woman stepped forward. She had already cleaned most of the blood from her face and now seemed to be trying to look as though nothing had happened. That was Allison. She would not be seen at anything less than her best for a moment longer than necessary.

Lilith nodded. "Well, I can see you're all right."

"Yes. Thank you." Allison hesitated. "Look, I really am grateful to you no matter what the truth turns out to be, but . . ."

"But?"

Allison looked down, then seemed to force herself to face Lilith again. "There isn't any nice way of saying this, but I've got to ask. Are you really human?"

Lilith stared at her, tried to raise indignation, but managed only weariness. How many times would she have to answer that question? And why did she bother? Would her words ease anyone's suspicions?

"This would be so goddamn much easier if I weren't human," she said. "Think about it. If I weren't human, why the hell would I care whether you got raped?"

She turned once more toward her room, then stopped, turned back, remembering. "I'm Awakening ten more people tomorrow. The final ten."

12

There was a shuffling of people. Some avoided Lilith because they were afraid of her—afraid she was not human, or not human enough. Others came to her because they believed that she would win. They did not know what that would mean, but they thought it would be better to be with her than to have her as an enemy.

Her core group, Joseph, Tate and Gabriel, Leah and Wray did not change. Peter's core group shifted. Victor was added. He was a strong personality and he had been Awake longer than most people. That encouraged a few of the newer people to follow him.

Peter himself was replaced by Curt. Peter's broken arm kept him quiet, sullen, and usually alone in his room. Curt was brighter and more physically impressive anyway. He would probably have led the group from the first if he had moved a little faster.

Peter's arm remained broken, swollen, painful and useless for two days. On the night of the second day, he was healed. He slept late, missed breakfast, but when he awoke, his arm was no longer broken—and he was a badly frightened man. He could not simply pass off two days of debilitating pain as illusion or trickery. The bones of his arm had been broken, and badly broken. Everyone who looked at it had seen the displacement, the swelling, the discoloration. Everyone had seen that he could not use his hand.

Now everyone saw a whole arm, undistorted, normal, and a hand that worked easily and well. Peter's own people looked askance at him.

Following lunch on the day of his healing, Lilith told the people carefully censored stories of her life among the Oankali. Peter did not stay to listen.

"You need to hear these things more than the others do," she told him later. "The Oankali will be a shock even if you're prepared. They fixed your arm while you were asleep because they didn't want you terrified and fighting them while they tried to help you."

"Tell them how grateful I am," he muttered.

"They want sanity, not gratitude," she said. "They want— and I want—you to be bright enough to survive."

He stared at her with contempt so great that it made his face almost unrecognizable.

She shook her head, spoke softly. "I hurt you because you were trying to hurt another person. No one else has hurt you at all. The Oankali have saved your life. Eventually, they'll send you back to Earth to make a new life for yourself." She paused. "A little thought, Pete. A little sanity."

She got up to leave him. He said nothing to her, only watched her with hatred and contempt. "Now there are forty-three of us," she said. "The Oankali could show themselves anytime. Don't do anything that will make them keep you here alone."

She left him, hoping he would begin to think. Hoping, but not believing.

Five days after Peter's healing, the evening meal was drugged.

Lilith was not warned. She ate with the others, sitting off to one side with Joseph. She was aware as she ate of growing relaxation, a particular kind of comfort that made her think of—

She sat up straight. What she felt now she had felt before only when she was with Nikanj, when it had established a neural link with her.

And the sweet fog of anticipation dissipated. Her body seemed to shrug it off and she was alert again. Nearby, other people still spoke to one another, laughing a little more than they had before. Laughter had never quite disappeared from the group, though at times it had been rare. There had been more fighting, more bed-hopping and less laughter for the past few days.

Now men and women had begun to hold hands, to sit closer to one another. They slipped arms around one another and sat together probably feeling better than they had since they had been Awakened. It was unlikely that any of them could shake off the feeling the way Lilith had. No ooloi had modified them.

She looked around to see whether the Oankali were coming in yet. There was no sign of them. She turned to Joseph who was sitting next to her frowning.

"Joe?"

He looked at her. The frown smoothed away and he reached for her.

She let him draw her closer, then spoke into his ear. "The Oankali are about to come in. We've been drugged."

He shook off the drug. "I thought . . ." He rubbed his face. "I thought something was wrong." He breathed deeply, then looked around. "There," he said softly.

She followed the direction of his gaze and saw that the wall between the food cabinets was rippling, opening. In at least eight places, Oankali were coming in.

"Oh no," Joseph said, stiffening, looking away. "Why didn't you leave me comfortably drugged?"

"Sorry," she said, and rested her head on his arm. He had had only one brief experience with one Oankali. Whatever happened might be almost as hard on him as it was on the others. "You're modified," she said. "I don't think the drug could have held you once things got interesting."

More Oankali came through the openings. Lilith counted twenty-eight altogether. Would that be enough to handle forty-three terrified humans when the drug wore off?

People seemed to react to the nonhuman presence in slow motion. Tate and Gabriel stood up together, leaning on each other, staring at the Oankali. An ooloi approached them and they drew back. They were not terrified as they could have been, but they were frightened.

The ooloi spoke to them and Lilith realized it was Kahguyaht.

She stood up, staring at the trio. She could not distinguish individual words in what Kahguyaht was saying, but its tone was not one she would have associated with Kahguyaht. The tone was quiet, calming, oddly compelling. It was a tone Lilith had learned to associate with Nikanj.

Somewhere else in the room, a scuffle broke out. Curt, in spite of the drug, had attacked the ooloi that approached him. All the Oankali present were ooloi.

Peter tried to go to Curt's aid, but behind him, Jean screamed, and he turned back to help her.

Beatrice fled from her ooloi. She managed to run several steps before it caught her. It wrapped one sensory arm around her and she collapsed unconscious.

Around the room, other people collapsed—all the fighters, all the runners. No form of panic was tolerated.

Tate and Gabriel were still awake. Leah was awake, but Wray was unconscious. An ooloi seemed to be calming her, probably assuring her that Wray was all right.

Jean was still awake in spite of her momentary panic, but Peter was down.

Celene was awake and frozen in place. An ooloi touched her, then jerked away as though in pain. Celene had fainted.

Victor Dominic and Hilary Ballard were awake and together, holding one another, though they had shown no interest in one another until now.

Allison screamed and threw food at her ooloi, then turned and ran. Her ooloi caught her, but kept her conscious, probably because she did not struggle. She went rigid, but seemed to listen as her ooloi spoke soothingly.

Elsewhere in the room, small groups of people, supporting one another, confronted the ooloi without panic. The drug had quieted them just enough. The room was a scene of quiet, strangely gentle chaos.

Lilith watched Kahguyaht with Tate and Gabriel. The ooloi was sitting down now, facing them, talking to them, even giving them time to stare at the way its joints bent and the way its sensory tentacles followed movement. When it moved, it moved very slowly. When it spoke, Lilith could hear none of the hectoring contempt or amused tolerance that she was used to.

"You know that one?" Joseph asked.

"Yes. It's one of Nikanj's parents. I never got along with it."

Across the room, Kahguyaht's head tentacles swept in her direction for a moment and she knew it had heard. She considered saying more, giving it an earful—figuratively.

But before she could begin, Nikanj arrived. It stood before

Joseph and looked at him critically. "You're doing very well," it said. "How do you feel?"

"I'm all right."

"You will be." It glanced at Tate and Gabriel. "Your friends won't be, I think. Not both of them, anyway."

"What? Why not?"

Nikanj rustled its tentacles. "Kahguyaht will try. I warned it, and it admits I have a talent for humans, but it wants them badly. The woman will survive, but the man may not."

"Why!" Lilith demanded.

"He may choose not to. But Kahguyaht is skillful. Those two humans are the calmest in the room apart from you two." It focused for a moment on Joseph's hands, on the fact that he had gouged one with the nails of the other and that the gouged hand was dripping blood onto the floor.

Nikanj shifted its attention, even turning its body away from Joseph. Its instinct was to help, to heal a wound, stop pain. Yet it knew enough to let Joseph go on hurting himself for now.

"What are you doing, foretelling the future?" Joseph asked. His voice was a harsh whisper. "Gabe will kill himself?"

"Indirectly, he might. I hope not. I can't foretell anything. Maybe Kahguyaht will save him. He's worth saving. But his past behavior says he will be hard to work with." It reached out and took Joseph's hands, apparently unable to stand the gouging any longer.

"You were only given a weak, ooloi-neutral drug in your food," it told him. "I can help you with something better."

Joseph tried to pull away, but it ignored his effort. It examined the hand he had injured, then further tranquilized him, all the while talking to him quietly.

"You know I won't hurt you. You're not afraid of being hurt or of pain. And your fear of my strangeness will pass eventually. No, be still. Let your body go limp. Let it relax. If your body is relaxed, it will be easier for you to handle your fear. That's it. Lean back against this wall. I can help you maintain this state without blurring your intellect. You see?"

Joseph turned his head to look at Nikanj, then turned away, his movements slow, almost languid, belying the emotion behind them. Nikanj moved to sit next to him and maintain its hold on him. "Your fear is less than it was," it said. "And even what you feel now will pass quickly."

Lilith watched Nikanj work, knowing that it would drug Joseph only lightly—perhaps stimulate the release of his own endorphins and leave him feeling relaxed and slightly high. Nikanj's words, spoken with quiet assurance, only reinforced new feelings of security and well-being.

Joseph sighed. "I don't understand why the sight of you should scare me so," Joseph said. He did not sound frightened. "You don't look that threatening. Just . . . very different."

"Different *is* threatening to most species," Nikanj answered. "Different is dangerous. It might kill you. That was true to your animal ancestors and your nearest animal relatives. And it's true for you." Nikanj smoothed its head tentacles. "It's safer for your people to overcome the feeling on an individual basis than as members of a large group. That's why we've handled this the way we have." It looked around at individuals and pairs of humans, each with an ooloi.

Nikanj focused on Lilith. "It would have been easier for you to be handled this way—with drugs, with an adult ooloi."

"Why wasn't I?"

"You were being prepared for me, Lilith. Adults believed you would be best paired with me during my subadult stage. Jdahya believed he could bring you to me without drugs, and he was right."

Lilith shuddered. "I wouldn't want to go through anything like that again."

"You won't. Look at your friend Tate."

Lilith turned and saw that Tate had extended a hand to Kahguyaht. Gabriel grabbed it and hauled it back, arguing.

Tate said only a few words while Gabriel said many, but after a while, he let her go. Kahguyaht had not moved or spoken. It waited. It let Tate look at it again, perhaps build up her courage again. When she extended her hand again, it seized the hand in a coil of sensory arm in a move that seemed impossibly swift, yet gentle, nonthreatening. The arm moved like a striking cobra, yet there was that strange gentleness. Tate did not even seem startled.

"How can it move that way?" Lilith murmured.

"Kahguyaht was afraid she would not have the courage to finish the gesture," Nikanj said. "It was right, I think."

"I drew back any number of times."

"Jdahya had to make you do all the work yourself. He couldn't help."

"What will happen now?" Joseph asked.

"We'll stay with you for several days. When you're used to us, we'll take you to the training floor we've created—the forest." It focused on Lilith. "For a little while, you won't have any duties. I could take you and your mate outside for a while, show him more of the ship."

Lilith looked around the room. There were no more struggles, no manifest terror. People who could not control themselves were unconscious. Others were totally focused on their ooloi and suffering through confused combinations of fear and drug-induced well-being.

"I'm the only human who has any idea what's going on," she said. "Some of them might want to talk to me."

Silence.

"Yeah. What about it, Joe? Want to look around outside?"

He frowned. "What just didn't get said?"

She sighed. "The humans here aren't going to want us near them for a while. In fact, you may not want them near you. It's a reaction to the ooloi drugs. So we can stay here and be ignored or we can go outside."

Nikanj coiled the end of one sensory arm around her wrist, prompting her to consider a third possibility. She said nothing, but the eagerness that suddenly blossomed in her was so intense, it was suspicious.

"Let go!" she said.

It released her, but was now completely focused on her. It

had felt her body's leap of response to its wordless suggestion—or to its chemical suggestion.

"Did you do that?" she demanded. "Did you . . . inject
something."

"Nothing." It wrapped its free sensory arm around her
neck. "Oh, but I will 'inject something.' We can go out later."
It stood up, bringing them both up with it.

"What?" Joseph said as he was hauled to his feet. "What's
happening?"

No one answered him, but he did not resist being guided
into Lilith's bedroom. As Lilith sealed the doorway, he asked
again, "What's going on?"

Nikanj slid its sensory arm from Lilith's neck. "Wait," it
told her. Then it focused on Joseph, releasing him, but not
moving away. "The second time will be the hardest for you. I
left you no choice the first time. You could not have understood what there was to choose. Now you have some small
idea. And you have a choice."

He understood now. "No!" he said sharply. "Not again."

Silence.

"I'd rather have the real thing!"

"With Lilith?"

"Of course." He looked as though he would say something
more, but he glanced at Lilith and fell silent.

"Rather with any human than with me," Nikanj supplied
softly.

Joseph only stared at it.

"And yet I pleased you. I pleased you very much."

"Illusion!"

"Interpretation. Electrochemical stimulation of certain
nerves, certain parts of your brain . . . What happened was
real. Your body knows how real it was. Your interpretations
were illusion. The sensations were entirely real. You can have
them again—or you can have others."

"No!"

"And all that you have, you can share with Lilith."

Silence.

"All that she feels, she'll share with you." It reached out and caught his hand in a coil of sensory arm. "I won't hurt you. And I offer a oneness that your people strive for, dream of, but can't truly attain alone."

He pulled his arm free. "You said I could choose. I've made my choice!"

"You have, yes." It opened his jacket with its many-fingered true hands and stripped the garment from him. When he would have backed away, it held him. It managed to lie down on the bed with him without seeming to force him down. "You see. Your body has made a different choice."

He struggled violently for several seconds, then stopped. "Why are you doing this?" he demanded.

"Close your eyes."

"What?"

"Lie here with me for a while and close your eyes."

"What are you going to do?"

"Nothing. Close your eyes."

"I don't believe you."

"You're not afraid of me. Close your eyes."

Silence.

After a long while, he closed his eyes and the two of them lay together. Joseph held his body rigid at first, but slowly, as nothing happened, he began to relax. Sometime later his breathing evened and he seemed to be asleep.

Lilith sat on the table, waiting, watching. She was patient and interested. This might be her only chance ever to watch close up as an ooloi seduced someone. She thought it should have bothered her that the "someone" in this case was Joseph. She knew more than she wanted to about the wildly conflicting feelings he was subject to now.

Yet, in this matter, she trusted Nikanj completely. It was enjoying itself with Joseph. It would not spoil its enjoyment by hurting him or rushing him. In a perverse way, Joseph too was probably enjoying himself, though he could not have said so.

Lilith was dozing when Nikanj stroked Joseph's shoulders, rousing him. His voice roused her.

"What are you doing?" he demanded.

"Waking you."

"I wasn't asleep!"

Silence.

"My god," he said after a while. "I did fall asleep, didn't I? You must have drugged me."

"No."

He rubbed his eyes, but made no effort to get up.

"Why didn't you . . . just do it?"

"I told you. This time you can choose."

"I've chosen! You ignored me."

"Your body said one thing. Your words said another." It moved a sensory arm to the back of his neck, looping one coil loosely around his neck. "This is the position," it said. "I'll stop now if you like."

There was a moment of silence, then Joseph gave a long sigh. "I can't give you—or myself—permission," he said. "No matter what I feel, I can't."

Nikanj's head and body became mirror smooth. The change was so dramatic that Joseph jumped and drew back. "Does that . . . amuse you somehow?" he asked bitterly.

"It pleases me. It's what I expected."

"So . . . what happens now?"

"You are very strong-willed. You can hurt yourself as badly as you think necessary to achieve a goal or hold to a conviction."

"Let go of me."

It smoothed its tentacles again. "Be grateful, Joe. I'm not going to let go of you."

Lilith saw Joseph's body stiffen, struggle, then relax, and she knew Nikanj had read him correctly. He neither struggled nor argued as Nikanj positioned him more comfortably against its body. Lilith saw that he had closed his eyes again, his face peaceful. Now he was ready to accept what he had wanted from the beginning.

Silently, Lilith got up, stripped off her jacket, and went to the bed. She stood over it, looking down. For a moment, she saw Nikanj as she had once seen Jdahya—as a totally alien being, grotesque, repellant beyond mere ugliness with its night crawler body tentacles, its snake head tentacles, and its tendency to keep both moving, signaling attention and emotion.

She froze where she stood and had all she could to keep from turning and running away.

The moment passed, left her almost gasping. She jumped when Nikanj touched her with the tip of a sensory arm. She stared at it for a moment longer wondering how she had lost her horror of such a being.

Then she lay down, perversely eager for what it could give her. She positioned herself against it, and was not content until she felt the deceptively light touch of the sensory hand and felt the ooloi body tremble against her.

13

Humans were kept drugged for days—drugged, and guarded, each individual or pair by an ooloi.

"Imprinting is the best word for what they're doing," Nikanj told Joseph. "Imprinting, chemical and social."

"What you're doing to me!" Joseph accused.

"What I'm doing to you, what I've done to Lilith. It has to be done. No one will be returned to Earth without it."

"How long will they be drugged?"

"Some are not heavily drugged now. Tate Marah isn't. Gabriel Rinaldi is." It focused on Joseph. "You aren't. You know."

Joseph looked away. "No one should be."

"In the end, no one will be. We dull your natural fear of strangers and of difference. We keep you from injuring or killing us or yourselves. We teach you more pleasant things to do."

"That's not enough!"

"It's a beginning."

14

Peter's ooloi proved that ooloi were not infallible. Drugged, Peter was a different man. For perhaps the first time since his Awakening, he was at peace, not fighting even with himself, not trying to prove anything, joking with Jean and their ooloi about his arm and the fighting.

Lilith, hearing this later, wondered what there was to laugh at in that incident. But the ooloi-produced drugs could be potent. Under their influence, Peter might have laughed at anything. Under their influence, he accepted union and pleasure. When that influence was allowed to wane and Peter began to think, he apparently decided he had been humiliated and enslaved. The drug seemed to him to be not a less painful way of getting used to frightening nonhumans, but a way of turning him against himself, causing him to demean himself in alien perversions. His humanity was profaned. His manhood was taken away.

Peter's ooloi should have noticed that at some point what Peter said and the expression he assumed ceased to agree with what his body told it. Perhaps it did not know enough about human beings to handle someone like Peter. It was older than Nikanj—more a contemporary of Kahguyaht. But it was not as perceptive as either of them—and perhaps not as bright.

Sealed in Peter's room, alone with Peter, it allowed itself to be attacked, pounded by Peter's bare fists. Unfortunately for Peter, he hit a sensitive spot with his first hammering blow, and triggered the ooloi's defensive reflexes. It gave him a lethal sting before it could regain control of itself and he collapsed in convulsions. His own contracting muscles broke several of his bones, then he went into shock.

The ooloi tried to help him once it had recovered from the worst of its own pain, but it was too late. He was dead. The ooloi sat down beside his body, its head and body tentacles drawn into hard lumps. It did not move or speak. Its cool flesh grew even cooler, and it seemed to be as dead as the human it was apparently mourning.

There were no Oankali on watch above. Peter might have been saved if there had been. But the great room was full of ooloi. Where was the need to keep watch?

By the time one of these ooloi noticed Jean sitting alone and forlorn outside the sealed room, it was too late. There was nothing to do but take Peter's body out and send for the ooloi's mates. The ooloi remained catatonic.

Jean, still lightly drugged, frightened, and alone, retreated from the people clustering around the room. She stood apart and watched as the body was carried out. Lilith noticed her, approached her, knowing she couldn't help, but hoping at least to give comfort.

"No!" Jean said, backing toward a wall. "Get away!"

Lilith sighed. Jean was going through a prolonged period of ooloi-induced reclusiveness. All of the humans who had been kept heavily drugged were this way—unable to tolerate the nearness of anyone except their human mate and the ooloi who had drugged them. Neither Lilith nor Joseph had experienced this extreme reaction. Lilith had hardly noticed any reaction at all beyond an increased aversion to Kahguyaht back when Nikanj matured and bound her to it. More recently, Joseph had reacted by simply staying close to Lilith and Nikanj for a couple of days. Then his reaction passed. Jean's was far from passing. What would happen to her now?

Lilith looked around for Nikanj. She spotted it in a cluster of ooloi, went to it and laid a hand on its shoulder.

It focused on her without turning or breaking the various

sensory tentacle and sensory arm contacts it had with the others. She spoke to the point of a thin cone of head tentacles.

"Can't you help Jean?"

"Help is coming for her."

"Look at her! She's going to break before it gets here."

The cone focused on Jean. She had wedged herself into a corner. Now she stood crying silently and looking around in confusion. She was a tall, strongly built woman. Now, though, she looked like a large child.

Nikanj detached itself from the other ooloi, apparently ending whatever communication was going on. The other ooloi relaxed away from one another. They went to their various human charges who stood waiting for them in widely separated ones and twos. The moment the news of the death had gone around, every human except Lilith and Jean had been drugged heavily. Nikanj had refused to drug Lilith. It trusted her to control her own behavior and the other ooloi trusted it. As for Jean, there was no one present who could drug her without harming her.

Nikanj closed to within about ten feet of Jean. It stopped there and waited until she saw it.

She trembled, but did not try to cringe farther into her corner.

"I won't come closer," Nikanj said softly. "Others will come to help you. You aren't alone."

"But . . . But I am alone," she whispered. "They're dead. I saw them."

"One is dead," Nikanj corrected, keeping its voice low.

She hid her face in her hands and shook her head from side to side.

"Peter is dead," Nikanj told her, "but Tehjaht is only . . . injured. And you have siblings coming to help."

"What?"

"They'll help you."

She sat down on the floor, head down, voice muffled when she spoke. "I've never had any brothers or sisters. Not even before the war."

"Tehjaht has mates. They'll take care of you."

"No. They'll blame me . . . because Tehjaht is hurt."

"They'll help you." Very softly. "They'll help both you and Tehjaht. *They will help.*"

She frowned, looking more childlike than ever as she tried to understand. Then her face changed. Curt, heavily drugged, edged along the wall toward her. He kept himself comfortably far from Nikanj, but moved a little too close to Jean. She cringed back from him.

Curt shook his head, took a step backward. "Jeanie?" he called, his heavy voice sounding too loud, sounding drunk.

Jean jumped, but said nothing.

Curt faced Nikanj. "She's one of ours! We should be the ones to take care of her!"

"It isn't possible," Nikanj said.

"*It should be possible!* It should be! Why isn't it?"

"Her bonding with her ooloi is too strong, too heavily reinforced—as yours is with your ooloi. Later when the bond is more relaxed, you'll be able to go near her again. Later. Not now."

"Goddammit, she needs us now!"

"No."

Curt's ooloi came up to him, took him by the arm. Curt would have pulled away, but suddenly his strength seemed to leave him. He stumbled, fell to his knees. Nearby, Lilith looked away. Curt was as unlikely to forgive any humbling as Peter had been. And he would not always be drugged. He would remember.

Curt's ooloi helped Curt to his feet and led him away to the room he now shared with it and with Celene. As he left, the wall opened at the far end of the room and a male and female Oankali came in.

Nikanj gestured to the pair and they came toward it. They held on to one another, walking as though wounded, as though holding one another up. They were two when they should have been three, missing an essential part.

The male and female made their way to Nikanj, and past it

to Jean. Frightened, Jean stiffened. Then she frowned as though something had been said, and she had not quite heard.

Lilith watched sadly, knowing that the first signals Jean received were olfactory. The male and female smelled good, smelled like family, all brought together by the same ooloi. When they took her hands, they felt right. There was a real chemical affinity.

Jean seemed still to be afraid of the two strangers, but she was also relieved. They were what Nikanj had said they would be. People who could help. Family.

She let them lead her into the room where Tehjaht sat frozen. No words had been spoken. Strangers of a different species had been accepted as family. A human friend and ally had been rejected.

Lilith stood staring after Jean, hardly aware of Joseph's coming to stand beside her. He was drugged, but the drug had only made him reckless.

"Peter was right," he said angrily.

She frowned. "Peter? Right to try to kill? Right to die?"

"He died human! And he almost managed to take one of them with him!"

She looked at him. "So what? What's changed? On Earth we can change things. Not here."

"Will we want to by then? What will we be, I wonder? Not human. Not anymore."

IV

THE TRAINING FLOOR

1

The training room was brown and green and blue. Brown, muddy ground was visible through thin, scattered leaf litter. Brown, muddy water flowed past the land, glittering in the light of what seemed to be the sun. The water was too laden with sediment to appear blue, though above it, the ceiling—the sky—was a deep, intense blue. There was no smoke, no smog, only a few clouds—remains of a recent rain.

Across the wide river, there was the illusion of a line of trees on the opposite bank. A line of green. Away from the river, the predominant color was green. Above was the very real green canopy—trees of all sizes, many burdened with a profusion of other life: bromeliads, orchids, ferns, mosses, lichens, lianas, parasitic vines, plus a generous complement of insect life and a few frogs, lizards, and snakes.

One of the first things Lilith had learned during her own earlier training period was not to lean against the trees.

There were few flowers, and those mainly bromeliads and orchids, high in the trees. On the ground, a colorful stationary object was likely to be a leaf or some kind of fungus. Green was everywhere. The undergrowth was thin enough to walk through without difficulty except near the river where in some places a machete was essential—and not yet permitted.

"Tools will come later," Nikanj told Lilith. "Let the humans get used to being here now. Let them explore and see for themselves that they are in a forest on an island. Let them begin to feel what it's like to live here." It hesitated. "Let them settle more firmly into their places with their ooloi. They can tolerate one another now. Let them learn that it isn't shameful to be together with one another and with us."

It had gone with Lilith to the riverbank at a place where a great piece of earth had been undercut and had fallen into the river, taking several trees and much undergrowth with it. There was no trouble here in reaching the water, though there was a sharp drop of about ten feet. At the edge of the drop was one of the giants of the island—a huge tree with buttresses that swept well over Lilith's head and, like walls, separated the surrounding land into individual rooms. In spite of the great variety of life that the tree supported, Lilith stood between a pair of buttresses, two-thirds enclosed by the tree. She felt enveloped in a solidly Earthly thing. A thing that would soon be undercut as its neighbors had been, that would soon fall into the river and die.

"They'll cut the trees down, you know," she said softly. "They'll make boats or rafts. They think they're on Earth."

"Some of them believe otherwise," Nikanj told her. "They believe because you do."

"That won't stop the boat building."

"No. We won't try to stop it. Let them row their boats to the walls and back. There's no way out for them except the way we offer: to learn to feed and shelter themselves in this environment—to become self-sustaining. When they've done that, we'll take them to Earth and let them go."

It knew they would run, she thought. It must know. Yet it talked about mixed settlements, human and Oankali—trade-partner settlements within which ooloi would control the fertility and "mix" the children of both groups.

She looked up at the sloping, wedge-shaped buttresses. Semi-enclosed as she was, she could not see Nikanj or the river. There was only brown and green forest—the illusion of wilderness and isolation.

Nikanj left her the illusion for a while. It said nothing, made no sound. Her feet tired and she looked around for something to sit on. She did not want to go back to the others any sooner than she had to. They could tolerate one another again now;

the most difficult phase of their bonding was over. There was very little drugging still going on. Curt and Gabriel were still drugged along with a few others. Lilith worried about these. Oddly, she also admired them for being able to resist conditioning. Were they strong, then? Or simply unable to adapt?

"Lilith?" Nikanj said softly.

She did not answer.

"Let's go back."

She had found a dry, thick liana root to sit on. It hung like a swing, dropping down from the canopy, then curving upward again to lock itself into the branches of a nearby smaller tree before dropping to the ground and digging in. The root was thicker than some trees and the few insects on it looked harmless. It was an uncomfortable seat—twisted and hard— but Lilith was not yet ready to leave it.

"What will you do with the humans who can't adapt?" she asked.

"If they aren't violent, we'll take them to Earth with the rest of you." Nikanj came around the buttress, destroying her sense of solitude and home. Nothing that looked and moved as Nikanj did could come from home. She got up wearily and walked with it.

"Have the ants bitten you?" it asked.

She shook her head. It did not like her to conceal small injuries. It considered her health very much its business, and looked after her insect bites—especially her mosquito bites— at the end of each day. She thought it would have been easier to have left the mosquitoes out of this small simulation of Earth. But Oankali did not think that way. A simulation of a tropical forest of Earth had to be complete with snakes, centipedes, mosquitoes and other things Lilith would have preferred to live without. Why should the Oankali worry, she thought cynically. Nothing bit them.

"There are so few of you," Nikanj said as they walked. "No one wants to give up on any of you."

She had to think back to realize what it was talking about.

"Some of us thought we should hold off bonding with you

until you were brought here," it told her. "Here it would have been easier for you to band together, become a family."

Lilith glanced at it uneasily, but said nothing. Families had children. Was Nikanj saying children should be conceived and born here?

"But most of us couldn't wait," it continued. It wrapped a sensory arm around her neck loosely. "It might be better for both our peoples if we were not so strongly drawn to you."

2

Tools, when they were finally handed out, were waterproof tarpaulins, machetes, axes, shovels, hoes, metal pots, rope, hammocks, baskets, and mats. Lilith spoke privately with each of the most dangerous humans before they were given their tools.

One more try, she thought wearily.

"I don't care what you think of me," she told Curt. "You're the kind of man the human race is going to need down on Earth. That's why I woke you. I want you to live to get down there." She hesitated. "Don't go Peter's way, Curt."

He stared at her. Only recently free of the drug, only recently capable of violence, he stared.

"Make him sleep again!" Lilith told Nikanj. "Let him forget! Don't give him a machete and wait for him to use it on someone."

"Yahjahyi thinks he'll be all right," Nikanj said. Yahjahyi was Curt's ooloi.

"Does it?" Lilith said. "What did Peter's ooloi think?"

"It never told anyone what it thought. As a result, no one realized it was in trouble. Incredible behavior. I said it would be better if we weren't so drawn to you."

She shook her head. "If Yahjahyi thinks Curt is all right, it's deluding itself."

"We've observed Curt and Yahjahyi," Nikanj said. "Curt will go through a dangerous time now, but Yahjahyi is ready. Even Celene is ready."

"Celene!" Lilith said with contempt.

"You did a good job matching them. Much better than with Peter and Jean."

"I didn't match Peter and Jean. Their own temperaments did—like fire and gasoline."

". . . yes. Anyway, Celene is not ready to lose another mate. She'll hold on to him. And Curt, since he sees her as much more vulnerable than she is, will have good reason not to risk himself, not to chance leaving her alone. They'll be all right."

"They won't," Gabriel told her later. He too was free of the drug, finally, but he was handling it better. Kahguyaht, who had been so eager to push Lilith, coerce her, ridicule her, seemed to be infinitely patient with Tate and Gabriel.

"Look at things from Curt's point of view," Gabriel said. "He's not in control even of what his own body does and feels. He's taken like a woman and. . . . No, don't explain!" He held up his hand to stop her from interrupting. "He knows the ooloi aren't male. He knows all the sex that goes on is in his head. It doesn't matter. It doesn't fucking matter! Someone else is pushing all his buttons. He can't let them get away with that."

Honestly frightened, Lilith asked, "How have you . . . made your peace with it?"

"Who says I have?"

She stared at him. "Gabe, we can't lose you, too."

He smiled. Beautiful, perfect, white teeth. They made her think of some predator. "I don't take the next step," he said, "until I see where I'm standing now. You know I still don't believe this isn't Earth."

"I know."

"A tropical forest in a space ship. Who'd believe that?"

"But the Oankali. You can see that they're not of Earth."

"Sure. But they're here now on what sure looks, sounds, and smells like Earth."

"It isn't."

"So you say. Sooner or later I'll find out for myself."

"Kahguyaht could show you things that would make you sure now. They might even convince Curt."

"Nothing will convince Curt. Nothing will reach him."

"You think he'll do what Peter did?"

"Much more efficiently."

"Oh god. Did you know they put Jean back into suspended animation? She won't even remember Peter when she wakes up."

"I heard. That will make it easier on her when they put her with another guy, I guess."

"Is that what you would want for Tate?"

He shrugged, turned, and walked away.

3

Lilith taught all the humans to make thatch shingles and place them in overlapping rows on rafters so that they would not leak. She showed them the best trees to cut for flooring and frame. They all worked several days to construct a large thatch-roofed cabin on stilts, well above the river's high-water mark. The cabin was a twin to the one they had all squeezed into so far—the one Lilith and the ooloi had constructed when the ooloi brought them all through the miles of corridors to the training room.

The ooloi left this second construction strictly to the humans. They watched or sat talking among themselves or disappeared on errands of their own. But when the work was finished they brought in a small feast to celebrate.

"We won't provide food for much longer," one of them told the group. "You'll learn to live on what grows here and to cultivate gardens."

No one was surprised. They had already been cutting hands of green bananas from existing trees and hanging them from beams or from the porch railing. As the bananas ripened, the humans discovered they had to compete with the insects for them.

A few people had also been cutting pineapples and picking papayas and breadfruits from existing trees. Most people did not like the breadfruit until Lilith showed them the seeded form of the fruit, the breadnut. When they roasted the seeds as she instructed and ate them, they realized they had been eating them all along back in the great room.

They had pulled sweet cassava from the ground and dug up the yams Lilith had planted during her own training.

Not it was time for them to begin planting their own crops.

And, perhaps, now it was time for the Oankali to begin to see what they would harvest in their human crop.

Two men and a woman took their allotted tools and vanished into the forest. They did not really know enough yet to be on their own, but they were gone. Their ooloi did not go after them.

The group of ooloi put their head tentacles and sensory arms together for a moment and seemed to come to a very fast agreement: None of them would pay any attention to the three missing people.

"No one has escaped," Nikanj told Joseph and Lilith when they asked what would be done. "The missing people are still on the island. They're being watched."

"Watched through all these trees?" Joseph demanded.

"The ship is keeping track of them. If they're hurt, they'll be taken care of."

Other humans left the settlement. As the days passed, some of their ooloi seemed acutely uncomfortable. They kept to themselves, sat rock still, their head and body tentacles drawn into thick, dark lumps that looked, as Leah said, like grotesque tumors. These ooloi could be shouted at, rained on, tripped over. They never moved. When their head tentacles ceased to follow the movements of those around them, their mates arrived to tend them.

Male and female Oankali came out of the forest and took charge of their particular ooloi. Lilith never saw any of them called, but she saw one pair arrive.

She had gone alone to a place on the river where there was a heavily laden breadnut tree. She had climbed the tree, not only to get the fruit, but to enjoy the solitude and the beauty of the tree. She had never been much of a climber even as a child, but during her training, she had developed climbing skill and confidence—and a love of being so close to something so much of Earth.

From the tree, she saw two Oankali come out of the water. They did not seem to swim in toward land, but simply stood up near shore and walked in. Both focused on her for a moment, then headed inland toward the settlement.

She had watched them in utter silence, but they had known she was there. One more male and female, come to rescue a sick, abandoned ooloi.

Would it give the humans a feeling of power to know that they could make their ooloi feel sick and abandoned? Ooloi did not endure well when bereft of all those who carried their particular scent, their particular chemical marker. They lived. Metabolisms slowed, they retreated deep within themselves until called back by their families or, less satisfactorily, by another ooloi behaving as a kind of physician. So why didn't they go to their mates when their humans left? Why did they stay and get sick?

Lilith walked back to the settlement, a long crude basket filled with breadnuts on her back. She found the male and female ministering to their ooloi holding it between them and entangling its head and body tentacles with their own. Wherever the three touched, tentacles joined them. It was an intimate, vulnerable position, and other ooloi lounged nearby, guarding without seeming to guard. There were also a few humans watching. Lilith looked around the settlement, wondering how many of the humans not present would not come back from their day of wandering or food gathering. Did those who left come together on some other part of the island? Had they built a shelter? Were they building a boat? A wild thought struck her: What if they were right? What if they somehow were on Earth? What if it were possible to row a boat to freedom? What if, in spite of all she had seen and felt, this was some kind of hoax? How would it be perpetrated? *Why* would it be perpetrated? Why would the Oankali go to so much trouble?

No. She did not understand why the Oankali had done some of what they had done, but she believed the basics. The ship. The Earth, waiting to be recolonized by its people. The Oankali's price for saving the few remaining fragments of humanity.

But more people were leaving the settlement. Where were they? What if—The thought would not let her alone no matter what facts she felt she knew. *What if the others were right?*

Where had the doubt come from?

That evening as she brought in a load of firewood, Tate blocked her path.

"Curt and Celene are gone," she said quietly. "Celene let it slip to me that they were leaving."

"I'm surprised it took them so long."

"I'm surprised Curt didn't brain an Oankali before he left."

Nodding in agreement, Lilith stepped around her and put down her load of wood.

Tate followed and again planted herself in Lilith's path.

"What?" Lilith asked.

"We're going too. Tonight." She kept her voice very low—though no doubt more than one Oankali heard her.

"Where?"

"We don't know. Either we'll find the others or we won't. We'll find something—or make something."

"Just the two of you?"

"Four of us. Maybe more."

Lilith frowned, not knowing how to feel. She and Tate had become friends. Wherever Tate was going, she would not escape. If she did not injure herself or anyone else, she would probably be back.

"Listen," Tate said, "I'm not just telling you for the hell of it. We want you to go with us."

Lilith steered her away from the center of the camp. The Oankali would hear no matter what they did, but there was no need to involve other humans.

"Gabe has already talked to Joe," Tate said. "We want—"

"Gabe what!"

"Shut up! You want to tell everyone? Joe said he'd go. Now what about you?"

Lilith stared at her hostilely. "What about me?"

"I need to know now. Gabe wants to leave soon."

"If I leave with you, we'll leave after breakfast tomorrow morning."

Tate, being Tate, said nothing. She smiled.

"I didn't say I was going. All I mean is that there's no reason to sneak away in the night and step on a coral snake or something. It's pitch black out there at night."

"Gabe thinks we'll have more time before they discover we're gone."

"Where's his mind—and yours? Leave tonight and they'll notice you're gone by tomorrow morning—if you don't wake everyone on your way out by tripping over something or someone. Leave tomorrow morning and they won't notice you're gone until tomorrow night at dinner." She shook her head. "Not that they'll care. They haven't so far. But if you want to slip away, at least do it in a way that will give you a chance to find shelter before nightfall—or in case it rains."

"When it rains," Tate said. "It always rains sooner or later. We thought . . . maybe once we were clear of this place, we'd cross the river, head north, keep heading north until we found a dryer, cooler climate."

"If we are on Earth, Tate, considering what was done to

Earth and especially to the northern hemisphere, south would be a better direction."

Tate shrugged. "You don't get a vote unless you come with us."

"I'll talk to Joe."

"But—"

"And you ought to get Gabe to help you with your acting. I haven't said a thing you and Gabe hadn't already thought of. Neither of you is stupid. And you, at least, are no good at bull-shitting people."

Characteristically, Tate laughed. "I used to be." She sobered. "Okay, yeah. We've pretty much worked out the best way of doing it—tomorrow morning and south and with someone who probably knows how to stay alive in this country better than anyone but the Oankali."

There was a silence.

"We really are on an island, you know," Lilith said.

"No, I don't *know*," Tate answered. "But I'm willing to take your word for it. We'll have to cross the river."

"And in spite of what we see on what seems to be the other side, I believe we'll find a wall over there."

"In spite of the sun, the moon and the stars? In spite of the rain and the trees that have obviously been here for hundreds of years?"

Lilith sighed. "Yes."

"All because the Oankali said so."

"And because of what I saw and felt before I Awoke you."

"What the Oankali let you see and made you feel. You wouldn't believe some of the stuff Kahguyaht has made me feel."

"Wouldn't I?"

"I mean, you can't trust what they do to your senses!"

"I knew Nikanj when it was too young to do anything to my senses without my being aware of it."

Tate looked away, stared toward the river where the glint of water could still be seen. The sun—artificial or real—had not quite vanished and the river looked browner than ever.

"Look," she said, "I don't mean anything by this, but I have
to say it. You and Nikanj . . ." She let her voice die, abruptly
looked at Lilith as though demanding a response. "Well?"

"Well, what?"

"You're closer to him—to it—than we are to Kahguyaht.
You . . ."

Lilith stared at her silently.

"Hell, all I mean is, if you won't go with us, don't try to stop
us."

"Has anyone tried to stop anyone from leaving?"

"Just don't say anything. That's all."

"Maybe you are stupid," Lilith said softly.

Tate looked away again and shrugged. "I promised Gabe I'd
get you to promise."

"Why?"

"He thinks if you give your word, you'll keep it."

"Otherwise, I'll run and tell, right?"

"I'm beginning not to care what you do."

Lilith shrugged, turned and started back toward camp. It
seemed to take Tate several seconds to see that she meant it. Then
she ran after Lilith, pulled her back away from the camp.

"All right, I'm sorry you're insulted," Tate rasped. "Now
are you going or aren't you?"

"You know the breadnut tree up the bank—the big one?"

"Yes?"

"If we're going, we'll meet you there after breakfast tomorrow."

"We won't wait long."

"Okay."

Lilith turned and walked back to camp. How many Oankali
had heard the exchange? One? A few? All of them? No matter.
Nikanj would know in minutes. So it would have time to send
for Ahajas and Dichaan. It would not have to sit and go catatonic like the others.

In fact, she still wondered why the others had not done it.
Surely they had known that their chosen humans were leaving.
Kahguyaht would know. What would it do?

Something occurred to her suddenly—a memory of tribal people sending their sons out to live for a while alone in the forest or desert or whatever as a test of manhood.

Boys of a certain age who had been taught how to live in the environment were sent out to prove what they had learned.

Was that it? Train the humans in the basics, then let them go out on their own when they were ready?

Then why the catatonic ooloi?

"Lilith?"

She jumped, then stopped and let Joseph catch up with her. They walked together to the fire where people were sharing baked yams and Brazil nuts from a tree someone had stumbled upon.

"Did you talk to Tate?" he asked.

She nodded.

"What did you tell her?"

"That I'd talk to you."

Silence.

"What do you want to do?" she asked.

"Go."

She stopped, turned to look at him, but his face told her nothing.

"Would you leave me?" she whispered.

"Why would you stay? To be with Nikanj?"

"Would you leave me?"

"*Why would you stay?*" The whispered words had the impact of a shout.

"Because this is a ship. Because there's nowhere to run."

He looked up at the bright half moon and at the first scattering of stars. "I've got to see for myself," he said softly. "This *feels* like home. Even though I've never been in a tropical forest before in my life, but this smells and tastes and looks like home."

". . . I know."

"I've got to see!"

"Yes."

"Don't make me leave you."

She seized his hand as though it were an animal about to escape.

"Come with us!" he whispered.

She closed her eyes, shutting out the forest and the sky, the people talking quietly around the fire, the Oankali, several physically joined in silent conversation. How many of the Oankali had heard what she and Joseph were saying? None of them behaved as though they had heard.

"All right," she said softly. "I'll go."

4

Joseph and Lilith found no one waiting at the breadnut tree after breakfast the next morning. Lilith had seen Gabriel leave camp, carrying a large basket, his ax, and his machete as though intending to chop wood. People did that as they saw need just as Lilith took her own machete, ax, and baskets and went to gather forest foods when she saw need. She took people with her when she wanted to teach and went alone when she wanted to think.

This morning only Joseph was with her. Tate had left camp before breakfast. Lilith suspected that she might have gone to one of the gardens Lilith and Nikanj's family had planted. There she could dig cassava or yams or cut papayas, bananas, or pineapple. It would not help much. They would soon have to live on what they found in the forest.

Lilith carried roasted breadnuts both because she liked them and because they were a good source of protein. She also carried yams, beans, and cassava. At the bottom of her basket she carried extra clothing, a hammock of light, strong Oankali cloth, and a few sticks of dry tinder.

"We won't wait much longer," Joseph said. "They should be here. Maybe they've come and gone."

"More likely they'll be here as soon as they decide we weren't followed. They'll want to be sure I haven't sold them out, told the Oankali."

Joseph looked at her, frowned. "Tate and Gabe?"

"Yes."

"I don't think so."

She shrugged.

"Gabe said you should get out for your own good. He said he'd heard people beginning to talk against you again—now that they can think for themselves again."

"I'll be going toward the dangerous ones, Joe, not away from them. So will you."

He stared at the river for a while, then put his arm around her. "Do you want to go back?"

"Yes. But we won't."

He did not argue. She resented his silence, but accepted it. He wanted to go that badly. His feeling that he was on Earth was that strong.

Sometime later, Gabriel led Tate, Leah, Wray, and Allison to the breadnut tree. He stopped, stared at Lilith for a moment. She was certain he had heard all she had said.

"Let's go," she said.

They headed upriver by mutual consent since no one really wanted to head back toward camp. They stayed near the river to avoid getting lost. This meant occasionally hacking their way through undergrowth and aerial roots, but no one seemed to mind.

In the humidity, everyone perspired freely. Then it began to rain. Beyond walking more carefully in the mud, no one paid any attention. The mosquitoes bothered them less. Lilith slapped at a persistent one. There would be no Nikanj tonight to heal her insect bites, no gentle, multiple touches of sensory tentacles and sensory hands. Was she the only one who would miss them?

The rain ceased eventually. The group walked on until the

sun was directly overhead. Then they sat on the wet trunk of a fallen tree, ignoring fungi and brushing away insects. They ate breadnuts and the ripest of the bananas Tate had brought. They drank from the river, having long ago learned to ignore the sediment. It couldn't be seen in the handfuls of water that they drank, and it was harmless.

There was strangely little conversation. Lilith went aside to relieve herself and when she stepped clear of the tree that had concealed her, every eye was on her. Then abruptly everyone found something else to notice—one another, a tree, a piece of food, their fingernails.

"Oh god," Lilith muttered. And more loudly: "Let's talk, people." She stood before the fallen tree that they either sat or leaned on. "What is it?" she asked. "Are you waiting for me to desert you and go back to the Oankali? Or maybe you think I have some magic way of signaling them from here? What is it you suspect me of?"

Silence.

"What is it, Gabe?"

He met her gaze levelly. "Nothing." He spread his hands. "We're nervous. We don't know what's going to happen. We're scared. You shouldn't have to take the brunt of our feelings, but . . . but you're the different one. Nobody knows how different."

"She's here!" Joseph said, moving to stand beside her. "That should tell you how much like us she is. Whatever we risk, she risks it too."

Allison slid down off the log. "What is it we risk?" she demanded. She spoke directly to Lilith. "What will happen to us?"

"I don't know. I've guessed, but my guesses aren't worth much."

"Tell us!"

Lilith looked at the others, saw them all waiting. "I think these are our final tests," she said. "People leave camp when they feel ready. They live as best they can. If they can sustain themselves here, they can sustain themselves on Earth. That's why people have been allowed to walk away. That's why no one chases them."

"We don't know that no one chases them," Gabriel said.

"No one is chasing us."

"We don't even know that."

"When will you let yourself know it?"

He said nothing. He stared upriver with an air of impatience.

"Why did you want me on this trip, Gabe? Why did you personally want me here?"

"I didn't. I just—"

"Liar."

He frowned, glared at her. "I just thought you deserved a chance to get away from the Oankali—if you wanted it."

"You thought I might be useful! You thought you'd eat better and be better able to survive out here. You didn't think you were doing me a favor, you thought you were doing yourself one. It could work out that way." She looked around at the others. "But it won't. Not if everyone's sitting around waiting for me to play Judas." She sighed. "Let's go."

"Wait," Allison said as people were getting up. "You still think we're on a ship, don't you?" she asked Lilith.

Lilith nodded. "We are on a ship."

"Does anyone else here think so?" Allison demanded.

Silence.

"I don't know where we are," Leah said. "I don't see how all this could be part of a ship, but whatever it is, wherever it is, we're going to explore it and figure it out. We'll know soon."

"But she already knows," Allison insisted is a ship no matter what the truth is. So wh

Lilith opened her mouth to answer but "She's here because I wanted her here. I w place as badly as you all do. And I want h

Lilith wished she had come from behin tended not to notice all the eyes and all the picion.

"Is that it?" Gabriel asked. "You came because Joe asked you to?"

"Yes," she said softly.

"Otherwise you would have stayed with the Oankali?"

"I would have stayed at camp. After all, I know I can live out here. If these are final tests, I've already passed mine."

"And what kind of grade did the Oankali give you?" It was probably the most honest question he had ever asked her—filled with hostility, suspicion, and contempt.

"It was a pass-fail course, Gabe. A live-die course." She turned and began walking upriver, breaking trail. After a while, she heard them following.

5

Upriver was the oldest part of the island, the part with the greatest number of huge old trees, many with broad buttresses. This land had once been connected to the mainland—had become first a peninsula, then an island as the river changed course and cut through the connecting neck of land. Or that was what was supposed to have happened. That was the Oankali illusion. Or was it an illusion?

Lilith found her moments of doubt coming more often as she walked. She had not been along this bank of the river. Like the Oankali, she had not worried about getting lost. She and Nikanj had walked through the interior several times, and she had found it easier to look up at the green canopy and believe herself within a vast room.

But the river seemed so large. As they followed the bank, the bank changed, seemed nearer, seemed more heavily forested more deeply eroded there, ranged from low bluffs to flat t slipped into the river, blending almost seamlessly with

its reflection. She could pick out individual trees—treetops anyway. Those that towered above the canopy.

"We should stop for the night," she said when the sun told
her it was late afternoon. "We should make camp here and tomorrow, we should start to build a boat."

"Have you been here before?" Joseph asked her.

"No. But I've been near here. The opposite bank is as close
to us as it gets in this area. Let's see what we can do about shelter. It's going to rain again."

"Wait a minute," Gabriel said.

She looked at him and knew what was coming. She had
taken charge out of habit. Now she would hear about it.

"I didn't invite you along to tell us what to do," he said.
"We're not in the prison room now. We don't take orders from
you."

"You brought me along because I had knowledge you didn't
have. What do you want to do? Keep walking until it's too late
to put up a shelter? Sleep in the mud tonight? Find a wider sec-
tion of river to cross?"

"I want to find the others—if they're still free."

Lilith hesitated for a moment in surprise. "And if they're together." She sighed. "Is that what the rest of you want?"

"I want to get as far from the Oankali as I can," Tate said.
"I want to forget what it feels like when they touch me."

Lilith pointed. "If that's land over there instead of some kind
of illusion, then that's your goal. Your first goal anyway."

"We find the others first!" Gabriel insisted.

Lilith looked at him with interest. He was in the open now.
Probably in his mind he was in some kind of struggle with her.
He wanted to lead and she did not—yet she had to. He could
easily get someone killed.

"If we build a shelter now," she said, "I'll find the others tomorrow if they're anywhere nearby." She held up her hand to
stop the obvious objection. "One or all of you can come with
me and watch if you want to. It's just that I can't get lost. If I
leave you and you don't move, I'll be able to find you again. If
we all travel together, I can bring you back to this spot. After

all, it's just possible that some or all of the others have already crossed the river. They've had time."

People were nodding.

"Where do we camp?" Allison asked.

"It's early," Leah protested.

"Not to me it isn't," Wray said. "Between the mosquitoes and my feet, I'm glad to stop."

"The mosquitoes will be bad tonight," Lilith told him. "Sleeping with an ooloi was better than any mosquito repellant. Tonight, they'll probably eat us alive."

"I can stand it," Tate said.

Had she hated Kahguyaht so much? Lilith wondered. Or was she only beginning to miss it and trying to defend herself against her own feelings?

"We can clear here," she said aloud. "Don't cut those two saplings. Wait a minute." She looked to see if either young tree were home to colonies of stinging ants. "Yes, these are all right. Find two more of this size or a little bigger and cut them. And cut aerial roots. Thin ones to use as rope. Be careful. If anything stings or bites you out here . . . We're on our own. You could die. And don't go out of sight of this area. It's easier to get lost than you think."

"But you're so good you can't get lost," Gabriel said.

"Good has nothing to do with it. I have an eidetic memory and I've had more time to get used to the forest." She had never told them why she had an eidetic memory. Every Oankali change she had told them about had diminished her credibility with them.

"Too good to be true," Gabriel said softly.

They chose the highest ground they could find and built a shelter. They believed they would be using it for a few days, at least. The shelter was wall-less—no more than a frame with a roof. They could hang hammocks from it or spread mats beneath it on mattresses of leaves and branches. It was just large enough to keep everyone out of the rain. They roofed it with the tarpaulins some of them had brought. Then they used branches to sweep the ground beneath clean of leaves, twigs and fungi.

Wray managed to get a fire going with a bow Leah had brought along, but he swore he would never do it again. "Too much work," he said.

Leah had brought corn from the garden. It was dark when they roasted it along with some of Lilith's yams. They ate these along with the last of the breadnuts. The meal was filling, though not satisfying.

"Tomorrow we can fish," Lilith told them.

"Without even a safety pin, a string, and a stick?" Wray said.

Lilith smiled. "Worse than that. The Oankali wouldn't teach me how to kill anything, so the only fish I caught were the ones stranded in some of the little streams. I cut a slender, straight sapling pole, sharpened one end, hardened it in the fire, and taught myself to spear fish. I actually did it—speared several of them."

"Ever try it with bow and arrow?" Wray asked.

"Yes. I was better with the spear."

"I'll try it," he said. "Or maybe I can even put together a jungle version of a safety pin and string. Tomorrow, while the rest of you look for the others, I'll start learning to fish."

"*We'll* fish," Leah said.

He smiled and took her hand—then let it go in almost the same motion. His smile faded and he stared into the fire. Leah looked away into the darkness of the forest.

Lilith watched them, frowning. What was going on? Was it just trouble between them—or was it something else?

It began to rain suddenly, and they sat dry and united by the darkness and the noise outside. The rain poured down and the insects took shelter with them, biting them and sometimes flying into the fire which had been built up again for light and comfort once the cooking was done.

Lilith tied her hammock to two crossbeams and lay down. Joseph hung his hammock near her—too near for a third person to lie between them. But he did not touch her. There was no privacy. She did not expect to make love. But she was bothered by the care he took not to touch her. She reached out and touched his face to make him turn toward her.

Instead, he drew away. Worse, if he had not drawn away, she would have. His flesh felt wrong somehow, oddly repellant. It had not been this way when he came to her before Nikanj moved in between them. Joseph's touch had been more than welcome. He had been water after a very long drought. But then Nikanj had come to stay. It had created for them the powerful threefold unity that was one of the most alien features of Oankali life. Had that unity now become a necessary feature of their human lives? If it had, what could they do? Would the effect wear off?

An ooloi needed a male and female pair to be able to play its part in reproduction, but it neither needed nor wanted two-way contact between that male and female. Oankali males and females never touched each other sexually. That worked fine for them. It could not possibly work for human beings.

She reached out and took Joseph's hand. He tried to jerk away reflexively, then he seemed to realize something was wrong. He held her hand for a long, increasingly uncomfortable moment. Finally it was she who drew away, shuddering with revulsion and relief.

6

The next morning just after dawn, Curt and his people found the shelter.

Lilith started awake, knowing that something was not right. She sat up awkwardly in the hammock and put her feet on the ground. Near Joseph, she saw Victor and Gregory. She turned toward them, relieved. Now there would be no need to look for the others. They could all get busy building the boat or raft they would need to cross the river. Everyone would find out for certain whether the other side was forest or illusion.

She looked around to see who else had arrived. That was when she saw Curt.

An instant later, Curt hit her across the side of the head with the flat of his machete.

She dropped to the ground, stunned. Nearby, she heard Joseph shout her name. There was the sound of more blows.

She heard Gabriel swearing, heard Allison scream.

She tried desperately to get up, and someone hit her again. This time she lost consciousness.

Lilith awoke to pain and solitude. She was alone in the small shelter she had helped build.

She got up, ignoring her aching head as best she could. It would stop soon.

Where was everyone?

Where was Joseph? He would not have deserted her even if the others did.

Had he been taken away by force? If so, why? Had he been injured and left as she had been?

She stepped out of the shelter and looked around. There was no one. Nothing.

She looked for some sign of where they had gone. She knew nothing in particular about tracking, but the muddy ground did show marks of human feet. She followed them away from the camp. Eventually, she lost them.

She stared ahead, trying to guess which way they had gone and wondering what she would do if she found them. At this point, all she really wanted to do was see that Joseph was all right. If he had seen Curt hit her, he would surely have tried to intervene.

She remembered now what Nikanj had said about Joseph having enemies. Curt had never liked him. Nothing had happened between the two of them in the great room or at the settlement. But what if something had happened now?

She must go back to the settlement and get help from the

Oankali. She must get nonhumans to help her against her own people in a place that might or might not be on Earth.

Why couldn't they have left her Joseph? They had taken her machete, her ax, her baskets—everything except her hammock and her extra clothing. They could at least have left Joseph to see that she was all right. He would have stayed to do that if they had let him.

She walked back to the shelter, collected her clothing and hammock, drank water from a small, clear stream that fed into the river, and started back toward the settlement.

If only Nikanj were still there. Perhaps it could spy on the human camp without the humans' knowing, without fighting. Then if Joseph were there, he could be freed . . . if he wanted to be. Would he want it? Or would he choose to stay with the others who were trying to do the thing she had always wanted them all to do? *Learn and run.* Learn to live in this country, then lose themselves in it, go beyond the reach of the Oankali. Learn to touch one another as human beings again.

If they were on Earth as they believed, they might have a chance. If they were aboard a ship, nothing they did would matter.

If they were aboard a ship, Joseph would definitely be restored to her. But if they were on Earth . . .

She walked quickly, taking advantage of the path cleared the day before.

There was a sound behind her, and she turned quickly. Several ooloi emerged from the water and waded onto the bank to thrash their way through the thick bank undergrowth.

She turned and went back to them, recognizing Nikanj and Kahguyaht among them.

"Do you know where they've gone?" she asked Nikanj.

"We know," it said. It settled a sensory arm around her neck.

She put her hand to the arm, securing it where it was, welcoming it in spite of herself. "Is Joe all right?"

It did not answer, and that frightened her. It released her and led her through the trees, moving quickly. The other ooloi followed, all of them silent, all clearly knowing where they were going and probably knowing what they would find there.

Lilith no longer wanted to know.

She kept their fast pace easily, staying close to Nikanj. She almost slammed into it when it stopped without warning near a fallen tree.

The tree had been a giant. Even on its side, it was high and hard to climb, rotten and covered with fungi. Nikanj leaped onto it and off the other side with an agility Lilith could not match.

"Wait," it said as she began to climb the trunk. "Stay there." Then it focused on Kahguyaht. "Go on," it urged. "There could be more trouble while you wait here with me."

Neither Kahguyaht nor any of the other ooloi moved. Lilith noticed Curt's ooloi among them, and Allison's and—

"Come over now, Lilith."

She climbed over the trunk, jumped down on the other side. And there was Joseph.

He had been attacked with an ax.

She stared, speechless, then rushed to him. He had been hit more than once—blows to the head and neck. His head had been all but severed from his body. He was already cold.

The hatred that someone must have felt for him . . . "Curt?" she demanded of Nikanj. "Was it Curt?"

"It was us," Nikanj said very softly.

After a time, she managed to turn from the grisly corpse and face Nikanj. "What?"

"Us," Nikanj repeated. "We wanted to keep him safe, you and I. He was slightly injured and unconscious when they took him away. He had fought for you. But his injuries healed. Curt saw the flesh healing. He believed Joe wasn't human."

"*Why didn't you help him!*" she screamed. She had begun to cry. She turned again to see the terrible wounds and did not understand how she could even look at Joseph's body so mutilated, dead. She had had no last words from him, no memory of fighting alongside him, no chance to protect him. Her last memory was of him flinching away from her too-human touch.

"I'm more different than he was," she whispered. "Why didn't Curt kill me?"

"I don't believe he meant to kill anyone," Nikanj said. "He was angry and afraid and in pain. Joseph had injured him when he hit you. Then he saw Joseph healing, saw the flesh mending itself before his eyes. He screamed. I've never heard a human scream that way. Then he . . . used his ax."

"Why didn't you help?" she demanded. "If you could see and hear everything, why—"

"We don't have an entrance near enough to this place."

She made a sound of anger and despair.

"And there was no sign that Curt meant to kill. He blames you for almost everything, yet he didn't kill you. What happened here was . . . totally unplanned."

She had stopped listening. Nikanj's words were incomprehensible to her. Joseph was dead—hacked to death by Curt. It was all some kind of mistake. Insanity!

She sat on the ground beside the corpse, first trying to understand, then doing nothing at all; not thinking, no longer crying. She sat. Insects crawled over her and Nikanj brushed them off. She did not notice.

After a time, Nikanj lifted her to her feet, managing her weight easily. She meant to push it away, make it let her alone. It had not helped Joseph. She did not need anything from it now. Yet she only twisted in its grasp.

It let her pull free and she stumbled back to Joseph. Curt had walked away and left him as though he were a dead animal. He should be buried.

Nikanj came to her again, seemed to read her thoughts. "Shall we pick him up on our way back and have him sent to Earth?" it asked. "He can end as part of his homeworld."

Bury him on Earth? Let his flesh be part of the new beginning there? "Yes," she whispered.

It touched her experimentally with a sensory arm. She glared at it, wanting desperately to be let alone.

"No!" it said softly. "No, I let you alone once, the two of you, thinking you could look after one another. I won't let you alone now."

She drew a deep breath, accepted the familiar loop of sensory arm around her neck. "Don't drug me," she said. "Leave me . . . leave me what I feel for him, at least."

"I want to share, not mute or distort."

"Share? Share my feelings now?"

"Yes."

"*Why?*"

"Lilith . . ." It began to walk and she walked beside it automatically. The other ooloi moved silently ahead of them. "Lilith, he was mine too. You brought him to me."

"You brought him to me."

"I would not have touched him if you had rejected him."

"I wish I had. He'd be alive."

Nikanj said nothing.

"Let me share what you feel," she said.

It touched her face in a startlingly human gesture. "Move the sixteenth finger of your left strength hand," it said softly. One more case of Oankali omniscience: *We understand your feelings, eat your food, manipulate your genes. But we're too complex for you to understand.*

"Approximate!" she demanded. "Trade! You're always talking about trading. Give me something of yourself!"

The other ooloi focused back toward them and Nikanj's head and body tentacles drew themselves into lumps of some negative emotion. Embarrassment? Anger? She did not care. Why should it feel comfortable about parasitizing her feelings for Joseph—her feelings for anything? It had helped set up a human experiment. One of the humans had been lost. What did it feel? Guilty for not having been more careful with valuable subjects? Or were they even valuable?

Nikanj pressed the back of her neck with a sensory hand—

warning pressure. It would give her something then. They
stopped walking by mutual consent and faced one another.

It gave her . . . a new color. A totally alien, unique, nameless
thing, half seen, half felt or . . . tasted. A blaze of something
frightening, yet overwhelmingly, compelling.

Extinguished.

A half known mystery beautiful and complex. A deep, impossibly sensuous promise.

Broken.

Gone.

Dead.

The forest came back around her slowly and she realized she
was still standing with Nikanj, facing it, her back to the waiting ooloi.

"That's all I can give you," Nikanj said. "That's what I feel.
I don't even know whether there are words in any human language to speak of it."

"Probably not," she whispered. After a moment, she let herself hug it. There was some comfort even in cool, gray flesh.
Grief was grief, she thought. It was pain and loss and despair—an abrupt end where there should have been a continuing.

She walked more willingly with Nikanj now, and the other
ooloi no longer isolated them in front or behind.

7

Curt's camp boasted a bigger shelter, not as well made. The
roof was a jumble of palm leaves—not thatch, but branches
crisscrossed and covering one another. No doubt it leaked.
There were walls, but no floor. There was an indoor fire, hot

and smoky. That was the way the people looked. Hot, smoky, dirty, angry.

They gathered outside the shelter with axes, machetes, and clubs, and faced the cluster of ooloi. Lilith found herself standing with aliens, facing hostile, dangerous humans.

She drew back. "I can't fight them," she said to Nikanj. "Curt, yes, but not the others."

"We'll have to fight if they attack," Nikanj said. "But you stay out of it. We'll be drugging them heavily—fighting to subdue without killing in spite of their weapons. Dangerous."

"No closer!" Curt called.

The Oankali stopped.

"This is a human place!" Curt continued. "It's off limits to you and your animals." He stared at Lilith, held his ax ready.

She stared back, afraid of the ax, but wanting him. Wanting to kill him. Wanting to take the ax from him and beat him to death with her own hands. Let him die here and rot in this alien place where he had left Joseph.

"Do nothing," Nikanj whispered to her. "He has lost all hope of Earth. He's lost Celene. She'll be sent to Earth without him. And he's lost mental and emotional freedom. Leave him to us."

She could not understand it at first—literally could not comprehend the words it spoke. There was nothing in her world but a dead Joseph and an obscenely alive Curt.

Nikanj held her until it too had to be acknowledged as part of her world. When it saw that she looked at it, struggled against it instead of simply struggling toward Curt, it repeated its words until she heard them, until they penetrated, until she was still. It never made any attempt to drug her, and it never let her go.

Off to one side, Kahguyaht was speaking to Tate. Tate stood well back from it, holding a machete and staying close to Gabriel who held an ax. It was Gabriel who had convinced her to abandon Lilith. It had to be. And what had convinced Leah? Practicality? A fear of being abandoned alone, left as much an outcast as Lilith?

Lilith found Leah and stared at her, wondering. Lilith looked away. Then her attention was drawn back to Tate.

"Go away," Tate was pleading in a voice that did not sound like her. "We don't want you! I don't want you! Let us alone!" She sounded as though she would cry. In fact, tears streamed down her face.

"I have never lied to you," Kahguyaht told her. "If you manage to use your machete on anyone, you'll lose Earth. You'll never see your homeworld again. Even this place will be denied to you." It stepped toward her. "Don't do this Tate. We're giving you the thing you want most: Freedom and a return home."

"We've got that here," Gabriel said.

Curt came to join him. "We don't need anything else from you!" he shouted.

The others behind him agreed loudly.

"You would starve here," Kahguyaht said. "Even in the short time you've been here, you've had trouble finding food. There isn't enough, and you don't yet know how to use what there is." Kahguyaht raised its voice, spoke to all of them. "You were allowed to leave us when you wished so that you could practice the skills you'd learned and learn more from each other and from Lilith. We had to know how you would behave after leaving us. We knew you might be injured, but we didn't think you would kill one another."

"We didn't kill a human being," Curt shouted. "We killed one of your animals!"

"We?" Kahguyaht said mildly. "And who helped you kill him?"

Curt did not answer.

"You beat him," Kahguyaht continued, "and when he was unconscious, you killed him with your ax. You did it alone, and in doing it, you've exiled yourself permanently from your Earth." It spoke to the others. "Will you join him? Will you be taken from this training room and placed with Toaht families to live the rest of your lives aboard the ship?"

The faces of some of the others began to change—doubts beginning or growing.

Allison's ooloi went to her, became the first to touch the human it had come to retrieve. It spoke very quietly. Lilith could not hear what it said, but after a moment, Allison sighed and offered it her machete.

It declined the knife with a wave of one sensory arm while settling the other arm around her neck. It drew her back behind the line of Oankali where Lilith stood with Nikanj. Lilith stared at her, wondering how Allison could turn against her. Had it only been fear? Curt could frighten just about anyone if he worked at it. And this was Curt with an ax—an ax he had already used on one man . . .

Allison met her gaze, looked away, then faced her again. "I'm sorry," she whispered. "We thought we could avoid bloodshed by going along with them, doing what they said. We thought . . . I'm sorry."

Lilith turned away, tears blurring her vision again. Somehow, she had been able to put Joseph's death aside for a few minutes. Allison's words brought it back.

Kahguyaht stretched out a sensory arm to Tate but Gabriel snatched her away.

"We don't want you here!" he grated. He thrust Tate behind him.

Curt shouted—a wordless scream of rage, a call to attack. He lunged at Kahguyaht and several of his people joined his attack, lunging at the other ooloi with their weapons.

Nikanj thrust Lilith toward Allison and plunged into the fighting. Allison's ooloi paused only long enough to say, "Keep her out of this!" in rapid Oankali. Then it, too, joined the fight.

Things happened almost too quickly to follow. Tate and the few other humans who seemed to want nothing more than to get clear found themselves caught in the middle. Wray and Leah, half supporting one another, stumbled out of the fighting between a pair of ooloi who seemed about to be slashed by three machete-wielding humans. Lilith realized suddenly that

Leah was bleeding, and she ran to help get her away from the danger.

The humans shouted. The ooloi did not make a sound. Lilith saw Gabriel swing at Nikanj, narrowly missing it, saw him raise his ax again for what was clearly intended to be a death blow. Then Kahguyaht drugged him from behind.

Gabriel made a small gasp of sound—as though there were not enough strength in him to force out a scream. He collapsed.

Tate screamed, grabbed him, and tried to drag him clear of the fighting. She had dropped her machete, was clearly no threat.

Curt had not dropped his ax. It gave him a long, deadly reach. He swung it like a hatchet, controlling it easily in spite of its weight, and no ooloi risked being hit by it.

Elsewhere a man did manage to swing his ax through part of an ooloi's chest, leaving a gaping wound. When the ooloi fell, the man closed in for the kill, aided by a woman with a machete.

A second ooloi stung them both from behind. As they fell, the injured ooloi got up. In spite of the cut it had taken, it walked over to where Lilith's group waited. It sat down heavily on the ground.

Lilith looked at Allison, Wray, and Leah. They stared at the ooloi, but made no move toward it. Lilith went to it, noticing that it focused on her sharply in spite of its wound. She suspected the wound would not have stopped it from stinging her to unconsciousness or death if it felt threatened.

"Is there anything I can do to help?" she asked. Its wound was just about where its heart would have been if it had been human. It was oozing thick clear fluid and blood so bright red that it seemed false. Movie blood. Poster-paint blood. Such a terrible wound should have been awash in bodily fluids, but the ooloi seemed to be losing very little.

"I'll heal," it said in its disconcertingly calm voice. "This isn't serious." It paused. "I never believed they would try to kill us. I never knew how hard it would be not to kill them."

"You should have known," Lilith said. "You've had plenty of time to study us. What did you think would happen when you told us you were going to extinguish us as a species by tampering genetically with our children?"

The ooloi focused on her again. "If you had used a weapon, you could probably have killed at least one of us. These others couldn't, but you could."

"I don't want to kill you. I want to get away from you. You know that."

"I know you think that."

It turned its attention from her and began doing something to its wound with its sensory arms.

"Lilith!" Allison called.

Lilith looked back at her, then looked where she was pointing.

Nikanj was down, writhing on the ground as no ooloi had so far. Kahguyaht abruptly stopped fencing with Curt, lunged under his ax, hit him, and drugged him. Curt was the last human to go down. Tate was still conscious, still holding Gabriel, who was unconscious from Kahguyaht's sting. Some distance away, Victor was conscious, weaponless, making his way to the injured ooloi near Lilith—Victor's ooloi, she realized.

Lilith did not care how the two would meet. They could both take care of themselves. She ran toward Nikanj, avoiding the sensory arms of another ooloi who might have stung her.

Kahguyaht was already kneeling beside Nikanj, speaking to it low-voiced. It fell silent as she knelt on Nikanj's opposite side. She saw Nikanj's wound at once. Its left sensory arm had been hacked almost off. The arm seemed to be hanging by little more than a length of tough gray skin. Clear fluid and blood spurted from the wound.

"My god!" Lilith said. "Can it . . . can it heal?"

"Perhaps," Kahguyaht answered in its insanely calm voice. She hated their voices. "But you must help it."

"Yes, of course, I'll help. What shall I do?"

"Lie beside it. Hold it and hold the sensory arm in place so that it can reattach—if it will."

"Reattach?"

"Get your clothing off. It may be too weak to burrow through clothing."

Lilith stripped, refusing to think how she would look to the humans still conscious. They would be certain now that she was a traitor. Stripping naked on the battlefield to lie down with the enemy. Even the few who had accepted her might turn on her now. But she had just lost Joseph. She could not lose Nikanj too. She could not simply watch it die.

She lay down beside it and it strained toward her silently. She looked up for more instructions from Kahguyaht, but Kahguyaht had gone away to examine Gabriel. Nothing important going on for it here. Only its child, horribly wounded.

Nikanj penetrated her body with every head and body tentacle that could reach her, and for once it felt the way she had always imagined it should. It hurt! It was like abruptly being used as a pincushion. She gasped, but managed not to pull away. The pain was endurable, was probably nothing to what Nikanj was feeling—however it experienced pain.

She reached twice for the nearly severed sensory arm before she could make herself touch it. It was covered with slimy bodily fluids and white, blue-gray, and red-gray tissues hung from it.

She grasped it as best she could and pressed it to the stump it had been hacked from.

But surely more was necessary than this. Surely the heavy, complex, muscular organ could not reattach itself with no aid but the pressure of a human hand.

"Breathe deeply," Nikanj said, hoarsely. "Keep breathing deeply. Use both hands to hold my arm."

"You're plugged into my left arm," she gasped.

Nikanj made a harsh, ugly sound. "I have no control. I'll have to let you go completely, then begin again. If I can."

Several seconds later, tens of dozens of "needles" were withdrawn from Lilith's body. She rearranged Nikanj as gently as she could so that its head was on her shoulder and she could reach the nearly severed limb with both hands. She could support it and hold it where it belonged. She could rest one of her own arms on the ground and the other across Nikanj's body. This was a position she could hold for a while as long as no one disturbed her.

"All right," she said, bracing for the pincushion effect again. Nikanj did nothing.

"Nikanj!" she whispered, frightened.

It stirred, then penetrated her flesh so abruptly in so many places—and so painfully—that she cried out. But she managed not to move beyond an initial reflexive jerk.

"Breathe deeply," it said. "I . . . I'll try not to hurt you anymore."

"It's not that bad. I just don't see how this can help you."

"Your body can help me. Keep breathing deeply."

It said nothing more, made no sound of its own pain. She lay with it, eyes closed most of the time, and let the time pass, let herself lose track of it. From time to time, hands touched her. The first time she felt them, she looked to see what they were doing and realized that they were Oankali hands, brushing insects from her body.

Much later when she had lost track of time she was surprised to open her eyes to darkness; she felt someone lift her head and slip something under it.

Someone had covered her body with cloth. Spare clothing? And someone had wedged cloth under the parts of her body that seemed to need easing.

She heard talking, listened for human voices, and could not distinguish any. Parts of her body went numb, then underwent their own painful reawakening with no effort on her part. Her arms ached, then were eased, though she never changed position. Someone put water to her lips and she drank between gasps.

She could hear her own breathing. No one had to remind her to breathe deeply. Her body demanded it. She had begun breathing through her mouth. Whoever was looking after her noticed this and gave her water more often. Small amounts to wet her mouth. The water made her wonder what would happen if she had to go to the bathroom, but the problem never occurred.

Bits of food were put into her mouth. She did not know what it was, could not taste it, but it seemed to strengthen her.

At some point she recognized Ahajas, Nikanj's female mate as the owner of the hands that gave her food and water. She was confused at first and wondered whether she had been moved out of the forest and back to the quarters the family shared. But when it was light, she could still see the forest canopy—real trees burdened with epiphytes and lianas. A rounded termite nest the size of a basketball hung from a branch just above her. Nothing like that existed in the orderly, self-manicured Oankali living areas.

She drifted away again. Later she realized she was not always conscious. Yet she never felt as though she had slept. And she never let go of Nikanj. She could not let go of it. It had frozen her hands, her muscles into position as a kind of living cast to hold it while it healed.

At times her heart beat fast, thundering in her ears as though she had been running hard.

Dichaan took over the task of giving her food and water and protecting her from insects. He kept flattening his head and body tentacles when he looked at Nikanj's wound. Lilith managed to look at it to see what was pleasing him.

There first seemed nothing to be pleased about. The wound oozed fluids that turned black and stank. Lilith was afraid that some kind of infection had set in, but she could do nothing. At least none of the local insects seemed attracted to it—and none of the local microorganisms, probably. More likely Nikanj had brought whatever caused its infection into the training room with it.

The infection seemed to heal eventually, though clear fluid

continued to leak from the wound. Not until it stopped completely did Nikanj let her go.

She began to rouse slowly, began to realize that she had not been fully conscious for a long time. It was as though she were Awakening again from suspended animation, this time without pain. Muscles that should have screamed when she moved after lying still for so long made no protest at all.

She moved slowly, straightening her arms, stretching her legs, arching her back against the ground. But something was missing.

She looked around, suddenly alarmed, and found Nikanj sitting beside her, focusing on her.

"You're all right," it said in its normal neutral voice. "You'll feel a little unsteady at first, but you're all right."

She looked at its left sensory arm. The healing was not yet complete. There was still visible what looked like a bad cut—as though someone had slashed at the arm and managed only a flesh wound.

"Are you all right?" she asked.

It moved the arm easily, normally, used it to stroke her face in an acquired human gesture.

She smiled, sat up, steadied herself for a moment, then stood up and looked around. There were no humans in sight, no Oankali except Nikanj, Ahajas, and Dichaan. Dichaan handed her a jacket and a pair of pants, both clean. Cleaner than she was. She took the clothing, and put it on reluctantly. She was not as dirty as she thought she should have been, but she still wanted to wash.

"Where are the others?" she asked. "Is everyone all right?"

"The humans are back at the settlement," Dichaan said. "They'll be sent to Earth soon. They've been shown the walls here. They know they're still aboard the ship."

"You should have shown them the walls on their first day here."

"We will do that next time. That was one of the things we had to learn from this group."

"Better yet, prove to them they're in a ship as soon as they're

Awakened," she said. "Illusion doesn't comfort them for long. It just confuses them, helps them make dangerous mistakes. I had begun to wonder myself where we really were."

Silence. Stubborn silence.

She looked at Nikanj's still-healing sensory arm. "Listen to me," she said. "Let me help you learn about us, or there'll be more injuries, more deaths."

"Will you walk through the forest," Nikanj asked, "or shall we go the shorter way beneath the training room?"

She sighed. She was Cassandra, warning and predicting to people who went deaf whenever she began to warn and predict. "Let's walk through the forest," she said.

It stood still, keenly focused on her.

"What?" she asked.

It looped its injured sensory arm around her neck. "No one has ever done what we did here. No one has ever healed a wound as serious as mine so quickly or so completely."

"There was no reason for you to die or be maimed," she said. "I couldn't help Joseph. I'm glad I could help you—even though I don't have any idea how I did it."

Nikanj focused on Ahajas and Dichaan. "Joseph's body?" it said softly.

"Frozen," Dichaan said. "Waiting to be sent to Earth."

Nikanj rubbed the back of her neck with the cool, hard tip of its sensory arm. "I thought I had protected him enough," it said. "It should have been enough."

"Is Curt still with the others?"

"He's asleep."

"Suspended animation?"

"Yes."

"And he'll stay here? He'll never get to Earth?"

"Never."

She nodded. "That isn't enough, but it's better than nothing."

"He has a talent like yours," Ahajas said. "The ooloi will use him to study and explore the talent."

"Talent . . . ?"

"You can't control it," Nikanj said, "but we can. Your body knows how to cause some of its cells to revert to an embryonic stage. It can awaken genes that most humans never use after birth. We have comparable genes that go dormant after metamorphosis. Your body showed mine how to awaken them, how to stimulate growth of cells that would not normally regenerate. The lesson was complex and painful, but very much worth learning."

"You mean . . ." She frowned. You mean my family problem with cancer, don't you?"

"It isn't a problem anymore," Nikanj said, smoothing its body tentacles. "It's a gift. It has given me my life back."

"Would you have died?"

Silence.

After a while, Ahajas said, "It would have left us. It would have become Toaht or Akjai and left Earth."

"Why?" Lilith asked.

"Without your gift, it could not have regained full use of the sensory arm. It could not have conceived children." Ahajas hesitated. "When we heard what had happened, we thought we had lost it. It had been with us for so little time. We felt . . . Perhaps we felt what you did when your mate died. There seemed to be nothing at all ahead for us until Ooan Nikanj told us that you were helping it, and that it would recover completely."

"Kahguyaht behaved as though nothing unusual were happening," Lilith said.

"It was frightened for me," Nikanj said. "It knows you dislike it. It thought any instructions from it beyond the essential would anger or delay you. It was badly frightened."

Lilith laughed bitterly. "It's a good actor."

Nikanj rustled its tentacles. It took its sensory arm from Lilith's neck and led the group toward the settlement.

Lilith followed automatically, her thoughts shifting from Nikanj to Joseph to Curt. Curt whose body was to be used to teach the ooloi more about cancer. She could not make herself

ask whether he would be conscious and aware during these experiments. She hoped he would be.

8

It was nearly dark when they reached the settlement. People
were gathered around fires, talking, eating. Nikanj and its mates
were welcomed by the Oankali in a kind of gleeful silence—a
confusion of sensory arms and tentacles, a relating of experience
by direct neural stimulation. They could give each other whole
experiences, then discuss the experience in nonverbal conversation. They had a whole language of sensory images and accepted
signals that took the place of words.

Lilith watched them enviously. They didn't lie often to humans because their sensory language had left them with no
habit of lying—only of withholding information, refusing contact.

Humans, on the other hand, lied easily and often. They
could not trust one another. They could not trust one of their
own who seemed too close to aliens, who stripped off her
clothing and lay down on the ground to help her jailer.

There was silence at the fire where Lilith chose to sit. Allison, Leah and Wray, Gabriel and Tate. Tate gave her a baked
yam and, to her surprise, baked fish. She looked at Wray.

Wray shrugged. "I caught it with my hands. Crazy thing to
do. It was half as big as I am. But it swam right up to me just
begging to be caught. The Oankali claimed I could have been
caught myself by some of the things swimming in the river—
electric eels, piranha, caiman . . . They brought all the worst
things from Earth. Nothing bothered me, though."

"Victor found a couple of turtles," Allison said. "Nobody

knew how to cook them so they cut the meat up and roasted it."

"How was it?" Lilith asked.

"They ate it." Allison smiled. "And while they were cooking it and eating it, the Oankali kept away from them."

Wray grinned broadly. "You don't see any of them around this fire either, do you?"

"I'm not sure," Gabriel answered.

Silence.

Lilith sighed. "Okay, Gabe, what have you got? Questions, accusations or condemnations?"

"Maybe all three."

"Well?"

"You didn't fight. You chose to stand with the Oankali!"

"Against you?"

Angry silence.

"Where were you standing when Curt hacked Joseph to death?"

Tate laid her hand on Lilith's arm. "Curt just went crazy," she said. She spoke very softly. "No one thought he would do anything like that."

"He did it," Lilith said. "And you all watched."

They picked at their food silently for a while, no longer enjoying the fish, sharing it with people from other fires who came offering Brazil nuts, pieces of fruit or baked cassava.

"Why did you take your clothes off?" Wray demanded suddenly. "Why did you lie down on the ground with an ooloi in the middle of the fighting?"

"The fighting was over," Lilith said. "You know that. And the ooloi I lay down with was Nikanj. Curt had all but severed one of its sensory arms. I think you know that, too. I let it use my body to heal itself."

"But why should you want to help it?" Gabriel whispered harshly. "Why didn't you just let it die?" Every Oankali in the area must have heard him.

"What good would that do?" she demanded. "I've k
Nikanj since it was a child. Why should I let it die

stuck with some stranger? How would that help me or you or anyone here?"

He drew back from her. "You've always got an answer. And it never quite rings true."

She went over in her mind the things she could have said to him about his own tendency not to ring true. Ignoring them all, she asked, "What is it, Gabe? What do you believe I can do or could have done to set you free on Earth one minute sooner?"

He did not answer, but he remained stubbornly angry. He was helpless and in a situation he found intolerable. Someone must be to blame.

Lilith saw Tate reach out to him, take his hand. For a few seconds they clung to the tips of one another's fingers, reminding Lilith of nothing so much as a very squeamish person suddenly given a snake to hold. They managed to let one another go without seeming to recoil in revulsion, but everyone knew what they felt. Everyone had seen. That was something else Lilith had to answer for, no doubt.

"What about *that*!" Tate demanded bitterly. She shook the hand Gabriel had touched as though to shake it clean of something. "What do we do about that?"

Lilith let her shoulders slump. "I don't know. It was the same for Joseph and me. I never got around to asking Nikanj what it had done to us. I suggest you ask Kahguyaht."

Gabriel shook his head. "I don't want to see him . . . *it*, let alone ask it anything."

"Really?" asked Allison. Her voice was so full of honest
abriel only glared at her.

aid. "Not really. He wishes he hated
es to hate it. But in the fighting, it was
kill. And here, now, it's me he blames and
Dankali set me up to be the focus of blame
lon't hate Nikanj. Maybe I can't. We're all
at least as far as our individual ooloi are

Gabriel stood up. He loomed over Lilith, glaring down. The camp had gone quiet, everyone watching him.

"I don't give a shit what you feel!" he said. "You're talking about your feelings, not mine. Strip and screw your Nikanj right here for everyone to see, why don't you. We know you're their whore! Everybody here knows!"

She looked at him, abruptly tired, fed up. "And what are you when you spend your nights with Kahguyaht?"

She believed for a moment that he would attack her. And, for a moment, she wanted him to.

Instead, he turned and stalked away toward the shelters. Tate glared at Lilith for a moment, then went after him.

Kahguyaht left the Oankali fire and came over to Lilith. "You could have avoided that," it said softly.

She did not look up at it. "I'm tired," she said. "I resign." "What?"

"I quit! No more scapegoating for you; no more being seen as a Judas goat by my own people. I don't deserve any of this."

It stood over her for a moment longer, then went after Gabriel and Tate. Lilith looked after it, shook her head, and laughed bitterly. She thought of Joseph, seemed to feel him beside her, hear him telling her to be careful, asking her what was the point in turning both peoples against her.

There was no point. She was just tired. And Joseph was not there.

9

People avoided Lilith. She suspected they saw her either as a traitor or as a ticking bomb.

She was content to be let alone. Ahajas and Dichaan asked her if she wanted to go home with them when they left, but she declined the offer. She wanted to stay in an Earthlike setting until she went to Earth. She wanted to stay with human beings even though for a time, she did not love them.

She chopped wood for the fire, gathered wild fruits for meals or casual eating, even caught fish by trying a method she remembered reading about. She spent hours binding together strong grass stems and slivers of split cane, fashioning them into a long, loose cone that small fish could swim into, but not out of. She fished the small streams that flowed into the river and eventually provided most of the fish the group ate. She experimented with smoking it and had surprisingly good results. No one refused the fish because she had caught it. On the other hand, no one asked how she made her fish traps—so she did not tell them. She did no more teaching unless people came to her and asked questions. This was more punishing to her than to the Oankali since she had discovered that she liked teaching. But she found more gratification in teaching one willing student than a dozen resentful ones.

Eventually people did begin to come to her. A few people. Allison, Wray and Leah, Victor. . . . She shared her knowledge of fish traps with Wray finally. Tate avoided her—perhaps to please Gabriel, perhaps because she had adopted Gabriel's way of thinking. Tate had been a friend. Lilith missed her, but somehow could not manage any bitterness against her. There was no other close friend to take Tate's place. Even the people who came to her with questions did not trust her. There was only Nikanj.

Nikanj never tried to make her change her behavior. She had the feeling it would not object to anything she did unless she began hurting people. She lay with it and its mates at night and it pleasured her as it had before she met Joseph. She did not want this at first, but she came to appreciate it.

Then she realized she was able to touch a man again and find pleasure in it.

"Are you so eager to match me with someone else?" she asked Nikanj. That day she had handed Victor an armload of cassava cuttings for planting and she had been surprised, briefly pleased at the feel of his hand, as warm as her own.

"You're free to find another mate," Nikanj told her. "We'll be Awakening other humans soon. I wanted you to be free to choose whether or not to mate."

"You said we would be put down on Earth soon."

"You stopped teaching here. People are learning more slowly. But I think they'll be ready soon." Before she could question it further, other ooloi called it away to swim with them. That probably meant it was leaving the training room for a while. Ooloi liked to use the underwater exits whenever they could. Whenever they were not guiding humans.

Lilith looked around the camp, saw nothing that she wanted to do that day. She wrapped smoked fish and baked cassava in a banana leaf and put it into one of her baskets with a few ripe bananas. She would wander. Later, she would probably come back with something useful.

It was late when she headed back, her basket filled with bean pods that provided an almost candy-sweet pulp and palm fruit that she had been able to cut from a small tree with her machete. The bean pods—inga, they were called—would be a treat for everyone. Lilith did not like this particular kind of palm fruit as much, but others did.

She walked quickly, not wanting to be caught in the forest after dark. She thought she could probably find her way home in the dark, but she did not want to have to. The Oankali had made this jungle too real. Only they were invulnerable to the things whose bite or sting or sharp spines were deadly.

It was almost too dark to see under the canopy when she arrived back at the settlement.

Yet at the settlement, there was only one fire. This was a time for cooking and talking and working on baskets, nets, and other small things that could be done mindlessly while people enjoyed one another's company. But there was only one fire—and only one person near it.

As she reached the fire, the person stood up, and she saw that it was Nikanj. There was no sign of anyone else.

Lilith dropped her basket and ran the last few steps into camp. "Where are they?" she demanded. "Why didn't someone come to find me?"

"Your friend Tate says she's sorry for the way she behaved," Nikanj told her. "She wanted to talk to you, says she would have done it within the next few days. As it happened, she didn't have a few more days here."

"Where is she?"

"Kahguyaht has enhanced her memory as I have yours. It thinks that will help her survive on Earth and help the other humans."

"But . . ." She stepped closer to it, shaking her head. "But what about me? I did all you asked. I didn't hurt anyone. *Why am I still here!*"

"To save your life." It took her hand. "I was called away today to hear the threats that had been made against you. I had already heard most of them. Lilith, you would have wound up like Joseph."

She shook her head. No one had threatened her directly. Most people were afraid of her.

"You would have died," Nikanj repeated. "Because they can't kill us, they would have killed you."

She cursed it, refusing to believe, yet on another level, believing, knowing. She blamed it and hated it and wept.

"You could have waited!" she said finally. "You could have called me back before they left."

"I'm sorry," it said.

"Why didn't you call me? *Why?*"

It knotted its head and body tentacles in distress. "You could have reacted very badly. With your strength, you could have injured or killed someone. You could have earned a place alongside Curt." It relaxed the knots and let its tentacles hang limp. "Joseph is gone. I didn't want to risk losing you too."

And she could not go on hating it. Its words reminded her too much of her own thoughts when she lay down to help it in spite of what other humans might think of her. She went to one of the cut logs that served as benches around the fire and sat down.

"How long do I have to stay here?" she whispered. "Do they ever let the Judas goat go?"

It sat beside her awkwardly, wanting to fold itself onto the log, but not finding enough room to balance there.

"Your people will escape us as soon as they reach Earth," it told her. "You know that. You encouraged them to do it—and of course, we expected it. We'll tell them to take what they want of their equipment and go. Otherwise they might run away with less than they need to live. And we'll tell them they're welcome to come back to us. All of them. Any of them. Whenever they like."

Lilith sighed. "Heaven help anyone who tries."

"You think it would be a mistake to tell them?"

"Why bother asking me what I think?"

"I want to know."

She stared into the fire, got up and pulled a small log onto it. She would not do this again soon. She would not see fire or collect inga and palm fruit or catch a fish . . .

"Lilith?"

"Do you want them to come back?"

"They will come back eventually. They must."

"Unless they kill one another."

Silence.

"Why must they come back?" she asked.

It turned its face away.

"They can't even touch one another, the men and the women. Is that it?"

"That will pass when they've been away from us for a while. But it won't matter."

"Why not?"

"They need us now. They won't have children without us. Human sperm and egg will not unite without us."

She thought about that for a moment, then shook her head. "And what kind of children would they have with you?"

"You haven't answered," it said.

"What?"

"Shall we tell them they can come back to us?"

"No. And don't be too obvious about helping them get away either. Let them decide for themselves what they'll do. Otherwise people who decide later to come back will seem to be obeying you, betraying their humanity for you. That could get them killed. You won't get many back, anyway. Some will think the human species deserves at least a clean death."

"Is it an unclean thing that we want, Lilith?"

"Yes!"

"Is it an unclean thing that I have made you pregnant?"

She did not understand the words at first. It was as though it had begun speaking a language she did not know.

"You . . . what?"

"I have made you pregnant with Joseph's child. I wouldn't have done it so soon, but I wanted to use his seed, not a print. I could not make you closely enough related to a child mixed from a print. And there's a limit to how long I can keep sperm alive."

She was staring at it, speechless. It was speaking as casually as though discussing the weather. She got up, would have backed away from it, but it caught her by both wrists.

She made a violent effort to break away, realized at once that she could not break its grip. "You said—" She ran out of breath and had to start again. "You said you wouldn't do this. You said—"

"I said not until you were ready."

"I'm not ready! I'll never be ready!"

"You're ready now to have Joseph's child. Joseph's daughter."

". . . daughter?"

"I mixed a girl to be a companion for you. You've been very lonely."

"Thanks to you."

"Yes. But a daughter will be a companion for a long time."

"It won't be a daughter." She pulled again at her arms, but it would not let her go. "It will be a thing—not human." She stared down at her own body in horror. "It's inside me, and it isn't human!"

Nikanj drew her closer, looped a sensory arm around her throat. She thought it would inject something into her and make her lose consciousness. She waited almost eager for the darkness.

But Nikanj only drew her down to the log bench again. "You'll have a daughter," it said. "And you are ready to be her mother. You could never have said so. Just as Joseph could never have invited me into his bed—no matter how much he wanted me there. Nothing about you but your words reject this child."

"But it won't be human," she whispered. "It will be a thing. A monster."

"You shouldn't begin to lie to yourself. It's a deadly habit. The child will be yours and Joseph's. Ahajas' and Dichaan's. And because I've mixed it, shaped it, seen that it will be beautiful and without deadly conflicts, it will be mine. It will be my first child, Lilith. First to be born, at least. Ahajas is also pregnant."

"Ahajas?" When had it found the time? It had been everywhere.

"Yes. You and Joseph are parents to her child as well." It used its free sensory arm to turn her head to face it. "The child that comes from your body will look like you and Joseph."

"I don't believe you!"

"The differences will be hidden until metamorphosis."

"Oh god. That too."

"The child born to you and the child born to Ahajas will be siblings."

"The others won't come back for this," she said. "I wouldn't have come back for it."

"Our children will be better than either of us," it continued. "We will moderate your hierarchical problems and you will lessen our physical limitations. Our children won't destroy themselves in a war, and if they need to regrow a limb or to change themselves in some other way they'll be able to do it. And there will be other benefits."

"But they won't be human," Lilith said. "That's what matters. You can't understand, but that *is* what matters."

Its tentacles knotted. "The child inside you matters." It released her arms, and her hands clutched uselessly at one another.

"This will destroy us," she whispered. "My god, no wonder you wouldn't let me leave with the others."

"You'll leave when I do—you, Ahajas, Dichaan, and our children. We have work to do here before we leave." It stood up. "We'll go home now. Ahajas and Dichaan are waiting for us."

Home? she thought bitterly. When had she last had a true home? When could she hope to have one. "Let me stay here," she said. It would refuse. She knew it would. "This is as close to Earth as it seems you'll let me come."

"You can come back here with the next group of humans. Come home now."

She considered resisting, making it drug her and carry her back. But that seemed a pointless gesture. At least she would get another chance with a human group. A chance to teach them . . . but not a chance to be one of them. Never that. Never?

Another chance to say, "*Learn and run!*"

She would have more information for them this time. And they would have long, healthy lives ahead of them. Perhaps they could find an answer to what the Oankali had done to them. And perhaps the Oankali were not perfect. A few fertile people might slip through and find one another. Perhaps. *Learn and run!* If she were lost, others did not have to be. Humanity did not have to be.

She let Nikanj lead her into the dark forest and to one of the concealed dry exits.

ADULTHOOD
RITES

To Lynn—
write!

I

LO

1

He remembered much of his stay in the womb.

While there, he began to be aware of sounds and tastes. They meant nothing to him, but he remembered them. When they recurred, he noticed.

When something touched him, he knew it to be a new thing—a new experience. The touch was first startling, then comforting. It penetrated his flesh painlessly and calmed him. When it withdrew, he felt bereft, alone for the first time. When it returned, he was pleased—another new sensation. When he had experienced a few of these withdrawals and returns, he learned anticipation.

He did not learn pain until it was time for him to be born.

He could feel and taste changes happening around him—the slow turning of his body, then later the sudden headfirst thrust, the compression first of his head, then gradually along the length of his body. He hurt in a dull, distant way.

Yet he was not afraid. The changes were right. It was time for them. His body was ready. He was propelled along in regular pulses and comforted from time to time by the touch of his familiar companion.

There was light!

Vision was first a blaze of shock and pain. He could not escape the light. It grew brighter and more painful, reached its maximum as the compression ended. No part of his body was free from the sharp, raw brilliance. Later, he would recall it as heat, as burning.

It cooled abruptly.

Something muted the light. He could still see, but seeing was no longer painful. His body was rubbed gently as he lay submerged in something soft and comforting. He did not like the rubbing. It made the light seem to jerk and vanish, then leap back to visibility. But it was the familiar presence that touched him, held him. It stayed with him and helped him endure the rubbing without fear.

He was wrapped in something that touched him everywhere except his face. He did not like the heavy feel of it, but it shut out the light and did not hurt him.

Something touched the side of his face, and he turned, mouth open, to take it. His body knew what to do. He sucked and was rewarded by food and by the taste of flesh as familiar as his own. For a time, he assumed it was his own. It had always been with him.

He could hear voices, could even distinguish individual sounds, though he understood none of them. They captured his attention, his curiosity. He would remember these, too, when he was older and able to understand them. But he liked the soft voices even without knowing what they were.

"He's beautiful," one voice said. "He looks completely Human."

"Some of his features are only cosmetic, Lilith. Even now his senses are more dispersed over his body than yours are. He is . . . less Human than your daughters."

"I'd guessed he would be. I know your people still worry about Human-born males."

"They were an unsolved problem. I believe we've solved it now."

"His senses are all right, though?"

"Of course."

"That's all I can expect, I guess." A sigh. "Shall I thank you for making him look this way—for making him seem Human so I can love him? . . . for a while."

"You've never thanked me before."

". . . no."

"And I think you go on loving them even when they change."

"They can't help what they are . . . what they become. You're sure everything else is all right, too? All the mismatched bits of him fit together as best they can?"

"Nothing in him is mismatched. He's very healthy. He'll have a long life and be strong enough to endure what he must endure."

2

He was Akin.

Things touched him when this sound was made. He was given comfort or food, or he was held and taught. Body to body understanding was given to him. He came to perceive himself as himself—individual, defined, separate from all the touches and smells, all the tastes, sights, and sounds that came to him. He was Akin.

Yet he came to know that he was also part of the people who touched him—that within them, he could find fragments of himself. He was himself, and he was those others.

He learned quickly to distinguish between them by taste and touch. It took longer for him to know them by sight or smell, but taste and touch were almost a single sensation for him. Both had been familiar to him for so long.

He had heard differences in voices since his birth. Now he began to attach identities to those differences. When, within days of his birth, he had learned his own name and could say it aloud, the others taught him their names. These they repeated when they could see that they had his attention. They let him watch their mouths shape the words. He came to understand quickly that each of them could be called by one or both of two groups of sounds.

Nikanj Ooan, Lilith Mother, Ahajas Ty, Dichaan Ishliin, and

the one who never came to him even though Nikanj Ooan had taught him that one's touch and taste and smell. Lilith Mother had shown him a print image of that one, and he had scanned it with all his senses: Joseph Father.

He called for Joseph Father and, instead, Nikanj Ooan came and taught him that Joseph Father was dead. Dead. Ended. Gone away and not coming back. Yet he had been part of Akin, and Akin must know him as he knew all his living parents.

Akin was two months old when he began to put together simple sentences. He could not get enough of being held and taught.

"He's quicker than most of my girls," Lilith commented as she held him against her and let him drink. It could have been difficult to learn from her smooth, unhelpful skin except that it was as familiar as his own—and superficially like his own. Nikanj Ooan taught him to use his tongue—his least Human visible organ—to study Lilith when she fed him. Over many feedings, he tasted her flesh as well as her milk. She was a rush of flavors and textures—sweet milk, salty skin smooth in some places, rough in others. He concentrated on one of the smooth places, focused all his attention on probing it, perceiving it deeply, minutely. He perceived the many cells of her skin, living and dead. Her skin taught him what it meant to be dead. Its dead outer layer contrasted sharply with what he could perceive of the living flesh beneath. His tongue was as long and sensitive and malleable as the sensory tentacles of Ahajas and Dichaan. He sent a filament of it into the living tissue of her nipple. He had hurt her the first time he tried this, and the pain had been channeled back to him through his tongue. The pain had been so sharp and startling that he withdrew, screaming and weeping. He refused to be comforted until Nikanj showed him how to probe without causing pain.

"That," Lilith had commented, "was a lot like being stabbed with a hot, blunt needle."

"He won't do it again," Nikanj had promised.

Akin had not done it again. And he had learned an important lesson: He would share any pain he caused. Best, then, to be careful and not cause pain. He would not know for months how unusual it was for an infant to recognize the pain of another person and recognize himself as the cause of that pain.

Now he perceived, through the tendril of flesh he had extended into Lilith, expanses of living cells. He focused on a few cells, on a single cell, on the parts of that cell, on its nucleus, on chromosomes within the nucleus, on genes along the chromosomes. He investigated the DNA that made up the genes, the nucleotides of the DNA. There was something beyond the nucleotides that he could not perceive—a world of smaller particles that he could not cross into. He did not understand why he could not make this final crossing—if it were the final one. It frustrated him that anything was beyond his perception. He knew of it only through shadowy ungraspable feelings. When he was older he came to think of it as a horizon, always receding when he approached it.

He shifted his attention from the frustration of what he could not perceive to the fascination of what he could. Lilith's flesh was much more exciting than the flesh of Nikanj, Ahajas, and Dichaan. There was something wrong with hers—something he did not understand. It was both frightening and seductive. It told him Lilith was dangerous, though she was also essential. Nikanj was interesting but not dangerous. Ahajas and Dichaan were so alike he had to struggle to perceive differences between them. In some ways Joseph had been like Lilith. Deadly and compelling. But he had not been as much like Lilith as Ahajas was like Dichaan. In fact, though he had clearly been Human and native to this place, this *Earth*, like Lilith, he had not been Lilith's relative. Ahajas and Dichaan were brother and sister, like most Oankali male and female mates. Joseph was unrelated, like Nikanj—but although Nikanj was Oankali, it was also ooloi, not male or female. Ooloi were supposed to be unrelated to their male and female mates so that they could focus their attention on their mates' genetic differences and construct children without making dangerous mistakes of overfamiliarity and overconfidence.

"Be careful," he heard Nikanj say. "He's studying you again."

"I know," Lilith answered. "Sometimes I wish he'd just nurse like Human babies."

Lilith rubbed Akin's back, and the flickering of light between and around her fingers broke his concentration. He withdrew his flesh from hers, then released her nipple and looked at her. She closed clothing over her breast but went on holding him on her lap. He was always glad when people held him and talked to each other, allowing him to listen. He had already learned more words from them than he had yet had occasion to use. He collected words and gradually assembled them into questions. When his questions were answered, he remembered everything he was told. His picture of the world grew.

"At least he isn't any stronger or faster in physical development than other babies," Lilith said. "Except for his teeth."

"There have been babies born with teeth before," Nikanj said. "Physically, he'll look his Human age until his metamorphosis. He'll have to think his way out of any problems his precocity causes."

"That won't do him much good with some Humans. They'll resent him for not being completely Human and for looking more Human than their kids. They'll hate him for looking much younger than he sounds. They'll hate him because they haven't been allowed to have sons. Your people have made Human-looking male babies a very valuable commodity."

"We'll allow more of them now. Everyone feels more secure about mixing them. Before now, too many ooloi could not perceive the necessary mixture. They could have made mistakes and their mistakes could be monsters."

"Most Humans think that's what they've been doing."

"Do you still?"

Silence.

"Be content, Lilith. One group of us believed it would be best to dispense with Human-born males altogether. We could construct female children for Human females and male children for Oankali females. We've done that until now."

"And cheated everyone. Ahajas wants daughters, and I want sons. Other people feel the same way."

"I know. And we control children in ways we should not to make them mature as Oankali-born males and Human-born females. We control inclinations that should be left to individual children. Even the group that suggested we go on this way knows we shouldn't. But they were afraid. A male who's Human enough to be born to a Human female could be a danger to us all. We must try though. We'll learn from Akin."

Akin felt himself held closer to Lilith. "Why is he such an experiment?" she demanded. "And why should Human-born men be such a problem? I know most prewar men don't like you. They feel you're displacing them and forcing them to do something perverted. From their point of view, they're right. But you could teach the next generation to love you, no matter who their mothers are. All you'd have to do is start early. Indoctrinate them before they're old enough to develop other opinions."

"But . . ." Nikanj hesitated. "But if we had to work that blindly, that clumsily, we couldn't have trade. We would have to take your children from you soon after they were born. We wouldn't dare trust you to raise them. You would be kept only for breeding—like nonsentient animals."

Silence. A sigh. "You say such god-awful things in such a gentle voice. No, hush, I know it's the only voice you've got. Nika, will Akin survive the Human males who will hate him?"

"They won't hate him."

"They will! He isn't Human. Un-Human women are offensive to them, but they don't usually try to hurt them, and they do sleep with them—like a racist sleeping with racially different women. But Akin . . . They'll see him as a threat. Hell, he *is* a threat. He's one of their replacements."

"Lilith, they will not hate him." Akin felt himself lifted from Lilith's arms and held close to Nikanj's body. He gasped at the lovely shock of contact with Nikanj's sensory tentacles, many of which held him while others burrowed painlessly into his flesh. It was so easy to connect with Nikanj and to learn. "They will see him as beautiful and like themselves," Nikanj said. "By the time he's old enough for his body to reveal what he actually is, he'll be an adult and able to hold his own."

"Able to fight?"

"Only to save his life. He'll tend to avoid fighting. He'll be like Oankali-born males now—a solitary wanderer when he's not mated."

"He won't settle down with anyone?"

"No. Most Human males aren't particularly monogamous. No construct males will be."

"But—"

"Families will change, Lilith—are changing. A complete construct family will be a female, an ooloi, and children. Males will come and go as they wish and as they find welcome."

"But they'll have no homes."

"A home like this would be a prison to them. They'll have what they want, what they need."

"The ability to be fathers to their kids?"

Nikanj paused. "They might choose to keep contact with their children. They won't live with them permanently—and no construct, male or female, young or old, will feel that as a deprivation. It will be normal to them, and purposeful, since there will always be many more females and ooloi than males." It rustled its head and body tentacles. "Trade means change. Bodies change. Ways of living must change. Did you think your children would only *look* different?"

3

Akin spent some part of the day with each of his parents. Lilith fed him and taught him. The others only taught him, but he went to them all eagerly. Ahajas usually held him after Lilith.

Ahajas was tall and broad. She carried him without seeming to notice his weight. He had never felt weariness in her. And he knew she enjoyed carrying him. He could feel pleasure the moment she sank filaments of her sensory tentacles into him. She was the first person to be able to reach him this way with more than simple emotions. She was the first to give him multisensory images and signaling pressures and to help him understand that she was speaking to him without words. As he grew, he realized that Nikanj and Dichaan also did this. Nikanj had done it even before he was born, but he had not understood. Ahajas had reached him and taught him quickly. Through the images she created for him, he learned about the child growing within her. She gave him images of it and even managed to give it images of him. It had several presences: all its parents except Lilith. And it had him. Sibling.

He knew he would be male when he grew up. He understood male, and female, and ooloi. And he knew that because he would be male, the unborn child who would begin its life seeming much less Human than he did would eventually become female. There was a balance, a naturalness to this that pleased him. He should have a sister to grow up with—a sister but not an ooloi sibling. Why? He wondered whether the child inside Ahajas would become ooloi, but Ahajas and Nikanj both assured him it would not. And they would not tell him how they knew. So this sibling should become a sister. It would take years to develop sexually, but he already thought of it as "she."

Dichaan usually took him once Ahajas had returned him to

Lilith and Lilith had fed him. Dichaan taught him about strangers.

First there were his older siblings, some born to Ahajas and becoming more Human, and some born to Lilith and becoming more Oankali. There were also children of older siblings, and finally, frighteningly, unrelated people. Akin could not understand why some of the unrelated ones were more like Lilith than Joseph had been. And none of them were like Joseph.

Dichaan read Akin's unspoken confusion.

"The differences you perceive between Humans—between groups of Humans—are the result of isolation and inbreeding, mutation, and adaptation to different Earth environments," he said, illustrating each concept with quick multiple images. "Joseph and Lilith were born in very different parts of this world—born to long separated peoples. Do you understand?"

"Where are Joseph's kind?" Akin asked aloud.

"Now there are villages of them to the southwest. They're called Chinese."

"I want to see them."

"You will. You can travel to them when you're older." He ignored Akin's rush of frustration. "And someday I'll take you to the ship. You'll be able to see Oankali differences, too." He gave Akin an image of the ship—a vast sphere made up of huge, still-growing, many-sided plates like the shell of a turtle. In fact, it was the outer shell of a living being. "There," Dichaan said, "you'll see Oankali who will never come to Earth or trade with Humans. For now, they tend the ship in ways that require a different physical form." He gave Akin an image, and Akin thought it resembled a huge caterpillar.

Akin projected silent questioning.

"Speak aloud," Dichaan told him.

"Is it a child?" Akin asked, thinking of the changes caterpillars underwent.

"No. It's adult. It's larger than I am."

"Can it talk?"

"In images, in tactile, bioelectric, and bioluminescent signals, in pheromones, and in gestures. It can gesture with ten limbs at once. But its throat and mouth parts won't produce speech. And it is deaf. It must live in places where there is a great deal of noise. My parents' parents had that shape."

This seemed terrible to Akin—Oankali forced to live in an ugly form that did not even allow them to hear or speak.

"What they are is as natural to them as what you are is to you," Dichaan told him. "And they are much closer to the ship than we can be. They're companions to it, knowing its body better than you know your own. When I was a little older than you are now, I wanted to be one of them. They let me taste a little of their relationship with the ship."

"Show me."

"Not yet. It's a very powerful thing. I'll show you when you're a little older."

Everything was to happen when he was older. He must wait! He must always wait! In frustration, Akin had stopped speaking. He could not help hearing and remembering all that Dichaan told him, but he would not speak to Dichaan again for days.

Yet it was Dichaan who began leaving him in the care of his older sisters, letting him begin to investigate them—while they thoroughly investigated him. His favorite among them was Margit. She was six years old—too small to carry him long, but he was content to ride on her back or sit on her lap for as long as she could handle him comfortably. She did not have sensory tentacles like his Oankali-born sisters, but she had clusters of sensitive nodules that would probably be tentacles when she grew up. She could match some of these to the smooth, invisible sensory patches on his skin, and the two of them could exchange images and emotions as well as words. She could teach him.

"You should be careful," she said as she took him to shelter in their family house, away from a hard afternoon rain. "Your eyes don't track a lot of the time. Can you see with them?"

He thought about this. "I can," he said, "but I don't always. Sometimes it's easier to see things from other parts of my body."

"When you're older, you'll be expected to turn your face and body toward people when you talk to them. Even now, you should look at Humans with your eyes. If you don't, they yell at you or repeat things because they're not sure they have your attention. Or they start to ignore you because they think you're ignoring them."

"No one's done that to me."

"They will. Just wait until you get past the stage when they try to talk stupid to you."

"Baby talk, you mean?"

"Human talk!"

Silence.

"Don't worry," she said after a while. "It's them I'm mad at, not you."

"Why?"

"They blame me for not looking like them. They can't help doing it, and I can't help resenting it. I don't know which is worse—the ones who cringe if I touch them or the ones who pretend it's all right while they cringe inside."

"What does Lilith feel?" Akin asked only because he already knew the answer.

"For her, I might as well look the way you do. I remember when I was about your age, she would wonder how I would find a mate, but Nikanj told her there would be plenty of males like me by the time I grew up. She never said anything after that. She tells me to stick with the constructs. I do, mostly."

"Humans like me," he said. "I guess because I look like them."

"Just remember to look at them with your eyes when they talk to you or you talk to them. And be careful about tasting them. You won't be able to get away with that for much longer. Besides, your tongue doesn't look Human."

"Humans say it shouldn't be gray, but they don't realize how different it really is."

"Don't let them guess. They can be dangerous, Akin. Don't show them everything you can do. But . . . hang around them when you can. Study their behavior. Maybe you can collect things about them that we can't. It would be wrong if anything that they are is lost."

"Your legs are going to sleep," Akin observed. "You're tired. You should take me to Lilith."

"In a little while."

She did not want to give him up, he realized. He did not mind. She was, Humans said, gray and warty—more different than most Human-born children. And she could hear as well as any construct. She caught every whisper whether she wanted to or not, and if she were near Humans, they soon began to talk about her. "If she looks this bad now, what will she look like after metamorphosis?" they would begin. Then they would speculate or pity her or condemn her or laugh at her. Better a few more minutes of peace alone with him.

Her full Human name was Margita Iyapo Domonkos Kaal-nikanjlo. Margit. She had all four of his living parents in common with him. Her Human father, though, was Vidor Domonkos, not the dead Joseph. Vidor—some people called him Victor—had moved to a village several miles upriver when he and Lilith tired of one another. He came back two or three times a year to see Margit. He did not like the way she looked, yet he loved her. She had seen that he did, and Akin was certain she had read his emotion correctly. He had never met Vidor himself. He had been too young for contact with strangers during the man's last visit.

"Will you tell Vidor to let me touch him when he comes to see you again?" Akin asked.

"Father? Why?"

"I want to find you in him."

She laughed. "He and I have a lot in common. He doesn't like having anyone explore him, though. Says he doesn't need anything burrowing through his skin." She hesitated. "He means that. He only let me do it once. Just talk to him if you meet him, Akin. In some ways he can be just as dangerous as any other Human."

"Your father?"

"Akin . . . *All of them!* Haven't you explored any of them?

Can't you feel it?" She gave him a complex image. He understood it only because he had explored a few Humans himself. Humans were a compelling, seductive, deadly contradiction. He felt drawn to them, yet warned against them. To touch a Human deeply—to taste one—was to feel this.

"I know," he said. "But I don't understand."

"Talk to Ooan. It knows and understands. Talk to Mother, too. She knows more than she likes to admit."

"She's Human. You don't think she's dangerous, too, do you?"

"Not to us." She stood up with him. "You're getting heavier. I'll be glad when you learn to walk."

"Me, too. How old were you when you walked?"

"Just over a year. You're almost there."

"Nine months."

"Yes. It's too bad you couldn't learn walking as easily as you learned talking." She returned him to Lilith, who fed him and promised to take him into the forest with her.

Lilith gave him bits of solid food now, but he still took great comfort in nursing. It frightened him to realize that someday she would not let him nurse. He did not want to grow that old.

4

Lilith put him on her back in a cloth sack and took him to one of the village gardens. This particular garden was some distance upriver from the village, and Akin enjoyed the long walk through the forest. There were new sounds, smells, and sights on each trip. Lilith would often stop to let him touch or taste new things or to let him view and memorize deadly things. He had discovered that his fingers were sensitive enough to taste which plants were harmful—if his sense of smell did not warn him before he touched.

"That's a good talent," Lilith said when he told her. "At least you're not likely to poison yourself. Be careful how you touch things, though. Some plants do damage on contact."

"Show me those," Akin said.

"I will. We clear them out of the area when we see them, but they always find their way back. I'll take you with me next time we decide to cull them."

"Does cull mean the same as clear?"

"Cull means to clear selectively. We only take out the plants with contact poisons."

"I see." He paused, trying to understand the new scent he had detected. "There's someone between us and the river," he whispered suddenly.

"All right." They had reached the garden. She bent over a cassava plant and pretended to find it hard to pull up so that she could move casually around to face the river. They could not see the water from where they were. There was plenty of ground between themselves and the river—and plenty of cover.

"I can't see them," she said. "Can you?" She had only her eyes to look with, but her senses were sharper than those of other Humans—somewhere between Human and construct.

"It's a man," Akin said. "He's hidden. He's Human and a stranger." Akin breathed in the adrenaline bite of the man's scent. "He's excited. Maybe afraid."

"Not afraid," she said softly. "Not of a woman pulling cassavas and carrying a baby. I hear him now, moving around near the big Brazil nut tree."

"Yes, I hear!" Akin said excitedly.

"Keep quiet! And hold on. I might have to move fast."

The man had stopped moving. Suddenly, he stepped into view, and Akin saw that he had something in his hands.

"Shit!" Lilith whispered. "Bow and arrow. He's a resister."

"You mean those sticks he's holding?"

"Yes. They're weapons."

"Don't turn that way. I can't see him."

"And he can't see you. Keep your head down!"

He realized then that he was in danger. Resisters were Humans who had decided to live without the Oankali—and thus without children. Akin had heard that they sometimes stole construct children, the most Human-looking construct children they could find. But that was stupid because they had no idea what the child might be like after metamorphosis. Oankali never let them keep the children anyway.

"Do you speak English?" Lilith called, and Akin, straining to look over her shoulder, saw the man lower his bow and arrow.

"English is the only Human language spoken here," Lilith said. It comforted Akin that she neither sounded nor smelled frightened. His own fear diminished.

"I heard you talking to someone," the man said in slightly accented English.

"Hold tight," Lilith whispered.

Akin grasped the material of the cloth sack in which she carried him. He held on with hands and legs, wishing he were stronger.

"My village isn't far from here," she said to the man. "You'll be welcome there. Food. Shelter. It's going to rain soon."

"*Who were you talking to!*" the man demanded, coming nearer.

"My son." She gestured toward Akin.

"What? The baby?"

"Yes."

The man came closer, peering at Akin. Akin peered back over Lilith's shoulder, curiosity overwhelming the last of his fear. The man was shirtless, black-haired, clean-shaven, and stocky. His hair was long and hung down his back. He had cut it off in a straight line across his forehead. Something about him reminded Akin of the picture he had seen of Joseph. This man's eyes were narrow like Joseph's, but his skin was almost as brown as Lilith's.

"The kid looks good," he said. "What's wrong with him?"

She stared at him. "Nothing," she said flatly.

The man frowned. "I don't mean to offend you. I just . . . Is he really as healthy as he looks?"

"Yes."

"I haven't seen a baby since back before the war."

"I'd guessed that. Will you come back to the village with us? It isn't far."

"How is it you were allowed to have a boy?"

"How is it your mother was allowed to have a boy?"

The man took a final step toward Lilith and was abruptly too close. He stood very straight and tried to intimidate her with his stiff, angry posture and his staring eyes. Akin had seen Humans do that to one another before. It never worked with constructs. Akin had never seen it work with Lilith. She did not move.

"I'm Human," the man said. "You can see that. I was born before the war. There's nothing Oankali about me. I have two parents, both Human, and no one told them when and whether they could have kids and what the sex of those kids would be. *Now, how is it you were allowed to have a boy?*"

"I asked for one." Lilith reached out, snatched the man's bow, and broke it over her knee before the man was fully aware of what had happened. Her move had been almost too swift for him to follow even if he had been expecting it.

"You're welcome to food and shelter for as long as you like," she said, "but we don't allow weapons."

The man stumbled back from her. "I mistook you for Human," he said. "My god, you look Human."

"I was born twenty-six years before the war," she said. "I'm Human enough. But I have other children in that village. You won't take weapons among them."

He looked at the machete hanging from her belt.

"It's a tool," she said. "We don't use them on each other."

He shook his head. "I don't care what you say. That was a heavy bow. No Human woman should have been able to take it from me and break it that way."

She walked away from him, unsheathed her machete, and

cut a pineapple. She picked it up carefully, slashed off most of its spiky top, and cut two more.

Akin watched the man while Lilith put her cassavas and pineapples into her basket. She cut a stalk of bananas, and once she was certain they were free of snakes and dangerous insects, she handed them to the man. He took a quick step back from her.

"Carry these," she said. "They're all right. I'm glad you happened along. The two of us will be able to carry more." She cut several dozen ribbons of quat—an Oankali vegetable that Akin loved—and tied it into a bundle with thin lianas. She also cut fat stalks of scigee, which the Oankali had made from some war-mutated Earth plant. Humans said it had the taste and texture of the flesh of an extinct animal—the pig.

Lilith bound the scigee stalks and fastened the bundle behind her just above her hips. She swung Akin to one side and carried her full basket on the other.

"Can you watch him without using your eyes?" she whispered to Akin.

"Yes," Akin answered.

"Do it." And she called to the man, "Come. This way." She walked away down the path to the village, not waiting to see whether the man would follow. It seemed for a while that the man would stay behind. The narrow path curved around a huge tree, and Akin lost sight of him. There was no sound of his following. Then there was a burst of sound—hurrying feet, heavy breathing.

"Wait!" the man called.

Lilith stopped and waited for him to catch up. He was, Akin noticed, still carrying the stalk of bananas. He had thrown it over his left shoulder.

"Watch him!" Lilith whispered to Akin.

The man came close, then stopped and stared at her, frowning.

"What the matter?" she asked.

He shook his head. "I just don't know what to make of you," he said.

Akin felt her relax a little. "This is your first visit to a trading village, isn't it?" she said.

"Trading village? So that's what you call them."

"Yes. And I don't want to know what you call us. But spend some time with us. Maybe you'll accept our definition of ourselves. You came to find out about us, didn't you?"

He sighed. "I guess so. I was a kid when the war started. I still remember cars, TV, computers . . . I do remember. But those things aren't real to me anymore. My parents . . . All they want to do is go back to the prewar days. They know as well as I do that that's impossible, but it's what they talk about and dream about. I left them to find out what else there might be to do."

"Both your parents survived?"

"Yeah. They're still alive. Hell, they don't look any older than I do now. They could still join a . . . one of your villages and have more kids. They won't though."

"And you?"

"I don't know." He looked at Akin. "I haven't seen enough to decide yet."

She reached out to touch his arm in a gesture of sympathy.

He grabbed her hand and held it at first as though he thought she would try to pull away. She did not. He held her wrist and examined the hand. After a time he let her go.

"Human," he whispered. "I always heard you could tell by the hands—that the . . . the others would have too many fingers or fingers that bend in un-Human ways."

"Or you could just ask," she said. "People will tell you; they don't mind. It's not the kind of thing anyone bothers to lie about. Hands aren't as reliable as you think."

"Can I look at the baby's?"

"No more than you are now."

He drew a long breath. "I wouldn't hurt a kid. Even one that wasn't quite Human."

"Akin isn't quite Human," she said.

"What's wrong with him?"

"Not a thing."

"I mean . . . What's different about him?"

"Internal differences. Rapid mental development. Perceptual differences. At metamorphosis, he'll begin to look different, though I don't know how different."

"Can he talk?"

"All the time. Come on."

He followed her along the path, and Akin watched him through light-sensitive patches on the skin of his shoulder and arm.

"Baby?" the man said peering at him.

Akin, remembering what Margit had told him, turned his head so that he faced the man. "Akin," he said. "What's your name?"

The man let his mouth fall open. "How old are you?" he demanded.

Akin stared at him silently.

"Don't you understand me?" the man asked. He had a jagged scar on one of his shoulders, and Akin wondered what had made it.

The man slapped at a mosquito with his free hand and spoke to Lilith. "How old is he?"

"Tell him your name," she said.

"What?"

She said nothing more.

The man's smallest toe was missing from his right foot, Akin noticed. And there were other marks on his body—scars, paler than the rest of his skin. He must have hurt himself often and had no ooloi to help him heal. Nikanj would never have left so many scars.

"Okay," the man said. "I give up. My name is Augustino Leal. Everybody calls me Tino."

"Shall I call you that?" Akin asked.

"Sure, why not? Now, how the hell old are you?"

"Nine months."

"Can you walk?"

"No, I can stand up if there's something for me to hold on

to, but I'm not very good at it yet. Why did you stay away from the villages for so long? Don't you like kids?"

"I . . . don't know."

"They aren't all like me. Most of them can't talk until they're older."

The man reached out and touched his face. Akin grasped one of the man's fingers and drew it to his mouth. He tasted it quickly with a snakelike flick of his tongue and a penetration too swift, too slight to notice. He collected a few living cells for later study.

"At least you put things in your mouth the way babies used to," he said.

"Akin," Lilith said, cautioning.

Suppressing his frustration, he let the man's finger go. He would have preferred to investigate further, to understand more of how the genetic information he read had been expressed and to see what nongenetic factors he could discover. He wanted to try to read the man's emotions and to find the marks the Oankali had left in him when they collected him from postwar Earth, when they repaired him and stored him away in suspended animation.

Perhaps later he would have the chance.

"If the kid is this smart now, what's he going to be like as an adult?" Tino asked.

"I don't know," Lilith told him. "The only adult male constructs we have so far are Oankali-born—born to Oankali mothers. If Akin is like them, he'll be bright enough, but his interests will be so diverse and, in some cases, so just plain un-Human that he'll wind up keeping to himself a lot."

"Doesn't that bother you?"

"There's nothing I can do about it."

"But . . . you didn't have to have kids."

"As it happens, I did have to. I had two construct kids by the time they brought me down from the ship. I never had a chance to run off and pine for the good old days!"

The man said nothing. If he stayed long, he would learn that Lilith had these flares of bitterness sometimes. They never seemed to affect her behavior, though often they frightened people. Margit had said, "It's as though there's something in her trying to get out. Something terrible." Whenever the something seemed on the verge of surfacing, Lilith went alone into the forest and stayed away for days. Akin's oldest sisters said they used to worry that she would leave and not come back.

"They forced you to have kids?" the man asked.

"One of them surprised me," she said. "It made me pregnant, then told me about it. Said it was giving me what I wanted but would never come out and ask for."

"Was it?"

"Yes." She shook her head from side to side. "Oh, yes. But if I had the strength not to ask, it should have had the strength to let me alone."

5

The rain had begun by the time they reached the village, and Akin enjoyed the first few warm drops that made their way through the forest canopy. Then they were indoors—followed by everyone who had seen Lilith arrive with a stranger.

"They'll want your life story," Lilith told him softly. "They want to hear about your village, your travels; anything you know may be news to us. We don't get that many travelers. And later, when you've eaten and talked and whatever, they'll try to drag you off to their beds. Do what you like. If you're too tired for any of this now, say so, and we'll save your party until tomorrow."

"You didn't tell me I would have to entertain," he said, staring at the inpouring of Humans, constructs, and Oankali.

"You don't have to. Do what you like."

"But . . ." He looked around helplessly, cringed away from

an Oankali-born unsexed construct child who touched him with one of the sensory tentacles growing from its head.

"Don't scare him," Akin told it from Lilith's back. He spoke in Oankali. "There aren't any of us where he comes from."

"Resister?" the child asked.

"Yes. But I don't think he means any harm. He didn't try to hurt us."

"What does the kid want?" Tino asked.

"It's just curious about you," Lilith told him. "Do you want to talk to these people while I put together a meal?"

"I guess so. I'm not a good storyteller, though."

Lilith turned to the still gathering crowd. "All right," she said loudly. And when they had quieted: "His name is Augustino Leal. He comes from a long way away, and he says he feels like talking."

People cheered.

"If anyone wants to go home to get something to eat or drink, we'll wait."

Several Humans and constructs left, ordering her not to let anything begin without them. An Oankali took Akin from her back. Dichaan. Akin flattened against him happily, sharing what he had learned of the new Human.

"You like him?" Dichaan asked by way of tactile signals shaded with sensory images.

"Yes. He's a little afraid and dangerous. Mother had to take his weapon. But he's mostly curious. He's so curious he feels like one of us."

Dichaan projected amusement. Maintaining his sensory link with Akin, he watched Lilith give Tino something to drink. The man tasted the drink and smiled. People had gathered around him, sitting on the floor. Most of them were children, and this seemed to put him at ease in one way—he was no longer afraid—and excite him in another. His eyes focused on one child after another, examining the wide variety of them.

"Will he try to steal someone?" Akin asked silently.

"If he did, Eka, it would probably be you." Dichaan softened the statement with amusement, but there was a serious-

ness beneath it that Akin did not miss. The man probably
meant no harm, was probably not a child thief. But Akin
should be careful, should not allow himself to be alone with
Tino.

People brought food, shared it among themselves and with
Lilith as they accepted what she offered. They fed their own
children and each other's children as usual. A child who could
walk could get bits of food anywhere.

Lilith prepared Tino and her younger children dishes of flat
cassava bread layered with hot scigee and quat alongside hot,
spicy beans. There were slices of pineapple and papaya for
dessert. She fed Akin small amounts of quat mixed with cassava. She did not let him nurse until she had settled down with
everyone else to talk and listen to Tino.

"They named our village Phoenix before my parents reached
it," Tino told them. "We weren't original settlers. We came in
half-dead from the forest—we'd eaten something bad, some
kind of palm fruit. It was edible, all right, but only if you
cooked it—and we hadn't. Anyway, we stumbled in, and the
people of Phoenix took care of us. I was the only child they
had—the only Human child they'd seen since before the war.
The whole village sort of adopted me because . . ." He
stopped, glanced at a cluster of Oankali. "Well, you know.
They wanted to find a little girl. They thought maybe the few
kids who hadn't gone through puberty before they were set
free might be fertile together when they grew up." He stared
at the nearest Oankali, who happened to be Nikanj. "True or
false?" he asked.

"False," Nikanj said softly. "We told them it was false. They
chose not to believe."

Tino stared at Nikanj—gave it a look that Akin did not understand. The look was not threatening, but Nikanj drew its
body tentacles up slightly into the beginnings of a prestrike
threat gesture. Humans called it knotting up or getting knotty.
They knew it meant getting angry or otherwise upset. Few of
them realized it was also a reflexive, potentially lethal gesture.
Every sensory tentacle could sting. The ooloi could also sting

with their sensory arms. But at least they could sting without killing. Male and female Oankali and constructs could only kill. Akin could kill with his tongue. This was one of the first things Nikanj had taught him not to do. Let alone, he might have discovered his ability by accident and killed Lilith or some other Human. The thought of this had frightened him at first, but he no longer worried about it. He had never seen anyone sting anyone.

Even now, Nikanj's body language indicated only mild upset. But why should Tino upset it at all? Akin began to watch Nikanj instead of Tino. As Tino spoke, all of Nikanj's long head tentacles swung around to focus on him. Nikanj was intensely interested in this newcomer. After a moment, it got up and made its way over to Lilith. It took Akin from her arms.

Akin had finished nursing and now flattened obligingly against Nikanj, giving what he knew Nikanj wanted: genetic information about Tino. In trade, he demanded to have explained the feelings Nikanj had expressed with its indrawn sensory tentacles.

In silent, vivid images and signals, Nikanj explained. "That one wanted to stay with us when he was a child. We couldn't agree to keep him, but we hoped he would come to us when he was older."

"You knew him then?"

"I handled his conditioning. He spoke only Spanish then. Spanish is one of my Human languages. He was only eight years old and not afraid of me. I didn't want to let him go. Everyone knew his parents would run when we released them. They would become resisters and perhaps die in the forest. But I couldn't get a consensus. We aren't good at raising Human children, so no one wanted to break up the family. And even I didn't want to force them all to stay with us. We had prints of them. If they died or kept resisting we could fashion genetic copies of them to be born to trader Humans. They wouldn't be lost to the gene pool. We decided that might have to be enough."

"Tino recognized you?"

"Yes, but in a very Human way, I think. I don't believe he understands why I caught his attention. He doesn't have complete access to memory."

"I don't understand that."

"It's a Human thing. Most Humans lose access to old memories as they acquire new ones. They know how to speak, for instance, but they don't recall learning to speak. They keep what experience has taught them—usually—but lose the experience itself. We can retrieve it for them—enable them to recall everything—but for many of them, that would only create confusion. They would remember so much that their memories would distract them from the present."

Akin received an impression of a dazed Human whose mind so overflowed with the past that every new experience triggered the reliving of several old ones, and those triggered others.

"Will I get that way?" he asked fearfully.

"Of course not. No construct is that way. We were careful."

"Lilith isn't that way, and she remembers everything."

"Natural ability, plus some changes I made. She was chosen very carefully."

"How did Tino find you again? Did you bring him here before you let him go? Did he remember?"

"This place didn't exist when we let his family and a few others go. He was probably following the river. Did he have a canoe?"

"I don't think so. I don't know."

"If you follow the river and keep your eyes open, you'll find villages."

"He found Mother and me."

"He's Human—and he's a resister. He wouldn't want to just walk into a village. He would want to have a look at it first. And he was lucky enough to meet some harmless villagers—people who might introduce him into the village safely or who could let him know why he should avoid the village."

"Mother isn't harmless."

"No, but she finds it convenient to seem harmless."

"What kind of village would he avoid?"

"Other resister villages, probably. Resister villages—especially widely separated ones—are dangerous in different ways. Some of them are dangerous to one another. A few become dangerous to us, and we have to break them up. Human diversity is fascinating and seductive, but we can't let it destroy them—or us."

"Will you keep Tino here?"

"Do you like him?"

"Yes."

"Good. Your mother doesn't yet, but she might change her mind. Perhaps he'll want to stay."

Akin, curious about adult relationships, used all his senses to perceive what went on between his parents and Tino.

First there was Tino's story to be finished.

"I don't know what to tell you about our village," he was saying. "It's full of old people who look young—just like here, I guess. Except here you have kids. We worked hard, getting things as much like they used to be as possible. That's what kept everyone going. The idea that we could use our long lives to bring back civilization—get things ready for when they found a girl for me or discovered some way to get kids of their own. They believed it would happen. I believed. Hell, I believed more than anyone.

"We did salvaging and quarrying in the mountains. I was never allowed to go. They were afraid something would happen to me. But I helped build the houses. Real houses, not huts. We even had glass for the windows. We made glass and traded it with other resister villages. One of them came in with us when they saw how well we were doing. That almost doubled our numbers. They had a guy about three years younger than me, but no young women.

"We made a town. We even had a couple of mills for power. That made building easier. We built like crazy. If you were really busy, you didn't have to think that maybe you were doing it all for nothing. Maybe all we were going to do was sit in our handsome houses and pray in our nice church and watch everybody not getting old.

"Then in one week, two guys and a woman hung themselves. Four others just disappeared. It would hit us like that—like a disease that one person caught and spread. We never had one suicide or one murder or one disappearance. Somebody else always caught the disease. I guess I finally caught it. Where do people go when they disappear? Someplace like this?" He looked around, sighed, then frowned. His tone changed abruptly. "You people have all the advantages. The Oankali can get you anything. Why do you live this way?"

"We're comfortable," Akin's oldest sister Ayre said. "This isn't a terrible way to live."

"It's primitive! You live like savages! I mean . . ." He lowered his voice. "I'm sorry. I didn't mean to say that. It's just that . . . I don't know any polite way to ask this: Why don't you at least build real houses and get rid of these shacks! You should see what we have! And . . . Hell, you have spaceships. *How can you live this way!*"

Lilith spoke softly to him. "How many of those real houses of yours were empty when you left, Tino?"

He faced her angrily. "My people never had a chance! They didn't make the war. They didn't make the Oankali. And they didn't make themselves sterile! But you can be damn sure that everything they did make was good and it worked and they put their hearts into it. Hey, I thought, 'If we made a town, the . . . traders . . . must have made a city!' And what do I find? A village of huts with primitive gardens. This place is hardly even a clearing!" His voice had risen again. He looked around with disapproval. "You've got kids to plan for and provide for, and you're going to let them slide right back to being cavemen!"

A Human woman named Leah spoke up. "Our kids will be okay," she said. "But I wish we could get more of your people to come here. They're as close to immortal as a Human being has ever been, and all they can think of to do is build useless houses and kill one another."

"It's time we offered the resisters a way back to us," Ahajas said. "I think we've been too comfortable here."

Several Oankali made silent gestures of agreement.

"Leave them alone," Tino said. "You've done enough to them! I'm not going to tell you where they are!"

Nikanj, still holding Akin, got up and moved through the seated people until it could sit with no one between itself and Tino. "None of the resister villages are hidden from us," it said softly. "We wouldn't have asked you where Phoenix was. And we don't mean to focus on Phoenix. It's time for us to approach all the resister villages and invite them to join us. It's only to remind them that they don't have to live sterile, pointless lives. We won't force them to come to us, but we will let them know they're still welcome. We let them go originally because we didn't want to hold prisoners."

Tino laughed bitterly. "So everyone here is here of their own free will, huh?"

"Everyone here is free to leave."

Tino gave Nikanj another of his unreadable looks and turned deliberately so that he faced Lilith. "How many men are there here?" he asked.

Lilith looked around, found Wray Ordway who kept the small guest house stocked with food and other supplies. This was where newly arrived men lived until they paired off with one of the village women. It was the only house in the village that had been built of cut trees and palm thatch. Tino might sleep there tonight. Wray kept the guest house because he had chosen not to wander. He had paired with Leah and apparently never tired of her. The two of them with their three Oankali mates had nine Human-born daughters and eleven Oankali-born children.

"How many men have we got now, Wray?" Lilith asked.

"Five," he said. "None in the guest house, though. Tino can have it all to himself if he wants."

"Five men." Tino shook his head. "No wonder you haven't built anything."

"We build ourselves," Wray said. "We're building a new

way of life here. You don't know anything about us. Why don't you ask questions instead of shooting off your mouth!"

"What is there to ask? Except for your garden—which barely looks like a garden—you don't grow anything. Except for your shacks, you haven't built anything! And as for building yourselves, the Oankali are doing that. You're their clay, that's all!"

"They change us and we change them," Lilith said. "The whole next generation is made up of genetically engineered people, Tino—constructs, whether they're born to Oankali or to Human mothers." She sighed. "I don't like what they're doing, and I've never made any secret of it. But they're in this with us. When the ships leave, they're stuck here. And with their own biology driving them, they can't not blend with us. But some of what makes us Human will survive, just as some of what makes them Oankali will survive." She paused, looked around the large room. "Look at the children here, Tino. Look at the construct adults. You can't tell who was born to whom. But you can see some Human features on every one of them. And as for the way we live . . . well, we're not as primitive as you think—and not as advanced as we could be. It was all a matter of how much like the ship we wanted our homes to be. The Oankali made us learn to live here without them so that if we did resist, we could survive. So that people like your parents would have a choice."

"Some choice," Tino muttered.

"Better than being a prisoner or a slave," she said. "They should have been ready for the forest. I'm surprised they ate the palm fruit that made them sick."

"We were city people, and we were hungry. My father didn't believe something could be poison raw but okay to eat cooked."

Lilith shook her head. "I was a city person, too, but there were some things I was willing not to learn from experience." She returned to her original subject. "Anyway, once we had learned to live in the forest on our own, the Oankali told us we didn't have to. They meant to live in homes as comfortable as the ones they had on the ship, and we were free to do the same. We accepted their offer. Believe me, weaving thatch and tying logs together with lianas doesn't hold any more fascination for me than it does for you—and I've done my share of it."

"This place has a thatched roof," Tino argued. "In fact, it looks freshly thatched."

"Because the leaves are green? Hell, they're green because they're alive. We didn't build this house, Tino, we grew it. Nikanj provided the seed; we cleared the land; everyone who was going to live here trained the walls and made them aware of us."

Tino frowned. "What do you mean, 'aware' of you? I thought you were telling me it was a plant."

"It's an Oankali construct. Actually, it's a kind of larval version of the ship. A neotenic larva. It can reproduce without growing up. It can also get a lot bigger without maturing sexually. This one will have to do that for a while. We don't need more than one."

"But you've got more than one. You've got—"

"Only one in this village. And a lot of that one is underground. What you see of it appears to be houses, grasses, shrubs, nearby trees, and, to some extent, riverbank. It allows some erosion, traps some newly arrived silt. Its inclination, though, is to become a closed system. A ship. We can't let it do that here. We still have a lot of growing to do ourselves."

Tino shook his head. He looked around at the large room, at the people watching, eating, feeding children, some small children stretched out asleep with their heads on adults' laps.

"Look up, Tino."

Tino jumped at the sound of Nikanj's soft voice so close to him. He seemed about to move away, shrink away. He had probably not been this close to an Oankali since he was a child. Somehow, he managed to keep still.

"Look up," Nikanj repeated.

Tino looked up into the soft yellow glow of the ceiling.

"Didn't you even wonder where the light was coming

from?" Nikanj asked. "Is that the ceiling of a primitive dwelling?"

"It wasn't like that when I came in," Tino said.

"No. It wasn't as much needed when you came in. There was plenty of light from outside. Look at the smooth walls. Look at the floor. Feel the floor. I don't think a floor of dead wood would be as comfortable. You'll have a chance to make comparisons if you choose to stay in the guest house. It really is the rough wood and thatch building you thought this was. It has to be. Strangers wouldn't be able to control the walls of the true houses here."

Wray Ordway said mildly, "Nika, if that man sleeps in the guest house tonight, I'll lose all faith in you."

Nikanj's body went helplessly smooth, and everyone laughed. The glass-smooth flattening of head and body tentacles normally indicated humor or pleasure, Akin knew, but what Nikanj was feeling now was neither of those emotions. It was more like a huge, consuming hunger, barely under control. If Nikanj had been Human, it would have been trembling. After a moment it managed to return its appearance to normal. It focused a cone of head tentacles on Lilith, appealing to her. She had not laughed, though she was smiling.

"You people are not nice," she said, keeping her smile. "You should be ashamed. Go home now, all of you. Have interesting dreams."

6

Tino watched in confusion as people began to leave. Some of them were still laughing—at a joke Tino was not sure he understood, not sure he wanted to understand. Some stopped to talk to the woman who had brought him into the village. Lilith

her name was. Lilith. Unusual name loaded with bad conno-
tations. She should have changed it. Almost anything would
have been better.

Three Oankali and several children clustered around her,
talking to the departing guests. Much of the conversation was
in some other language—almost certainly Oankali, since Lilith
had said the villagers had no other Human languages in common.

The group, family and guests, was a menagerie, Tino
thought. Human; nearly Human with a few visible sensory
tentacles; half-Human, gray with strangely jointed limbs and
some sensory tentacles; Oankali with Human features con-
trasting jarringly with their alienness; Oankali who might possibly be part Human; and Oankali like the ooloi who had
spoken to him, who obviously had no Humanity at all.

Lilith amid the menagerie. He had liked her looks when he
spotted her in the garden. She was an amazon of a woman, tall
and strong, but with no look of hardness to her. Fine, dark
skin. Breasts high in spite of all the children—breasts full of
milk. He had never before seen a woman nursing a child. He
had almost had to turn his back on her to stop himself from
staring as Lilith fed Akin. The woman was not beautiful. Her
broad, smooth face was usually set in an expression of solem-
nity, even sadness. It made her look—and Tino winced at the
thought—it made her look saintly. A mother. Very much a
mother. And something else.

And she had no man, apparently. She had said Akin's father
was long dead. Was she looking for someone? Was that what
all the laughter was about? After all, if he stayed with Lilith,
he would also be staying with her Oankali family, with the
ooloi whose reaction had provoked so much laughter. Especially with that ooloi. And what would that mean?

He was looking at it when the man Lilith had called Wray
came up to him.

"I'm Wray Ordway," he said. "I live here permanently.
Come around when you can. Anyone here can head you toward my house." He was a small, blond man with nearly col-

orless eyes that caught Tino's attention. Could anyone really see out of such eyes? "Do you know Nikanj?" the man asked.

"Who?" Tino asked, though he thought he knew.

"The ooloi who spoke to you. The one you're watching."

Tino stared at him with the beginnings of dislike.

"I think it recognized you," Wray said. "It's an interesting creature. Lilith thinks very highly of it."

"Is it her mate?" Of course it was.

"It's one of her mates. She hasn't had a man stay with her for a long time, though."

Was this Nikanj the mate who had forced pregnancy on her? It was an ugly creature with too many head tentacles and not enough of anything that could be called a face. Yet there was something compelling about it. Perhaps he had seen it before. Perhaps it was the last ooloi he had seen before he and his parents had been set down on Earth and let go. That ooloi . . . ?

A very Human-looking young woman brushed past Tino on her way out. Tino's attention was drawn to her, and he stared as she walked away. He saw her join another very similar young woman, and the two both turned to look at him, smile at him. They were completely alike, pretty, but so startling in their similarity that he was distracted from their beauty. He found himself searching his memory for a word he had had no occasion to use since childhood.

"Twins?" he asked Wray.

"Those two? No." Wray smiled. "They were born within a day of one another, though. One of them should have been a boy."

Tino stared at the well-shaped young women. "Neither of them is in any way like a boy."

"Do you like them?"

Tino glanced at him and smiled.

"They're my daughters."

Tino froze, then shifted his gaze from the girls uneasily. "Both?" he asked after a moment.

"Human mother, Oankali mother. Believe me, they weren't identical when they were born. I think they are now because

Tehkorahs wanted to make a point—that the nine children Leah and I have produced are true siblings of the children of our Oankali mates."

"Nine children?" Tino whispered. "Nine?" He had lived since childhood among people who would almost have given their lives to produce one child.

"Nine," Wray confirmed. "And listen." He stopped, waited until Tino's eyes focused on him. "Listen, I wouldn't want you to get the wrong idea. Those girls wear more clothing than most constructs because they have concealable differences. Neither of them is as Human as she looks. Let them alone if you can't accept that."

Tino looked into the pale, blind-seeming eyes. "What if I can accept it?"

Wray looked at the two girls, his expression gentling. "That's between you and them." The girls were exchanging words with Nikanj. Another ooloi came up to them, and as the exchange continued, it put one strength arm around each girl.

"That's Tehkorahs," Wray said, "my ooloi mate. That's Tehkorahs being protective, I think. And Nikanj . . . being impatient if anyone can believe that."

Tino watched the two ooloi and the two girls with interest. They did not seem to be arguing. In fact, they had ceased to speak at all—or ceased to speak aloud. Tino suspected they were still communicating somehow. There had always been a rumor that Oankali could read minds. He had never believed it, but clearly something was happening.

"One thing," Wray said softly. "Listen."

Tino faced him questioningly.

"You can do as you please here. As long as you don't hurt anyone, you can stay or go as you like; you can choose your own friends, your own lovers. No one has the right to demand anything from you that you don't want to give." He turned and walked away before Tino could ask what this really meant when it came to the Oankali.

Wray joined his daughters and Tehkorahs and led them out of the house. Tino found himself watching the young women's hips. He did not realize until they were gone that Nikanj and Lilith had come over to him.

"We'd like you to stay with us," Lilith said softly. "At least for the night."

He looked at her lineless face, her cap of dark hair, her breasts, now concealed beneath a simple gray shirt. He had had only a glimpse of them as she had settled herself to nurse Akin.

She took his hand, and he remembered seizing her hand to examine it. She had large, strong, calloused hands, warm and Human. Almost unconsciously, he turned his back to Nikanj. What did it want? Or rather, how did it go about getting what it wanted? What did the ooloi actually do to Humans? What would it want of him? And did he really want Lilith badly enough to find out?

But why had he left Phoenix if not for this?

But so quickly? Now?

"Sit with us," Lilith said. "Let's talk for a while." She drew him toward a wall—toward the place they had sat when he spoke to the people. They sat cross-legged—or the two Humans crossed their legs—their bodies forming a tight triangle. Tino watched the other two Oankali in the room as they herded the children away. Akin and the small gray child who now held him clearly wanted to stay. Tino could see that, though neither child was speaking English. The larger of the two Oankali lifted both children easily and managed to interest them in something else. All three vanished with the others through a doorway that seemed to grow shut behind them— the way doorways had closed so long ago aboard the ship. The room was sealed and empty except for Tino, Lilith, and Nikanj.

Tino made himself look at Nikanj. It had folded its legs under it the way the Oankali did. Many of its head tentacles were trained on him, seeming almost to be straining toward him. He suppressed a shudder—not a response of fear or disgust. Those feelings would not have surprised him. He felt . . . He did not know what he felt about this ooloi.

"It was you, wasn't it?" he asked suddenly.

"Yes," Nikanj admitted. "You're unusual. I've never known a Human to remember before."

"To remember his conditioning?"

Silence.

"To remember his conditioner," Tino said nodding. "I don't think anyone could forget his conditioning. But . . . I don't know how I recognized you. I met you so long ago, and . . . well, I don't mean to offend you, but I still can't tell your people apart."

"You can. You just don't realize it yet. That's unusual, too. Some Humans never learn to recognize individuals among us."

"What did you do to me back then?" he demanded. "I've never . . . never felt anything like that before or since."

"I told you then. I checked you for disease and injury, strengthened you against infection, got rid of any problems I found, programmed your body to slow its aging processes after a certain point, and did whatever else I could to improve your chances of surviving your reintroduction to Earth. Those are the things all conditioners did. And we all took prints of you—read all that your bodies could tell us about themselves and created a kind of blueprint. I could make a physical copy of you even if you hadn't survived."

"A baby?"

"Yes, eventually. But we prefer you to any copy. We need cultural as well as genetic diversity for a good trade."

"Trade!" Tino said scornfully. "I don't know what I'd call what you're doing to us, but it isn't trade. Trade is when two people agree to an exchange."

"Yes."

"It doesn't involve coercion." — being forced to do something

"We have something you need. You have something we need."

"We didn't need anything before you got here!"

"You were dying."

Tino said nothing for a moment. He looked away. The war was an insanity he had never understood, and no one in

Phoenix had been able to explain it to him. At least, no one had been able to give him a reason why people who had excellent reasons to suppose they would destroy themselves if they did a certain thing chose to do that thing anyway. He thought he understood anger, hatred, humiliation, even the desire to kill a man. He had felt all those things. But to kill everyone . . . almost to kill the Earth . . . There were times when he wondered if somehow the Oankali had not caused the war for their own purposes. How could sane people like the ones he had left behind in Phoenix do such a thing—or, how could they let insane people gain control of devices that could do so much harm? If you knew a man was out of his mind, you restrained him. You didn't give him power.

"I don't know about the war," Tino admitted. "It's never made sense to me. But . . . maybe you should have left us alone. Maybe some of us would have survived."

"Nothing would have survived except bacteria, a few small land plants and animals, and some sea creatures. Most of the life that you see around you we reseeded from prints, from collected specimens from our own creations, and from altered remnants of things that had undergone benign changes before we found them. The war damaged your ozone layer. Do you know what that is?"

"No."

"It shielded life on Earth from the sun's ultraviolet rays. Without its protection, above-ground life on Earth would not have been possible. If we had left you on Earth, you would have been blinded. You would have been burned—if you hadn't already been killed by other expanding effects of the war—and you would have died a terrible death. Most animals did die, and most plants, and some of us. We're hard to kill, but your people had made their world utterly hostile to life. If we had not helped it, it couldn't have restored itself so quickly. Once it was restored, we knew we couldn't carry on a normal trade. We couldn't let you breed alongside us, coming to us only when you saw the value of what we offered. Stabilizing a trade that way takes too many generations. We needed to free you—the least dangerous of you anyway. But we couldn't let your numbers grow. We couldn't let you begin to become what you were."

"You believe we would have had another war?"

"You would have had many others—against each other, against us. Some of the southern resister groups are already making guns."

Tino digested that silently. He had known about the guns of the southerners, had assumed they were to be used against the Oankali. He had not believed people from the stars would be stopped by a few crude firearms, and he had said so, making himself unpopular with those of his people who wanted to believe—needed to believe. Several of these had left Phoenix to join the southerners.

"What will you do about the guns?" he asked.

"Nothing, except to those who actually do try to shoot us. Those go back to the ship permanently. They lose Earth. We've told them that. So far, none of them have shot us. A few have shot one another, though."

Lilith looked startled. "You're letting them do that?"

Nikanj focused a cone of tentacles on her. "Could we stop them, Lilith, really?"

"You used to try!"

"Aboard the ship, here in Lo, and in the other trade villages. Nowhere else. We control the resisters only if we cage them, drug them, and allow them to live in an unreal world of drug-stimulated imaginings. We've done that to a few violent Humans. Shall we do it to more?"

Lilith only stared at it, her expression unreadable.

"You won't do that?" Tino asked.

"We won't. We have prints of all of you. We would be sorry to lose you, but at least we would save something. We will be inviting your people to join us again. If any are injured or crippled or even sick in spite of our efforts, we'll offer them our help. They're free to accept our help yet stay in their villages. Or they can come to us." It aimed a sharp cone of head tentacles at Tino. "You've known since I sent you back to your parents years ago that you could choose to come to us."

Tino shook his head, spoke softly. "I seem to remember that I didn't want to go back to my parents. I asked to stay with you. To this day, I don't know why."

"I wanted to keep you. If you'd been a little older . . . But we've been told and shown that we aren't good at raising fully Human children." It shifted its attention for a moment to Lilith, but she looked away. "You had to be left with your parents to grow up. I thought I wouldn't see you again."

Tino caught himself staring at the ooloi's long, gray sensory arms. Both arms seemed relaxed against the ooloi's sides, their ends coiled, spiraling upward so that they did not touch the floor.

"They always look a little like elephants' trunks to me," Lilith said.

Tino glanced at her and saw that she was smiling—a sad smile that became her somehow. For a moment, she was beautiful. He did not know what he wanted from the ooloi—if he wanted anything. But he knew what he wanted from the woman. He wished the ooloi were not there. And as soon as the thought occurred to him, he rejected it. Lilith and Nikanj were a pair somehow. Without Nikanj, she would not have been as desirable. He did not understand this, but he accepted it.

They would have to show him what was to happen. He would not ask. They had made it clear they wanted something from him. Let *them* ask.

"I was thinking," Tino said, referring to the sensory arms, "that I don't know what they are."

Nikanj's body tentacles seemed to tremble, then solidify into discolored lumps. They sank into themselves the way the soft bodies of slugs seemed to when they drew themselves up to rest.

Tino drew back a little in revulsion. God, the Oankali were ugly creatures. How had Human beings come to tolerate them so easily, to touch them and allow them to . . .

Lilith took the ooloi's right sensory arm between her hands and held it even when Nikanj seemed to try to pull away. She stared at it, and Tino knew there must be some communication. Did the Oankali share mind-reading abilities with their pet Humans? Or was it mind reading? Lilith spoke aloud.

"Slow," she whispered. "Give him a moment. Give me a moment. Don't defeat your own purpose by hurrying."

For a moment, Nikanj's lumps looked worse—like some grotesque disease. Then the lumps resolved themselves again into slender gray body tentacles no more grotesque than usual. Nikanj drew its sensory arm from Lilith's hands, then stood up and went to a far corner of the room. There it sat down and seemed almost to turn itself off. Like something carved from gray marble, it became utterly still. Even its head and body tentacles ceased to move.

"What was all that?" Tino demanded.

Lilith smiled broadly. "For the first time in my life, I had to tell it to be patient. If it were Human, I would say it was infatuated with you."

"You're joking!"

"I am," she said. "This is worse than infatuation. I'm glad you feel something for it, too, even though you don't yet know what."

"Why has it gone to sit in that corner?"

"Because it can't quite bring itself to leave the room, though it knows it should—to let the two of us be Human for a little while. Anyway, I don't think you really want it to leave."

"Can it read minds? Can you?"

She did not laugh. At least she did not laugh. "I've never met anyone, Oankali or Human, who could read minds. It can stimulate sensations and send your thoughts off in all sorts of directions, but it can't read those thoughts. It can only share the new sensations they produce. In effect, it can give you the most realistic and the most pleasurable dreams you've ever experienced. Nothing you've known before can match it—except perhaps your conditioning. And that should tell you why you're here, why you were bound to seek out a trade village sooner or later. Nikanj touched you when you were too young to have any defenses. And what it gave you, you won't ever quite forget—or quite remember, unless you feel it again. You want it again. Don't you."

It was not a question. Tino swallowed and did not bother with an answer. "I remember drugs," he said, staring at nothing. "I never took any. I was too young before the war. I remember other people taking them and maybe going crazy for a little while or maybe just being high. I remember that they got addicted, that they got hurt sometimes or killed . . ."

"This isn't just a drug."

"What then?"

"Direct stimulation of the brain and nervous system." She held up her hand to stop him from speaking. "There's no pain. They hate pain more than we do, because they're more sensitive to it. If they hurt us, they hurt themselves. And there are no harmful side effects. Just the opposite. They automatically fix any problems they find. They get real pleasure from healing or regenerating, and they share that pleasure with us. They weren't as good at repairs before they found us. Regeneration was limited to wound healing. Now they can grow you a new leg if you lose one. They can even regenerate brain and nervous tissue. They learned that from us, believe it or not. We had the ability, and they knew how to use it. They learned by studying our cancers, of all things. It was cancer that made Humanity such a valuable trade partner."

Tino shook his head, not believing. "I saw cancer kill both my grandfathers. It's nothing but a filthy disease."

Lilith touched his shoulder, let her hand slide down his arm in a caress. "So that's it. That's why Nikanj is so attracted to you. Cancer killed three close relatives of mine, including my mother. I'm told it would have killed me if the Oankali hadn't done some work on me. It's a filthy disease to us, but to the Oankali, it's the tool they've been looking for for generations."

"What will it do to me that has to do with cancer?"

"Nothing. It just finds you a lot more attractive than it does most Humans. What can you do with a beautiful woman that you can't do with an ugly one? Nothing. It's just a matter of preference. Nikanj and every other Oankali already have all the information they need to use what they've learned from us. Even the constructs can use it once they're mature. But people like you and me are still attractive to them."

"I don't understand that."

"Don't worry about it. I'm told our children will understand them, but we won't."

"Our children will be them."

"You accept that?"

It took him a moment to realize what he had said. "No! I don't know. Yes, but—" He closed his eyes. "I don't know."

She moved closer to him, rested warm, calloused hands on his forearms. He could smell her. Crushed plants—the way a fresh-cut lawn used to smell. Food, pepper and sweet. Woman. He reached out to her, touched the large breasts. He could not help himself. He had wanted to touch them since he had first seen them. She lay down on her side, drawing him down facing her. It occurred to him a moment later that Nikanj was behind him. That she had deliberately positioned him so that Nikanj would be behind him.

He sat up abruptly, turned to look at the ooloi. It had not moved. It gave no sign that it was even alive.

"Lie here with me for a while," she said.

"But—"

"We'll go to Nikanj in a little while. Won't we."

"I don't know." He lay down again, now glad to keep his back to it. "I still don't understand what it does. I mean, so it gives me good dreams. How? And what else will it do? Will it use me to make you pregnant?"

"Not now. Akin is too young. It . . . might collect some sperm from you. You won't be aware of it. When they have the chance, they stimulate a woman to ovulate several eggs. They collect the eggs, store them, collect sperm, store it. They can keep sperm and eggs viable and separate in their bodies for decades. Akin is the child of a man who died nearly thirty years ago."

"I heard there was a time limit—that they could only keep sperm and eggs alive for a few months."

"Progress. Before I left the ship, someone came up with a new method of preservation. Nikanj was one of the first to learn it."

Tino looked at her closely, searched her smooth, broad face. "So you're what? In your fifties?"

"Fifty-five."

He sighed, shook his head against the arm he had rested it on. "You look younger than I do. I've at least got a few gray hairs. I remember I used to worry that I really was the Human the Oankali had failed with, fertile and aging normally, and that all I'd really get out of it was old."

"Nikanj wouldn't have failed with you."

She was so close to him that he couldn't help touching her, moving his fingers over the fine skin. He drew back, though, when she mentioned the ooloi's name.

"Can't it go?" he whispered. "Just for a while."

"It chooses not to," she said in a normal voice. "And don't bother whispering. It can hear your heartbeat from where it's sitting. It can hear your subvocalizations—the things you . . . say to yourself in words but not quite out loud. That may be why you thought it could read minds. And it obviously will not go away."

"Can we?"

"No." She hesitated. "It isn't Human, Tino. This isn't like having another man or woman in the room."

"It's worse."

She smiled wearily, leaned over him, and kissed him. Then she sat up. "I understand," she said. "I felt the way you do once. Maybe it's just as well." She hugged herself and looked at him almost angrily. Frustration? How long had it been for her? Well, the damned ooloi could not *always* be there. *Why* wouldn't it go away, wait its turn? Failing that, why was he so shy of it? Its presence did bother him more than another Human's would have. Much more.

"We'll join Nikanj, Tino, once I've told you one more

thing," she said. "That is, we'll join it if you decide you still want anything to do with me."

"With you? But it wasn't you I was having trouble with. I mean—"

"I know. This is something else—something I'd rather never mention to you. But if I don't, someone else will." She drew a deep breath. "Didn't you wonder about me? About my name?"

"I thought you should have changed it. It isn't a very popular name."

"I know. And changing it wouldn't do much good. Too many people know me. I'm not just someone stuck with an unpopular name, Tino. I'm the one who made it unpopular. I'm Lilith Iyapo."

He frowned, began to shake his head, then stopped. "You're not the one who . . . who . . ."

"I awakened the first three groups of Humans to be sent back to Earth. I told them what their situation was, what their options were, and they decided I was responsible for it all. I helped teach them to live in the forest, and they decided it was my fault they had to give up civilized life. Sort of like blaming me for the goddamn war! Anyway, they decided I had betrayed them to the Oankali, and the nicest thing some of them called me was Judas. Is that the way you were taught to think of me?"

"I . . . Yes."

She shook her head. "The Oankali either seduced them or terrified them, or both. I, on the other hand, was nobody. It was easy for them to blame me. And it was safe.

"So now and then when we get ex-resisters traveling through Lo and they hear my name, they assume I have horns. Some of the younger ones have been taught to blame me for everything—as though I were a second Satan or Satan's wife or some such idiocy. Now and then one of them will try to kill me. That's one of the reasons I'm so touchy about weapons here."

He stared at her for a while. He had watched her closely as

she spoke, trying to see guilt in her, trying to see the devil in her. In Phoenix, people had said things like that—that she was possessed of the devil, that she had sold first herself, then Humanity, that she was the first to go willingly to an Oankali bed to become their whore and to seduce other Humans . . .

"What do your people say about me?" she asked.

He hesitated, glanced at Nikanj. "That you sold us."

"For what currency?"

There had always been some debate about that. "For the right to stay on the ship and for . . . powers. They saw you were born Human, but the Oankali made you like a construct."

She made a sound that she may have intended as a laugh. "I begged to go to Earth with the first group I awakened. I was supposed to have gone. But when the time came, Nika wouldn't let me. It said the people would kill me once they got me away from the Oankali. They probably would have. And they would have felt virtuous and avenged."

"But . . . you are different. You're very strong, fast . . ."

"Yes. That wasn't the Oankali way of paying me off. It was their way of giving me some protection. If they hadn't changed me a little, someone in the first group would have killed me while I was still awakening people. I'm somewhere between Human and construct in ability. I'm stronger and faster than most Humans, but not as strong or as fast as most constructs. I heal faster than you could, and I'd recover from wounds that would kill you. And of course I can control walls and raise platforms here in Lo. All Humans who settle here are given that ability. That's all. Nikanj changed me to save my life, and it succeeded. Instead of killing me, the first group I awakened killed Akin's father, the man I had paired with . . . might still be with. One of them killed him. The others watched, then went on following that one."

There was a long silence. Finally Tino said, "Maybe they were afraid."

"Is that what you were told?"

"No. I didn't know about that part at all. I even heard . . . that . . . perhaps you didn't like men at all."

She threw back her head in startling, terrible laughter. "Oh, god. Which of my first group is in Phoenix?"

"A guy named Rinaldi."

"Gabe? Gabe and Tate. Are they still together?"

"Yes. I didn't realize . . . Tate never said anything about being with him then. I thought they had gotten together here on Earth."

"I awoke them both. They were my best friends for a while. Their ooloi was Kahguyaht—ooan Nikanj."

"What Nikanj?"

"Nikanj's ooloi parent. It stayed aboard the ship with its mates and raised another trio of children. Nikanj told it Gabe and Tate wouldn't be leaving the resisters any time soon. It was finally willing to acknowledge Nikanj's talent, and it couldn't bring itself to accept other Humans."

Tino looked at Nikanj. After a while, he got up and went over to it, sat down opposite it. "What is your talent?" he asked.

Nikanj did not speak or acknowledge his presence.

"Talk to me!" he demanded. "I know you hear."

The ooloi seemed to come to life slowly. "I hear."

"What is your talent!"

It leaned toward him and took his hands in its strength hands, keeping its sensory arms coiled. Oddly, the gesture reminded him of Lilith, was much like what Lilith tended to do. He did not mind, somehow, that now hard, cool gray hands held his.

"I have a talent for Humans," it said in its soft voice. "I was bred to work with you, taught to work with you, and given one of you as a companion during one of my most formative periods." It focused for a moment on Lilith. "I know your bodies, and sometimes I can anticipate your thinking. I knew that Gabe Rinaldi couldn't accept a union with us when Kahguyaht wanted him. Tate could have, but she would not leave Gabe for an ooloi—no matter how badly she wanted to.

And Kahguyaht would not simply keep her with it when the others were sent to Earth. That surprised me. It always said there was no point in paying attention to what Humans said. It knew Tate would eventually have accepted it, but it listened to her and let her go. And it wasn't raised as I was in contact with Humans. I think your people affect us more than we realize."

"I think," Lilith said quietly, "that you may be better at understanding us than you are at understanding your own people."

It focused on her, its body tentacles smoothed to invisibility against its flesh. That meant it was pleased, Tino remembered. Pleased or even happy. "Ahajas says that," it told her. "I don't think it's true, but it may be."

Tino turned toward Lilith but spoke to Nikanj. "Did you make her pregnant against her will?"

"Against one part of her will, yes," Nikanj admitted. "She had wanted a child with Joseph, but he was dead. She was . . . more alone than you could imagine. She thought I didn't understand."

"It's your fault she was alone!"

"It was a shared fault." Nikanj's head and body tentacles hung limp. "We believed we had to use her as we did. Otherwise we would have had to drug newly awakened Humans much more than was good for them because we would have had to teach them everything ourselves. We did that later because we saw . . . that we were damaging Lilith and the others we tried to use.

"In the first children, I gave Lilith what she wanted but could not ask for. I let her blame me instead of herself. For a while, I became for her a little of what she was for the Humans she had taught and guided. Betrayer. Destroyer of treasured things. Tyrant. She needed to hate me for a while so that she could stop hating herself. And she needed the children I mixed for her."

Tino stared at the ooloi, needing to look at it to remind himself that he was hearing an utterly un-Human creature. Finally, he looked at Lilith.

She looked back, smiling a bitter, humorless smile. "I told you it was talented," she said.

"How much of that is true?" he asked.

"How should I know!" She swallowed. "All of it might be. Nikanj usually tells the truth. On the other hand, reasons and justifications can sound just as good when they're made up as an afterthought. Have your fun, then come up with a wonderful-sounding reason why it was the right thing for you to do."

Tino pulled away from the ooloi and went to Lilith. "Do you hate it?" he asked.

She shook her head. "I have to leave it to hate it. Sometimes I go away for a while—explore, visit other villages, and hate it. But after a while, I start to miss my children. And, heaven help me, I start to miss it. I stay away until staying away hurts more than the thought of coming . . . home."

He thought she should be crying. His mother would never have contained that much passion without tears—would never have tried. He took her by the arms, found her stiff and resistant. Her eyes rejected any comfort before he could offer it.

"What shall I do?" he asked. "What do you want me to do?"

She hugged him suddenly, holding him hard against her. "Will you stay?" she said into his ear.

"Shall I?"

"Yes."

"All right." She was not Lilith Iyapo. She was a quiet, expressive, broad face. She was dark, smooth skin and warm, work-calloused hands. She was breasts full of milk. He wondered how he had resisted her earlier.

And what about Nikanj? He did not look at it, but he imagined he felt its attention on him.

"If you decide to leave," Lilith said, "I'll help you."

He could not imagine wanting to leave her.

Something cool and rough and hard attached itself to his

upper arm. He froze, not having to look to know it was one of the ooloi's sensory arms.

It stood close to him, one sensory arm on him and one on Lilith. They *were* like elephants' trunks, those arms. He felt Lilith release him, felt Nikanj drawing him to the floor. He let himself be pulled down only because Lilith lay down with them. He let Nikanj position his body alongside its own. Then he saw Lilith sit up on Nikanj's opposite side and watch the two of them solemnly.

He did not understand why she watched, why she did not take part. Before he could ask, the ooloi slipped its sensory arm around him and pressed the back of his neck in a way that made him shudder, then go limp.

He was not unconscious. He knew when the ooloi drew closer to him, seemed to grasp him in some way he did not understand.

He was not afraid.

The splash of icy-sweet pleasure, when it reached him, won him completely. This was the half-remembered feeling he had come back for. This was the way it began.

Before the long-awaited rush of sensation swallowed him completely, he saw Lilith lie down alongside the ooloi, saw the second sensory arm loop around her neck. He tried to reach out to her across the body of the ooloi, to touch her, touch the warm Human flesh. It seemed to him that he reached and reached, yet she remained too far away to touch.

He thought he shouted as the sensation deepened, as it took him. It seemed that she was with him suddenly, her body against his own. He thought he said her name and repeated it, but he could not hear the sound of his own voice.

7

Akin took his first few steps toward Tino's outstretched hands. He learned to take food from Tino's plate, and he rode on Tino's back whenever the man would carry him. He did not forget Dichaan's warning not to be alone with Tino, but he did not take it seriously. He came to trust Tino very quickly. Eventually everyone came to trust Tino.

Thus, as it happened, Akin was alone with Tino when a party of raiders came looking for children to steal.

Tino had gone out to cut wood for the guest house. He was not yet able to perceive the borders of Lo. He had gotten into the habit of taking Akin along to spot for him after breaking an ax he had borrowed from Wray Ordway on a tree that was not a tree. The Lo entity shaped itself according to the desires of its occupants and the patterns of the surrounding vegetation. Yet it was the larval form of a space-going entity. Its hide and its organs were better protected than any living thing native to Earth. No ax or machete could mark it. Until it was older, no native vegetation would grow within its boundaries. That was why Lilith and a few other people had gardens far from the village. Lo would have provided good food from its own substance—the Oankali could stimulate food production and separate the food from Lo. But most Humans in the village did not want to be dependent on the Oankali. Thus, Lo had a broad fringe of Human-planted gardens, some in use and some fallow. Akin had had, at times, to keep Tino from tramping right into them, then realizing too late that he had slashed his way through food plants and destroyed someone's work. It was as though he could not see at all.

Akin could not help knowing when he passed the borders of Lo. Even the smell of the air was different. The vegetation that touched him made him cringe at first because it was abruptly not-home. Then, for exactly the same reason, it drew him, called to him with its strangeness. He deliberately let Tino walk farther than was necessary until something he had not tasted before chanced to brush across his face.

"Here," he said, tearing leaves from the sapling that had touched him. "Don't cut that tree, but you can cut any of the others."

Tino put him down and grinned at him. "May I?" he said.

"I like this one," Akin said. "When it's older, I think we'll be able to eat from it."

"Eat what?"

"I don't know. I've never seen one like this before. But even if it doesn't bear fruit, the leaves are good to eat. My body likes them."

Tino rolled his eyes toward the forest canopy and shook his head. "Everything goes into your mouth," he said. "I'm surprised you haven't poisoned yourself ten times."

Akin ignored this and began investigating the bark on the sapling and looking to see what insects or fungi might be eating it and what might be eating them. Tino had been told why Akin put things in his mouth. He did not understand, but he never tried to keep things out of Akin's mouth the way other visitors did. He could accept without understanding. Once he had seen that a strange thing did no harm, he no longer feared it. He said Akin's tongue looked like a big gray slug, but somehow this did not seem to bother him. He allowed himself to be probed and studied when he carried Akin about. Lilith worried that he was concealing disgust or resentment, but he could not have concealed such strong emotions even from Akin. He certainly could not have concealed them from Nikanj.

"He's more adaptable than most Humans," Nikanj had told Akin. "So is Lilith."

"He calls me 'son'," Akin said.

"I've heard."

"He won't go away, will he?"

"He won't go. He's not a wanderer. He was looking for a home where he could have a family, and he's found one."

Now Tino began to chop down a small tree. Akin watched

for a moment, wondering why the man enjoyed such activity. He did enjoy it. He had volunteered to do it. He did not like gardening. He did not like adding to Lo's library—writing down his prewar memories for later generations. Everyone was asked to do that if they stayed even for a short while in Lo. Constructs wrote about their lives as well, and Oankali, who would not write anything, though they were capable of writing, told their stories to Human writers. Tino showed no interest in any of this. He chopped wood, he worked with Humans who had established a fish farm and with constructs who raised altered bees, wasps, earthworms, beetles, ants, and other small animals that produced new foods. He built canoes and traveled with Ahajas when she visited other villages. She traveled by boat for his sake, though most Oankali swam. She had been surprised to see how easily he accepted her, had recognized his fascination with her pregnancy. Both Ahajas and Akin tried to tell him what it was like to touch the growing child and feel its response, it's recognition, it's intense curiosity. The two had talked Nikanj into trying to simulate the sensation for him. Nikanj had resisted the idea only because Tino was not one of the child's parents. But when Tino asked, the ooloi's resistance vanished. It gave Tino the sensation—and held him longer than was necessary. That was good, Akin thought. Tino needed to be touched more. It had been painfully hard for him when he discovered that his entry into the family meant he could not touch Lilith. This was something Akin did not understand. Human beings liked to touch one another—needed to. But once they mated through an ooloi, they could not mate with each other in the Human way—could not even stroke and handle one another in the Human way. Akin did not understand why they needed this, but he knew they did, knew it frustrated and embittered them that they could not. Tino had spent days screaming at or not speaking at all to Nikanj, screaming at or not speaking to Lilith, sitting alone and staring at nothing. Once he left the village for three days, and Dichaan followed him and led him back when he was ready to return. He could have gone away until the effects of his mating with Nikanj had passed from his body. He could have found another village and a sterile Human-only mating. He had had several of those, though. Akin had heard him speak of them during those first few bad days. They were not what he wanted. But neither was this. Now he was like Lilith. Very much attached to the family and content with it most of the time, yet poisonously resentful and bitter some-times. But only Akin and the rest of the younger children of the house worried that he might leave permanently. The adults seemed certain he would stay.

Now he cut the tree he had felled into pieces and cut lianas to bundle the wood. Then he came to collect Akin. He stopped abruptly and whispered. "My god!"

Akin was tasting a large caterpillar. He had allowed it to crawl onto his forearm. It was, in fact, almost as large as his forearm. It was bright red and spotted with what appeared to be tufts of long, stiff black fur. The tufts, Akin knew, were deadly. The animal did not have to sting. It had only to be touched on one of the tufts. The poison was strong enough to kill a large Human. Apparently Tino knew this. His hand moved toward the caterpillar, then stopped.

Akin split his attention, watching Tino to see that he made no further moves and tasting the caterpillar gently, delicately, with his skin and with a flick of his tongue to its pale, slightly exposed underside. Its underside was safe. It did not poison what it crawled on.

It ate other insects. It even ate small frogs and toads. Some ooloi had given it the characteristics of another crawling crea-ture—a small, multilegged, wormlike peripatus. Now both caterpillar and peripatus could project a kind of glue to snare prey and hold it until it could be consumed.

The caterpillar itself was not good to eat. It was too poison-ous. The ooloi who had assembled it had not intended that it be food for anything while it was alive, though it might be killed by ants or wasps if it chose to hunt in one of the trees protected by these. It was safe, though, in the tree it had chosen. Its kind would give the tree a better chance to mature and produce food.

Akin held his arm against the trunk of the sapling and carefully maneuvered the caterpillar into crawling back to it. The moment it had left his arm, Tino snatched him up, shouting at him.

"*Never* do anything so crazy again! *Never!* That thing could kill you! It could kill me!"

Someone grabbed him from behind.

Someone else grabbed Akin from his arms.

Now, far too late, Akin saw, heard, and smelled the intruders. Strangers. Human males with no scent of the Oankali about them. Resisters. Raiders. Child thieves!

Akin screamed and twisted in the arms of his captor. But physically, he was still little more than a baby. He had let his attention be absorbed by Tino and the caterpillar, and now he was caught. The man who held him was large and strong. He held Akin without seeming to notice Akin's struggles.

Meanwhile, four men had surrounded Tino. There was blood on Tino's face where someone had hit him, cut him. One of the four had a piece of gleaming silver metal around one of his fingers. That must have been what had cut Tino.

"Hold it!" one of Tino's captors said. "This guy used to be Phoenix." He frowned at Tino. "Aren't you the Leal kid?"

"I'm Augustino Leal," Tino said, holding his body very straight. "I was Phoenix. I was Phoenix before you ever heard of it!" His voice did not tremble, but Akin could see that his body was trembling slightly. He looked toward his ax, which now lay on the ground several feet from him. He had leaned it against a tree when he came to get Akin. His machete, though, had still been at his belt. Now it was gone. Akin could not see where it had gone.

The raiders all had long wood-and-metal sticks, which they now pointed at Tino. The man holding Tino also had such a stick, strapped across his back. These were weapons, Akin realized. Clubs—or perhaps guns? And these men knew Tino.

One of them knew Tino. And Tino did not like that one. Tino was afraid. Akin had never seen him more afraid.

The man who held Akin had put his neck within easy reach of Akin's tongue. Akin could sting him, kill him. But then what would happen? There were four other men.

Akin did nothing. He watched Tino, hoping the man would know what was best.

"There were no guns in Phoenix when I left," Tino was saying. So the sticks were guns.

"No, and you didn't want there to be any, did you?" the same man asked. He made a point of jabbing Tino with his gun.

Tino began to be a little less afraid and more angry. "If you think you can use those to kill the Oankali, you're as stupid as I thought you were."

The man swung his gun up so that its end almost touched Tino's nose.

"Is it Humans you mean to kill?" Tino asked very softly. "Are there so many Humans left? Are our numbers increasing so fast?"

"You've joined the traitors!" the man said.

"To have a family," Tino said softly. "To have children." He looked at Akin. "To have at least part of myself continue."

The man holding Akin spoke up. "This kid is as human as any I've seen since the war. I can't find anything wrong with him."

"No tentacles?" one of the four asked.

"Not a one."

"What's he got between his legs?"

"Same thing you've got. Little smaller, maybe."

There was a moment of silence, and Akin saw that three of the men were amused and one was not.

Akin was afraid to speak, afraid to show the raiders his un-Human characteristics: his tongue, his ability to speak, his intelligence. Would these things make them let him alone or make them kill him? In spite of his months with Tino, he did not know. He kept quiet and began trying to hear or smell any Lo villager who might be passing nearby.

"So we take the kid," one of the men said. "What do we do with him?" He gestured sharply toward Tino.

Before anyone could answer, Tino said, "No! You can't take him. He still nurses. If you take him, he'll starve!"

The men looked at one another uncertainly. The man holding Akin suddenly turned Akin toward him and squeezed the sides of Akin's face with his fingers. He was trying to get Akin's mouth open. Why?

It did not matter why. He would get Akin's mouth open, then be startled. He was Human and a stranger and dangerous. Who knew what irrational reaction he might have. He must be given something familiar to go with the unfamiliar. Akin began to twist in the man's arm and to whimper. He had not cried so far. That had been a mistake. Humans always marveled at how little construct babies cried. Clearly a Human baby would have cried more.

Akin opened his mouth and wailed.

"Shit!" muttered the man holding him. He looked around quickly as though fearing someone might be attracted by the noise. Akin, who had not thought of this, cried louder. Oankali had hearing more sensitive than most Humans realized.

"Shut up!" the man shouted, shaking him. "Good god, it's got the ugliest goddamn gray tongue you ever saw! Shut up, you!"

"He's just a baby," Tino said. "You can't get a baby to shut up by scaring him. Give him to me." He had begun to step toward Akin, holding his arms out to take him.

Akin reached toward him, thinking that the resisters would be less likely to hurt the two of them together. Perhaps he could shield Tino to some degree. In Tino's arms he would be quiet and cooperative. They would see that Tino was useful.

The man who had first recognized Tino now stepped behind him and smashed the wooden end of his gun into the back of Tino's head.

Tino dropped to the ground without a cry, and his attacker hit him again, driving the wood of the gun down into Tino's head like a man killing a poisonous snake.

Akin screamed in terror and anguish. He knew Human anatomy well enough to know that if Tino were not dead, he would die soon unless an Oankali helped him.

And there was no Oankali nearby.

The resisters left Tino where he lay and strode away into the forest, carrying Akin who still screamed and struggled.

II

PHOENIX

1

Dichaan slipped from the deepest part of the broad lake, shifted from breathing in water to breathing in air, and began to wade to shore.

Humans called this an oxbow lake—one that had originally been part of the river. Dichaan had kept the Lo entity from engulfing it so far because the entity would have killed the plant life in it and that would have eventually killed the animal life. Even with help, Lo could not have been taught to provide what the animals needed in a form they would accept before they died of hunger. The only useful thing the entity could have provided at once was oxygen.

But now the entity was changing, moving into its next growth stage. Now it could learn to incorporate Earth vegetation, sustain it, and benefit from it. On its own, it would learn slowly, killing a great deal, culling native vegetation for that vegetation's ability to adapt to the changes it made.

But the entity in symbiotic relationship with its Oankali inhabitants could change faster, adapting itself and accepting adapted plant life that Dichaan and others had prepared.

Dichaan stepped on shore through a natural corridor between great profusions of long, thick, upright prop roots that would slowly be submerged when the rainy season began and the water rose.

Dichaan had made his way out of the mud, his body still savoring the taste of the lake—rich in plant and animal life—when he heard a cry.

He stood utterly still, listening, his head and body tentacles slowly swinging around to focus on the direction of the sound.

Then he knew where it was and who it was, and he began to run. He had been underwater all morning. What had been happening in the air?

Leaping over fallen trees, dodging around dangling lianas, undergrowth, and living trees, he ran. He spread his body tentacles against his skin. This way the sensitive parts of the tentacles could be protected from the thin underbrush that lashed him as he ran through it. He could not avoid it all and still move quickly.

He splashed through a small stream, then scrambled up a steep bank.

He came to a bundle of small logs and saw where a tree had been cut. The scent of Akin and of strange Human males was there. Tino's scent was there—very strong.

And now Tino cried out weakly, making only a shadow of the sound Dichaan had heard at the lake. It hardly seemed a Human sound at all, yet to Dichaan, it was unmistakably Tino. His head tentacles swept around, seeking the man, finding him. He ran to him where he lay, concealed by the broad, wedge-shaped buttresses of a tree.

His hair was stuck together in solid masses of blood, dirt, and dead leaves. His body twitched, and he made small sounds.

Dichaan folded to the ground, first probed Tino's wounds with several head tentacles, then lay down beside him and penetrated his body wherever possible with filaments from head and body tentacles.

The man was dying—would die in a moment unless Dichaan could keep him alive. It had been good having a Human male in the family. It had been a balance found after painful years of imbalance, and no one had felt the imbalance more than Dichaan. He had been born to work with a Human male parallel—to help raise children with the aid of such a person, and yet he had had to limp along without this essential other. How were children to learn to understand the Human male side of themselves—a side they all possessed whatever their eventual sex?

Now, here was Tino, childless and unused to children, but quickly at ease with them, quickly accepted by them.

Now, here was Tino, nearly dead at the hands of his own kind.

Dichaan linked with his nervous system and kept his heart beating. The man was a beautiful, terrible physical contradiction, as all Humans were. He was a walking seduction, and he would never understand why. He would not be lost. He could not be another Joseph.

There was some brain damage. Dichaan could perceive it, but he could not heal it. Nikanj would have to do that. But Dichaan could keep the damage from growing worse. He stopped the blood loss, which was not as bad as it looked, and made certain the living brain cells had intact blood vessels to nourish them. He found damage to the skull and perceived that the damaged bone was exerting abnormal pressure on the brain. This, he did not tamper with. Nikanj would handle it. Nikanj could do it faster and more certainly than a male or female could.

Dichaan waited until Tino was as stable as he could be, then left him for a moment. He went to the edge of Lo to one of the larger buttresses of a pseudotree and struck it several times in the code of pressures he would have used to supplement exchanged sensory impressions. The pressures would normally be used very rapidly, soundlessly, against another person's flesh. It would take a moment for this drumming to be perceived as communication. But it would be noticed. Even if no Oankali or construct heard it, the Lo entity would pick up the familiar groups of vibrations. It would alert the community the next time someone opened a wall or raised a platform.

Dichaan pounded out the message twice, then went back to Tino and lay down to monitor him and wait.

Now there was time to think about what he had been too late to prevent.

Akin was gone—had been gone for some time. His abductors had been Human males—resisters. They had run toward the river. No doubt they had already headed up- or downriver toward their village—or perhaps they had crossed the river and traveled over land. Either way, their scent trail would probably vanish along the river. He had included in his message instructions to search for them, but he was not hopeful. All resister villages had to be searched. Akin would be found. Phoenix in particular would be checked, since it had once been Tino's home. But would men from Phoenix have hated Tino so much? He did not seem to be the kind of man people could know and still hate. The people of Phoenix who had watched him grow up as the village's only child must have felt as parents toward him. They would have been more likely to abduct him along with Akin.

Akin.

They would not hurt him—not intentionally. Not at first. He still nursed, but he did it more for comfort than for nutrition. He had an Oankali ability to digest whatever he was given and make the most of it. If they fed him what they ate, he would satisfy his body's needs.

Did they know how intelligent he was? Did they know he could talk? If not, how would they react when they found out? Humans reacted badly to surprise. He would be careful, of course, but what did he know of angry, frightened, frustrated Humans? He had never been near even one person who might hate him, who might even hurt him when they discovered that he was not as Human as he looked.

2

Upriver.

The Humans had a long, smooth, narrow canoe, light and easy to row. Two pairs of men took turns at the oars, and the boat cut quickly through the water. The current was not strong. Working in relay as they were, the men never slowed to rest.

Akin had screamed as loudly as he could as long as there had been any chance of his being heard. But no one had come. He was quiet now, exhausted and miserable. The man who had caught him still held him, had once dangled him by his feet and threatened to dunk him in the river if he did not be quiet. Only the intervention of the other men had stopped him from doing this. Akin was terrified of him. The man honestly did not seem to understand why murder and abduction should disturb Akin or stop him from following orders.

Akin stared at the man's broad, bearded, red face, breathed his sour breath. His was a bitter, angry face whose owner might hurt him for acting like a baby, yet might kill him for acting like anything else. The man held him as disgustedly as he had once seen another man hold a snake. Was he as alien as a snake to these people?

The bitter man looked down, caught Akin staring. "What the hell are you looking at?" he demanded.

Akin ceased to watch the man with his eyes, but kept him in view with other light-sensitive parts of his body. The man stank of sweat and of something else. Something was wrong with his body—some illness. He needed an ooloi. And he would never go near one.

Akin lay very still in his arms and, somehow, eventually, fell asleep.

He awoke to find himself lying between two pairs of feet on a piece of soggy cloth at the bottom of the boat. Water sloshing on him had awakened him.

He sat up cautiously, knowing before he moved that the current was stronger here and that it was raining. Raining hard. The man who had been holding Akin began to bail water from the boat with a large gourd. If the rain continued or got worse, surely they would stop.

Akin looked around at the land and saw that the banks were high and badly eroded—cliffs with vegetation spilling over the edges. He had never seen such things. He was farther from

home than he had ever been, and still traveling. Where would
they take him? . . . into the hills? . . . into the mountains?

The men gave up their effort and rowed for the bank. The
water was gray-brown and rough, and the rain was coming
down harder. They did not quite make it to shore before the
canoe sank. The men cursed and jumped out to pull the boat
onto a broad mud flat, while Akin stayed where he was, all but
swimming. They dumped the boat, tipping both him and the
water over one side, laughing when he slid along the mud.

One of them grabbed him by a leg and tried to hand him to
the man who had captured him.

His captor would not take him. "You babysit for a while,"
the man said. "Let him piss on you."

Akin was barely able to stop himself from speaking out in
indignation. He had not urinated on anyone for months—not
since his family had been able to make him understand that he
should not, that he should warn them when he needed to urinate or move his bowels. He would not have urinated even on
these men.

"No thanks," said the man holding Akin by the foot. "I just
rowed the damn boat god knows how many miles while you
sat there and watched the scenery. Now you can watch the
kid." He put Akin down on the mud flat and turned to help
carry the boat to a place where they might be able to make
their way up the bank. The mud flat was exactly that—a sliver
of soft, wet, bare silt collected only just above the water. It was
neither safe nor comfortable in the downpour. And night was
coming. Time to find a place to camp.

Akin's babysitter stared at Akin with cold dislike. He rubbed
his stomach, and, for a moment, pain seemed to replace his
general displeasure. Perhaps his stomach hurt him. How stupid to be sick and know where there was healing and decide to
stay sick.

Abruptly, the man grabbed Akin, lifted him by one arm,
thrust him under one of the man's own long, thick arms, and
followed the others up the steep, muddy trail.

Akin shut his eyes during the climb. His captor was not

surefooted. He kept falling but somehow never fell on Akin or dropped him. He did, however, hold him so tightly that Akin could hardly breathe, so tightly the man's fingers hurt and bruised him. He whimpered and sometimes cried out, but most of the time he tried to keep quiet. He feared this man as he had never before feared anyone. This man who had been eager to dunk him in water that might contain predators, who had gripped him and shaken him and threatened to punch him because he was crying, this man who was apparently willing to endure pain rather than go to someone who would heal him and ask nothing of him—this man might kill him before anyone could act to stop him.

At the top of the bluff, Akin's captor threw him down. "You can walk," the man muttered.

Akin sat still where he had landed, wondering whether Human babies had been thrown about this way—and if so, how they had survived? Then he followed the men as quickly as he could. If he were mature, he would run away. He would go back to the river and let it take him home. If he were mature he could breathe underwater and fend off predators with a simple chemical repellant—the equivalent of a bad smell.

But then, if he were mature, the resisters would not want him. They wanted a helpless infant—and they had very nearly gotten one. He could think, but his body was so small and weak that he could not act. He would not starve in the forest, but he might be poisoned by something that bit or stung him unexpectedly. Near the river, he might be eaten by an anaconda or a caiman.

Also, he had never been alone in the forest before.

As the men drew away from him, he grew more and more frightened. He fell several times but refused to cry again. Finally, exhausted, he stopped. If the men meant to leave him, he could not prevent them. Did they carry off construct children to abandon in the forest?

He urinated on the ground, then found a bush with edible, nutritious leaves. He was too small to reach the best possible food sources—sources the men could have reached but probably could not recognize. Tino had known a great deal, but he did not know much about the forest plants. He ate only obvious things—bananas, figs, nuts, palm fruit—wild versions of things his people grew in Phoenix. If a thing did not look or taste familiar to him, he would not eat it. Akin would eat anything that would not poison him and that would help to keep him alive. He was eating an especially nutritious gray fungus when he heard one of the men coming back for him.

He swallowed quickly, muddied one hand deliberately, and wiped it over his face. If he were simply dirty, the men would pay no attention. But if only his mouth were dirty, they might decide to try to make him throw up.

The man spotted him, cursed him, snatched him up, and carried him under one arm to where the others were building a shelter.

They had found a relatively dry place, well protected by the forest canopy, and they had swept it clean of leaf litter. They had stretched latex-sealed cloth from a pair of small trees to the ground. This cloth had apparently been in the boat, out of Akin's sight. Now they were cutting small branches and sapling trees for flooring. At least they did not plan to sleep in the mud.

They built no fire. They ate dry food—nuts, seeds, and dry fruit mixed together, and they drank something that was not water. They gave Akin a little of the drink and were amused to see that once he had tasted it, he would not take it again.

"It didn't seem to bother him, though," one of them said. "And that stuff is strong. Give him some food. Maybe he can handle it. He's got teeth, right?"

"Yeah."

He had been born with teeth. They gave him some of their food, and he ate slowly, one small fragment at a time.

"So that Phoenix we killed was lying," Akin's captor said. "I thought he might be."

"I wonder if it was really his kid."

"Probably. It looks like him."

"Jesus. I wonder what he had to do to get it. I mean, he didn't just fuck a woman."

"You know what he did. If you didn't know, you would have died of old age or disease by now."

Silence.

"So what do you think we can get for the kid?" a new voice asked.

"Whatever we want. A boy, almost perfect? Whatever they've got. He's so valuable I wonder if we shouldn't keep him."

"Metal tools, glass, good cloth, a woman or two . . . And this kid might not even live to grow up. Or he might grow up and grow tentacles all over. So what if he looks good now. Doesn't mean a thing."

"And I'll tell you something else," Akin's captor put in. "Our chances, any man's chances of seeing that kid grow up are rat shit. The worms are going to find him sooner or later, dead or alive. And the village they find him in is fucked."

Someone else agreed. "The only way is to get rid of him fast and get out of the area. Let someone else worry about how to hold him and how not to wind up dead or worse."

Akin went out of the shelter, found a place to relieve himself and another place—a clearing where one of the larger trees had recently fallen—where the rain fell heavily enough for him to wash himself and to catch enough water to satisfy his thirst.

The men did not stop him, but one of them watched him. When he reentered the shelter, wet and glistening, carrying broad, flat wild banana leaves to sleep on, the men all stared at him.

"Whatever it is," one of them said, "it isn't as Human as we thought. Who knows what it can do? I'll be glad to get rid of it."

"It's just what we knew it was," Akin's captor said. "A mongrel baby. I'll bet it can do a lot more that we haven't seen."

"I'll bet if we walked off and left it here it would survive and get home," the man who had killed Tino said. "And I'll bet if we poisoned it, it wouldn't die."

An argument broke out over this as the men passed around their alcoholic drink and listened to the rain, which stopped then began again.

Akin grew more afraid of them, but even his fear could not keep him awake after a while. He had been relieved to know that they would trade him away to some other people—to Phoenix, perhaps. He could find Tino's parents. Perhaps they would imagine that he looked like Tino, too. Perhaps they would let him live with them. He wanted to be among people who did not grab him painfully by a leg or an arm and carry him as though he had no more feeling than a piece of dead wood. He wanted to be among people who spoke to him and cared for him instead of people who either ignored him or drew away from him as though he were a poisonous insect or laughed at him. These men not only frightened him, they made him agonizingly lonely.

Sometime after dark, Akin awoke to find someone holding him and someone else trying to put something in his mouth.

He knew at once that the men had all had too much of their alcoholic drink. They stank of it. And their speech was thicker, harder to understand.

They had begun a small fire somehow, and in the light of it Akin could see two of them sprawled on the floor, asleep. The other three were busy with him, trying to feed him some beans they had mashed up.

He knew without his tongue touching the mashed beans that they were deadly. They were not to be eaten at all. Mashed as they were, they might incapacitate him before he could get rid of them. Then they would surely kill him.

He struggled and cried out as best he could without opening his mouth. His only hope, he thought, was to awaken the sleeping men and let them see how their trade goods were being destroyed.

But the sleeping men slept on. The men who were trying to feed him the beans only laughed. One of them held his nose and pried his mouth open.

In desperation, Akin vomited over the intruding hand.

The man jumped back cursing. He fell over one of the sleeping men and was thrown off into the fire.

There was a terrifying confusion of shouting and cursing and the shelter stank of vomit and sweat and drink. Men struggled with one another, not knowing what they were doing. Akin escaped outside just before they brought the shelter down.

Frightened, confused, lonely almost to sickness, Akin fled into the forest. Better to try to get home. Better to chance hungry animals and poisonous insects than to stay with these men who might do anything, any irrational thing. Better to be completely alone than lonely among dangerous creatures that he did not understand.

But it was aloneness that really frightened him. The caimans and the anacondas could probably be avoided. Most stinging or biting insects were not deadly.

But to be alone in the forest . . .

He longed for Lilith, for her to hold him and give him her sweet milk.

3

The men realized quickly that he was gone.

Perhaps the pain of the fire and the wild blows, the collapse of the shelter, and the sudden wash of rain brought them to their senses. They scattered to search for him.

Akin was a small, frightened animal, unable to move quickly or coordinate his movements well. He could hear and occasionally see them, but he could not get away from them quickly enough. Nor could he be as quiet as he wished. Fortunately, the rain hid his clumsiness.

He moved inland—deeper into the forest, into the darkness where he could see and the Humans could not. They glowed with body heat that they could not see. Akin glowed with it as well and used it and the heat-light from the vegetables to guide him. For the first time in his life, he was glad Humans did not have this ability.

They found him without it.

He fled as quickly as he could. The rain ceased, and there were only insect and frog noises to conceal his mistakes. Apparently these were not enough. One of the men heard him. He saw the man jerk around to look. He froze, hoping he would not be seen, half-covered as he was by the leaves of several small plants.

"Here he is!" the man shouted. "I've found him!"

Akin scrambled away past a large tree, hoping the man would trip in the dangling lianas or run into a buttress. But beyond the tree was another man blundering toward the sound of the shout. He almost certainly did not see Akin. He did not seem even to see the tree. He tripped over Akin, fell against the tree, then twisted around, both arms extended, and swept them before him almost in swimming motions. Akin was not quick enough to escape the groping hands.

He was caught, felt roughly all over, then lifted and carried.

"I've got him," the man yelled. "He's all right. Just wet and cold."

Akin was not cold. His normal body temperature was slightly lower than the man's though, so his skin would always feel cool to Humans.

Akin rested against the man wearily. There was no escape. Not even at night when his ability to see gave him an advantage. He could not run away from grown men who were determined to keep him.

What could he do then? How could he save himself from their unpredictable violence? How could he live at least until they sold him?

He put his head against the man's shoulder and closed his eyes. Perhaps he could not save himself. Perhaps there was nothing for him to do but wait until they killed him.

The man who was carrying him rubbed his back with a free

hand. "Poor kid. Shaking like hell. I hope those fools haven't made you sick. What do we know about taking care of a sick kid—or for that matter, a well one."

He was only muttering to himself, but he was at least not blaming Akin for what had happened. And he had not picked Akin up by an arm or a leg. That was a pleasant change. Akin wished he dared ask the man not to stroke him. Being stroked across the back was very much like being rubbed across eyes that could not protect themselves by closing.

Yet the man meant to be kind.

Akin looked at the man curiously. He had the shortest, brightest hair and beard of the group. Both were copper-colored and striking. He had not been the one to hit Tino. He had been asleep when his friends had tried to poison Akin. In the boat, he had been behind Akin, rowing, resting, or bailing. He had paid little attention to Akin beyond momentary curiosity. Now, though, he held Akin comfortably, supporting his body, and letting him hold on instead of clutching him and squeezing out his breath. He had stopped the rubbing now, and Akin was comfortable. He would stay close to this man if the man would let him. Perhaps with this man's help, he would survive to be sold.

4

Akin slept the rest of the night with the red-haired man. He simply waited until the man adjusted his sleeping mat under the newly built shelter and lay down. Then Akin crawled onto the mat and lay beside him. The man raised his head, frowned at Akin, then said, "Okay, kid, as long as you're housebroken."

The next morning while the red-haired man shared his

sparse breakfast with Akin, his original captor vomited blood and collapsed.

Frightened, Akin watched him from behind the red-haired man. This should *not* be happening. *It should not be happening!* Akin hugged himself, trembling, panting. The man was in pain, bleeding, sick, and all his friends could do was help him lie flat and turn his head to one side so that he did not reswallow the blood.

Why didn't they find an ooloi? How could they just let their friend bleed? He might bleed too much and die. Akin had heard of Humans doing that. They could not stop themselves from hemorrhaging without help. Akin could do this within his own body, but he did not know how to teach the skill to a Human. Perhaps it could not be taught. And he could not do it for anyone else the way the ooloi could.

One of the men went down to the river and got water. Another sat with the sick man and wiped away the blood—though the man continued to bleed.

"Jesus," the red-haired man said, "he's never been that bad before." He looked down at Akin, frowned, then picked Akin up and walked away toward the river. They met the man who had gone for water coming back with a gourdful.

"Is he all right?" the man asked, stopping so quickly he spilled some of his water.

"He's still throwing up blood. I thought I'd get the kid away."

The other man hurried on, spilling more of his water.

The red-haired man sat on a fallen tree and put Akin down beside him.

"Shit!" he muttered to himself. He put one foot on the tree trunk, turning away from Akin.

Akin sat, torn, wanting to speak, yet not daring to, almost sick himself about the bleeding man. It was *wrong* to allow such suffering, *utterly wrong* to throw away a life so unfinished, unbalanced, unshared.

The red-haired man picked him up and held him, peering

into his face worriedly. "You're not getting sick, too, are you?" he asked. "Please, God, no."

"No," Akin whispered.

The man looked at him sharply. "So you can talk. Tilden said you ought to know a few words. Being what you are, you probably know more than a few, don't you?"

"Yes."

Akin did not realize until later that the man had not expected an answer. Human beings talked to trees and rivers and boats and insects the way they talked to babies. They talked to be talking, but they believed they were talking to uncomprehending things. It upset and frightened them when something that should have been mute answered intelligently. All this, Akin realized later. Now he could only think of the man vomiting blood and perhaps dying *so* incomplete. And the red-haired man had been kind. Perhaps he would listen.

"He'll die," Akin whispered, feeling as though he were using shameful profanity.

The red-haired man put him down, stared at him with disbelief.

"An ooloi would stop the bleeding and the pain," Akin said. "It wouldn't keep him or make him do anything. It would just heal him."

The man shook his head, let his mouth sag open. "What the hell are you?" There was no longer kindness or friendliness in his voice. Akin realized he had made a mistake. How to recoup? Silence? No, silence would be seen as stubbornness now, perhaps punished as stubbornness.

"*Why should your friend die?*" he asked with all the passionate conviction he felt.

"He's sixty-five," the man said, drawing away from Akin. "At least he's been awake for sixty-five years in all. That's a decent length of time for a Human being."

"But he's sick, in pain."

"It's just an ulcer. He had one before the war. The worms fixed it, but after a few years it came back."

"It could be fixed again."

"I think he'd cut his own throat before he'd let one of those things touch him again. I know I would."

Akin looked at the man, tried to understand his new expression of revulsion and hatred. Did he feel these things toward Akin as well as toward the Oankali? He was looking at Akin.

"What the hell are you?" he said.

Akin did not know what to say. The man knew what he was.

"How old are you really?"

"Seventeen months."

"Crap! Jesus, what are the worms doing to us? What kind of mother did you have?"

"I was born to a Human woman." That was what he really wanted to know. He did not want to hear that Akin had two female parents just as he had two male parents. He knew this, though he probably did not understand it. Tino had been intensely curious about it, had asked Akin questions he was too embarrassed to ask his new mates. This man was curious, too, but it was like the kind of curiosity that made some Humans turn over rotting logs—so they could enjoy being disgusted by what lived there.

"Was that Phoenix your father?"

Akin began to cry in spite of himself. He had thought of Tino many times, but he had not had to speak of him. It hurt to speak of him. "How could you hate him so much and still want me? He was Human like you, and I'm not, but one of you killed him."

"He was a traitor to his own kind. He chose to be a traitor."

"He never hurt other Humans. He wasn't even trying to hurt anyone when you killed him. He was just afraid for me."

Silence.

"How can what he did be wrong if I'm valuable?"

The man looked at him with deep disgust. "You may not be valuable."

Akin wiped his face and stared his own dislike back at this man who defended the killing of Tino, who had never harmed him. "I will be valuable to you," he said. "All I have to do is be quiet. Then you can be rid of me. And I can be rid of you."

The man got up and walked away.

Akin stayed where he was. The men would not leave him. They would come this way when they went down to the river. He was frightened and miserable and shaking with anger. He had never felt such a mix of intense emotions. And where had his last words come from? They made him think of Lilith when she was angry. Her anger had always frightened him, yet here it was inside him. What he had said was true enough, but he was not Lilith, tall and strong. It might have been better for him not to speak his feelings.

Yet there had been some fear in the red-haired man's expression before he went away.

"Human beings fear difference," Lilith had told him once. "Oankali crave difference. Humans persecute their different ones, yet they need them to give themselves definition and status. Oankali seek difference and collect it. They need it to keep themselves from stagnation and overspecialization. If you don't understand this, you will. You'll probably find both tendencies surfacing in your own behavior." And she had put her hand on his hair. "When you feel a conflict, try to go the Oankali way. Embrace difference."

Akin had not understood, but she had said, "It's all right. Just remember." And of course, he had remembered every word. It was one of the few times she had encouraged him to express Oankali characteristics. But now . . .

How could he embrace Humans who, in their difference, not only rejected him but made him wish he were strong enough to hurt them?

He climbed down from his log and found fungi and fallen fruit to eat. There were also fallen nuts, but he ignored them because he could not crack them. He could hear the men talking occasionally, though he could not hear what they said. He was afraid to try to run away again. When they caught him this time, they might beat him. If Red-Hair told them how well he could talk and understand, they might want to hurt him.

When he had eaten his fill he watched several ants, each the size of a man's forefinger. These were not deadly, but adult Humans found their sting agonizing and debilitating. Akin was gathering his courage to taste one, to explore the basic structure of it, when the men arrived, snatched him up, and stumbled and slipped down the path to the river. Three men carried the boat. One man carried Akin. There was no sign of the fifth man.

Akin was placed alone on the fifth seat in the center of the boat. No one spoke to him or paid any particular attention to him as they threw their gear into the boat, pushed the boat into deeper water, and jumped in.

The men rowed without speaking. Tears streamed down the face of one. Tears for a man who seemed to hate everyone, and who had apparently died because he would not ask an ooloi for help.

What had they done with his body? Had they buried it? They had left Akin alone for a long time—long enough, perhaps, even to escape if he had dared. They were getting a very late start in spite of their knowledge that they were being pursued. They had had time to bury a body.

Now they were dangerous. They were like smoldering wood that might either flare into flames or gradually cool and become less deadly. Akin made no sound, hardly moved. He must not trigger a flaring.

5

Dichaan helped Ahajas to a sitting position, then placed himself behind her so that she could rest against him if she wished. She never had before. But she needed him near her, needed contact with him during this one act—the birth of her child. She needed all her mates near her, touching her, needed to be able to link into them and feel the parts of her child that had come from them. She could survive without this contact, but that would not be good for her or for the child. Solitary births produced children with tendencies to become ooloi. It was too soon for construct ooloi. Such a child would have been sent to the ship to grow up among Lo relatives there.

Lilith had accepted this. She had shared all Ahajas's births as Ahajas had shared all of hers. She knelt now beside Dichaan, slightly behind Ahajas. She waited with false patience for the child to find its way out of Ahajas's body. First Tino had had to be transported to the ship for healing. He would probably not die. He would heal physically and emotionally during a short period in suspended animation. He might, however, lose some of his memory.

Then, when he was gone and Lilith was ready to join those already looking for Akin, Ahajas's child decided to be born. That was the way with children, Human or Oankali. When their bodies were ready, they insisted on being born. Eleven months for the Human-born instead of their original nine. Fifteen months for the Oankali-born instead of the original eighteen. Humans were so quick about everything. Quick and potentially deadly. Construct births on both sides had to be more carefully conventional than Human or Oankali births. Missing parents had to be simulated by the ooloi. The world had to be introduced very slowly after the child had gotten to know its parents. Lilith could not simply assist at the birth, then leave. Nikanj had all it could do simulating Joseph and being itself for the child. More would be uncertain—unsafe for the construct child.

Nikanj sat searching with its sensory arms for the place from which the child would eventually emerge. Lilith's Human way of giving birth was simpler. He child emerged from an existing orifice—the same one each time. Its birth hurt Lilith, but

Nikanj always took away her pain. Ahajas had no birth orifice. Her child had to make its own way out of her body.

This did not hurt Ahajas, but it weakened her momentarily, made her want to sit down, made her focus her whole attention on following the child's progress, helping it if it
seemed in distress. It was the duty of her mates to protect her
from interference and reassure her that they were with her—
all part of her child that was part of her. All interconnected,
all united—a network of family into which each child should
fall. This should be the best possible time for a family. But
with Tino badly injured and Akin abducted, it was a time of
confused feelings. The moments of union and anticipation
were squeezed between moments of fear for Akin and worry
that the Tino they got back might not know them or want
them.

Surely the raiders would not hurt Akin. Surely . . .

But they did not belong to any resister village. That much
had already been learned. They were nomads—traveling
traders when they had trade goods, raiders when they had
nothing. Would they try to keep Akin and raise him to be one
of them, use his Oankali senses against the Oankali? Others
had tried that before them, but they had never tried it with a
child so young. They had never tried it with a Human-born
male child, since there had been none before Akin. That worried Dichaan most. He was Akin's only living same-sex parent,
and he felt uncertain, apprehensive, and painfully responsible.
Where in the vast rain forest was the child? He probably could
not escape and return home as so many others had before him.
He simply did not have the speed or the strength. He must
know that by now, and he must know he had to cooperate
with the men, make them value him. *If* he were still alive, he
must know.

The child would emerge from Ahajas's left side. She lay
down on her right side. Dichaan and Lilith moved to maintain
contact while Nikanj stroked the area of slowly rippling flesh.
In tiny circular waves, the flesh withdrew itself from a central
point, which grew slowly to show a darker gray—a temporary

orifice within which the child's head tentacles could be seen moving slowly. These tentacles had released the substance that began the birth process. They were responsible now for the way Ahajas's flesh rippled aside.

Nikanj exposed one of its sensory hands, reached into the orifice, and lightly touched the child's head tentacles.

Instantly, the head tentacles grasped the sensory arm—the familiar thing amid so much strangeness. Ahajas, feeling the sudden movement and understanding it, rolled carefully onto her back. The child knew now that it was coming into an accepting, welcoming place. Without that small contact, its body would have prepared it to live in a harsher place—an environment less safe because it contained no ooloi parent. In truly dangerous environments, ooloi were likely to be killed trying to handle hostile new forms of life. That was why children who had no ooloi parents to welcome them at birth tended to become ooloi themselves when they matured. Their bodies assumed the worst. But in order for them to mature in the assumed hostile environment, they had to become unusually hardy and resilient early. This child, though, would not have to undergo such changes. Nikanj was with it. And someday it would probably be female to balance Akin—if Akin returned in time to influence it.

Nikanj caught the child as it slipped easily through its birth orifice. It was gray with a full complement of head tentacles, but only a few small body tentacles. It had a startlingly Human face—eyes, ears, nose, mouth—and it had a functioning sair orifice at its throat surrounded by pale, well-developed tentacles. The tentacles quivered slightly as the child breathed. That meant the small Human nose was probably only cosmetic.

It had a full set of teeth, as many construct newborns did, and unlike Human-born constructs, it would be using them at once. It would be given small portions of what everyone else ate. And once it had shown to Nikanj's satisfaction that it was not likely to poison itself, it would have the freedom to eat whatever it found edible—to graze, as the Humans said.

Akin might be doing that now to keep himself alive—grazing or browsing on whatever he could find. The resisters might or might not feed him. If they simply let him feed himself in the forest, it would be enough. Humans, though, were always frightened when they saw a young child putting something strange in its mouth. If the raiders were conscientious, normal Humans, they might kill him.

6

The river branched and branched, and the men never seemed in doubt about which branch to take. The journey seemed endless. Five days. Ten days. Twelve days. . . .

Akin said nothing as they traveled. He had made one mistake. He was afraid to make another. The red-haired man, whose name was Galt, never told anyone about his talking. It was as though the man did not quite believe he had heard Akin speak. He kept away from Akin as much as he could, never spoke to him, hardly spoke of him. The three others swung Akin around by his arms and legs or shoved him with their feet or carried him when necessary.

It took Akin days to realize that the men were not, in their own minds, treating him cruelly. There were no more drunken attempts to poison him, and no one hit him. They did hit each other occasionally. Twice, a pair of them rolled in the mud, punching and clutching at one another. Even when they did not fight, they cursed each other and cursed him.

They did not wash themselves often enough, and sometimes they stank. They talked at night about their dead comrade Tilden and about other men they had traveled with and raided with. Most of these, it seemed, were also dead. So many men, uselessly dead.

When the current grew too strong against them, they hid the boat and began to walk. The land was rising now. It was still rain forest, but it was climbing slowly into the hills. There, they hoped to trade Akin to a rich resister village called Hillmann where the people spoke German and Spanish. Tilden had been the group's German speaker. His mother, someone said, had been German. The men believed it was necessary to speak German because the majority of the people in the village were German, and they were likely to have the best trade goods. Yet only one other man, Damek, the man who had hit Tino, spoke any German at all. And he spoke only a little. Two people spoke Spanish—Iriarte and Kaliq. Iriarte had lived in a place called Chile before the war. The other, Kaliq, had spent years in Argentina. It was decided that bargaining would be done in Spanish. Many of the Germans spoke their neighbors' language. The traders would pretend not to know German, and Damek would listen to what he was not supposed to hear. Villagers who thought they could not be understood might talk too much among themselves.

Akin looked forward to seeing and hearing different kinds of Humans. He had heard and learned some Spanish from Tino. He had liked the sound of it when Tino had gotten Nikanj to speak it to him. He had never heard German at all. He wished that someone other than Damek spoke it. He avoided Damek as best he could, remembering Tino. But the thought of meeting an entirely new people was almost enticing enough to ease his grief and his disappointment at not being taken to Phoenix, where he believed he would have been welcomed by Tino's parents. He would not have pretended to them to be Tino's son, but if the color of his skin and the shape of his eyes reminded them of Tino, he would not have been sorry. Perhaps the Germans would not want him.

The four resisters and Akin approached Hillmann through fields of bananas, papaya trees, pineapple plants, and corn. The fields looked well kept and fruitful. They looked more impressive to Akin than Lilith's gardens because they were so much larger and so many more trees had been cut down. There was a great deal of cassava and rows of something that had not yet come up. Hillmann must have lost a great deal of top soil to the rain in all those long, neat rows. How long could they farm this way before the land was ruined and they had to move? How much land had they already ruined?

The village was two neat rows of thatched-roof wooden houses on stilts. Within the village, several large trees had been preserved. Akin liked the way the place looked. There was a calming symmetry to it.

But there were no people in it.

Akin could see no one. Worse, he could hear no one. Humans were noisy even when they tried not to be. These Humans, though, should be talking and working and going about their lives. Instead, there was absolutely no sound of them. They were not hiding. They were simply gone.

Akin stared at the village from the arms of Iriarte and wondered how long it would take the men to realize that something was wrong.

Iriarte seemed to notice first. He stopped, stood staring straight ahead. He glanced at Akin whose face was so close to his own, saw that Akin had turned in his arms and was also staring with his eyes.

"What is it?" he asked as though expecting Akin to answer. Akin almost did—almost forgot himself and spoke aloud. "Something is crazy here," Iriarte said to the others.

Immediately Kaliq took the opposite position. "It's a nice place. Still looks rich. There's nothing wrong."

"No one is here," Iriarte said.

"Why? Because they don't rush out to meet us? They're around somewhere, watching."

"No. Even the kid noticed something."

"Yes," Galt agreed. "He did. I was watching him. His kind are supposed to see and hear better than we are." He gave Akin a look of suspicion. "What we walk into, you walk into with us, kid."

"For godsake," Damek said, "he's a baby. He doesn't know anything. Let's go."

He had gone out several steps ahead before the others began to follow. He drew even farther ahead, showing his scorn for their caution, but he drew neither bullets nor arrows. There was no one to shoot him. Akin rested his chin on Iriarte's shoulder and savored the strange pale scents—all pale now. Humans had been gone from this place for several days. There was food spoiling in some of the houses. The scent of that grew stronger as they neared the village. Many men, a few women, spoiling food, and agoutis—the small rodents that some resisters ate.

And Oankali.

Many Oankali had been here several days ago. Did it have anything to do with Akin's abduction? No. How could it? The Oankali would not empty a village on his account. If someone in the village had harmed him, they would certainly find that person, but they would not bother anyone else. And this emptying may have occurred before he was abducted.

"There's nobody here," Damek said. He had stopped, finally, in the middle of the village, surrounded by empty houses.

"I told you that a long time ago," Iriarte muttered. "I think it's okay for us, though. The kid was nervous before, but he's relaxed now."

"Put him down," Galt said. "Let's see what he does."

"If he's not nervous, maybe we ought to be." Kaliq looked around warily, peered through the open doorway of a house. "Oankali did this. They must have."

"Put the kid down," Galt repeated. He had ignored Akin for most of Akin's captivity, but seemed to forget or deny Akin's precocity. Now he seemed to want something.

Iriarte put Akin down, though Akin would have been content to stay in the man's arms. But Galt seemed to expect something. Best to give him something and keep him quiet. Akin turned slowly, drawing breaths over his tongue. Something unusual but not likely to stimulate fear or anger.

Blood in one direction. Old human blood, dry on dead wood. No. It would do no good to show them that.

An agouti nearby. Most of these had gone—apparently either carried away by the villagers or released into the forest. This one was still in the village, eating the seedpods that had fallen from one of the few remaining trees. Best not to make the men notice it. They might shoot it. They craved meat. Within the last few days, they had caught, cooked, and eaten several fish, but they talked a great deal about real meat—steaks and chops and roasts and burgers . . .

A faint smell of the kind of vegetable dye Humans at Lo used to write with. Writing. Books. Perhaps the people of Hillmann had left some record of the reason for their leaving.

Without speaking, the men followed Akin to the house that smelled strongest of the dye, the ink, Lilith called it. She used it so often that the smell of it made Akin see her in his mind and almost cry with wanting her.

"Just like a bloodhound," Damek said. "He doesn't waste a step."

"He eats mushrooms and flowers and leaves," Kaliq said inconsequentially. "It's a wonder he hasn't poisoned himself."

"What's that got to do with anything? What's he found?" Iriarte picked up a large book that Akin had been trying to reach. The paper, Akin could see, was heavy and smooth. The cover was of polished, dark-stained wood.

"Shit," Iriarte muttered. "It's in German." He passed the book to Damek.

Damek rested the book on the little table and turned pages slowly. "*Ananas . . . bohnen . . . bananen . . . mangos. . . .* This is just stuff about crops. I can't read most of it, but it's . . . records. Crop yields, farming methods . . ." He turned several more pages to the end of the book. "Here's some Spanish, I think."

Iriarte came back to look. "Yeah. It says . . . shit. Ah, shit!"

Kaliq pushed forward to look. "I don't believe this," he said after a moment. "Someone was forced to write this!"

"Damek," Iriarte said, gesturing. "Look at this German shit

up here. The Spanish says they gave it up. The Oankali invited them again to join the trade villages, and they voted to do it. To have Oankali mates and kids. They say, 'Part of what we are will continue. Part of what we are will go to the stars someday. That seems better than sitting here, rotting alive or dying and leaving nothing. How can it be a sin for the people to continue?' " Iriarte looked at Damek. "Does it say anything like that in German?"

Damek studied the book for so long that Akin sat down on the floor to wait. Finally Damek faced the others, frowning. "It says just about that," he told them. "But there are two writers. One says 'We're joining the Oankali. Our blood will continue.' But the other one says the Oankali should be killed—that to join with them is against God. I'm not sure, but I think one group went to join the Oankali and another went to kill the Oankali. God knows what happened."

"They just walked away," Galt said. "Left their homes, their crops . . ." He began looking through the house to see what else had been left. Trade goods.

The other men scattered through the village to carry on their own searches. Akin looked around to be certain he was unobserved, then went out to watch the agouti. He had not seen one close up before. Lilith claimed they looked like a cross between deer and rats. Nikanj said they were larger now than they had been before the war, and they were more inclined now to seek out insects. They had lived mainly on fruits and seeds before, though even then they took insects as well. This agouti was clearly more interested in the insect larvae that infested the seedpods than in the pods themselves. Its forelegs ended in tiny hands, and it sat back on its haunches and used the hands to pluck out the white larvae. Akin watched it, fascinated. It looked at him, tensed for a moment, then selected another seedpod. Akin was smaller than it was. Apparently it did not see him as a threat. He stooped near it and watched it. He inched closer, wanting to touch it, see how the furred body felt.

To his amazement, the animal let him touch it, let him stroke the short fur. He was surprised to find that the fur did not feel like hair. It was smooth and slightly stiff in one direction and rough in the other. The animal moved away when he rubbed its fur against the grain. It sniffed his hand and stared at him for a moment. It clutched a large, half-eaten larva in its hands.

An instant later the agouti flew sideways in a roar of Human-made thunder. It landed on its side some distance from Akin, and it made small, useless running motions with its feet. It could not get up.

Akin saw at once that it was Galt who had shot the animal. The man looked at Akin and smiled. Akin understood then that the man had shot the inoffensive animal not because he was hungry for its meat, but because he wanted to hurt and frighten Akin.

Akin went to the agouti, saw that it was still alive, still strug-gling to run. Its hind feet did not work, but its forefeet made small running steps through the air. There was a gaping hole in its side.

Akin bent to its neck and tasted it, then, for the first time, deliberately injected his poison. A few seconds later, the agouti stopped struggling and died.

Galt stepped up and nudged the animal with his foot.

"It was beginning to feel terrible pain," Akin said. "I helped it die." He swayed slightly, even though he was seated on the ground. He had tasted the agouti's life and its pain, but all he could give it was death. If he had not gone near it, Galt might never have noticed it. It might have lived.

He hugged himself, trembling, feeling sick.

Galt nudged him with a foot, and he fell over. He picked himself up and stared at the man, wanting desperately to be away from him.

"How come you only talk to me?" Galt asked.

"First because I wanted to help Tilden," Akin whispered quickly. The others were coming. "Now because I have to . . . have to help you. You shouldn't eat the agouti. The poison I gave it would kill you."

Akin managed to dodge the vicious kick Galt aimed at his head. Iriarte picked Akin up and held him protectively.

"You fool, you'll kill him!" Iriarte shouted.

"Good riddance," Galt yelled back. "Shit, there's plenty of trade goods here. We don't need that mongrel bastard!"

Kaliq had come up to stand beside Iriarte. "What have you found here that we could trade for a woman?" he demanded.

Silence.

"That boy is to us what gold used to be," Kaliq spoke softly now.

"In fact," Iriarte said, "he's more valuable to us than you are."

"He can talk!" Galt shouted.

Kaliq took a step closer to him. "Man, I don't care if he can fly! There are people who'll pay *anything* for him. He *looks* okay, that's what's important."

Iriarte looked at Akin. "Well, he always knew he could understand us better than any normal kid his age. What did he say?"

Galt drew his mouth into a thin smile. "After I shot the agouti, he bit it on the neck, and it died. He told me not to eat it because he had poisoned it."

"Yeah?" Iriarte held Akin away from him and stared. "Say something, kid."

Akin was afraid the man would drop him if he spoke. He was also afraid he would lose Iriarte as a protector—as he had lost Galt. He tried to look as frightened as he felt, but he said nothing.

"Give him to me," Galt said. "I'll make him talk."

"He'll talk when he gets ready," Iriarte said. "Hell, I had seven kids before the war. They'd talk all the time until you wanted them to."

"Listen, I'm not talking about baby talk!"

"I know. I believe you. Why does it bother you so?"

"He can talk as well as you can!"

"So? It's better than being covered with tentacles or gray skin. It's better than being without eyes or ears or a nose. Kaliq is right. It's looks that are important. But you know as well as I do that he isn't Human, and it's *got* to come out somehow."

"He claims to be poison," Galt said.

"He may be. The Oankali are."

"So you go on holding him next to your neck. You do that."

To Akin's surprise, Iriarte did just that. Later, when he was alone with Akin, he said, "You don't have to talk if you don't want to." He ran a hand across Akin's hair. "I think I'd rather you didn't, really. You look so much like one of my kids, it hurts."

Akin accepted this silently.

"Don't kill anything else," he said. "Even if it's suffering, let it alone. Don't scare these guys. They get crazy."

7

At Siwatu village, the people looked much like Lilith. They spoke English, Swahili, and a scattering of other languages. They examined Akin and wished very much to buy him, but they would not send one of the village women away with foreign men. The women took Akin and fed him and bathed him as though he could do nothing for himself. Several of them believed that their breasts could be made to produce milk if they kept Akin with them.

The men were so fascinated with him that his captors became frightened. They took him and stole out of the village one moonless night. Akin did not want to go. He liked being with the women who knew how to lift him without hurting him and who gave him interesting food. He liked the way they smelled and the softness of their bosoms and their voices, high and empty of threat.

But Iriarte carried him away, and he believed that if he cried out, the man might be killed. Certainly some people would be killed. Perhaps it would only be Galt who kicked at him whenever he was nearby and Damek who had clubbed Tino down. But more likely, it would be all four of his abductors and several village men. He might die himself. He had seen that men could go mad when they were fighting. They could do things that afterward amazed and shamed them.

Akin let himself be carried to the raiders' canoes. They had two now—the one they had begun with and a light, new one found in Hillmann. Akin was put into the new one between two balanced mounds of trade goods. Behind one mound Iriarte rowed. In front of the other, Kaliq rowed. Akin was glad, at least, not to have to worry about Galt's feet or his oar. And he continued to avoid Damek when he could, though the man showed him friendliness. Damek acted as though Akin had not seen him club Tino down.

8

There were Oankali in Vladlengrad. Galt saw them through the rain at yet another branching of the river. They were far away, and Akin himself did not see them at first—gray beings, slipping from gray water into the shadow of the trees on the bank, and all this through heavy rain.

The man ignored their weariness to row hard into the left fork of the river, leaving the right fork to Vladlengrad and the Oankali.

The men rowed until they were completely exhausted. Finally, reluctantly, they dragged themselves and their boats onto a low bank. They concealed their boats, ate smoked fish and dried fruit from Siwatu, and drank a mild wine. Kaliq held Akin and gave him some of the wine. Akin discovered that he liked it, but he drank only a little. His body did not like the disorientation it caused and would have expelled a larger amount. When he had eaten the food Kaliq had given him, he went out to graze. While he was out, he gathered several large nuts in a wide leaf and took them back to Kaliq.

"I've seen these," Kaliq said, examining one. "I think they're one of the new postwar species. I wondered whether they were good to eat."

"I wouldn't eat them," Galt said. "Anything that wasn't here before the war. I don't need."

Kaliq took two of the nuts in one hand and squeezed. Akin could hear the shells cracking. When he opened his hand, several small round nuts rolled around amid the shell fragments. Kaliq offered them to Akin, and Akin took most of them gratefully. He ate them with such obvious enjoyment that Kaliq laughed and ate one of them himself. He chewed slowly, tentatively.

"It tastes like . . . I don't know." He ate the rest. "It's very good. Better than anything I've had for a long time." He settled to breaking and eating the rest while Akin brought another leafful to Iriarte. There were not many good nuts on the ground. Most were insect-infested. He checked each one with his tongue to make sure they were all right. When Damek went out and gathered nuts of his own, almost every one was infested with insect larvae. This made him stare at Akin with suspicion and doubt. Akin watched him without facing him, watched him without eyes until he shrugged and threw the last of his nuts away in disgust. He looked at Akin once more and spat on the ground.

9

Phoenix.

The four resisters had been avoiding it, they said, because

they knew it was Tino's home village. The Oankali would check it first, perhaps stay there the longest. But Phoenix was also the richest resister village they knew of. It sent people into the hills to salvage metal from prewar sites and had people who knew how to shape the metal. It had more women than any other village because it traded metal for them. It grew cotton and made soft, comfortable clothing. It raised and tapped not only rubber trees, but trees that produced a form of oil that could be burned in their lamps without refinement. And it had fine, large houses, a church, a store, vast farms . . .

It was, the raiders said, more like a prewar town—and less like a group of people who have given up, whose only hope was to kill a few Oankali before they died.

"I almost settled there once," Damek said when they had hidden the canoes and begun their single-file walk toward the hills and Phoenix. Phoenix was many days south of Hillmann on a different branch of the river, but it, too, was located closer to the mountains than most trader and resister villages. "I swear," Damek continued, "they've got everything there but kids."

Iriarte, who was carrying Akin, sighed quietly. "They'll buy you, niño," he said. "And if you don't frighten them, they'll treat you well."

Akin moved in the man's arms to show that he was listening. Iriarte had developed a habit of talking to him. He seemed to accept movement as sufficient response.

"Talk to them," Iriarte whispered. "I'm going to tell them you can talk and understand like a much older kid, and you do it. It's no good pretending to be something you aren't and then scaring them with what you really are. You understand?"

Akin moved again.

"Tell me, niño. Speak to me. I don't want to make a fool of myself."

"I understand," Akin whispered into his ear.

He held Akin away from him for a moment and stared at him. Finally he smiled, but it was a strange smile. He shook his head and held Akin against him again. "You still look like one of my kids," he said. "I don't want to give you up."

Akin tasted him. He made the gesture very quick, deliberately placing his mouth against the man's neck in the way that Humans called kissing. Iriarte would feel a kiss and nothing more. That was good. He thought a Human who felt as he did might have expressed the feeling with a kiss. His own need was to understand Iriarte better and keep that understanding. He wished he dared to study the man in the leisurely, thorough way he had studied Tino. What he had now was an impression of Iriarte. He could have given an ooloi the few cells he had taken from Iriarte, and the ooloi could have used the information to build a new Iriarte. But it was one thing to know what the man was made of and another to know how the parts worked together—how each bit was expressed in function, behavior, and appearance.

"You'd better watch that kid," Galt called from several steps behind. "A kiss from him could be the same as a kiss from a bushmaster."

"That man had three children before the war," Iriarte whispered. "He liked you. You shouldn't have frightened him."

Akin knew this. He sighed. How could he avoid scaring people? He had never seen a Human baby. How could he behave as one? Would it be easier to avoid scaring villagers who knew he could talk? It should be. After all, Tino had not been afraid. Curious, suspicious, startled when an un-Human-looking child touched him, but not frightened. Not dangerous.

And the people of Phoenix were his people.

Phoenix was larger and more beautiful than Hillmann. The houses were large and colored white or blue or gray. They had the glass windows Tino had boasted of—windows that glittered with reflected light. There were broad fields and storage buildings and an ornate structure that must have been the church. Tino had described it to Akin and tried to make Akin understand what it was for. Akin still did not understand, but he could repeat Tino's explanation if he had to. He could even say his prayers. Tino had taught him, thinking it scandalous that he had not known them before.

Human men worked in the fields, planting something. Human men came out of their houses to look at the visitors. There was a faint scent of Oankali in the village. It was many days old—searchers who had come and searched and waited and finally left. None of the searchers had been members of his family.

Where were his parents looking?

And in this village, where were the Human women?

Inside. He could smell them in their houses—could smell their excitement.

"Don't say a word until I tell you to," Iriarte whispered.

Akin moved to show that he had heard, then twisted in Iriarte's arms to face the large, well-built, low-stilted house they were walking toward and the tall, lean man who awaited them in the shade of its roof in what seemed to be a partially enclosed room. The walls were only as high as the man's waist, and the roof was held up by regularly spaced, rounded posts. The half-room reminded Akin of a drawing he had seen by a Human Lo woman, Cora: great buildings whose overhanging roofs were supported by huge, ornately decorated, round posts.

"So that's the kid," the tall man said. He smiled. He had a short, well-tended black beard and short hair, very black. He wore a white shirt and short pants, displaying startlingly hairy arms and legs.

A small blond woman came from the house to stand beside him. "My god," she said, "that's a beautiful child. Isn't there anything wrong with him?"

Iriarte walked up several steps and put Akin into the woman's arms. "He is beautiful," Iriarte told her quietly. "But he has a tongue you'll have to get used to—in more than one way. And he is very, very intelligent."

"And he is for sale," the tall man said, his eyes on Iriarte. "Come in, gentlemen. My name is Gabriel Rinaldi. This is my wife Tate."

The house was cool and dark and sweet-smelling inside. It smelled of herbs and flowers. The blond woman took Akin into another room with her and gave him a chunk of pineapple to eat while she poured some drinks for the guests.

"I hope you won't wet the floor," she said, glancing at him.

"I won't," he said impulsively. Something made him want to talk to this woman. He had wanted to speak to the women of Siwatu, but he had been afraid. He was never alone with one of them. He had feared their group reaction to his un-Human aspect.

The woman looked at him, eyes momentarily wide. Then she smiled with only the left side of her mouth. "So that's what the raider meant about that tongue of yours." She lifted him and put him on a counter so that she could talk to him without bending or stooping. "What's your name?"

"Akin." No one else had asked his name during his captivity. Not even Iriarte.

"Ah-keen," she pronounced. "Is that right?"

"Yes."

"How old are you?"

"Seventeen months." Akin thought for a moment. "No, eighteen now."

"Very, very intelligent," Tate said, echoing Iriarte. "Shall we buy you, Akin?"

"Yes, but . . ."

"But?"

"They want a woman."

Tate laughed. "Of course they do. We might even find them one. Men aren't the only ones who get itchy feet. But, Jesus, four men! She'd better have another itchy part or two."

"What?"

"Nothing, little one. Why do you want us to buy you?"

Akin hesitated, said finally, "Iriarte likes me and so does Kaliq. But Galt hates me because I look more Human than I am. And Damek killed Tino." He looked at her blond hair, knowing she was no relative of Tino's. But perhaps she had known him, liked him. It would be hard to know him and not like him. "Tino used to live here," he said. "His whole name is Augustino Leal. Did you know him?"

"Oh, yes." She had become very still, totally focused on Akin. If she had been Oankali, all her head tentacles would have been elongated toward him in a cone of living flesh. "His parents are here," she said. "He . . . couldn't have been your father. You look like him, though."

"My Human father is dead. Tino took his place. Damek called him a traitor and killed him."

She closed her eyes, turned her face away from Akin. "Are you sure he's dead?"

"He was alive when they took me away, but the bones of his head had been broken with the wooden part of Damek's gun. There was no one around to help him. He must have died."

She took Akin down from the counter and hugged him. "Did you like him, Akin?"

"Yes."

"We loved him here. He was the son most of us never had. I knew he was going, though. What was there for him in a place like this? I gave him a packet of food to take with him and aimed him toward Lo. Did he reach it?"

"Yes."

She smiled again with only half her mouth. "So you're from Lo. Who's your mother?"

"Lilith Iyapo." Akin did not think she would have liked hearing Lilith's long Oankali name.

"Son of a bitch!" Tate whispered. "Listen, Akin, don't say that name to anyone else. It may not matter anymore, but don't say it."

"Why?"

"Because there are people here who don't like your mother. There are people here who might hurt you because they can't get at her. Do you understand?"

Akin looked into her sun-browned face. She had very blue eyes—not like Wray Ordway's pale eyes, but a deep, intense color. "I don't understand," he said, "but I believe you."

"Good. If you do that, we'll buy you. I'll see to it."

"At Siwatu, the raiders took me away because they were afraid the men were going to try to steal me."

"Don't you worry. Once I drop this tray and you in the living room, I'll see to it that they don't go anywhere until our business with them is done."

She carried the tray of drinks and let Akin walk back to her husband and the resisters. Then she left them.

Akin climbed onto Iriarte's lap, knowing he was about to lose the man, missing him already.

"We'll have to have our doctor look at him," Gabriel Rinaldi was saying. He paused. "Let me see your tongue, kid."

Obligingly, Akin opened his mouth. He did not stick his tongue out to its full extent, but he did nothing to conceal it.

The man got up and looked for a moment, then shook his head. "Ugly. And he's probably venomous. The constructs usually are."

"I saw him bite an agouti and kill it," Galt put in.

"But he's never made any effort to bite any of us," Iriarte said with obvious irritation. "He's done what he's been told to do. He's taken care of his own toilet needs. And he knows better than we do what's edible and what isn't. Don't worry about his picking up things and eating them. He's been doing that since we took him—seeds, nuts, flowers, leaves, fungi . . . and he's never been sick. He won't eat fish or meat. I wouldn't force him to if I were you. The Oankali don't eat it. Maybe it would make him sick."

"What I want to know," Rinaldi said, "is just how un-Human he is . . . mentally. Come here, kid."

Akin did not want to go. Showing his tongue was one thing. Deliberately putting himself in hands that might be unfriendly was another. He looked up at Iriarte, hoping the man would not let him go. Instead Iriarte put him down and gave him a shove toward Rinaldi. Reluctantly, he edged toward the man.

Rinaldi got up impatiently and lifted Akin into his arms. He sat down, turned Akin about on his lap looking at him, then held Akin facing him. "Okay, they say you can talk. So talk."

Again Akin turned to look at Iriarte. He did not want to

begin talking in a room full of men when talking had already made one of those men hate him.

Iriarte nodded. "Talk, niño. Do as he says."

"Tell us your name," Rinaldi said.

Akin caught himself smiling. Twice now, he had been asked his name. These people seemed to care who he was, not just what he was. "Akin," he said softly.

"Ah-keen?" Rinaldi frowned down at him. "Is that a Human name?"

"Yes."

"What language?"

"Yoruba."

"Yor— . . . what? What country?"

"Nigeria."

"Why should you have a Nigerian name? Is one of your parents Nigerian?"

"It means *hero*. If you put an *s* on it, it means *brave boy*. I'm the first boy born to a Human woman on Earth since the war."

"That's what the worms hunting for you said," Rinaldi agreed. He was frowning again. "Can you read?"

"Yes."

"How can you have had time to learn to read?"

Akin hesitated. "I don't forget things," he said softly.

The raiders looked startled. "Ever?" Damek demanded. "Anything?"

Rinaldi only nodded. "That's the way the Oankali are," he said. "They can bring out the ability in Humans when they want to—and when the Humans agree to be useful to them. I thought that was the boy's secret."

Akin, who had considering lying, was glad he had not. He had always found it easy to tell the truth and difficult to make himself lie. He could lie very convincingly, though, if lying would keep him alive and spare him pain among these men. It was easier, though, to divert questions—as he had diverted the question about his parents.

"Do you want to stay here, Akin?" Rinaldi asked.

"If you buy me, I'll stay," Akin said.

"Shall we buy you?"

"Yes."

"Why?"

Akin glanced at Iriarte. "They want to sell me. If I have to be sold, I'd like to stay here."

"Why?"

"You aren't afraid of me, and you don't hate me. I don't hate you, either."

Rinaldi laughed. Akin was pleased. He had hoped to make the man laugh. He had learned back in Lo that if he made Humans laugh, they were more comfortable with him—though, of course, in Lo, he had never been exposed to people who might injure him simply because he was not Human.

Rinaldi asked his age, the number of languages he spoke, and the purpose of his long, gray tongue. Akin withheld information only about the tongue.

"I smell and taste with it," he said. "I can smell with my nose, too, but my tongue tells me more." All true, but Akin had decided not to tell anyone what else his tongue could do. The idea of his tasting their cells, their genes, might disturb them too much.

A woman called a doctor came in, took Akin from Rinaldi, and began to examine, poke, and probe his body. She did not talk to him, though Rinaldi had told her he could talk.

"He's got some oddly textured spots on his back, arms, and abdomen," she said. "I suspect they're where he'll grow tentacles in a few years."

"Are they?" Rinaldi asked him.

"I don't know," Akin said. "People never know what they'll be like after metamorphosis."

The doctor stumbled back from him with a wordless sound.

"I told you he could talk, Yori."

She shook her head. "I thought you meant . . . baby talk."

"I meant like you and me. Ask him questions. He'll answer."

"What can you tell me about the spots?" she asked.

"Sensory spots. I can see and taste with most of them." And he could complete sensory connections with anyone else who had sensory tentacles or spots. But he would not talk to Humans about that.

"Does it bother you when we touch them?"

"Yes. I'm used to it, but it still bothers me."

Two women came into the room and called Rinaldi away.

A man and woman came in to look at Akin—just to stand and stare at him and listen as he answered the doctor's questions. He guessed who they were before they finally spoke to him.

"Did you really know our son?" the woman asked. She was very small. All the women he had seen so far were almost tiny. They would have looked like children alongside his mother and sisters. Still, they were gentle and knew how to lift him without hurting him. And they were neither afraid of him nor disgusted by him.

"Was Tino your son?" he asked the woman.

She nodded, mouth pulled tight. Small lines had gathered between her eyes. "Is it true?" she asked. "Have they killed him?"

Akin bit his lips, suddenly caught by the woman's emotion. "I think so. Nothing could save him unless an Oankali found him quickly—and no Oankali heard when I screamed for help."

The man stepped close to Akin, wearing an expression Akin had never seen before—yet he understood it. "Which one of them killed him?" the man demanded. His voice was very low, and only Akin and the two women heard. The doctor, slightly behind the man, shook her head. Her eyes were like his Human father Joseph's had been—more narrow than round. Akin had been waiting for a chance to ask her whether she was Chinese. Now, though, her eyes were big with fear. Akin knew fear when he saw it.

"One who died," Akin lied quietly. "His name was Tilden. He had a sickness that made him bleed and hurt and hate everyone. The other men called it an ulcer. One day, he threw up too much blood, and he died. I think the others buried him. One of them took me away so I wouldn't see."

"You know that he's dead? You're sure?"

"Yes. The others were angry and sad and dangerous for a long time after that. I had to be very careful."

The man stared at him for a long time, trying to see what any Oankali would have known at a touch, what this man would never know. He had loved Tino, this man. How could Akin, even without the doctor's warning, send him with his bare hands to face a man who had a gun, who had three friends with guns?

Tino's father turned from Akin and went to the other side of the room, where both Rinaldis, the two women who had come in, and the four raiders were talking, shouting, gesturing. They had, Akin realized, begun the business of trading for him. Tino's father was smaller than most of the men, but when he stalked into their midst, everyone stopped talking. Perhaps it was the look on the man's face that made Iriarte finger the rifle beside him.

"Is there one of you called Tilden?" Tino's father asked. His voice was calm and soft.

The raiders did not answer for a moment. Then, ironically, it was Damek who said, "He died, mister. That ulcer of his finally got him."

"Did you know him?" Iriarte asked.

"I would like to have met him," Tino's father said. And he walked out of the house. Tate Rinaldi looked over at Akin, but no one else seemed to pay attention to him. Attention shifted from Tino's father back to the subject of the trade. Tino's mother smoothed back Akin's hair and looked into his face for a moment.

"What was my son to you?" she asked.

"He took the place of my dead Human father."

She closed her eyes for a moment, and tears ran down her face. Finally she kissed his cheek and went away.

"Akin," the doctor said softly, "did you tell them the truth?"

Akin looked at her and decided not to answer. He wished he had not told Tate Rinaldi the truth. She had sent Tino's parents to him. It would have been better not to meet them at all until the raiders had gone away. He had to remember, had to keep reminding himself how dangerous Human beings were.

"Never tell them," Yori whispered. His silence had apparently told her enough. "There has been enough killing. We die and die and no one is born." She put her hands on either side of his face and looked at him, her expression shifting from pain to hatred to pain to something utterly unreadable. She hugged him suddenly, and he was afraid she would crush him or scratch him with her nails or thrust him away from her and hurt him. There was so much suppressed emotion in her, so much deadly tension in her body.

She left him. She spoke for a few moments with Rinaldi, then left the house.

10

Bargaining went on into the night. People ate and drank and told stories and tried to outtrade one another. Tate gave Akin what she called a decent vegetarian meal, and he did not tell her that it was not decent at all. It did not contain nearly enough protein to satisfy him. He ate it, then slipped out a door at the back of the house and supplemented his meal with peas and seed from her garden. He was eating these things when the shooting began inside.

The first shot startled him so much that he fell over. As he stood up, there were more shots. He took several steps toward the house, then stopped. If he went in, someone might shoot him or step on him or kick him. When the shooting stopped, he would go in. If Iriarte or Tate called him, he would go in.

There was the noise of furniture smashing—heavy bodies thrown about, people shouting, cursing. It was as though the people inside intended to destroy both the house and themselves.

Other people rushed into the house, and the sounds of fighting increased, then died.

When there had been several moments of silence, Akin went up the steps and into the house, moving slowly but not quietly. He made small noises deliberately, hoping he would be heard and seen and known not to be dangerous.

He saw first broken dishes. The clean, neat room where Tate had given him pineapple and talked to him was now littered with broken dishes and broken furniture. He had to move very carefully to avoid cutting his feet. His body healed faster than the bodies of Humans, but he found injuring himself just as painful as they seemed to.

Blood.

He could smell it strongly enough to be frightened. Someone must be dead with so much blood spilled.

In the living room, there were people lying on the floor and others tending them. In one corner, Iriarte lay untended.

Akin ran toward the man. Someone caught him before he could reach Iriarte and picked him up in spite of his struggles and cries.

Rinaldi.

Akin yelled, twisted, and bit the man's thumb.

Rinaldi dropped him, shouting that he had been poisoned—which he had not—and Akin scrambled to Iriarte.

But Iriarte was dead.

Someone had struck him several times across the body with what must have been a machete. He had gaping, horrible wounds, some spilling entrails onto the floor.

Akin screamed in shock and frustration and grief. When he came to know a man, the man died. His Human father was dead without Akin ever knowing him except through Nikanj. Tino was dead. Now Iriarte was dead. His years had been cut off unfinished. His Human children had died in the war, and his construct children, created from material the ooloi had collected long ago, would never know him, never taste him and find themselves in him.

Why?

Akin looked around the room. Yori and a few others were doing what they could for the injured, but most of the people in the room were just staring at Akin or at Gabriel Rinaldi.

"He's not poisoned!" Akin said with disgust. "You're the ones who kill people, not me!"

"He's all right?" Tate said. She was standing with her husband, looking frightened.

"Yes." He looked at her for a moment, then looked again at Iriarte. He looked around, saw that Galt also appeared to be dead, hacked about the head and shoulders. Yori was working over Damek. What irony if Damek lived while Iriarte died for the murder Damek had committed.

Tino's murder *must* be the reason for all this.

On the floor near Damek lay Tino's father, wounded in his left thigh, his left arm, and his right shoulder. His wife was weeping over him, but he was not dead. A man was using something other than water to clean away blood from the shoulder wound. Another man was holding Tino's father down.

There were other wounded and dead around the room. Akin found Kaliq dead behind a long cushion-covered wooden bench. He had only one wound, bloody but small. It was a chest wound, probably involving his heart.

Akin sat beside him while others in the house helped the injured and carried out the dead. No one came for Kaliq while he sat there. Behind him, someone began to scream. Akin looked back and saw that it was Damek. Akin tried not to feel the anguish that came to him reflexively when he saw a Human suffering. One part of his mind screamed for an ooloi to save this irreplaceable Human, this man whom some ooloi somewhere had made prints of, but whom no Oankali or construct truly knew.

Another part of his mind hoped Damek would die. Let him suffer. Let him scream. Tino had not even had time to scream.

Tino's father did not scream. He grunted. Bits of metal were cut from his flesh while he held a piece of folded cloth between his teeth and grunted.

Akin came out of his corner to look at one of the bits of metal—a gray pellet covered with the blood of Tino's father.

Tate came over to him and picked him up. To his own surprise, he held on to her. He put his head on her shoulder and did not want to be put down.

"Don't you bite me," she said. "If you want to get down, you tell me. Bite me and I'll bounce you off a wall."

He sighed, feeling alone even in her arms. She was not the haven he had needed. "Put me down," he said.

She held him away from her and looked at him. "Really?"

Surprised, he looked back. "I thought you didn't want to hold me."

"If I didn't want to hold you, I wouldn't have picked you up. I just want us to understand each other. Okay?"

"Yes."

And she held him to her again and answered his questions, told him about bullets and how they were fired from guns, how Tino's father Mateo had come with his friends to take revenge on the raiders in spite of their guns. There were no guns in Phoenix before the raiders arrived.

"We voted not to have them," she said. "We have enough things to hurt each other with. Now . . . well, we've got our first four. I'll bury the damned things if I get the chance."

She had taken him in among the broken dishes and sat him on the counter. He watched while she lit a lamp. The lamp reminded him suddenly, painfully, of the guest house back in Lo.

"You want anything else to eat?" she asked.

"No."

"No, what?"

"No . . . what?"

"Shame on Lilith. 'No, thank you,' little one. Or 'Yes, please.' Understand?"

"I didn't know resisters said those things."

"In my house they do."

"Did you tell Mateo who killed Tino?"

"God, no. I was afraid you told him. I forgot to tell you to keep that to yourself."

"I told him the man who killed Tino was dead. One of the raiders really did die. He was sick. I thought if Mateo believed it was that one, he wouldn't hurt anyone else."

She nodded. "That should have worked. You're brighter than I thought. And Mateo is crazier than I thought." She sighed. "Hell, I don't know. I never had any kids. I don't know how I would have reacted if I had one and someone killed him."

"You shouldn't have told Tino's parents anything at all until the raiders were gone," Akin said quietly.

She looked at him, then looked away. "I know. All I said was that you had known Tino and that he had been killed. Of course they wanted to know more, but I told them to wait until we had settled you in—that you were just a baby, after all." She looked at him again, frowning, shaking her head. "I wonder what the hell you really are."

"A baby," he said. "A Human-Oankali construct. I wish I were something more because the Oankali part of me scares people, but it doesn't help me when they try to hurt me."

"I'm not going to hurt you."

Akin looked at her, then looked toward the room in which Iriarte lay dead.

Tate made herself very busy cleaning up the broken dishes and glass.

11

Both Damek and Mateo lived.

Akin avoided both of them and stayed with the Rinaldis.

Tino's mother Pilar wanted him, seemed to believe she had a right to him since her son was dead. But Akin did not want to be near Mateo, and Tate knew it. Tate wanted him herself. She also felt guilty about the shooting, about her misjudgment. Akin trusted her to fight for him. He did not want to chance making an enemy of Pilar.

Other women fed him and held him when they could. He tried to speak to them or at least be heard speaking before they could get their hands on him. This made some of them back away from him. It kept them all from talking baby talk to him—most of the time. It also kept them from making fools of themselves and later resenting him for it. It forced them to either accept him for what he was or reject him.

And it had been Tate's idea.

She reminded him of his mother, though the two were physical opposites. Pink skin and brown, blond hair and black, short stature and tall, small-boned and large. But they were alike in the way they accepted things, adapted to strangeness, thought quickly, and turned situations to their advantage. And they were both, at times, dangerously angry and upset for no apparent reason. Akin knew that Lilith sometimes hated herself for working with the Oankali, for having children who were not fully Human. She loved her children, yet she felt guilt for having them.

Tate had no children. She had not cooperated with the Oankali. What did she feel guilt for? What drove her sometimes when she stalked away into the forest and stayed for hours?

"Don't worry about it," Gabe told him when he asked. "You wouldn't understand."

Akin suspected that he himself did not understand. He watched her sometimes in a way that made Akin think he was trying hard to understand her—and failing.

Gabe had accepted Akin because Tate wanted him to. He did not particularly like Akin. "The mouth," he called Akin. And he said when he thought Akin could not hear: "Who the hell needs a baby that sounds like a midget?"

Akin did not know what a midget was. He thought it must be a kind of insect until one of the village women told him it was a Human with a glandular disorder that caused him to remain tiny even as an adult. After he had asked the question, several people in the village never called him anything except midget.

He had no worse trouble than that in Phoenix. Even the people who did not like him were not cruel. Damek and Mateo recuperated out of his sight. And he had begun at once to try to convince Tate to help him escape and go home.

He had to do something. No one seemed to be coming for him. His new sibling must be born by now and bonding with other people. It would not know it had a brother, Akin. It would be a stranger when he finally saw it. He tried to tell Tate what this would mean, how completely wrong it would be.

"Don't worry about it," Tate told him. They had gone out to pick pummelos—Tate to pick the fruit and Akin to graze, but Akin stayed close to her. "The kid's just a newborn now," Tate continued. "Even construct kids can't be born talking and knowing people. You'll have time to get acquainted with it."

"This is the time for bonding," Akin said, wondering how he could explain such a personal thing to a Human who deliberately avoided all contact with the Oankali. "Bonding happens shortly after birth and shortly after metamorphosis. At other times . . . bonds are only shadows of what they could be. Sometimes people manage to make them, but usually they don't. Late bonds are never what they should be. I'll never know my sister the way I should."

"Sister?"

Akin looked away, not wanting to cry but not able to stop a few silent tears. "Maybe it won't be a sister. It should be, though. It would be if I were there." He looked up at her suddenly and thought he read sympathy in her face.

"Take me home!" he whispered urgently. "I'm not really finished with my own bonding. My body was waiting for this new sibling."

She frowned at him. "I don't understand."

"Ahajas let me touch it, let me be one of its presences. She let me recognize it and know it as a sibling still forming. It would be the sibling closest to me—closest to my age. It should be the sibling I grow up with, bond with. We . . . we won't be right . . ." He thought for a moment. "We won't be complete without each other." He looked up at her hopefully.

"I remember Ahajas," she said softly. "She was so big . . . I thought she was male. Then Kahguyaht, our ooloi, told me Oankali females are like that. 'Plenty of room inside for children,' it said. 'And plenty of strength to protect the children, born and unborn.' Gabe asked what males did if females did all that. 'They seek out new life,' it said. 'Males are seekers and collectors of life. What ooloi and females *can* do, males *must* do.' Gabe thought that meant ooloi and females could do without males. Kahguyaht said no, it meant the Oankali as a people would eventually die without males. I don't think Gabe ever believed that." She sighed. She had been thinking aloud, not really talking to Akin. She jumped when Akin spoke to her.

"Kahguyaht ooan Nikanj?" he asked.

"Yes," she said.

He stared at her for several seconds. "Let me taste you," he said finally. She could consent or refuse. She would not be frightened or disgusted or dangerous.

"How would you do that?" she asked.

"Pick me up."

She stooped and lifted him into her arms.

"Would you sit down and let me do it without making you tired?" he asked. "I know I'm heavy to you."

"Not that heavy."

"It won't hurt or anything," he said. "People only feel it when the ooloi do it. Then they like it."

"Yeah. Go ahead and do it."

He was surprised that she was not afraid of being poisoned. She leaned against a tree and held him while he tasted her neck, studied her.

"Regular little vampire," he heard her say before he was lost in the taste of her. There were echoes of Kahguyaht in her.

Nikanj had shared its memory of its own ooloi parent, had let Akin study that memory so thoroughly that Akin felt he knew Kahguyaht.

Tate herself was fascinating—very unlike Lilith, unlike Joseph. She was somewhat like Leah and Wray, but not truly like anyone he had tasted. There was something truly strange about her, something wrong.

"You're pretty good," she said when he drew back and looked into her face. "You found it, didn't you?"

"I found . . . something. I don't know what it is."

"A nasty little disease that should have killed me years ago. Something I apparently inherited from my mother. Though at the time of the war, we were only beginning to suspect that she had inherited it. Huntington's disease, it was called. I don't know what the Oankali did for me, but I never had any symptoms of it."

"How do you know that's what it is?"

"Kahguyaht told me."

That was good enough.

"It was a . . . wrong gene," he said. "It drew me and I had to look at it. Kahguyaht didn't want it ever to start to work. I don't think it will—but you should be near Kahguyaht so that it could keep watch. It should have replaced that gene."

"It said it would if we stayed with it. It said it would have to watch me for a while if it did any real tampering. I . . . couldn't stay with it."

"You wanted to."

"Did I?" She shifted him in her arms, then put him down.

"You still do."

"Have you had all you wanted to eat out here?"

"Yes."

"You follow me, then. I've got this fruit to carry." She stooped and lifted the large basket of fruit to her head. When she was satisfied with its placement, she stood up and turned back toward the village.

"Tate?" he called.

"What?" She did not look at him.

"It went back to the ship, you know. It's still Dinso. It will have to come to Earth sometime. But it did not want to live here with any of the Humans it could have. I never knew why before."

"Nobody ever mentioned us?"

Us, Akin thought. Tate and Gabe. They had both known Kahguyaht. And Gabe was probably the reason Tate had not gone to Kahguyaht. "Kahguyaht would come back if Nikanj called it," he said.

"You really didn't know about us?" she insisted.

"No. But the walls in Lo aren't like the walls here. You can't hear through Lo walls. People seal themselves in and no one knows what they're saying."

She stopped, put one hand up to balance the basket, then stared down at him. "Good god!" she said.

It occurred to him then that he should not have let her know he could hear through Phoenix walls.

"What is Lo!" she demanded. "Is it just a village, or . . ."

Akin did not know what to say, did not know what she wanted.

"Do the walls really seal?" she asked.

"Yes, except at the guest house. You've never been there?"

"Never. Traders and raiders have told us about it, but never that it was . . . What is it, for godsake! A baby ship?"

Akin frowned. "It could be someday. There are so many on Earth, though. Maybe Lo will be one of the males inside one of those that become ships."

"But . . . but someday it will leave Earth?"

Akin knew the answer to this question, but he realized he must not give it. Yet he liked her and found it difficult to lie to her. He said nothing.

"I thought so," she said. "So someday the people of Lo—or their descendants—will be in space again, looking for some other people to infect or afflict or whatever you call it."

"Trade."

"Oh, yeah. The goddamn gene trade! And you want to know why I can't go back to Kahguyaht."

She walked away, leaving him to make his own way back to the village. He made no effort to keep up with her, knowing he could not. The little she had guessed had upset her enough to make her not care that he, valuable being that he was, was left alone in the groves and gardens where he might be stolen. How would she have reacted if he had told her all he knew— that it was not only the descendants of Humans and Oankali who would eventually travel through space in newly mature ships. It was also much of the substance of Earth. And what was left behind would be less than the corpse of a world. It would be small, cold, and as lifeless as the moon. Maturing Chkahichdahk left nothing useful behind. They had to be worlds in themselves for as long as it took the constructs in each one to mature as a species and find another partner species to trade with.

The salvaged Earth would finally die. Yet in another way, it would live on as single-celled animals lived on after dividing. Would that comfort Tate? Akin was afraid to find out.

He was tired, but he had nearly reached the houses when Tate returned for him. She had already put away her basket of fruit. Now she picked him up without a word and carried him back to her home. He fell asleep in her arms before they reached it.

12

No one came for him.

No one would take him home or let him go.

He felt both unwanted and wanted too much. If his parents could not come because of his sibling's birth, then others should have come. His parents had done this kind of service for other families, other villages who had had their children stolen. People helped each other in searching for and recovering children.

And yet, his presence seemed to delight the people of Phoenix. Even those who were disturbed by the contrast between his tiny body and his apparent maturity grew to like having him around. Some always had a bit of food ready for him. Some asked question after question about his life before he was brought to them. Others liked to hold him or let him sit at their feet and tell him stories of their own prewar lives. He liked this best. He learned not to interrupt them with questions. He could learn afterward what kangaroos, lasers, tigers, acid rain, and Botswana were. And since he remembered every word of their stories, he could easily think back and insert explanations where they should go.

He liked it less when people told him stories that were clearly not true—stories peopled by beings called witches or elves or gods. Mythology, they said; fairy tales.

He told them stories from Oankali history—past partnerships that contributed to what the Oankali were or could become today. He had heard such stories from all three of his Oankali parents. All were absolutely true, yet the Humans believed almost none of them. They liked them anyway. They would gather around close so that they could hear him. Sometimes they let their work go and came to listen. Akin liked the attention, so he accepted their fairy tales and their disbelief in his stories. He also accepted the pairs of short pants that Pilar Leal made for him. He did not like them. They cut off some of his perception, and they were harder than skin to clean once they were soiled. Yet it never occurred to him to ask anyone else to wash them for him. When Tate saw him washing them, she gave him soap and showed him how to use it on them. Then she smiled almost gleefully and went away.

People let him watch them make shoes and clothing and paper. Tate persuaded Gabe to take him up to the mills—one where grain was ground and one where wooden furniture, tools, and other things were being made. The man and woman there were making a large canoe when Akin arrived.

"We could build a textile mill," Gabe told him. "But foot-powered spinning wheels, sewing machines, and looms are enough. We already make more than we need, and people need to do some things at their own pace with their own designs."

Akin thought about this and decided he understood it. He had often watched people spinning, weaving, sewing, making things they did not need in the hope of being able to trade with villages that had little or no machinery. But there was no urgency. They could stop in the middle of what they were doing and come to listen to his stories. Much of their work was done simply to keep them busy.

"What about metal?" he asked.

Gabe stared down at him. "You want to see the blacksmith's shop?"

"Yes."

Gabe picked him up and strode off with him. "I wonder how much you really understand," he muttered.

"I usually understand," Akin admitted. "What I don't understand, I remember. Eventually I understand."

"Jesus! I wonder what you'll be like when you grow up."

"Not as big as you," Akin said wistfully.

"Really? You know that?"

Akin nodded. "Strong, but not very big."

"Smart, though."

"It would be terrible to be small and foolish."

Gabe laughed. "It happens," he said. "But probably not to you."

Akin looked at him and smiled himself. He was still pleased when he could make Gabe laugh. It seemed that the man was beginning to accept him. It was Tate who had suggested that Gabe take him up the hill and show him the mills. She pushed them together when she could, and Akin understood that she wanted them to like each other.

But if they did what would happen when his people finally

came for him? Would Gabe fight? Would he kill? Would he die?

Akin watched the blacksmith make a machete blade, heating, pounding, shaping the metal. There was a wooden crate of machete blades in one corner. There were also scythes, sickles, axes, hammers, saws, nails, hooks, chains, coiled wire, picks . . . And yet there was no clutter. Everything, work tools and products, had their places.

"I work here sometimes," Gabe said. "And I've helped salvage a lot of our raw materials." He glanced at Akin. "You might get to see the salvage site."

"In the mountains?"

"Yeah."

"When?"

"When things start to get warm around here."

It took Akin several seconds to realize that he was not talking about the weather. He would be hidden at the salvage site when his people came looking for him.

"We've found artifacts of glass, plastic, ceramic, and metal. We've found a lot of money. You know what money is?"

"Yes. I've never seen any, but people have told me about it."

Gabe reached into his pocket with his free hand. He brought out a bright, golden disk of metal and let Akin hold it. It was surprisingly heavy for its size. On one side was something that looked like a large letter *t* and the words, "He is risen. We shall rise." On the other side there was a picture of a bird flying up from fire. Akin studied the bird, noticing that it was a kind he had never seen pictured before.

"Phoenix money," Gabe said. "That's a phoenix rising from its own ashes. A phoenix was a mythical bird. You understand?"

"A lie," Akin said thoughtlessly.

Gabe took the disk from him, put it back into his pocket and put Akin down.

"Wait!" Akin said. "I'm sorry. I call myths that in my mind. I didn't mean to say it out loud."

Gabe looked down at him. "If you're always going to be

small, you ought to learn to be careful with that word," he said.

"But . . . I didn't say *you* were lying."

"No. You said my dream, the dream of everyone here, was a lie. You don't even know what you said."

"I'm sorry."

Gabe stared at him, sighed, and picked him up again. "I don't know," he said. "Maybe I ought to be relieved."

"At what?"

"That in some ways you really are just a kid."

13

Weeks later, traders arrived bringing two more stolen children. Both appeared to be young girls. The traders took away not a woman but as many metal tools and as much gold as they could carry, plus books that were more valuable than gold. Two couples in Phoenix worked together with occasional help from others to make paper and ink and print the books most likely to be desired by other villages. Bibles—using the memories of every village they could reach, Phoenix researchers had put together the most complete Bible available. There were also how-to books, medical books, memories of prewar Earth, listings of edible plants, animals, fish, and insects and their dangers and advantages, and propaganda against the Oankali.

"We can't have kids, so we make all this stuff," Tate told Akin as they watched the traders bargain for a new canoe to carry all their new merchandise in. "Those guys are now officially rich. For all the good it will do them."

"Can I see the girls?" Akin asked.

"Why not? Let's go over."

She walked slowly and let him follow her over to the Wilton house where the girls were staying. Macy and Kolina Wilton had been quick enough to seize both children for themselves. They were one half of Phoenix's publishers. They would probably be expected to give up one child to another couple, but for now they were a family of four.

The girls were eating roasted almonds and cassava bread with honey. Kolina Wilton was spooning a salad of mixed fruit into small bowls for them.

"Akin," she said when she saw him. "Good. These little girls don't speak English. Maybe you can talk to them."

They were brown girls with long, thick black hair and dark eyes. They wore what appeared to be men's shirts, belted with light rope and cut off to fit them. The bigger of the two girls had already managed to free her arms from the makeshift garment. She had a few body tentacles around her neck and shoulders, and confining them was probably blinding, itching torment. Now all her small tentacles focused on Akin, while the rest of her seemed to go on concentrating on the food. The smaller girl had a cluster of tentacles at her throat, where they probably protected a sair breathing orifice. That meant her small, normal-looking nose was probably ornamental. It might also mean the girl could breathe underwater. Oankali-born, then, in spite of her human appearance. That was unusual. If she was Oankali-born, then she was *she* only by courtesy. She could not know yet what her sex would be. But such children, if they had Human-appearing sex organs at all, tended to look female. The children were perhaps three and four years old.

"You'll have to go into their gardens and into the forest to find enough protein," Akin told them in Oankali. "They try, but they never seem to give us enough."

Both girls climbed down from their chairs, came to touch him and taste him and know him. He became so totally focused on them and on getting to know them that he could not perceive anything else for several minutes.

They were siblings—Human-born and Oankali-born. The

smaller one was Oankali-born and the more androgenous-looking of the two. It would probably become male in response to its sibling's apparent femaleness. Its name, it had signaled, was Shkaht—Kaalshkaht eka Jaitahsokahldahktohj aj Dinso. It was a relative. They were both relatives through Nikanj, whose people were Kaal. Happily, Akin gave Shkaht the Human version of his own name, since the Oankali version did not give enough information about Nikanj. Akin Iyapo Shing Kaalnikanjlo.

Both children knew already that he was Human-born and expected to become male. That made him an object of intense curiosity. He discovered that he enjoyed their attention, and he let them investigate him thoroughly.

". . . not like kids at all," one of the Humans was saying. "They're all over each other like a bunch of dogs." Who was speaking? Akin made himself focus on the room again, on the Humans. Three more had come into the room. The speaker was Neci, a woman who had always seen him as a valuable property, but who had never liked him.

"If that's the worst thing they do, we'll get along fine with them," Tate said. "Akin, what are their names?"

"Shkaht and Amma," Akin told her. "Shkaht is the younger one."

"What kind of name is Shkaht?" Gabe said. He had come in with Neci and Pilar.

"An Oankali name," Akin said.

"Why? Why give her an Oankali name?"

"Three of her parents are Oankali. So are three of mine." He would not tell them Shkaht was Oankali-born. He would not let Shkaht tell them. What if they found out and decided they only wanted the Human-born sibling? Would they trade Shkaht away later or return her to the raiders? Best to let them go on believing that both Amma and Shkaht were Human-born and truly female. He must think of them that way himself so that his thoughts did not become words and betray him. He had already warned both children that they must not tell this particular truth. They did not understand yet, but they had agreed.

"What languages do they speak?" Tate asked.

"They want to know what languages you speak," Akin said in Oankali.

"We speak French and Twi," Amma said. "Our Human father and his brothers come from France. They were traveling in our mother's country when the war came. Many people in her country spoke English, but in her home village people spoke mostly Twi."

"Where was her village?"

"In Ghana. Our mother comes from Ghana."

Akin relayed this to Tate.

"Africa again," she said. "It probably didn't get hit at all. I wonder whether the Oankali have started settlements there. I thought people in Ghana all spoke English."

"Ask them what trade village they're from," Gabe said.

"From Kaal," Akin said without asking. Then he turned to the children. "Is there more than one Kaal village?"

"There are three," Shkaht said. "We're from Kaal-Osei."

"Kaal-Osei," Akin relayed.

Gabe shook his head. "Kaal . . ." He looked at Tate, but she shook her head.

"If they don't speak English there," she said, "nobody we know would be there."

He nodded. "Talk to them, Akin. Find out when they were taken and where their village is—if they know. Can they remember things the way you can?"

"All constructs remember."

"Good. They're going to stay with us, so start teaching them English."

"They're siblings. Very close. They need to stay together."

"Do they? We'll see."

Akin did not like that. He would have to warn Amma and Shkaht to get sick if they were separated. Crying would not work. The Humans had to be frightened, had to think they might lose one or two of their new children. They had now what they had probably never had before: children they thought might eventually be fertile together. From what he had heard about resisters, he had no doubt that some of them really believed they could soon breed new, Human-trained, Human-looking children.

"Let's go outside," he told them. "Are you still hungry?"

"Yes." They spoke in unison.

"Come on. I'll show you where the best things grow."

14

The next day, all three children were arranged in backpacks and carried toward the mountains. They were not allowed to walk. Gabe carried Akin atop a bundle of supplies, and Tate walked behind, carrying even more supplies. Amma rode on Macy Wilton's back and surreptitiously tasted him with one of her small body tentacles. She had a normal Human tongue, but each of her tentacles would serve her as well as Akin's long, gray Oankali tongue. Shkaht's throat tentacles gave her a more sensitive sense of smell and taste than Akin, and she could use her hands for tasting. Also, she had slender, dark tentacles on her head, mixed with her hair. She could see with these. She could not see with her eyes. She had learned, though, to seem to look at people with her eyes—to turn and face them and to move her slender head tentacles as she moved her head so that Humans were not disturbed by her hair seeming to crawl about. She would have to be very careful because Humans, for some reason, liked to cut people's hair. They cut their own, and they had cut Akin's. Even back in Lo, men in particular either cut their own hair or got others to cut it. Akin did not want to think about what it might feel like to have sensory tentacles cut off. Nothing could hurt worse. Nothing would be more likely to cause an Oankali or a construct to sting reflexively, fatally.

The Humans walked all day, stopping for rest and food only once at noon. They did not talk about where they were going or why, but they walked quickly, as though they feared pursuit.

They were a party of twenty, armed, in spite of Tate's efforts, with the four guns of Akin's captors. Damek was still alive, but he could not walk. He was being cared for back at Phoenix. Akin suspected that he had no idea what was going on—that his gun was gone, that Akin was gone. What he did not know, he could not resent or tell.

That night the Humans erected tents and made beds of blankets and branches or bamboo—whatever they could find. Some stretched hammocks between trees and slept outside the tents since they saw no sign of rain. Akin asked to sleep outside with someone and a woman named Abira simply reached out of her hammock and lifted him in. She seemed glad to have him in spite of the heat and humidity. She was a short, very strong woman who carried a pack as heavy as those of men half again her size, yet she handled him with gentleness.

"I had three little boys before the war," she said in her strangely accented English. She had come from Israel. She gave his head a quick rub—her favorite caress—and went to sleep, leaving him to find his own most comfortable position.

Amma and Shkaht slept together on their own bed of blanket-covered bamboo. Humans valued them, fed them, sheltered them, but they did not like the girls' tentacles—would not deliberately allow themselves to be touched by the small sensory organs. Amma had only managed to taste Macy Wilton because she was riding on his back and her tentacles were able to burrow through the clothing he had put between himself and her.

No Human wanted to sleep with them. Even now Neci Roybal and her husband Stancio were whispering about the possibility of removing the tentacles while the girls were young.

Alarmed, Akin listened carefully.

"They'll learn to do without the ugly little things if we take them off while they're so young," Neci was saying.

"We have no proper anesthetics," the man protested. "It would be cruel." He was his wife's opposite, quiet, steady, kind. People tolerated Neci for his sake. Akin avoided him in order to avoid Neci. But Neci had a way of saying a thing and saying a thing over and over until other people began to say it—and believe it.

"They won't feel much now," she said. "They're so young . . . And those little worm things are so small. Now is the best time to do it."

Stancio said nothing.

"They'll learn to use their Human senses," Neci whispered. "They'll see the world as we do and be more like us."

"Do you want to cut them?" Stancio asked. "Little girls. Almost babies."

"Don't talk foolishness. It can be done. They'll heal. They'll forget they ever had tentacles."

"Maybe they'd grow back."

"Cut them off again!"

There was a long silence.

"How many times, Neci," the man said finally. "How many times would you torture children? Would you torture them if they had come from your body? Will you torture them now because they did not?"

Nothing more was said. Akin thought Neci cried a little. She made small, wordless sounds. Stancio made only regular breathing sounds. After a time, Akin realized he had fallen asleep.

15

They spent days walking through forest, climbing forested hills. But it was cooler now, and Akin and the girls had to fight off attempts to clothe them more warmly. There was still plenty to eat, and their bodies adjusted quickly and easily to the temperature change. Akin went on wearing the short pants Pilar Leal had made for him. There had been no time for clothing to be made for the girls, so they wore lengths of cloth wrapped around their waists and tied at the top. This was the only clothing they did not deliberately shed and lose.

Akin had begun sleeping with them on the second night of the journey. They needed to learn more English and learn it quickly. Neci was doing as Akin had expected—saying over and over to different people in quiet, intense conversation that the girls' tentacles should be removed now, while they were young, so that they would look more Human, so that they would learn to depend on their Human senses and perceive the world in a Human way. People laughed at her behind her back, but now and then, Akin heard them talking about the tentacles—how ugly they were, how much better the girls would look without them . . .

"Will they cut us?" Amma asked him when he told them. All her tentacles had flattened invisibly to her flesh.

"They might try," Akin said. "We have to stop them from trying."

"How?"

Shkaht touched him with one of her small, sensitive hands. "Which Humans do you trust?" she asked. She was the younger of the two, but she had managed to learn more.

"The woman I live with. Tate. Not her husband. Just her. I'm going to tell her the truth."

"Can she really do anything?"

"She can. She might not. She does . . . strange things some- times. She . . . The worst thing she might do now is nothing."

"What's wrong with her?"

"What's wrong with them all? Haven't you noticed?"

". . . yes. But I don't understand."

"I don't either, really. But it's the way they have to live. They want kids, so they buy us. But we still aren't their kids. They want to have kids. Sometimes they hate us because they can't. And sometimes they hate us because we're part of the Oankali and the Oankali are the ones who won't let them have kids."

"They could have dozens of kids if they stop living by them- selves and join us."

"They want kids the way they used to have them before the war. Without the Oankali."

"Why?"

"It's their way." He lay in a jumble with them so that sen- sory spot found sensory spot, so that the girls were able to use their sensory tentacles and he was able to use his tongue. They were almost unaware that the conversation had ceased to be vocal. Akin had already learned that Humans consid- ered them to be asleep half-atop one another when they lay this way.

"There won't be any more of them," he said, trying to pro- ject the sensations of aloneness and fear he believed the Hu- mans felt. "Their kind is all they've ever known or been, and now there won't be any more. They try to make us like them, but we won't ever be really like them, and they know it."

The girls shuddered, broke contact briefly, minutely. When they touched him again they seemed to communicate as one person.

"We are them! And we are the Oankali. You know. If they could perceive, they would know!"

"If they could perceive, they would be us. They can't and they aren't. We're the best of what they are and the best of what the Oankali are. But because of us, they won't exist any- more."

"Oankali Dinso and Toaht won't exist anymore."

"No. But Akjai will go away unchanged. If the Human-Oankali construct doesn't work here or with the Toaht, Akjai will continue."

"Only if they find some other people to blend with." This came distinctly from Amma.

"Humans had come to their own end," Shkaht said. "They were flawed and overspecialized. If they hadn't had their war, they would have found another way to kill themselves."

"Perhaps," Akin admitted. "I was taught that, too. And I can see the conflict in their genes—the new intelligence put at the service of ancient hierarchical tendencies. But . . . they didn't have to destroy themselves. They certainly don't have to do it again."

"How could they not?" Amma demanded. All that she had learned, all that the bodies of her own Human parents had shown her told her he was talking nonsense. She had not been among resister Humans long enough to begin to see them as a truly separate people.

Yet she must understand. She would be female. Someday, she would tell her children what Humans were. And she did not know. He was only beginning to learn himself.

He said with intensity, with utter certainty, "There should be a Human Akjai! There should be Humans who don't change or die—Humans to go on if the Dinso and Toaht unions fail."

Amma was moving uncomfortably against him, first touching, then breaking contact as though it hurt her to know what he was saying, but her curiosity would not let her stay away. Shkaht was still, fastened to him by slender head tentacles, trying to absorb what he was saying.

"You're here for this," she said aloud softly. Her voice startled him, though he did not move. She had spoken in Oankali, and her communication, like his, had the feel of intensity and truth.

Amma linked more deeply into both of them, giving them her frustration. She did not understand.

"He is being left here," Shkaht explained silently. She deliberately soothed her sibling with her own calm certainly. "They want him to know the Humans," she said. "They would not have sent him to them, but since he's here and not being hurt, they want him to learn so that later he can teach."

"What about us?"

"I don't know. They couldn't come for us without taking him. And they probably didn't know where we would be sold—or even whether we would be sold. I think we'll be left here until they decide to come for him—unless we're in danger."

"We're in danger now," Amma whispered aloud.

"No. Akin will talk to Tate. If Tate can't help us, we'll disappear some night soon."

"Run away?"

"Yes."

"The Humans would catch us!"

"No. We'd travel at night, hide during the day, take to the nearest river when it's safe."

"Can you breathe underwater?" Akin asked Amma.

"Not yet," she answered, "but I'm a good swimmer. I always went in whenever Shkaht did. If I get into trouble, Shkaht helps—links with me and breathes for me."

As Akin's sibling would have been able to help him. He withdrew from them, reminded by their unity of his own solitude. He could talk to them, communicate with them nonvocally, but he could never have the special closeness with them that they had with each other. Soon he would be too old for it—if he wasn't already. And what was happening to his sibling?

"I don't believe they're leaving me with the Humans deliberately," he said. "My parents wouldn't do that. My Human mother would come alone if no one would come with her."

Both girls were back in contact with him at once. "No!" Shkaht was saying. "When resisters find women alone, they keep them. We saw it happen at a village where our captors tried to trade us."

"What did you see?"

"Some men came to the village. They lived there, but they had been traveling. They had a woman with them, her arms tied with rope and a rope tied around her neck. They said they had found her and she was theirs. She screamed at them, but no one knew her language. They kept her."

"No one could do that to my mother," Akin said. "She wouldn't let them. She travels alone whenever she wants to."

"But how would she find you alone? Maybe every resister village she went to would try to tie her up and keep her. Maybe if they couldn't they would hurt her or kill her with guns."

Maybe they would. They seemed to do such things so easily. Maybe they already had.

Some communication he did not catch passed between Amma and Shkaht. "You have three Oankali parents," Shkaht whispered aloud. "They know more about resisters than we do. They wouldn't let her go alone, would they? If they couldn't stop her, they would go with her, wouldn't they?"

". . . yes," Akin answered, feeling no certainty at all. Amma and Shkaht did not know Lilith, did not know how she became so frightening sometimes that everyone stayed away from her. Then she vanished for a while. Who knew what might happen to her while she roamed the forests alone?

The girls had placed him between them. He did not realize until it was too late that they were calming him with their own deliberate calm, soothing him, putting themselves and him to sleep.

Akin awoke the next day still miserable, still frightened for his mother and lonely for his sibling. Yet he went to Tate and asked her to carry him for a while so that he could talk to her.

She picked him up at once and took him to the small, fast-running stream where the camp had gotten its water.

"Wash," she said, "and talk to me here. I don't want people watching the two of us whispering together."

He washed and told her about Neci's efforts to have Amma's

and Shkaht's tentacles removed. "They would grow back," he said. "And until they did, Shkaht wouldn't be able to see at all or breathe properly. She would be very sick. She might die. Amma probably wouldn't die, but she would be crippled. She wouldn't be able to use any of her senses to their full advantage. She wouldn't be able to recognize smells and tastes that should be familiar to her—as though she could touch them, but not grasp them—until her tentacles grew back. They would always grow back. And it would hurt her to have them cut off—maybe the way it would hurt you to have your eyes cut out."

Tate sat on a fallen log, ignoring its fungi and its insects. "Neci has a way of convincing people," she said.

"I know," he said. "That's why I came to you."

"Gabe said something to me about a little surgery on the girls. Are you sure it was Neci's idea?"

"I heard her talking about it on the first night after we left Phoenix."

"God." Tate sighed. "And she won't quit. She never quits. If the girls were older, I'd like to give her a knife and tell her to go try it." She stared at Akin. "And since neither of those two is an ooloi, I assume that would be fatal to her. Wouldn't it, Akin?"

". . . yes."

"What if the girls were unconscious?"

"It wouldn't matter. Even if they . . . Even if they were dead and hadn't been dead very long, their tentacles would still sting anyone who tried to cut them or pull them."

"Why didn't you tell me that instead of telling me how badly the girls would be hurt?"

"I didn't want to scare you. We don't want to scare anyone."

"No? Well, sometimes it's a good thing to scare people. Sometimes fear is all that will keep them from doing stupid things."

"You're going to tell them?"

"In a way. I'm going to tell them a story. Gabe and I once

saw what happened to a man who injured an Oankali's body tentacles. That was back on the ship. There are other people in Phoenix who remember, but none of them are with us here. Your mother was with us then, Akin, though I don't intend to mention her."

Akin looked away from her, stared across the stream bed, and wondered if his mother were still alive.

"Hey," Tate said. "What's the matter?"

"You should have taken me home," he said bitterly. "You say you know my mother. You should have taken me back to her."

Silence.

"Shkaht says men in resister villages tie up women when they catch them, and they keep them. My mother probably knows that, but she would look for me anyway. She wouldn't let them keep her, but they might shoot her or cut her."

More silence.

"You should have taken me home." He was crying openly now.

"I know," she whispered. "And I'm sorry. But I can't take you home. You mean too much to my people." She had crossed her arms in front of her, the fingers of each hand curved around an elbow. She had made a bar against him like the wooden bars she used to secure her doors. He went to her and put his hands on her arms.

"They won't let you keep me much longer," he said. "And even if they did . . . Even if I grew up in Phoenix and Amma and Shkaht grew up there, you would still need an ooloi. And there are no construct ooloi."

"You don't know what we'll need!"

This surprised him. How could she think he did not know? She might wish he did not know, but of course he did. "I've known since I touched my sibling," he said. "I couldn't have said it then, but I knew we were two-thirds of a reproductive unit. I know what that means. I don't know how it feels. I don't know how threes of adults feel when they come together to mate. But I know there must be three, and one of those three must be an ooloi. My body knows that."

She believed him. Her face said she believed him.

"Let's get back," she said.

"Will you help me get home?"

"No."

"But why?"

Silence.

"Why!" He pulled futilely at her locked arms.

"Because . . ." She waited until he remembered to turn his face up to meet her gaze. "Because these are my people. Lilith has made her choice, and I've made mine. That's something you'll probably never understand. You and the girls are hope to these people, and hope is something they haven't had for more years than I want to think about."

"But it's not real. We can't do what they want."

"Do yourself a favor. Don't tell them."

Now he did not have to remind himself to stare at her.

"Your people will come for you, Akin. I know that, and so do you. I like you, but I'm not good at self-delusion. Let my people hope while they can. Keep quiet." She drew a deep breath. "You'll do that, won't you?"

"You've taken my sibling from me," he said. "You've kept me from having what Amma and Shkaht have, and that's something you don't understand or even care about. My mother might die because you keep me here. You know her, but you don't care. And if you don't care about my people, why should I care about yours?"

She looked downward, then gazed into the running water. Her expression reminded him of Tino's mother's expression when she asked if her son were dead. "No reason," she said finally. "If I were you, I'd hate our guts." She unbarred her arms and picked him up, put him on her lap. "We're all you've got, though, kid. It shouldn't be that way, but it is."

She stood up with him, holding him tighter than necessary, and turned to see Gabe coming toward them.

"What's going on?" he asked. Akin thought later that he

looked a little frightened. He looked uncertain, then relieved, yet slightly frightened—as though something bad still might happen.

"He had some things to tell me," Tate said. "And we have work to do."

"What work?" He took Akin from her as they walked back toward camp, and there was somehow more to the gesture than simply relieving her of a burden. Akin had seen this odd tension in Gabe before, but he did not understand it.

"We have to see to it that our little girls aren't forced to kill anyone," Tate said.

16

The salvage site that was their destination was a buried town. "Smashed and covered by the Oankali," Gabe told Akin. "They didn't want us living here and remembering what we used to be."

Akin looked at the vast pit the salvage crew had dug over the years, excavating the town. It had not been wantonly smashed as Gabe believed. It had been harvested. One of the shuttles had partially consumed it. The small ship-entities fed whenever they could. There was no faster way to destroy a town than to land a shuttle on it and let the shuttle eat its fill. Shuttles could digest almost anything, including the soil itself. What the people of Phoenix were digging through were leavings. Apparently these were enough to satisfy their needs.

"We don't even know what this place used to be called," Gabe said bitterly.

Piles of metal, stone, and other materials lay scattered about. Salvagers were tying some things together with jute rope so that they could be carried. They all stopped their work, though, when they saw the party of newcomers. They gathered around first, shouting and greeting people by name, then falling silent as they noticed the three children.

Men and women, covered with sweat and dirt, clustered around to touch Akin and make baby-talk noises at him. He did not surprise them by speaking to them, although both girls were trying out their new English on their audience.

Gabe knelt down, slipped out of his pack, then lifted Akin free. "Don't goo-goo at him," he said to a dusty woman salvager who was already reaching for him. "He can talk as well as you can—and understand everything you say."

"He's beautiful!" the woman said. "Is he ours? Is he—"

"We got him in trade. He's more Human-looking than the girls, but that probably doesn't mean anything. He's construct. He's not a bad kid, though."

Akin looked up at him, recognizing the compliment—the first he had ever received from Gabe, but Gabe had turned away to speak to someone else.

The salvager picked Akin up and held him so that she could see his face. "Come on," she said. "I'll show you a damn big hole in the ground. Why don't you talk like your friends? You shy?"

"I don't think so," Akin answered.

The woman looked startled, then grinned. "Okay. Let's go take a look at something that probably used to be a truck."

The salvagers had hacked away thick, wild vegetation to dig their hole and to plant their crops along two sides of it, but the wild vegetation was growing back. People with hoes, shovels, and machetes had been clearing it away. Now they were talking with newly arrived Humans or getting acquainted with Amma and Shkaht. Three Humans trailed after the woman who carried Akin, talking to each other about him and occasionally talking to him.

"No tentacles," one of them said, stroking his face. "So Human. So beautiful . . ."

Akin did not believe he was beautiful. These people liked him simply because he looked like them. He was comfortable with them, though. He talked to them easily and ate the bits of food they kept giving him and accepted their caresses, though he did not enjoy them any more than he ever had. Humans needed to touch people, but they could not do so in ways that were pleasurable or useful. Only when he felt lonely or frightened was he glad of their hands, their protection.

They passed near a broad trench, its sides covered with grass. At its center flowed a clear stream. No doubt there were wet seasons when the entire riverbed was filled, perhaps to overflowing. The wet and dry seasons here would be more pronounced than in the forest around Lo. There, it rained often no matter what the season was supposed to be. Akin knew about such things because he had heard adults talk about them. It was not strange to see this shrunken river. But when he looked up as he was carried toward the far end of the pit, he saw for the first time between the green hills to the distant, snow-covered peaks of the mountains.

"Wait!" Akin shouted as the salvager—Sabina, her name was—would have carried him on toward the house on the far side of the hole. "Wait, let me look."

She seemed pleased to do this. "Those are volcanic," she said. "Do you know what that means?"

"A broken place in the Earth where hot liquid rock comes up," Akin said.

"Good," she said. "Those mountains were pushed up and built by volcanic activity. One of them went off last year. Not close enough to us to matter, but it was exciting. It still steams now and then, even though it's covered with snow. Do you like it?"

"Dangerous," he said. "Did the ground shake?"

"Yes. Not much here, but it must have been pretty bad there. I don't think there are any people living near there."

"Good. I like to look at it, though. I'd like to go there some day to understand it."

"Safer to look from here." She took him on to the short row of houses where salvagers apparently lived. There was a flattened rectangular metal frame—Sabina's "truck" apparently. It

looked useless. Akin had no idea what Humans had once done
with it, but now it could only be cut up into metal scrap and
eventually forged into other things. It was huge and would
probably yield a great deal of metal. Akin wondered how the
feeding shuttle had missed it.

"I'd like to know how the Oankali smashed it flat this way,"
another woman said. "It's as though a big foot stepped on it."

Akin said nothing. He had learned that people did not really
want him to give them information unless they asked him directly—or unless they were so desperate they didn't care where
their information came from. And information about the
Oankali tended to frighten or anger them no matter how they
received it.

Sabina put him down, and he looked more closely at the
metal. He would have tasted it if he had been alone. Instead,
he followed the salvagers into one of the houses. It was a
solidly built house, but it was plain, unpainted, roofed with
sheets of metal. The guest house at Lo was a more interesting
building.

But inside there was a museum.

There were stacks of dishes, bits of jewelry, glass, metal.
There were boxes with glass windows. Behind the windows
was only a blank, solid grayness. There were massive metal
boxes with large, numbered wheels on their doors. There were
metal shelves, tables, drawers, bottles. There were crosses like
the one on Gabe's coin—crosses of metal, each with a metal
man hanging from them. Christ on the cross, Akin remembered. There were also pictures of Christ rapping with his
knuckles on a wooden door and others of him pulling open his
clothing to reveal a red shape that contained a torch. There
was a picture of Christ sitting at a table with a lot of other
men. Some of the pictures seemed to move as Akin viewed
them from different angles.

Tate, who had reached the house before him, took one of
the moving pictures—a small one of Christ standing on a hill
and talking to people—and handed it to Akin. He moved it
slightly in his hand, watching the apparent movement of

Christ, whose mouth opened and closed and whose arm moved up and down. The picture, though scratched, was hard and flat—made of a material Akin did not understand. He tasted it—then threw it hard away from him, disgusted, nauseated.

"Hey!" one of the salvagers yelled. "Those things are valuable!" The man retrieved the picture, glared at Akin, then glared at Tate. "What the hell would you give a thing like that to a baby for anyway?"

But both Tate and Sabina had stepped quickly to see what was wrong with Akin.

Akin went to the door and spat outside several times, spat away pure pain as his body fought to deal with what he had carelessly taken in. By the time he was able to talk and tell what was wrong, he had everyone's attention. He did not want it, but he had it.

"I'm sorry," he said. "Did the picture break?"

"What's the matter with you?" Tate said with unmistakable concern.

"Nothing now. I got rid of it. If I were older, I could have handled it better—made it harmless."

"The picture—the plastic—was harmful to you?"

"The stuff it was made of. Plastic?"

"Yes."

"It's so sealed and covered with dirt that I didn't feel the poison before I tasted it. Tell the girls not to taste it."

"We won't," Amma and Shkaht said in unison, and Akin jumped. He did not know when they had come in.

"I'll show you later," he said in Oankali.

They nodded.

"It was . . . more poison packed tight together in one place than I've ever known. Did Humans make it that way on purpose?"

"It just worked out that way," Gabe said. "Hell, maybe that's why the stuff is still here. Maybe it's so poisonous—or so useless—that not even the microbes would eat it. Nonbiodegradable, I think the prewar word was."

Akin looked at him sharply. The shuttle had not eaten the plastic. And the shuttle could eat anything. Perhaps the plastic, like the truck, had simply been overlooked. Or perhaps the shuttle had found it useless as Gabe had said.

"Plastics used to kill people back before the war," a woman said. "They were used in furniture, clothing, containers, appliances, just about everything. Sometimes the poisons leached into food or water and caused cancer, and sometimes there was a fire and plastics burned and gassed people to death. My pre-war husband was a fireman. He used to tell me."

"I don't remember that," someone said.

"I remember it," someone else contradicted. "I remember a house fire in my neighborhood where everybody died trying to get out because of poison gas from burning plastics."

"My god," Sabina said, "should we be trading this stuff?"

"We can trade it," Tate said. "The only place that has enough of it to be a real danger is right here. Other people need things like this—pictures and statues from another time, something to remind them what we were. What we are."

"Why did people use it so much if it killed them?" Akin asked.

"Most of them didn't know how dangerous it was," Gabe said. "And some of the ones who did know were making too damn much money selling the stuff to worry about fire and contamination that might or might not happen." He made a wordless sound—almost a laugh, although Akin could detect no humor in it. "That's what Humans are, too, don't forget. People who poison each other, then disclaim all responsibility. In a way, that's how the war happened."

"Then . . ." Akin hesitated. "Then why don't you paint new pictures and make statues from wood or metal?"

"It wouldn't be the same for them," Shkaht said in Oankali. "They really do need the old things. Our Human father got one of the little crosses from a traveling resister. He always wore it on a cord around his neck."

"Was it plastic?" Akin asked.

"Metal. But prewar. Very old. Maybe it even came from here."

"Independent resisters take our stuff to your villages?" Tate asked when Akin translated.

"Some of them trade with us," Akin said. "Some stay for a while and have children. And some only come to steal children."

Silence. The Humans went back to their trade goods, broke into groups, and began exchanging news.

Tate showed Akin the house where he was to sleep—a house filled with mats and hammocks, cluttered with small objects the salvagers had dug up, and distinguished by a large, cast-iron woodstove. It made the one in Tate's kitchen seem child-sized.

"Stay away from that," Tate said. "Even when it's cold. Make a habit of staying away from it, you hear?"

"All right. I wouldn't touch anything hot by accident, though. And I'm finally too old to poison, so—"

"You just poisoned yourself!"

"No. I was careless, and it hurt, but I wouldn't have gotten very sick or died. It was like when you hit your toe and stumbled on the trail. It didn't mean you don't know how to walk. You were just careless."

"Yeah. That may or may not be a good analogy. You stay away from the stove anyway. You want something to eat or has everyone already stuffed you with food?"

"I'll have to get rid of some of what I've already eaten so that I can eat some more protein."

"Want to eat with us or would you rather go out and eat leaves?"

"I'd rather go out and eat leaves."

She frowned at him for a second, then began to laugh. "Go," she said. "And be careful."

17

Neci Roybal wanted one of the girls. And she had not given up the idea of having both girls' tentacles removed. She had begun again to campaign for that among the salvagers. The tentacles looked more like slugs than worms most of the time, she said. It was criminal to allow little girls to be afflicted with such things. Girl children who might someday be the mothers of a new Human race ought to look Human—ought to see Human features when they looked in the mirror . . .

"They're not Oankali," Akin heard her tell Abira one night. "What happened to the man Tate and Gabe knew—that might only happen with Oankali."

"Neci," Abira told her, "if you go near those kids with a knife, and they don't finish you, I will."

Others were more receptive. A pair of salvagers named Senn converted quickly to Neci's point of view. Akin spent much of his third night at the salvage camp lying in Abira's hammock, listening as in the next house Neci and Gilbert and Anne Senn strove to convert Yori Shinizu and Sabina Dobrowski. Yori, the doctor, was obviously the person they hoped would remove the girls' tentacles.

"It's not just the way the tentacles look," Gil said in his soft voice. Everyone called him Gil. He had a soft, ooloilike voice. "Yes, they are ugly, but it's what they represent that's important. They're alien. Un-Human. How can little girls grow up to be Human women when their own sense organs betray them?"

"What about the boy?" Yori asked. "He has the same alien senses, but they're located in his tongue. We couldn't remove that."

"No," Anne said, soft-voiced like her husband. She looked and sounded enough like him to be his sister, but Humans did not marry their siblings, and these two had been married be-

fore the war. They had come from a place called Switzerland
and had been visiting a place called Kenya when the war happened. They had gone to look at huge, fabulous animals, now
extinct. In her spare time, Anne painted pictures of the animals
on cloth or paper or wood. Giraffes, she called them, lions, elephants, cheetahs . . . She had already shown Akin some of her
work. She seemed to like him.

"No," she repeated. "But the boy must be taught as any
child should be taught. It's wrong to let him always put things
into his mouth. It's wrong to let him eat grass and leaves like
a cow. It's wrong to let him lick people. Tate says he calls it
tasting them. It's disgusting."

"She lets him give in to any alien impulse," Neci said. "She
had no children before. I heard there was some sickness in her
family so that she didn't dare have children. She doesn't know
how to care for them."

"The boy loves her," Yori said.

"Because she spoils him," Neci said. "But he's young. He
can learn to love other people."

"You?" Gil asked.

"Why not me! I had two children before the war. I know
how to bring them up."

"We also had two," Anne said. "Two little girls." She gave
a low laugh. "Shkaht and Amma look nothing like them, but
I would give anything to make one of those girls my daughter."

"With or without tentacles?" Sabina said.

"If Yori would do it, I would want them removed."

"I don't know whether I'd do it," Yori said. "I don't believe
Tate was lying about what she saw."

"But what she saw was between a Human and an adult
Oankali," Anne said. "These are children. Almost babies. And
they're almost Human."

"They *look* almost Human," Sabina put in. "We don't know
what they really are."

"Children," Anne said. "They're children."

Silence.

"It should be done," Neci said. "Everyone knows it should

be done. We don't know how to do it yet, but, Yori, you should be finding out how. You should study them. You came along to guard their health. Doesn't that mean you should spend time with them, get to know more about them?"

"That won't help," Yori said. "I already know they're venomous. Perhaps I could protect myself, and perhaps I couldn't. But . . . this is cosmetic surgery, Neci. Unnecessary. And I'm no surgeon anyway. Why should we risk the girls' health and my life just because they have what amounts to ugly birthmarks? Tate says the tentacles grow back, anyway." She drew a deep breath. "No, I won't do it. I wasn't sure before, but I am now. I won't do it."

Silence. Sounds of moving about, someone walking—Yori's short, light steps. Sound of a door being opened.

"Good night," Yori said.

No one wished her a good night.

"It's not that complicated," Neci said moments later. "Especially not with Amma. She has so few tentacles—eight or ten—and they're so small. Anyone could do it—with gloves for protection."

"I couldn't do it," Anne said. "I couldn't use a knife on anyone."

"I could," Gil said. "But . . . if only they weren't such little girls."

"Is there any liquor here?" Neci asked. "Even that foul cassava stuff the wanderers drink would do."

"We make the corn whiskey here, too," Gil said. "There's always plenty. Too much."

"So we give it to the girls and then do it."

"I don't know," Sabina said. "They're so young. And if they get sick . . ."

"Yori will care for them if they get sick. She'll care for them, even if she doesn't like what we've done. And it will be done, as it should be."

"But—"

"It *must* be done! We must raise Human children, not aliens who don't even understand how we see things."

Silence.

"Tomorrow, Gil? Can it be done tomorrow?"

"I . . . don't know. . . ."

"We can collect the kids when they're out eating plants. No one will notice for a while that they're gone. Sabina, you'll get the liquor, won't you?"

"I—"

"Are there very sharp knives here? It should be done quickly and cleanly. And we'll need clean cloths for bandages, gloves for all of us, just in case, and that antiseptic Yori has. I'll get that. There probably won't be any infection, but we won't take chances." She stopped abruptly, then spoke one word harshly. "Tomorrow!"

Silence.

Akin got up, managed to struggle out of the hammock. Abira awoke, but only mumbled something and went back to sleep. Akin headed toward the next room where Amma and Shkaht shared a hammock. They met him coming out. All three linked instantly and spoke without sound.

"We have to go," Shkaht said sadly.

"You don't," Akin argued. "They're only a few, and not that strong. We have Tate and Gabe, Yori, Abira, Macy and Kolina. They would help us!"

"They would help us tomorrow. Neci would wait and recruit and try again later."

"Tate could talk to the salvagers the way she talked to the camp on the way up here. People believe her when she talks."

"Neci didn't."

"Yes she did. She just wants to have everything her way—even if her way is wrong. And she's not very smart. She's seen me taste metal and flesh and wood, but she thinks gloves will protect her hands from being tasted or stung when she cuts you."

"Plastic gloves?"

Surprised, Akin thought for a moment. "They might have gloves made of some kind of plastic. I haven't seen plastic that soft, but it could exist. But once you understand the plastic it can't hurt you."

"Neci probably doesn't realize that. You said she wasn't smart. That makes her more dangerous. Maybe if other people stop her from cutting us tomorrow, she'll get angrier. She'll want to hurt us just to prove she can."

After a time, Akin agreed. "She would."

"We have to go."

"I want to go with you!"

Silence.

Frightened, Akin linked more deeply with them. "Don't leave me here alone!"

More silence. Very gently, they held him between them and put him to sleep. He understood what they were doing and resisted them angrily at first, but they were right. They had a chance without him. They were stronger, larger, and could travel faster and farther without rest. Communication between them was quicker and more precise. They could act almost as though they shared a single nervous system. Only paired siblings and adult mates came to know each other that well. Akin would hamper them, probably get them recaptured. He knew this, and they could feel his contradictory feelings. They knew he knew. Thus, there was no need to argue. He must simply accept the reality.

He accepted it finally and allowed them to send him into a deep sleep.

18

He slept naked on the floor until Tate found him the next morning. She awoke him by lifting him and was startled when he grabbed her around the neck and would not let go.

He did not cry or speak. He tasted her but did not study her. Later he realized he had actually tried to become her, to join with her as he might with his closest sibling. It was not possible. He was reaching for a union the Humans had denied him. It seemed to him that what he needed was just beyond his grasp, just beyond that final crossing he could not make, as with his mother. As with everyone. He could know so much and no more, feel so much and no more, join so close and no closer.

Desperately, he took what he could get. She could not comfort him or even know how deeply he perceived her. But she could, simply by permitting the attachment, divert his attention from himself, from his own misery.

Aside from her original jerk of surprise, Tate did not try to detach him. He did not know what she did. All his senses were focused on the worlds within the cells of her body. He did not know how long he was frozen to her, not thinking, not knowing or caring what she did as long as she did not disturb him.

When he finally drew away from her, he found that she was sitting on a mat on the floor, leaning against a wall. She had gone on holding him on her arm and resting her arm on her knees. Now as he straightened and reoriented himself, she took his chin between her fingers and turned his face toward hers.

"Are you all right?" she asked.

"Yes."

"What was it?"

He said nothing for a moment, looked around the room.

"Everyone's at breakfast," she said. "I've had my regularly scheduled lecture about how I spoil you and a little extra to boot. Now, why don't you tell me exactly what happened."

She put him down beside her and stared down at him, waiting. Clearly she did not know the girls were gone. Perhaps no one had noticed yet, thanks to the morning grazing habits of all three children. He could not tell. Amma and Shkaht should have as much of a start as possible.

"It's too late for me to bond with my sibling," he said truthfully. "I was thinking about that last night. I was feeling . . . Lonely wouldn't really be the right word. This was more like . . . something died." Every word was true. His answer was simply incomplete. Amma and Shkaht had started his feelings—their union, their leaving . . .

"Where are the girls?" Tate asked.

"I don't know."

"Have they gone, Akin?"

He looked away. Why was she always so hard to hide things from? Why did he hesitate so to lie to her?

"Good god," she said, and started to get up.

"Wait!" Akin said. "They were going to cut them this morning. Neci and her friends were going to grab them while they were eating and hide them and cut off their sensory tentacles."

"The hell they were!"

"They were! We heard them last night! Yori wouldn't help them, but they were going to do it anyway. They were going to give them corn whiskey and—"

"Moonshine?"

"What?"

"They were going to make the girls drunk?"

"They couldn't."

Tate frowned. "Were they going to give them the moonshine—the whiskey?"

"Yes. But it wouldn't make them drunk. I've seen drunk Humans. I don't think anything we could drink would make us like that. Our bodies would reject the drink."

"What would it have done to them?"

"Make them vomit or urinate a lot. It isn't strong or deadly. Probably they would just pass it through almost unchanged. They would urinate a lot."

"That stuff's damn strong."

"I mean . . . I mean it's not a deadly poison. Humans can drink it without dying. We can drink it without vomiting it up wrapped in part of our flesh to keep it from injuring us."

"So it wouldn't hurt them—just in case Neci caught them."

"It wouldn't hurt them. They wouldn't like it, though. And Neci hasn't caught them."

"How do you know?"

"I've heard her. She's been asking people where the girls are. No one's seen them. She's getting worried."

Tate stared at nothing, believing, absorbing. "We wouldn't have let her do it. All you had to do was tell me."

"You would have stopped her this time," he agreed. "She would have kept trying. People believe her after a while. They do what she wants them to."

She shook her head. "Not this time. Too many of us were against her on this. Little girls, for godsake! Akin, we could waste days searching for them, but you could track them faster with your Oankali hearing and sight."

"No."

"Yes. Oh, yes! How far do you think those girls will get before something happens to them? They're not much bigger than you are. They'll die out there!"

"I wouldn't. Why should they?"

Silence. She frowned down at him. "You mean you could get home from here?"

"I could if no Humans stopped me."

"And you think no Humans will stop the girls?"

"I think . . . I think they're afraid. I think they're frightened enough to sting."

"Oh, god."

"What if someone were going to cut your eyes out, and you had a gun?"

"I thought the new species was supposed to be above that kind of thing."

"They're afraid. They only want to go home. They don't want to be cut."

"No." She sighed. "Get dressed. Let's go to breakfast. The riot should be starting any time now."

"I don't think they'll find the girls."

"If what you say is true, I hope they don't. Akin?"

He waited, knowing what she would ask.

"Why didn't they take you with them?"

"I'm too small." He walked away from her, found his pants in the next room, and put them on. "I couldn't work with them the way they could work with each other. I would have gotten them caught."

"You wanted to go?"

Silence. If she did not know he had wanted to go, wanted desperately to go, she was stupid. And she was not stupid.

"I wonder why the hell your people don't come for you," she said. "They must know better than I do what they're putting you through."

"What *they're* putting me through?" he asked, amazed.

She sighed. "We, then. Whatever good that admission does you. Oankali drove us to become what we are. If they hadn't tampered with us, we'd have children of our own. We could live in our own ways, and they could live in theirs."

"Some of you would attack them," Akin said softly. "I think some Humans would have to attack them."

"Why?"

"Why did Humans attack one another?"

Suddenly there was shouting outside.

"Okay," Tate said. "They've realized the girls are gone. They'll be here in a moment."

Almost before she had finished speaking, Macy Wilton and Neci Roybal were at the door, looking around the room.

"Have you seen the girls?" Macy demanded.

Tate shook her head. "No, we haven't been out."

"Did you see them at all this morning?"

"No."

"Akin?"

"No." If Tate thought it was best to lie, then he would lie— although neither of them had begun lying yet.

"I heard you were sick, Akin," Neci said.

"I'm all right now."

"What made you sick?"

He stared at her with quiet dislike, wondering what it might be safe to say.

Tate spoke up with uncharacteristic softness. "He had a dream that upset him. A dream about his mother."

Neci raised an eyebrow skeptically. "I didn't know they dreamed."

Tate shook her head, smiled slightly. "Neci, why not? He's at least as Human as you are."

The woman drew back. "You should be out helping to search for the girls!" she said. "Who knows what's happened to them!"

"Maybe someone decided to follow your advice, grab them, and cut off their sensory tentacles."

"What!" demanded Macy. He had gone into the room where he and the girls and his wife had slept. Now he came out, staring at Tate.

"She has an obscene sense of humor," Neci said.

Tate made a wordless sound. "These days, I have no sense of humor at all where you're concerned." She looked at Macy. "She was still pushing to have the girls' tentacles amputated. She's been talking to the salvagers about it." Now she looked directly at Neci. "Deny it."

"Why should I? They would be better off without them— more Human!"

"Just as much better off as you would be without your eyes! Let's go look for them, Macy. I hope to god they never heard the things Neci's been saying."

Amazed, Akin followed her out. She had put the blame for the girls' flight exactly where it belonged without involving him at all. She left him with a salvager who had injured his knee and joined the search as though she had every expectation of finding the girls quickly.

19

Amma and Shkaht were not found. They were simply gone—perhaps found by other resisters, perhaps safe in some trade village. Most of the resisters seemed to think they were dead—eaten by caimans or anacondas, bitten by poisonous snakes or insects. The idea that such young children could find their way to safety seemed completely impossible to them.

And most of the resisters blamed Neci. Tate seemed to find that satisfying. Akin did not care. If Neci left him alone, he was content with her. And she did leave him alone—but only after planting the idea that he must be watched more carefully. She was not the only one who believed this, but she was the only one to suggest that he be kept out of the pit, kept away from the river, be harnessed and tied outside the cabins when everyone was too busy to watch him.

He would not have stood for that. He would have stung the rope or chain that they tied him with until it rotted or corroded through, and he would have run away—up the mountain, not down. They might not find him higher up. He would probably not make it back to Lo. He was too far from it now, and there were so many resister villages between it and him that he would probably be picked up once he headed down from the hills. But he would not stay with people who tied him.

He was not tied. He was watched more closely than before, but it seemed the resisters had as great an aversion to tying or confining people as he did.

Neci finally left with a group of salvagers going home—men and women carrying wealth on their backs. They took two of the guns with them. There had been a general agreement among new salvagers and old that Phoenix would begin to manufacture guns. Tate was against it. Yori was so strongly against it that she threatened to move to another resister village. Nevertheless, guns would be made.

"We've got to protect ourselves," Gabe said. "Too many of the raiders have guns now, and Phoenix is too rich. Sooner or later, they'll realize it's easier to steal from us than carry on honest trade."

Tate slept several nights alone or with Akin once the decision was made. Sometimes she hardly slept at all, and Akin wished he could comfort her the way Amma and Shkaht had comforted him. Sleep could be a great gift. But he could have given it only with the help of a close Oankali-born sibling.

"Would raiders begin raiding you the way they raid us?" he asked her one night as they lay together in a hammock.

"Probably."

"Why haven't they already?"

"They have occasionally—trying to steal metal or women. But Phoenix is a strong town—plenty of people willing to fight if they have to. There are smaller, weaker settlements that are easier pickings."

"Are guns really a bad idea, then?"

In the dark she tried to stare at him. She couldn't have seen him—although he saw her clearly. "What do you think?" she asked.

"I don't know. I like a lot of the people in Phoenix. And I remember what raiders did to Tino. They didn't have to. They just did it. Later, though, while I was with them, they didn't really seem . . . I don't know. Most of the time, they were like the men in Phoenix."

"They probably came from someplace like Phoenix—some village or town. They got sick of one pointless, endless existence and chose another."

"Pointless because resisters can't have children?"

"That's it. It means a lot more than I could ever explain to you. We don't get old. We don't have kids, and nothing we do means shit."

"What would it mean . . . if you had a kid like me?"

"We have got a kid like you. You."

"You know what I mean."

"Go to sleep, Akin."

"Why are you afraid of guns?"

"They make killing too easy. Too impersonal. You know what that means?"

"Yes. I'll ask if you say something I don't understand."

"So we'll kill more of each other than we already do. We'll learn to make better and better guns. Someday, we'll take on the Oankali, and that will be the end of us."

"It would. What do you want to happen instead?"

Silence.

"Do you know?"

"Not extinction," she whispered. "Not extinction in any form. As long as we're alive, we have some chance."

Akin frowned, trying to understand. "If you had kids in the old way, your prewar way, with Gabe, would that mean you and Gabe were becoming extinct?"

"It would mean we weren't. Our kids would be Human like us."

"I'm Human like you—and Oankali like Ahajas and Dichaan."

"You don't understand."

"I'm trying to."

"Are you?" She touched his face. "Why?"

"I need to. It's part of me, too. It concerns me, too."

"Not really."

Abruptly he was angry. He hated her soft condescension. "Then why am I here! Why are you here! You and Gabe would be down in Phoenix if it didn't concern me. I would be back in Lo. Oankali and Human have done what Human male and female used to do. And they made me and Amma and Shkaht, and they're no more extinct than you would be if you had kids with Gabe!"

She turned slightly—turned her back to him as much as she could in a hammock. "Go to sleep, Akin."

But he did not sleep. It was his turn to lie awake thinking. He understood more than she thought. He recalled his argument with Amma and Shkaht that Humans should be permitted their own Akjai division—their own hedge against disaster and true extinction. Why should it be so difficult? There were, according to Lilith, bodies of land surrounded by vast amounts of water. Humans could be isolated and their ability to reproduce in their own way restored to them. But then what would happen when the constructs scattered to the stars, leaving the Earth a stripped ruin. Tate's hopes were in vain.

Or were they?

Who among the Oankali was speaking for the interests of resister Humans? Who had seriously considered that it might not be enough to let Humans choose either union with the Oankali or sterile lives free of the Oankali? Trade-village Humans said it, but they were so flawed, so genetically contradictory that they were often not listened to.

He did not have their flaw. He had been assembled within the body of an ooloi. He was Oankali enough to be listened to by other Oankali and Human enough to know that resister Humans were being treated with cruelty and condescension.

Yet he had not even been able to make Amma and Shkaht understand. He did not know enough yet. These resisters had to help him learn more.

20

Akin was with the people of Phoenix for over a year. He spent most of this time in the hills, watching the salvaging and taking part when the salvagers would let him. One of the men set him to cleaning small, decorative items—jewelry, figurines, small bottles, jars, eating utensils. He knew he was given the job mainly to keep him from underfoot, but the work pleased him. He tasted everything before he cleaned it and afterward. Often he found Human leavings protected within containers. There were bits of hair, skin, nail. From some of these he salvaged lost Human genetic patterns that ooloi could re-create if they needed the Human genetic diversity. Only an ooloi could tell him what was useful. He memorized everything to give to Nikanj someday.

Once Sabina caught him tasting the inside of a small bottle. She tried to snatch the bottle away. Fortunately, he managed to dodge her hands and withdraw the thin, searching filaments of his tongue before she broke them. She should have gone back to Phoenix when her group left. She had done her share of what she called grubbing in the dirt, but she had stayed. Akin believed she had stayed because of him. He had not forgotten that she had been willing to take part in cutting off Amma's and Shkaht's tentacles. But she seemed brighter than Neci, more able, more willing to learn.

"What was this called?" he asked her once there was no chance of her injuring him.

"It was a perfume bottle. You keep it out of your mouth."

"Where were you going?" he asked.

"What?"

"If you have time, I'll tell you why I put things in my mouth."

"All kids put things in their mouths—and sometimes they poison themselves."

"I *must* put things in my mouth to understand them. And I must try to understand them. Not to try would be like having hands and eyes and yet always being tied and blindfolded. It would make me . . . not sane."

"Oh, but—"

"And I'm too old now to poison myself. I could drink the fluid that used to be in this bottle and nothing would happen. It would pass through me quickly, almost unchanged, because it isn't very dangerous. If it were very dangerous, my body would either change its structure and neutralize it or . . . contain it in a kind of sealed flesh bottle and expel it. Do you see?"

"I . . . understand what you're saying, but I'm not sure I believe you."

"It's important that you understand. Especially you."

"Why?"

"Because just now, you almost hurt me a lot. You could have injured me more than any poison could. And you could have made me sting you. If I did that, you would die. That's why."

She had drawn back from him. Her face had changed slightly. "You always look so normal . . . sometimes I forget."

"Don't forget. But don't hate me either. I've never stung anyone, and I don't ever want to."

Some of the wariness left her eyes.

"Help me learn," he said. "I want to know the Human part of myself better."

"What can I teach you?"

He smiled. "Tell me why Human kids put things in their mouths. I've never known."

21

He made them all his teachers. He told only Tate what he meant to do. When she had heard, she looked at him then shook her head sadly. "Go ahead," she said. "Learn all you can about us. It can't do any harm. But afterward, I think you'll find you have a few more things to learn about the Oankali, too."

He worried about that. No other resister could have made him worry about the Oankali. But Tate had been almost a relative. She would have been an ooloi relative if she had stayed with Kahguyaht and its mates. He felt her to be almost a relative now. He trusted her. Yet he could not give up his own belief that he could someday speak for the resisters.

"Shall I tell them there must be Akjai Humans?" he asked her. "Would you be willing to begin again, isolated somewhere far from here?" Where, he could not imagine, but *somewhere*!

"If it were a place where we could live, and if we could have children." She drew a breath, wet her lips. "We would do anything for that. Anything."

There was an intensity that he had never heard before in her voice. And there was something else. He frowned. "Would you go?"

She had come over to watch him scrub a piece of colorful mosaic—a square of bright bits of glass fitted together to make a red flower against a blue field.

"That's beautiful," Tate said softly. "There was a time when I would have thought it was cheap junk. Now, it's beautiful."

"Would you go?" Akin asked again.

She turned and walked away.

22

Gabe took him away from his tasting and cleaning for a while—took him higher into the hills where the great mountains in the distance could be seen clearly. One of them smoked and steamed into the blue sky and was somehow very beautiful—a pathway deep into the Earth. A breathing place. A kind of joint where great segments of the Earth's crust came together. Akin could look at the huge volcano and understand a little better how the Earth worked—how it would work until it was broken and divided between departing Dinso groups.

Akin chose the edible plants he thought would taste best to

Gabe and introduced the man to them. In return, Gabe told him about a place called New York and what it had been like to grow up there. Gabe talked more than he ever had—talked about acting, which Akin did not understand at all at first.

Gabe had been an actor. People gave him money and goods so that he would pretend to be someone else—so that he would take part in acting out a story someone had made up.

"Didn't your mother ever tell you any stories?" he asked Akin.

"Yes," Akin said. "But they were true."

"She never told you about the three bears?"

"What's a bear?"

Gabe looked first angry, then resigned. "I still forget sometimes," he said. "A bear is just one more large, extinct animal. Forget it."

That night in a small, half-ruined stone shelter before a campfire, Gabe became another person for Akin. He became an old man. Akin had never seen an old man. Most of the old Humans who had survived the war had been kept aboard the ship. The oldest were dead by now. The Oankali had not been able to extend their lives for more than a few years, but they kept them healthy and free of pain for as long as possible.

Gabe became an old man. His voice became heavier, thicker. His body seemed heavier, too, and painfully weary, bent, yet hard to bend. He was a man whose daughters had betrayed him. He was sane, and then not sane. He was terrifying. He was another person altogether. Akin wanted to get up and run out into the darkness.

Yet he sat still, spellbound. He could not understand much of what Gabe said, though it seemed to be English. Somehow, though, he felt what Gabe seemed to want him to feel. Surprise, anger, betrayal, utter bewilderment, despair, madness. . . .

The performance ended, and Gabe was Gabe again. He turned his face upward and laughed aloud. "Jesus," he said. "*Lear* for a three-year-old. Damn. It felt good, anyway. It's been so long. I didn't know I remembered all that stuff."

"Don't you do that for the people in Phoenix?" Akin asked timidly.

"No. I never have. Don't ask me why. I don't know. I farm now or I work metal. I dig up junk from the past and turn it into stuff people can use today. That's what I do."

"I liked the acting. It scared me at first, and I couldn't understand a lot of it, but . . . It's like what we do—constructs and Oankali. It's like when we touch each other and talk with feelings and pressures. Sometimes you have to remember a feeling you haven't had for a long time and bring it back so you can transmit it to someone else or use a feeling you have about one thing to help someone understand something else."

"You do that?"

"Yes. We can't do it very well with Humans. The ooloi can, but males and females can't."

"Yeah." He sighed and lay down on his back. They had cleared some of the plant growth and rubble from the stone floor of the shelter and could wrap themselves in their blankets and lie on it in comfort.

"What was this place?" Akin asked, looking up at the stars through the roofless building. Only the overhang of the hill provided any shelter at all if it happened to rain that night.

"Don't know," Gabe said. "It could have been some peasant's house. I suspect it goes back further, though. I think it's an old Indian dwelling. Maybe even Inca or some related people."

"Who were they?"

"Short brown people. Probably looked something like Tino's parents. Something like you, maybe. They were here for thousands of years before people who look like me or Tate got here."

"You and Tate don't look alike."

"No. But we're both descended from Europeans. Indians were descended from Asians. The Incas are the ones everyone thinks of for this part of the world, but there were a lot of different groups. To tell the truth, I don't think we're far enough into the mountains to be seeing Inca ruins. This is a damn old place, though." He pulled his mouth into a smile. "Old and Human."

They walked for many days, exploring, finding other ruined dwellings, describing a great circle back to the salvage camp. Akin never asked why Gabe took him on the long trip. Gabe never volunteered an explanation. He seemed pleased that Akin insisted on walking most of the time and usually managed to keep up. He willingly tried eating plants Akin recommended and liked some of them well enough to take them back as small plants, seeds, stalks, or tubers. Akin guided him in this, too.

"What can I take back that will grow?" Gabe would say. He could not know how much this pleased Akin. What he and Gabe were doing was what the Oankali always did—collect life, travel and collect and integrate new life into their ships, their already vast collection of living things, and themselves.

He studied each plant very carefully, telling Gabe exactly what he must do to keep the plant alive. Automatically, he kept within himself a memory of genetic patterns or a few dormant cells from each sample. From these, an ooloi could recreate copies of the living organism. Ooloi liked cells from or memories of several individuals within a species. For the Humans, Akin saw that Gabe took seed when there was seed. Seed could be carried in a leaf or a bit of cloth tied with a twist of grass. And it would grow. Akin would see to that. Even without an ooloi to help, he could taste a plant and read its needs. With its needs met, it would thrive.

"This is about the happiest I've ever seen you," Gabe remarked as they neared the salvage camp.

Akin grinned at him but said nothing. Gabe would not want to know that Akin was collecting information for Nikanj. It was enough for him to know that he had pleased Akin very much.

Gabe did not smile back, but only because he made an obvious effort not to.

When they reached camp a few days later, Gabe met Tate

with none of the odd anxiety he often showed when she had been out of his sight for a while.

23

Ten days after Akin and Gabe returned, a new salvage team arrived to take their turn at the dig. While both teams were still on the site, the Oankali arrived.

They were not seen. There was no outcry among the Humans. Akin was busy scrubbing a small, ornate crystal vase when he noticed the Oankali scent.

He put the vase down carefully in a wooden box lined with cloth—a box used for especially delicate, especially beautiful finds. Akin had never broken one of these. There was no reason to break one now.

What should he do? If Humans spotted the Oankali, there might be fighting. Humans could so easily provoke the lethal sting reflex of the Oankali. What to do?

He spotted Tate and called to her. She was digging very carefully around something large and apparently delicate. She was digging with what looked like a long, thin knife and a brush made of twigs. She ignored him.

He went to her quickly, glad there was no one near her to hear.

"I have to go," he whispered. "They're here."

She almost stabbed herself with the knife. "Where!"

"That way." He looked east but did not point.

"Of course."

"Walk me out there. People will notice if I get too far from camp alone."

"Me? No!"

"If you don't, someone might get killed."

"If I do, I might get killed!"

"Tate."

She looked at him.

"You know they won't hurt you. You know. Help me. Your people are the ones I'm trying to save."

She gave him a look so hostile that he stumbled back from her. Abruptly she grabbed him, picked him up, and began walking east.

"Put me down," he said. "Let me walk."

"Shut up!" she said. "Just tell me when I'm getting close to them."

He realized belatedly that she was terrified. She could not have been afraid of being killed. She knew the Oankali too well for that. What then?

"I'm sorry," he whispered. "You were the only one I dared to ask. It will be all right."

She took a breath and put him down, held his hand. "It won't be all right," she said. "But that's not your fault."

They went over a rise, out of sight of the camp. There, several Oankali and two Humans waited. One of the Humans was Lilith. The other . . . looked like Tino.

"Oh, Jesus God!" Tate whispered as she caught sight of the Oankali. She froze. Akin thought she might turn and run, but somehow she managed not to move. Akin wanted to go to his family, but he too kept very still. He did not want to leave Tate standing alone and terrified.

Lilith came over to him. She moved so quickly that he had no time to react before she was there, bending, lifting him, hugging him so hard it hurt.

She had not made a sound. She let Akin taste her neck and feel the utter security of flesh as familiar as his own.

"I've been waiting for you for so *long*," he whispered finally.

"I've been looking for you for so long," she said, her voice hardly sounding like her voice at all. She kissed his face and stroked his hair and finally held him away from her. "Three years old," she said. "So big. I kept worrying that you wouldn't remember me—but I knew you would. I knew you would."

He laughed at the impossible notion of his forgetting her and looked to see whether she was crying. She was not. She was examining him—his hands and arms, his legs . . .

A shout made them both look up. Tate and the other Human stood facing one another. The sound had been Tate shouting Tino's name.

Tino was smiling at her uncertainly. He did not speak until she took him by the arms and said, "Tino, don't you recognize me? Tino?"

Akin looked at Tino's expression, and he knew he did not recognize her. He was alive, but something was the matter with him.

"I'm sorry," Tino said. "I've had a head injury. I remember a lot of my past, but . . . some things are still coming back to me."

Tate looked at Lilith. Lilith looked back with no sign of friendliness. "They tried to kill him when they took Akin," she said. "They clubbed him down, fractured his skull so badly he nearly did die."

"Akin said he was dead."

"He had good reason to think so." She paused. "Was it worth his life for you to have my son?"

"She didn't do it," Akin said quickly. "She was my friend. The men who took me tried to sell me in a lot of places before . . . before Phoenix wanted to buy me."

"Most of the men who took him are dead," Tate said. "The survivor is paralyzed. There was a fight." She glanced at Tino. "Believe me, you and Tino are avenged."

The Oankali began communicating silently among themselves as they heard this. Akin could see his Oankali parents among them, and he wanted to go to them, but he also wanted to go to Tino, wanted to make the man remember him, wanted to make him sound like Tino again.

"Tate . . . ?" Tino said staring at her. "Is it . . . ? Are you . . . ?"

"It's me," she said quickly. "Tate Rinaldi. You did half of your growing up in my house. Tate and Gabe. Remember?"

"Kind of." He thought for a moment. "You helped me. I was going to leave Phoenix and you said . . . you told me how to get to Lo."

Lilith looked surprised. "You did?" she asked Tate.

"I thought he would be safe in Lo."

"He should have been." Lilith drew a deep breath. "That was our first raid in years. We'd gotten careless."

Ahajas, Dichaan, and Nikanj detached themselves from the other Oankali and came over to the Human group. Akin could not wait any longer. He reached toward Dichaan, and Dichaan took him and held him for several minutes of relief and reacquaintance and joy. He did not know what the Humans said while he and Dichaan were locked together by as many of Dichaan's sensory tentacles as could reach him and by Akin's own tongue. Akin learned how Dichaan had found Tino and struggled to keep him alive and got home only to discover that Ahajas's child was soon to be born. The family could not search. But others had searched. At first.

"Was I left among them for so long so that I could study them?" Akin asked silently.

Dichaan rustled his free tentacles in discomfort. "There was a consensus," he said. "Everyone came to believe it was the right thing to do except us. We've never been alone that way before. Others were surprised that we didn't accept the general will, but they were wrong. They were wrong to even want to risk you!"

"My sibling?"

Silence. Sadness. "It remembers you as something there then not there. Nakanj kept you in its thoughts for a while, and the rest of us searched. As soon as we could leave it, we began searching. No one would help us until now."

"Why now?" Akin asked.

"The people believed you had learned enough. They knew they had deprived you of your sibling."

"It's . . . too late for bonding." He knew it was.

"Yes."

"There was a pair of construct siblings here."

"We know. They're all right."

"I saw what they had, how it was for them." He paused for a moment remembering, longing. "I'll never have that." Without realizing it, he had begun to cry.

"Eka, you'll have something very like it when you mate. Until then, you have us." Dichaan did not have to be told how little this was. It would be long years before Akin was old enough to mate. And bonding with parents was not the same as bonding with a close sibling. Nothing he had touched was as sweet as that bonding.

Dichaan gave him to Nikanj, and Nikanj coaxed from him all the information he had discovered about plant and animal life, about the salvage pit. This could be given with great speed to an ooloi. It was the work of ooloi to absorb and assimilate information others had gathered. They compared familiar forms of life with what had been or should be. They detected changes and found new forms of life that could be understood, assembled, and used as they were needed. Males and females went to the ooloi with caches of biological information. The ooloi took the information and gave in exchange intense pleasure. The taking and the giving were one act.

Akin had experienced mild versions of this exchange with Nikanj all his life, but this experience taught him he had known nothing about what an ooloi could take and give until now. Locked to Nikanj, he forgot for a time the pain of being denied bonding with his sibling.

When he was able to think again, he understood why people treasured the ooloi. Males and females did not collect information only to please the ooloi or get pleasure from them. They collected it because the collecting felt necessary to them and pleased them.

But, still, they did know that at some point an ooloi must take the information and coordinate it so that the people could use it. At some point, an ooloi must give them the sensation that only an ooloi could give. Even Humans were vulnerable to this enticement. They could not deliberately gather the kind of specific biological information the ooloi wanted, but they could share with an ooloi all that they had recently eaten, breathed, or absorbed through their skins. They could share any changes in their bodies since their last contact with the ooloi. They did not understand what they gave the ooloi. But they knew what the ooloi gave them. Akin understood exactly what he was giving to Nikanj. And for the first time, he began to understand what an ooloi could give him. It did not take the place of an ongoing closeness like Amma's and Shkaht's. Nothing could do that. But this was better than anything he had ever known. It was an easing of pain for now and a foreshadowing of healing for the distant, adult future.

Sometime later, Akin became aware again of the three Humans. They were sitting on the ground talking to one another. On the hill behind them, the hill that concealed them from the salvage camp, Gabe stood. Apparently, none of the Humans had seen him yet. All the Oankali must be aware of him. He was watching Tate, no doubt focusing on her yellow hair.

"Don't say anything," Nikanj told him silently. "Let them talk."

"He's her mate," Akin whispered aloud. "He's afraid she'll come with us and leave him."

"Yes."

"Let me go and get him."

"No, Eka."

"He's a friend. He took me all around the hills. It was because of him that I had so much information to give you."

"He's a resister. I won't give him the chance to use you as a hostage. You don't realize how valuable you are."

"He wouldn't do it."

"What if he simply picked you up and stepped over the hill and called his friends. There are guns in that camp, aren't there?"

Silence. Gabe might do such a thing if he thought he was losing both Akin and Tate. He might. Just as Tino's father had gathered his friends and killed so many even though he believed nothing he could do would bring Tino back or even properly avenge him.

"Come with us!" Lilith was saying. "You like kids? Have some of your own. Teach them everything you know about what Earth used to be."

"That's not what you used to say," Tate said softly.

Lilith nodded. "I used to think you resisters would find an answer. I hoped you would. But, Jesus, your only answer has been to steal kids from us. The same kids you're too good to have yourselves. What's the point?"

"We thought . . . we thought they would be able to have children without an ooloi."

Lilith took a deep breath. "No one does it without the ooloi. They've seen to that."

"I can't come back to them."

"It's not bad," Tino said. "It's not what I thought."

"I know what it is! I know exactly what it is. So does Gabe. And I don't think anything I could say would make him go through that again."

"Call him," Lilith said. "He's there on the hill."

Tate looked up, saw Gabe. She stood up. "I have to go."

"Tate!" Lilith said urgently.

Tate looked back at her.

"Bring him to us. Let's talk. What harm can it do?"

But Tate would not. Akin could see that she would not. "Tate," he called to her.

She looked at him, then looked away quickly.

"I'll do what I said I would," he told her. "I don't forget things."

She came over to him, and kissed him. The fact that Nikanj was still holding him seemed not to bother her.

"If you ask," Nikanj said, "my parents will come from the ship. They haven't found other Human mates."

She looked at Nikanj but did not speak to it. She walked away up the hill and over it, not stopping even to speak to Gabe. He followed her, and both disappeared over the hill.

III

CHKAHICHDAHK

1

The boy wanders too much," Dichaan said as he sat sharing a meal with Tino. "It's too early for the wandering phase of his life to begin." Dichaan ate with his fingers from a large salad of fruits and vegetables that he had prepared himself. Only he knew best what he felt like eating and exactly what his current nutritional needs were.

Tino ate a corn and bean dish and had beside him a sliced melon with sweet orange flesh and dishes of fried plantains and roasted nuts. He was, Dichaan thought, paying more attention to his food than to what Dichaan was saying.

"Tino, listen to me!"

"I hear." The man swallowed and licked his lips. "He's twenty, 'Chaan. If he weren't showing some independence by now, I would be the one who was worried."

"No." Dichaan rustled his tentacles. "His Human appearance is deceiving you. His twenty years are like . . . like twelve Human years. Less in some ways. He isn't fertile now. He won't be until his metamorphosis is complete."

"Four or five more years?"

"Perhaps. Where does he go, Tino?"

"I won't tell you. He's asked me not to."

Dichaan focused sharply on him. "I haven't wanted to follow him."

"Don't follow him. He isn't doing any harm."

"I'm his only same-sex parent. I should understand him better. I don't because his Human inheritance makes him do things that I don't expect."

"What would a twenty-year-old Oankali be doing?"

"Developing an affinity for one of the sexes. Beginning to know what it would become."

"He knows that. He doesn't know how he'll look, but he knows he'll become male."

"Yes."

"Well, a twenty-year-old Human male in a place like this would be exploring and hunting and chasing girls and showing off. He'd be trying to see to it that everyone knew he was a man and not a kid anymore. That's what I was doing."

"Akin is still a kid, as you say."

"He doesn't look like one, in spite of his small size. And he probably doesn't feel like one. And whether he's fertile or not, he's damned interested in girls. And they don't seem to mind."

"Nikanj said he would go through a phase of quasi-Human sexuality."

Tino laughed. "This must be it, then."

"Later he'll want an ooloi."

"Yeah. I can understand that, too."

Dichaan hesitated. He had come to the question he most wanted to ask, and he knew Tino would not appreciate his asking. "Does he go to the resisters, Tino? Are they the reason for his wandering?"

Tino looked startled, then angry. "If you knew, why did you ask?"

"I didn't know. I guessed. He must stop!"

"No."

"They could kill him, Tino! They kill each other so easily!"

"They know him. They look after him. And he doesn't go far."

"You mean they know him as a construct man?"

"Yes. He's picked up some of their languages. But he hasn't hidden his identity from them. His size disarms them. Nobody that small could be dangerous, they think. On the other hand, that means he's had to fight a few times. Some guys think if he's small, he's weak, and if he's weak, he's fair game."

"Tino, he is too valuable for this. He's teaching us what a Human-born male can be. There are still so few like him because we're too unsure to form a consensus—"

"Then learn from him! Let him alone and learn!"

"Learn what? That he enjoys the company of resisters? That he enjoys fighting?"

"He doesn't enjoy fighting. He had to learn to do it in self-defense, that's all. And as for the resisters, he says he has to know them, has to understand them. He says they're part of him."

"What is there still for him to learn?"

Tino straightened his back and stared at Dichaan. "Does he know everything about the Oankali?"

". . . no." Dichaan let his head and body tentacles hang limp. "I'm sorry. The resisters don't seem very complex—except biologically."

"Yet they resist. They would rather die than come here and live easy, pain-free lives with you."

Dichaan put his food aside and focused a cone of head tentacles on Tino. "Is your life pain-free?"

"Sometimes—biologically."

He did not like Dichaan to touch him. It had taken Dichaan a while to realize that this was not because Dichaan was Oankali, but because he was male. He touched hands with or threw an arm around other Human males, but Dichaan's maleness disturbed him. He had finally gone to Lilith for help in understanding this.

"You're one of his mates," she had told him solemnly. "Believe me, 'Chaan, he never expected to have a male mate. Nikanj was difficult enough for him to get used to."

Dichaan didn't see that Tino had found it difficult to get used to Nikanj. People got used to Nikanj very quickly. And in the long, unforgettable group matings, Tino had not seemed to have any difficulty with anyone. Though afterward, he did tend to avoid Dichaan. Yet Lilith did not avoid Ahajas.

Dichaan got up from his platform, left his salad, and went

to Tino. The man started to draw back, but Dichaan took his arms.

"Let me try to understand you, Chkah. How many children have we had together? Be still."

Tino sat still and allowed Dichaan to touch him with a few long, slender head tentacles. They had had six children together. Three boys from Ahajas and three girls from Lilith. The old pattern.

"You chose to come here," Dichaan said. "And you've chosen to stay. I've been very glad to have you here—a Human father for the children and a Human male to balance group mating. A partner in every sense. Why does it hurt you to stay here?"

"How could it not hurt?" Tino asked softly. "And how could you not know? I'm a traitor to my people. Everything I do here is an act of betrayal. Someday, my people won't exist at all, and I will have helped their destroyers. I've betrayed my parents . . . everyone." His voice had all but vanished even before he finished speaking. His stomach hurt him, and he was developing a pain in his head. He got very bad pains in his head sometimes. And he would not tell Nikanj. He would go away by himself and suffer. If someone found him, he might curse them. He would not struggle against help, though.

Dichaan moved closer to the platform on which Tino sat. He penetrated the flesh of the platform—of the Lo entity—and asked it to send Nikanj. It liked doing such things. Nikanj always pleasured it when it passed along such a message.

"Chkah, does Lilith feel the way you do?" he asked Tino.

"Do you really not know the answer to that?"

"I know she did at first. But she knows that resisters' genes are just as available to us as any other Human genes. She knows there are no resisters, living or dead, who are not already parents to construct children. The difference between them and her—and you—is that you have decided to act as parents."

"Does Lilith really believe that?"

"Yes. Don't you?"

Tino looked away, head throbbing. "I guess I believe it. But it doesn't matter. The resisters haven't betrayed themselves or their Humanity. They haven't helped you do what you're doing. They may not be able to stop you, but they haven't helped you."

"If all Humans were like them, our construct children would be much less Human, no matter how they looked. They would know only what we could teach them of Humans. Would that be better?"

"I tell myself it wouldn't," Tino said. "I tell myself there's some justification for what I'm doing. Most of the time, I think I'm lying. I wanted kids. I wanted . . . the way Nikanj makes me feel. And to get what I wanted, I've betrayed everything I once was."

Dichaan moved Tino's food off his platform and told him to lie down. Tino only looked at him. Dichaan rustled his body tentacles uncomfortably. "Nikanj says you prefer to endure your pain. It says you need to make yourself suffer so that you can feel that your people are avenged and you've paid your debt to them."

"That's shit!"

Nikanj came through a wall from the outside. It looked at the two of them and shot them a bad smell.

"He insists on hurting himself," Dichaan said. "I wonder if he hasn't convinced Akin to hurt himself, too."

"Akin does as he pleases!" Tino said. "He understands what I feel better than either of you could, but it's not what he feels. He has his own ideas."

"You aren't part of his body," Nikanj said, pushing him backward so that he would lie down. He did lie down this time. "But you're part of his thoughts. You've done more than Lilith would have to make him feel that the resisters have been wronged and betrayed."

"Resisters *have* been wronged and betrayed," Tino said. "I never told Akin that, though. I never had to. He saw it for himself."

"You're working on another ulcer," Nikanj said.

"So what?"

"You want to die. And yet you want to live. You love your children and your parents and that is a terrible conflict. You even love us—but you don't think you should." It climbed onto the platform and lay down alongside Tino. Dichaan touched the platform with his head tentacles, encouraging it to grow, to broaden and make room for him. He was not needed, but he wanted to know firsthand what happened to Tino.

"I remember Akin telling me about a Human who bled to death from ulcers," he said to Nikanj. "One of his captors."

"Yes. He gave the man's identity. I found the ooloi who had conditioned the man and learned that he had had ulcers since adolescence. The ooloi tried to keep him for his own sake, but the man wouldn't stay."

"What was his name?" Tino demanded.

"Joseph Tilden. I'm going to put you to sleep, Tino."

"I don't care," Tino muttered. After a time, he drifted off to sleep.

"What did you say to him?" Nikanj asked Dichaan.

"I asked him about Akin's disappearances."

"Ah. You should have asked Lilith."

"I thought Tino would know."

"He does. And it disturbs him very much. He thinks Akin is more loyal to Humanity than Tino himself. He doesn't understand why Akin is so focused on the resisters."

"I didn't realize how focused he was," Dichaan admitted. "I should have."

"The people deprived Akin of closeness with his sibling and handed him a compensating obsession. He knows this."

"What will he do?"

"Chkah, he's your child, too. What do you think he'll do?"

"Try to save them—what's left of them—from their empty, unnecessary deaths. But how?"

Nikanj did not answer.

"It's impossible. There's nothing he can do."

"Maybe not, but the problem will occupy him until his metamorphosis. Then I hope the other sexes will occupy him."

"But there must be more to it than that!"

Nikanj smoothed its body tentacles in amusement. "Anything to do with Humans always seems to involve contradictions." It paused. "Examine Tino. Inside him, so many very different things are working together to keep him alive. Inside his cells, mitochondria, a previously independent form of life, have found a haven and trade their ability to synthesize proteins and metabolize fats for room to live and reproduce. We're in his cells too now, and the cells have accepted us. One Oankali organism within each cell, dividing with each cell, extending life, and resisting disease. Even before we arrived, they had bacteria living in their intestines and protecting them from other bacteria that would hurt or kill them. They could not exist without symbiotic relationships with other creatures. Yet such relationships frighten them."

"Nika . . ." Dichaan deliberately tangled his head tentacles with those of Nikanj. "Nika, we aren't like mitochondria or helpful bacteria, and they know it."

Silence.

"You shouldn't lie to them. It would be better to say nothing."

"No, it wouldn't. When we keep quiet, they suppose it's because the truth is terrible. I think we're as much symbionts as their mitochondria were originally. They could not have evolved into what they are without mitochondria. Their earth might still be inhabited only by bacteria and algae. Not very interesting."

"Is Tino going to be all right?"

"No. But I'll take care of him."

"Can't you do something to stop him from hurting himself?"

"I could make him forget some of his past again."

"No!"

"You know I wouldn't. I wouldn't even if I hadn't seen the pleasant, empty man he was before his memories came back. I wouldn't do it. I don't like to tamper with them that way. They lose too much of what I value in them."

"What will you do, then? You just go on repairing him until finally he leaves us and maybe kills himself?"

"He won't leave us."

It meant it would not let him go, *could* not. Ooloi could be that way when they found a Human they were strongly attracted to. Nikanj certainly could not let Lilith go, no matter how much it let her wander.

"Will Akin be all right?"

"I don't know."

Dichaan detached himself from Nikanj and sat up, folding his legs under him. "I'm going to separate him from the resisters."

"Why?"

"Sooner or later, one of them will kill him. We've collected their guns twice since they took him. They always make more, and the new ones are always more effective. Greater range, greater accuracy, greater safety for the Humans using them . . . Humans are too dangerous. And they're only one part of him. Let him learn what else he is."

Nikanj drew its body tentacles in, upset, but it said nothing. If it had favorites among its children, Akin was one of them. It had no same-sex children, and that was a real deprivation. Akin was unique, and when he was at home, he spent much of his time with Nikanj. But Dichaan was still his same-sex parent.

"Not for long, Chkah," Dichaan said softly. "I won't keep him from you long. And he'll bring you all the changes he finds in Chkahichdahk."

"He always brings me things," Nikanj whispered. It seemed to relax, accepting Dichaan's decision. "He goes out of his way to find unusual things to taste and bring back. There's so little time until he metamorphoses and begins giving all his acquisitions to his mates."

"A year," Dichaan said. "I'll bring him back in only a year." He lay down again to comfort Nikanj and was not surprised to find that the ooloi needed comfort. It had been upset by the way Tino continually took his frustration and confusion out on his own body. Now it was even more upset. It was to lose a year of Akin's childhood. In its home with its large family all around, it felt alone and tired.

Dichaan linked himself into the nervous system of the ooloi. He could feel his own deep family bond stimulating Nikanj's. These bonds expanded and changed over the years, but they did not weaken. And they never failed to capture Nikanj's most intense interest.

Later Dichaan would tell Lo to signal the ship and have it send a shuttle. Later he would tell Akin it was time for him to learn more about the Oankali side of his heritage.

2

Sometimes it seemed to Akin that his world was made up of tight units of people who treated him kindly or coldly as they chose, but who could not let him in, no matter how much they might want to.

He could remember a time when blending into others seemed not only possible but inevitable—when Tiikuchahk was still unborn and he could reach out and taste it and know it as his closest sibling. Now, though, because he had not been able to bond with it, it was perhaps his least interesting sibling. He had spent as little time as possible with it.

Now it wanted to go to Chkahichdahk with him.

"Let it go and let me stay here," he had told Dichaan.

"It is alone, too," Dichaan had answered. "You and it both need to learn more about what you are."

"I know what I am."

"Yes. You are my same-sex child, near his metamorphosis."

Akin had not been able to answer this. It was time for him to listen to Dichaan, learn from him, prepare to be a mature male. He felt strongly inclined to obey.

Yet he had lost himself in the forest for days, resisting the inclination and deeply resenting it each time it returned to nag him.

No one came after him. And no one seemed surprised when he came home. The shuttle had eaten a new clearing waiting for him.

He stood staring at it. It was a great green-shelled thing—a male itself to the degree that the ship-entities could be of one sex or the other. Each one had the capacity to become female. But as long as it received a controlling substance from the body of Chkahichdahk, it would remain small and male. It would extend the reach of Chkahichdahk by investigating planets and moons of solar systems, bringing back information, supplies of minerals, life. It would carry passengers and work with them in exploration. And it would ferry people to the ship and back.

Akin had never been inside one. He would not be allowed to link into one's nervous system until he was an adult. So much had to wait until he was an adult.

When he was an adult, he could speak for the resisters. Now, his voice could be ignored, would not even be heard without the amplification provided by one of the adult members of his family. He remembered Nikanj's stories of its own childhood—of being right, knowing it was right, and yet being ignored because it was not adult. Lilith had occasionally been hurt during those years because people did not listen to Nikanj, who knew her better than they did.

Akin would not make Nikanj's mistake. He had decided that long ago. But now . . . Why had Dichaan decided to send him to Chkahichdahk? Was it only to keep him out of danger or was there some other reason?

He moved closer to the shuttle, waiting to go inside but wanting first to walk around the thing, look at it, appreciate it with the senses he and the Humans shared.

It looked from every angle like a perfectly symmetrical high hill. Once it was airborne, it would be spherical. Its shell plates would slide around and lock—three layers of them—and nothing would get in or out.

"Akin."

He looked around without moving his body and saw Ahajas coming from the direction of Lo. Everyone else made some noise when they walked, but Ahajas, larger, taller than almost everyone else, seemed to flow along, sixteen-toed feet hardly seeming to touch the ground. If she did not want to be heard, no one heard her. Females had to be able to hide if possible and to fight if hiding was impossible or useless. Nikanj had said that.

He would not see Nikanj for a year. Perhaps longer.

She came towering over him, then folded herself into a sitting position opposite him the way some Humans used to stoop or kneel to talk to him when he was younger. Now his head and hers were at the same level.

"I wanted to see you before you left. You might not still be a child when you come back."

"I will be." He put his hand in among her head tentacles and felt them grasp and penetrate. "I'm still years away from changing."

"Your body can change faster than you think. The stress of having to adjust to a new environment could make things go more quickly. You should see everyone now."

"I don't want to."

"I know. You don't want to leave so you don't want to say goodbye. You didn't even go to your resister friends."

She didn't smell them on him. He had been particularly embarrassed to realize that she and others knew by scent when he had been with a woman. He washed, of course, but still they knew.

"You should have gone to them. You might change a great deal during your metamorphosis. Humans don't accept that easily."

"Lilith?"

"You know better. In spite of the things she says, I've never seen her reject one of her children. But would you want to leave without seeing her?"

Silence.

"Come on, Eka." She released his hand and stood up.

He followed her back to the village, feeling resentful and manipulated.

3

An outdoor feast was arranged for him. The people stopped their activities and came together in the center of the village for him and for Tiikuchahk. Tiikuchahk seemed to enjoy the party, but Akin simply endured it. Margit, who was known to be on the verge of her metamorphosis, came to sit beside him. She was still his favorite sibling, although she spent more time with her own paired sibling. She held out a gray hand to him, and he almost took it between his own before he noticed what she was showing him. She had always had too many fingers for a Human-born child—seven on each hand. But the hand she held out to him now had only five long, slender, gray fingers.

He stared at her, then carefully took the offered hand and examined it. There was no wound, no scars.

"How . . . ?" he asked.

"I woke up this morning, and they were gone. Nothing left but the nail and some shriveled, dead skin."

"Did your hand hurt?"

"It felt fine. It still does. I'm sleepy, but that's all so far." She hesitated. "You're the first person I've told."

He hugged her and was barely able to stop himself from crying. "I won't even know you when I come back. You'll be someone else, probably mated and pregnant."

"I may be mated and pregnant, but you'll know me. I'll see to that!"

He only looked at her. Everyone changed, but, irrationally, he did not want her to change.

"What is it?" Tiikuchahk asked.

Akin did not understand why he did it, but after looking to see that it was all right with Margit, he took her hand and showed it to Tiikuchahk.

Tiikuchahk, who looked a great deal more Human than Margit did in spite of being Oankali-born, began to cry. It kissed her hand and let it go sadly. "Things are going to change too much while we're gone," it said, silent tears sliding down its gray face. "We'll be strangers when we come back." Its few small sensory tentacles tightened into lumps against its body, making it look the way Akin felt.

Now others wanted to know what was wrong, and Lilith came to them, looking as though she already knew.

"Margit?" she said softly.

Margit held up her hands and smiled. "I thought so," Lilith said. "Now this is your party, too. Come on." She led Margit away to show others.

Akin and Tiikuchahk got up together without speaking. They did sometimes act in unison in the way of paired siblings, but the phenomenon always startled them and somehow never gave the comfort it seemed to give to sibling pairs who had bonded properly in infancy. Now, though, they moved together toward Ayre, their oldest sister. She was a construct adult—the oldest construct adult in Lo—and she had been watching them, training several head tentacles on them as she sat talking to one of Leah's Oankali-born sons. She had been born in Chkahichdahk. She had passed her metamorphosis on Earth, mated, and borne several children. The things that they still faced, she had already survived.

"Sit with me," Ayre said as they came up to her. "Sit here." She positioned them on either side of her. She immediately tangled her long head tentacles with Tiikuchahk's. Akin had come to find having only one true sensory tentacle, and that one in his mouth, very inconvenient. Resisters liked it because they did not have to look at it, but it inhibited communication with Oankali and constructs. He had quickly grown too large to be held in someone's arms.

But Ayre, being Ayre, simply took him under one arm and pulled him against her so that it was easy for him to link with her as she used her body tentacles to link with him.

"We don't know what will happen to us," both he and Tiikuchahk said in silent unison. It was a cry of fear from both of them and, for Akin, also a cry of frustration. Time was being stolen from him. He knew the people and languages of a Chinese resister village, an Igbo village, three Spanish-speaking villages made up of people from many countries, a Hindu village, and two villages of Swahili-speaking people from different countries. So many resisters. Yet there were so many more. He had been driven out of, of all things, a village of English-speaking people because he was browner than the villagers were. He did not understand this, and he had not dared to ask anyone in Lo. But still, there were resisters he had never seen, resisters whose ideas he had not heard, resisters who believed their only hope was to steal construct children or to die as a species. There were stories now of a village whose people had gathered in their village square and drunk poison. No one Akin had talked to knew the name of this village, but everyone had heard about it.

Would there be any Humans left to save when he was finally old enough to have his opinions respected?

And would he still look Human enough to persuade them?

Or was all that foolishness? Would he truly be able to help them at all, no matter what happened? The Oankali would not stop him from doing anything they did not consider harmful. But if there were no consensus, they would not help him. And he could not help the Humans alone.

He could not, for instance, give them a ship entity. As long as they remained Human enough to satisfy their beliefs, they could not communicate with a ship. Some of them insisted on believing the ships were not alive—that they were metal things that anyone could learn to control. They had not understood at all when Akin tried to explain that ships controlled themselves. You either joined with them, shared their experiences, and let them share yours, or there was no trade. And without trade, the ships ignored your existence.

"You know you must help each other," Ayre said.

Akin and Tiikuchahk drew back reflexively.

"You can't be what you should have been, but you can help each other." Akin could not miss the certainty Ayre felt. "You're both alone. You'll both be strangers. And you're like one pea cut in half. Let yourselves depend on each other a little."

Neither Akin nor Tiikuchahk responded.

"Is a pea cut in half one wounded thing or two?" she asked softly.

"We can't heal each other," Tiikuchahk said.

"Metamorphosis will heal you, and it may be closer than you think."

And they were afraid again. Afraid of changing, afraid of returning to a changed, unrecognizable home. Afraid of going to a place even less their own than the one they were leaving. Ayre sought to divert them. "Ti, why do you want to go to Chkahichdahk?" she asked.

Tiikuchahk did not want to answer the question. Both Akin and Ayre received only a strong negative feeling from it.

"There are no resisters there," Ayre said. "That's it, isn't it?"

Tiikuchahk said nothing.

"Has Ahajas said you would be female?" Ayre asked.

"Not yet."

"Do you want to be?"

"I don't know."

"You think you might want to be male?"

"Maybe."

"If you want to be male, you should stay here. Let Akin go. Spend your time with Dichaan and Tino and with your sisters.

Male parents, female siblings. Your body will know how to respond."

"I want to see Chkahichdahk."

"You could wait. See it after you change."

"I want to go with Akin." There was the strong negative
again. It had said what it had not wanted to say.

"Then you will probably be female."

Sadness. "I know."

"Ti, maybe you want to go with Akin because you're still
trying to heal the old wound. As I said, there are no resisters
on Chkahichdahk. No bands of Humans to distract him and
use so much of his time." She shifted her attention to Akin.
"And you. Since you must go, how do you feel about having
Ti go with you?"

"I don't want it to go." No lie could be told successfully in
this intimate form of communication. The only way to avoid
unpleasant truths was to avoid communication—to say nothing. But Tiikuchahk already knew he did not want it to go with
him. Everyone knew. It repelled him and yet drew him in such
an incomprehensible, uncomfortable way that he did not like
to be near it at all. And it felt the same things he did. It should
have been glad to see him go away.

Ayre shuddered. She did not break the contact between
them, but she wanted to. She could feel the deep attraction-
repulsion between them. She tried to overcome the conflicting
emotions with her own calm, with feelings of unity that she recalled with her own paired sibling. Akin recognized the feeling.
He had noticed it before in others. It did nothing to calm his
own confusion of feelings.

Ayre broke contact with them. "Ti is right. You should go
up together," she said, rustling her head tentacles uncomfortably. "You have to resolve this. It's disgusting that the people
chose to let this happen to you."

"We don't know how to resolve it," Akin said, "except to
wait for metamorphosis."

"Find an ooloi. A subadult. That's something you can't do
here. I haven't seen a subadult down here for years."

"I've never seen one," Tiikuchahk said. "They come down after their second metamorphosis. What can they do before then?"

"Focus the two of you away from each other without even trying. You'll see. Even before they grow up, they're . . . interesting."

Akin stood up. "I don't want an ooloi. That makes me think about mating. Everything is going too fast."

Ayre sighed and shook her head. "What do you think you've been doing with those resister women?"

"That was different. Nothing could happen. I even told them nothing could happen. They wanted to do it anyway—in case I was wrong."

"You and Ti find yourselves an ooloi. If it isn't mature it can't mate—but it can help you."

They left her, found themselves both seeking out then starting toward Nikanj. At that point, Akin deliberately pulled himself out of synchronization with Tiikuchahk. It was a grating synchronization that kept happening by accident and feeling the way the saw mill in Phoenix had once sounded when something went badly wrong with the saw and the mill had to be shut down for days.

He stopped, and Tiikuchahk went on. It stumbled, and he knew it felt the same tearing away that he did. Things had always been this way for them. He knew it was usually glad when he left the village for weeks or months. Sometimes it would not stay with the family when he was home but went to other families, where it found being alone, being an outsider, more endurable.

Humans had no idea how completely Oankali and construct society was made up of groups of two or more people. Tate did not know what she had done when she refused to help him get back to Lo and Tiikuchahk. Perhaps that was why in all his travels, he had never returned to Phoenix.

He went to Lilith, as someone began calling for a story. She was sitting alone, ignoring the call, although people liked her stories. Her memory supplied her with the smallest details of prewar Earth, and she knew how to put everything together in ways that made people laugh or cry or lean forward, listening, fearful of missing the next words.

She looked up at him, and said nothing when he sat down next to her.

"I wanted to say goodbye," he said softly.

She seemed tired. "I was thinking about Margit growing up, you and Ti going. . . . But you should go." She took his hand and held it. "You should know the Oankali part of yourselves, too. But I can hardly stand the thought of losing what may be the last year of your childhood."

"I hoped I would reach more of the resisters," he said.

She said nothing. She did not talk to him about his trips to the resisters. She cautioned him sometimes, answered questions if he asked. And he could see that she worried about him. But she volunteered nothing—nor did he. Once, when she had left the village on one of her solitary treks, he had followed her, found her sitting on a log waiting for him when he finally caught her. They traveled together for several days, and she told him her story—why her name was an epithet among English-speaking resisters, how they blamed her for what the Oankali had done to them because she was the person the Oankali had chosen to work through. She had had to awaken groups of Humans from suspended animation and help them understand their new situation. Only she could speak Oankali then. Only she could open and close walls and use her Oankali-enhanced strength to protect herself and others. That was enough to make her a collaborator, a traitor in the minds of her own people. It had been safe to blame her, she said. The Oankali were powerful and dangerous, and she was not.

Now she faced him. "You couldn't possibly reach all the resisters," she said. "If you want to help them, you already have the information you need from them. Now you need to learn more about the Oankali. Do you see?"

He nodded slowly, his skin itching where there were sensory

spots but no tentacles to coil tight and express the tension he felt.

"If there is anything you can do, now is the time to find out what it is and how to do it. Learn all you can."

"I will." He compared her long, brown hand to his own and wondered how there could be so little visible difference. Perhaps the first sign of his metamorphosis would be new fingers growing or old ones losing their flat Human nails. "I hadn't really thought of the trip being useful."

"Make it useful!"

"Yes." He hesitated. "Do you really believe I can help?"

"Do you?"

"I have ideas."

"Save them. You've been right to keep quiet about them so far."

It was good to hear her confirming what he had believed. "Will you come to the ship with me?"

"Of course."

"Now."

She looked out at the party, at the village. People had clustered at the guest house where someone was telling a story, and another group had gotten out flutes, drums, guitars, and a small harp. Their music would soon either drive the storytellers into one of the houses or, more likely, bring them into the singing and dancing.

Oankali did not like music. They began to withdraw into the houses—to save their hearing, they said. Most constructs enjoyed music as much as Humans did. Several Oankali-born construct males had become wandering musicians, more than welcome at any trade village.

"I'm not in a mood for singing or dancing or stories," he said. "Walk with me. I'll sleep at the ship tonight. I've said my goodbyes."

She stood up, towering over him in a way that made him feel oddly secure. No one spoke to them or joined them as they left the village.

4

Chkahichdahk. Dichaan went up with Akin and Ti-ikuchahk. The shuttle could simply have been sent home. It had eaten its fill and been introduced to several people who had reached adulthood recently. It was content and needed no guiding. But Dichaan went with them anyway. Akin was glad of this. He needed his same-sex parent more than he would have admitted.

Tiikuchahk seemed to need Dichaan, too. It stayed close to him in the soft light of the shuttle. The shuttle had made them a plain gray sphere within itself and left them to decide whether they wanted to raise platforms or bulkheads. The air would be kept fresh, the shuttle efficiently supplying them with the oxygen it produced and taking away the carbon dioxide they exhaled for its own use. It could also use any waste they produced, and it could feed them anything they could describe, just as Lo could. Even a child with only one functional sensory tentacle could describe foods he had eaten and ask for dupli-cate foods. The shuttle would synthesize them as Lo would have.

But only Dichaan could truly link with the shuttle and, through its senses, share its experience of flying through space. He could not share what he experienced until he had detached himself from the shuttle. Then he held Akin immobile as though holding an infant and showed him open space.

Akin seemed to drift, utterly naked, spinning on his own axis, leaving the wet, rocky, sweet-tasting little planet that he had always enjoyed and going back to the life source that was wife, mother, sister, haven. He had news for her of one of their children—of Lo.

But he was in empty space—surrounded by blackness, feed-ing from the impossibly bright light of the sun, falling away from the great blue curve of the Earth, aware over all the body of the great number of distant stars. They were gentle touches, and the sun was a great, confining hand, gentle but inescapable. No shuttle could travel this close to a star, then escape its gravitational embrace. Only Chkahichdahk could do that, powered by its own internal sun—its digestion utterly efficient, wasting nothing.

Everything was sharp, starkly clear, intense beyond enduring. Everything pounded the senses. Impressions came as blows. He was attacked, beaten, tormented . . .

And it ended.

Akin could not have ended it. He lay now, weak with shock, no longer annoyed at Dichaan's holding him, needing the support.

"That was only a second," Dichaan was saying. "Less than a second. And I cushioned it for you."

Gradually, Akin became able to move and think again. "Why is it like that?" he demanded.

"Why does the shuttle feel what it feels? Why do we experience its feelings so intensely? Eka, why do *you* feel what you feel? How would a coati or an agouti receive your feelings?"

"But—"

"It feels as it feels. Its feelings would hurt you, perhaps injure or kill you if you took them directly. Your reactions would confuse it and throw it off course."

"And when I'm an adult, I'll be able to perceive through it as you do?"

"Oh, yes. We never trade away our abilities to work with the ships. They're more than partners to us."

"But . . . what do we do for them, really? They allow us to travel through space, but they could travel without us."

"We build them. They are us, too, you know." He stroked a smooth, gray wall, then linked into it with several head tentacles. He was asking for food, Akin realized. Delivery would take a while, since the shuttle stored nothing. Foods were stored when Humans were brought along because some shuttles were not as practiced as they might be in assembling foods that tasted satisfying to Humans. They had never poisoned anyone or left anyone malnourished. But sometimes Humans found the food they produced so odd-tasting that the Humans chose to fast.

"They began as we began," Dichaan continued. He touched Akin with a few long-stretched head tentacles, and Akin moved closer again to receive an impression of Oankali in one of their earliest forms, limited to their home world and the life that had originated there. From their own genes and those of many other animals, they fashioned the ancestors of the ships. Their intelligence, when it was needed, was still Oankali. There were no ooloi ships, so their seed was always mixed in Oankali ooloi.

"And there are no construct ooloi," Akin said softly.

"There will be."

"When?"

"Eka . . . when we feel more secure about you."

Silenced, Akin stared at him. "Me alone?"

"You and the others like you. By now, every trade village has one. If you had done your wandering to trade villages, you'd know that."

Tiikuchahk spoke for the first time. "Why should it be so hard to get construct males from Human females? And why are Human-born males so important?"

"They must be given more Human characteristics than Oankali-born construct males," Dichaan answered. "Otherwise, they could not survive inside their Human mothers. And since they must be so Human and still male, and eventually fertile, they must come dangerously close to fully Human males in some ways. They bear more of the Human Contradiction than any other people."

The Human Contradiction again. The Contradiction, it was more often called among Oankali. Intelligence and hierarchical behavior. It was fascinating, seductive, and lethal. It had brought Humans to their final war.

"I don't feel any of that in me," Akin said.

"You're not mature yet," Dichaan said. "Nikanj believes you are exactly what it intended you to be. But the people must see the full expression of its work before they are ready to shift their attention to construct ooloi and maturity for the new species."

"Then it will be an Oankali species," Akin said softly. "It will grow and divide as Oankali always have, and it will call itself Oankali."

"It will be Oankali. Look within the cells of your own body. You are Oankali."

"And the Humans will be extinct, just as they believe."

"Look within your cells for them, too. Your cells in particular."

"But we will be Oankali. They will only be . . . something we consumed."

Dichaan lay back, relaxing his body and welcoming Tiikuchahk, who immediately lay beside him, some of its head tentacles writhing into his.

"You and Nikanj," he said to Akin. "Nikanj tells the Humans we are symbionts, and you believe we are predators. What have you consumed, Eka?"

"I'm what Nikanj made me."

"What has it consumed?"

Akin stared at the two of them, wondering what communion they shared that he took no part in. But he did not want another painful, dissonant blending with Tiikuchahk. Not yet. That would happen soon enough by accident. He sat watching them, trying to see them both as a resister might. They slowly became alien to him, became ugly, became almost frightening.

He shook his head suddenly, rejecting the illusion. He had created it before, but never so deliberately or so perfectly.

"They are consumed," he said quietly. "And it was wrong and unnecessary."

"They live, Eka. In you."

"Let them live in themselves!"

Silence.

"What are we that we can do this to whole peoples? Not predators? Not symbionts? What then?"

"A people, growing, changing. You're an important part of that change. You're a danger we might not survive."

"I'm not going to hurt anyone."

"Do you think the Humans deliberately destroyed their civilization?"

"What do you think I will destroy?"

"Nothing. Not you personally, but human-born males in general. Yet we must have you. You're part of the trade. No trade has ever been without danger."

"Do you mean," Akin said, frowning, "that this new branch of the Oankali that we're intended to become could wind up fighting a war and destroying itself?"

"We don't think so. The ooloi have been very careful, checking themselves, checking each other. But if they're wrong, if they've made mistakes and missed them, Dinso will eventually be destroyed. Toaht will probably be destroyed. Only Akjai will survive. It doesn't have to be war that destroys us. War was only the quickest of the many destructions that faced Humanity before it met us."

"It should have another chance."

"It has. With us." Dichaan turned his attention to Tiikuchahk. "I haven't let you taste the ship's perceptions. Shall I?"

Tiikuchahk hesitated, opening its mouth so that they would know it meant to speak aloud. "I don't know," it said finally. "Shall I taste it, Akin?"

Akin was surprised to be asked. This was the first time Tiikuchahk had spoken directly to him since they had entered the ship. Now he examined his own feelings, searching for an answer. Dichaan had upset him, and he resented being pulled to another subject so abruptly. Yet Tiikuchahk had not asked a frivolous question. He should answer.

"Yes," he said. "Do it. It hurts, and you won't like it, but there's something more in it than pain, something you won't feel until afterward. I think maybe . . . maybe it's a shadow of the way it will be for us when we're adult and able to perceive directly. It's worth what it costs, worth reaching for."

5

Akin and Tiikuchahk were asleep when the shuttle reached Chkahichdahk. Dichaan awoke them with a touch and led them out into a pseudocorridor that was exactly the same color as the inside of the shuttle. The pseudocorridor was low and narrow—just large enough for the three of them to walk through, single file. It closed behind them. Akin, following last, could see the walls sphinctering together just a few steps behind him. The movement fascinated him. No structure in Lo was massive enough to move this way, creating a temporary corridor to guide them through a thick layer of living tissue. And the flesh must be opening ahead of them. He tried to look past Tiikuchahk and Dichaan and see the movement. He caught sight of it now and then. That was the trouble with being small. He was not weak, but nearly everyone he knew was taller and broader than he was—and always would be. During metamorphosis, Tiikuchahk, if it became female, would almost double its size. But he would be male, and metamorphosis made little difference in the size of males.

He would be small and solitary, Nikanj had said shortly after his birth. He would not want to stay in one place and be a father to his children. He would not want anything to do with other males.

He could not imagine such a life. It was not Human or Oankali. How could he be able to help the resisters if he were so solitary?

Nikanj knew a great deal, but it did not know everything. Its children were always healthy and intelligent. But they did not always do what it wanted or expected them to. It had better luck sometimes predicting what Humans would do under a given set of circumstances. Surely it did not know as much as it thought it did about what Akin would do as an adult.

"This is a bad way to bring Humans in," Dichaan was saying as they walked. "Most of them are disturbed at being so closed in. If you ever have to bring any in, have the shuttle take you as close as possible to one of the true corridors and get them into that corridor as quickly as possible. They don't like the flesh movement either. Try to keep them from seeing it."

"They see it at home," Tiikuchahk said.

"Not this massive kind of movement. Lilith says it makes her think of being swallowed alive by some huge animal. At least she can stand it. Some Humans go completely out of control and hurt themselves—or try to hurt us." He paused. "Here's a true corridor. Now we ride."

Dichaan led them to a tilio feeding station and chose one of the large, flat animals. The three of them climbed onto it, and Dichaan touched several head tentacles to it. The animal was curious and sent up pseudotentacles to investigate them.

"This one's never carried an Earth-born construct before," Dichaan said. "Taste it. Let it taste you. It's harmless."

It reminded Akin of an agouti or an otter, although it was brighter than either of those animals. It carried them through other riders and through pedestrians—Oankali, construct, and Human. Dichaan had told it where he wanted to go, and it found its way without trouble. And it enjoyed meeting strange-tasting visitors.

"Will we have these animals on Earth eventually?" Tiikuchahk asked.

"We'll have them when we need them," Dichaan said. "All our ooloi know how to assemble them."

Assemble was the right word, Akin thought. The tilio had been fashioned from the combined genes of several animals. Humans put animals in cages or tied them to keep them from straying. Oankali simply bred animals who did not want to stray and who enjoyed doing what they were intended to do. They were also pleased to be rewarded with new sensations or pleasurable familiar sensations. This one seemed particularly interested in Akin, and he spent the journey telling it about Earth and about himself—giving it simple sensory impressions. Its delight with these gave him as much pleasure as he gave the tilio. When they reached the end of their journey, Akin hated to leave the animal. Dichaan and Tiikuchahk waited patiently while he detached himself from it and gave it a final touch of farewell.

"I liked it," he said unnecessarily as he followed Dichaan through a wall and up a slope toward another level.

Without turning, Dichaan focused a cone of head tentacles on him. "It paid a great deal of attention to you. More than to either of us. Earth animals pay attention to you, too, don't they?"

"They let me touch them sometimes, even let me taste them. But if someone else is with me, they run away."

"You can train here to look after animals—to understand their bodies and keep them healthy."

"Ooloi work?"

"You can be trained to do it. Everything except controlling their breeding. And ooloi must mix their young."

Of course. You controlled both animals and people by controlling their reproduction—controlling it absolutely. But perhaps Akin could learn something that would be of use to the resisters. And he liked animals.

"Would I be able to work with shuttles or with Chkahichdahk?" he asked.

"If you choose to, after you change. There will be a need for people to do that kind of work during your generation."

"You told me once that people who work with the ship had to look different—really different."

"That change won't be needed on Earth for several generations."

"Working with animals won't affect the way I look at all?"

"Not at all."

"I want to do it then." After a few steps, he looked back at Tiikuchahk. "What will you do?"

"Find us an ooloi subadult," it said.

He would have walked faster if he had known the way. He wanted to get away from Tiikuchahk. The thought of it finding an ooloi—even an immature one—to unite the two of them, even briefly, was disturbing, almost disgusting.

"I meant what work will you do?"

"Gather knowledge. Collect information on Toaht and Akjai changes that have taken place since Dinso settled on Earth. I don't think I would be allowed to do much more. You know what your sex will be. It's as though you were never really eka. But I am."

"You won't be prevented from learning work," Dichaan said. "You won't be taken seriously, but no one will stop you from doing what you choose. And if you want help, people will help you."

"I'll gather knowledge," Tiikuchahk insisted. "Maybe while I'm doing that, I'll see some work that I want to do."

"This is Lo aj Toaht," Dichaan said, leading them into one of the vast living areas. Here grew great treelike structures bigger than any tree Akin had ever seen on Earth. Lilith had said they were as big as high-rise office buildings, but that had meant nothing to Akin. They were living quarters, storage space, internal support structures, and providers of food, clothing, and other desired substances such as paper, waterproof covering, and construction materials. They were not trees but parts of the ship. Their flesh was the same as the rest of the ship's flesh.

When Dichaan touched his head tentacles to what appeared to be the bark of one of them, it opened as walls opened at home, and inside was a familiar room, empty of resister-style furniture but containing several platforms grown for sitting or for holding containers of food. The walls and platforms were all a pale yellow-brown.

As the three of them entered, the wall on the opposite side of the room opened, and three Oankali Akin had never seen before came in.

Akin drew air over his tongue and his sense of smell told

him that the male and female newcomers were Lo—close relatives, in fact. The ooloi must be their mate. There was no scent of family familiarity to it at all as there would have been if it had been ooan Dichaan. These were not parents, then. But they were relatives. Dichaan's brother and sister and their ooloi mate, perhaps.

The adults came together silently, head and body tentacles tangling together, locking together in intense feeling. After a time, probably after feelings and communications had slowed, cooled to something a child could tolerate, they drew Ti-ikuchahk in, handling and examining it with great curiosity. It examined them as well and made their acquaintance. Akin envied it its head tentacles. When the adults released it and took him into their midst, he could taste only one of them at a time, and there was no time to savor them all as he wished. Children and resisters were easier to cope with.

Yet these people welcomed him. They could see themselves in him and see his alien Humanity. The latter fascinated them, and they chose to take the time to perceive themselves through his senses.

The ooloi was particularly fascinated by him. Taishokaht its name was—Jahtaishokahtlo lel Surohahwahj aj Toaht. He had never touched a Jah ooloi before. It was shorter and stockier than ooloi from the Kaal or Lo. In fact, it was built rather like Akin himself, although it was taller than Akin. Everyone was taller than Akin. There was a feeling of intensity and confidence to the ooloi and a feeling almost of humor—as though he amused it very much, but it liked him.

"You don't know what an intricate mix you are," it told him silently. "If you're the prototype for Human-born males, there are going to be a great many of us who settle for daughters only from our Human mates. And that would be a loss."

"There are several others now," Dichaan told it aloud. "Study him. Maybe you'll mix the first for Lo Toaht."

"I don't know whether I'd want to."

Akin, still in contact with it, broke the contact and drew back to look at it. It wanted to. It wanted to badly. "Study me all you want," he said. "But share what you learn with me as much as you can."

"Trade, Eka," it said with amusement. "I'll be interested to see how much you can perceive."

Akin was not sure he liked the ooloi. It had a soft, paper-dry voice and an attitude that irritated Akin. The ooloi did not care that Akin was clearly going to be male and was close to metamorphosis. To it, he was eka: sexless child. Child trying to make adult bargains. Amusing. But that was what Dichaan had promised Tiikuchahk. They would be helped and taught with a certain lack of seriousness. In a sense, they would be humored. Children who lived in the safety of the ship did not have to grow up as quickly as those on Earth. Except for young ooloi who underwent two metamorphoses with their subadult years between, everyone was allowed a long, easy childhood. Even the ooloi were not seriously challenged until they proved they were to be ooloi—until they reached the subadult stage. No one abducted them in infancy or carried them around by their arms and legs. No one threatened them. They did not have to keep themselves alive among well-meaning but ignorant resisters.

Akin looked at Dichaan. "How can it be good for me to be treated as though I were younger than I am?" he asked. "What lesson is condescension supposed to teach me about this group of my people?"

He would not have spoken so bluntly if Lilith had been with him. She insisted on more respect for adults. Dichaan, though, simply answered his questions as he had expected. "Teach them who you are. Now they only know what you are. Both of you." He focused for a moment on Tiikuchahk. "You're here to teach as well as to learn." Which was just about what Taishokaht had said, but Taishokaht had said it as though to a much younger child.

At that moment, for no reason he could understand, Tiikuchahk touched him, and they fell into their grating, dissonant near-synchronization.

"This is what we are, too," he said to Taishokaht—only to

hear the same words coming from Tiikuchahk. "This is what we need help with!"

The three Oankali tasted them, then drew back. The female, Suroh, drew her body tentacles tight against her and seemed to speak for all of them.

"We heard about that trouble. It's worse than I thought."

"It was wrong to separate them," Dichaan said softly.

Silence. What was there to say? The thing had been done by consensus years before. Adults of Earth and Chkahichdahk had made the decision.

"I know a Tiej family with an ooloi child," Suroh said. There could be no boy children, no girl children among the Oankali, but a subadult ooloi was often referred to as an ooloi child. Akin had heard the words all his life. Now adults would find an ooloi child for him and for Tiikuchahk. The thought made him shudder.

"My closest siblings have an ooloi child," Taishokaht said. "It's young, though. Just through its first metamorphosis."

"Too young," Dichaan said. "We need one who understands itself. Shall I stay and help choose?"

"We'll choose," the male said, smoothing his body tentacles flat against his skin. "There's more than one problem to be solved here. You've brought us something very interesting."

"I've brought you my children," Dichaan said quietly.

At once the three of them touched him, reassured him directly, drawing Akin and Tiikuchahk in to let him know that they had a home here, that they would be cared for.

Akin wanted desperately to go back to his true home. When food was served, he did not eat. Food did not interest him. When Dichaan left, it was all Akin could do to keep himself from following and demanding to be taken home to Earth. Dichaan would not have taken him. And no one present would have understood why he was making the gesture. Nikanj would understand, but Nikanj was back on Earth. Akin looked at the Toaht ooloi and saw that it was paying no attention to him.

Alone, and more lonely than he had been since the raiders abducted him, he lay down on his platform and went to sleep.

6

"Are you afraid?" Taishokaht asked. "Humans are always afraid of them."

"I'm not afraid," Akin said. They were in a large, dark, open area. The walls glowed softly with the body heat of Chkahichdahk. There was only body heat to see by here, deep inside the ship. Living quarters and travel corridors were above—or Akin thought of their direction as above. He had passed through areas where gravity was less, even where it was absent. Words like *up* and *down* were meaningless, but Akin could not keep himself from thinking them.

He could see Taishokaht by its body heat—less than his own and greater than that of Chkahichdahk. And he could see the other person in the room.

"I'm not afraid," he repeated. "Can this one hear?"

"No. Let it touch you. Then taste the limb it offers."

Akin stepped toward what his sense of smell told him was an ooloi. His sight told him it was large and caterpillarlike, covered with smooth plates that made a pattern of bright and dark as body heat escaped between the plates rather than through them. From what Akin had heard, this ooloi could seal itself within its shell and lose little or no air or body heat. It could slow its body processes and induce suspended animation so that it could survive even drifting in space. Others like it had been the first to explore the war-ruined Earth.

It had mouth parts vaguely like those of some terrestrial insects. Even if it had possessed ears and vocal cords, it could not have formed anything close to Human or Oankali speech.

Yet it was as Oankali as Dichaan or Nikanj. It was as Oankali as any intelligent being constructed by an ooloi to incorporate the Oankali organelle within its cells. As Oankali as Akin himself.

It was what the Oankali had been, one trade before they found Earth, one trade before they used their long memories and their vast store of genetic material to construct speaking, hearing, bipedal children. Children they hoped would seem more acceptable to Human tastes. The spoken language, an ancient revival, had been built in genetically. The first Human captives awakened had been used to stimulate the first bipedal children to talk—to "remember" how to talk.

Now, most of the caterpillarlike Oankali were Akjai like the ooloi that stood before Akin. It or its children would leave the vicinity of Earth physically unchanged, carrying nothing of Earth or Humanity with it except knowledge and memory.

The Akjai extended one slender forelimb. Akin took the limb between his hands as though it were a sensory arm—and it seemed to be just that, although Akin learned in the first instant of contact that this ooloi had six sensory limbs instead of only two.

Its language of touch was the one Akin had first felt before his birth. The familiarity of this comforted him, and he tasted the Akjai, eager to understand the mixture of alienness and familiarity.

There was a long period of getting to know the ooloi and understanding that it was as interested in him as he was in it. At some point—Akin was not certain when—Taishokaht joined them. Akin had to use sight to find out for certain whether Taishokaht had touched him or touched the Akjai. There was an utter blending of the two ooloi—greater than any blending Akin had perceived between paired siblings. This, he thought, must be what adults achieved when they reached for a consensus on some controversial subject. But if it was, how did they continue to think at all as individuals? Taishokaht and Kohj, the Akjai, seemed completely blended, one nervous system communicating within itself as any nervous system did.

"I don't understand," he communicated.

And, just for an instant, they showed him, brought him into that incredible unity. He could not even manage terror until the moment had ended.

How did they not lose themselves? How was it possible to break apart again? It was as though two containers of water had been poured together, then separated—each molecule returned to its original container.

He must have signaled this. The Akjai responded. "Even at your stage of growth, Eka, you can perceive molecules. We perceive subatomic particles. Making and breaking this contact is no more difficult for us than clasping and releasing hands is for Humans."

"Is that because you're ooloi?" Akin asked.

"Ooloi perceive and, within reproductive cells, manipulate. Males and females only perceive. You'll understand soon."

"Can I learn to care for animals while I'm so . . . limited?"

"You can learn a little. You can begin. First, though, because you don't have adult perception, you must learn to trust us. What we let you feel, briefly, wasn't such a deep union. We use it for teaching or for reaching a consensus. You must learn to tolerate it a little early. Can you do that?"

Akin shuddered. "I don't know."

"I'll try to help you. Shall I?"

"If you don't, I won't be able to do it. It scares me."

"I know that. You won't be so afraid now."

It was delicately controlling his nervous system, stimulating the release of certain endorphins in his brain—in effect, causing him to drug himself into pleasurable relaxation and acceptance. His body was refusing to allow him to panic. As he was enfolded in a union that felt more like drowning than joining, he kept jerking toward panic only to have the emotion smothered in something that was almost pleasure. He felt as though something were crawling down his throat and he could not manage a reflexive cough to bring it up.

The Akjai could have helped him more, could have suppressed all discomfort. It did not, Akin realized, because it was already teaching. Akin strove to control his own feelings, strove to accept the self-dissolving closeness.

Gradually, he did accept it. He discovered he could, with a shift of attention, perceive as the Akjai perceived—a silent, mainly tactile world. It could see—see far more than Akin could in the dim room. It could see most forms of electromagnetic radiation. It could look at a wall and see great differences in the flesh, where Akin saw none. And it knew—could see—the ship's circulatory system. It could see, somehow, the nearest outside plates. As it happened, the nearest outside plates were some distance above their heads where Akin's Earth-trained senses told him the sky should be. The Akjai knew all this and more simply by sight. Tactilely, though, it was in constant contact with Chkahichdahk. If it chose to, it could know what the ship was doing in any part of the huge shipbody at any time. In fact, it did know. It simply did not care because nothing required its attention. All the many small things that had gone wrong or that seemed about to go wrong were being attended to by others. The Akjai could know this through the contact of its many limbs with the floor.

The startling thing was, Taishokaht knew it, too. The thirty-two toes of its two bare feet told it exactly what the Akjai's limbs told it. He had never noticed Oankali doing this at home. He had certainly never done it himself with his very Human, five-toed feet.

He was no longer afraid.

No matter how closely he was joined to the two ooloi, he was aware of himself. He was equally aware of them and their bodies and their sensations. But, somehow, they were still themselves, and he was still himself. He felt as though he were a floating, disembodied mind, like the souls some resisters spoke of in their churches, as though he looked from some impossible angle and saw everything, including his own body as it leaned against the Akjai. He tried to move his left hand and saw it move. He tried to move one of the Akjai's limbs, and once he understood the nerves and musculature, the limb moved.

"You see?" the Akjai said, its touches feeling oddly like Akin touching his own skin. "People don't lose themselves. You can do this."

He could. He examined the Akjai's body, comparing it to Taishokaht's and to his own. "How can Dinso and Toaht people give up such strong, versatile bodies to trade with Humans?" he asked.

Both ooloi were amused. "You only ask that because you don't know your own potential," the Akjai told him. "Now I'll show you the structure of a tilio. You don't know it even as completely as a child can. When you understand it, I'll show you the things that go wrong with it and what you can do about them."

7

Akin lived with the Akjai as it traveled around the ship. The Akjai taught him, withholding nothing that he could absorb. He learned to understand not only the animals of Chkahich-dahk and Earth, but the plants. When he asked for information on the resisters' bodies, the Akjai found several visiting Dinso ooloi. It learned in a matter of minutes all that they could teach it. Then it fed the information to Akin in a long series of lessons.

"Now you know more than you realize," the Akjai said when it had given its information on Humans. "You have information you won't even be able to use until after your own metamorphosis."

"I know more than I thought I could learn," Akin said. "I

know enough to heal ulcers in a resister's stomach or cuts or puncture wounds in flesh and in organs."

"Eka, I don't think they'll let you."

"Yes, they will. At least, they will until I change. Some will."

"What do you want for them, Eka? What would you give them?"

"What you have. What you are." Akin sat with his back against the Akjai's curved side. It could touch him with several limbs and give him one sensory limb to signal into. "I want a Human Akjai," he told it.

"I've heard that you did. But your kind can't exist alongside them. Not separately. You know that."

Akin took the slender, glowing limb from his mouth and looked at it. He liked the Akjai. It had been his teacher for months now. It had taken him into parts of the ship that most people never saw. It had enjoyed his fascination and deliberately suggested new things that he might be interested in learning. He was, it said, more energetic than the older students it had had.

It was a friend. Perhaps he could talk to it, reach it as he had not been able to reach his family. Perhaps he could trust it. He tasted the limb again.

"I want to make a place for them," he said. "I know what will happen to Earth. But there are other worlds. We could change the second one or the fourth one—make one of them more like Earth. A few of us could do it. I've heard that there is nothing living on either world."

"There's nothing living there. The fourth world could be more easily transformed than the second."

"It could be done?"

"Yes."

"It was so obvious. . . . I thought I might be wrong, thought I had missed something."

"Time, Akin."

"Get things started and turn them over to the resisters. They need metal, machinery, things they can control."

"No."

Akin focused his whole attention on the Akjai. It was not saying, no, the Humans could not have their machines. Its signals did not communicate that at all. It was saying, no, Humans did not need machines.

"We can make it possible for them to live on the fourth world," it said. "They wouldn't *need* machines. If they wanted them, they would have to build them themselves."

"I would help. I would do whatever was needed."

"When you change, you'll want to mate."

"I know. But—"

"You don't know. The urge is stronger than you can understand now."

"It's . . ." He projected amusement. "It's pretty strong now. I know it will be different after metamorphosis. If I have to mate, I have to mate. I'll find people who'll work with me on this. There must be others that I can convince."

"Find them now."

Startled, Akin said nothing for a moment. Finally he asked, "Do you mean I'm close to metamorphosis now?"

"Closer than you think. But that isn't what I meant."

"You agree with me that it can be done? The resisters can be transplanted? Their Human-to-Human fertility can be restored?"

"It's possible if you can get a consensus. But if you get a consensus, you may find that you've chosen your life's work."

"Wasn't that work chosen for me years ago?"

The Akjai hesitated. "I know about that. The Akjai had no part in the decision to leave you so long with the resisters."

"I didn't think you had. I've never been able to talk about it to anyone I felt had taken part—who had chosen to break me from my nearest sibling."

"Yet you'll do the work that was chosen for you?"

"I will. But for the Humans and for the Human part of me. Not for the Oankali."

"Eka . . ."

"Shall I show you what I can feel, *all* I can feel with Tiikuchahk, my nearest sibling? Shall I show you all I've ever had with it? All Oankali, all constructs have something that Oankali and constructs came together and decided to deny me."

"Show me."

Again Akin was startled. But why? What Oankali would decline a new sensation? He remembered for it all the jarring, tearing dissonance of his relationship with Tiikuchahk. He duplicated the sensations in the Akjai's body along with the revulsion they made him feel and the need he felt to avoid this person whom he should have been closest to.

"I think it almost wants to be male to avoid any sexual feelings for me," he finished.

"Keeping you separated was a mistake," the Akjai agreed. "I can see now why it was done, but it was a mistake."

Only Akin's family had ever said that before. They had said it because he was one of them, and it hurt them to see him hurt. It hurt them to see the family unbalanced by paired siblings who had failed to pair. People who had never had close siblings or whose closest siblings had died did not damage the balance as much as close siblings who had failed to bond.

"You should go back to your relatives," the Akjai said. "Make them find a young ooloi for you and your sibling. You should not go through metamorphosis with so much pain cutting you off from your sibling."

"Ti was talking about finding a young ooloi before I left to study with you. I don't think I could stand to share an ooloi with it."

"You will," the Akjai said. "You must. Go back now, Eka. I can feel what you're feeling, but it doesn't matter. Some things hurt. Go back and reconcile with your sibling. Then come to me and I'll find new teachers for you—people who know the processes of changing a cold, dry, lifeless world into something Humans might survive on."

The Akjai straightened its body and broke contact with him. When Akin stood still, looking at it, not wanting to leave it, it turned and left him, opening the floor beneath itself and surging into the hole it had made. Akin let the hole seal itself, knowing that once it was sealed he would not find the Akjai again until it wished to be found.

8

The ooloi subadult was a relative of Taishokaht. Jahdehki-aht, its personal name was at this stage of its life. Dehkiaht. It had been living with Taishokaht's family and Tiikuchahk, waiting for him to return from the Akjai.

The young ooloi looked sexless but did not smell sexless. It would not develop sensory arms until its second metamorphosis. That made its scent all the more startling and disturbing.

Akin had never been aroused by the scent of an ooloi before. He liked them, but only resister and construct women had interested him sexually. What could an immature ooloi do for anyone sexually, anyway?

Akin took a step back the moment he caught the ooloi scent. He looked at Tiikuchahk who was with the ooloi, who had introduced it eagerly.

There was no one else in the room. Akin and Dehkiaht stared at each other.

"You aren't what I thought," it whispered. "Ti told me, showed me . . . and I still didn't understand."

"What didn't you understand?" Akin asked, taking another step backward. He did not want to feel so drawn to anyone who was clearly already on good terms with Tiikuchahk.

"That you are a kind of subadult yourself," Dehkiaht said. "Your growth stage now is more like mine than like Ti's."

That was something no one had said before. It almost distracted him from the ooloi's scent. "I'm not fertile yet, Nikanj says."

"Neither am I. But it's so obvious with ooloi that no one could make a mistake."

To Akin's amazement, he laughed. Just as abruptly, he sobered. "I don't know how this works."

Silence.

"I didn't want it to work before. I do now." He did not look at Tiikuchahk. He could not avoid looking at the ooloi, although he feared it would see that his motives for wanting success had little to do with it or Tiikuchahk. He had never felt as naked as he did before this immature ooloi. He did not know what to do or say.

It occurred to him that he was reacting exactly as he had the first time he realized a resister woman was trying to seduce him.

He took a deep breath, smiled, and shook his head. He sat down on a platform. "I'm reacting very Humanly to an un-Human thing," he said. "To your scent. If you can do anything to suppress it, I wish you would. It's confusing the hell out of me."

The ooloi smoothed its body tentacles and folded itself onto a platform. "I didn't know constructs talked about hell."

"We say what we've grown up hearing. Ti, what does its scent do to you?"

"I like it," Tiikuchahk said. "It makes me not mind that you're in the room."

Akin tried to consider this through the distracting scent. "It makes me hardly notice that you're in the room."

"See?"

"But . . . It . . . I don't want to feel like this all the time if I can't do anything about it."

"You're the only one here who *could* do anything about it," Dehkiaht said.

Akin longed to be back with his Akjai teacher, an adult ooloi who had never made him feel this way. No adult ooloi had made him feel this way.

Dehkiaht touched him.

He had not noticed the ooloi coming closer. Now he

jumped. He felt himself more eager than ever for a satisfaction the ooloi could not give. Knowing this, he almost pushed Dehkiaht away in frustration. But Dehkiaht was ooloi. It did have that incredible scent. He could not push it or hit it. Instead, he twisted away from it. It had touched him only with its hand, but even that was too much. He had moved across the room to an outside wall before he could stop. The ooloi, clearly surprised, only watched him.

"You don't have any idea what you're doing, do you?" he said to it. He was panting a little.

"I think I don't," it admitted. "And I can't control my scent yet. Maybe I can't help you."

"No!" Tiikuchahk said sharply. "The adults said you could help—and you do help me."

"But I hurt Akin. I don't know how to stop hurting him."

"Touch him. Understand him the way you've understood me. Then you'll know how."

Tiikuchahk's voice stopped Akin from urging the ooloi to go. Tiikuchahk sounded . . . not just frightened but desperate. It was his sibling, as tormented by the situation as he was. And it was a child. Even more a child than he was—younger and truly eka.

"All right," he said unhappily. "Touch me, Dehkiaht. I'll hold still."

It held still itself, watching him silently. He had almost injured it. If he had fled from it only a little less quickly, he would have caused it a great deal of pain. And it probably would have stung him reflexively and caused him a great deal of pain. It needed more than Akin's words to assure it that he would not do such a thing again.

He made himself walk over to it. Its scent made him want to run to it and grab it. Its immaturity and its connection with Tiikuchahk made him want to run the other way. Somehow, he crossed the room to it.

"Lie down," it told him. "I'll help you sleep. When I'm finished, I'll know whether I can help you in any other way."

Akin lay down on the platform, eager for the relief of sleep.

The light touches of the ooloi's head tentacles were an almost unendurable stimulant, and sleep was not as quick in coming as it should have been. He realized, finally, that his state of arousal was making sleep impossible.

The ooloi seemed to realize this at the same time. It did something Akin was not quick enough to catch, and Akin was abruptly no longer aroused. Then he was no longer awake.

9

Akin awoke alone.

He got up feeling slightly drowsy but unchanged and wandered through the Lo Toaht dwelling, looking for Tiikuchahk, for Dehkiaht, for anyone. He found no one until he went outside. There, people went about their business as usual, their surroundings looking like a gentle, incredibly well-maintained forest. True trees did not grow as large as the ship's treelike projections, but the illusion of rolling, forested land was inescapable. It was, Akin thought, too tame, too planned. No grazing here for exploring children. The ship gave food when asked. Once it was taught how to synthesize a food, it never forgot. There were no bananas or papayas or pineapples to pick, no cassava to pull, no sweet potatoes to dig, no growing, living things except appendages of the ship. Perfect "sweet potatoes" could be made to grow on the pseudotrees if an Oankali or a construct adult asked it of Chkahichdahk.

He looked up at the limbs above him and saw that nothing other than the usual hairlike, green, oxygen-producing tentacles hung from the huge pseudotrees.

Why was he thinking about such things? Homesickness? Where were Dehkiaht and Tiikuchahk? Why had they left him?

He put his face to the pseudotree he had emerged from and probed with his tongue, allowing the ship to identify him so that it would give him any message they had left.

The ship complied. "Wait," the message said. Nothing more. They had not abandoned him, then. Most likely, Dehkiaht had taken what it had learned from Akin to some adult ooloi for interpretation. When it came back to him it would probably still smell tormenting. An adult would have to change it—or change him. It would have been simpler for adults to find a solution for him and Tiikuchahk directly.

He went back in to wait and knew at once that Dehkiaht, at least, had already returned.

He could have found it without sight. In fact, its scent overwhelmed his senses so completely that he could hardly see, hear, or feel anything. This was worse than before.

He discovered that his hands were on the ooloi, grasping it as though he expected it to be taken from him, as though it were his own personal property.

Then, gradually, he was able to let go of it, able to think and focus on something other than its enveloping scent. He realized he was lying down again. Lying alongside Dehkiaht, pressed against it, and comfortable.

Content.

Dehkiaht's scent was still interesting, still enticing, but no longer overwhelming. He wanted to stay near the ooloi, felt possessive of it, but was not so totally focused on it. He liked it. He had felt this way about resister women who let him make love to them and who saw him as something other than a container of sperm they hoped might prove fertile.

He breathed deeply and enjoyed the many light touches of Dehkiaht's head and body tentacles.

"Better," he whispered. "Will I stay this way, or will you have to keep readjusting me?"

"If you stayed this way, you'd never do any work," the ooloi said, flattening its free tentacles in amusement. "This is good, though. Especially after the other. Tiikuchahk is here."

"Ti?" Akin raised his head to look over the ooloi's body. "I didn't . . . I don't feel you."

It gave him a Human smile. "I feel you, but no more than I do anyone else I'm near."

Feeling oddly bereft, Akin reached over Dehkiaht to touch it.

Dehkiaht seized his hand and put it back at his side.

Surprised, Akin focused all his senses on it. "Why should you care whether I touch Ti? You aren't mature. We aren't mated."

"Yes. I do care, though. It would be better if you don't touch each other for a while."

"I . . . I don't want to be bound to you."

"I couldn't bind you. That's why you confused me so. I went back to my parents to show them what I had learned about you and ask their advice. They say you can't be bound. You were not constructed to be bound."

Akin moved against Dehkiaht, wanting to move closer, welcoming the inadequate strength arm the ooloi put around him. It was not an Oankali thing to put strength arms around people or to caress with strength hands. Someone must have told Dehkiaht that Humans and constructs found such gestures comforting.

"I've been told that I would wander," he said. "I wander now when I'm on Earth, but I always come home. I'm afraid that when I'm adult, I won't have a home."

"Lo will be your home," Tiikuchahk said.

"Not the way it will be yours." It would almost certainly be female and become part of a family like the one he had been raised in. Or it would mate with a construct male like him or his Oankali-born brothers. Even then, it would have an ooloi and children to live with. But who would he live with? His parents' home would remain the only true home he knew.

"When you're adult," Dehkiaht said, "you'll feel what you can do. You'll feel what you want to do. It will seem good to you."

"How would you know!" Akin demanded bitterly.

"You aren't flawed. I noticed even before I went to my parents that there was a wholeness to you—a strong wholeness. I don't know whether you'll be what your parents wanted you to be, but whatever you become, you'll be complete. You'll have within yourself everything you need to content yourself. Just follow what seems right to you."

"Walk away from mates and children?"

"Only if it seems right to you."

"Some Human men do it. It doesn't seem right to me, though."

"Do what seems right. Even now."

"I'll tell you what seems right to me. You both should know. It's what seemed right to me since I was a baby. And it will be right, no matter how my mating situation turns out."

"Why should we know?"

This was not the question Akin had expected. He lay still, silent, thoughtful. Why, indeed? "If you let go of me, will I go out of control again?"

"No."

"Let go, then. Let me see if I still want to tell you."

Dehkiaht released him, and he sat up, looking down at the two of them. Tiikuchahk looked as though it belonged beside the ooloi. And Dehkiaht looked . . . felt frighteningly necessary to him, too. Looking at it made him want to lie down again. He imagined returning to Earth without Dehkiaht, leaving it to another pair of mates. They would mature and keep it, and the scent of them and the feel of them would encourage its body to mature quickly. When it was mature, they would be a family. A Toaht family if it stayed aboard the ship.

It would mix construct children for other people.

Akin got down from the bed platform and sat beside it. It was easier to think down there. Before today, he had never had sexual feelings for an ooloi—had not had any idea how such feelings would affect him. The ooloi said it could not bind him to it. Adults apparently wanted to be bound by an ooloi—to be joined and woven into a family. Akin felt confused about what he wanted, but he knew he did not want Dehkiaht stimulated to maturity by other people. He wanted it on Earth with him. Yet he did not want to be bound to it. How much of what he felt was chemical—simply a result of Dehkiaht's provoking scent and its ability to comfort his body?

"Humans are freer to decide what they want," he said softly.

"They only think they are," Dehkiaht replied.

Yes. Lilith was not free. Sudden freedom would have terrified her, although sometimes she seemed to want it. Sometimes she stretched the bonds between herself and the family. She wandered. She still wandered. But she always came home. Tino would probably kill himself if he were freed. But what about the resisters? They did terrible things to each other because they could not have children. But before the war—during the war—they had done terrible things to each other even though they could have children. The Human Contradiction held them. Intelligence at the service of hierarchical behavior. They were not free. All he could do for them, if he could do anything, was to let them be bound in their own ways. Perhaps next time their intelligence would be in balance with their hierarchical behavior, and they would not destroy themselves.

"Will you come to Earth with us?" he asked Dehkiaht.

"No," Dehkiaht said softly.

Akin stood up and looked at it. Neither it nor Tiikuchahk had moved. "No?"

"You can't ask for Tiikuchahk, and Tiikuchahk doesn't know yet whether it will be male or female. So it can't ask for itself."

"I didn't ask you to promise to mate with us when we're all adult. I asked you to come to Earth. Stay with us for now. Later, when I'm adult, I intend to have work that will interest you."

"What work?"

"Giving life to a dead world, then giving that world to the resisters."

"The resisters? But—"

"I want to establish them as Akjai Humans."

"They won't survive."

"Perhaps not."

"There's no perhaps. They won't survive their Contradic-tion."

"Then let them fail. Let them have the freedom to do that, at least."

Silence.

"Let me show them to you—not just their interesting bodies and the way they are here and in the trade villages on Earth. Let me show them to you as they are when there are no Oankali around."

"Why?"

"Because you should at least know them before you deny them the assurance that Oankali always claim for themselves." He climbed onto the platform and looked at Tiikuchahk. "Will you take part?" he asked it.

"Yes," it said solemnly. "This will be the first time since be-fore I was born that I'll be able to take impressions from you without things going wrong."

Akin lay down next to the ooloi. He drew close to it, his mouth against the flesh of its neck, its many head and body tentacles linked with him and with Tiikuchahk. Then, care-fully, in the manner of a storyteller, he gave it the experience of his abduction, captivity, and conversion. All that he had felt, he made it feel. He did what he had not known he could do. He overwhelmed it so that for a time it was, itself, both cap-tive and convert. He did to it what the abandonment of the Oankali had done to him in his infancy. He made the ooloi un-derstand on an utterly personal level what he had suffered and what he had come to believe. Until he had finished, neither it nor Tiikuchahk could escape.

But when he had finished, when he had let him go, they both left him. They said nothing. They simply got up and left him.

10

The Akjai spoke to the people for Akin. Akin had not realized it would do this—an Akjai ooloi telling other Oankali that there must be Akjai Humans. It spoke through the ship and had the ship signal the trade villages on Earth. It asked for a consensus and then showed the Oankali and construct people of Chkahichdahk what Akin had shown Dehkiaht and Tiikuchahk.

As soon as the experience ended, people began objecting to its intensity, objecting to being so overwhelmed, objecting to the idea that this could have been the experience of such a young child . . .

No one objected to the idea of a Human Akjai. For some time, no one mentioned it at all.

Akin perceived what he could through the Akjai, drawing back whenever the transmission was too fast or too intense. Drawing back felt like coming up for air. He found himself gasping, almost exhausted each time. But each time he went back, needing to feel what the Akjai felt, needing to follow the responses of the people. It was rare for children to take part in a consensus for more than a few seconds. No child who was not deeply concerned would want to take part for longer.

Akin could feel the people avoiding the subject of Akjai Humans. He did not understand their reactions to it: a turning away, a warding off, a denial, a revulsion. It confused him, and he tried to communicate his confusion to the Akjai.

The Akjai seemed at first not to notice his wordless questioning. It was fully occupied with its communication with the people. But suddenly, gently, it clasped Akin to it so that he would not break contact. It broadcast his bewilderment, letting people know they were experiencing the emotions of a construct child—a child too Human to understand their reactions naturally. A child too Oankali and too near adulthood to disregard.

They feared for him, that this search for a consensus would be too much for a child. The Akjai let them see that it was protecting him but that his feelings must be taken into account. The Akjai focused on the adult constructs aboard the ship. It pointed out that the Human-born among them had had to learn the Oankali understanding of life itself as a thing of inexpressible value. A thing beyond trade. Life could be changed, changed utterly. But not destroyed. The Human species could cease to exist independently, blending itself into the Oankali. Akin, it said, was still learning this.

Someone else cut in: Could Humans be given back their independent lives and allowed to ride their Contradiction to their deaths? To give them back their independent existence, their fertility, their own territory was to help them breed a new population only to destroy it a second time.

Many answers blended through the ship into one: "We've given them what we can of the things they value—long life, freedom from disease, freedom to live as they wish. We can't help them create more life only to destroy it."

"Then let me and those who choose to work with me do it," Akin told them through the Akjai. "Give us the tools we need, and let us give the Humans the things they need. They'll have a new world to settle—a difficult world even after we've prepared it. Perhaps by the time they've learned the skills and bred for the strengths to settle it, the Contradiction will be less. Perhaps this time their intelligence will stop them from destroying themselves."

There was nothing. A neurosensory equivalent of silence. Denial.

He reached through the Akjai once more, struggling against sudden exhaustion. Only the Akjai's efforts kept him conscious. "Look at the Human-born among you," he told them. "If your flesh knows you've done all you can for Humanity, their flesh should know as mine does that you've done almost nothing. Their flesh should know that resister Humans must survive as a separate, self-sufficient species. Their flesh should know that Humanity must live!"

He stopped. He could have gone on, but it was time to stop. If he had not said enough, shown them enough, if he had not guessed accurately about the Human-born, he had failed. He must try again later when he was an adult, or he must find people who would help him in spite of the majority opinion. That would be difficult, perhaps impossible. But it must be tried.

As he realized he was about to be cut off, shielded by the Akjai, he felt confusion among the people. Confusion, dissension.

He had reached some of them, perhaps caused Human-born constructs to start to think, start to examine their Human heritage as they had not before. Toaht constructs could have little reason to pay close attention to their own Humanity. He would go to them if opinion went against him. He would seek them out and teach them about the people they were part of. He would go to them even if opinion did not go against him. Aboard the ship, they were the group most likely to help him.

"Sleep," the Akjai advised him. "You're too young for all this. I'll argue for you now."

"Why?" he asked. He was almost asleep, but the question was like an itch in his mind. "Why do you care so when my own kin-group doesn't care?"

"Because you're right," the Akjai said. "If I were Human, little construct, I would be a resister myself. All people who know what it is to end should be allowed to continue if they can continue. Sleep."

The Akjai coiled part of its body around him so that he lay in a broad curve of living flesh. He slept.

11

Tiikuchahk and Dehkiaht were with him when he awoke. The Akjai was there, too, but he realized it had not been with him continually. He had a memory of it going away and coming back with Tiikuchahk and Dehkiaht. As Akin took in his surroundings, he saw the Akjai draw Dehkiaht into an alarming embrace, lifting the ooloi child and clasping it in over a dozen limbs.

"They wanted to learn about one another," Tiikuchahk said. These were the first words it had spoken to him since he caused it to experience his memories.

He sat up and focused on it questioningly.

"You shouldn't have been able to grab us and hold us that way," it said. "Dehkiaht and its parents say no child should be able to do that."

"I didn't know I could do it."

"Dehkiaht's parents say it's a teaching thing—the way adults teach subadult ooloi sometimes when the ooloi have to learn something they aren't really ready for. They've never heard of a subadult male."

"But Dehkiaht says that's what I am."

"It is what you are. Human-born construct females could be called subadults too, I guess. But you're a first. Again."

"I'm sorry you didn't like what I did. I'll try not to do it again."

"Don't. Not to me. The Akjai says you learned it here."

"I must have—without realizing it." He paused, watching Tiikuchahk. It was sitting next to him in apparent comfort. "Is it all right between us?"

"Seems to be."

"Will you help me?"

"I don't know." It focused narrowly on him. "I don't know what I am yet. I don't even know what I want to be."

"Do you want Dehkiaht?"

"I like it. It helped us, and I feel better when it's around. If I were like you, I would probably want to keep it."

"I do."

"It wants you, too. It says you're the most interesting person it's known. I think it will help you."

"If you become female, you could join us—mate with it."

"And you?"

He looked away from it. "I can't imagine how I would feel to have it and not you. What I've felt of it was . . . partly you."

"I don't know. No one knows yet what I'll be. I can't feel what you feel yet."

He managed to stop himself from arguing. Tiikuchahk was right. He still occasionally thought of it as female, but its body was neuter. It could not feel as he did. He was amazed at his own feelings, although they were natural. Now that Tiikuchahk was no longer a source of irritation and confusion, he could begin to feel about it the way people tended to feel about their closest siblings. He did not know whether he truly wanted to have it as one of his mates—or whether a wandering male of the kind he was supposed to be could be said to have mates. But the idea of mating with it felt right, now. It, Dehkiaht, and himself. That was the way it should be.

"Do you know what the people have decided?" he asked.

Tiikuchahk shook its head Humanly. "No."

After a time, Dehkiaht and the Akjai separated, and Dehkiaht climbed to the Akjai's long, broad back.

"Come join us," Dehkiaht called.

Akin got up and started toward it. Behind him, though, Tiikuchahk did not move.

Akin stopped, turned to face it. "Are you afraid?" he asked.

"Yes."

"You know the Akjai won't hurt you."

"It will hurt me if it thinks hurting me is necessary."

That was true. The Akjai had hurt Akin in order to teach him—and had taught Akin much more than he realized.

"Come anyway," Akin said. He wanted to touch Tiikuchahk now, draw it to him, comfort it. He had never before wanted to do such a thing. And in spite of the impulse, he found he was not willing to touch it now. It would not want him to. Dehkiaht would not want him to.

He went back to it and sat next to it. "I'll wait for you," he said.

It focused on him, head tentacles knotting miserably. "Join them," it said.

He said nothing. He sat with it, comfortably patient, wondering whether it feared the joining because it might find itself making decisions it did not feel ready to make.

Dehkiaht simply lay down on the Akjai's back, and the Akjai squatted, resting on its belly, waiting. Humans said no one knew how to wait better than the Oankali. Humans, perhaps remembering their earlier short life spans, tended to hurry without reason.

He did not know how much time had passed when Tiikuchahk stood up and he roused and stood up beside it. He focused on it, and when it moved, he followed it to the Akjai and Dehkiaht.

The Akjai drew its body into the familiar curve and welcomed Tiikuchahk and Akin to sit or lie against it. The Akjai gave each a sensory arm and gave Dehkiaht one too when it slid down one of the plates to settle beside them.

Now Akin learned for the first time what the people had decided. He felt now what he had not been able to feel before. That the people saw him as something they had helped to make.

He was intended to decide the fate of the resisters. He was intended to make the decision the Dinso and the Toaht could not make. He was intended to see what must be done and convince others.

He had been abandoned to the resisters when they took him so that he could learn them as no adult could, as no Oankaliborn construct could, as no construct who did not look quite Human could. Everyone knew the resisters' bodies, but no one knew their thinking as Akin did. No one except other Humans. And they had not been allowed to convince Oankali to do the profoundly immoral, antilife thing that Akin had decided must be done. The people had suspected what he would decide—had feared it. They would not have accepted it if he had not been able to stir confusion and some agreement among constructs, both Oankali-born and Human-born.

They had deliberately rested the fate of the resisters—the fate of the Human species—on him.

Why? Why not on one of the Human-born females? Some of them were adults before he was born.

The Akjai supplied him with the answer before he was aware of having asked the question. "You're more Oankali than you think, Akin—and far more Oankali than you look. Yet you're very Human. You skirt as close to the Contradiction as anyone has dared to go. You're as much of them as you can be and as much of us as your ooan dared make you. That leaves you with your own contradiction. It also made you the most likely person to choose for the resisters—quick death or long, slow death."

"Or life," Akin protested.

"No."

"A chance for life."

"Only for a while."

"You're certain of that . . . and yet you spoke for me?"

"I'm Akjai. How can I deny another people the security of an Akjai group? Even though for this people it's a cruelty. Understand that, Akin; it *is* a cruelty. You and those who help you will give them the tools to create a civilization that will destroy itself as certainly as the pull of gravity will keep their new world in orbit around its sun."

Akin felt absolutely no sign of doubt or uncertainty in the Akjai. It meant what it was saying. It believed it knew factually that Humanity was doomed. Now or later.

"It's your life work to decide for them," the Akjai continued, "and then to act on your decision. The people will allow you to do what you believe is right. But you're not to do it in ignorance."

Akin shook his head. He could feel the attention of Tiikuchahk and Dehkiaht on him. He thought for some time,
trying to digest the indigestible certainty of the Akjai. He had
trusted it, and it had not failed him. It did not lie. It could be
mistaken, but only if all Oankali were mistaken. Its certainty
was an Oankali certainty. A certainty of the flesh. They had
read Human genes and reviewed Human behavior. They knew
what they knew.

Yet . . .

"I can't not do it," he said. "I keep trying to decide not to
do it, and I can't."

"I'll help you do it," Dehkiaht said at once.

"Find a female mate that you can be especially close to," the
Akjai told it. "Akin will not stay with you. You know that."

"I know."

Now the Akjai turned its attention to Tiikuchahk. "You are
not as much a child as you want to be."

"I don't know what I'll be," it said.

"What do you feel about the resisters?"

"They took Akin. They hurt him, and they hurt me. I don't
want to care about them."

"But you do care."

"I don't want to."

"You're part Human. You shouldn't carry such feelings for
such a large group of Humans."

Silence.

"I've found teachers for Akin and Dehkiaht. They'll teach
you, too. You'll learn to prepare a lifeless world for life."

"I don't want to."

"What do you want to do?"

"I . . . don't know."

"Then do this. The knowledge won't harm you if you decide
not to use it. You need to do this. You've taken refuge too long
in doing nothing at all."

And that was that. Somehow, Tiikuchahk could not bring itself to go on arguing with the Akjai. Akin was reminded that
in spite of the way the Akjai looked, it was an ooloi. With

scent and touch and neural stimulation, ooloi manipulated people. He focused warily on Dehkiaht, wondering whether he would know when it began to move him with things other than words. The idea disturbed him, and for the first time, he looked forward to wandering.

IV

HOME

1

For a time, Earth seemed wild and strange to Akin—a profusion of life almost frightening in its complexity. On Chkahich-dahk, there was only a potential profusion stored in people's memories and in seed, cell, and gene-print banks. Earth was still a huge biological bank itself, balancing its own ecology with little Oankali help.

Akin could do nothing on the fourth planet—Mars, the Humans called it—until after his metamorphosis. His training too had gone as far as it could until his metamorphosis. His teachers had sent him home. Tiikuchahk, now at peace with him and with itself, seemed glad to come home. And Dehkiaht had simply attached itself to Akin. When Dichaan came for Akin and Tiikuchahk, even he did not suggest leaving Dehkiaht behind.

Once they reached Earth, however, Akin had to get away from Dehkiaht, away from everyone for a while. He wanted to see some of his resister friends before his metamorphosis—before he changed beyond recognition. He had to let them know what had happened, what he had to offer them. Also, he needed respected Human allies. He first thought of people he had visited during his wanderings—men and women who knew him as a small, nearly Human man. But he did not want to see them. Not yet. He felt drawn toward another place—a place where the people would hardly know him. He had not been there since his third year. He would go to Phoenix—to Gabe and Tate Rinaldi, where his obsession with the resisters had begun.

He settled Dehkiaht with his parents and noticed that Tiikuchahk seemed to be spending more and more time with Dichaan. He watched this sadly, knowing that he was losing his closest sibling for the second time, the final time. If it chose later to help with the changing of Mars, it would not do so as a mate or a potential mate. It was becoming male.

He went to see Margit, who was brown now and mated and pregnant and content.

He asked his parents to find a female mate for Dehkiaht.

Then he left for Phoenix. He especially wanted to see Tate again while he still looked Human. He wanted to tell her he had kept his promise.

2

Phoenix was still more a town than a village, but it was a shabbier town. Akin could not help comparing Phoenix as he remembered it to Phoenix now.

There was trash in the street. Dead weeds, food waste, scrap wood, cloth, and paper. Some of the houses were obviously vacant. A couple of them had been partially torn down. Others seemed ready to fall down.

Akin walked into town openly as he had always walked into resister settlements. He had been shot doing this only once. That once had been nothing more than a painful nuisance. A Human would have died. Akin had simply run away and healed himself. Lilith had warned him that he must not let resisters see how his body healed—that the sight of wounds healing before their eyes could frighten them. And Humans were most dangerous, most unpredictable when they were afraid.

There were rifles pointed at him as he walked down the street of Phoenix. So Phoenix was armed now. He could see guns and people through the windows, although it seemed the people were trying not to be seen. A few people working or loitering in the street stared at him. At least two were too drunk to notice him.

Hidden guns and open drunkenness.

Phoenix was dying. One of the drunken men was Macy Wilton, who had acted as father to Amma and Shkaht. The other was Stancio Roybal, husband of Neci, the woman who had wanted to amputate Amma's and Shkaht's sensory tentacles. And where were Kolina Wilton and Neci? How could they let their mates—their husbands—lie in the mud half-conscious or unconscious?

And where was Gabe?

He reached the house that he had shared with Tate and Gabe, and for a moment he was afraid to climb the stairs to the porch and rap his knuckles against the door Human-fashion. The house was shut and looked well-kept, but . . . who might live there now?

A man with a gun came out onto the porch and looked down. Gabe.

"You speak English?" he demanded, pointing his rifle at Akin.

"I always have, Gabe." He paused, giving the man time to look at him. "I'm Akin."

The man stood staring at him, peering first from one angle, then moving slightly to peer from another. Akin had changed after all, had grown up. Gabe looked the same.

"I worried that you would be in the hills or out at another village," Akin said. "I never thought to worry that you might not recognize me. I've come back to keep a promise I made to Tate."

Gabe said nothing.

Akin sighed and settled to wait. It was not likely that anyone would shoot him as long as he stood still, hands in sight, unthreatening.

Men gathered around Akin, waiting for some sign from Gabe.

"Check him," Gabe said to one of them.

The man rubbed rough hands over Akin's body. He was
Gilbert Senn. He and his wife Anne had once stood with Neci,
feeling that sensory tentacles should be removed. Akin did not
speak to him. Instead, he waited, eyes on Gabe. Humans
needed the steady, visible gaze of eyes. Males respected it. Females found it sexually interesting.

"He says he's that kid we bought almost twenty years ago,"
Gabe said to the men. "He says he's Akin."

The men stared at Akin with hostility and suspicion. Akin
gave no indication that he saw this.

"No worms," one man said. "Shouldn't he have them by
now?"

No one answered. Akin did not answer because he did not
want to be told to be quiet. He wore only a pair of short pants
as he had when these people knew him. Insects no longer bit
him. He had learned to make his body unpalatable to them.
He was a dark, even brown, small, but clearly not weak. And
clearly not afraid.

"Are you an adult?" Gabe asked him.

"No," he said softly.

"Why not?"

"I'm not old enough."

"Why did you come here?"

"To see you and Tate. You were my parents for a while."

The rifle wavered slightly. "Come closer."

Akin obeyed.

"Show me your tongue."

Akin smiled, then showed his tongue. It did not look any
more Human now than it had when Gabe had first seen it.

Gabe drew back, then took a deep breath. He let the rifle
point toward the ground. "So it is you."

Almost shyly, Akin extended a hand. Human beings often
shook one another's hands. Several had refused to shake his.

Gabe took the hand and shook it, then seized Akin by both
shoulders and hugged him. "I don't believe it," he kept saying.
"I don't fucking believe it.

"It's okay," he told the other men. "It's really him!"

The men watched for a moment longer, then began to drift away. Watching them without turning, Akin got the impression that they were disappointed—that they would have preferred to beat him, perhaps kill him.

Gabe took Akin into the house, where everything looked the same—cool and dark and clean.

Tate lay on a long bench against a wall. She turned her head to look at him, and he read pain in her face. Of course, she did not recognize him.

"She took a fall," Gabe said. There was deep pain in his voice. "Yori's been taking care of her. You remember Yori?"

"I remember," Akin said. "Yori once said she'd leave Phoenix if the people here made guns."

Gabe gave him an odd look. "Guns are necessary. Raids taught everyone that."

"Who . . . ?" Tate asked. And then, amazingly, "Akin?"

He went to her, knelt beside her, and took her hand. He did not like the slightly sour smell of her or the lines around her eyes. How much harm had been done to her? How much help would she and Gabe tolerate?

"Akin," he echoed. "How did you fall? What happened?"

"You're the same," she said, touching his face. "I mean, you're not grown up yet."

"No. But I have kept my promise to you. I've found . . . I've found what may be the answer for your people. But tell me how you got hurt."

He had forgotten nothing about her. Her quick mind, her tendency to treat him like a small adult, the feeling she projected of being not quite trustworthy—just unpredictable enough to make him uneasy. Yet he had accepted her, liked her from his first moments with her. It troubled him more than he could express that she seemed so changed now. She had lost weight, and her coloring, like her scent, had gone wrong. She was too pale. Almost gray. Her hair, too, seemed to be graying. It was much less yellow than it had been. And she was far too thin.

"I fell," she said. Her eyes were the same. They examined

his face, his body. She took one of his hands and looked at it. "My god," she whispered.

"We were exploring," Gabe said. "She lost her footing, fell down a hill. I carried her back to Salvage." He paused. "The old camp's a town itself now. People live there permanently. But they don't have their own doctor. Some of them helped me bring her down to Yori. That was . . . That was bad. But she's getting better now." She was not. He knew she was not.

She had closed her eyes. She knew it as well as he did. She was dying.

Akin touched her face so that she would open her eyes. Humans seemed almost not to be there when they closed their eyes. They could close off all visual awareness and shut themselves too completely within their own flesh. "When did it happen?" he asked.

"God. Two, almost three months ago."

She had suffered that long. Gabe had not found an ooloi to help her. Any ooloi would have done it at no cost to the Humans. Even some males and females could help. He believed he could. It was clear that she would die if nothing was done.

What was the etiquette of asking to save someone's life in an unacceptable way? If Akin asked in the wrong way, Tate would die.

Best not to ask at all. Not yet. Perhaps not at all. "I came back to tell you I'd kept my promise to you," he said. "I don't know if you and the others can accept what I have to offer, but it would mean restored fertility and . . . a place of your own."

Now her eyes were wide and intent on him. "What place?" she whispered. Gabe had come to stand near them and stare down.

"Where!" he demanded.

"It can't be here," Akin said. "You would have to build whole new towns in a new environment, learn new ways to live. It would be hard. But I've found people—other constructs—to help me make it possible."

"Akin, where?" she whispered.

"Mars," he said simply. They stared at him, wordless. He

did not know what they might know about Mars, so he began to reassure them. "We can enable the planet to support Human life. We'll start as soon as I'm mature. The work has been given to me. No one else felt the need to do it as strongly as I did."

"Mars?" Gabe said. "Leave Earth to the Oankali? All of Earth?"

"Yes." Akin turned his face toward Gabe again. The man must understand as quickly as possible that Akin was serious. He needed to have reason to trust Akin with Tate. And Tate needed a reason to continue to live. It had occurred to Akin that she might be weary of her long, pointless life. That, he realized, was something that would not occur to the Oankali. They would not understand even if they were told. Some would accept without understanding. Most would not.

Akin turned his face to Tate again. "They left me with you for so long so that you could teach me whether what they had done with you was right. They couldn't judge. They were so . . . disturbed by your genetic structure that they couldn't do, couldn't even consider doing what I will do."

"Mars?" she said. "Mars?"

"I can give it to you. Others will help me. But . . . you and Gabe have to help me convince resisters."

She looked up at Gabe. "Mars," she whispered, and managed to shake her head.

"I've studied it," Akin told them. "With protection, you could live there now, but you would have to live underground or inside some structure. There's too much ultraviolet light, an atmosphere of carbon dioxide, and no liquid water. And it's cold. It will always be colder than it is here, but we can make it warmer than it is now."

"How?" Gabe asked.

"With modified plants and, later, modified animals. The Oankali have used them all before to make lifeless planets livable."

"Oankali plants?" Gabe demanded. "Not Earth plants?"

Akin sighed. "If something the Oankali have modified belongs to them, then you and all your people belong to them now."

Silence.

"The modified plants and animals work much faster than anything that could be found on Earth naturally. We need them to prepare the way for you relatively quickly. The Oankali won't allow your fertility to be restored here on Earth. You're older now than most Humans used to get. You can still live a long time, but I want you to leave as soon as possible so that you can still raise children there the way my mother has here and teach them what they are."

Tate's eyes had closed again. She put one hand over them, and Akin restrained an impulse to move it away. Was she crying?

"We've lost almost everything already," Gabe said. "Now we lose our world and everything on it."

"Not everything. You'll be able to take whatever you want. And plant life from Earth will be added as the new environment becomes able to support it." He hesitated. "The plants that grow here . . . Not many of them will grow there outdoors. But a lot of the mountain plants will eventually grow there."

Gabe shook his head. "All that in our lifetimes?"

"If you keep yourselves safe, you'll live about twice as long as you already have. You'll live to see plants from Earth growing unprotected on Mars."

Tate took her hand away from her face and looked at him. "Akin, I probably won't live another month," she said. "Before now, I didn't want to. But now . . . Can you get help for me?"

"No!" Gabe protested. "You don't need help. You'll be okay!"

"I'll be dead!" She managed to glare at him. "Do you believe Akin?" she asked.

He looked from her to Akin, stared at Akin as he answered. "I don't know."

"What, you think he's lying?"

"I don't know. He's just a kid. Kids lie."

"Yes. And men lie. But don't you think you can lie to me after all these years. If there's something to live for, I want to live! Are you saying I should die?"

"No. Of course not."

"Then let me get the only help available. Yori had given up on me."

Gabe looked as though he still wanted to protest, but he only looked at her. After a time, he spoke to Akin. "Get someone to help her," he said. Akin could recall hearing him curse in that same tone of voice. Only Humans could do that: say, "Get someone to help her," with their mouths, and "Damn her to hell!" with their voices and bodies.

"I can help her," Akin said.

And both Humans were suddenly looking at him with a suspicion he didn't understand at all.

"I asked for training," he said. "Why are you looking at me that way?"

"If you aren't ooloi," Gabe said, "how can you heal anyone?"

"I told you, I asked to be taught. My teacher was ooloi. I can't do everything it could do, but I can help your flesh and your bones heal. I can encourage your organs to repair themselves, even if they wouldn't normally."

"I've never heard that males could do that," Gabe said.

"An ooloi could do it better. You would enjoy what it did. The safest thing for me to do is make you sleep."

"That's what you'd do if you were an ooloi child, isn't it?" Tate asked.

"Yes. But it's what I'll always do, even as an adult. Ooloi change and become physically able to do more."

"I don't want more done," Tate said. "I want to be healed— healed of everything. And that's all."

"I can't do anything else."

Gabe made a short, wordless sound. "You can still sting, can't you?"

Akin suppressed an urge to stand up, to face Gabe. His body

was almost tiny compared to Gabe's. Even if he had been larger, physical confrontation would have been pointless. He simply stared at the man.

After a time, Gabe came closer and bent to face Tate. "You really want to let him do this?"

She sighed, closed her eyes for a moment. "I'm dying. Of course I'm going to let him do it."

And he sighed, stroked her hair lightly. "Yeah." He turned to glare at Akin. "All right, do whatever it is you do."

Akin did not speak or move. He continued to watch Gabe, resenting the man's attitude, knowing that it did not come only from fear for Tate.

"Well?" Gabe said, standing straight and looking down. Tall men did this. They meant to intimidate. Some of them wanted to fight. Gabe simply intended to make a point he was in no position to make.

Akin waited.

Tate said, "Get out of here, Gabe. Leave us alone for a while."

"Leave you with him!"

"Yes. Now. I'm sick of feeling like shit that's been stepped in. Go."

He went. It was better for him to go because she wanted it than for him to give in to Akin. Akin would have preferred to let him go silently, but he did not dare.

"Gabe," he said as the man was going outside.

Gabe stopped but did not turn.

"Guard the door. An interruption could kill her."

Gabe closed the door behind him without speaking. Immediately, Tate let her breath out in a kind of moan. She looked at the door, then at Akin. "Do I have to do anything?"

"No. Just put up with having me on that bench with you."

This did not seem to disturb her. "You're small enough," she said. "Come on."

He was no smaller than she was.

Carefully, he settled himself between her and the wall. "I

still have only my tongue to work with," he said. "That means this will look like I'm biting you on the neck."

"You used to do that whenever I'd let you."

"I know. Apparently, though, it looks more threatening or more suspicious now."

She tried to laugh.

"You don't think he'll come in, do you? It really could kill you if someone tried to pull us apart."

"He won't. He learned a long time ago not to do things like that."

"Okay. You won't sleep as quickly as you would with an ooloi because I can't sting you unconscious. I have to convince your body to do all the work. Keep still now."

He put one arm around her to keep her in position when she lost consciousness, then put his mouth to the side of her neck. From then on, he was aware only of her body—its injured organs and poorly healed fractures . . . and its activation of her old illness, her Huntington's disease. Did she know? Had the disease caused her to fall? It could have. Or she could have fallen deliberately in the hope of escaping the disease.

She had strained and bruised the ligaments in her back. She had dislocated one of the disks of cartilage between the vertebrae of her neck. She had broken her left kneecap badly. Her kidneys were damaged. Both kidneys. How had she managed to do that? How far had she fallen?

Her left wrist had been broken but had been set and had almost healed. There were also two rib fractures, nearly healed.

Akin lost himself in the work—the pleasure—of finding injuries and stimulating her body's own healing ability. He stimulated her body to produce an enzyme that turned off the Huntington's gene. The gene would eventually become active again. She *must* have an ooloi take care of the disease permanently before she left Earth. He could not replace the deadly gene or trick her body into using genes she had not used since before her birth. He could not help her create new ova clean of the Huntington's gene. What he had already done to suppress the gene was as much as he dared to do.

3

Gabe's interruption of Akin's healing produced the only serious disruption in his memory Akin ever experienced. All he recalled of it later was abrupt agony.

In spite of his warning to Gabe, in spite of Tate's reassurance, Gabe came into the room before the healing was complete. Akin learned later that Gabe returned because hours had passed without a sound from Akin or Tate. He was afraid for Tate, afraid something had gone wrong, and suspicious of Akin.

He found Akin apparently unconscious, his mouth still against Tate's neck. Akin did not even seem to breathe. Nor did Tate. Her flesh was cool—almost cold—and that frightened Gabe. He believed she was dying, feared she might already be dead. He panicked.

First he tried to pull Tate free, alerting Akin on some level that something was wrong. But Akin's attention was too much on Tate. He had only begun to disengage when Gabe hit him.

Gabe was afraid of Akin's sting. He would not grasp Akin and try to pull him away from Tate. Instead, he tried to knock Akin away with quick, hard punches.

The first blow all but tore Akin loose. It hurt him more than he had ever been hurt, and he could not help passing some of his pain on to Tate.

Yet he managed not to poison her. He did not know when she began to scream. He continued automatically to hold her. That and the fact that he was stronger than the larger Gabe enabled him to withdraw from Tate's nervous system and then from her body without being badly injured—and without killing. Later he was amazed that he had done this. His teacher had warned him that males did not have the control to do such things. Oankali males and females avoided healing not only because they were not needed as healers but because they were more likely than ooloi to kill by accident. They could be driven to kill unintentionally by interruptions and even by their subjects if things went wrong. Even Gabe should have been in danger. Akin should have struck at him blindly, reflexively.

Yet he did not.

His body coiled into a painfully tight fetal knot and lay vulnerable and more completely unconscious than it had ever been.

4

When Akin became able to perceive the world around him again he discovered that he could not move or speak. He lay frozen, aware that sometimes there were Humans around him. They looked at him, sat with him sometimes, but did not touch him. For some time he did not know who they were—or where he was. Later, he compared this period with his earliest infancy. It was a time he remembered but took no part in. But even as an infant, he had been fed and washed and held. Now no hand touched him.

He slowly became aware that two people did talk to him. Two females, both Human, one small and yellow-haired and pale. One slightly larger, dark-haired, and sun-browned.

He was glad when they were with him.

He dreaded their coming.

They aroused him. Their scents reached deep into him and drew him to them. Yet he could not move. He lay, being drawn and drawn and utterly still. It was torment, but he preferred it to solitude.

The females talked to him. After a while, he came to know that they were Tate and Yori. And he remembered all that he knew of Tate and Yori.

Tate sat close to him and said his name. She told him how well she felt and how her crops were growing and what different people in the settlement were doing. She did her sewing and her writing while sitting with Akin. She kept a journal.

Yori kept one, too. Yori's became a study of him. She told him so. He was in metamorphosis, she said. She had never seen metamorphosis before, but she had heard it described. Already there were small, new sensory tentacles on his back, on his head, on his legs. His skin was gray now, and he was losing his hair. She said he must find a way to tell them if he wished to be touched. She said Tate was all right, and Akin must find a way to communicate. She said anything he asked would be done for him. She would see to it. She said he must not worry about being alone because she would see that someone was always with him.

This comforted him more than she could know. People in metamorphosis had little tolerance for solitude.

Gabe sat with him. Gabe and the two women had lifted the bench he lay on and carried it and him into a small sunlit room.

Sometimes Gabe tempted him with food or water. He could not know that the scent of the women tempted Akin more strongly than anything Gabe could place near him. He would have wanted food before he fell asleep if he had gone into metamorphosis normally. He would have eaten, then slept. He had heard that ooloi did not sleep straight through much of their second metamorphosis. Lilith had told him that Nikanj slept most of the time, but woke up now and then to eat and talk. Eventually it would fall into another deep sleep. Males and females slept through most of their one metamorphosis. They did not eat, drink, urinate, or defecate. The women stirred Akin, focused his attention, but the smells of food and water did not interest him. He noticed them because they were intermittent. They were environmental changes that he could not fail to notice.

Gabe brought him plants, and he realized after a while that the plants were some of those that he had enjoyed eating when he was younger, upon which Gabe had seen him grazing. The man remembered. That pleased him and eased the sudden shock when, one day, Gabe touched him.

There was no warning. As Gabe had decided to come into the room and separate Akin and Tate, he now decided to do one of the things Yori had told him and Tate not to do.

He simply placed his hand on Akin's back and shook Akin.

After a moment, Akin shuddered. His small, new sensory tentacles moved for the first time, elongating reflexively toward the touching hand.

Gabe jerked his hand away. He would not have been hurt, but he did not know that, and Akin could not tell him. Gabe did not touch him again.

Pilar and Mateo Leal took their turns sitting with Akin. Tino's parents. Mateo had killed people Akin had cared for very much. For a time, his presence made Akin intensely uncomfortable. Then, because he had no choice, Akin adjusted.

Kolina Wilton sat with him sometimes but never spoke to him. One day, to his surprise, Macy Wilton sat with him. So the man was not always lying drunk in the street.

Macy came back several times. He carved things of wood while he sat with Akin, and the smells of his woods were an announcement of his coming. He began to talk to Akin—to speculate about what had happened to Amma and Shkaht, to speculate about children he might someday father, to speculate about Mars.

This told Akin for the first time that Gabe and Tate had spread the story, the hope that he had brought.

Mars.

"Not everyone wants to go," Macy said. "I think they're crazy if they stay here. I'd give anything to see homo sap have another chance. Lina and I will go. And don't you worry about those others!"

At once, Akin began to worry. There was no way to hurry metamorphosis. Bringing it on so traumatically had nearly killed him. Now there was nothing to do but wait. Wait and know that when Humans disagreed, they sometimes fought, and when they fought, all too often they killed one another.

5

Akin's metamorphosis dragged on. He was silent and motionless for months as his body reshaped itself inside and out. He heard and automatically remembered argument after argument over his mission, his right to be in Phoenix, the Human right to Earth. There was no resolution. There was cursing, shouting, threats, fighting, but no resolution. Then, on the day his silence ended, there was a raid. There was shooting. One man was killed. One woman was carried off.

Akin heard the noise but did not know what was happening. Pilar Leal was with him. She stayed with him until the shooting was over. Then she left him for a few moments to see that her husband was all right. When she returned, he was trying desperately to speak.

Pilar gave a short, startled scream, and he knew he must be doing something that she could see. He could see her, hear her, smell her, but he was somehow distant from himself. He had no image of himself and was not sure whether he was causing any part of his body to move. Pilar's reaction said he was.

He managed to make a sound and knew that he had made it. It was nothing more than a hoarse croak, but he had done it deliberately.

Pilar crept toward him, stared at him, *"Está despierto?"* she demanded. Was he awake?

"Sí," he said, and gasped and coughed. He had no strength. He could hear himself, but he still felt distanced from his body. He tried to straighten it and could not.

"Do you have pain?" she asked.

"No. Weak. Weak."

"What can I do? What can I get for you?"

He could not answer for several seconds. "Shooting," he said finally. "Why?"

"Raiders. Dirty bastards! They took Rudra. They killed her husband. We killed two of them."

Akin wanted to slip back into the refuge of unconsciousness. They were not killing each other over the Mars decision, but they were killing each other. There always seemed to be reason for Humans to kill each other. He would give them a new world—a hard world that would demand cooperation and intelligence. Without either, it would surely kill them. Could even Mars distract them long enough for them to breed their way out of their Contradiction?

He felt stronger and tried to speak to Pilar again. He discovered she was gone. Yori was with him now. He had slept. Yes, he had a stored memory of Yori coming in, Pilar reporting that he had spoken, Pilar going out. Yori speaking to him, then understanding that he was asleep.

"Yori?"

She jumped, and he realized she had fallen asleep herself. "So you are awake," she said.

He took a deep breath. "It isn't over. I can't move much yet."

"Should you try?"

He attempted a smile. "I am trying." And a moment later, "Did they get Rudra back?" He had not known the woman, though he remembered seeing her during his stay in Phoenix. She was a tiny brown woman with straight black hair that would have swept the ground if she had not bound it up. She and her husband were Asians from a place called South Africa.

"Men went after her. I don't think they're back yet."

"Are there many raids?"

"Too many. More all the time."

"Why?"

"Why? Well, because we're flawed. Your people said so."

He had not heard her speak so bitterly before.

"There were not so many raids before."

"People had hope here when you were a baby. We were more formidable. And . . . our men had not begun raiding then."

"Phoenix men raiding?"

"Humanity extinguishing itself in boredom, hopelessness, bitterness . . . I'm surprised we've lasted this long."

"Will you go to Mars, Yori?"

She looked at him for several seconds. "It's true?"

"Yes. I have to prepare the way. After that, Humanity will have a place of its own."

"What will we do with it, I wonder?"

"Work hard to keep it from killing you. You'll be able to live there when I've prepared it, but your lives will be hard. If you're careless or can't work together, you'll die."

"We can have children?"

"I can't arrange that. You'll have to let an ooloi do it."

"But it will be done!"

"Yes."

She sighed. "Then I'm going." She watched him for a moment. "When?"

"Years from now. Some of you will go early, though. Some of you must see and understand what I do so that you'll understand from the beginning how your new world works."

She sat watching him silently.

"And I need help with other resisters," he said. He strained for a moment, trying to lift a hand, trying to unknot his body. It was as though he had forgotten how to move. Yet this did not concern him. He knew he was simply trying to rush things that could not be rushed. He could talk. That had to be enough.

"I probably look a lot less Human than I did," he continued. "I won't be able to approach people who used to know me. I don't like being shot or having to threaten people. I need Humans to talk to other Humans and gather them in."

"You're wrong."

"What?"

"You need mostly Oankali for that. Or adult constructs."

"But—"

"You need people who won't be shot on sight. Sane people only shoot Oankali by accident. You need people who won't be taken prisoner and everything they say ignored. That's the way Human beings are now. Shoot the men. Steal the women. If you have nothing better to do, go raid your neighbors."

"That bad?"

"Worse."

He sighed. "Will you help me, Yori?"

"What shall I do?"

"Advise me. I'll need Human advisors."

"From what I've heard, your mother should be one of them."

He tried to read her still face. "I didn't realize you knew who she was."

"People tell me things."

"I've chosen a good advisor, then."

"I don't know. I don't think I can leave Phoenix except with the group that goes to Mars. I've trained others, but I'm the only formally trained doctor. That's a joke, really. I was a psychiatrist. But at least I have formal training."

"What's a psychiatrist?"

"A doctor who specializes in the treatment of mental illness." She gave a bitter laugh. "The Oankali say people like me dealt with far more physical disorders than we were capable of recognizing."

Akin said nothing. He needed someone like Yori who knew the resisters and who seemed not to be afraid of the Oankali. But she must convince herself. She must see that helping Humanity move to its new world was more important than setting broken bones and treating bullet wounds. She probably already knew this, but it would take time for her to accept it. He changed the subject.

"How do I look, Yori? How much have I changed?"

"Completely."

"What?"

"You look like an Oankali. You don't sound like one, but if I didn't know who you were, I would assume you were a small Oankali. Perhaps a child."

"Shit!"

"Will you change any more?"

"No." He closed his eyes. "My senses aren't as sharp as they will be. But the shape I have is the shape I will have."

"Do you mind, really?"

"Of course I mind. Oh, god. How many resisters will trust me now? How many will even believe I'm a construct?"

"It doesn't matter. How many of them trust each other? And they know they're Human."

"It's not like that everywhere. There are resister settlements close to Lo that don't fight so much."

"You might have to take them, then, and give up on some of the people here."

"I don't know if I can do that."

"I can."

He looked at her. She had placed herself so that he could see her with his eyes even though he could not move. She would go back to Lo with him. She would advise him and observe the metamorphosis of Mars.

"Do you need food yet?" she asked.

The idea disgusted him. "No. Soon, perhaps, but not now."

"Do you need anything?"

"No. But thank you for seeing that I was never left alone."

"I had heard it was important."

"Very. I should begin to move in a few more days. I'll still need people around."

"Anyone in particular?"

"Did you choose the people who've been sitting with me— other than the Rinaldis, I mean?"

"Tate and I did."

"You did a good job. Will they all immigrate to Mars, do you think?"

"That's not why we chose them."

"Will they immigrate?"

After a while she nodded. "They will. So will a few others."

"Send me the others—if you don't think my looks now will scare them."

"They've all seen Oankali before."

Did she mean to insult him? he wondered. She spoke in such a strange tone. Bitterness and something else. She stood up.

"Wait," he said.

She paused, not changing expression.

"My perception isn't what it will be eventually. I don't know what's wrong."

She stared at him with unmistakable hostility. "I was thinking that so many people have suffered and died," she said. "So many have become . . . unsalvageable. So many more will be lost." She stopped, breathed deeply. "Why did the Oankali cause this? Why didn't they offer us Mars years ago?"

"They would never offer you Mars. I offer you Mars."

"*Why?*"

"Because I'm part of you. Because I say you should have one more chance to breed yourselves out of your genetic Contradiction."

"And what do the Oankali say?"

"That you can't grow out of it, can't resolve it in favor of intelligence. That hierarchical behavior selects for hierarchical behavior, whether it should or not. That not even Mars will be enough of a challenge to change you." He paused. "That to give you a new world and let you procreate again would . . . would be like breeding intelligent beings for the sole purpose of having them kill one another."

"That wouldn't be our purpose," she protested.

He thought about that for a moment, wondered what he should say. The truth or nothing. The truth. "Yori, Human purpose isn't what you say it is or what I say it is. It's what your biology says it is—what your genes say it is."

"Do you believe that?"

". . . yes."

"Then why—"

"Chance exists. Mutation. Unexpected effects of the new environment. Things no one has thought of. The Oankali can make mistakes."

"Can we?"

He only looked at her.

"Why are the Oankali letting you do this?"

"I want to do it. Other constructs think I should. Some will help me. Even those who don't think I should understand why I want to. The Oankali accept this. There was a consensus. The Oankali won't help, except to teach. They won't set foot on Mars once we've begun. They won't transport you." He tried to think of a way to make her understand. "To them, what I'm doing is terrible. The only thing that would be more terrible would be to murder you all with my own hands."

"Not reasonable," she whispered.

"You can't see and read genetic structure the way they do. It isn't like reading words on a page. They feel it and know it. They . . . There's no English word for what they do. To say they know is completely inadequate. I was made to perceive this before I was ready. I understand it now as I couldn't then."

"And you'll still help us."

"I'll still help. I have to."

She left him. The expression of hostility was gone from her face when she looked back at him before closing the wooden door. She looked confused, yet hopeful.

"I'll send someone to you," she said, and closed the door.

6

Akin slept and knew only peripherally that Gabe came in to sit with him. The man spoke to him for the first time, but he did not awaken to answer. "I'm sorry," Gabe said once he was certain Akin was asleep. He did not repeat the words or explain them.

Gabe was still there some time later when the noise began outside. It wasn't loud or threatening, but Gabe went out to see what had happened. Akin awoke and listened.

Rudra had been rescued, but she was dead. Her captors had beaten and raped her until she was so badly hurt that her rescuers could not get her home alive. They had not even been able to catch or kill any of her captors. They were tired and angry. They had brought back Rudra's body to be buried with her husband. Two more people lost. The men cursed all raiders and tried to figure out where this group had come from. Where should the reprisal raid take place?

Someone—not Gabe—brought up Mars.

Someone else told him to shut up.

A third person asked how Akin was.

"Fine," Gabe said. There was something wrong with the way he said it, but Akin could not tell what it was.

The men were silent for a while.

"Let's have a look at him," one of them said suddenly.

"He didn't steal Rudra or kill Mehtar," Gabe said.

"Did I say he did? I just want to look at him."

"He looks like an Oankali now. Just like an Oankali. Yori says he's not too thrilled about that, but there's nothing he can do about it."

"I heard they could change their shapes after metamorphosis," someone said. "I mean, like those chameleon lizards that used to be able to change color."

"They hoped to use something they got from us to be able to do that," Gabe said. "Cancer, I think. But I haven't seen any sign that they've been able to do it."

It could not be done. It would not be tried until people felt more secure about constructs like Akin—Human-born males—whom they thought were most likely to cause trouble. It could not be done until there were construct ooloi.

"Let's all go see him." That voice again. The same man who

had suggested before that he wanted to see Akin. Who was he? Akin thought for a moment, searching his memory.

He did not know the man.

"Hold on," Gabe was saying. "This is my home. You don't just goddamn walk in when you feel like it!"

"What are you hiding in there? We've all seen the goddamn leeches before."

"Then you don't need to see Akin."

"It's just one more worm come to feed on us."

"He saved my wife's life," Gabe said. "What the hell did you ever save?"

"Hey, I just wanted to look at him . . . make sure he's okay."

"Good. You can look at him when he's able to get up and look back at you."

Akin began to worry at once that the other man would find his way into the house. Obviously, Humans were strongly tempted to do things they were warned not to do. And Akin was more vulnerable now than he had been since infancy. He could be tormented from a distance. He could be shot. If an attacker was persistent enough, Akin could be killed. And at this moment, he was alone. No companion. No guardian.

He began trying to move again—trying desperately. But only his new sensory tentacles moved. They writhed and knotted helplessly.

Then Tate came in. She stopped, stared at the many moving sensory tentacles, then settled down in the chair Gabe had occupied. Across her lap, she held a long, dull-gray rifle.

"You heard that crap, didn't you?" she said.

"Yes," he whispered.

"I was afraid you would. Relax. Those people know us. They won't come in here unless they're feeling suicidal." She had been so strongly against guns once. Yet she held the thing in her lap as though it were a friend. And he had to be glad she did, glad of her protection. Confused, he kept silent until she said, "Are you all right?"

"I'm afraid someone will be killed on my account."

She said nothing for a while. Finally she asked, "How soon before you can walk?"

"A few days. Three or four. Maybe."

"I hope that will be soon enough. If you're mobile, they won't dare give you trouble. You look thoroughly Oankali."

"When I can walk, I'll leave."

"We're going with you. It's past time for us to leave this place."

He looked at her and thought he smiled.

She laughed. "I wondered if you could do that."

He realized then by the sudden muting of his senses that his new sensory tentacles had flattened against his body, had smoothed like a second skin and seemed more painted on than real. He had seen this all his life in Oankali and constructs. Now, it felt utterly natural to do it himself.

She touched him.

He saw her reach out, felt the warmth of her hand long before she laid it on his shoulder and rubbed it over the smooth tentacles. For a second, he was able to keep them smooth. Then they locked into her hand. Her femaleness tormented him more than ever, but he could only taste it, savor it. Even if she had been interested in him sexually, he would have been helpless.

"Let go," she said. She was not frightened or angry. She simply waited for him to let her go. She had no idea how difficult it was for him to draw his sensory tentacles back, to break the deep, frustrating contact.

"What was that all about?" she asked when she had her hand back.

He was not quick enough to think of an innocuous answer before she began to laugh.

"I thought so," she said. "We should definitely get you home. Do you have mates waiting?"

Chagrined, he said nothing.

"I'm sorry. I didn't mean to embarrass you. It's been a long time since I was an adolescent."

"Humans called me that before I changed."

"Young adult, then."

"How can you condescend to me and still follow me?"

She smiled. "I don't know. I haven't worked out my feelings toward the new you yet."

Something about her manner was a lie. Nothing she said was a direct lie, but there was something wrong.

"Will you go to Mars, Tate, or stay on Earth?" he asked.

She seemed to pull back from him without moving.

"You'll be as free to stay as you will be to go." She had Oankali mates who would be overjoyed to have her stay. If she did not, they might never settle on Earth.

"Truce," Tate said quietly.

He wished she were Oankali so that he could show her he meant what he was saying. He had not spoken in response to her condescension, as she clearly believed. He had responded instead to the falseness of her manner. But communication with Humans was always incomplete.

"Goddamn you," Tate said softly.

"What?"

She looked away from him. She stood up, paced across to a window, and stared out. She stood to one side, making it difficult for anyone outside to see her. But there was no one outside that window. She paced around the room, restless, grim.

"I thought I'd made my decision," she said. "I thought leaving here would be enough for now."

"It is," Akin said. "There's no hurry. You don't have to make any other decisions yet."

"Who's patronizing whom?" she said bitterly.

More misunderstanding. "Take me literally," Akin said. "Assume that I mean exactly what I say."

She looked at him with disbelief and distrust.

"You *can* decide later," he insisted.

After a while she sighed. "No," she said, "I can't."

He did not understand, so he said nothing.

"That's my problem, really," she continued. "I don't have a choice anymore. I have to go."

"You don't."

She shook her head. "I made my choice a long time ago—the way Lilith made hers. I chose Gabe and Phoenix and Humanity. My own people disgust me sometimes, but they're still my people. I have to go with them."

"Do you?"

"Yes."

She sat down again after a while and put the gun on her lap and closed her eyes.

"Tate?" he said, when she seemed calm.

She opened her eyes but said nothing.

"Does the way I look now bother you?"

The question seemed to annoy her at first. Then she shrugged. "If anyone had asked me how I would feel if you changed so completely, I would have said it would upset me, at least. It doesn't. I don't think it bothers the others either. We all watched you change."

"What about those who didn't watch?"

"To them you'll be an Oankali, I think."

He sighed. "There'll be fewer immigrants because of me."

"Because of us," she said.

Because of Gabe, she meant.

"He thought I was dead, Akin. He panicked."

"I know."

"I've talked to him. We'll help you gather people. We'll go to the villages—alone, with you, or with other constructs. Just tell us what you want us to do."

His sensory tentacles smoothed again with pleasure. "Will you let me improve your ability to survive injuries and heal?" he asked. "Will you let someone correct your Huntington's disease genetically?"

She hesitated. "The Huntington's?"

"You don't want to pass that on to your children."

"But genetic changes . . . That will mean time with an ooloi. A lot of time."

"The disease had become active, Tate. It was active when I healed you. I thought perhaps . . . you had noticed."

"You mean I'm going to get sick with it? Crazy?"

"No. I fixed it again. A temporary fix. The deactivation of a gene that should have been replaced long ago."

"I . . . couldn't have gone through that."

"The disease may be the reason you fell."

"Oh my god," she whispered. "That's the way it happened with my mother. She kept falling. And she had . . . personality changes. And I read that the disease causes brain damage—irreversible . . ."

"An ooloi can reverse it. It isn't serious yet, anyway."

"Any brain damage is serious!"

"It can be repaired."

She looked at him, clearly wanting to believe.

"You can't introduce this to the Mars colony. You know you can't. It would spread through the population in a few generations."

"I know."

"You'll let it be corrected, then?"

"Yes." The word was hardly more than a moving of her lips, but Akin saw it and believed her.

Relieved and surprisingly tired, he drifted off to sleep. With her help and the help of others in Phoenix, he had a chance of making the Mars colony work.

7

When he awoke, the house was aflame.

He thought at first that the sound he heard was rain. The smoke scent forced him to recognize it as fire. There was no one with him. The room was dark, and he had only a stored memory of Macy Wilton sitting beside him, a short, thick gun across his knees. A double-barreled gun of a type Akin had not seen before. He had gotten up and gone to investigate a strange noise just outside the house. Akin replayed his memory of the noise. Even asleep, he had heard what Macy probably had not.

People whispering.

"Don't pour that there. Throw it against the wall where it will do some good. And throw it on the porch."

"Shut up. They're not deaf in there."

Footsteps, oddly unsteady.

"Go pour some under the mongrel's window, Babe."

Footsteps coming closer to Akin's window—almost stumbling closer. And someone fell. That was the sound Macy heard: a grunt of pain and a body landing heavily.

Akin knew all this as soon as he was fully awake. And he knew the people outside had been drinking. One of them was the man who had wanted to get past Gabe to see Akin.

The other was Neci. She had graduated from attempting mutilation to attempting murder.

What had happened to Macy? Where were Tate and Gabe? How could the fire make so much noise and light and not awaken everyone? It had crept up outside one window now. The windows were high off the ground. The fire he could see must already be eating its way through the wall and floor.

He began to shout Tate's name, Gabe's name. He could move a little now, but not enough to make a difference.

No one came.

The fire ate its way into the room, making choking smoke that Akin discovered he could breathe easier if he did not breathe through his mouth. He had a sair at his throat now, surrounded by large and strong sensory tentacles. These moved automatically to filter the smoke from the air he breathed.

But, still, no one came to help him. He would burn. He had no protection against fire.

He would die. Neci and her friend would destroy Human chances at a new world because they were drunk and out of their minds.

He would end.

He shouted and choked because he did not quite understand

yet how to talk through a familiar orifice and breathe through an unfamiliar one.

Why was he being left to burn? People heard him. They must have heard! He could hear them now—running, shouting, their sounds blending into the snapping and roaring of the fire.

He managed to fall off the bed.

Landing was only a small shock. His sensory tentacles automatically protected themselves by flattening into his body. Once he was on the wood floor, he tried to roll toward the door.

Then he stopped, trying to understand what his senses were telling him. Vibrations. Someone coming.

Someone running toward the room he was in. Gabe's footsteps.

He shouted, hoping to guide the man in the smoke. He saw the door open, felt hands on him.

With an effort that was almost painful, Akin managed not to sink his sensory tentacles into the man's flesh. The man's touch was like an invitation to investigate him with enhanced adult senses. But now was not the time for such things. He must do all he could not to hinder Gabe.

He let himself become a thing—a sack of vegetables to be thrown over someone's shoulder. For once, he was glad to be small.

Gabe fell once, coughing, seared by the heat. He dropped Akin, picked him up, and again threw him over one shoulder.

The front door was blocked by sheets of fire. The back would be blocked in a moment. Gabe kicked it open and ran down the steps, for a moment actually plunging through flames. His hair caught fire, and Akin shouted at him to put it out.

Gabe stopped once he was clear of the house, dropped Akin into the dirt, and collapsed, beating at himself and coughing.

The tree they had stopped under had caught fire from the house. They had to move again, quickly, to avoid burning branches. Once Gabe had put out his own fire, he picked Akin up and staggered farther away toward the forest.

"Where are you going?" Akin asked him.

He did not answer. It seemed all he could do to breathe and move.

Behind them, the house was totally engulfed. Nothing could be alive in there now.

"Tate!" Akin said suddenly. Where was she? Gabe would never save him and leave Tate to burn.

"Ahead," Gabe wheezed.

She was all right, then.

Gabe fell again, this time half-atop Akin. Hurt, Akin locked into him in helpless reflex. He immediately paralyzed the man, stopping significant messages of movement between the brain and the rest of the body.

"Lie still," he said, hoping to give Gabe the illusion of choice. "Just lie there and let me help you."

"You can't help yourself," Gabe whispered, struggling to breathe, to move.

"I can help myself by healing you! If you fall on me again, I might sting you. Now shut up and stop trying to move. Your lungs are damaged and you're burned." The lung damage was serious and could kill him. The burns were only very painful. Yet Gabe would not be quiet.

"The town . . . Can they see us?"

"No. There's a cornfield between us and Phoenix now. The fire is still visible, though. And it's spreading." At least one other house was burning now. Perhaps it had caught from the burning tree.

"If it doesn't rain, half the town might burn. Fools."

"It isn't going to rain. Now be quiet, Gabe."

"If they catch us, they'll probably kill us!"

"What? Who?"

"People from town. Not everybody. Just troublemakers."

"They'll be too busy trying to put out the fire. It hasn't rained for days. They chose the wrong season for all this. Just be quiet and let me help you. I won't make you sleep, so you might feel something. But I won't hurt you."

"I hurt so bad already, I probably wouldn't know if you did."

Akin interrupted the messages of pain that Gabe's nerves
were sending to his brain and encouraged his brain to secrete
specific endorphins.

"Jesus Christ!" the man said, gasping, coughing. For him
the pain had abruptly ceased. He felt nothing. It was less confusing for him that way. For Akin, it meant sudden, terrible
pain, then slow alleviation. Not euphoria. He did not want
Gabe drunk on his own endorphins. But the man could be
made to feel good and alert. It was almost like making music—
balancing endorphins, silencing pain, maintaining sobriety. He
made simple music. Ooloi made great harmonies, interweav-
ing people and sharing pleasure. And ooloi contributed substances of their own to the union. Akin would feel that soon
when Dehkiaht changed. For now, there was the pleasure of
healing.

Gabe began to breathe easier as his lungs improved. He did
not notice when his flesh began to heal. Akin let the useless
burned flesh slough off. Gabe would need water and food
soon. Akin would finish by stimulating feelings of hunger and
thirst in the man so that he would be willing to eat or drink
whatever Akin could spot for him. It was especially important
that he drink soon.

"Someone's coming," Gabe whispered.

"Gilbert Senn," Akin said into his ear. "He's been searching
for some time. If we're still, he may not find us."

"How do you know it's—?"

"Footsteps. He still sounds the same as he did when I was
here before. He's alone."

Silently Akin finished his work and withdrew the filaments
of his sensory tentacles from Gabe. "You can move now," he
whispered. "But don't."

Akin could move too, a little more, although he doubted
that he could walk.

Abruptly Gilbert Senn found them—all but stumbled over
them in the moonlight and the firelight. He leaped back, his
rifle aimed at them.

Gabe sat up. Akin used Gabe to pull himself up and managed not to fall when he let go. He could hurry everyone's bodily processes but his own. Gilbert Senn looked at him, then carefully avoided looking at him. He lowered the rifle.

"Are you all right, Gabe?" he asked.

"I'm fine."

"You're burned."

"I was." Gabe glanced at Akin.

Gilbert Senn carefully did not look at Akin. "I see." He turned toward the fire. "I wish that hadn't happened. We would never have burned your home."

"For all I know, you did," Gabe muttered.

"Neci did," Akin said quickly. "She and the man who wanted to get into the house to see me. I heard them."

The rifle came up again, aimed only at Akin this time. "You will be quiet," he said.

"If he dies, we all die," Gabe said softly.

"We all die no matter what. Some of us choose to die free!"

"There will be freedom on Mars, Gil."

The corners of Gilbert Senn's mouth turned down. Gabe shook his head. To Akin he said, "He believes your Mars idea is a trick. A way of gathering in the resisters easily to use them on the ship or in the Oankali villages on Earth. A lot of people feel that way."

"*This* is my world," Gilbert Senn said. "I was born here, and I'll die here. And if I can't have Human children—fully Human children—I'll have no children at all."

This was a man who would have helped cut sensory tentacles from Amma and Shkaht. He had not wanted to do such things to children, to females, but he honestly believed it was the right thing to do.

"Mars is not for you," Akin told him.

The gun wavered. "What?"

"Mars isn't for anyone who doesn't want it. It will be hard work, risk, and challenge. It will be a Human world someday. But it will never be Earth. You need Earth."

"You think your childish psychology will influence me?"

"No," Akin said.

"I don't want to hear it from you or from Yori."

"If you kill me now, no Humans will go to Mars."

"None will go anyway."

"Humanity will live or die by what you do now."

"No!"

The man wanted to shoot Akin. Perhaps he had never wanted anything as much. He might even have come into the field hoping to find Akin and shoot him. Now he could not shoot Akin because Akin might possibly somehow be telling the truth.

After a long time, Gilbert Senn turned and went back toward the fire.

After a moment, Gabe stood up and shook himself. "If that was psychology, it was damn good," he said.

"It was literal truth," Akin told him.

"I was afraid it might be. Gil almost shot you."

"I thought he might."

"Could he have killed you?"

"Yes, with enough ammunition and enough persistence. Or perhaps he could have made me kill him."

He bent to pick Akin up. "You've made yourself too valuable to take risks like that. I know guys who wouldn't have hesitated." He shook himself again, shaking Akin. "God, what's this stuff you've smeared me with? Goddamn slimy shit!"

Akin did not answer.

"What is it?" Gabe insisted. "It stinks."

"Cooked flesh."

Gabe shuddered and said nothing.

8

Tate waited at the edge of the forest amid a cluster of other people. Mateo and Pilar Leal were there. How would Tino take seeing them again? How would they take seeing him with Nikanj? Would he stay with his mates and his children or go with his parents' people? It was not likely that Nikanj could let him go or that he could survive long without Nikanj. Mars might even make Tino's choice of the Oankali more acceptable to Tino. He would no longer be helping Humanity breed itself out of existence. But he would not be helping it shape its new world either.

Yori was there, standing with Kolina Wilton and Stancio Roybal. Sober now, Stancio looked tired and ill. There were people Akin did not recognize—new people. There was Abira—an arm reaching out of a hammock, lifting him in.

"Where's Macy?" Gabe asked as he put Akin down.

"He hasn't come," Kolina answered. "We hoped he was helping you with Akin."

"He went out when he heard Neci and her friend setting the fire," Akin said. "I lost track of him after that."

"Was he hurt?" Kolina demanded.

"I don't know. I'm sorry."

She thought about this for a moment. "We have to wait for him!"

"We'll wait," Tate said. "He knows where to meet us."

They moved deeper into the forest as the light from the fire grew brighter.

"My home is burning," Abira said as everyone watched. "I didn't think I would have to watch my home burn again."

"Just be glad you aren't in it," one of the strangers said. Akin knew at once that this man disliked Abira. Humans would carry their dislikes with them to be shut up together on Mars.

The fire burned through the night, but Macy did not come. A few other people arrived. Yori had asked most of them to come. It was she who kept others from shooting them as they were spotted. If they shot anyone, they would have to leave quickly before the sound drew enemies.

"I have to go back," Kolina said finally.

No one said anything. Perhaps they had been waiting for this.

"They could be holding him," Tate said finally. "They could be waiting for you."

"No. Not with the fire. They wouldn't think about me."

"There are those who would. The kind who would hold you and sell you if they thought they could get away with it."

"I'll go," Stancio said. "Probably no one's even noticed that I've left town. I'll find him."

"I can't leave without him," she said.

"But we have to leave soon," Gabe said. "Gil Senn nearly killed Akin back there in the field. If he gets another chance, he might pull the trigger. I know there are others who wouldn't hesitate, and they'll be out hunting as soon as it's light."

"Someone give me a gun," Stancio said.

One of the strangers handed him one.

"I want one, too," Kolina said. She was staring at the fire, and when Yori thrust a rifle at her, she took it without turning her head. "Keep Akin safe," she said.

Yori hugged her. "Keep yourself safe. Bring Macy to us. You can find the way."

"North to the big river, then east along the river. I know."

No one said anything to Stancio, so Akin called him over. Gabe had propped Akin against a tree, and now Stancio squatted before him, clearly not bothered by his appearance.

"Would you let me check you?" Akin asked. "You don't look well, and for this you may need to be . . . very healthy."

Stancio shrugged. "I don't have anything you can cure."

"Let me have a look. It won't hurt."

Stancio stood up. "Is this Mars thing real?"

"It's real. Another chance for Humanity."

"You see to that, then. Don't worry about me." He put his gun on his shoulder and walked with Kolina back toward the fire.

Akin watched them until they disappeared around the edge of the cornfield. He never saw either of them again.

After a while, Gabe lifted him, hung him over one shoulder, and began to walk. Akin would be able to walk himself tomorrow or the day after. For now, he watched from Gabe's shoulder as the others fell in, single file. They headed north toward the river. There, they would turn east toward Lo. In less time than they probably realized, some of them would be aboard shuttles headed for Mars, there to watch the changes begin and be witnesses for their people.

He was perhaps the last to see the smoke cloud behind them and Phoenix still burning.

IMAGO

To Irie Isaacs

I

METAMORPHOSIS

1

I slipped into my first metamorphosis so quietly that no one noticed. Metamorphoses were not supposed to begin that way. Most people begin with small, obvious, physical changes—the loss of fingers and toes, for instance, or the budding of new fingers and toes of a different design.

I wish my experience had been that normal, that safe.

For several days, I changed without attracting attention. Early stages of metamorphosis didn't normally last for days without bringing on deep sleep, but mine did. My first changes were sensory. Tastes, scents, all sensations suddenly became complex, confusing, yet unexpectedly seductive.

I had to relearn everything. River water, for instance: when I swam in it, I noticed that it had two distinctive major flavors—hydrogen and oxygen?—and many minor flavors. I could separate out and savor each one individually. In fact, I couldn't help separating them. But I learned them quickly and accepted them in their new complexity so that only occasional changes in minor flavors demanded my attention.

Our river water at Lo always came to us clouded with sediment. "Rich," the Oankali called it. "Muddy," the Humans said, and filtered it or let the silt settle to the bottom before they drank it. "Just water," we constructs said, and shrugged. We had never known any other water.

As quickly as I could, I learned again to understand and accept my sensory impressions of the people and things around me. The experience absorbed so much of my attention that I didn't understand how my family could fail to see that something unusual was happening to me. But beyond mentioning that I was daydreaming too much, even my parents missed the signs.

They were, after all, the wrong signs. No one was expecting them, so no one noticed when they appeared.

All five of my parents were old when I was born. They didn't look any older than my adult sisters and brothers, but they had helped with the founding of Lo. They had grandchildren who were old. I don't think I had ever surprised them before. I wasn't sure I liked surprising them now. I didn't want to tell them. I especially didn't want to tell Tino, my Human father. He was supposed to stay with me through my metamorphosis—since he was my same-sex Human parent. But I did not feel drawn to him as I should have. Nor did I feel drawn to Lilith, my birth mother. She was Human, too, and what was happening to me was definitely not a Human thing. Strangely I didn't want to go to my Oankali father, Dichaan, either, and he was my logical choice after Tino. My Oankali mother, Ahajas, would have talked to one of my fathers for me. She had done that for two of my brothers who had been afraid of metamorphosis—afraid they would change too much, lose all signs of their Humanity. That could happen to me, though I had never worried about it. Ahajas would have talked to me and for me, no matter what my problem was. Of all my parents, she was the easiest to talk to. I would have gone to her if the thought of doing so had been more appealing—or if I had understood why it was so unappealing. What was wrong with me? I wasn't shy or afraid, but when I thought of going to her, I felt first drawn, then . . . almost repelled.

Finally there was my ooloi parent, Nikanj.

It would tell me to go to one of my same-sex parents—one of my fathers. What else could it say? I knew well enough that I was in metamorphosis, and that that was one of the few things ooloi parents could not help with. There were still some Humans who insisted on seeing the ooloi as some kind of male-female combination, but the ooloi were no such thing. They were themselves—a different sex altogether.

So I went to Nikanj only hoping to enjoy its company for a

while. Eventually it would notice what was happening to me and send me to my fathers. Until it did, I would rest near it. I was tired, sleepy. Metamorphosis was mostly sleep.

I found Nikanj inside the family house, talking to a pair of Human strangers. The Humans were standing back from Nikanj. The female was almost sheltering behind the male, and the male was making a painful effort to appear courageous. Both looked alarmed when they saw me open a wall and step through into the room. Then, as they got a look at me, they seemed to relax a little. I looked very Human—especially if they compared me to Nikanj, who wasn't Human at all.

The Humans smelled most obviously of sweat and adrenaline, food and sex. I sat down on the floor and let myself work out the complex combinations of scents. My new awareness wouldn't allow me to do anything else. By the time I was finished, I thought I would be able to track those two Humans through anything.

Nikanj paid no attention to me except to notice me when I came in. It was used to its children coming and going as they chose, used to all of us spending time with it, learning whatever it was willing to teach us.

It had an incredibly complex scent because it was ooloi. It had collected within itself not only the reproductive material of other members of the family but cells of other plant and animal species that it had dealt with recently. These it would study, memorize, then either consume or store. It consumed the ones it knew it could re-create from memory, using its own DNA. It kept the others alive in a kind of stasis until they were needed.

Its most noticeable underscent was Kaal, the kin group it was born into. I had never met its parents, but I knew the Kaal scent from other members of the Kaal kin group. Somehow, though, I had never noticed that scent on Nikanj, never separated it out this way.

The main scent was Lo, of course. It had mated with Oankali of the Lo kin group, and on mating, it had altered its own scent as an ooloi must. The word "ooloi" could not be translated directly into English because its meaning was as complex as Nikanj's scent. "Treasured stranger." "Bridge." "Life trader." "Weaver." "Magnet."

Magnet, my birth mother says. People are drawn to ooloi and can't escape. She couldn't, certainly. But then, neither could Nikanj escape her or any of its mates. The Oankali said the chemical bonds of mating were as difficult to break as the habit of breathing.

Scents . . . The two visiting Humans were longtime mates and smelled of each other.

"We don't know yet whether we want to emigrate," the female was saying. "We've come to see for ourselves and for our people."

"You'll be shown everything," Nikanj told them. "There are no secrets about the Mars colony or travel to it. But right now the shuttles allotted to emigration are all in use. We have a guest area where Humans can wait."

The two Humans looked at one another. They still smelled frightened, but now both were making an effort to look brave. Their faces were almost expressionless.

"We don't want to stay here," the male said. "We'll come back when there's a ship."

Nikanj stood up—unfolded, as Humans say. "I can't tell you when there'll be a ship," it said. "They arrive when they arrive. Let me show you the guest area. It isn't like this house. Humans built it of cut wood."

The pair stumbled back from Nikanj.

Nikanj's sensory tentacles flattened against its body in amusement. It sat down again. "There are other Humans waiting in the guest area," it told them gently. "They're like you. They want their own all-Human world. They'll be traveling with you when you go." It paused, looked at me. "Eka, why don't you show them?"

I wanted to stay with it now more than ever, but I could see that the two Humans were relieved to be turned over to someone who at least looked Human. I stood up and faced them.

"This is Jodahs," Nikanj told them, "one of my younger children."

The female gave me a look that I had seen too often not to recognize. She said, "But I thought . . ."

"No," I said to her, and smiled. "I'm not Human. I'm a Human-born construct. Come out this way. The guest area isn't far."

They did not want to follow me through the wall I opened until it was fully open—as though they thought the wall might close on them, as though it would hurt them if it did.

"It would be like being grasped gently by a big hand," I told them when we were all outside.

"What?" the male asked.

"If the wall shut on you. It couldn't hurt you because you're alive. It might eat your clothing, though."

"No, thanks!"

I laughed. "I've never seen that happen, but I've heard it can."

"What's your name?" the female asked.

"All of it?" She looked interested in me—smelled sexually attracted, which made her interesting to me. Human females did tend to like me as long as I kept my few body tentacles covered by clothing and my few head tentacles hidden in my hair. The sensory spots on my face and arms looked like ordinary skin, though they didn't feel ordinary.

"Your Human name," the female said. "I already know . . . Eka and Jodahs, but I'm not sure which to call you."

"Eka is just a term of endearment for young children," I told her, "like lelka for married children and Chka between mates. Jodahs is my personal name. The Human version of my whole name is Jodahs Iyapo Leal Kaalnikanjlo. My name, the surnames of my birth mother and Human father, and Nikanj's name beginning with the kin group it was born into and ending with the kin group of its Oankali mates. If I were Oankali-born or if I gave you the Oankali version of my name, it would be a lot longer and more complicated."

"I've heard some of them," the female said. "You'll probably drop them eventually."

"No. We'll change them to suit our needs, but we won't drop them. They give very useful information, especially when people are looking for mates."

"Jodahs doesn't sound like any name I've heard before," the male said.

"Oankali name. An Oankali named Jodahs died helping with the emigration. My birth mother said he should be remembered. The Oankali don't have a tradition of remembering people by naming kids after them, but my birth mother insisted. She does that sometimes—insists on keeping Human customs."

"You look very Human," the female said softly.

I smiled. "I'm a child. I just look unfinished."

"How old are you?"

"Twenty-nine."

"Good god! When will you be considered an adult?"

"After metamorphosis." I smiled to myself. Soon. "I have a brother who went through it at twenty-one, and a sister who didn't reach it until she was thirty-three. People change when their bodies are ready, not at some specific age."

She was silent for some time. We reached the last of the true houses of Lo—the houses that had been grown from the living substance of the Lo entity. Humans without Oankali mates could not open walls or raise table, bed, or chair platforms in such houses. Left alone in our houses, these Humans were prisoners until some construct, Oankali, or mated Human freed them. Thus, they had been given first a guest house, then a guest area. In that area they had built their dead houses of cut wood and woven thatch. They used fire for light and cooking and occasionally they burned down one of their houses. Houses that did not burn became infested with rodents and insects which ate the Human's food and bit or stung the Humans themselves. Periodically Oankali went in and drove the non-

Human life out. It always came back. It had been feeding on
Humans, eating their food, and living in their buildings since
long before the Oankali arrived. Still the guest area was rea-
sonably comfortable. Guests ate from trees and plants that
were not what they appeared to be. They were extensions of
the Lo entity. They had been induced to synthesize fruits and
vegetables in shapes, flowers, and textures that Humans recognized. The foods grew from what appeared to be their
proper trees and plants. Lo took care of the Humans' wastes,
keeping their area clean, though they tended to be careless
about where they threw or dumped things in this temporary
place.

"There's an empty house there," I said, pointing.

The female stared at my hand rather than at where I
pointed. I had, from a Human point of view, too many fingers
and toes. Seven per. Since they were part of distinctly Human-
looking hands and feet, Humans didn't usually notice them at
once.

I held my hand open, palm up so that she could see it, and
her expression flickered from curiosity and surprise through
embarrassment back to curiosity.

"Will you change much in metamorphosis?" she asked.

"Probably. The Human-born get more Oankali and the
Oankali-born get more Human. I'm first-generation. If you
want to see the future, take a look at some of the third- and
fourth-generations constructs. They're a lot more uniform
from start to finish."

"That's not our future," the male said.

"Your choice," I said.

The male walked away toward the empty house. The female
hesitated. "What do you think of our emigration?" she asked.

I looked at her, liking her, not wanting to answer. But such
questions should be answered. Why, though, were the
Human females who insisted on asking them so often small,
weak people? The Martian environment they were headed
for was harsher than any they had known. We would see that
they had the best possible chance to survive. Many would

live to bear children on their new world. But they would suffer so. And in the end, it would all be for nothing. Their own
genetic conflict had betrayed and destroyed them once. It
would do so again.

"You should stay," I told the female. "You should join us."

"Why?"

I wanted very much not to look at her, to go away from her.
Instead I continued to face her. "I understand that Humans
must be free to go," I said softly. "I'm Human enough for my
body to understand that. But I'm Oankali enough to know
that you will eventually destroy yourselves again."

She frowned, marring her smooth forehead. "You mean another war?"

"Perhaps. Or maybe you'll find some other way to do it.
You were working on several ways before your war."

"You don't know anything about it. You're too young."

"You should stay and mate with constructs or with
Oankali," I said. "The children we construct are free of inher-
ent flaws. What we build will last."

"You're just a child, repeating what you've been told!"

I shook my head. "I perceive what I perceive. No one had to
tell me how to use my senses any more than they had to tell
you how to see or hear. There is a lethal genetic conflict in Humanity, and you know it."

"All we know is what the Oankali have told us." The male
had come back. He put his arm around the female, drawing
her away from me as though I had offered some threat. "They
could be lying for their own reasons."

I shifted my attention to him. "You know they're not," I
said softly. "Your own history tells you. Your people are intelligent, and that's good. The Oankali say you're potentially one
of the most intelligent species they've found. But you're also
hierarchical—you and your nearest animal relatives and your
most distant animal ancestors. Intelligence is relatively new to
life on Earth, but your hierarchical tendencies are ancient. The
new was too often put at the service of the old. It will be again.
You're bright enough to learn to live on your new world, but

you're so hierarchical you'll destroy yourselves trying to dominate it and each other. You might last a long time, but in the end, you'll destroy yourselves."

"We could last a thousand years," the male said. "We did all right on Earth until the war."

"You could. Your new world will be difficult. It will demand most of your attention, perhaps occupy your hierarchical tendencies safely for a while."

"We'll be free—us, our children, their children."

"Perhaps."

"We'll be fully Human and free. That's enough. We might even get into space again on our own someday. Your people might be dead wrong about us."

"No." He couldn't read the gene combinations as I could. It was as though he were about to walk off a cliff simply because he could not see it—or because he, or rather his descendants, would not hit the rocks below for a long time. And what were we doing, we who knew the truth? Helping him reach the cliff. Ferrying him to it.

"We might outlast your people here on Earth," he said.

"I hope so," I told him. His expression said he didn't believe me, but I meant it. We would not be here—the Earth he knew would not be here—for more than a few centuries. We, Oankali and construct, were space-going people, as curious about other life and as acquisitive of it as Humans were hierarchical. Eventually we would have to begin the long, long search for a new species to combine with to construct new lifeforms. Much of Oankali existence was spent in such searches. We would leave this solar system in perhaps three centuries. I would live to see the leave-taking myself. And when we broke and scattered, we would leave behind a lump of stripped rock more like the moon than like his blue Earth. He did not know that. He would never know it. To tell him would be a cruelty.

"Do you ever think of yourself or your kind as Human?" the female asked. "Some of you look so Human."

"We feel our Humanity. It helps us to understand both you

and the Oankali. Oankali alone could never have let you have your Mars colony."

"I heard they were helping!" the male said. "Your . . . your parent said they were helping!"

"They help because of what we constructs tell them: that you should be allowed to go even though you'll eventually destroy yourselves. The Oankali believe . . . the Oankali *know to the bone* that it's wrong to help the Human species regenerate unchanged because it *will* destroy itself again. To them it's like deliberately causing the conception of a child who is so defective that it must die in infancy."

"They're wrong. Someday we'll show them how wrong."

It was a threat. It was meaningless, but it gave him some slight satisfaction. "The other Humans here will show you where to gather food," I said. "If you need anything else, ask one of us." I turned to go.

"So goddamn patronizing," the male muttered.

I turned back without thinking. "Am I really?"

The male frowned, muttered a curse, and went back into the house. I understood then that he was just angry. It bothered me that I sometimes made them angry. I never intended to.

The female stepped to me, touched my face, examined a little of my hair. Humans who hadn't mated among us never really learned to touch us. At best, they annoyed us by rubbing their hands over sensory spots, and once their hands found the spots they never liked them.

The female jerked her hand back when her fingers discovered the one below my left ear.

"They're a little like eyes that can't close to protect themselves," I said. "It doesn't exactly hurt us when you touch them, but we don't like you to."

"So what? You have to teach people how to touch you?"

I smiled and took her hand between my own. "Hands are always safe," I said. I left her standing there, watching me. I could see her through sensory tentacles in my hair. She stood there until the male came out and drew her inside.

2

I went back to Nikanj and sat near it while it took care of family matters, while it met with people from the Oankali homeship, Chkahichdahk, which circled the Earth out beyond the orbit of the moon, while it exchanged information with other ooloi or took biological information from my siblings. We all brought Nikanj bits of fur, flesh, pollen, leaves, seeds, spores, or other living or dead cells from plants or animals that we had questions about or that were new to us.

No one paid any attention to me. There was an odd comfort in that. I could examine them all with my newly sharpened senses, see what I had never seen before, smell what I had never noticed. I suppose I seemed to doze a little. For a time, Aaor, my closest sibling—my Oankali-born sister—came to sit beside me. She was the child of my Oankali mother, and not yet truly female, but I had always thought of her as a sister. She looked so female—or she had looked female before I began to change. Now she . . . Now it looked the way it always should have. It looked eka in the true meaning of the word—a child too young to have developed sex. That was what we both were—for now. Aaor smelled eka. It could literally go either way, become male or female. I had always known this, of course, about both of us. But now, suddenly, I could no longer even think of Aaor as she. It probably would be female someday, just as I would probably soon become the male I appeared to be. The Human-born rarely change their apparent sex. In my family, only one Human-born had changed from apparent female to actual male. Several Oankali-born had changed, but most knew long before their metamorphosis that they felt more drawn to become the opposite of what they seemed.

Aaor moved close and examined me with a few of its head and body tentacles. "I think you're close to metamorphosis," it said. It has not spoken aloud. Children learned early that it was ill mannered to speak aloud among themselves if others nearby were having ongoing vocal conversations. We spoke through touch signals, signs, and multisensory illusions transmitted through head or body tentacles—direct neural stimulation.

"I am," I answered silently. "But I feel . . . different."

"Show me."

I tried to re-create my increased sensory awareness for it, but it drew away.

After a time, it touched me again lightly. In tactile signals only, it said, "I don't like it. Something's wrong. You should show Dichaan."

I did not want to show Dichaan. That was odd. I hadn't minded showing Aaor. I felt no aversion to showing Nikanj— except that it would probably send me to my fathers.

"What about me disturbs you?" I asked Aaor.

"I don't know," it answered. "But I don't like it. I've never felt it before. Something is wrong." It was afraid, and that was odd. New things normally drew its attention. This new thing repelled it.

"It isn't anything that will hurt you," I said. "Don't worry."

It got up and went away. It didn't say anything. It just left. That was out of character. Aaor and I had always been close. It was only three months younger than I was, and we'd been together since it was born. It had never walked away from me before. You only walk away from people you could no longer communicate with.

I went over to Nikanj. It was alone now. One of our neighbors had just left it. It focused a cone of its long head tentacles on me, finally noticing that there was something different about me.

"Metamorphosis, Eka?"

"I think so."

"Let me check. Your scent is . . . strange."

The tone of its voice was strange. I had been around when siblings of mine went into metamorphosis. Nikanj had never sounded quite that way.

It wrapped the tip of one sensory arm around my arm and extended its sensory hand. Sensory hands were ooloi appendages. Nikanj did not normally use them to check for metamorphosis. It could have used its head or body tentacles just like anyone else, but it was disturbed enough to want to be more precise, more certain.

I tried to feel the filaments of the sensory hand as they slipped through my flesh. I had never been able to before, but I felt them clearly now. There was no pain, of course. No communication. But I felt as though I had found what I had been looking for. The deep touch of the sensory hand was air after a long, blundering swim underwater. Without thinking I caught its second sensory arm between my hands.

Something went wrong then. Nikanj didn't sting me. It wouldn't do that. But something happened. I startled it. No, I shocked it profoundly—and it transmitted to me the full impact of that shock. Its multisensory illusions felt more real than things that actually happened, and this was worse than an illusion. This was a sudden, swift cycling of its own intense surprise and fear. From me to it to me. Closed loop.

I lost focus on everything else. I wasn't aware of collapsing or of being caught in Nikanj's two almost Human-looking strength arms. Later, I examined my latent memories of this and knew that for several seconds I had been simply held in all four of Nikanj's arms. It had stood utterly still, frozen in shock and fear.

Finally, its shock ebbing, its fear growing, it put me on a broad platform. It focused a sharp cone of head tentacles on me and stood rock still again, observing. After a time it lay down beside me and helped me understand why it was so upset.

But by then, I knew.

"You're becoming ooloi," it said quietly.

I began to be afraid for myself. Nikanj lay alongside me. Its head and body tentacles did not touch me. It offered no comfort or reassurance, no movement, no sign that it was even conscious.

"Ooan?" I said. I hadn't called it that for years. My older
siblings called our parents by their names, and I had begun
early to imitate them. Now, though, I was afraid. I did not
want "Nikanj." I wanted "Ooan," the parent I had most often
gone to or been carried to for healing or teaching. "Ooan,
can't you change me back? I still *look* male."

"You know better," it said aloud.

"But . . ."

"You were never male, no matter how you looked. You were
eka. You know that."

I said nothing. All my life, I had been referred to as "he" and
treated as male by my Human parents, by all the Humans in
Lo. Even Oankali sometimes said "he." And everyone had assumed that Dichaan and Tino were to be my same-sex parents.
People were supposed to feel that way so that I would be prepared for the change that should have happened.

But the change had gone wrong. Until now, no construct
had become ooloi. When people reached adulthood and were
ready to mate, they went to the ship and found an Oankali
ooloi or they signaled the ship and an Oankali ooloi was sent
down.

Human-born males were still considered experimental and
potentially dangerous. A few males from other towns had been
sterilized and exiled to the ship. Nobody was ready for a construct ooloi. Certainly nobody was ready for a Human-born
construct ooloi. Could there be a more potentially deadly
being?

"Ooan!" I said desperately.

It drew me against it, its head and body tentacles touching,
then penetrating my flesh. Its sensory arm coiled around me so
that the sensory hand could seat itself at the back of my neck.
This was the preferred ooloi grip with Humans and with many
constructs. Both brain and spinal cord were easily accessible to
the slender, slender filaments of the sensory hand.

For the first time since I stopped nursing, Nikanj drugged
me—immobilized me—as though it could not trust me to be

still. I was too frightened even to be offended. Maybe it was right not to trust me.

Still, it did not hurt me. And it did not calm me. Why should it calm me? I had good reason to be afraid.

"I should have noticed this," it said aloud. "I should have . . . I constructed you to look very male—so male that the females would be attracted to you and help convince you that you *were* male. Until today, I thought they had. Now I know I was the one who was convinced. I deceived myself into carelessness and blindness."

"I've always felt male," I said. "I've never thought about being anything else."

"I should have sent you to spend more time with Tino and Dichaan." It paused for a moment, rustled its unengaged body tentacles. It did that when it was thinking. A dozen or so body tentacles rubbed together sounded like wind blowing through the trees. "I liked having you around too much," it said. "All my children grow up and turn away from me, turn to their same-sex parents. I thought you would, too, when the time came."

"That's what I thought. I never wanted to do it, though."

"You didn't want to go to your fathers?"

"No. I only left you when I knew I would be in the way."

"I never felt that you were in the way."

"I tried to be careful."

It rustled its tentacles again, repeated, "I should have noticed. . . ."

"You were always lonely," I said. "You had mates and children, but to me, you always tasted . . . empty in some way—as though you were hungry, almost starving."

It said nothing for some time. It did not move, but I felt safely enveloped by it. Some Humans tried to give you that feeling when they hugged you and irritated your sensory spots and pinched your sensory tentacles. Only the Oankali could give it, really. And right now, only Nikanj could give it to me. In all its long life, it had had no same-sex child. It had used all its tricks to protect us from becoming ooloi. It had used all its tricks to keep itself agonizingly alone.

I think I had always known how lonely it was. Surely, of my five parents, I had always loved it best. Apparently my body had responded to it in the way an Oankali child's would. I was taking on the sex of the parent I had felt most drawn to.

"What will happen to me?" I asked after a long silence.

"You're healthy," it said. "Your development is exactly right. I can't find any flaw in you."

And that meant there was no flaw. It was a good ooloi. Other ooloi came to it when they had problems beyond their perception or comprehension.

"What will happen?" I repeated.

"You'll stay with us."

No qualification. It would not allow me to be sent away. Yet it had agreed with other Oankali a century before that any accidental construct ooloi must be sent to the ship. There it could be watched, and any damage it did could be spotted and corrected quickly. On the ship, its every move could be monitored. On Earth, it might do great harm before anyone noticed.

But Nikanj would not allow me to be sent away. It had said so.

3

Quickly Nikanj called all my parents together. I would sleep soon. Metamorphosis is mostly deep sleep while the body changes and matures. Nikanj wanted to tell the others while I was still awake.

My Human mother came in, looked at Nikanj and me, then walked over to me and took my hands. No one had said anything aloud, but she knew something was wrong. She certainly knew that I was in metamorphosis. She had seen that often enough.

She looked closely at me, holding her face near mine, since her eyes were her only organs of sight. Then she looked at Nikanj. "What's wrong with him? This isn't just metamorphosis."

Through her hands, I had begun to study her flesh in a way I never had before. I knew her flesh better than I knew anyone's, but there was something about it now—a flavor, a texture I had never noticed.

She took her hands from me abruptly and stepped away. "Oh, good god. . . ."

Still, no one had spoken to her. Yet she knew.

"What is it?" my Human father asked.

My mother looked at Nikanj. When it did not speak, she said, "Jodahs . . . Jodahs is becoming ooloi."

My Human father frowned. "But that's impos—" He stopped, followed my mother's gaze to Nikanj. "It's impossible, isn't it?"

"No," Nikanj said softly.

He went to Nikanj, stood stiffly over it. He looked more frightened than angry. "*How could you let this happen?*" he demanded. "Exile, for godsake! Exile for your own child!"

"No, Chka," Nikanj whispered.

"Exile! It's your law, you ooloi!"

"No." It focused a cone of head tentacles on its Oankali mates. "The child is perfect. My carelessness has allowed it to become ooloi, but I haven't been careless in any other way." It hesitated. "Come. Know for certain. Know for the people."

My Oankali mother and father joined with it in a tangle of head and body tentacles. It did not touch them with its sensory arms, did not even uncoil the arms until Dichaan took one arm and Ahajas took the other. In unison, then, all three focused cones of head tentacles on my two Human parents. The Humans glared at them. After a time, Lilith went to the Oankali, but did not touch them. She turned and held one arm out to Tino. He did not move.

"Your law!" he repeated to Nikanj.

But it was Lilith who answered. "Not law. Consensus. They agreed to send accidental ooloi to the ship. Nika believes it can change the agreement."

"Now? In the middle of everything?"

"Yes."

"What if it can't?"

Lilith swallowed. I could see her throat move. "Then maybe we'll have to leave Lo for a while—live apart in the forest."

He went to her, looked at her the way he does sometimes when he wants to touch her, maybe to hold her the way Humans hold each other in the guest area. But Humans who accept Oankali mates give up that kind of touching. They don't give up wanting to do it, but once they mate Oankali, they find each other's touch repellent.

Tino shifted his attention to Nikanj. "Why don't you talk to me? Why do you leave her to tell me what's going on?"

Nikanj extended a sensory arm toward him.

"No! Goddamnit, talk to me! Speak aloud!"

". . . all right," Nikanj whispered, its body bent in an attitude of deep shame.

Tino glared at it.

"I cannot restore . . . your same-sex child to you," it said.

"Why did you do this? How could you do it?"

"I made a mistake. I only realized earlier today what I had allowed to happen. I . . . I would not have done it deliberately, Chka. Nothing could have made me do it. It happened because after so many years I had begun to relax about our children. Things have always gone well. I was careless."

My Human father looked at me. It was as though he looked from a long way away. His hands moved, and I knew he wanted to touch me, too. But if he did, it would go wrong the way it had earlier with my mother. They couldn't touch me anymore. Within families, people could touch their same-sex children, their unsexed children, their same-sex mates, and their ooloi mates.

Now, abruptly, my Human father turned and grasped the sensory arm Nikanj offered. The arm was a tough, muscular organ that existed to contain and protect the essential ooloi sensory and reproductive organs. It probably could not be injured by bare Human hands, but I think Tino tried. He was angry and hurt, and that made him want to hurt others. Of my two Human parents, only he tended to react this way. And now the only being he could turn to for comfort was the one who had caused all his trouble. An Oankali would have opened a wall and gone away for a while. Even Lilith would have done that. Tino tried to give pain. Pain for pain.

Nikanj drew him against its body and held him motionless as it comforted him and spoke silently with him. It held him for so long that my Oankali parents raised platforms and sat on them to wait. Lilith came to share my platform, though she could have raised her own. My scent must have disturbed her, but she sat near me and looked at me.

"Do you feel all right?" she said.

"Yes. I'll fall asleep soon, I think."

"You look ready for it. Does my being here bother you?"

"Not yet. But it must bother you."

"I can stand it."

She stayed where she was. I could remember being inside her. I could remember when there was nothing in my universe except her. I found myself longing to touch her. I hadn't felt that before. I had never before been unable to touch her. Now I discovered a little of the Human hunger to touch where I could not.

"Are you afraid?" Lilith asked.

"I was. But now that I know I'm all right, and that you'll all keep me here, I'm fine."

She smiled a little. "Nika's first same-sex child. It's been so lonely."

"I know."

"We all knew," Dichaan said from his platform. "All the

ooloi on Earth must be feeling the desperation Nikanj felt. The people are going to have to change the old agreement before more accidents happen. The next one might be a flawed ooloi."

A flawed natural genetic engineer—one who could distort or destroy with a touch. Nothing could save it from confinement on the ship. Perhaps it would even have to be physically altered to prevent it from functioning in any way as an ooloi. Perhaps it would be so dangerous that it would have to spend its existence in suspended animation, its body used by others for painless experimentation, its consciousness permanently shut off.

I shuddered and lay down again. At once, both Nikanj and Tino were beside me, reconciled, apparently, by their concern for me. Nikanj touched me with a sensory arm, but did not expose the sensory hand. "Listen, Jodahs."

I focused on it without opening my eyes.

"You'll be all right here. I'll stay with you. I'll talk to the people from here, and when you've reached the end of this first metamorphosis, you'll remember all that I've said to them— and all they've said." It slipped a sensory arm around my neck and the feel of it there comforted me. "We'll take care of you," it said.

Later, it stripped my clothing from me as I floated atop sleep, a piece of straw floating on a still pond. I could not slip beneath the surface yet.

Something was put into my mouth. It had the flavor and texture of chunks of pineapple, but I knew from tiny differences in its scent that it was a Lo creation. It was almost pure protein—exactly what my body needed. When I had eaten several pieces, I was able to slip beneath the surface into sleep.

4

Metamorphosis is sleep. Days, weeks, months of sleep broken by a few hours now and then of waking, eating, talking. Males and females slept even more, but they had just the one metamorphosis. Ooloi go through this twice.

There were times when I was aware enough to watch my body develop. A sair was growing at my throat so that I would eventually be able to breathe as easily in water as in air. My nose was not absorbed into my face, but it became little more than an ornament.

I didn't lose my hair, but I grew many more head and body tentacles. I would not develop sensory arms until my second metamorphosis, but my sensitivity had already been increased, and I would soon be able to give and receive more complex multisensory illusions, and handle them much faster.

And something was growing between my hearts.

Because I was Human-born, my internal arrangement was basically Human. Ooloi are careful not to construct children who provoke uncontrollable immune reactions in their birth mothers. Even two hearts seem radical to some Humans. Sometimes they shoot us where they think a heart should be—where their own hearts are—then run away in panic because that kind of thing doesn't stop us. I don't think many Humans have seen what the Oankali look like inside—or what we constructs look like. Two hearts are just double the Human allotment. But the organ now growing between my hearts was not Human at all.

Every construct had some version of it. Males and females used it to store and keep viable the cells of unfamiliar living things that they sought out and brought home to their ooloi mate or parent. In ooloi, the organ was larger and more complex. Within it, ooloi manipulated molecules of DNA more deftly than Human women manipulated the bits of thread they used to sew their cloth. I had been constructed inside such an organ, assembled from the genetic contributions of my two mothers and my two fathers. The construction itself and a single Oankali organelle was the only ooloi contribution to my existence. The organelle had divided within each of my cells as the cells divided. It had become an essential part of my body. We were what we were because of that organelle. It made us collectors and traders of life, always learning, always changing in every way but one—that one organelle. Ooloi said we *were* that organelle—that the original Oankali had evolved through that organelle's invasion, acquisition, duplication, and symbiosis. Sometimes on worlds that had no intelligent, carbon-based life to trade with, Oankali deliberately left behind large numbers of the organelle. Abandoned, it would seek a home in the most unlikely indigenous life-forms and trigger changes— evolution in spurts. Hundreds of millions of years later, perhaps some Oankali people would wander by and find interesting trade partners waiting for them. The organelle made or found compatibility with life-forms so completely dissimilar that they were unable even to perceive one another as alive.

Once I had been all enclosed within Nikanj in a mature version of the organ I was growing between my hearts. That, I did not remember. I came to consciousness within my Human mother's uterus.

Yashi, the ooloi called their organ of genetic manipulation. Sometimes they talked about it as though it were another person. "I'm going out to taste the river and the forest. Yashi is hungry and twisting for something new."

Did it really twist? I probably wouldn't find out until my second metamorphosis when my sensory arms grew. Until then, yashi would enlarge and develop to become only a little more useful than that of a male or a female.

Other Oankali organs began to develop now as genes, dormant since my conception, became active and stimulated the growth of new, highly specialized tissues. Adult ooloi were more different than most Humans realized. Beyond their insertion of the Oankali organelle, they made no genetic contribution to their children. They left their birth families and mated with strangers so that they would not be confronted with too much familiarity. Humans said familiarity bred contempt. Among the ooloi, it bred mistakes. Male and female siblings could mate safely as long as their ooloi came from a totally different kin group.

So, for an ooloi, a same-sex child was as close as it would ever come to seeing itself in its children.

For that reason among others, Nikanj shielded me.

I felt as though it stood between me and the people so that they could not get past it to take me away.

I absorbed all that happened in the room with me, and all that came through the platform to me from Lo.

"*How can we trust you?*" the people demanded of Nikanj. Their messages reached us through Lo, and reached Lo either directly from our neighbors or by way of radio signals from other towns relayed to Lo by the ship. And we heard from people who lived on the ship. A few messages came from nearby towns that could make direct underground contact with Lo. The messages were all essentially the same. "*How can we possibly trust you? No one else has made such a dangerous mistake.*"

Through Lo, Nikanj invited the people to examine it and its findings as though it were some newly discovered species. It invited them to know all that it knew about me. It endured all the tests people could think of and agree on. But it kept them from touching me.

In spite of its mistakes, it was my same-sex parent. Since it said I must not be disturbed in metamorphosis, and since they were not yet convinced that it had lost all competence, they would not disturb me. Humans thought this sort of thing was a matter of authority—who had authority over the child. Constructs and Oankali knew it was a matter of physiology. Nikanj's body "understood" what mine was going through—what it needed and did not need. Nikanj let me know that I was all right and reassured me that I wasn't alone. In the way of Oankali and construct same-sex parents, it went through metamorphosis with me. It knew exactly what would disturb me and what was safe. Its body knew, and no one would argue with that knowledge. Even Human same-sex parents seemed to reach an empathy with their children that the people respected. Without that empathy, some developing males and females had had a strange time of it. One of my brothers was completely cut off from the family and from Oankali and construct companionship during his metamorphosis. He reacted to his unrelated, all-Human companions by losing all visible traces of his own Human heritage. He survived all right. The Humans had taken care of him as best they could. But after metamorphosis he had had to accept people treating him as though he were an entirely different person. He was Human-born, but our Human parents didn't recognize him at all when he came home.

"I don't want to push you toward the Human or the Oankali extreme," Nikanj said once when the people gave it a few hours of peace. It talked to me often, knowing that whether I was conscious or not, I would hear and remember. Its presence and its voice comforted me. "I want you to develop as you should in every way. The more normal your changes are, the sooner the people will accept you as normal."

It had not yet convinced the people to accept anything about me. Not even that I should be allowed to stay on Earth and live in Lo through my subadult stage and second metamorphosis. The consensus now was that I should be brought up to the ship as soon as I had completed this first metamorphosis. Subadults were still seen as children, but they could work as ooloi in ways that did not involve reproduction. Subadults could not only heal or cause disease, but they could cause genetic changes—mutations—in plants and animals. They could do anything that could be done without mates. They could be unintentionally deadly, changing insects and microorganisms in unexpected ways.

"I don't want to hurt anything," I said toward the end of my months-long change when I could speak again. "Don't let me do any harm."

"No harm, Oeka," Nikanj said softly. It had lain down beside me as it often did so that while I slept, it could be with me, yet sink its head and body tentacles into the platform—the flesh of Lo—and communicate with the people. "There is no flaw in you," it continued. "You should be aware of everything you do. You can make mistakes, but you can also perceive them. And you can correct them. I'll help you."

Its words gave a security nothing else could have. I had begun to feel like one of the dormant volcanoes high in the mountains beyond the forest—like a thing that might explode anytime, destroying whatever happened to be nearby.

"There is something that you must be aware of, though," Nikanj said.

"Yes?"

"You will be complete in ways that male and female constructs have not been. Eventually you and others like you will awaken dormant abilities in males and females. But you, as an ooloi, can have no dormant abilities."

"What will it mean . . . to be complete?"

"You'll be able to change yourself. What we can do from one generation to the next—changing our form, reverting to earlier forms or combinations of forms—you'll be able to do within yourself. Superficially, you may even be able to create new forms, new shells for camouflage. That's what we intended."

"If I can change my shape . . ." I focused narrowly on Nikanj. "Could I become male?"

Nikanj hesitated. "Do you still want to be male?"

Had I ever wanted to be male? I had just assumed I *was* male, and would have no choice in the matter. "The people wouldn't be as hard on you if I were male."

It said nothing.

"They haven't accepted me yet," I argued. "They could go on rejecting me until the family had to leave Lo—all because of me."

It continued to focus on me silently. There were times when I envied Humans their ability to shut off their sight by closing their eyes, shut off their understanding by some conscious act of denial that was beyond me.

I closed my throat, then drew and released a noisy, Human breath by mouth. It wasn't necessary now when I wasn't talking, but it filled time.

"I have too many feelings," I said. "I want to be your same-sex child, but I don't want to cause the family trouble."

"What do you want for yourself?"

Now I could not speak. I would hurt it, no matter what I said.

"Oeka, I must know what you want, what you feel, and for your own sake, you must tell me. It will be better for you if the people only see you through me until your metamorphosis is complete."

It was right. The thought of a lot of other people interfering with me now was frightening, terrifying. I hadn't known it would be, but it was. "I wouldn't want to give up being what I am," I said. "I . . . I want to be ooloi. I really want it. And I wish I didn't. How can I want to cause the family so much trouble?"

"You want to be what you are. That's healthy and right for you. What we do about it is our decision, our responsibility. Not yours."

I might not have believed this if a Human had said it. Humans said one thing with their bodies and another with their mouths and everyone had to spend time and energy figuring out what they really meant. And once we did understand them, the Humans got angry and acted as though we had stolen thoughts from their minds.

Nikanj, on the other hand, meant what it said. Its body and its mouth said the same things. It believed that I should want to be what I was. But . . .

"Ooan, could I change if I wanted to?"

It smoothed its head and body tentacles flat against its skin, accepting my curiosity with amusement. "Not now. But when you're mature, you'll be able to cause yourself to look male. You wouldn't be satisfied with a male sexual role, though, and you wouldn't be able to make a male contribution to reproduction."

I tried to move, tried to reach toward it, but I was still too weak. Talking was exhausting, most other movement was impossible. My head tentacles swept toward it.

It moved closer and let me touch it, let me examine its flesh so that I could begin to understand the difference between its flesh and my own. I would be the most extreme version of a construct—not just a mix of Human and Oankali characteristics, but able to use my body in ways that neither Human nor Oankali could. Synergy.

I studied a single cell of Nikanj's arm, comparing it with cells of my own. Apart from my Human admixture, the main difference seemed to be that certain genes of mine had activated and caused my metamorphosis. I wondered what might happen if these genes activated in Nikanj. It was mature. Were there other changes it might undergo?

"Stop," Nikanj said quietly. It signaled silently and spoke aloud. Its silent signal felt urgent. What was I doing?

"Look what you've done." Now it spoke only silently.

I reexamined the cell I had touched and realized that somehow I had located and activated the genes I had been curious about. These genes were trying to activate others of their kind in other cells, trying to cause Nikanj's body to begin the secretion of inappropriate hormones that would cause inappropriate growth.

What would grow?

"Nothing would grow in me," Nikanj said, and I realized it had perceived my curiosity. "The cell will die. You see?"

The cell died as I watched.

"I could have kept it alive," Nikanj said. "By a conscious act, I could have prevented my body from rejecting it. Without you, though, I could not have activated the dormant genes. My body rejects that kind of behavior as . . . deeply self-destructive."

"But it didn't seem wrong or dangerous," I said. "It just felt . . . out of place."

"Out of place, out of its time. In a Human, that could be enough to kill."

I couldn't think of anything to say. My curiosity burned away in fear.

"When you touch them, never withdraw without checking to see whether you've done harm."

"I won't touch them at all."

"You won't be able to resist them."

It didn't doubt or guess or suspect. It knew. "What shall I do?" I whispered aloud. It couldn't be wrong about such things. It had lived too long, seen too much.

"For now you can only be careful. After your second metamorphosis, you'll mate and you won't be quite so interested in investigating people who aren't your mates."

"But that could be two or three years from now."

"Less, I think. Your body feels as though it will develop quickly now. Until it has, you know how careful you'll have to be."

"I don't know whether I can do it. To be so careful of every touch . . ."

"Only deep touches." Touches that penetrated flesh with sensory tentacles or, later, sensory arms. Only Humans could be satisfied with less than deep touches.

"I don't see how I can be that careful," I said. "But I have to."

"Yes."

"Then I'll do it."

It touched my head tentacles with several of its own, agreeing. Then it examined the rest of my body closely, again checking for dangerous flaws, gathering information for the people. I relaxed and let it work, and it said instantly, "No!"

"What?" I asked. I really hadn't done anything this time. I knew I hadn't.

"Until you know yourself a great deal better, you can't afford to relax that way while you're in contact with another person. Not even with me. You're too competent, too well able to make tiny, potentially deadly changes in genes, in cells, in organs. What males, females, and even some ooloi must struggle to perceive, you can't fail to perceive on one level or another. What they must be taught to do, what they must strain to do, you can do almost without thought. You have all the sensitivity I could give you, and that's a great deal. And you have the latent abilities of your Human ancestors. In you, those abilities are no longer latent. That's why you were able to activate genes in me that even I can't reawaken. That's why the Humans are such treasure. They've given us regenerative abilities we had never been able to trade for before, even though we've found other species that had such abilities. I'm here because a Human was able to share such ability with me."

It meant Lilith, my birth mother. Every child in the family had heard that story. One of Nikanj's sensory arms had been all but severed from its body, but Lilith allowed it to link into her body and activate certain of her highly specialized genes. It used what it learned from these to encourage its own cells to grow and reattach the complex structures of the arm. It could not have done this without the triggering effect of Lilith's genetic help.

Lilith's ability had run in her family, although neither she nor her ancestors had been able to control it. It had either lain dormant in them or come to life in insane, haphazard fashion and caused the growth of useless new tissue. New tissue gone obscenely wrong.

Humans called this condition cancer. To them, it was a hated disease. To the Oankali, it was treasure. It was beauty beyond Human comprehension.

Nikanj might have died without Lilith's help. If it had lived, maimed, it could not have functioned as an ooloi. Its mates would have had to find another ooloi. They were young then. They might have survived the break and managed to accept someone else. But then we wouldn't exist—we, the children Nikanj had constructed gene by gene, chromosome by chromosome. A different ooloi would have chosen a different mix, would have manufactured a different series of genes to patch the created whole together and make it viable. All our construct uniqueness was the work of our ooloi parent. Until Nikanj's mistake with me, it had been known for the beauty of its children. It had shared all that it knew about mixing construct children, and it had probably saved other people from pain, trouble, and deadly error. It had been able to do all this because, thanks to Lilith, it had two functioning sensory arms.

"You could give Humans back their cancers," it said, rousing me from my thoughts. "Or you could affect them genetically. You could damage their immune systems, cause neurological disorders, glandular problems. . . . You could give them diseases they don't have names for. You could do all that with just a moment's inattention." It paused, wholly focused on me. "Humans will attract you and seduce you without realizing what they're doing. But they'll have no defense against you. And you're probably as sexually precocious as any Human-born construct."

"I don't have sensory arms," I said. "What can I do sexually until they grow?" I had nothing between my legs anymore. No one could see me naked and mistake me for male—or female. I was an ooloi subadult, and I would be one for years—or perhaps only for months if Nikanj was right about the speed of my maturing.

"You'll be able to take pleasure in new sensation," Nikanj said. "Especially in the complex, frightening, promising taste of Humans. I didn't enjoy them often when I was subadult because I could give little in return. I tasted Lilith when I could heal her or make necessary changes. But I couldn't give pleasure until I was adult. You may be able to give it now with sensory tentacles."

I drew my sensory tentacles tight against me, wondering. There had been that Human couple I met just before I fell asleep months ago. They were on their way to Mars by now. But what would they have tasted like? The female might have let me find out. But the male . . . ? How did any ooloi seduce Human males? Males were suspicious, hostile, dangerous. I suddenly wanted very much to taste one. I had touched my

Human father and other mated males before my change, but I wasn't as perceptive then. I wanted to touch an unmated stranger—perhaps a potential mate.

"Precocious," Nikanj said flatly. "Stick to constructs for a while. They aren't defenseless. But even they can be hurt. You can damage them so subtly that no one notices the problem until it becomes serious. Be more careful than you have ever been."

"Will they let me touch them?"

"I don't know. The people haven't decided yet."

I thought about what it might be like to spend all my subadulthood alone in the forest with only my parents and unmated siblings as company. A shudder went through my body and Nikanj touched its sensory tentacles to mine, concerned.

"I want them to accept me," I said unnecessarily.

"Yes. I can see that any exile could be hard on you, bad for you. But . . . perhaps Chkahichdahk exile would be least hard. My parents are still there. They would take you in."

Ship exile. "You said you wouldn't let them take me!"

"I won't. You'll stay with us for as long as you want to stay."

It meant as long as I was not more miserable alone with the family than it believed I would be if I were cut off from the family and sent to the ship. Humans tended to misunderstand ooloi when ooloi said things like that. Humans thought the ooloi were promising that they would do nothing until the Humans said they had changed their minds—told the ooloi with their mouths, in words. But the ooloi perceived all that a living being said—all words, all gestures, and a vast array of other internal and external bodily responses. Ooloi absorbed everything and acted according to whatever consensus they discovered. Thus ooloi treated individuals as they treated groups of beings. They sought a consensus. If there was none, it meant the being was confused, ignorant, frightened, or in some other way not yet able to see its own best interests. The ooloi gave information and perhaps calmness until they could perceive a consensus. Then they acted.

If, someday, Nikanj saw that I needed mates more than I needed my family, Nikanj would send me to the ship no matter what I said.

5

As the days passed, I grew stronger. I hoped, I wished, I pleaded with myself for Nikanj to have no reason ever to seek a consensus within me. If only the people would trust me, perceive that I was no more interested in using my new abilities to hurt other living things than I was in hurting myself.

Unfortunately I often did both. Every day, at least, Nikanj had to correct some harm that I had done to Lo—to the living platform on which I lay. Lo's natural color was gray-brown. Beneath me, it turned yellow. It developed swellings. Rough, diseased patches appeared on it. Its odor changed, became foul. Parts of it sloughed off. Sometimes it developed deep, open sores.

And all that I did to Lo, I also did to myself. But it was Lo that I felt guilty about. Lo was parent, sibling, home. It was the world I had been born into. As an ooloi, I would have to leave it when I mated. But woven into its genetic structure and my own was the unmistakable Lo kin group signature. I would have done anything to avoid giving Lo pain.

I got up from my platform as soon as I could and collected dead wood to sleep on.

Lo ate the wood. It was not intelligent enough to reason with—would not be for perhaps a hundred years. But it was self-aware. It knew what was part of it and what wasn't. I was part of it—one of its many parts. It would not have me with it, yet so distant from it, separated by so much dead matter. It preferred whatever pain I gave it to the unnatural itch of apparent rejection.

So I went on giving it pain until I was completely recovered. By then, I knew as well as anyone else that I had to go. The people still wanted me to go to Chkahichdahk because the ship was a much older, more resistant organism. It was as able as most ooloi to protect and heal itself. Lo would be that resistant someday, but not for more than a century. And on the ship, I could be watched by many more mature ooloi.

Or I could go into exile here on Earth—before I did more harm to Lo or to someone in Lo. Those were my only choices. Through Lo, Nikanj had kept a check on the air of my room. It had seen that I did not change the microorganisms I came into contact with. And outside, insects avoided me as they avoided all Oankali and constructs. The people would permit me Earth exile, then.

With no real discussion, we prepared to go. My Human parents made packs for themselves, wrapping Lo cloth hammocks around prewar books, tools, extra clothing, and food from Lilith's garden—food grown in the soil of Earth, not from the substance of Lo. Both Lilith and Tino knew that their Oankali mates would provide for all their physical needs, yet they could not easily accept being totally dependent. This was a characteristic of adult Humans that the Oankali never understood. The Oankali simply accepted it as best they could and were pleased to see that we constructs understood.

I went to my Human mother and watched her assemble her pack. I did not touch her—had not touched any Human since my metamorphosis ended. As a reminder of my unstable condition, I had developed a rough, crusty growth on my right hand. I had deliberately reabsorbed it twice, but each night it grew again. I saw Lilith staring at it.

"It will heal," I told her. "Nikanj will help me with it."

"Does it hurt?" she asked.

"No. It just feels . . . *wrong*. Like a weight tied there where it shouldn't be."

"Why is it wrong?"

I looked at the growth. It was red and broken in places, crusty with distorted flesh and dried blood. It always seemed to be bleeding a little. "I caused it," I said, "but I don't understand how I did it. I fixed a couple of obvious problems, but the growth keeps coming back."

"How are you otherwise?"

"Well, I think. And once Ooan shows me how to take care of this growth, I'll remember."

I think my scent was beginning to bother. She stepped away, but looked at me as though she wanted to touch me. "How can I help you?" she asked.

"Make a pack for me."

She looked surprised. "What shall I put in it?"

I hesitated, afraid my answer would hurt her. But I wanted the pack, and only she could put it together as I wished. "I may not live here again," I said.

She blinked, looked at me with the pain I had hoped not to see.

"I want Human things," I said. "Small Human things that you and Tino would leave behind. And I want yams from your garden—and cassava and fruit and seed. Samples of all the seed or whatever is needed to grow your plants."

"Nikanj could give you cell samples."

"I know. . . . But will you?"

"Yes."

I hesitated again. "I would have to leave Lo anyway, you know. Even without this exile, I couldn't mate here where I'm related to almost everyone."

"I know. But it will be a while before you mate. And if you were leaving to do that, we'd see you again. If you have to go to the ship . . . we may not."

"I belong to this world," I said. "I intend to stay. But even so, I want something of yours and Tino's."

"All right."

We looked at one another as though we were already saying goodbye—as though only I were leaving. I did leave her then, to take a final walk around Lo to say goodbye to the people I had spent my life with. Lo was more than a town. It was a family group. All the Oankali males and females were related in some way. All constructs were related except the few males who drifted in from other towns. All the ooloi had become part of Lo when they mated here. And any Human who stayed long in a relationship with an Oankali family was related more closely than most Humans realized.

It was hard to say goodbye to such people, to know that I might not see them again.

It was hard not to dare to touch them, not to allow them to touch me. But I would certainly do to some of them what I kept doing to Lo—change them, damage them as I kept changing and damaging myself. And because I was ooloi and construct, theoretically I could survive more damage than they could. I was to let Nikanj know if I touched anyone.

Everywhere I went, ooloi watched me with a terrible mixture of suspicion and hope, fear and need. If I didn't learn control, how long would it be before they could have same-sex children? I could hurt them more than anyone else they knew. The sharp, attentive cones of their head tentacles followed me everywhere and weighed on me like logs. If there were anything I would be glad to be away from, it was their intense, sustained attention.

I went to our neighbor Tehkorahs, an ooloi whose Human mates were especially close to my Human parents. "Do you think I should go into exile on the ship?" I asked it.

"Yes." Its voice was softer than most soft ooloi voices. It preferred not to speak aloud at all. But signs were sterile without touch to supplement them, and even Tehkorahs would not touch me. That hurt because it was ooloi and safe from anything I was likely to do. "Yes," it repeated uncharacteristically.

"Why! You know me. I won't touch people. And I'll learn control."

"If you can."

". . . yes."

"There are resisters in the forest. If you're out there long enough, they'll find you."

"Most of them have emigrated."

"Many. Not most."

"I won't touch them."

"Of course you will."

I opened my mouth, then closed it in the face of Tehkorahs's certainty. There was no reserve in it, no concealment. It was speaking what it believed was the truth.

After a time, it said, "How hungry are you?"

I didn't answer. It wasn't asking me how badly I wanted food, but when I'd last been touched. Just before I would have walked away, it held out all four arms. I hesitated, then stepped into its embrace.

It was not afraid of me. It was a forest fire of curiosity, longing, and fear, and I stood comforted and reassured while it examined me with every sensory tentacle that could reach me and both sensory arms.

We fed each other. My hunger was to be touched and its was to know everything firsthand and understand it all. Observing it, I understood that it was looking mainly for reassurance of its own. It wanted to see from an understanding of my body that I would gain control. It wanted me to be a clear success so that it would know it would be allowed to have its own same-sex children. Soon.

When it let me go, it was still uncomprehending. "You were very hungry," it said. "And that after only a day or two of being avoided." It knotted its head and body tentacles hard against its flesh. "You know something of what we can do, we ooloi, but I think you had no idea how much we need contact with other people. And you seem to need it more than we do. Spend more time with your paired sibling or you could become dangerous."

"I don't want to hurt Aaor."

"Nikanj will heal it until you learn to. If you learn to."

"I still don't want to hurt it."

"I don't think you can do it much harm. Not being able to go to anyone for comfort, though, can make you like the lightning—mindless and perhaps deadly."

I looked at it, my own head tentacles swept forward, focused. "What did you learn when you examined me? You weren't satisfied. Does that mean you think I can't learn control?"

"I don't know whether you can or not. I couldn't tell. Nikanj says you can, but that it will be hard. I don't know what it sees to draw that conclusion. Perhaps it only sees its first same-sex child."

"Do you still think I should go to the ship?"

"Yes. For your sake. For everyone's." It rubbed its right hand, and I saw that it had developed a duplicate of my crusty, running tumor.

"I'm sorry," I said. "Do you know what I did wrong to cause that?"

"A combination of things. I don't understand all of them yet. You should take this to Nikanj, *now.*"

"Will you be all right?"

"Yes."

I looked at it, missing it already—a smaller than average pale gray ooloi from the Jah kin group. It uncoiled one sensory arm and touched a sensory spot on my face. It could see the spots—as I could now. Their texture was slightly rougher than the skin around them. Tehkorahs made the contact a sharp, sweet shock of pleasure that washed over me like a sudden, cool rain. It ebbed slowly away. A goodbye.

6

It was raining when we left. Pouring. A brief waterfall from the sky. Lilith said rains like this happened to remind us that we lived in a rain forest. She had been born in a desert place called Los Angeles. She loved sudden, drenching rains.

There were eleven of us. My five parents, Aaor and me, Oni and Hozh, Ayodele and Yedik. These last four were my youngest siblings. They could have been left behind with some of our adult siblings, but they didn't want to stay. I didn't blame them. I wouldn't have wanted to part with our parents at that premetamorphosal state either. Even now, between metamorphoses, I needed them. And the family would have felt wrong without the younger siblings. My parents had only one pair per decade now. Ordinarily they would already have begun the next pair. But during the months of my metamorphosis, they had decided to wait until they could return to Lo—with or without me.

We headed first toward Lilith's garden to gather a few more fresh fruits and vegetables. I think she and Tino just wanted to see it again.

"It's time to rest this land anyway," Lilith said as we walked. She changed the location of her garden every few years, and let the forest reclaim the land. With these changes and with her habit of using fertilizer and river mud, she had used and reused the land beyond Lo for a century. She abandoned her gardens only when Lo grew too close to them.

But this garden had been destroyed.

It had not simply been raided. Raids happened occasionally. Resisters were afraid to raid Oankali towns—afraid the Oankali would begin to see them as real threats and transfer them permanently to the ship. But Lilith's gardens were clearly not Oankali. Resisters knew this and seemed to feel free to steal fruit or whole plants from them. Lilith never seemed to mind. She knew resisters thought of her—of any mated Human—as a traitor to Humanity, but she never seemed to hold it against them.

This time almost everything that had not been stolen had been destroyed. Melons had been stomped or smashed against the ground and trees. The line of papaya trees in the center of the garden had been broken down. Beans, peas, corn, yams, cassava, and pineapple plants had been uprooted and trampled. Nearby nut, fig, and breadfruit trees that were nearly a century old had been hacked and burned, though the fire had not destroyed most of them. Banana trees had been hacked down.

"Shit!" Lilith whispered. She stared at the destruction for a moment, then turned away and went to the edge of the garden clearing. There, she stood with her back to us, her body very straight. I thought Nikanj would go to her, offer comfort. Instead, it began gathering and trimming the least damaged cassava stalks. These could be replanted. Ahajas found an undamaged stalk of ripening bananas and Dichaan found and unearthed several yams, though the aboveground portions of the plants had been broken and scattered. Oankali and constructs could find edible roots and tubers easily by sitting on the ground and burrowing into it with the sensory tentacles of their legs. These short body tentacles could extend to several times their resting length.

It was Tino who went to Lilith. He walked around her, stood in front of her, and said, "What the hell? You know you'll have other gardens."

She nodded.

His voice softened. "I think we met in this one. Remember?"

She nodded again, and some of the rigidity went out of her posture. "How many kids ago was that?" she asked softly. The humor in her voice surprised me.

"More than I ever expected to have," he said. "Perhaps not enough, though."

And she laughed. She touched his hair, which he wore long and bound with a twist of grass into a long tail down his back. He touched hers—a soft black cloud around her face. They could touch each other's hair without difficulty because hair was essentially dead tissue. I had seen them touch that way before. It was the only way left to them.

"As much as I've loved my gardens," she said, "I never raised them just for myself or for us. I wanted the resisters to take what they needed."

Tino looked away, found himself staring at the downed papaya trees, and turned his head again. He had been a resister—

had spent much of his life among people who believed that Humans who mated with Oankali were traitors, and that anything that could be done to harm them was good. He had left his people because he wanted children. The Mars colony did not exist then. Humans either came to the Oankali or lived childless lives. Lilith had told me once that Tino did not truly let go of his resister beliefs until the Mars colony was begun and his people could escape the Oankali. She had never been a resister. She had been placed with Nikanj when it was about my age. She did not understand at the time what that meant, and no one told her. Nikanj said she did not stop trying to break away until one of my brothers convinced the people to allow resisting Humans to settle on Mars.

In one way, the Mars colony freed both my Human parents to find what pleasure they could find in their lives. In another it hadn't helped at all. They still feel guilt, feel as though they've deserted their people for aliens, as though they still suspect that they are the betrayers the resisters accused them of being. No Human could see the genetic conflict that made them such a volcanic species—so certain to destroy themselves. Thus, perhaps no Human completely believed it.

"I was always glad when they took whole plants," Lilith was saying, "Something to feed them now and something to transplant later."

"There are some peanuts here that survived," Tino said. "Do you want them?" He bent to pull a few of the small plants from the loose soil I had watched Lilith prepare for them.

"Leave them," she said. "I have some." She turned back to face the garden, watched the Oankali members of the family place what they had gathered on a blanket of overlapping banana leaves. Ahajas stopped Oni from eating a salvaged papaya and sent her to tell Lo what had happened and that the food was being left. Oni was Human-born, and so deceptively Human-looking that I had gone on thinking of her as female—though it would be more than ten years before she would have any sex at all.

"Wait," Lilith said.

Oni stopped near her, stood looking up at her.

Lilith walked over to Dichaan. "Will you go instead?" she asked him.

"The people who did this are gone, Lilith," he told her. "They've been gone for over a day. There's no sound of them, no fresh scent."

"I know. But . . . just for my peace of mind, will you go?"

"Yes." He turned and went. He would go only to the edge of Lo where some of the trees and smaller plants were not what they appeared to be. There he could signal Lo by touch, and Lo would pass the message on exactly to the next several people to open a wall or request food or in some other way come into direct contact with the Lo entity. Lo would pass the message on eight or ten times, then stop and store the message away. It couldn't forget any more than we could, but unless someone requested the memory, it would never bother anyone with it again. Humans could neither leave nor receive such messages. Even though Lilith and a few others had learned some of what they called Oankali codes, their fingers were not sensitive enough to receive messages or fine and penetrating enough to send them.

Oni watched Dichaan go, then returned to Hozh, who had finished her papaya. She stood close to him. He was no more male than she female, but it was easier to go on thinking of them the way I always had. The two of them slipped automatically into silent communication. Whenever they stood close together that way, Hozh's sensory tentacles immediately found Oni's sensory spots—she had very few sensory tentacles of her own—and established communication. Paired siblings.

Watching them made me lonely, and I looked around for Aaor. I caught it watching me. It had avoided me carefully since I got up from my metamorphosis. I had let it keep its distance in spite of what Tehkorahs had told me because Aaor obviously did not want contact. It did not seem to need me as much as I needed it. As I watched, it turned away from me and focused its attention on a large beetle.

Lilith and Tino joined the family group where it had settled to wait for Dichaan. "This is just the beginning," Lilith said to no one in particular. "We'll be meeting people like the ones who destroyed this garden. Sooner or later they'll spot us and come after us."

"You have your machete," Nikanj said.

It could not have gotten more attention if it had screamed. I focused on it to the exclusion of everything, felt pulled around to face it. Oankali did not suggest violence. Humans said violence was against Oankali beliefs. Actually it was against their flesh and bone, against every cell of them. Humans had evolved from hierarchical life, dominating, often killing other life. Oankali had evolved from acquisitive life, collecting and combining with other life. To kill was not simply wasteful to the Oankali. It was as unacceptable as slicing off their own healthy limbs. They fought only to save their lives and the lives of others. Even then, they fought to subdue, not to kill. If they were forced to kill, they resorted to biological weapons collected genetically on thousands of worlds. They could be utterly deadly, but they paid for it later. It cost them so dearly that they had no history at all of striking out in anger, frustration, jealousy, or any other emotion, no matter how keenly they felt it. When they killed even to save life, they died a little themselves.

I knew all this because it was as much a part of me as it was of them. Life was treasure. The only treasure. Nikanj was the one who had made it part of me. How could Nikanj be the one to suggest that anyone kill?

". . . Nika?" Ahajas whispered. She sounded the way I felt. Uncomprehending, disbelieving.

"They have to protect their lives and the family," Nikanj whispered. "If this were only a journey, we could guard them. We've guarded them before. But we're leaving home. We'll live cut off from others for . . . I don't know, perhaps a long time. There will be times when we aren't with them. And there are resisters who would kill them on sight."

"I don't want anyone to die because of me," I said. "I thought we were leaving to save life."

It focused on me, reached out a sensory arm, and drew me to its side. "We're leaving because the forest is the only place where we can live together as a family," it said. "No one will die because of you."

"But—"

"If they die, it will only be because they work very hard to make us kill them."

My siblings and other parents began to focus away from it. It had never said such things before. I stared at it and saw what they had missed. It was almost making itself sick with this talk. It would have been happier holding its hand in fire.

"There are easier ways to say these things," it admitted. "But some things shouldn't be said easily." It hesitated as Dichaan rejoined us. "We will leave the group only in pairs. We won't leave if it isn't necessary. You children—all of you—look out for one another. There will be new things everywhere to taste and understand. If your sibling is tasting something, you stand guard. If you see or smell Humans, hide. If you're caught in the open, run—even if it means being shot. If you're brought down, scream. Make as much noise as you can. Don't let them carry you away. Struggle. Make yourselves inconvenient to hold. If they seem intent on killing you, sting."

My siblings stood with head and body tentacles hanging undirected. The stings of males, females, and children were lethal.

"Once you're free, come to me or call me. I may be able to save whoever you've stung." It paused. "These are terrible things. If you stay with the group and stay alert, you won't have to do them."

They began to come alive again, focusing a few tentacles on it and understanding why it was speaking so bluntly to them. We were all hard to kill. Even our Human parents had been modified, made strong, more able to survive injury. The main danger was in being overwhelmed and abducted. Once we were taken away from the family, anything could be done to us. Perhaps Oni and Hozh would only be adopted for a time by Humans who were desperate for children. The rest of us looked too much like adult Humans—or adult Oankali. Those who looked female would be raped. Those who looked male would be killed. The Humans would have all the time they needed to beat, cut, and shoot us until we died. Unless we killed them.

Best never to get into such a position.

Nikanj focused on Lilith and Tino for several seconds, but said nothing. It knew them. It knew they would make every effort not to kill their own people—and it knew they would resent being told to take care. I had seen Oankali make the mistake of treating Humans like children. It was an easy mistake to make. Most Humans were more vulnerable than their own half-grown children. The Oankali tried to take care of them. The Humans reacted with anger, resentment, and withdrawal. Nikanj's way was better.

Nikanj focused for a moment on me. I still stood next to it, a coil of its right sensory arm around my neck. With its left sensory arm, it gestured to Aaor.

"No!" I whispered.

It ignored me. Aaor came toward us slowly, its whole body echoing my "no." It was afraid of me. Afraid of being hurt?

"Do you understand what you feel?" Nikanj asked when Aaor was close enough for it to loop its left sensory arm around Aaor's neck.

Aaor shook its head Humanly. "No. I don't want to avoid Jodahs. I don't know why I do it."

"I understand," Nikanj said. "But I don't know whether I can help you. This is something new."

That caught Aaor's attention. Anything new was of interest.

"Think, Eka. When has an ooloi ever had a paired sibling?"

I almost missed seeing Aaor's surprise, I was so involved with my own. Of course ooloi did not have paired siblings in the usual sense. In Oankali families, females had three children, one right after the other. One became male, one female, and one ooloi. Their own inclinations decided which became which. The male and the female metamorphosed and found an unrelated ooloi to mate with. The ooloi still had its subadult phase to mature through. It was still called a child—the only child who knew its sex. And it was alone until it neared its second metamorphosis and found mates. I should have had only my parents around me now. But where would that leave Aaor?

"Stop running away from one another," Nikanj said. "Find out what's comfortable for you. Do what your bodies tell you is right. This is a new relationship. You'll be finding the way for others as well as for yourselves."

"If it touches me, you'll have to heal it," I said.

"I know." It flattened its head and body tentacles in something other than amusement. "Or at least, I think I know. This is new to me, too. Aaor, come to me every day for examination and healing. Come even if you believe nothing is wrong. Jodahs can make very subtle, important changes. Come immediately if you feel pain or if you notice anything wrong."

"Ooan, help me understand it," Aaor said. "Let me reach it through you."

"Shall I?" Nikanj asked me silently.

"Yes," I answered in the same way.

It wove us into seamless neurosensory union.

And it was as though Aaor and I were touching again with nothing between us. I savored Aaor's unique taste. It was like part of me, long numb, long out of touch, yet so incredibly welcome back that I could only submerge myself in it.

Aaor said nothing to me. It only wanted to know me again—know me as an ooloi. It wanted to understand as deeply as it could the changes that had taken place in me. And I came to understand from it without words how lonely it had been, how much it wanted me back. It was totally unnatural for paired siblings to be near one another, and yet avoid touching.

Aaor asked wordlessly for release, and Nikanj released us both. For a second I was aware only of frog and insect sounds, the rain dropping from the trees, the sun breaking through the clouds. No one in the family moved or spoke. I hadn't realized they were all focused on us. I started to look around, then Aaor stepped up to me and touched me. I reached for it with every sensory tentacle I had, and its own more numerous tentacles strained toward me. This was normal. This was what paired siblings were supposed to be able to do whenever they wanted to.

For a moment relief overwhelmed me again. My underarms itched just about where my sensory arms would grow someday. If I had already had the arms, I couldn't have kept them off Aaor.

"It's about time," Ahajas said. "You two look after each other."

"Let's go." Tino said.

We followed him out of the ruined garden, moving single file through the forest. He knew of a place that sounded as though it would make a good campsite—plenty of space, far from other settlements of any kind. Everyone's fear was that I would make changes in the plant and animal life. These changes could spread like diseases—could actually be diseases. The adults in the family did not know whether they could detect and disarm every change. Sooner or later other people would have to deal with some of them. The idea was for us to isolate ourselves, to minimize and localize any cleaning up that would have to be done later. The place Tino had found years before was an island—a big island with a new growth of cecropia trees at one end and a mix of old growth over the rest. It was moving slowly downstream the way river islands did—mud taken from one end was deposited downstream at the other. All the adults remembered a place like this created aboard the ship and used to train Humans to live in the forest. None of them had liked it. Now they were headed for the real thing—because of me.

Sometime during the afternoon, Aaor's underarms began to itch and hurt. By the time it went to Nikanj for healing, swellings had begun to appear. I had apparently caused Aaor's unsexed, immature body to try to grow sensory arms. Instead, it was growing potentially dangerous tumors.

"I'm sorry," I said when Nikanj had finished with it.

"Just figure out what you did wrong," it said unhappily. "Find out how to avoid doing it again."

That was the problem. I hadn't been aware of doing anything to Aaor. If I had felt myself doing it, I would have stopped myself. I thought I had been careful. I was like a blind Human, trampling what I could not see. But a blind Human's eyesight could be restored. What I was missing was something I had never had—or at least, something I had never discovered.

"Learn as quickly as you can so we can go home," Aaor said.

I focused on the trail ahead—on scenting or hearing strangers. I couldn't think of anything to say.

7

The island should have been three days' walk upriver. We thought we might make it in five days, since we had to circle around Pascual, an unusually hostile riverine resister settlement. People from Pascual were probably the ones who had destroyed Lilith's garden. Now we would go far out of our way to avoid repaying them. Too many of them might not survive contact with me.

We never thought we were in danger from Pascual because its people knew better than most resisters what happened to anyone who attacked us. Their village, already shrunken by emigration, would be gassed, and the attackers hunted out by scent. They would be found and exiled to the ship. There, if they had killed, they would be kept either unconscious or drugged to pleasure and contentment. They would never be allowed to awaken completely. They would be used as teaching aids, subjects for biological experiments, or reservoirs of Human genetic material. The people of Pascual knew this, and thus committed only what Lilith called property crimes. They stole, they burned, they vandalized. They had not come as close to Lo as the garden before. They had confined their attentions to travelers.

We did not understand how extreme their behavior had become until we met some of them on our first night away from Lo. We stopped walking at dusk, cooked and ate some of the food Lilith and Tino had brought, and hung our hammocks between trees. We didn't bother erecting a shelter, since the adults agreed that it wasn't going to rain.

Only Nikanj cleared a patch of ground and spread its hammock on the bare earth. Because of the connections it had to make with sensory arms and tentacles, it was not comfortable sharing a hanging hammock with anyone. It wanted us to feel free to come to it with whatever wounds, aches, or pains we had developed. It gestured to me first, though I had not intended to go to it at all.

"Come every night until you learn to control your abilities," it told me. "Observe what I do with you. Don't drowse."

"All right."

It could not heal without giving pleasure. People tended simply to relax and enjoy themselves with it. Instead, this time I observed, as it wished, saw it investigate me almost cell by cell, correcting the flaws it found—flaws I had not noticed. It was as though I had gained an understanding of the complexity of the outside world and lost even my child's understanding of my inner self. I used to notice quickly when something was wrong. Now my worst problem was uncontrolled, unnecessary cell division. Cancers. They began and grew very quickly—many, many times faster than they could have in a Human. I was supposed to be able to control and use them in myself and in others. Instead, I couldn't even spot my own when they began. And they began with absolutely no conscious encouragement from me.

"Do you see?" Nikanj asked.

"Yes. But I didn't before you showed me."

"I've left one."

I hunted for it and after some time found it growing in my throat, where it would surely kill me if it were allowed to continue. I did not readjust the genetic message of the cells and deactivate the part that was in error. That was what Nikanj had done to the others, but I did not trust my ability to follow its example. I might accidentally reprogram other genes. Instead, I destroyed the few malignant cells.

Then I put my head against Nikanj, let my head tentacles link with its own. I spoke to it silently.

"I'm not learning. I don't know what to do."

"Wait."

"I don't want to keep being dangerous, hurting Aaor, being afraid of myself."

"Give yourself time. You're a new kind of being. There's never been anyone like you before. But there's no flaw in you. You just need time to find out more about yourself."

Its certainty fed me. I rested against it for a while, enjoying the easy, safe contact—my only one now. It nudged me after a while, and I went back to my hammock. Lilith was lying with it when the resisters made themselves known to us.

First they screamed. A female Human screamed again and again, first cursing someone, then begging, then making hoarse, wordless noises. There were also male voices—at least three of them shouting, laughing, cursing.

"Real and not real," Dichaan said when the screaming began.

"What is it?" Oni demanded.

"The female is being hurt now," Nikanj said. "And she's afraid. But something is wrong about this. Her first screams were false. She was not afraid then."

"If she's being hurt now, that's enough!" Tino said. He was on his feet, staring at Nikanj, his posture all urgency and anger.

"Stay here," Nikanj said. It stood up and grasped Tino with all four arms. "Protect the children." It shook him once for emphasis, then ran into the forest. Ahajas and Dichaan followed. Oankali were much less likely to be killed even if the shouting Humans made a serious effort.

Our Human parents gathered us together and drew us into thicker forest, where we could see and resisters could not. Lilith and Tino had been modified so that, like us, they could see by infrared light—by heat. For us all, the living forest was full of light.

And the air was full of scents. Humans coming. Not close yet, but coming. Several of them. Eight, nine of them. Males.

Lilith and Tino freed their machetes and backed us farther into the forest.

"Do nothing unless they come after us," Lilith said. "If they do come, run. If they catch you, kill."

She sounded like Nikanj. But from Nikanj, the words had sounded like cries of pain. From her they were cries of fear. She feared for us. I could not remember ever seeing her afraid for herself. Years before, concealed high in a tree, I watched her fight off three male resisters who wanted to rape her. She hadn't been afraid once she saw that they weren't aware of me. She even managed not to hurt them much. They ran away, believing she was a construct.

The resisters who were hunting us now would not run from us, and both Lilith and Tino knew it. They watched as the resisters discovered the camp, tried to tear down the hammocks, tried to burn them. But Lo cloth would not burn, and no normal Human could cut or tear it.

They stole Lilith's and Tino's packs, hacked down the smaller trees we'd tied our hammocks to, ground exposed food into the dirt, and set fire to the trees. They looked for us in the light of the fire, but they were afraid to venture too far into the forest, afraid to scatter too much yet, afraid to seem to huddle together. Perhaps they knew what would happen to them if they found us. Perhaps destroying our belongings would be enough—though they did have guns.

They had not gotten the pack Lilith had made for me. While she and Tino were gathering my siblings, I had grabbed my pack and run with it. I meant to help if there was fighting. I wouldn't run with my younger siblings. But I also meant to keep what might be my last bit of Lo. No one would steal it.

The fire spread slowly, and the resisters had to leave our campsite. They went back into the trees the way they'd come. We stayed where we were, knowing that the river was nearby. We would run for that if we had to.

But the fire did not spread far. It singed a few standing trees and consumed the few that had been cut. My Oankali parents came back wounded and already healing, carrying a living burden.

The danger seemed past. We smelled nothing except smoke, heard nothing except the crackling of the dying fire and natural sounds. We went out to meet the three Oankali.

As I stepped into the open, into the firelight, I was in front of my Human parents and my siblings. That was good because as an ooloi, I was theoretically more able to survive gunshot wounds than any of them. Now I would find out whether that was true.

I was shot three times. The first two shots came from slightly different directions at almost the same instant. To me, they were a single blow, slamming into me, spinning me all the way around. The first two shots hit me in the left shoulder and left lower back. The third hit me in the chest as I spun. It knocked me down.

I rolled and came to my feet just in time to see my Oankali parents go after the resisters. The resisters stopped firing abruptly and scattered. I could hear them—nine males fleeing in nine directions, knowing that three Oankali could not catch them all.

Nikanj and Dichaan each caught one of them. Ahajas, larger, and apparently unwounded, caught two. Each of those caught had fired their rifles. They smelled of the powder they used to shoot. They also smelled terrified. They were being held by the people they feared most. They struggled desperately. One of them wept and cursed and stank more than the others. This was one of those held by Ahajas.

Silently Nikanj took that one from Ahajas and passed her

the one he'd caught. The male who had been given to Nikanj began to scream. Blood spilled out of his nose, though no one had touched his face.

Nikanj touched his neck with a sensory tentacle and injected calmness.

The male shouted, "No, no, no, no." But the last "no" was a whimper. He drew a deep breath, choked on his own blood, and coughed several times. After a while, he was quiet and calm. Nikanj let him wipe his nose on the cloth of his shirt at the shoulder. Nikanj touched his neck once more and the male smiled. Nikanj took him to a large tree and made him sit down against it.

"Stay there," Nikanj said.

The male looked at it, smiled, and nodded. Even in the leaping fire shadows, he looked peaceful, relaxed.

"Run!" one of his companions shouted to him.

The male put his head back against the tree and closed his eyes. He wasn't unconscious. He was just too comfortable, too relaxed to worry about anything.

Nikanj went to each prisoner and gave comfort and calmness. When there was no need for anyone to hold them, it came to examine me.

I had sat down against a tree myself, glad for the support it gave. I was having a lot of pain, but I had already expelled the two bullets that hadn't gone all the way through me and I had stopped the bleeding. By the time Nikanj reached me, I was slowly, carefully encouraging my body to repair itself. I had never been injured this badly before, but my body seemed to be handling it. Here was its chance to grow tissue quickly to fulfill need rather than to cause trouble.

"Good," Nikanj said. "You don't need me right now." It stood back from me. "Is anyone else hurt?"

No one was except the Human woman my Oankali parents had rescued. I could have used some help with my pain, but Nikanj had perceived that and ignored it. It wanted to see what I could do on my own.

Nikanj went to the bloody, unconscious Human woman and lay down beside her.

The woman had been beaten about the face, and from her scent, two males had recently had sex with her. I was too involved with my own healing to detect anything else.

Aaor came to sit next to me. It did not touch me, but I was glad it was there. My other siblings and Dichaan kept watch for resisters.

Ahajas spoke to one of the captives—the one who had been so frightened.

"Why did you attack us?" she asked, sitting down in front of him.

The male stared at her, seemed to examine her very carefully with his eyes. Finally he reached out and touched a sensory tentacle on her arm. Ahajas allowed this. He had not been able to hurt her when she captured him. Now that he was drugged, he was not likely even to try.

After a time, he let the tentacle go as though he did not like it. Humans compared ooloi sensory arms to the appendages of extinct animals—elephant trunks. They compared sensory tentacles to large worms or snakes—like the slender, venomous vine snakes of the forest, perhaps, though sensory tentacles could be much more dangerous, more sensitive, and more flexible than vine snakes, and they were not independent at all.

"You were coming to raid us," the male said. "One of our hunters saw you and warned us."

"We would not have attacked you," Ahajas protested. "We've never done such a thing."

"Yes. We were warned. A gang of Oankali and half-Oankali coming to take revenge for the garden."

"Did you destroy the garden?"

"Some of us did. Not me." That was true. People drugged the way he was did not bother to lie. It didn't occur to them. "We thought your animals shouldn't have real Human food."

"Animals . . . ?"

"Those!" He waved a hand toward Lilith and Tino.

Ahajas had known. She had simply wanted to know

whether he would say it. He looked with interest at Oni and Ayodele. Since my metamorphosis, they were the most Human-looking members of the family. Children born of Lilith-the-animal.

Aaor and I got up in unison and moved to the other side of the tree we had been leaning against. I was still in pain and I had to watch my healing flesh closely to see that it did not go wrong. It could go very wrong it I kept paying attention to the captive and his offensive nonsense.

8

Sometime later the rescued female made a small, wordless noise, and without thinking, I left Aaor and went over to where she lay on the ground alongside Nikanj. I stood, looking down at them. The female was completely unconscious now, and Nikanj was busy healing her. I almost lay down on her other side, but Lilith called my name, and I stopped. I stood where I was, confused, not knowing why I stood there, but not wanting to leave.

Some of Nikanj's body tentacles lifted toward me. Gradually it detached itself from the female and focused on me. It sat up and extended its sensory tentacles toward me. "Let me see what you've done for yourself," it said.

I stepped around the female, who was still unconscious, and let Nikanj examine me.

"Good," it said after a moment. "Flawless." It was clearly surprised.

"Let me touch her," I said.

"I haven't finished with her." Nikanj smoothed its tentacles flat to its body. "There's work for you to do if you want it."

I did. That was exactly what I wanted. Yet I knew I shouldn't have been allowed to touch her. I hesitated, focusing sharply on Nikanj.

"I'll have to check her afterward," it said. "You'll find you won't like that. But for the sake of her health, I have to do it. Now go ahead. Help her."

I lay down alongside the female. I don't think I could have refused Nikanj's offer. The pull of the female, injured, alone, and in no way related to me was overwhelming.

I might still be too young to give her pleasure. That disturbed me, but there was nothing I could do about it. When I had something to work with besides sensory tentacles, I could give great pleasure. Now, at least, I could give relief from pain.

The female's face, head, breasts, and abdomen were bruised from blows and would be painful if I woke her. I could find no other injuries. Nikanj had not left me anything serious. I went to work on the bruises.

I held the female close to me and sank as many head and body tentacles into her as I could, but I couldn't get over the feeling that I was somehow not close enough to her, not linked deeply enough into her nervous system, that there was something missing.

Of course there was—and there would be until my second metamorphosis. I understood the feeling, but I couldn't make it go away. I had to be especially careful not to hold her too tightly, not to interfere with her breathing.

The beauty of her flesh was my reward. A foreign Human as incredibly complex as any Human, as full of the Human Conflict—dangerous and frightening and intriguing—as any Human. She was like the fire—desirable and dangerous, beautiful and lethal. Humans never understood why Oankali found them so interesting.

I took my time finishing with the woman. No one hurried me. It was a real effort for me to move aside and let Nikanj check her. I didn't want it to touch her. I didn't want to share her with it. I had never felt that way before.

I stood with my arms tightly folded and my attention on the now silent male prisoners. I think Nikanj worked quickly for my sake. After a very short time, it stood up and said, "I think she's inspired you to get control of your abilities. Stay with her until she wakes. Don't call me unless she seems likely to hurt herself or to run away."

"Was she working with them?" I asked, gesturing with head tentacles toward the males.

"She was a captive of their friends. I don't think she knew what was going to happen to her." It hesitated. "They've learned that false screams won't lure us away. Her first screams sounded false because she wasn't frightened yet. Probably they told her to scream. Then they began to beat her."

The female moaned. Nikanj turned and went to help Lilith and Tino, who had begun to pull undamaged Lo cloth hammocks and pieces of clothing from the ashes. The fire had not gone completely out, but it was burning down rather than spreading. We didn't seem to be in any danger. I went over and borrowed one of Tino's salvaged shirts. He rarely wore them himself, but now, for a while, they would conceal some of my new body tentacles. The more familiar I seemed to the female, the less likely she would be to panic. I was gray-brown now. She would know I was a construct. But not such a startling construct.

She awoke, sat up abruptly, looked around in near panic.

"You're safe," I said to her. "You're not hurt and no one here will hurt you."

She drew back from me, scrambled away, then froze when she saw my parents and siblings.

"You're safe," I repeated. "The people who hurt you are not here."

That seemed to catch her attention. After all, Humans had injured her, not Oankali. She looked around more carefully, jumped when she saw the Human males sitting nearby.

"They can't hurt you," I said. "Even if they've hurt you before, they can't now."

She stared at me, watched my mouth as I spoke.

"What's your name?" I asked.

She didn't answer.

I sighed, watched her for a while without speaking. She understood me. It was as though it had suddenly occurred to her to pretend not to understand. I had spoken to her in English and her responses had shown me she understood. She had very black hair that reminded me of Tino's. But hers was loose and uncombed, hanging lank around her narrow, angular brown face. She had not gotten enough to eat for many days. Her body had told me that clearly. But for most of her life, she had been comfortably well nourished. Her body was small, quick, harder muscled than most Human female bodies. Not only had it done hard work, it was probably comfortable doing hard work. It liked to move quickly and eat frequently. It was hungry now.

I went to the tree I had leaned against while I was healing. I'd left my pack there. I found it and brought it back to where the female sat on her knees, watching me. From it I gave her two bananas and a handful of shelled nuts. She didn't even make a pretense of not wanting them.

I watched her eat and wondered what it would be like to be in contact with her while she ate. How did the food taste and feel to her?

"Why are you staring at me?" she demanded. Fast, choppy English like the firing of guns.

"My name is Jodahs," I offered. "What's yours?"

"Marina Rivas. I want to go to Mars."

I looked away from her, suddenly weary. One more small, thin-boned female to be sacrificed to Human stubbornness. I recalled from examining her that she had never had a child. That was good because her narrow hips were not suitable to bearing children. If her fertility were restored and nothing else changed, she would surely die trying to give birth to her first child. She could be changed, redesigned. I wouldn't trust myself to do such substantial work, but she must have it done.

"Were you on your way to Lo?" I asked.

"Yes. The ships leave from there, don't they?"

"Yes."

"You're from there?"

"Yes."

"Can I go back with you?"

"We'll see that you get there. Did your people beat you because you wanted to go to Mars?" Such things had happened. Some resisters killed their "deserters," as they called those who wanted to emigrate.

"Do they look like my people!" the female demanded harshly. "I was on my way to Lo. When I passed their village, they took me from my canoe and raped me and called me stupid names and made me stay in their pigsty village. The men kept me shut up in an animal pen and they raped me. The women spat on me and put dirt or shit in my food because the men raped me."

There was so much hatred and anger in her face and voice that I drew back. "I know Humans do such things," I said. "I understand the biological reasons why they do them, but . . . I've never seen them done."

"Good. Why should you? Do you have anything else to eat?"

I gave her what I had. She needed it.

"Where did you live before the war?" I asked. She was brown and narrow-eyed and her English was accented in a way I had not heard before. I had siblings who looked a little like her—children of Lilith's first postwar mate who had come from China. He had been killed by people like the resisters who had shot me.

Aaor came up and stood close so that it could link with me. It was intensely curious about the female. The female stared at it with equal curiosity, but spoke to me.

"I'm from Manila." Her voice had gone harsh again, as though the words hurt her. "What can that mean to you?"

"The Philippines?" I asked.

She looked surprised. "What do you know about my country?"

I thought for a moment, remembering. "That it was made up of islands, warm and green—some of them like this, I think." I gestured toward the forest. "That it could have fed everyone easily, but didn't because some Humans took more than they needed. That it took no part in the last war, but it died anyway."

"Everything died," the female said bitterly. "But how do you know even that much? Have you known another Filipina?"

"No, but a few people from the Philippines have come through Lo. Some of my adult siblings told me about them."

"Do you know any names?"

"No."

She sighed. "Maybe I'll see them on Mars. Who is this?" She looked at Aaor.

"My closest sibling, Aaor."

She stared at us both and shook her head. "I could almost stay," she said. "It doesn't seem as bad as it once did—the Oankali, the idea of . . . different children. . . ."

"You should stay," I told her. "Mars may not be green during your lifetime. You won't be able to go outside the shelters unprotected. Mars is cold and dry."

"Mars is Human. Now."

I said nothing.

"I'm tired," she said after a while. "Does anyone care if I sleep?"

I cleared some ground for her and spread a piece of Lo cloth on it.

"You two are children, aren't you?" she asked Aaor.

"Yes," Aaor answered.

"So? Will you be a woman someday?"

"I don't know."

"I don't understand that. It bothers me more than most things about you people. Come and lie here. I know your kind like to touch everyone. If you want to, you can touch me."

I took that to include me, too, and pressed two pieces of Lo cloth edge-to-edge so that we could have a wider sleeping mat.

"I didn't invite you," she said to me. "You look too much like a man."

"I'm not male," I said.

"I don't care. You look male."

"Let it sleep here," Aaor said. "The insects won't come near you with one of us on either side."

She stared at me. "Really? You scare the bugs away?"

"Our scent repels them."

She sniffed, trying to smell us. In fact, she did smell me—unconsciously. I smelled ooloi. Interesting, perhaps attractive to an unmated person.

"All right," she said. "I've never yet caught an Oankali or a construct in a lie. Come and sleep here. You're honestly not male?"

"I'm honestly not male."

"Come keep the bugs off, then."

We kept the bugs off and kept her warm and investigated her thoroughly, though we were careful not to touch her in any way that would alarm her. I thought hands would alarm her, so I only touched her with my longest sensory tentacles. This startled her at first, but once she realized she wasn't being hurt, she put up with our curiosity. She never knew that I helped her fall asleep.

And I never knew how it happened that during the night she moved completely out of contact with Aaor and against me so that I could reach her with most of my head and body tentacles.

I discovered that I had slightly altered the structure of her pelvis during the night. I hadn't intended to try such a thing. It wouldn't have occurred to me to try it. Yet it was done. The female could bear children now.

I detached myself from her and sat up, missing the feel of her at once. It was dawn and my parents were already up. Nikanj and Ahajas were cooking something in a suspended pot made of layers of Lo cloth. Lilith was looking through the ashes of the night's fire. Tino and Dichaan where out of sight, but I could hear and smell them nearby. Last night, once my attention was on Marina Rivas, I had almost stopped sensing them. I had not known then how completely she had absorbed my attention.

Nikanj left the belly of cloth and its weight of cooking food—nut porridge. The Humans would not want it until they had tasted it. Then they would not be able to get enough of it. It might actually contain some nuts from wild trees. Lilith or Tino might have gathered some. More likely, though, all the nuts had been synthesized by Nikanj and Ahajas from the substance of Ahajas's body. We could eat a great many things that Humans could not or would not touch. Then we could use what we'd eaten to create something more palatable for Humans. My Human parents shrugged and said this was no more than Lo did every day—which was true. But resisters were always repelled if they knew. So we didn't tell them unless they asked directly.

Nikanj came over to me and checked me carefully.

"You're all right," it said. "You're doing fine. The female is good for you."

"She's going to Mars."

"I heard."

"I wish I could keep her here."

"She's very strong. I think she'll survive Mars."

"I changed her a little. I didn't mean to, but—"

"I know. I'm going to check her very thoroughly just before we leave her, but from what I've seen in you, you did a good job. I wish she were not so old. If she were younger, I would help you persuade her to stay."

She was as old as my Human mother. She might live a century more here on Earth where there was plenty to eat and drink and breathe, where there were Oankali to repair her injuries. I could live five times that long—unless I mated with someone like Marina. Then I would live only as long as I could keep her alive.

"If she were younger, I would persuade her myself," I said.

Nikanj coiled a sensory arm around my neck briefly, then went to give the male captives their morning drugging. Best to do that before they woke.

Marina was already awake and looking at me. "There's

food," I said. "It doesn't look very interesting, but it tastes good."

She extended a hand. I took it and pulled her to her feet. Four bowls from Lo had been salvaged from the fire. We took two of them down to the river, washed them, washed ourselves, and swam a little. This was my first experience with breathing underwater. I slipped into it so naturally and comfortably that I hardly noticed that I was doing something new.

I heard Marina's voice calling me and I realized I'd drifted some distance downstream. I turned and swam back to her. She had not taken off her clothing—short pants that had once been longer and a ragged shirt much too big for her.

I had taken off mine. She had stared at me then. Now she stared again. No visible genitals. In fact, no reproductive organs at all.

"I don't understand," she said as I walked out of the water. "You must not care what I see or you wouldn't have undressed. I don't understand how you can have . . . nothing."

"I'm not an adult."

"But . . ."

I put my shorts and Tino's shirt back on.

"Why do you wear clothes?"

"For Humans. Don't you feel more comfortable now?"

She laughed. I hadn't heard her laugh before. It was a harsh, sharp shout of joy. "I feel more comfortable!" she said. "But take your clothes off if you want to. What difference does it make?"

My underarms itched painfully. Because there was nothing else for me to do, I took her hand, picked up the bowls, and headed back toward camp and breakfast.

She walked close to me and didn't shrink away from my sensory tentacles.

"I don't think you have to worry about becoming a woman," she said.

"No."

"You're almost a man now."

I stepped in front of her and stopped. She stopped obligingly and watched me, waiting.

"I'm not male. I never will be. I'm ooloi."

She almost leaped away from me. I saw the shadow of abrupt movement, not quite completed in her muscles. "How *can* you be?" she demanded. "You have two arms, not four."

"So far," I said.

She stared at my arms. "You . . . You're truly ooloi?"

"Yes."

She shook her head. "No wonder I had dreams about you last night."

"Oh? Did you like them?"

"Of course I liked them. I liked you. And I shouldn't have. You look too male. Nothing male should have been appealing to me last night—after what those bastards did to me. Nothing male should be appealing to me for a long, long time."

"You're healed."

"Yes. You did that?"

"Part of it."

"There's more to healing than just closing wounds."

"You're healed."

She looked at me for a time, then looked away at the trees. "I must be," she said.

"More than healed."

She put her head to one side. "What?"

"When your fertility is restored, you'll be able to have children without trouble. You couldn't have done that before."

Her expression changed to one of remembered pain. "My mother died when I was born. People said she should have had a cesarean, you know?"

"Yes."

"She didn't. I don't know why."

"You need to be changed a little genetically so that your daughters will be able to give birth safely."

"Can you do that?"

"I won't have time. We'll be escorting you and the male prisoners to Lo today. I'm not experienced enough to do that kind of work anyway."

"Who'll do it?"

"An adult ooloi."

"No!"

"Yes," I said, taking her by the arms. "Yes. You can't condemn your daughters to die the way your mother did. Why do adult ooloi frighten you?"

"They don't frighten me. My response to them frightens me. I feel . . . as though I'm not in control of myself anymore. I feel drugged—as though they could make me do anything."

"You won't be their prisoner. And you won't be dealing with unmated ooloi. The ooloi who changes you won't want anything from you."

"I would rather have you do it—or someone like you."

"I'm a construct ooloi. The first one. There is no one else like me."

She looked at me for a little longer, then pulled me closer to her and drew a long, weary breath. "You're beautiful, you know? You shouldn't be, but you are. You remind me of a man I knew once." She sighed again. "Damn."

9

Back to Lo.

We gave the drugged prisoners to the people of Lo. A house would be grown for them from the substance of Lo and they would not be let out of it until a shuttle came for them. Then they would be transferred to the ship. They understood what was to happen to them, and even drugged, they asked to be spared, to be released. The one who had called Lilith and Tino animals began to cry. Nikanj drugged him a little more and he seemed to forget why he had been upset. That would be his life now. Once he was aboard the ship, one ooloi would drug him regularly. He would come to look forward to it—and he would not care what else was done with him.

I took Marina to the guest area before Nikanj was free to check her. I didn't want to watch it examine her. I got the impression that it was perfectly willing not to touch her. There must have been too much of my scent on her to make her seem still alone and unrelated.

She kissed me before I left her. I think it was an experiment for her. For me it was an enjoyment. It let me touch her a little more, sink filaments of sensory tentacles into her along the lengths of our bodies. She liked that. She shouldn't have. I was supposed to be too young to give pleasure. She liked it anyway.

"I'll send someone to change you genetically," I said after a time. "Don't be afraid. Let your children have the same chance you have."

"All right."

I held her a little longer, then left her. I asked Tehkorahs to check her and make the necessary adjustment.

It stood with Wray Ordway, its male Human mate, and Wray smiled and gave me a look of understanding and amusement. He was one of the few people in Lo to speak for me when the exile decision was being made. "A child is a child," he said through Tehkorahs. "The more you treat it like a freak, the more it will behave like one." I think people like him eased things for me. They made Earth exile feel less objectionable to the truly frightened people who wanted me safely shut away on the ship.

"You know I'll take care of the female," Tehkorahs said. "She seemed to like you very much."

I felt my head and body tentacles flatten to my skin in remembered pleasure. "Very much."

Wray laughed. "I told you it would be sexually precocious—just like the construct males and females."

Tehkorahs looped a sensory tentacle around his neck. "I'm not surprised. Every gene trade brings change. Jodahs, let me check you. The female won't want to see me for a while. You've left too much of yourself with her."

I stepped close to it and it released Wray and examined me quickly, thoroughly. I felt its surprise before it let me go. "You're much more in control now," it said. "I can't find anything wrong with you. And if your memories of the female are accurate—"

"Of course they are!"

"Then I probably won't find anything wrong with her either. Except for the genetic problem."

"She'll cooperate when you're ready to correct that."

"Good. You look like her, you know."

"What?"

"Your body has been striving to please her. You're more brown now—less gray. Your face is changed subtly."

"You look like a male version of her," Wray said. "She probably thought you were very handsome."

"She said so," I admitted amid Wray's laughter. "I didn't know I was changing."

"All ooloi change a little when they mate," Tehkorahs said. "Our scents change. We fit ourselves into our mates' kin group. You may fit in better than most of us—just as your descendants will fit more easily when they find a new species for the gene trade."

If I ever had descendants.

The next day, the family gathered new supplies and left Lo for the second time. I had had one more night to sleep in the family house. I slept with Aaor the way I always used to before my metamorphosis. I think I made it as lonely as I felt myself now that Marina was gone. And that night I gave Aaor, Lo, and myself large, foul-smelling sores.

II

EXILE

1

We didn't stop at the island we had intended to live on. It was too close to Pascual. Living there would have made us targets for more Human fear and frustration. We followed the river west, then south, traveling when we wanted to, resting when we were tired—drifting, really. I was restless, and drifting suited me. The others simply seemed not content with any likely campsite we found. I suspected that they wouldn't be content again until they returned to Lo to stay.

We edged around Human habitations very carefully. Humans who saw us either stared from a distance or followed us until we left their territory. None approached us.

Twelve days from Lo, we were still drifting. The river was long with many tributaries, many curves and twists. It was good to walk along the shaded forest floor, following the sound and smell of it, and thinking about nothing at all. My fingers and toes became webbed on the third day, and I didn't bother to correct them. I was wet at least as often as I was dry. My hair fell out and I developed a few more sensory tentacles. I stopped wearing clothing, and my coloring changed to gray-green.

"What are you doing?" my Human mother asked. "Letting your body do whatever it wants to?" Her voice and posture expressed stiff disapproval.

"As long as I don't develop an illness," I said.

She frowned. "I wish you could see yourself through my eyes. Deformity is as bad as illness."

I walked away from her. I had never done that before.

Fifteen days out of Lo, someone shot at us with arrows.

Only Lilith was hit. Nikanj caught the archer, drugged him unconscious, destroyed all his weapons, and changed the color of his hair. It had been deep brown. It would be colorless from now on. It would look all white. Finally Nikanj encouraged his face to fall into the permanent creases that this male's behavior and genetic heritage had dictated for his old age. He would look much older. He would not be weaker or in any way infirm, but appearances were important to Humans. When this male awoke—sometime the next day—his eyes and his fingers would tell him he had paid a terrible price for attacking us. More important, his people would see. They would misunderstand what they saw, and it would frighten them into letting us alone.

Lilith had no special trouble with the arrow. It damaged one of her kidneys and gave her a great deal of pain, but her life was in no danger. Her improved body would have healed quickly even without Nikanj's help, since the arrow was not poisoned. But Nikanj did not leave her to heal herself. It lay beside her and healed her completely before it returned to whiten the drugged archer's hair and wrinkle his face. Mates took care of one another.

I watched them, wondering who I would take care of. Who would take care of me?

Twenty-one days out, the bed of our river turned south and we turned with it. Dichaan veered off the trail, and left us for some time, and came back with a male Human who had broken his leg. The leg was grotesque—swollen, discolored, and blistered. The smell of it made Nikanj and me look at one another.

We camped and made a pallet for the injured Human. Nikanj spoke to me before it went to him.

"Get rid of your webbing," it said. "Try to look less like a frog or you'll scare him."

"Are you going to let me heal him?"

"Yes. And it will take a while for you to do it right. Your first regeneration. . . . Go eat something while I ease his pain."

"Let me do that," I said. But it had already turned away and gone back to the male. The male's leg was worse than worth-less. It was poisoning his body. Portions of it were already dead. Yet the thought of taking it disturbed me.

Ahajas and Aaor brought me food before I could look around for it, and Aaor sat with me while I ate.

"Why are you afraid?" it said.

"Not exactly afraid, but . . . To take the leg . . ."

"Yes. It will give you a chance to grow something other than webbing and sensory tentacles."

"I don't want to do it. He's old like Marina. You don't know how I hated letting her go."

"Don't I?"

I focused on it. "I didn't think you did. You didn't say anything."

"You didn't want me to. You should eat."

When I didn't eat, it moved closer to me and leaned against me, linking comfortably into my nervous system. It had not done that for a while. It wasn't afraid of me anymore. It had not exactly abandoned me. It had allowed me to isolate my-self—since I seemed to want to. It let me know this in simple neurosensory impressions.

"I was lonely," I protested aloud.

"I know. But not for me." It spoke with confidence and con-tentment that confused me.

"You're changing," I said.

"Not yet. But soon, I think."

"Metamorphosis? We'll lose each other when you change."

"I know. Share the Human with me. It will give the two of us more time together."

"All right."

Then I had to go to the Human. I had to heal him alone. After that, Aaor and I could share him.

People remembered their ooloi siblings. I had heard Ahajas and Dichaan talk about theirs. But they had not seen it for decades. An ooloi belonged to the kin group of its mates. Its siblings were lost to it.

The Human male had lost consciousness by the time I lay

down beside him. The moment I touched him, I knew he must have broken his leg in a fall—probably from a tree. He had puncture wounds and deep bruises on the left side of his body. The left leg was, as I had expected, a total loss, foul and poisonous. I separated it from the rest of his body above the damaged tissue. First I stopped the circulation of bodily fluids and poisons to and from the leg. Then I encouraged the growth of a skin barrier at the hip. Finally I helped his body let go of the rotting limb.

When the leg fell away, I withdrew enough of my attention from the male to ask the family to get rid of it. I didn't want the male to see it.

Then I settled down to healing the many smaller injuries and neutralizing the poisons that had already begun to destroy the health of his body. I spent much of the evening healing him. Finally I focused again on his leg and began to reprogram certain cells. Genes that had not been active since well before the male was born had to be awakened and set to work telling the body how to grow a leg. A leg, not a cancer. The regeneration would take many days and would have to be monitored. We would camp here and keep the man with us until regeneration was complete.

It had been dark for some time when I detached myself from the male. My Human parents and my siblings were asleep nearby. Ahajas and Dichaan sat near one another guarding the camp and conversing aloud so softly that even I could not hear all they said. A Human intruder would have heard nothing at all. Oankali and construct hearing was so acute that some resisters imagined we could read their thoughts. I wished we could have so that I would have some idea how the male I had healed would react to me. I would have to spend as much time with him as new mates often spent together. That would be hard if he hated or feared me.

"Do you like him, Oeka?" Nikanj asked softly.

I had known it was behind me, sitting, waiting to check my work. Now it came up beside me and settled a sensory arm around my neck. I still enjoyed its touch, but I held stiff against it because I thought it would next touch the male.

"Thorny, possessive ooloi child," it said, pulling me against it in spite of my stiffness. "I must examine him this once. But if what you tell me and show me matches what I find in him, I won't touch him again until it's time for him to go—unless something goes wrong."

"Nothing will go wrong!"

"Good. Show me everything."

I obeyed, stumbling now and then because I understood the working of the male's body better than I understood the vocabulary, silent or vocal, for discussing it. But with neurosensory illusions, I could show it exactly what I meant.

"There are no words for some things," Nikanj told me as it finished. "You and your children will create them if you need them. We've never needed them."

"Did I do all right with him?"

"Go away. I'll find out for sure."

I went to sit with Ahajas and Dichaan and they gave me some of the wild figs and nuts they had been eating. The food did not take my mind off Nikanj touching the Human, but I ate anyway, and listened while Ahajas told me how hard it had been for Nikanj when its ooan Kahguyaht had had to examine Lilith.

"Kahguyaht said ooloi possessiveness during subadulthood is a bridge that helps ooloi understand Humans," she said. "It's as though Human emotions were permanently locked in ooloi subadulthood. Humans are possessive of mates, potential mates, and property because these can be taken from them."

"They can be taken from anyone," I said. "Living things can die. Nonliving things can be destroyed."

"But Human mates can walk away from one another," Dichaan said. "They never lose the ability to do that. They can leave one another permanently and find new mates. Humans can take the mates of other Humans. There's no physical bond.

No security. And because Humans are hierarchical, they tend to compete for mates and property."

"But that's built into them genetically," I said. "It isn't built into me."

"No," Ahajas said. "But, Oeka, you won't be able to bond with a mate—Human, construct, or Oankali—until you're adult. You can feel needs and attachments. I know you feel more at this stage than an Oankali would. But until you're mature, you can't form a true bond. Other ooloi can seduce potential mates away from you. So other ooloi are suspect."

That sounded right—or rather, it sounded true. It didn't make me feel any better, but it helped me understand why I felt like tearing Nikanj loose from the male and standing guard to see that it did not approach him again.

Nikanj came over to me after a while, smelling of the male, tasting of him when it touched me. I flinched in resentment.

"You've done a good job," it said. "How can you do such a good job with Humans and such a poor one with yourself and Aaor?"

"I don't know," I said bleakly. "But Humans steady me somehow. Maybe it's just that Marina and this male are alone—mateless."

"Go rest next to him. If you want to sleep, sleep linked with him so that he won't wake up until you do."

I got up to go.

"Oeka."

I focused on Nikanj without turning.

"Tino made crutches for him to use for the next few days. They're near his foot."

"All right." I had never seen a crutch, but I had heard of them from the Humans in Lo.

"There's clothing with the crutches. Lilith says put some of it on and give the rest to him."

Now I did turn to look at it.

"Put the clothing on, Jodahs. He's a resister male. It will be hard enough for him to accept you."

It was right, of course. I wasn't even sure why I had stopped wearing clothes—except perhaps that I didn't have anyone to wear them for. I dressed and lay down alongside the male.

2

The male and I awoke together. He saw me and tried at once to scramble away from me. I held him, spoke softly to him. "You're safe," I said. "No one will hurt you here. You're being helped."

He frowned, watched my mouth. I could read no understanding in his expression, though the softness of my voice seemed to ease him.

"*Español?*" I asked.

"*Português?*" he asked hopefully.

Relief. "*Sim, senhor. Falo português.*"

He sighed with relief of his own. "Where am I? What has happened to me?"

I sat up, but with a hand on his shoulder encouraged him to go on lying down. "We found you badly injured, alone in the forest. I think you had fallen from a tree."

"I remember . . . my leg. I tried to get home."

"You can go home in a few days. You're still healing now." I paused. "You did a great deal of damage to yourself, but we can fix it all."

"Who are you?"

"Jodahs Iyapo Leal Kaalnikanjlo. I'm the one who has to see that you walk home on two good legs."

"It was broken, my leg. Will it be crooked?"

"No. It will be new and straight. What's your name?"

"Excuse me. I am João. João Eduardo Villas da Silva."

"João, your leg was too badly injured to be saved. But your new leg has already begun to grow."

He groped in sudden terror for the missing leg. He stared at me. Abruptly he tried again to scramble away.

I caught his arms and held him still, held him until he stopped struggling. "You are well and healthy," I told him softly. "In a few days you will have a new leg. Don't do yourself any more harm now. You're all right."

He stared at my face, shook his head, stared again.

"It is true," I said. "A few days of crutches, then a whole leg again. Look at it."

He looked, twisting so that I could not see—as though he thought his body still held secrets from me.

"It doesn't look like a new leg," he said.

"It's only a few hours old. Give it time to grow."

He sat where he was and looked around at the rest of the family. "Who are you all? Why are you here?"

"We're travelers. One family from Lo, traveling south."

"My home is to the west in the hills."

"We won't leave you until you can go there."

"Thank you." He stared at me a little longer. "I mean no offense, but . . . I've met very few of your people—Human and not Human."

"Construct."

"Yes. But I don't know . . . Are you a man or a woman?"

"I'm not an adult yet."

"No? You appear to be an adult. You appear to be a young woman—too thin, perhaps, but very lovely."

I wasn't surprised this time. My body wanted him. My body sought to please him. What would happen to me when I had two or more mates? Would I be like the sky, constantly changing, clouded, clear, clouded, clear? Would I have to be hateful to one partner in order to please the other? Nikanj looked the same all the time and yet all four of my other parents treasured it. How well would my looks please anyone when I had four arms instead of two?

"No male or female could regenerate your leg," I told João. "I am ooloi."

It was as though the air between us became a crystalline

wall—transparent, but very hard. I could not reach him through it anymore. He had taken refuge behind it and even if I touched him, I would not reach him.

"You have nothing to fear from us," I said, meaning he had nothing to fear from me. "And even though I'm not adult, I can complete your regeneration."

"Thank you," he said from behind his cold new shield. "I'm very grateful." He was not. He did not believe me.

My head and body tentacles drew themselves into tight pre-strike coils, and I moved back from João. It would have been easier if he had leaped away from me the way Marina had almost done. Fear was easier to deal with than this . . . this cold rejection—this revulsion.

"Why do you hate me?" I whispered. "You would have died without an ooloi to save your life. Why do you hate me for saving your life?"

João's face underwent several changes. Surprise, regret, shame, anger, renewed hatred and revulsion. "I did not ask you to save me."

"Why do you hate me?"

"I know what you do—your kind. You take men as though they were women!"

"No! We—"

"Yes! Your kind and your Human whores are the cause of all our trouble! You treat all mankind as your woman!"

"Is that how I've treated you?"

He became sullen. "I don't know what you've done."

"Your body tells you what I've done." I sat for a time and looked at him with my eyes. When he looked away, I said, "That male over there is my Human father. The female is my Human mother. I came from her body. I didn't heal you so that you could insult these people."

He only stared at me. But there was doubt in him now. Lilith was putting something into a Lo cloth pot that she had suspended between two trees. She had not yet made a fire beneath it. Tino was some distance away cutting palm branches. We would build a shelter of sapling trees, Lo cloth, and palm branches and hang our hammocks in it. We had not done that for a while.

My Human parents must have looked much like the people of João's home village. When lone resisters had to live among us, they usually found themselves identifying with the mated Humans around them and choosing an Oankali or a construct "protector." They became temporary mates or temporary adopted siblings. Marina had chosen a kind of temporary mate status, staying with me and hardly speaking at all to anyone else except Aaor. That was what I wanted of João, too. But I would have to encourage him more, and at the same time convince him that his manhood was not threatened. I had heard that males often felt this way about ooloi. I would have to talk to Tino. He could help me understand the fear and ease it. Reason would clearly not be enough.

"No one will guard you," I told João. "You are not a prisoner. But I have to monitor your leg. If you leave before the regeneration is complete, before I make certain the growth process had stopped, you could wind up with a monstrous tumor. It would eventually kill you. If someone cut it away for you, it would grow again."

He did not want to believe me, but I had frightened him. I had intended to. All that I'd said was true.

I stood up and pointed. "Your crutches are there. And my Human mother has left you clean clothing." I paused. "Anyone here will give you any help you need if you don't insult them."

I wanted to hold my hand out to him, but all of his body language said he would not take it as Marina had. He sat where he was, staring at the place where his leg had been. He made no effort to get up.

I brought him a bowl of fruit and nut porridge and he only sat staring at it. I sat with him and ate mine, but he hardly moved. No, he moved once. When I touched him, he flinched and turned to stare at me. There was nothing in his expression except hatred.

I went away and bathed in the river. Aaor was with João

when I got back to camp. They were not talking, but the stiffness had gone out of João's back. Perhaps he was simply tired. I saw Aaor push the bowl of porridge toward him. He took the bowl and ate. When Aaor touched him, he did not flinch.

3

João chose Aaor. He accepted help from it and talked to it and caressed its small breasts once he realized that neither it nor anyone else minded this. The breasts did not represent true mammary glands. Aaor would probably lose them when it metamorphosed. Most constructs did, even when they became female. But João liked them. Aaor simply enjoyed the contact.

At night, João endured me. I think his greatest shame was that his body did not find me as repellent as he wanted to believe I was. This frightened him as much as it shamed him. Perhaps it told him what I had already realized—that given time he could learn to accept me, to enjoy me very much. I think he hated me more for that than for anything.

In twenty-one days João's leg had grown. I had made him eat huge amounts of food—had stimulated his appetite so that he could not stubbornly refuse meals. Also, I chemically encouraged him to be sedentary. He needed all his energy to grow his leg.

I had grown breasts myself, and developed an even more distinctly Human female appearance. I neither directed my body nor attempted to control it. It developed no diseases, no abnormal growths or changes. It seemed totally focused on João, who ignored it during the day, but caressed it at night and investigated it before I put him to sleep.

I kept him with me for three extra days to help him regain his strength and to be absolutely certain the leg had stopped growing and worked as well as his old one. It was smooth and soft-skinned and very pale. The foot was so tender that I folded lengths of Lo cloth and pressed them together to make sandals for him.

"I haven't worn anything on my feet since long before you were born," he told me.

"Wear these back to your home or you'll damage the new foot badly," I said.

"You're really going to let me go?"

"Tomorrow." It was our twenty-fifth night together. He still pretended to ignore me during the day, but it had apparently become so much trouble for him to manufacture hatred against me at night. He accepted what I did for him and he did not insult me. He didn't insult anyone. Once I found him telling Aaor, Lilith, and Tino about São Paulo, where he had been born. He had been only nineteen when the war came. He had been a student. He would have become a doctor like his father. "People shook their heads over the war at first," he told them. "They said it would kill off the north—Europe, Asia, North America. They said the northerners had lost their minds. No one realized we would suffer from sickness, hunger, blindness. . . ."

He had known I was listening. He hadn't cared, but he would not have volunteered to tell me anything of his past. He answered my questions, but he volunteered nothing.

The name of his resister village was São Paulo, in memory of his home city, which had once existed far to the east. He had just traveled back to the site of the city—through thick forests and hostile people, across many rivers. Before the war and the coming of the Oankali, São Paulo was a city of millions of Humans and the forests of buildings, large and small. But what the war and its aftermath had not destroyed, the Oankali fed to their shuttles. Shuttles ate whatever they landed on. There were a few ruins left, but the forest now covered most of what had been São Paulo.

João had talked about his past to Ahajas and Dichaan as

well. He avoided Nikanj, at least. I could accept everything he did as long as he avoided Nikanj.

"Tomorrow," he repeated now, lying beside me. He moved warningly, then sat up. I had told him always to move a little to warn me that he intended to change position or get up—in case I had sensory tentacles linked into him. He had ignored me once. The pain of that had made him scream aloud and roll himself into a tight fetal knot for some time, sweating and gasping. He hurt me as badly as he hurt himself, but I managed not to react as much. I never said anything, but he always made me a small, warning move after that.

He looked down at me. "I didn't believe you."

"Your leg is complete and strong. It's tender. You need to protect it. But you're whole. Why shouldn't you leave?"

His mouth said nothing. His face said he wasn't sure he wanted to go. He wasn't even sure he appreciated my telling him he could go. But his pride kept him silent.

"All right!" he said finally. "Tomorrow I go. Tomorrow morning."

I drew him down to our pallet and kissed his face, then his mouth. "I won't be glad to see you go," I said. "If you were younger . . ." I rubbed the back of his neck. My underarms didn't itch. They hurt.

"I didn't know my age was important," he said. He sighed. "I shouldn't care. I should be grateful. I haven't changed my opinion . . . of ooloi."

"You have, I think."

"No. I've only changed my feelings toward you. I wouldn't have believed I could do even that."

"Before you leave, go to Nikanj. Have it check you to be certain that I haven't missed anything."

"No!"

"It will only touch you for a moment. Only for a moment. Come to me afterward . . . to say goodbye."

"No. I can't let that thing touch me. I would rather trust you."

"It's one of my parents."

"I know. I mean no offense. But I cannot do that."

"I won't send you away to die from some mistake of mine that could have been corrected. You *will* let it touch you."

Silence.

"Do it for my sake, João. Don't leave me wondering whether I've killed you."

He sighed. After a moment, he nodded.

I put him to sleep. He did not realize it, but I was responsible for strengthening his aversion to Nikanj. No male or female who spent as much time with an ooloi as he had with me would feel comfortable touching another ooloi. João was not bound to me, but he was chemically oriented toward me and away from others. And adult ooloi could seduce him from me if he truly disliked me and was interested in finding another ooloi. But otherwise, he would stay with me. Lilith had begun this way with Nikanj.

The next morning, I took João to Nikanj. As I had promised, Nikanj touched him briefly, then let him go.

"You've done nothing wrong with him," he told me. "I wish he could stay and keep you from becoming a frog again." I was grateful that it spoke in English and João did not understand.

I gave João food and a hammock and my machete. He had lost whatever gear he had had with him when he fell.

"There are older Oankali who would mate with you," I told him. "They could give you pleasure. You could have children."

"Which of them would look like someone I used to dream about when I was young?" he asked.

"I don't really look like this, João. You know I don't. I didn't look this way when we met."

"You look like this for me," he said. "Tell me who else could do that?"

I shook my head. "No one."

"You see?"

"Then go to Mars. Find someone who does really look this way. Have Human children."

"I've thought about Mars. It seemed a fantasy, though. To live on another world. . . ."

"Oankali have lived on many other worlds. Why shouldn't Humans live on at least one other?"

"Why should the Oankali have the one world that's ours?"

"They do have it. And you can't take it back from them. You can stay here and die uselessly, resisting. You can go to Mars and help found a new Human society. Or you can join us in the trade. We will go to the stars eventually. If you join us, your children will go with us."

He shook his head. "I don't know. I've been among Oankali before. We all have, we resisters. Oankali never made me doubt what I should do." He smiled. "Before I met you, Jodahs, I knew myself much better."

He went away undecided. "I don't even know what I want from you," he said as he was leaving. "It isn't the usual thing, certainly, but I don't want to leave you."

But, of course, he did leave.

4

Two days after João had gone, Aaor went into metamorphosis. It did not seem to edge in slowly as I had—though I had been so preoccupied with João that I could easily have missed the signs. It simply went to its pallet and went to sleep. I was the one who touched it and realized that it was in metamorphosis. And that it was becoming ooloi.

There would be two of us, then. Two dangerous uncertainties who might never be allowed to mate normally, who might spend the rest of our lives in one kind of exile or another.

We had not begun to travel again on the day João left us. Now we could not. There was no good reason to carry Aaor through the forest, forcing it to assimilate new sensations when it should be isolated and focusing inward on the growth and readjustment of its own body.

We could have put together a raft and traveled down the river to Lo in a fraction of the time it had taken us to reach this point. In an emergency, Nikanj could even signal for help. But what help? A shuttle to take us back to Lo, where we could not stay? A shuttle to take us to Chkahichdahk, where we did not want to go?

We sat grouped around the sleeping Aaor and agreed to do the only thing we really could do: move to higher ground to avoid the rainy season floods and build a more permanent house. My Human mother said it was time to plant a garden.

Nikanj and I stayed with Aaor while the others went to find the site of our new home.

"Do you realize you've already lost most of your hair?" Nikanj asked me as we sat on opposite sides of Aaor's sleeping body.

I touched my head. It still had a very thin covering of hair, but as Nikanj had said, I was nearly bald. Again. I had not noticed. Now I could see that my skin was changing, too, losing the softness it had taken on for João, losing its even brown coloring. I could not tell yet whether I would return to my natural gray-brown or take on the greenish coloring I'd had just before João.

"You should be at least as good at monitoring your own body as you are at monitoring a Human," Nikanj said.

"Will Aaor be like me?" I asked.

It let all its sensory tentacles hang limp. "I'm afraid it might be." It was silent for a while. "Yes, I believe it will be," it said finally.

"So now you have two same-sex children to need you . . . and to resent you."

It focused on me for a long time with an intensity that first puzzled me, then began to scare me. It had rested one sensory arm across Aaor's chest, examining, checking.

"Is it all right?" I asked.

"As much as you are." It rustled its tentacles. "Perfect, but imperfect. It has all that it should have. It can do all that it should be able to do. But that won't be enough. You'll have to go to the ship, Oeka. You and Aaor."

"No!" I felt the way I had once when an apparently friendly Human had hit me in the face.

"You need mates," it said softly. "No one will mate with you here except old Humans who would steal perhaps four fifths of your life. On the ship, you may be able to get young mates—perhaps even young Humans."

"And bring them back to Earth?"

"I don't know."

"I won't go then. I won't take the chance of being held there. I don't think Aaor will either."

"It will. You both will when it finishes its metamorphosis."

"No!"

"Oeka, you've seen it yourself. With a potential mate—even a very unsuitable one—your control is flawless. Without a potential mate, you have no control. You were surprised when I told you you were losing your hair. You've been surprised by your body again and again. Yet nothing it does should surprise you. Nothing it does should be beyond your control."

"But I didn't even grow that hair deliberately. I just . . . On some level I realized João would like it. I think I became all the things he liked, even though he never told me what they were."

"His body told you. His every look, his reactions, his touch, his scent. He never stopped telling you what he wanted. And since he was the sole focus of your attention, you gave him everything he asked for." It lay down beside Aaor. "We do that, Jodahs. We please them so that they'll stay and please us. You're better at it with Humans than I ever was. I was bred for this trade, but you, you're part of the trade. You can understand both Human and Oankali by looking inside yourself." It paused, rustled its tentacles. "I don't believe we would have had many resisters if we had made construct ooloi earlier."

"You think that, and you still want to send me away?"

"I believe it, yes. But no one else does. We must teach them."

"I don't want to teach—. We? We, Ooan?"

"For a while, we'll all relocate to the ship."

I almost said no again, but it wouldn't have paid any attention to me. When it began telling me what I *would* do, it had decided. Our interests—Aaor's and mine—and our needs would be best served on Chkahichdahk, even if we were never allowed to come home. The family would stay with us until we were adults, but then it would leave us on the ship. No more forests or rivers. No more wildness filled with things I had not yet tasted. The planet itself was like one of my parents. I would leave it, and I would gain nothing.

No, that wasn't true. I would gain mates. Eventually. Perhaps. Nikanj would do all it could to get the mates. There were young Humans born and raised on the ship because there had been so few salvageable Humans left after their war and their resulting disease and atmospheric disturbances. There had not been enough for a good trade. Also most of those who wanted to return to Earth had been allowed to return. That left the Toaht Oankali—those who wanted to trade and to leave with the ship—too few Human mates. They had been breeding more Humans as well as accepting violent ones from Earth. But even so, there were not enough for everyone who wanted them. Not yet. How likely would the Toaht be to let me mate with even one?

I shook my head. "Don't desert me, Ooan."

It focused on me, its manner questioning. "You know I won't."

"I won't go to Chkahichdahk. I won't take what they decide to give me and stay if they decide to keep me. I would rather stay here and mate with old Humans."

It did not shout at me as my Human parents would have. It did not tell me what I already knew. It did not even turn away from me.

"Lie here with me," it said softly.

I went over and lay down next to it, felt it link into me with more sensory tentacles than I had on my entire body. It looped a sensory arm around my neck.

"Such despair in you," it said silently. "You could not throw away so much life."

"Your life will be shorter because of Tino and Lilith," I told it. "Do you feel that you're throwing something away?"

"On Chikahichdahk, there are Humans who will live as long as you would normally."

"So many that a pair would be allowed to come to me? And what about Aaor?"

It began to feel despair of its own. "I don't know."

"But you don't think so. Neither do I."

"You know I'll speak for you."

"Ooan . . ."

"Yes. I know. I've produced two construct ooloi children. No one else has produced any. Who will listen to me?"

"Will anyone?"

"Not many."

"Why did you threaten to send me to Chkahichdahk, then?"

"You will go, Oeka. There's no place for you here, and you know it."

"No!"

"There's life there for you. *Life!*" It paused. "You're more adaptable than you think. I made you. I know. You could live there. You could find construct or Oankali mates and learn to be content with shipboard life."

I spoke aloud. "You're probably right. There used to be Humans who adapted to not being able to see or hear or walk or move. They adapted. But I don't think any of them chose to be so limited."

"But think!" It tightened its grip on me. "Where will you live with old Human mates? Will resisters let you join them in one of their villages? How many attacks on you will it take for them to force a lethal response from you? What will happen then? And, Jodahs, what will happen to your children—your Human children? Will you make them sterile or let them mate together without an ooloi and create deformity and disease? Will you try to force them to go to one of our villages? They may not want to join us any more than you want to go to

Chkahichdahk. They'll want the land and the people they know. And if you do a good job when you make them, they could outlive all other resisters. They could outlive this world. If they manage to elude us, they could die when we break the Earth and go our ways."

I withdrew from it, signaling it to withdraw from me. When the Earth was divided and the new ship entities scattered to the stars, Nikanj would be long dead. If I mated with an Old Human, I would be dead, too. I would not be able to safeguard my children even if they were willing, as adults, to be guided by a parent.

I went away from Nikanj, into the forest. I didn't go far. Aaor was helpless and Nikanj might need help protecting it. Aaor was more my paired sibling now than ever. Had it known what was happening to it? Had it wanted to be ooloi? Since it was Oankali-born, would it be willing to live on Chkahichdahk?

What difference would it make what Aaor wanted—or what I wanted? We would go to Chkahichdahk. And we would probably not be allowed to come home.

When my parents and siblings returned to move Aaor to the new home site they had chosen, I went down to the river, went in, and crossed.

I wandered for three days, my body green, scaly, and strange. No one came near me. I lived off the plants I found, picking and choosing according to the needs of my body. I ate everything raw. Humans liked fire. They valued cooked food much more than we did. Also, Humans were less able to get the nutrition they needed from the leaves, grasses, seeds, and fungi that were so abundant in the forest. We could digest what we needed from wood if we had to.

I wandered, tasting the forest, tasting the Earth that I would soon be taken from.

After three days, I went back to the family. I spent a couple of days sitting with Aaor, then left again.

That was my pattern during the rest of Aaor's metamorphosis. Sometimes I brought Nikanj a few cells of some plant or

animal that I had run across for the first time. We all did that—
brought the adult ooloi of the family living samples of whatever we encountered. Ooloi generally learned a great deal from
what their mates and unmated children brought them. And
whatever we gave Nikanj, it remembered. It could still recall
and re-create a rare mountain plant that one of my brothers
had introduced it to over fifty years before. Someday it was
supposed to duplicate the cells of its vast store of biological information and pass the copies along to its same-sex children.
We were to receive it when we were fully adult and mated.
What would that mean, really, for Aaor and me? Someday on
Chkahichdahk? Never?

I had always enjoyed bringing Nikanj things. I had enjoyed
sharing the pleasure it felt in new tastes, new sensations. Now
I needed contact with it more than ever. But I no longer enjoyed the contact. I didn't blame it for pointing out the obvious: that Aaor and I had to go to the ship. It was our same-sex
parent, doing its duty. But every time it touched me, all I could
feel was stress. Distress. Its own and mine. I brought out the
worst in it.

I began to stay away even longer.

I met resisters occasionally, but I looked so un-Human and
so un-Oankali most of the time that they fled. Twice they shot
me, then fled. But no matter how my body distorted itself, I
could always heal wounds.

My family never tried to control my goings and comings.
They accepted my feelings whether they understood them or
not. They wanted to help me, and suffered because they could
not. When I was at home I sat with them sometimes—with Ayodele and Yedik when they guarded at night. People guarded
in pairs except for Nikanj, who stayed with Aaor, and Oni and
Hozh, who were too young to guard.

But I could touch Oni and Hozh. I could touch Ayodele and
Yedik. They were still children, neutral-scented, and not yet
forbidden to me. When I came out of the forest, looking like
nothing anyone on Earth would recognize, one or the other
pair of them took me between them and stayed with me until

I looked like myself again. If I touched only one of them, I
would change that one, make it what I was. But if they both
stayed with me, they changed me.

"We shouldn't be able to do this to you," Yedik said as we
guarded one night.

"You make it easy for me not to wander," I told it. "My
body wanders. Even when I come home, it wants to go on
wandering."

"We shouldn't be able to stop it," Yedik insisted. "We
shouldn't influence you at all. We're too young."

"I want you to influence me." I looked from one of them to
the other. Ayodele looked female and Yedik looked male. I
hoped they would be more strongly influenced by the way they
looked than I had. Humans said they were beautiful.

"I can change myself," I told them. "But it's an effort. And
it doesn't last. It's easier to do as water does: allow myself to
be contained, and take on the shape of my containers."

"I don't understand," Ayodele said.

"You help me do what I want to do."

"What do Humans do?"

"Shape me according to their memories and fantasies."

"But—" They both spoke at once. Then, by mutual consent,
Ayodele spoke. "Then you're either out of control or contained by us or forced into a false Human shape."

"Not forced."

"When can you be yourself?"

I thought about that. I understood it because I remembered
being their age and having a strong awareness of the way my
face and body looked, and of that look being *me*. It never had
been, really.

"Changing doesn't bother me anymore," I said. "At least,
not this kind of deliberate, controlled changing. I wish it didn't
bother other people. I've never deformed plants or animals the
way people said I might."

"Just people," Yedik said quietly. "People and Lo."

"Lo was barely annoyed. It would have survived that war
the Humans killed each other with."

"It's part of you and vulnerable to you. You hurt it."

"I know. And I confused it. But I don't think I could injure it seriously if I tried—and I wouldn't try. As for people, have you noticed that the Humans, the people I'm supposed to be the greatest danger to, are the ones I've never hurt?"

Silence.

"Does it bother you to have me here with you?"

"It did," Ayodele said. "We thought your life must be terrible. We can feel your distress when we link with you."

"This is my place," I told them. "This world. I don't belong on the ship—except perhaps for a visit. People go there to absorb more of our past sometimes. I wouldn't mind that. But I can't live there. No matter what Ooan says, I can't live there. It's a finished place. The people are still making themselves, but the place . . ."

"It's still dividing in two to make a ship for the Toaht and a ship for the Akjai."

"And the two halves will be smaller finished places. No wildness. No newness. I'm Dinso like you, not Toaht or Akjai."

Again they were silent.

"You two sit together." I withdrew from them and started to get up.

They watched me with their eyes and their few sensory tentacles. Silently they took my hands and drew me down to sit between them again. They acted more in perfect unison than any of my siblings. Ahajas said they would certainly become mates if they developed as male and female. They did not want me between them. I made them uncomfortable because they wanted to help me and couldn't help much. On the other hand, they *did* want me between them because they could help a little, and they knew they would lose me soon, and they liked the way I made their bodies feel. I wasn't as able to make people feel good as Nikanj was, but I could give them something. And I was old enough to read internal and external body language and understand more of what they were feeling.

I liked that. I liked a lot of what I had been able to do recently. It was only the thought of going to Chkahichdahk, and being kept there, that made me feel caged and frantic.

The next morning that thought drove me into the forest again.

5

Aaor had a long metamorphosis. Eleven months. I was afraid every time I went home that it would be awake and the family would be building a raft.

I began to seek out Humans. I avoided large parties of them, but it was easy to find individuals and small groups.

I followed them silently, dissected and enjoyed their scents, listened to their conversations. Sometimes they became aware that they were being followed, though they never saw me. My coloring had darkened and I hid easily in the shadows. The forest understory was usually wet or at least damp, and it was easy for me to move silently. The Humans I followed often made much more noise than I did. I watched a Human hunter make so much noise that the feeding peccary he was stalking heard him and ran away. The Human went to the place where the peccary had been feeding and he cursed and kicked the fruit the animal had been feeding on. It never occurred to him to eat the fruit or to collect some for his people. I ate some when he was gone.

Once three people stalked me. I considered letting them catch me. But I circled around to have a look at them first, and I heard them talking about opening me up and seeing how I looked inside. Since they all had guns and machetes, I decided to avoid them. Three were too many for a subadult to subdue safely.

I was moving upriver—farther upriver than I had been before—well into the hills. The forest was less varied here, but I had no trouble finding enough to eat, and occasional plants and animals that were new to me. But I found few people in the hills. For several days, I found no one at all. No breeze brought me a Human scent.

I began to feel loneliness as an almost physical pain. I hadn't realized how much seeing Humans every few days had meant to me.

Now I had to go home. I didn't want to. Surely Aaor would be awake this time. The thought panicked me, brought back the caged feeling so strongly that I could not think.

I stayed where I was for a while, cleared a space, made a fire, though I did not need one. It comforted me and reminded me of Humans. I let the fire burn down and roasted several wild tubers in the coals. The smell of the food wasn't enough to mask the smell of the two Humans when they approached. No doubt it was the food smell that drew them.

They were a male and a female and they smelled . . . very strange. Wrong. Injured, perhaps. They were armed. I could smell gunpowder. They might shoot me. I decided to risk it. I would not move. I would let them surprise me.

My body at this time was covered with fingernail-sized, overlapping scales. It was also inclined to be quadrapedal, but I had resisted that. Hands were much more useful than clawed forefeet.

Now, while the Humans approached very carefully, very quietly, I prepared for them. My bald, scaly head and scaly face had to look more Human. I didn't have time to change the rest of me. I could look as though I were wearing unusual clothing, perhaps. In fact, I didn't wear clothing at all on these trips. It just got in the way.

The Humans kept to cover and circled around, watching me. They wanted to be behind me. I decided to play dead if they shot me. Best to lure them close and disarm them as quickly as possible.

Perhaps they would not shoot me. I used a stick to uncover one of the tubers and roll it out of the coals. It was too hot to eat, but I brushed it off and broke it open. It was well cooked, steaming hot, spicy, and sweet. It had not existed before the Humans had their war. Lilith said it was one of the few good-tasting mutations she had eaten. She called it an applesauce fruit. Apples were an extinct fruit that she had especially liked. She didn't like the taste of the tubers raw, but sometimes when she had baked one she went away by herself to eat it and remember a different time.

One of the Humans made a small noise behind me—a moan.

I ran a hand over my face. The hand was more clawlike than I would have preferred, but the face was clear and soft now. If it wasn't beautiful, it was, at least, not terrifying.

"Come join me," I said loudly. It felt unnatural to talk aloud. I hadn't spoken at all for about thirty days. "There's more food. You're welcome to it." I repeated the words in Spanish, Portuguese, and Swahili. Those, together with French and English, were the most widely known languages. Most people were fluent in at least one of them. Most survivors were from Africa, Australia, and South America.

The two Humans did not answer me. They did not move, but their heartbeats speeded up. They had heard me and they probably understood that I was talking to them. When had their heartbeats increased? I focused on my memories for a moment. My speaking at all had startled them, but my Spanish had excited them more. My other languages had provoked no further reaction. Spanish, then. I repeated my invitation in Spanish.

They did not come. I thought they understood, but they did not answer, and they remained hidden.

I took the rest of the tubers from the coals and put them on a platter of large leaves.

"They're yours if you would like them," I said. I cleared a place well away from the food and lay down to rest. I had not slept in two days. Humans liked regular periods of sleep—preferably at night. Oankali slept when they needed rest. I needed rest now, but I would not sleep until the Humans made some decision—either to go away or to come satisfy their hunger and their curiosity. But I could be still in the Oankali way. I could lie awake using the least possible energy, and as Lilith and Tino said, looking dead. I could do this very comfortably for much longer than most Humans would willingly sit and watch.

The male left cover first. I watched him with a few of my sensory tentacles. All his body language told me he meant to grab the food and run with it. I was prepared to let him do that until I got a good look at him.

He was diseased. His face was half obscured by a large growth. He wore no shirt and I could see that his back and chest were covered with tumorous growths, large and small. One of his eyes was completely covered. The other seemed endangered. If the facial tumor continued to grow, he would soon be unable to see.

I couldn't let him go. I don't think any ooloi could have let him go. No living being should be left to wander without care in his condition.

I waited until his attention was totally focused on the food. At first he kept flickering back and forth between the food and me. Finally, though, the food was in reach. He put out his hands to take it.

I had him before he realized I was up. At once, I turned him to face the female, whom I could see now. She was aiming a rifle at me. Let her aim it at him.

He struggled, first wildly, then with calculation, meaning to hurt me and get free. I held him still and investigated him quickly.

He had a genetic disorder. Its effects were worsening slowly. As I had suspected, he would be blind if it were allowed to continue. The disorder had deformed even the bones of his face. He was deaf in one ear. Eventually he would be deaf in the other. His spine was becoming involved. Already he could not turn his head freely. One shoulder was completely covered with fleshy growths. The arm was still useful, but it wouldn't be for long. And there was something else wrong. Something I didn't understand. This man was already dying. He was using up his life the way mice did, swallowing it in a few quick gulps, then dying. The disorder threatened to invade his brain and spine. But even without continued tumor growth, he would die in just a few decades. He was genetically programmed to use himself up obscenely quickly.

How could he have such a disorder? An ooloi had examined him before he was set free. Ooloi had examined every Human, correcting defects, slowing aging, strengthening resistance to disease. But perhaps the ooloi had only controlled the disorder—imperfectly—and not tried to correct it. Ooloi had done that with some genetic disorders. Such disorders were complicated and best corrected by mates. Resisters had been altered so that they could not have children without ooloi mates, and thus could not pass their disorder on. Controlling it should have been enough.

I spoke into the male's one good ear as I held him. "You'll be completely blind soon. After that you'll go deaf. Eventually you won't be able to use your right arm—and that's the arm you prefer to use. That's not all. That's not even the worst. Do you understand me?"

He had stopped struggling. Now he rocked back, trying to get a look at me in spite of his uncooperative neck.

"I can help you," I said. "I will help you if you let me. And if your friend doesn't shoot me." I would help him whether the female shot me or not, but I wanted to avoid being shot if I could. Bullet wounds hurt more than I wanted to think about, and I still wasn't very good at controlling my own pain.

The man was feeling calmer now. I did not dare drug him much. I could please him a little, relax him a little, but I could not put him to sleep. If he lost consciousness in my arms, the female would surely misunderstand, and shoot me.

"I can help," I repeated. "All I ask in return is that you not try to kill me."

"Why should you do anything?" he demanded. "Just let me go!"

I shifted to a more comfortable grip. "Why should you become more and more disabled?" I asked. "Why should you die when you can live and be well? Let me help you."

"Let go of me!"

"Will you stay, and at least hear me?"

He hesitated. "Yes. All right." His body was tense—ready to run.

I made a sighing sound so that he would hear it. "If you lie to me, I can't help knowing."

That frightened him and made him stiffly resentful in my grasp, but he said nothing.

The female came completely out of her cover and faced us. I kept the male's body between my own and her rifle. Looking at her, I had absolutely no doubt that she would shoot. But I needed a few moments more with the male before I could have anything serious to show them. The female had tumors, too, though hers were not as big as the male's. Her face, arms, and legs—all that was visible of her—were covered with small irregularly spaced growths.

"Let him go," she said quietly. "I won't shoot you if you let him go." That was true at least. She was afraid, but she meant what she said.

I nodded to her, then spoke to the male. "I haven't hurt you. What will you do if I let you go?"

Now the male gave a real sigh. "Leave."

"You're hungry. Take the food with you."

"I don't want it." He no longer trusted it—probably because I wanted him to have it.

"Do one thing for me before I let you go."

"What?"

"Move your neck."

I kept a firm hold on him, but drew back slightly to let him turn and twist the neck that had been all but frozen in place before I touched him. He swore softly.

"Tomás?" the female said, her voice filled with doubt.

"I can move it," he said unnecessarily. He had not stopped moving it.

"Does it hurt?"

"No. It just feels . . . normal. I had forgotten how it felt to move this way."

I let him go and spoke softly. "Perhaps when you've been blind for a while, you'll forget how it feels to see."

He almost fell turning to look at me. When he'd gotten a good look, he took a step back. "You won't touch me again until I see you heal yourself," he said. "What . . . Who are you?"

"Jodahs," I said. "I'm a construct, Human and Oankali."

He looked startled, then moved around so that he could get a look at all sides of me. "I never heard that they had scales." He shook his head. "My god, man, you must frighten more people than we do!"

I laughed. I could feel my sensory tentacles flattening against my scales. "I don't always look this way," I said. "If you stay to be healed, I'll begin to look more like you. More like the way you will look when you're healed."

"We can't be healed," the female said. "The tumors can be cut off, but they grow back. The disease . . . we were born with it. No one can heal it."

"I know you were born with it. You'll give it to at least some of your children if you decide to go where you can have them. I can correct the problem."

They looked at each other. "It isn't possible," the male said.

I focused on him. He had been such a pleasure to touch. Now there was no need to hurry back home. No need to hurry at anything. Two of them. Treasure.

"Move your neck," I said again.

The male moved it, shaking his misshapen head. "I don't understand," he said. "What did you say you were called?"

"Jodahs."

"I'm Tomás. This is Jesusa." No other names. Very deliberately, no other names. "Tell us how you did this."

I took sticks from the pile I had gathered and built up the fire. The two Humans obligingly sat down around it. The male picked up a baked tuber. The female caught his arm and looked at him, but he only grinned, broke open the tuber, and bit into it. His single visible eye opened wide in surprise and pleasure. The tuber was new to him. He ate a little more, then gave a piece to the female. She scooped out a little with one finger and tasted it. She did not take on the same look of surprised pleasure, but she ate, then examined the peeling carefully in the firelight. It was dark now for resisters. The sun had gone down.

"I haven't tasted this before. Is it only a lowland plant?"

"It grows here. I'll show you tomorrow morning."

There was a silence. Of course they would stay the night in this place. Where else could they go in the dark?

"You're from the mountains?" I asked softly.

More silence.

"I won't get to the mountains. I wish I could."

They were both eating tubers now, and they seemed content to eat and not talk. That was surprising. Nervousness alone should have made at least one of them talkative. How many times had they sat alone in the forest at night with a scaly construct?

"Will you let me begin to heal you tonight?" I asked Tomás.

"Thank you for healing my neck," Tomás said aloud while his entire body recoiled from me in tiny movements.

"It may fuse again if your disorder isn't cured."

He shrugged. "It wasn't that bad. Jesusa says it kept me working instead of looking around daydreaming."

Jesusa touched his forearm and smiled. "Nothing would keep you from daydreaming, brother."

Brother? Not mate—or husband, as the Humans would say. "Blindness will be bad," I said. "Deafness will be even worse."

"Why do you say he'll go blind or deaf?" Jesusa demanded. "He may not. You don't know."

"Of course I know. I couldn't touch him and not know. And I know there was a time when he could see out of his right eye and hear with his right ear. There was a time when the mass on his shoulder was smaller and his arm wasn't involved at all. He will be blind and deaf and without the use of his right arm—and he knows it. So do you."

There was a very long silence. I lay down on the cleared ground and closed my eyes. I could still see perfectly well, and most Humans knew it. Somehow, though, they felt more at ease when they were observed only with sensory tentacles. They *felt* unobserved.

"Why do you want to heal us?" Jesusa asked. "You waylay us, feed us, and want to heal us. Why?"

I opened my eyes. "I was feeling very lonely," I said. "I would have been glad to see . . . almost anyone. But when I realized you had something wrong, I wanted to help. I need to help. I'm not an adult yet, but I can't ignore illness. I'm ooloi."

Their mild reaction surprised me. I expected anything from João's prejudiced rejection to actually running away into the forest. Only ooloi interacted directly with Humans *and* produced children. Only ooloi interacted directly with Humans in an utterly non-Human way.

And only ooloi needed to heal. Males and females could learn to heal if they wanted to. Ooloi had no choice. We exist to make the people and to unite them and to maintain them.

Jesusa grabbed Tomás's hand and stared at me with terror. Tomás looked at her, touched his neck thoughtfully, and looked at her again. "So it isn't true, what they say," he whispered.

She gave him a look more forceful than a scream.

He drew back a little, touched his neck again, and said nothing else.

"I had thought . . ." Jesusa's voice shook and she paused for a moment. When she began again, the quiver was gone. "I thought that all ooloi had four arms—two with bones and two without."

"Strength arms and sensory arms," I said. "Sensory arms come with maturity. I'm not old enough to have them yet."

"You're a child? A child as big as an adult?"

"I'm as big as I'll get except for my sensory arms. But I still have to develop in other ways. I'm not exactly a child, though. Young children have no sex. They're potentially any sex. I'm definitely ooloi—a subadult, or as my parents would say, an ooloi child."

"Adolescent," Jesusa decided.

"No. Human adolescents are sexually mature. They can reproduce. I can't." I said this to reassure them, but they didn't seem to be reassured.

"How can you heal us if you're just a kid?" Tomás asked.

I smiled. "I'm old enough to do that." My gaze seemed to confuse him, but it only annoyed her. She frowned at me. She would be the difficult one. I looked forward to touching her, learning her body, curing the disorder she never should have had. Some ooloi had wronged her and Tomás more than I would have imagined was possible.

I changed the subject abruptly. "Tomorrow I'll show you some of the things you can eat here in the forest. The tuber was one of many. If you keep moving, the forest will sustain you very comfortably." I paused. "Can you see well enough to make pallets for yourselves or will you sleep on the bare ground?"

Tomás sighed and looked around. "Bare ground, I suppose. We'll do the local insects a good turn." The pupil of his eye was large, but I doubted that he could see beyond the light of the fire. The moon had not yet risen, and starlight was useful to Humans only in boats on the rivers. Very little of it reached the forest understory.

I got up and stepped around the fire to them. "Let me have your machete for a few moments."

Jesusa grabbed Tomás's arm to stop him, but he simply handed me the machete. I took it and went into the forest. Bamboo was plentiful in the area so I cut that and a few stalks from saplings. I would cover these with palm and wild banana leaves. I also took a stem of bananas. They could be cooked for breakfast. They weren't ripe enough for Humans to eat raw. And there was a nut tree nearby—not to mention more tubers. All this so close, and yet Tomás had been very hungry when I touched him.

"You haven't cut anything for yourself," Jesusa said as I

handed back the machete. It meant a great deal to her to get the knife back and to get a comfortable pallet to sleep on. She was still wary, but less obviously on edge.

"I'm used to the ground," I said. "No insect will bother me."

"Why?"

"I don't smell good to them. I would taste even worse."

She thought for a moment. "That would protect you against biting insects, but what about those that sting?"

"Even those. I smell offensive and dangerous. Humans don't notice my scent in any negative way, but insects always do."

"Oh, I would be willing to stink if it would keep them off me," Tomás said. "Can you make me immune to them?"

Jesusa turned to frown at him.

I smiled to myself. "No, I can't help you with that." Not until they let me sleep between them. But insects would bother them less while I healed them. If someday they mated with an adult ooloi, insects would hardly bother them at all. There was time enough for them to learn that. I lay down again beside the dying fire.

Jesusa and Tomás lay quietly, first awake, then drifting into sleep. I did not sleep, though I lay still, resting. The scent of the Humans was a mild torment to me because I could not touch them—would not touch them until they had learned to trust me. There was something strange about them—about Tomás, anyway—something I didn't yet understand. And my failure to understand was unusual. Normally if I touched someone to correct a flaw, I understood that person's body completely. I had to get my hands on Tomás again. And I had to touch Jesusa. But I wanted them to let me do it. Immature as I was, my scent must be working on them. And Tomás's healed neck must be working on him. He couldn't possibly like his growing disabilities—and surely other Humans did not like the way he looked. Humans cared very much how other people looked. Even Jesusa must seem grotesquely ugly to them—though neither Tomás nor Jesusa acted as though they cared how they looked. Very unusual. Perhaps it was because there were two of them. If they were siblings they had been together most of their lives. Perhaps they sustained one another.

6

They awoke just before dawn the next morning. Jesusa awoke first. She shook Tomás awake, then put a hand over his mouth so that he would not speak. He took her hand from his mouth and sat up. How much could they see? It was still fairly dark.

Jesusa pointed downriver through the forest.

Tomás shook his head, then glanced at me and shook his head again.

Jesusa pulled at him, both her face and her body language communicating pleading and terror.

He shook his head again, tried to take her arms. His manner was reassuring, but she evaded him. She stood up, looked down at him. He would not get up.

She sat down again, touching him, her mouth against his ear. It was more as though she breathed the words. I heard them, but I might not have if I hadn't been listening for them.

"For the others!" she whispered. "For *all* of the others, we *must* go!"

He shut his eyes for a moment, as though the soft words hurt him.

"I'm sorry," she breathed. "I'm so sorry."

He got up and followed her into the forest. He did not look at me again. When I couldn't see them any longer, I got up. I was well rested and ready to track them—to stay out of sight and listen and learn. They were going downriver as I had to do to get home. That was convenient, though the truth was, I would have followed them anywhere. And when I spoke to

them again, I would know the things they had not wanted me
to know.

I followed them for most of the day. Whatever was driving
them, it kept them from stopping for more than a few minutes
to rest. They ate almost nothing until the end of the day when,
with metal hooks they had not shown me, they managed to
catch a few small fish. The smell of these cooking was disgusting, but the conversation, at least, was interesting.

"We should go back," Tomás said. "We should cross the
river to avoid Jodahs, then we should go back."

"I know," Jesusa agreed. "Do you want to?"

"No."

"It will rain soon. Let's make a shelter."

"Once we're home, we'll never be free again," he said.
"We'll be watched all the time, probably shut up for a while."

"I know. Cut leaves from that plant and that one. They're
big enough for good roofing."

Silence. Sounds of a machete hacking. And sometime later,
Tomás's voice, "I would rather stay here and be rained on
every day and starve every other day." There was a pause. "I
would almost rather cut my own throat than go back."

"We will go back," Jesusa said softly.

"I know." Tomás sighed. "Who else would have us anyway—except Jodah's people."

Jesusa had nothing to say on that subject. They worked for
a while in silence, probably erecting their shelter. I didn't mind
being rained on, so I stretched out silently and lay with most
of my attention focused on the two Humans. If someone approached me from a different direction, I would notice, but if
people or animals were simply moving around nearby, not
coming in my direction, I would not be consciously aware of
them.

"We should have let Jodahs teach us about safe, edible
plants," Tomás said finally. "There's probably food all around
us, but we don't recognize it. I'm hungry enough to eat that big
insect right there."

Jesusa said, with amusement in her voice, "That is a very pretty red cockroach, brother. I don't think I'd eat it."

"At least there will be fewer insects when we get home."

"They'll separate us." Jesusa became grim again. "They'll make me marry Dario. He has a smooth face. Maybe we'll have mostly smooth-faced children." She sighed. "You'll choose between Virida and Alma."

"Alma," he said wearily. "She wants me. How do you think she will like leading me around? And how will we speak to one another when I'm deaf?"

"Hush, little brother. Why think about that?"

"You don't have to think about it. It won't happen to you." He paused, then continued with sad irony. "That leaves you free to worry about bearing child after child after child, watching most of them die, and being told by some smooth-faced elder who looks younger than you do that you're ready to do it all again—when she's never done it at all."

Silence.

"Jesusita."

"Yes?"

"I'm sorry."

"Why? It's true. It happened to Mama. It will happen to me."

"It may not be so bad. There are more of us now."

In a tone that made a lie of every word she said, Jesusa agreed. "Yes, little brother. Perhaps it will be better for our generation."

They were quiet for so long, I thought they wouldn't speak again, but he said, "I'm glad to have seen the lowland forest. For all its insects and other discomforts, it's a good place stuffed with life, drunk with life."

"I think the mountains better," she said. "The air is not so thick or so wet. Home is always better."

"Maybe not if you can't see it or hear it. I don't want that life, Jesusa. I don't think I can stand it. Why should I help give the people more ugly cripples anyway? Will my children thank me? I don't think they will."

Jesusa made no comment.

"I'll see that you get back," he said. "I promise you that."

"We'll both get back," she said with uncharacteristic harshness. "You know your duty as well as I know mine."

There was no more talk.

There was no more need for talk. *They were fertile!* Both of them. That was what I had spotted in Tomás—spotted, but not recognized. He was fertile, and he was young. *He was young!* I had never touched a Human like him before—and he had never touched an ooloi. I had thought his rapid aging was part of his genetic disorder, but I could see now that he was aging the way Humans had aged before their war—before the Oankali arrived to rescue the survivors and prolong their lives.

Tomás was probably younger than I was. They were both probably younger than I was. *I could mate with them!*

Young Humans, born on Earth, fertile among themselves. A colony of them, diseased, deformed, but breeding!

Life.

I lay utterly still. I had all I could do to keep myself from getting up, going to them at once. I wanted to bind them to me absolutely, permanently. I wanted to lie between them tonight. Now. Yet if I weren't careful, they would reject me, escape me. Worse, their hidden people would have to be found. I would have to betray them to my family, and my family would have to tell others. The settlement of fertile Humans would be found and the people in it collected. They would be allowed to choose Mars or union with us or sterility here on Earth. They could not be allowed to continue to reproduce here, then to die when we separated and left an uninhabitable rock behind.

No Human who did not decide to mate with us was told this last. They were given their choices and not told why.

What could Tomás and Jesusa be told? What should they be told to ease the knowledge that their people could not remain as they were? Obviously Jesusa, in particular, cared deeply about these people—was about to sacrifice herself for them. Tomás cared enough to walk away from certain healing when it was what he desperately wanted. Now, clearly, he was thinking about death, about dying. He did not want to reach his home again.

How could either of them mate with me, knowing what my people would do to theirs?

And how should I approach them? If they were potential mates and nothing more, I would go to them now. But once Jesusa understood that I knew their secret, her first question would be, "What will happen to our people?" She would not accept evasion. If I lied to her, she would learn the truth eventually, and I did not think she would forgive me for the lies. Would she forgive me for the truth?

When she and Tomás saw that they had given their people away, would they decide to kill me, to die themselves, or to do both?

7

The next day, Jesusa and Tomás crossed the river and began their journey home. I followed. I let them cross, waited until I could no longer see or hear them, then swam across myself. I swam upriver for a while, enjoying the rich, cool water. Finally I went up the bank and sorted their scent from the many.

I followed it silently, resting when they rested, grazing on whatever happened to be growing nearby. I had not decided what I would do, but there was comfort for me just being within range of their scent.

Perhaps I should follow them all the way to their home, see its location, and take news of it back to my family. Then other people, Oankali and construct, would do what was necessary. I would not be connected with it. But I also might not be allowed to mate with Jesusa and Tomás. I might be sent to the ship in spite of everything. Jesusa and Tomás might choose

Mars once others had healed them and explained their choices to them. Or they might mate with others. . . .

The more I followed them, the more I wanted them, and the more unlikely it seemed that I would ever mate with them.

After four days, I couldn't stand it any longer. I just joined them. If I could not have them as mates permanently, I could enjoy them for a while.

They had caught no fish that night. They had found wild figs and eaten them, but I doubted that these had satisfied them.

I found nuts and fruit for them, and root stalks that could be roasted and eaten. I wrapped all this in a crude basket I had woven of thin lianas and lined with large leaves. I could only do this by biting through the lianas in a way that would have disturbed the resisters, so I was glad they could not see me. A resister had said to me years before that we constructs and Oankali were supposed to be superior beings, but we insisted on acting like animals. Oddly both ideas seemed to disturb him.

I took my basket of food and went quietly into Jesusa and Tomás's camp. It was dark and they had built a small shelter and made a fire. Their fire still burned, but they had lain down on their pallets. Jesusa's even breathing said she was asleep, but Tomás lay awake. His eyes were open, but he did not see me until I was beside him.

Then before he could get up, before he could shout, I was down beside him, one hand over his mouth, the other grasping his hand and forcing it to maintain its hold on the machete, but to be still.

"Jodahs," I whispered, and he stopped struggling and stared at me.

"It *can't* be you!" he whispered when I let him speak. He remembered a scaly Jodahs, like a humanoid reptile. But I could not stay within range of their scent for four days and go on looking that way. Now I was brown-skinned and black-haired and I thought it was likely that I looked the way Tomás would when I healed him. He was the one I had touched and studied.

He let me take the machete from his hand and put it aside.

I already had several body tentacles linked into his nervous system. I put him to sleep so that I could take care of Jesusa before she awoke.

From the moment I said my name, he was never afraid. "Will you heal me?" he whispered in his last moments of consciousness.

"I will," I said. "Completely."

He closed his eye, trusting himself to me in a way that made it hard for me to withdraw from him and turn to attend to Jesusa.

When I did turn, it was almost too late. She was awake, her eyes full of confusion and terror. She drew back as I turned, and she almost pulled the trigger on the rifle she was holding.

"I'm Jodahs," I told her.

She shot me.

The bullet went through one of my hearts and I had all I could do to stop myself from lunging at her reflexively and stinging her to death. I grabbed the gun from her and threw it against a nearby tree. It broke into two pieces, the wooden stock splintering and separating from the metal, and the metal bending.

I grasped her wrists so she couldn't run. I couldn't trust myself to put her to sleep until I had my own problem under control.

She struggled and shouted for Tomás to wake up and help her. She managed to bite me twice, managed to kick me between the legs, then stopped her struggling for a moment to absorb the reality that I had only smooth skin between my legs, and that her kick did not bother me at all.

She twisted frantically and tried to gouge my eyes. I held on. I had to hold her. She couldn't see in the dark. She might run into the surrounding forest and hurt herself—or run toward the river and fall down the high, steep bluff there. Or perhaps she meant to try to shoot me again with what was left of the gun or use the machete on me. I could not let her hurt herself or hurt me again and perhaps make me kill her. Nothing would be more irrational than that.

She stopped struggling abruptly and stared at one of the bite wounds she had inflicted on my left arm. In the firelight, even Human eyes could see it. It was healing, and that seemed to fascinate her. She watched until there was no visible sign of injury. Just a little smeared blood and saliva.

"You're doing that inside," she said, "healing your wound."

I lay down, dragging her with me. She lay facing me, watching me with fear and distrust.

"I can heal myself as well as most adults," I said. "I'm not very good at controlling pain in myself, though."

She looked concerned, then deliberately hardened her expression. "What did you do to Tomás?"

"He's only asleep."

"No! He would have awakened."

"I drugged him a little. He didn't mind. I promised I would heal him."

"We don't want your healing!"

The worst of the pain from my wound was over. I relaxed in relief and drew a long breath. I let go of her hands and she drew them away, looked at them, then back to me.

I grinned at her. "You're not afraid of me now. And you don't want to hurt me again."

I could feel her face grow warmer. She sat up abruptly, very much against her own will. My scent was at work on her. She would probably have difficulty resisting it because she was not consciously aware of it.

"We truly don't want your healing," she repeated. "Though . . . I'm sorry I shot you." She sat still, looking down at me. "You look like Tomás, you know? You look the way he should look. You could be our brother—or perhaps our sister."

"Neither."

"I know. Why did you follow us?"

"Why did you run from me?"

She stared at the machete. She would have to get over or around both Tomás and me to get it.

"No, Jesusa," I said. "Stay here. Let me talk to you."

"You know about us, don't you?" she demanded.

"Yes."

"I knew you would—once you'd touched us both."

"I should have known from your scent alone. I let your disorder and my own inexperience confuse me. But, no, I didn't learn what I know from touching you just now. I learned it from following you and hearing you and Tomás talk."

Her face took on a look of outrage. "You listened? You hid in the bushes and listened to what I said to my brother!"

"Yes. I'm sorry. We don't usually do such things, but I needed to know about you. I needed to understand you."

"You needed nothing!"

"You were new to me. New, different, in need of help with your genetic disorder, and alone. You knew I could help you, yet you ran away. When you know us better, you may understand that it was as though you were dragging me by several ropes. The question wasn't whether I would follow you, but how long I could follow before I joined you again."

She shook her head. "I don't think I like your people if you're all compelled to do such things."

"It's been a century since anyone in my family has seen anyone like you. And you . . . perhaps you won't have to worry about attracting the attention of others of my people."

"What will you do, now that you know about us? What do you want of us?"

"That we must talk about," I said, "you, Tomás, and me. But I wanted to talk to you first."

"Yes?" she said.

I looked at her for some time, simply enjoying the look and the scent of her. She still might leave me. She no longer wanted to, but she was capable of causing herself pain if she thought it was the right thing to do.

"Lie here with me," I said, knowing she would not. Not yet.

"Why?" she asked, frowning.

"We're very tactile. We don't just enjoy contact, we need it."

"Not with me."

At least she did not move away from me. My left heart was

not yet healed so I did not get up. I took her hand and held it for a while, examined it with body tentacles. This startled her, but did not bring out the phobic terror some Humans are subject to when we touch them that way. Instead, she bent to get a better look at my body tentacles. They were widely scattered now, and the same brown as the rest of my skin. My head tentacles, all hidden in my hair now, were as black as my hair.

"Can you move them all at will?" she asked.

"Yes. As easily as you move your fingers. You've never seen them before, have you?"

"I've heard of them. All my life, I've heard that they were like snakes and the Oankali were covered with them."

"Some are. No Oankali has as few of them as I do now. Even I have the potential to develop a great many more."

She looked at her own arm and its dozens of small tumors. "Actually I think mine are uglier," she said.

I laughed and, with great relief, pulled her down beside me again. She didn't really mind. She was wary, but not afraid.

"You have to tell me what will happen," she said. "I'm afraid for my people. You have to tell me."

I put her head on my shoulder so that I could reach her with both head and body tentacles. She let me position her, then lay relaxed and alert against me. I eased her weariness, but did not let her become drowsy. She was younger than I had thought. She had never had a mate in the Human way. Now she never would. I felt as though I could absorb her into myself. And yet she seemed too far away. If I could just bring her closer, touch her with more sensory tentacles, touch her with . . . with what I did not yet possess.

"This is wonderful," she said. "But I don't know why it should be." She said nothing for a while. On her own, she discovered that if she touched me now with her hand, she felt the touch as though on her own skin, felt pleasure or discomfort just as she made me feel.

"Touch me," she said.

I touched her thigh, and her body flared with sexual feeling. This surprised and frightened her and she caught my free hand

and held it in her own. "You haven't told me anything," she said.

"In a way, I've told you everything," I said, "and all without words."

She let go of my hand and touched me again, let the sensation we shared guide her so that her fingertips slid around the bases of some of my sensory tentacles. She stopped an instant before I would have stopped her. The sensation was too intense.

She took my hand and put it on her breasts, and I remembered what it had been like to have breasts for João, and to drink from Lilith's breasts. Jesusa's breasts, covered by rough cloth that scratched against the top of my hand, were small and wonderfully sensitive. How had she become accustomed to the rough cloth? Probably she had never worn anything else.

She moaned and shared with me the pleasure of her body until I took my hand away and reluctantly detached from her.

"No!" she said.

"I know. We'll sleep together tonight. I have to talk to you, though, and I wanted you to experience a little of that first. I wanted you to live in my skin for a while."

She sat up and glanced at Tomás, who slept on. "Is that what you do?" she asked. She meant was that all I did.

"For now. When I'm an adult, I'll be able to do more. And also . . . even now, if I spend much time with you, I'll heal you. I can't help it."

"I can't go home if you heal me."

"Jesusa . . . that doesn't really matter."

"My people matter. They matter very much to me."

"Your people are tormenting themselves unnecessarily. They don't even know about the Mars colony, do they?"

"The what?"

"I thought not. And with their background in high-altitude living, they may be better suited to it than most Humans. The Mars colony is exactly what it sounds like: a colony of Humans living and reproducing on the planet Mars. We transport them and we've given them the tools to make Mars livable."

"Why?"

"There are no Oankali living on Mars. It's a Human world."

"*This* should be a Human world!"

"It isn't anymore. It won't ever be again."

Silence.

"That's a hard thing to think about, but it's true. Humans who are sent to Mars are healed completely of any disease or defect. They'll pass only good health on to their children."

"What else had been done to them?"

"Nothing. Not even what I've already done with you. Their healing won't be done by some hungry ooloi child. It will be done by people who are adult and mated and not especially interested in them. That's good if they want to go to Mars. That's safe."

"And I think what we did is not safe."

"Not safe at all."

"Then you must tell me what you want of me—and of Tomás?"

I turned my face away from her for a moment. I could still lose her. I stood a good chance of losing her. "You know what I want of you. Your people must have warned you. I want to mate with you. With both of you. I want you to stay with me."

"To . . . to marry? But you're . . . we're strangers."

"Are we? Not really. Not after what we've shared. I don't think one of your priests would make us a marriage ceremony, but Oankali and constructs don't have much of a ceremony. For us, mating is biological . . . neurochemical."

"I don't understand."

"Our bodies please one another and depend on one another. We keep one another well and make children together. We—"

"Have children with my brother!"

"Jesusa . . ." I shook my head. "Your flesh is so like his that I could transplant some of it to his body, and with only a small adjustment, it would live and grow on him as well as it does on you. Your people have been breeding brother to sister and parent to child for generations."

"Not anymore! We don't have to do that anymore!"

"Because there are more of you now—all closely related. Isn't that so?"

She said nothing.

"And unfortunately there was a mutation. Or perhaps one of your founding parents had a serious genetic defect that was controlled, but not corrected. That wouldn't have mattered if they'd had an ooloi to clear the way for them, but they didn't." I touched her face. "You have one now, so why should you be separated from Tomás?"

She drew back from me. "We've never touched one another that way!"

"I know."

"People had to do what they did in the past. Like the children of Adam and Eve. There wasn't anyone else."

"On Mars there are already a great many others. Why should your people want to stay here and breed dead children or disabled children? They should go to Mars or come to us. We would welcome them."

She shook her head slowly. "They told us you were of the devil."

Now it was my turn to keep quiet. She didn't believe in devils. In spite of her name, she probably didn't believe strongly in gods. She believed in her people and in what her senses told her.

"Your people won't be hurt," I assured her. "People who spend as much time as we do living inside one another's skins are very slow to kill. And if we injure people, we heal them."

"You should let them alone."

"No. We shouldn't."

"They own themselves. They don't belong to you."

"They can't survive as they are. Their gene pool is too small. It's only a matter of time before some disease or defect wipes them out." I stopped for a moment, thinking. "I'm Human enough to understand what they're trying to do. One of my brothers began the Mars colony because he understood the need of Humans to live as themselves, not to blend completely with the Oankali."

"You have brothers?" She was frowning at me as though it had never occurred to her that she and I had anything in common.

"I have brothers and sisters. I even have one ooloi sibling." Had it completed its first metamorphosis yet? Was the family simply waiting for me to return so that Aaor and I could begin our extraterrestrial exile? Let them wait.

I focused on Jesusa. I couldn't lie to her, yet I couldn't tell her everything. I was desperate to keep her and Tomás with me. The people would almost certainly not allow me to find Human mates on the ship, but they would not take away mates I had found on my own. And perhaps they would not exile me at all if they saw that with these two Humans, I was stable—not changing others, not changing myself except in a deliberate, controlled way. And Aaor could get mates from among Jesusa's people. It would want them. I had no doubt of that.

So what to do?

"My people will fight," Jesusa said.

"They'll be gassed and taken," I said. "My people like to get that kind of thing over quickly so that they don't have to hurt anyone."

She looked at me with anger—almost with hatred. "I won't tell you where my people are. I would drown myself before I would tell you."

"I wouldn't have asked."

"Why? How will you find out?"

"I won't. My people will. Once they know that your people exist, they'll find them."

She did not look toward the broken gun. She probably could not have seen it in the darkness now, but her body wanted to turn and look. Her hands wanted the gun. Her muscles twitched. If she killed me, no one would find out what I knew. No one would look for her hidden people.

I made up my mind abruptly. She had to know everything or she might die defending her people. She probably could not kill me, but she could force me to act reflexively and kill her.

"Jesusa," I said, "come over here."

She stared at me with hostility.

"Come. I'm going to tell you something my own Human mother didn't learn until she had given birth to two construct children. Your people are not usually told this at all. I . . . I should not tell it to you, but I think I have to. Come."

Her muscles wanted to move her toward me. My scent and her memory of comfort and pleasure drew her, but she moved deliberately away. "Tell me," she said. "Just tell me. Don't touch me again."

I said nothing for a while. It would be easier for her to believe what I said if we were in contact. Humans did not usually understand why being linked into our nervous systems enabled them to feel the truth of what we said, but they did feel it. Now she would not. All her body language told me she would not be persuaded.

Should she still be told?

Se had to be.

I spoke to her very softly. "You and your brother mean life to me." I paused. "And in a different way, I mean life to your people. They'll die if they stay where they are. *They'll all die.*"

"Some of us die. Some live." She shook her head. "I don't care what you say. Nothing will kill us if your people let us alone. We're strong enough to stand anything else."

"No."

"You don't know—"

"Jesusa! Listen." When she had settled into an angry silence, I told her what would happen to the Earth, what would be left of it when we were gone. "Nothing will be able to live on what we leave," I said. "If your people stay where they are and keep breeding, they'll be destroyed. Every one of them. There's life for them on Mars, and there's life here with us. But if they insist on staying where they are . . . they won't be allowed to keep having children. That way, by the time we break away from Earth, your people will have died of age."

She shook her head slowly as I spoke. "I don't believe you. Even your people can't destroy all the Earth."

"Not all of it, no. It's like . . . when you eat a piece of fruit that has an inedible core or inedible seeds. There will be a rocky core of the Earth left—a great mass of material, useful for mining, but not for living on. We'll be scattering in a great many ships. Each one will have to be self-sustaining in interstellar space perhaps for thousands of years."

"Self-sustaining in . . . ?"

"Just think of it as being beyond any possible help or dependable resupply."

"In space . . . between the stars. That's what you mean. No sun. Almost nothing."

"Yes."

"The elders who raised us when our mother died . . . they knew about such things. One used to write about them before the war to help others understand."

I said nothing. Let her think for a while.

She sat silent, frowning, sometimes shaking her head. After a while, she rubbed her face with both hands and moved to sit next to Tomás.

"Shall I wake him?" I asked.

She shook her head.

I went into the forest and brought back a few sticks of dry wood. The rain began just as I returned. Jesusa sat where I had left her, rocking back and forth a little. I hung the basket of food that I had brought on the stump of a branch that had been left on one of the support saplings. Jesusa was hungry, but she did not want to eat now. I could satisfy the needs of her body without getting her to eat. Linked with her, I could transfer nourishment to her.

I fed the fire, then went to sit with her, Tomás lying between us.

"I don't know what to think," she said softly. "My brother was going to die, you know." She stroked his black hair.

"Someone is always going to die." She paused. "He was going to kill himself as soon as he got me within sight of home. I don't know whether I could have stopped him this time."

"He tried before?" I asked.

She nodded. "That was the reason for this trip. To keep him alive a little longer." She looked at me solemn-faced. "We didn't need you to tell us he was becoming disabled. We've watched it happen to too many of our people. And . . . they just go on having children until they die or it becomes physically impossible." She touched his misshapen face. "Last year, he broke his leg and had to lie on his back with his leg splinted and attached to weights for weeks. He told the elders he didn't remember what happened. I told them he fell. They would have locked him up otherwise. We both knew he'd jumped. He meant to die. That long fall down to the river should have killed him. Thank god it didn't. I promised him we would make this trip before they married us off. I said when his leg was strong, we would slip away. He had wanted to do that for years. Only I knew. It was wrong, of course. Fertile young people risking themselves in the lowland forests, risking the welfare of everyone. . . . I did it for him. I didn't even want to come here." Tears streamed down her face, but she made no sound of crying, no move to wipe her face.

I reached over Tomás, caught her by the waist, and lifted her. She wasn't heavy at all. I put her down beside me so that I was between the two of them—where I belonged.

"You've saved him," I said. "You've saved his life and your people's lives. You've saved yourself from a life of unnecessary misery."

"Have I done so much good? Then how is it that my people would kill me if they found out?"

She believed me. It didn't make her feel any better, but she did believe.

"We can't go home," she said. "The elders always told us that if even one of your people learned the truth about us, they would find us, and the thing we were trying to rebuild would be destroyed."

"Perhaps it will only be healed and transported to Mars. Everyone who wants to go will be sent."

"They won't believe you. They wouldn't even believe me. Even if I went home now, when your people came to collect us, my people would know who had betrayed them."

"That's not what you've done. Anyway, I want you to stay with me."

She studied me, vertical frowns forming between her eyes where there was a small expanse of clear skin. "I don't know if I can do that," she said.

"You're with me now." I lay down and moved close against Tomás so that all the sensory tentacles on his side of my body could reach him. Linking into him was such a sharp, sweet shock that for a moment, I could not see. When the shock had traveled through me, I became aware of Jesusa watching. I reached up and pulled her down with us. She gasped as the contact was completed. Then she groaned and twisted her body so that she could bring more of it into contact with me. Tomás, not really awake yet, did the same, and we lay utterly submerged in one another.

8

By the next morning, most of Jesusa's small tumors had vanished, reabsorbed into her body. She was not truly healed yet, but her skin was soft and smooth for the first time since her early childhood. She cried as she ate the breakfast I prepared from my basket. She examined herself over and over.

Tomás's tumors had been bigger and would take longer to get rid of, but they had clearly begun to shrink.

We had all awakened together—which meant they had awakened when I did. I didn't want to take a chance on Jesusa rationalizing and running again, or worse, deciding to try to kill me again.

They awoke content and rested and in better physical shape than they'd been in for years. Both were fascinated by the obvious changes in Jesusa.

I lay between them, comfortably exhausted on a brand-new level. My body had been working hard all night on two people. And yet, I'd never felt this well, this complete before.

Jesusa, after touching her face and her arms and her legs and finding only smooth skin and beginning to cry, leaned down and kissed me.

"I have," Tomás said, "a very strange compulsion to do that, too." He kept his tone light, but there was real confusion behind it.

I sat up and kissed him, savoring the healing that had taken place so far. Invisible healing as well as shrinkage of visible tumors. His optic nerve was being restored—against the original genetic advice of his body. Insanely one bit of genetic information said the nerve was complete and the genes controlling its development were not to become active again. Yet his genetic disorder went on causing the growth of more and more useless, dangerous tissue on such finished organs and preventing them from carrying on their function.

Tomás had grown patches of hair on his face overnight. When I touched one of them, he smiled. "I have to shave," he said. "I'd grow a beard if I could, but when I tried, Jesusa said it looked like an alpaca sheared by a five-year-old-child."

I frowned. "Alpaca?"

"A highland animal. We raise them for wool to make clothing."

"Oh." I smiled. "I think your beard will grow more evenly when I've finished with you," I said.

"Do you think you'll ever do that?" he asked. "Finish with us?"

My free head and body tentacles tightened flat to my skin

with pleasurable sexual tension. "No," I said softly. "I don't think so."

He had to be told everything. He and Jesusa and I talked and rested all that day, then lay together to share the night. The next morning we began several days of walking—drifting, really—back toward my family's camp. We were in no hurry. I taught them to find and make safe use of wild forest foods. They talked about their people and worried about them. Jesusa talked with real horror about the breaking apart of the planet, but Tomás seemed less concerned.

"It isn't real to me," he said simply. "It will happen long after I'm dead. And if you're telling us the truth, Jodahs, there's nothing we can do to prevent it."

"Will you stay with me?" I asked.

He looked at Jesusa, and Jesusa looked away. "I don't know," he said softly.

"If you stay with me, you'll almost certainly live past the time of separation."

He stared at me, frowning, thinking. They both had their silent, thoughtful times.

We wandered downstream, walking and resting and enjoying one another for seven days. Seven very good days. Tomás's tumors vanished and the sight of his eye returned. His hearing improved. He looked at himself in the water of a small pond and said, "I don't know how I'll get used to being so beautiful."

Jesusa threw a handful of mud at him.

On the morning of our eighth day together, I was more tired than I should have been. I didn't understand why until I realized that the flesh under my arms itched more than usual, and that it was swollen a little. Just a little.

I was beginning my second metamorphosis. Soon, in the middle of the forest, far from even our temporary home, I would fall into a sleep so deep that Tomás and Jesusa would not be able to awaken me.

9

"Will you stay with me?" I asked Tomás and Jesusa as we ate that morning. I had not asked either of them that question since we began to travel together. I had slept in a cocoon of their bodies every night. Perhaps that had helped bring on the change. Oankali ooloi usually made the final change after they had found mates. Mates gave them the security to change. Mates would look after them while they were helpless and be there for them when they awoke. Now, looking at Jesusa and Tomás, I felt afraid, desperate. They had no idea how much I needed them.

Jesusa looked at Tomás, and Tomás spoke.

"I want to stay with you. I don't really know what that will mean, but I want it. There's no place else for me. But you want us both, don't you?"

"Want?" I whispered, and shook my head. "I need you both very much."

I think that surprised them. Jesusa leaned toward me. "You've known Human beings all your life," she said. "But we've never known anyone like you. And . . . you want me to have children with my brother."

Ah. "Touch him."

"What?"

I waited. They had not touched one another since their first night with me. They were not aware of it, but they were avoiding contact.

Tomás reached out toward Jesusa's arm. She flinched, then kept still. Tomás's hand did not quite reach her. He frowned, then drew back. He turned to face me.

"What is it?"

"Nothing harmful. You *can* touch her. You won't enjoy it, but you can do it. If she were drowning, you could save her."

Jesusa reached out abruptly and grasped his wrist. She held

on for a moment, both of them rigid with a revulsion they might not want to recognize. Tomás made himself cover her repellent hand with his own.

As abruptly as they had come together, they broke apart. Jesusa managed to stop herself from wiping her hand against her clothing. Tomás did not.

"Oh, god," she said. "What have you done to us?"

I got up, went around her to sit between them. I could still walk normally, but even those few steps were exhausting.

I took their hands, rested each of them on one of my thighs so that I would not have to maintain a grip. I linked into their nervous systems and brought them together as though they were touching one another. It was not illusion. They were in contact through me. Then I gave them a bit of illusion. I "vanished" for them. For a moment, they were together, holding one another. There was no one between them.

By the time Jesusa finished her scream of surprise, I was "back," and more exhausted than ever. I let them go and lay down.

"If you stay," I said, "what you do, you'll do through me. You literally won't touch one another."

"What's the matter with you?" Tomás asked. "You didn't feel the same just now."

"Oh, I'm not the same. I'm changing. Now, I'm maturing."

They did not understand. I saw concern and questioning on their faces, but no alarm. Not yet.

"My final metamorphosis is beginning now," I said. "It will last for several months."

Now they looked alarmed. "What will happen to you?" Jesusa asked. "What shall we do for you?"

"I'm sorry," I told her, "I had no idea it was so close. The first time, I had several days' warning. If it had happened that way this time, I would have been able to go into the river and get home without your help. I can't do that now."

"Did you think we would abandon you?" she demanded. "Is that why you asked us again to stay?"

"Not that you would walk away and leave me here, no. But that . . . you wouldn't wait."

"A few months?"

"As much as a year."

"We have to get you back to your people. We can't find enough food. . . ."

"Wait. Can you . . . will you make a raft? There are young cecropia trees just above the sandbar. Farther inland, there are plenty of lianas. If you can put something together while I'm awake, we can go downriver to my family's camp. I won't let you pass it. Then . . . if you want to leave me, my family won't try to hold you."

Jesusa moved to sit near my head. "Will you be all right if we leave?"

I looked at her for a long time before I could make myself answer. "Of course not."

She got up and walked a short distance away from me, kept her back to me. Tomás moved to where she had been and took my hand.

"We'll build the raft," he said. "We'll get you home." He thought for a moment. "I don't see why we can't stay until you finish your metamorphosis."

I closed my eyes, and I said nothing. Was that how Nikanj had done it a century before? Lilith had been with it when its second metamorphosis began. Had it been tempted to say, "If you stay with me now, you'll never leave?" Or had it simply never thought to say anything? It was Oankali. It had probably never thought to say anything. It wouldn't have been harboring any sexual feeling for her at that point. It had enjoyed her because she was so un-Oankali—different and dangerous and fascinating.

I felt those things myself about these two, but I felt more. As Nikanj had said, I was precocious.

I said nothing at all to Tomás. Someday he would curse me for my silence.

He went to Jesusa and said, "If we stay, we'll have a chance to see how their families work."

"I'm afraid to stay," she said.

"Afraid?"

She picked up the machete. "We should get started on the raft."

"Jesusita, why are you afraid?"

"Why aren't you?" she said. She looked at me, then at him. "This is an alien thing Jodahs wants of us. Certainly it's an un-Christian thing, an un-Human thing. *It's the thing we've been taught against all our lives.* How can we be accepting it or even considering it so easily?"

"Are you?" he asked quietly.

"Of course I am. So are you. You've said you want to stay."

"Yes, but—"

"Something is not right. Jodahs sleeps with us and heals us and pleasures us—and asks only for the opportunity to go on doing these things." She paused, shook her head. "When I think of leaving Jodahs, finding other Human beings, or perhaps going to the colony on Mars, my stomach knots. It wants us to stay and I want to stay and so do you, *and we shouldn't!* Something is wrong."

I fell asleep at that point. It was not deliberate, but it could not have been better timed. Second metamorphosis, I had been told, was not one long sleep as the first one had been. It was a series of shorter sleeps—sleeps several days long.

I frightened them. Jesusa thought first that I was faking, then that I was dead. Only when they were able to get some reaction from my body tentacles did they decide I was alive and probably all right. They carried me down to the river and left me under a tree while they found other, small trees to chop down with their machete. Slow, hard work. I perceived and remembered everything in latent memories, stored away for consideration later when I was conscious.

They took good care of me, moving me when they moved, keeping me near them. Without realizing it, they became a torment to me when they touched me, when I could smell them. But they were a much worse torment when they went too far away. My only salvation was the certainty that they would not abandon me and the knowledge that this, uncomfortable as it was, was normal. It would be the same if I were being cared for by a pair of Oankali or a pair of constructs. Nikanj had warned me. Helpless lust and unreasoning anxiety were just part of growing up.

I endured, grateful to Jesusa and Tomás for their loyalty.

The raft took four days to finish. Not only was the machete not the best tool for the job, but Jesusa and Tomás had never built such a thing before. They were not sure what would work and they would not load me onto a craft that would come apart in the water or one they could not control. They spent time learning to control it with long poles and with paddles. They worried that in some places the river might be too deep for poles. They worried about hostile people, too. We would be very visible on the river. People with guns could pick us off if they wanted to. What could we do about that?

I awoke as they were loading me and baskets of food onto the raft. Figs, nuts, bean pods with edible pulp, and several baked applesauce tubers.

"Are you all right?" Tomás asked when he saw my eyes open. He was carrying me toward the raft. I felt as though I could sink into him, merge with him, become him. Yet I felt as though he were days away from me and beyond my reach completely.

"Don't worry," he said. "I won't drop you. Jesusa might, but I won't."

"Don't say that!" Jesusa said quickly. "Jodahs may not know you're joking."

Tomás put me down on the raft. They had made a pallet for me there of large leaves covering soft grasses. I made myself relax and not clutch at Tomás as he put me down.

He sat down next to me for a moment. "Is there anything you need? You haven't eaten for days."

"People don't eat much during metamorphosis," I said. "On the other hand, eating can take my mind off . . . other things. Do you see the bush there with the deep green leaves?"

He looked around, then pointed.

"Yes, that one. Pull several branches of young leaves from it.
I eat the leaves."

"Truly? They're good for you?"

"Yes, but not for you, so don't ever eat them. I can digest
them and use their nutrients."

"Eat some nuts."

"No. You eat the nuts. Bring me the leaves."

He obeyed, though slowly.

I ate the first few leaves while he watched incredulously. "I
don't understand enough about you," he said.

"Because I eat leaves? I can eat almost anything. Some
things are more worth the effort than others."

"More than that. Something I've been trying to figure out.
How do you . . . ? I don't mean to offend you, but I can't figure this out on my own." He hesitated, looked around to see
where Jesusa was. She was out of sight among the trees. "How
do you shit?" he demanded. "How do you piss? You're all
closed up."

I laughed aloud. My Human mother had been with Nikanj
for almost a year before she asked that question. "We're very
thorough," I said. "What we leave behind would make poor
fertilizer—except for our ships. We shed what we don't need."

"The way we shed hair or dead skin?"

"Yes. At home, the ship or the town would take it as soon
as it was shed. Here, it's dust. I leave it behind when I sleep—
when I sleep normally, anyway. People in metamorphosis leave
almost nothing behind."

"I've never seen anything."

"Dust."

"And water?"

I smiled. "Easiest to shed when I'm in it, though I can sweat
as you do."

"And?"

"That's all. Think Tomás. When did you last see me drink
water? I can drink, of course, but normally I get all the mois-
ture I need from what I eat. We use everything that we take in
much more thoroughly than you do."

"Why aren't you ever covered in mud?"

"I do one thing at a time."

"And . . . our children would be like you?"

"Not at first. Human-born children look very Human at first. They eliminate in Human ways until metamorphosis." I changed the subject abruptly. "Tomás, I'm going to stay awake through as much of this trip as I can. I should be able to warn you if we're near people so that we can at least stay close to the opposite shore. And I'll have to stop you at my family's camp. You won't be able to see it from the river."

"All right," he said.

"If I do fall asleep, make camp. Wait for me to wake up. This is a very long river, and I'm not up to backtracking."

"All right," he repeated.

Jesusa arrived them. She had found a cacao tree the night before, and today had climbed it again for one last harvest. I had pointed a cacao tree out to her as we traveled together, and she had discovered she especially liked the pulp of the pods. She put her basket, stuffed with pods, onto the raft, then helped Tomás push off. They poled us into the current not far from shore.

"Listen," I said to them once the raft was moving easily.

Both glanced around to show me they were listening.

"If we're attacked or we have to abandon the raft for any reason, push me off into the water—whether I'm awake or not. I can breathe in the water and nothing that lives there will be interested in eating me. Get me out later if you can. If you can't, don't worry about me. Get yourselves out and keep each other safe. I'm much harder to kill than you are."

They didn't argue. Jesusa gave me an odd look, and I remembered her shooting me. Her gun had not been salvageable. The metal parts had been too damaged. Was she remembering how hard I was to kill—or how I had destroyed their most powerful weapon? After a time, she left poling the raft to Tomás. He seemed to have no trouble letting the current carry us and preventing us from drifting too close to either bank, where fallen trees and sandbars made progress slow and dangerous.

Jesusa sat with me and fed me cacao pulp and did not talk to me at all.

10

We drifted for days on the river.

I could not help with paddles or poles. It took all the energy I had just to stay awake. I could and did sit up and spot barely submerged sandbars for them and keep them aware of the general depth of the water. I kept quiet about the animals I could see in the water. The Humans could see almost nothing through the brown murk, but we often drifted past animals that would eat Human flesh if they could get it. Fortunately the worst of the carnivorous fish preferred slow, quieter waters, and were no danger to us.

It was the people who were dangerous.

Twice I directed Jesusa and Tomás away from potentially hostile people—Humans grouped on one side of the river or the other. Resisters still fought among themselves and sometimes robbed and murdered strangers.

I didn't scent the third group of Humans in time. And, unlike the first two, the third group spotted us.

There was a shot—a loud crack like the first syllable of a phrase of thunder. We all fell flat to the logs of the raft, Jesusa losing her pole as she fell.

She was wounded. I could smell the blood rushing out of her.

I lost myself then. I was not fully conscious anymore, but my latent memories told me later that I dragged myself toward her, my body still flat against the logs. From shore, the Humans fired several more times, and Tomás, unaware of Jesusa's injury, cursed them, cursed the current that was not moving us beyond their reach quickly enough, cursed his own broken rifle. . . .

I reached Jesusa, unconscious, bleeding from the abdomen, and I locked on to her.

I was literally unconscious now. There was nothing at work except my body's knowledge that Jesusa was necessary to it, and that she would die from her wound if it didn't help her. My body sought to do for her what it would have done for itself. Even if I had been conscious and able to choose, I could not have done more. Her right kidney and the large blood vessels leading to it had been severely damaged. Her colon had been damaged. She was bleeding internally and poisoning herself with bodily wastes. Fortunately she was unconscious or her pain might have caused her to move away before I could lock into her. Once I was in, though, nothing could have driven me off.

We drifted beyond the range and apparently beyond the interest of the resisters. I was regaining consciousness as Tomás crawled back to us. I saw him freeze as he noticed the blood, saw him look at us, saw him lunge toward us, rocking the raft, then stop just short of touching us.

"Is she alive?" he whispered.

It was an effort to speak. "Yes," I answered after a moment. I couldn't manage anything else.

"What can I do to help?"

One more word. "Home."

I was of no use at all to him after that. I had all I could do to keep Jesusa unconscious and alive while my own body insisted on continuing its development and change. I could not heal Jesusa quickly. I wasn't sure I could heal her at all. I had stopped the blood loss, stopped her bodily wastes from poisoning her. It seemed a very long time, though, before I was able to seal the hole in her colon and begin the complicated process of regenerating a new kidney. The wounded one was not salvageable. I used it to nourish her—which involved me breaking the kidney down to its useful components and feeding them to her intravenously. It was the most nutritious meal she had had in days. That was part of the problem. Neither she nor I was in particularly good condition. I worried that my efforts at regeneration would trigger her genetic disorder, and I tried to keep watch. It occurred to me that I could have left her with one kidney until I was through my metamorphosis and able to look after her properly. That was what I should have done.

I hadn't done it because on some level, I was afraid Nikanj would take care of her if I didn't. I couldn't stand to think of it touching her, or touching Tomás.

That one thought drove me harder than anything else could have. It almost caused me to let us pass my family's home site.

The scent of home and relatives got through to me somehow. "Tomás!" I called hoarsely. And when I saw that I had his attention, I pointed. "Home."

He managed to bring us to the bank some distance past my family's cabin. He waded to shore and pulled the raft as close to the bank as he could.

"There's no one around," he said. "And no house that I can see."

"They didn't want to be easily visible from the river," I said. I detached myself from Jesusa and examined her visually. No new tumors. Smooth skin beneath her ragged, bloody, filthy clothing. Smooth skin across her abdomen.

"Is she all right?" Tomás asked.

"Yes. Just sleeping now. I've lost track. How long has it been since she was shot?"

"Two days."

"That long . . . ?" I focused on him with sensory tentacles and saw evidence of the load of worry and work that he had carried. I could think of nothing sufficient to say to him. "Thank you for taking care of us."

He smiled wearily. "I'll go look for some of your people."

"No, they'll notice my scent if they haven't already. They'll be coming. Help Jesusa off, then come back for me. She can walk."

I shook her and she awoke—or half awoke. She cringed away when Tomás waded into the shallow water and reached for her. He drew back. After a while, she got up slowly, swayed, and followed Tomás's beckoning hand.

"Come on, Jesusita," he whispered. "Off the raft." He walked beside her through the water and up the bank where the ground was dry enough to be firm. There, she sat down and seemed to doze again.

When he came back for me, he held something in his fingers—held it up for me to see. An irregularly shaped piece of metal smaller than the end point of his smallest finger. It was the bullet I had caused Jesusa's body to expel.

"Throw it away," I said. "It almost took her from us."

He threw it far out into the river.

11

Some of my family is coming now," I said. Tomás had put me on the bank beside Jesusa. He had sat down beside me to rest. Now he became alert again.

"Tomás," I said softly.

He glanced at me.

"You won't feel comfortable about letting them get close to you or letting them surround you. Jesusa won't either. My family will understand that. And no one will touch you—except the children. You won't mind their touch."

He frowned, gave me a longer look. "I don't understand."

"I know. It has to do with your being with me, letting me heal you, letting me sleep with you. You'll feel . . . drawn to be with Jesusa and me and strongly repelled by others. The feeling won't last. It's normal, so don't let it worry you."

Lilith, Nikanj, and Aaor came out of the trees together. Aaor. It was awake and strong. The family must only have been waiting for me to get home. Exile—true exile—had been that close.

The three stood near enough to speak normally, but not near enough to make Tomás uncomfortable.

"I'm going to have to learn not to worry about you," Lilith said, smiling. "Welcome back." She had spoken in Oankali. She switched to Spanish, which meant she had heard me talking to Tomás. "Welcome," she said to him. "Thank you for caring for our child and bringing it home." She inserted the English "it" because in English the word was truly neuter. Spanish did not have a word that translated exactly. Spanish-speaking people usually handled the ooloi gender by ignoring it. They used masculine or feminine, whichever felt right to them—when they had to use anything.

I took Tomás's hand, felt it grip mine desperately, almost painfully, yet his face betrayed no sign of emotion.

"These are two of my parents," I told him, gesturing with my free hand. "Lilith is my birth mother and Nikanj is my same-sex parent. This third one is Aaor, my paired sibling." I enjoyed the sight of it for a moment. It was gray-furred now and, oddly, not that unusual-looking. Perhaps the other siblings helped it stay almost normal. "Aaor has been closer to me than my skin at times," I said. "I think it turned out to be more like me than it would have preferred."

Aaor, who was restraining itself with an obvious effort, said, "When I touch you, Jodahs, I won't let you go for at least a day."

I laughed, remembering its touch, realizing that I was eager to touch it, too, and understand exactly how it had changed. We would not be the same—Human-born and Oankali-born. Examining it would teach me more about myself by similarity and by contrast. And it would want even more urgently to know where I had found Jesusa and Tomás. If its own sense of smell had not recognized them as young and fertile—as mine had not when I met them—Nikanj would have let it know.

"I'll tell you everything," I said. "But put us somewhere dry, first, and feed us." I meant, and all three of them knew it, that Tomás and Jesusa should be given a dry place and food.

Nikanj rested a sensory arm on Aaor's shoulders and some of the straining eagerness went out of Aaor.

"What are you called?" Nikanj asked Tomás. It spoke very softly, yet that soft voice carried so well. Did I sound that way?

Tomás leaned forward, responding to the voice, then was barely able to keep himself from drawing back. He had never seen an Oankali before, and Nikanj, an adult ooloi, was especially startling. He stared, and then was ashamed and looked away. Then he stared again.

"What are you called?" Nikanj repeated.

"Tomás," he answered finally. "Tomás Serrano y Martín." He had not told me that much. He paused, then said, "This is Jesusa, my sister." He touched her hair the way my Human parents sometimes touched one another's hair. "She was shot."

Nikanj focused sharply on me.

"She's all right," I said. "She's exhausted because she hasn't been eating well for a while—and you know how hard I had to make her body work." I turned and shook her. "Jesusa," I whispered. "You're all right. Wake up. We've reached my family." I kept my hand on her shoulder, shook her again gently, wishing I could give her the kind of comfort I would have been able to give only a few days before. But I had had all I could do to save her life.

She opened her eyes, looked around, and saw Nikanj. She turned her face from it and whimpered—a sound I had not heard from her before.

"You're safe," I told her. "These people are here to help us. You're all right. No one will harm you."

She realized finally what I was saying. She fell silent and became almost still. She could not stop her trembling, but she

looked at me, then at Lilith, Aaor, and Nikanj. She made herself look longest at Nikanj.

"Excuse me," she said after a moment. "I . . . haven't seen
anyone like you before."

Nikanj's many sensory tentacles flattened smooth as its
body. "I haven't seen anyone like you for a century," it said.

At the sound of its voice, she looked startled. She turned to
look at me, then looked back at Nikanj. I introduced it along
with Lilith and Aaor.

"I'm pleased to meet you," Jesusa lied politely. She watched
Nikanj, fascinated, not knowing that it held its position of
amusement, of smoothness, extra long for her benefit. I went
smooth every time I laughed, but my few sensory tentacles
were not that visible even when they were not flattened. And I
did laugh. Nikanj did not.

"I'm amazed and pleased," Nikanj said. And to me in
Oankali, it said, "Where are they from?"

"Later," I said.

"Will they stay, Oeka?"

"Yes."

It focused on me, seemed to expect me to say more. I kept
quiet.

Aaor broke the silence. "You can't walk, can you?" it said
in Spanish. "We'll have to carry you."

Tomás stood up quickly. "If you'll show me the way," he
said, "I'll carry Jodahs." He hesitated for a moment beside Jesusa. "Sister, can you walk?"

"Yes." She stood up slowly, holding her ragged bloody
clothing together. She took a tentative step. "I feel all right,"
she said, "but . . . so much blood."

Aaor had turned to lead the way back to the cabin. Tomás
lifted me, and Jesusa walked close to him. I spoke to her from
his arms. "You'll have good food to eat here," I told her.
"You'll probably be a little hungrier than usual for a while because you're still regrowing part of yourself. Aside from that,
you're well."

She took my dangling hand and kissed it.

Tomás smiled. "If you really feel well, Jesusa, give it one more for me. You don't know what it brought you back from."

She looked ahead at Nikanj. "I don't know what it's brought me back to," she whispered.

"No one will hurt you here," I told her again. "No one will touch you or even come near you. No one will keep you from coming to me when you want to."

"Will they let me go?" she asked.

I turned my head so that I could look at her with my eyes. "Don't leave me," I said very softly.

"I'm afraid. I don't see how I can stay here with your . . . family."

"Stay with *me*."

"Your . . . relative. The Oankali one. . . ."

"Nikanj. My ooloi parent. It will never touch you." I would get that promise from it before I slept again.

"It's . . . ooloi, like you."

Ah. "No, not like me. It's Oankali. No Human admixture at all. Jesusa, my birth mother is as Human as you are. My Human father looks like a relative of yours. Even when I'm adult, I won't look the way Nikanj does. You'll never have reason to fear me."

"I fear you now because I still don't understand what's happening."

Tomás spoke up. "Jesusa, it saved you. It could hardly move, but it saved you."

"I know," she said. "I'm grateful. More grateful than I can say." She touched my face, then moved her hand to my hair and let her fingers slide expertly around the base of a group of sensory tentacles.

I shuddered with sudden pleasure and frustrated need.

"I'll try to stay until your metamorphosis is over," she said. "I owe you that and more. I promise to stay that long."

My mother turned her head and looked at Jesusa, then at me, looked long at me.

I met her gaze, but said nothing to her.

After a time, she turned back to the path. Her scent, as it reached me, said she was upset, under great stress. But like me, she said nothing at all.

12

We were given food. For a change, I actually needed it. Healing Jesusa had depleted my resources. I had no strength at all, and Jesusa fed me as she fed herself. She seemed to take some comfort in feeding me.

Jesusa and Tomás were given clean, dry clothing. They went to the river to wash themselves and came back to the house clean and content. They ate parched nuts and relaxed with my family.

"Tell us about your people," Aaor said as the sun went down and Dichaan put more wood on the fire. "I know there are things you don't want to tell us, but . . . tell us how your people came to exist. How did your fertile ancestors find one another?"

Jesusa and Tomás looked at each other. Jesusa looked apprehensive, but Tomás smiled. It was a tired, sad smile.

"Our first postwar ancestors never found one another," he said. "I'll tell you if you like."

"Yes!"

"Our elders were people who joined together because they could communicate," he said. "They all spoke Spanish. They were from Mexico and Peru and Spain and Chile and other countries. The First Mother was from Mexico. She was fifteen years old and traveling with her parents. There were others with them who knew this country and who said it would be best to live higher in the mountains. They were on the way up when the First Mother and her own mother were attacked.

They had left the group to bathe. The Mother never saw her attackers. She was hit from behind. She was raped—probably many times.

"When she regained consciousness, she was alone. Her mother was there, but she was dead. The First Mother was badly injured. She had to crawl and drag herself back to her people. They cared for her as best they could. Her father couldn't help her. He left her to others. He was so angry at what had been done to her and to her mother that eventually he left the group. The Mother awoke one morning and he was gone. She never saw him again.

"The people had already begun to make homes for themselves in the place they had chosen when they realized the Mother would have a child. No one had thought it was possible. People had tried to accept their sterility. They said it was better to have no children than . . . than to have un-Human children." Tomás looked down at his hands. When he raised his head, he found himself looking directly at Tino.

"My people said the same thing before I left them," Tino said. "They believed it. But it's a lie."

Tomás looked at Lilith, his gaze questioning.

"You know it's a lie," Lilith said quietly.

Tomás looked at me, then continued his story. "The people worried that the Mother's child might not be Human. No one had seen her attackers. No one knew who or what they had been."

Nikanj spoke up. "They could not have believed we would send them away sterile, then change our minds and impregnate one of them while killing another." Even with its soft mature-ooloi's voice, it managed to sound outraged.

Tomás was already able to look at it, speak to it. It had been careful not to notice when he studied it as he ate. Now he said, "They said you could do almost anything. Some of them said your powers came from the devil. Some said you *were* devils. Some were disgusted with that kind of talk. To them, you were only the enemy. They didn't believe you had raped the Mother. They believed the Mother could be their tool to defeat you.

They took her in and cared for her and fed her even when they didn't have enough to eat themselves. When her son was born, they helped her care for him and they showed him to everyone so that the people could see that he was perfect and Human. They called him Adan. The mother's name was María de la Luz. When Adan was weaned, they cared for him. They encouraged his mother to work in the gardens and help with the building and be away from her son. That way, when the time came, when Adan was thirteen years old, they were able to put mother and son together. By then, both had been taught their duty. And by then, everyone had realized that the Mother was not only fertile but mortal—as they seemed not to be. By the time her first daughter was born, the Mother looked older than some of those who had helped her raise her son.

"The Mother bore three daughters eventually. She died with the birth of her second son. That son was . . . seriously deformed. He had a hole in his back. People say you could see the spine. And he had other things wrong with him. He died and was buried with the Mother in a place . . . that is sacred to us. The people built a shrine there. Some have seen the Mother when they went there to think or to pray. They've seen her spirit." Tomás stopped and looked at the three Oankali. "Do you believe in spirits?"

"We believe in life," Ahajas said.

"Life after death?"

Ahajas smoothed her tentacles briefly in agreement. "When I'm dead," she said, "I will nourish other life."

"But I mean—"

"If I died on a lifeless world, a world that could sustain some form of life if it were tenacious enough, organelles within each cell of my body would survive and evolve. In perhaps a thousand million years, that world would be as full of life as this one."

". . . it would?"

"Yes. Our ancestors have seeded a great many barren worlds that way. Nothing is more tenacious than the life we are made of. A world of life from apparent death, from dissolution. That's what we believe in."

"Nothing more?"

Ahajas became smooth enough with amusement to reflect firelight. "No, Lelka. Nothing more."

He did not ask what "Lelka" meant, though he couldn't have known. It meant mated child—something parents called their adult children and mates of their children. I would have to ask her not to call him that. Not yet.

"When I was little," Tomás said, "I planted a tree at the Mother's shrine." He smiled, apparently remembering. "Some people wanted to pull it up. It grew so well, though, that no one touched it. People said the Mother must like having it there." He stopped and looked at Ahajas.

She nodded Humanly and watched him with interest and approval.

"The Mother had twenty-three grandchildren," he continued. "Fifteen survived. Among these were several who were deformed or who grew deformed. They were fertile, and not all of their children had the deformities. The deformed ones could not be spared. Sometimes smooth children with only a few dark spots on their skin had deformed young. One of our elders said this was a disorder that had been known before the war. He had known a woman who had it and who looked much the way I did before Jodahs healed me."

Everyone turned at once and focused on me.

"Ask me when his story is finished," I said. "I don't know a name for the disease anyway. I can only describe it."

"Describe it," Lilith said.

I looked at her and understood that she was asking me for more than a description of the disorder. Her face was set and grim, as it had been since Jesusa promised to stay with me through metamorphosis. She wanted to know what reason there might be apart from her love for me for not telling the Humans how bound to me they were becoming. She wanted to know why she should betray her own kind with silence.

"It was a genetic disorder," I said. "It affected their skin, their bones, their muscles, and their nervous systems. It made tumors—large ones on Tomás's face and upper body. His optic nerve was affected. The bones of his neck and one arm were affected. His hearing was affected. Jesusa was covered head to foot in small very visible tumors. They didn't impair her ability to move or to use her senses."

"I was very lucky," Jesusa said quietly. "I looked ugly, but people didn't care, because I could have children. I didn't suffer the way Tomás did."

Tomás looked at her. The look said more than even a shout of protest could have. "You suffered," he said. "And if not for Jodahs, you would have made yourself go back and suffer more. For the rest of your life."

She stared at the floor, then into the fire. There was no shyness in the gesture. She simply did not agree with him. The corners of her mouth turned slightly downward. As her brother began speaking again, I took her hand. She jumped, looked at me as though I were a stranger. Then she took my hand between her own and held it. I didn't think she had noticed that across the room from us Tino was holding one of Nikanj's sensory arms in exactly the same way.

"Sometimes," Tomás was saying, "people have only brown spots and no tumors. Sometimes they have both. And sometimes their minds are affected. Sometimes there are other troubles and they die. Children die." He let his voice vanish away.

"No more!" Lilith said. "That misery will soon be over for them."

Tomás turned to face her. "You must know they won't thank me or Jesusa for that. They'll hate us as traitors."

"I know."

"Was it that way for you?"

Lilith looked downward for a moment, moving only her eyes. "Has Jodahs told you about the Mars colony?"

"Yes."

"It didn't exist as an alternative for me."

"My people may not see it as an alternative either."

"If they're wise, they will." She looked at Nikanj. "Their

disorder does sound like something that was around before the war, if it matters. In the United States, people called it *neurofibromatosis*. I don't know the Spanish name for it. It could have occurred as a mutation in one or more of the Mother's children if no one had it until the third generation. I remember reading about a couple of especially horrible prewar cases. Sometimes the tumors became malignant. That would be a special attraction to Jodahs, I think. Ooloi can see great unused potential in that kind of thing."

"See it and smell it and taste it," Aaor said.

Everyone focused on it.

"I can change to look the way Jodahs does," it said. "There must be two more or at least one more sick Human among the Mother's people who would join me."

Silence. Jesusa and Tomás looked startled.

"You don't understand how strongly we're taught against you," Tomás said. "And most of us believe. Jesusa and I came down to the lowlands to see a little of the world before she began to have child after child, and before I became too crippled. No one else we know of had done such a thing. I don't think anyone else would."

"If I could reach them," Aaor said, "I could convince them."

I could see the hunger in it, the desperation. Ayodele and Yedik moved to sit on either side of it and ease its discomfort as best they could. They seemed to do this automatically, as though they had finally adapted to having ooloi siblings.

But Aaor was not comforted. "I'm one more mistake!" it said. "One more ooloi who shouldn't exist. There's no other place on Earth for me to find mates. And if their people are collected and given the choice of Mars, union with us, or sterility where they are, I'll never get near them! Even the ones who choose union with us will be directed to other mates. Mates who are not accidents."

"None of them will accept union," Jesusa said. "I know them. I know what they believe."

"But you don't know us well enough yet," Aaor said. "Did

you know what you would do . . . before Jodahs reached you?"

"I know I won't lead you or anyone else to my people," she told it. "If your people can find mine without us as Jodahs said, we can't stop you. But nothing you can say would make us help you."

"You don't understand!" it said, leaning toward her.

"I know that," she admitted, "and I'm sorry."

They said more as I drifted into sleep, but they found no common ground. Throughout the argument, Jesusa never let go of my hand. When Nikanj saw that I had fallen asleep, it said I should be taken to the small room that had been set aside for Aaor's metamorphosis.

"There are too many distractions for it out here," it told Jesusa and Tomás. "Too much stimulation. It should be isolated and allowed to focus inward on the changes its body must make."

"Does it have to be isolated from us?" Tomás asked.

"Of course not. The room is large enough for three, and Jodahs will always need the companionship of at least one person. If you both have to leave it for a while, tell Aaor or tell me. The room is over there." It pointed with a strength hand.

Tomás lifted my unconscious body, Jesusa helping him with me now that I was deadweight. I have a clear, treasured memory of the two of them carrying me into the small room. They did not know then that my memory went on recording everything my senses perceived even when I was unconscious. Yet they handled me with great gentleness and care, as they had from the beginning of my change. They did not know that this was exactly what Oankali mates did at these times. And they did not see Aaor watching them with a hunger that was so intense that its face was distorted and its head and body tentacles elongated toward us.

III

IMAGO

1

During my metamorphosis, Aaor lost its coat of gray fur. Its skin turned the same soft, bright brown as Jesusa's, Tomás's and my own. It grew long, black Human-looking hair and began to wear it as Tino wore his—bound with a twist of grass into a long tail down his back. I wore mine loose.

"Apart from that," Jesusa told me during one of my waking times, "the two of you could be twins."

Yet she avoided Aaor—as did Tomás. It smelled more like me than anyone else alive. But it did not smell exactly like me. Their Human noses had no trouble perceiving the difference. They didn't know that was what they were perceiving, but they avoided Aaor.

And it did not want to be avoided.

I found its loneliness and need agonizing when it touched me. It awoke me several times as I lay changing. It didn't mean to, but my body perceived it as an unhealed wound, and I could not rest until I had erased its pain and given . . . not healing, but momentary relief. What I gave was inadequate and short-lived, but Aaor came back for it again and again.

Once, lying linked with me, it asked if I could give it one of the young Humans.

I hurt it. I didn't mean to, but what it said provoked reaction before I could control myself. Direct neural stimulation. Pure pain. As pure as any sensation can be. I did manage not to loop the pain between us and keep it going. Yet afterward, Aaor needed more healing. I kept it with me to give it comfort and ease its loneliness. It stayed until I fell asleep.

I never gave Aaor a verbal answer to its question. It never

repeated the question. It seemed to realize that I could no longer separate myself deliberately from Tomás and Jesusa. They could still leave me, but they wouldn't. Jesusa took the promises she gave very seriously. She would not try to leave until I was on my feet again. And Tomás would not leave without her. By the time they were prepared to go, it would be too late.

My only fear was that someone in the family would tell them. My mother believed she should, but she had not, so far. She loved me, and yet, until now, she had been able to do nothing to help me. She had not been able to make herself destroy the only chance I was likely to get of having the mates I needed.

Yet she was weighted with guilt. One more betrayal of her own Human kind for people who were not Human, or not altogether Human. She spoke to Jesusa as a much older sister— or as a same-sex parent. She advised her.

"Listen to Jodahs," I heard her say on one occasion. "Listen carefully. It will tell you what it wants you to know. It won't lie to you. But it will withhold information. Once you've heard what it has to say, get away from it. Get out of the house. Go to the river or a short way into the forest. Do your thinking there about what it's told you, and decide what questions you still need answers to. Then come home and ask."

"Home?" Jesusa whispered so softly I almost failed to hear. They were outside the house, replacing the roof thatch. They were not near my room, but my mother probably knew I could hear them.

"You live here," my mother said. "That makes this home. It isn't a permanent home for any of us." She was good at evasion and withholding information herself.

"Would you go to Mars if you could?" Jesusa asked.

"Leave my family?"

"If you were as I am. If you had no family."

My mother did not answer for a long time. She sighed finally. "I don't know how to answer that. I'm content with these people. More than content. I lost my husband and my son before the war. They died in an accident. When the war came, I lost everything else. We all did, we elders, as you call us. I couldn't give up and die, but I expected almost nothing. Food and shelter, maybe. An absence of pain. Nikanj said it knew I needed children, so it took seed from the man I had then and made me pregnant. I didn't think I would ever forgive it for that."

"But . . . you have forgiven it?"

"I've understood it. I've accepted it. I wouldn't have believed I could do that much. Back when I met my first mature ooloi, Nikanj's parent Kahguyaht, I found it alien, arrogant, and terrifying. I hated it. I thought I hated all ooloi."

She paused. "Now I feel as though I've loved Nikanj all my life. Ooloi are dangerously easy to love. They absorb us, and we don't mind."

"Yes," Jesusa agreed, and I smiled. "I'm afraid, though, because I don't understand them. I'll go to Mars if I don't stay with Jodahs. I can understand settling a new place. I know what to expect from a Human husband."

"Look at my family, Jesusa—and realize you're only seeing six of our children. This is what you can expect if you mate with Jodahs. There's closeness here that I didn't have with the family I was born into or with my husband and son."

"But you have Oankali mates other than Nikanj."

"You will, too, eventually. With Jodahs, I mean. And your children will look much like mine. And half of them will be born to an Oankali female, but will inherit from all five of you."

After a time, Jesusa said, "Ahajas and Dichaan aren't so bad. They seem . . . very gentle."

"Good mates. I was with Nikanj before they were—like you with Jodahs. That's best, I think. An ooloi is probably the strangest thing any Human will come into contact with. We need time alone with it to realize it's probably also the best thing."

"Where would we live?"

"You and your new family? In one of our towns. I think any

one of them would eventually welcome the three of you. You'd be something brand-new—the center of a lot of attention. Oankali and constructs love new things."

"Jodahs says it had to go into exile because it was a new thing."

"Is that what it said, really?"

Silence. What was Jesusa doing? Searching her memory for exactly what I had said? "It said it was the first of its kind," she said finally. "The first construct ooloi."

"Yes."

"It said there weren't supposed to be any construct ooloi yet, so the people didn't trust it. They were afraid it would not be able to control itself as an ooloi must. They were afraid it would hurt people."

"It did hurt some people, Jesusa. But it's never hurt Humans. And it's never hurt anyone when it's had Humans with it."

"It told me that."

"Good. Because if it hadn't, I would have. It needs you more than Nikanj ever needed me."

"You want me to stay with it."

"Very much."

"I'm afraid. This is all so different. . . . How did you ever . . . ? I mean . . . with Nikanj. . . . How did you decide?"

My mother said nothing at all.

"You didn't have a choice, did you?"

"I did, oh, yes. I chose to live."

"That's no choice. That's just going on, letting yourself be carried along by whatever happens."

"You don't know what you're talking about," my mother said.

After that, there was no talk for a while. My mother had not shouted those last words, as some Humans would have. She had almost whispered them. Yet they carried such feeling, they would have silenced me, too—and I did know much of what my birth mother had survived. And it was so much more than she had said that Jesusa would not have wanted to hear it. Yet, in a way, in my mother's voice she had heard it. It was not until I had almost drifted off to sleep that they spoke again. Jesusa began.

"It's flattering to think that Jodahs needs us. It seems so powerful, so able to endure anything. At first I couldn't understand why it even wanted us. I was suspicious."

"It can endure a great deal of physical suffering. And it will have to if you leave it."

"There are other Humans for it to mate with."

"No, there aren't. There's Mars now. Resisters choose to go there. Ordinary resisters are too old for Jodahs anyway. As for the few young Humans born on the ship, they're rare and spoken for."

"So . . . what will happen to Jodahs if we leave?"

"I don't know. Just as I don't know what's going to happen to Aaor, period. It's Aaor that I'm most worried about now."

"It asked me if I would tell it where my people were—tell it alone so that it could go to them and try to persuade two of them to mate with it."

"What was your answer?"

"That they would kill it. They would kill it as soon as they realized what it was."

"And?"

"It said it didn't care. It said Jodahs had us, but it was starving."

"Did you tell it what it wanted to know?"

"I couldn't. Even if I didn't know how my people would greet it, I couldn't betray them that way. They'll already think of me as a traitor when the Oankali come for them."

"I know. Aaor knows, too, really. But it's desperate."

"Tomás says it asked him, too."

"That's unusual. Has it asked you more than once?"

"Three times."

"That goes beyond unusual. I'll talk to Nikanj about it."

"I don't mean to make trouble for it. I wish I could help it."

"It's already in trouble. And right now, Nikanj is probably the only one who can help it."

I stopped fighting sleep and let myself drift off. I would talk to Aaor when I awoke again. It was starving. I didn't know what I could do about that, but there must be something.

2

But I had no chance to talk to Aaor before my second metamorphosis ended. It left home as I had. It wandered, perhaps looking for some sign of Jesusa and Tomás's people.

It found only aged, hostile, infertile resisters who had nothing to offer it except bullets and arrows.

It changed radically: grew fur again, lost it, developed scales, lost them, developed something very like tree bark, lost that, then changed completely, lost its limbs, and went into a tributary of our river.

When it realized it could not force itself back to a Human or Oankali form, could not even become a creature of the land again, it swam home. It swam in the river near our cabin for three days before anyone realized what it was. Even its scent had changed.

I was awake, but not yet strong enough to get up. My sensory arms were fully developed, but I had not yet used them. By the time Oni and Hozh found Aaor in the river, I was just learning to coordinate them as lifting and handling limbs.

Hozh showed me what Aaor had become—a kind of near mollusk, something that had no bones left. Its sensory tentacles were intact, but it no longer had eyes or other Human sensory organs. Its skin, very smooth, was protected by a coating of slime. It could not speak or breathe air or make any sound at all. It had attracted Hozh's attention by crawling up the bank and forcing part of its body out of the water. Very difficult. Painful. Its altered flesh was very sensitive to sunlight.

"I would never have recognized it if I hadn't touched it," Hozh told me. "It didn't even smell the same. In fact, it hardly smelled at all."

"I don't understand that," I said. "It isn't an adult yet. How can it change its scent?"

"Suppressed. It suppressed its scent. I don't think it intended to."

"It doesn't sound as though it intended to become what it has in any way. When it can be brought to the house, tell Ooan to bring it to me."

"Ooan has taken it back into the water to help it change back. Ooan says it almost lost itself. It was becoming more and more what it appeared to be."

"Hozh, are Jesusa and Tomás around the house?"

"They're at the river. Everyone is."

"Ask them to come to me."

"Can you help Aaor?"

"I think so."

It went away. A short time later Jesusa and Tomás came to me and sat on either side of me. I thought about sitting up to say what I had to say to them, but that would have been exhausting, and there were other things I wanted to do with the energy I had.

"You saw Aaor?" I asked them.

Tomás nodded. Jesusa shuddered and said, "It was a . . . a great slug."

"I think we can help it," I said. "I wish it had come to me before it went away. I think we could have helped it even then."

"We?" Tomás said.

"One of you on one side of me and Aaor on the other. I think I can bring you and it together enough to satisfy it. I think I can do that with no discomfort to you." I touched each of them with a sensory arm. "In fact, I hope I can arrange things so that you enjoy it."

Tomás examined my left sensory arm, his touch bringing it

to life as nothing else could. "So you'll give Aaor a little pleasure," he said. "What good will that do?"

"Aaor wants Human mates. It *must* have mates of some
kind. Until it can get them, will you share what we have with
it?"

Jesusa took my right sensory arm and simply held it. "I
couldn't touch Aaor," she said.

"No need. I'll touch it. You touch me."

"Will it be changed back to what it was? Will Nikanj finish
changing it before it brings it to us?"

"It will not be a limbless slug when it's brought to us. But it
won't be what it was when it left us either. Nikanj will make it
a land creature again. That will take days. Nikanj won't even
bring it out of the river until it has developed bones again and
can support itself. By the time it's able to come to us, we'll be
ready for it."

Jesusa let go of my sensory arm. "I don't know whether I
can be ready for it. You didn't see it, Jodahs. You don't know
how it looked."

"Hozh showed me. Very bad, I know. But it's my paired sibling. It's also the only other being in existence that's like me. I
don't know what will happen to it if I don't help it."

"But Nikanj could—"

"Nikanj is our parent. It will do all it can. It did all it could
for me." I paused, watching her. "Jesusa, do you understand
that what happened to Aaor is what was in the process of happening to me when you found me?"

Tomás moved against me slightly. "You were still in control
of yourself," he said. "You were even able to help us."

"I never stayed away from home as long as Aaor has. As it
was, I don't think I would have gotten back without you. I
would have gone into the water or into the ground for my second metamorphosis. Our changes don't go well when we're
alone. I don't know what I would have become."

"You think Aaor is in its second metamorphosis?" Jesusa
asked.

"Probably."

"No one said so."

"They would have if you'd asked them. To them it was obvious. Once we get Aaor stabilized, it can finish its change in here. I'll be up soon."

"Where will we sleep?" Jesusa asked.

With me! I thought instantly. But I said, "In the main room. We can build a partition if you like."

"Yes."

"And we'll have to go on spending some of our time with Aaor. If we don't, its change will go wrong again."

"Oh, god," Jesusa whispered.

"Have the two of you eaten recently?"

"Yes," Tomás said. "We were having dinner with your Human parents when Oni and Hozh found Aaor."

"Good." They could share their meal with me and save me the trouble of eating. "Lie down with me."

They did that willingly enough. Jesusa cringed a little when for the first time I looped a sensory arm around her neck. When she was still, I settled into her with every sensory tentacle on her side of my body. I could not let her move again for a while.

Then with relief that was beyond anything I had ever felt with her, I extended my sensory hand, grasped the back of her neck with it, and sank filaments of it bloodlessly into her flesh.

For the first time, I injected—could not avoid injecting—my own adult ooloi substance into her.

By the neural messages I intercepted, I knew she would have convulsed if she had been able to move at all. She did shout, and for an instant I was distracted by the abrupt adrenaline scent of Tomás's alarm.

With my free sensory arm, I touched the skin of his face. "She's all right," I made myself say. "Wait."

Perhaps he believed me. Perhaps the expression on Jesusa's face reassured him. Whatever the reason, he grew calm and I focused completely on Jesusa. I should have gone into both of them at once, but this first time as an adult, I wanted to savor their individual essences separately.

Adult awareness felt sharper to me, finer and different in some way I had not yet defined. The smell-taste-feel of Jesusa, the rhythm of her heartbeat, the rush of her blood, the texture of her flesh, the easy, right, life-sustaining working of her organs, her cells, the smallest organelles within her cells—all this was a vast, infinitely absorbing complexity. The genetic error that had caused her and her people so much misery was as obvious to me as a single cloud in an otherwise clear sky. I was tempted to begin now to make repairs. Her body cells would be easy to alter, though the alteration would take time. The sex cells, though, the ova, would have to be replaced. Both her parents had the disorder and about three quarters of her own ova were defective. I would have to cause parts of her body to function as they had not since before her birth. Best to save that kind of work until later. Best simply to enjoy Jesusa now—the complex harmonies of her, the built-in danger of her genetically inevitable Human conflict: intelligence versus hierarchical behavior. There was a time when that conflict or contradiction—it was called both—frightened some Oankali so badly that they withdrew from contact with Humans. They became Akjai—people who would eventually leave the vicinity of Earth without mixing with Humans.

To me, the conflict was spice. It had been deadly to the Human species, but it would not be deadly to Jesusa or Tomás any more than it had been to my parents. My children would not have it at all.

Jesusa, solemn and questioning, beautiful on levels she would probably never understand, would surely be one of the mothers of those children.

I enjoyed her for a few moments more, especially enjoyed her pleasure in me. I could see how my own ooloi substance stimulated the pleasure centers of her brain.

"Monitor them very carefully," Nikanj had told me. "Give them as much as they can take, and no more. Don't hurt them, don't frighten them, don't overstimulate them. Start them slowly, and in only a little time, they will be more willing to give up eating than to give you up."

Jesusa had only begun to taste me—me as an adult—and I could see that this was true. She had liked me very much as a subadult. But what she felt now went beyond liking, beyond loving, into the deep biological attachment of adulthood. Literal, physical addiction to another person, Lilith called it. I couldn't think about it that coldly. For me it meant that soon Jesusa would not want to leave me, would not be able to leave me for more than a few days at a time.

It worked both ways, of course. Soon I would not be able to stand long separation from her. And she could hurt me by deliberately avoiding me. From what I knew of her, she would be willing to do this if she thought she had cause—even though she would inflict as much pain on herself as on me. Lilith had done that to Nikanj many times before the Mars colony was established.

Human males could be dangerous, and Human females frustrating. Yet I felt compelled to have both. So did Aaor, no doubt. If Jesusa and Tomás ever turned their worst Human characteristics against me, it would probably be on account of Aaor. I had no choice but to try to help it, and Jesusa and Tomás must help me with it. I did not know whether I could make the experience easy for them.

All the more reason to see that they enjoyed this experience. Jesusa grew pleasantly weary as I explored her and healed the few bruises and small wounds she had acquired. Her greatest enjoyment would happen when I brought her together with Tomás and shared the pleasure of each of them with the other, mingling with it my own pleasure in them both. When I could make an ongoing loop of this, we would drown in one another.

But that was for later. Now, without apparent movement, I caressed and lulled Jesusa into deep sleep.

"They will never understand what treasure they are," Nikanj had said to me once while it sat with me. "They see our differences—even yours, Lelka—and they wonder why we want them."

I detached myself from Jesusa, lingering for a moment over the salt taste of her skin. I had once heard my mother say to

Nikanj, "It's a good thing your people don't eat meat. If you did, the way you talk about us, our flavors and your hunger and your need to taste us, I think you would eat us instead of fiddling with our genes." And after a moment of silence, "That might even be better. It would be something we could understand and fight against."

Nikanj had not said a word. It might have been feeding on her even then—sharing bits of her most recent meal, taking in dead or malformed cells from her flesh, even harvesting a ripe egg before it could begin its journey down her fallopian tubes to her uterus. It stored some of the eggs and consumed the rest. I would have taken an egg from Jesusa if one had been ready. "We feed on them every day," Nikanj had said to me. "And in the process, we keep them in good health and mix children for them. But they don't always have to know what we're doing."

I turned to face Tomás, and without a word, he lay down beside me, and used his arms to pull me closer to him. When he had kissed me very thoroughly, he said, "Will I always have to wait?"

"Oh, no," I said, positioning him so that he would be comfortable. "Once I've tasted you this way, I doubt that I'll ever be able to keep you waiting again."

I looped one sensory arm around his neck, exposed my sensory hand. I paralyzed him as I had Jesusa, but left him an illusion of movement. "Males in particular need to feel that they're moving," Nikanj had told me. "You'll enjoy them more if you give them the illusion they're climbing all over you."

It was entirely right. And though I had not been able to collect an egg from Jesusa, I collected considerable sperm from Tomás. Much of it carried the defective gene and was useless for procreation. Protein. The rest of it I stored for future use.

Tomás was stronger than Jesusa. He lasted longer before he tired. Just before I put him to sleep, he said, "I never intended to let you get away from me. Now I know you never will."

I used his muscles to move us both close against Jesusa. There, with me wedged between them, the two could sleep and

I could rest and take a little more of their dinner. They wouldn't feel it. They could spare it, and I needed it to build strength fast now—for Aaor's sake.

3

Aaor was in its second metamorphosis. When Nikanj brought it to me after several days of reconstruction, it was not yet recognizable. Not like a Human or an Oankali or any construct I had ever seen.

Its skin was deep gray. Patches of it still glistened with slime. Aaor could not walk very well. It was bipedal again, but very weak, and its coordination had not returned as it should have.

It was hairless.

It could not speak aloud.

Its hands were webbed flippers.

"It keeps slipping away," Nikanj said. "I'd brought it almost back to normal, but it has no control left. The moment I release it, it drifts toward a less complex form."

It placed Aaor on the pallet we had prepared for it. Tomás had followed it in. Now he stood staring as Aaor's body retreated further and further from what it should have been. Jesusa had not come in at all.

"Can you help it?" Tomás asked me.

"I don't know," I said. I lay down alongside it, saw that it was watching me. Its reconstructed eyes were not what they should have been either. They were too small. They protruded too much. But it could see with them. It was staring at my sensory arms. I wrapped them both around it, wrapped my strength arms around it as well.

It was deeply, painfully afraid, desperately lonely and hungry for a touch it could not have.

"Lie down behind me, Tomás," I said, and saw with my sensory tentacles how he hesitated, how his throat moved when he swallowed. Yet he lay behind me, drew up close, and let me share him with Aaor as I had already shared him with Jesusa.

In spite of my efforts, there was no pleasure in the exercise. Something had gone seriously wrong with Aaor's body, as Nikanj had said. It kept slipping away from me—simplifying its body. It had no control of itself, but like a rock rolling downhill, it had inertia. Its body "wanted" to be less and less complex. If it had stayed unattended in the water for much longer, it would have begun to break down completely—individual cells each with its own seed of life, its own Oankali organelle. These might live for a while as single-cell organisms or invade the bodies of larger creatures at once, but Aaor as an individual would be gone. In a way, then, Aaor's body was trying to commit suicide. I had never heard of any carrier of the Oankali organism doing such a thing. We treasured life. In my worst moments before I found Jesusa and Tomás, such dissolution had not occurred to me. I didn't doubt that it would have happened eventually—not as something desirable, but as something inescapable, inevitable. We called our need for contact with others and our need for mates *hunger*. The word had not been chosen frivolously. One who could hunger could starve.

The people who had wanted me safely shut away on Chkahichdahk had been afraid not only of what my instability might cause me to do but of what my hunger might cause me to do. Dissolution had been one unspoken possibility. Dissolution in the river would be bound to affect—to infect— plants and animals. Infected animals would be drawn to areas like Lo, where ship organisms were growing. So would free-living cells be drawn to such places. Only a very few cells would end by causing trouble—causing diseases and mutations in plants, for instance.

Aaor wanted to continue living as Aaor. It tried to help me bring it back to a normal metamorphosis, but without words,

I discouraged its efforts. It had not even enough control to help in its own restoration.

Tomás wanted desperately to withdraw from me and from Aaor. I put him to sleep and kept him with me. His presence would help Aaor whether he was conscious or not.

For a day and a half, the three of us lay together, forcing Aaor's body to do what it no longer wanted to do. By the time Tomás and I got up to go to bathe and eat, Aaor looked almost as it had before it went away. Smooth brown skin, a sensory arm bud under each strength arm, a dusting of black hair on its head, fingers without webbing, speech.

"What am I going to do?" it asked just before we left it with Nikanj.

"We'll take care of you," I promised.

Without a word to each other, Tomás and I went to the river and scrubbed ourselves.

"I don't ever want to do that again," Tomás said as we emerged from the water.

I said nothing. The next day, as Aaor's body shape began to change in the wrong way, Tomás and I did it again. He didn't want to, but he looked at Aaor and me and reluctantly lay down alongside me.

The next time it happened, I called Jesusa. Afterward, at the river, she said, "I feel as though I've been crawled over by a lot of slugs!"

Aaor's body did not learn stability. Again and again, it had to be brought back from drifting toward dissolution. Working with Jesusa and Tomás, I could always bring it back, but I couldn't hold it. Our work was never finished.

"Why does it always feel so disgusting?" Jesusa demanded after a long session. We had washed. Now three of us shared a meal—something we weren't able to do very often.

"Two reasons," I said. "First, Aaor isn't me. Mated people don't want that kind of contact with ooloi who aren't their mates. The reasons are biochemical." I stopped. "Aaor smells wrong and tastes wrong to you. I wish I could mask that for you, but I can't."

"We never touch it, and yet I feel it," Jesusa said.

"Because it needs to feel you. I make you sleep because it doesn't need to feel your revulsion. You can't help feeling revulsion, I know, but Aaor doesn't need to share it."

"What's the second reason?" Tomás asked.

I hugged myself with my strength arms. "Aaor is ill. It should not keep sliding away from us the way it does. It should stabilize the way my siblings used to help me stabilize. But it can't." I looked at his face—thinner than it should have been, though he got plenty to eat. The effects of his sessions with Aaor were beginning to show. And Jesusa looked older than she should have. The vertical lines between her eyes had deepened and become set. When all this was over I would erase them.

She and Tomás looked at one another bleakly.

"What is it?" I asked.

Jesusa moved uncomfortably. "What will happen to Aaor?" she asked. "How long will we have to keep helping it?" She leaned back against the cabin wall. "I don't know how much longer I can stand it."

"If we can get it through metamorphosis," I said, "it might stabilize just because its body is mature."

"Do you think you would have without us?" Jesusa asked.

I didn't answer. After a moment, no answer was necessary.

"What will happen to it?" she insisted.

"Ship exile, probably. We'll take it back to Lo, and it will be sent to the ship. There it may find Oankali or construct mates who can stabilize it. Or perhaps it will finally be . . . be allowed to dissolve. Its life now is terrible. If it has nothing better to look forward to . . ."

They turned simultaneously and looked at each other again. They were paired siblings, after all, though they did not think in such terms. They were like Aaor and me. Between them a look said a great deal. That same look excluded me.

Jesusa took one of my sensory arms between her hands and coaxed out the sensory hand. She seemed to do this as naturally as my male and female parents did it with Nikanj. She rarely touched my strength arms now that my sensory arms had grown.

"Nikanj has talked to us about Aaor," she said softly.

I focused narrowly on her. "Nikanj?"

"It told us what you've just told us. It said Aaor probably would dissolve. Die."

"Not exactly die."

"Yes! Yes, die. It will not be Aaor any longer no matter how many of its cells live. Aaor will be gone!"

I was startled by her sudden vehemence. I resisted the impulse to calm her chemically because she did not want to be calmed.

"We know more about dying than you do," she said bitterly. "And, I tell you, I know death when I see it."

I put my strength arm around her, but could not think of anything to say.

Tomás spoke finally. "At home, she was made to help with the sick and the dying. She hated it, but people trusted her. They knew she would do what was necessary, no matter how she felt." He sighed. "Like you, I suppose. There must be something wrong with me—to love only serious, duty-bound people."

I smiled and extended my free sensory arm to him.

He came to sit with us and accepted the arm. No intensity now. Only comfort in being together. We'd had little of that lately.

"If Aaor had a chance to mate with a pair of Humans," Jesusa said, "would it survive?"

She felt frightened and sick to her stomach. She spoke as though the words had been beaten out of her. Both Tomás and I stared at her.

"Well, Jodahs? Would it?"

"Yes," I said. "Almost certainly."

She nodded. "What I was thinking is that if you could fix our faces back the way they were, we could go home. I can think of people who might be willing to join us once they know what we've found—what we've learned."

"We'd be locked up and bred!" Tomás protested.

"I don't think any elders or parents would have to see us. You were always good at coming and going without being seen when you thought you might be put to work."

"That was nothing. This is serious." He paused. "With a name like yours, sister, this isn't a role you should play."

She turned her face away from him, rested her head against my shoulder. "I don't want to do it," she said. "But why should Aaor die? We know our people will be taken and moved or absorbed or sterilized. It's too late to prevent that. How can we watch Aaor suffer and know it will probably die and just do nothing? It's true that our people will think badly of us when they find out that we've joined the Oankali. But they *will* find out eventually, no matter what."

"They'll kill us if they get the chance," Tomás said.

Jesusa shook her head. "Not if we look the way we used to look. Jodahs will have to change us back in every way. Even your neck must be stiff again. That will give us a chance to get out again sooner or later, even if we're caught." She thought for a moment. "They can't know yet what we've done, can they, Jodahs?"

"Not yet," I admitted. "Nikanj has avoided sending word to the ship or to any of the towns."

"Because it hoped we would do just what we're doing."

I nodded. "It would not ask either of you. It only hoped."

"And you?"

"I couldn't ask either. You had already refused. We understood your refusal."

She said nothing for a while. She sat utterly still, staring at the floor. Adrenaline flowed into her system, and she began to shake.

"Jesusa?" I said.

"I don't know if I can do it," she said. "You think you understand. You don't. You can't."

I held her and stroked her until she stopped shaking. Tomás touched her hair, reaching across me to do it, and making me want to grab his hand and stop him. Oankali male and female mates had no need to do this. I had to learn to endure it in Human mates.

"Shall we do it?" she asked him suddenly.

He drew back from her, looked from one of us to the other, then looked away.

She looked at me. "Shall we?" she asked.

I opened my mouth to say yes, she should, of course. Then I closed it. "I don't want you to destroy yourself," I said after a while. "I don't want to trade my sibling's life for yours." I felt what she felt. She could not give me multisensory illusions. Humans did not have that kind of control. But I could feel how tightly she held herself, how her stomach hurt her and her muscles ached. I had to keep stopping myself from giving her relief. She didn't need or want that from me now. Both my mother and Nikanj had warned me that not every pain should be immediately healed. Her body language would tell me when she wanted relief.

"I won't die," she whispered. "I'm not that fragile. Or maybe . . . not that lucky. If I can save your sibling, I will. But I think it would be easier for me to break several of my bones."

Now she and I both looked at Tomás.

He shook his head. "I hate that place," he said softly. "Full of pain and sickness and duty and false hope. I meant to die rather than see it again. You both know that."

I nodded. Jesusa made no move at all. She watched him.

"Yet I love those people," he said. "I don't want to do this to them. Isn't there any other way?"

"None that anyone's thought of," I said. "If you can do this, you'll save Aaor. If you can't, we'll get it to the ship and . . . hope for the best."

"We've already betrayed our people," Jesusa said softly. "We did that with you, Jodahs. All we're doing now is arguing about whether to bring two more of our people out early or let them all wait until the Oankali arrive."

"Is that all?" Tomás said with bitter irony.

"Will you go with me?" she asked.

He sighed. "Didn't I promise you I'd get you back there?"

He ran a hand through his own hair. After a moment he got up, and went outside.

4

There were complications.

We couldn't leave until Aaor's metamorphosis ended. Jesusa and Tomás thought I would give them back their disfigurement and they would go back to the mountains alone. They couldn't have done that, even if I had been willing to let them try. They couldn't leave me now.

I never told them they couldn't leave. They found out as Lilith had. When they had had all they could take of Aaor for a while, when they realized I could not be talked out of going with them to their mountain home, they went away on their own. They went together into the forest and stayed for several days. It was a foretaste for me of what I would suffer when they died.

I panicked when I realized they were gone. Tomás was supposed to spend the night with Aaor and me. The moment I thought about him, though, I realized he wasn't in camp. Neither was Jesusa. Their scent was beginning to fade.

Why? Where had they gone? Which way had they gone? I focused all my concentration on picking up their scent trail, finding out where their scent was strongest and freshest. Once I discovered the path they had taken into the forest, I would follow them.

Ahajas stopped me.

She was large and quiet and immensely comfortable to be near. Oankali females tended to be that way. I knew that sometimes after a session with Aaor, Nikanj went to her and literally seemed to grow into her body. She was so much larger, it looked like a child against her.

Now she blocked my path.

"Let them come back to you," she said quietly.

I stared at her with my eyes while my sensory tentacles all focused to the path Jesusa and Tomás had taken.

"I saw them leave," she said. "They took packs and machetes. They'll be all right, and in a few days, they'll be back."

"Resisters could capture them!" I said.

"Yes," she said. "But it isn't likely. They were on their own for a long time before they met you."

"But they—"

"They are as able as any Humans to take care of themselves. Lelka, you should have told them how they were bound to you."

"I was afraid to. I was afraid they'd do this."

"They probably would have. But now when they begin to need you and feel desperate and afraid, they won't know why."

"That's why I want to go after them."

"Speak to Lilith first. She used to do this, you know. Nikanj had to learn very young that she would stretch the cord until it almost strangled her. And if Nikanj went after her, she would curse it and hate it."

I knew that about Lilith. I went to her and stood near her for a while. She was drawing with black ink or dye on bark cloth. In Lo, other Humans had treasured her drawings— scenes of Earth before the war, of animals long extinct, of distant places, cities, the sea. . . . She did paintings, too, sometimes with dyes from plants. She had done little of that during our exile. Now she was returning to it, stripping bark from the limb of a nearby fig tree, preparing it and making her dye and her brushes and sharp sticks. She had told me once that it was something she did to calm herself. Something she did to make herself feel Human.

She patted the ground next to her, and I went over and cleared a space and sat down.

"They're gone," I said.

"I know," she said. She was drawing an outdoor family meal with all of us gathered and eating from gourd dishes and Lo bowls. All. My parents, my siblings—even Aaor as it had looked before it went into the forest—and Jesusa and Tomás. Everyone was completely recognizable, though it seemed to me they shouldn't have been. They were made up only of a few black lines.

"Your mates will never trust me or Tino again," she said. "That will be our reward for keeping quiet about what was happening to them."

"Shall I go after them?"

"Not now. In a few days. Go when your own feelings tell you they're suffering, maybe turning back. Meet them somewhere between here and wherever they've gone. Can you track them well enough to do that?"

"Yes."

"Do it, then. And don't expect them to behave as though they're glad to see you for any reasons except the obvious biological need."

"I know."

"They won't love or even like you for quite a while."

"Or trust me," I said miserably.

"That won't last. It's us they'll distrust and resent."

I moved around to face her. "They'll know you kept silent for me."

She smiled a bitter smile. "Pheromones, Lelka. Your scent won't let them hate you for long. They can hate us, though. I'm sorry for that. I like them. You're very lucky to have them."

I did as she said. And when I brought home my silent, resentful mates, they did as she had said they would. Tino and Tomás seemed to find some common ground by the time Aaor had completed its metamorphosis, but Jesusa held an unyielding grudge. She hardly spoke to my mother from then on. And when it was time for us to go, and she learned that Aaor had to go with us, she almost stopped speaking to me. That was another battle. Aaor did have to go. If we left it behind with only Nikanj to help it, it would not survive. I suspected it was surviving now only because of our combined efforts and its new hope of Human mates to bond with. I suspected, too, that Jesusa understood this. She never threatened to change her mind, to refuse us and leave Aaor to its fate. She was gentler with Aaor than she was with me. Contact with it through me was still torment for her, but its illness reached something in her that perhaps nothing else could. I, on the other hand, was both her comfort and torment. She stopped touching me. She accepted my touch, even enjoyed it as much as she ever had. But she stopped reaching out to me.

"You did wrong," Tomás told me when he had been watching us for a while. "If she wasn't so good at punishing you, I'd have to think of a way to do it myself."

"But you don't mind," I said. He had felt only relief when I met them in the forest and brought them home. Jesusa had been full of resentment and anger.

"She minds," he said. "She feels trapped and betrayed. I mind that."

"I know. I'm sorry. I was more afraid of losing you than you can imagine."

"I can see Aaor," he said. "I don't have to imagine."

"No. It was the two of you I wanted. Not just to avoid pain."

He looked at me for a moment, then smiled. "She'll forgive you eventually, you know. And she'll be very suspicious of why she's done it. And she'll be right. Won't she?"

I looped a sensory arm around his neck and did not bother to answer.

The rainy season was just ending when the four of us prepared to leave camp. Aaor was strong again—able to walk all day and live on whatever it ran across. And if we slept with it every two or three nights, it could hold its shape. Yet with us all around, it was hideously lonely, empty, almost blank. It could follow and care for itself—just barely. I had to touch it sometimes to rouse it. It was as though it were lost within itself, and only surfaced when we were in contact. It rarely spoke.

When we were ready to go, Nikanj stood between my Oankali parents to give me final advice and to say goodbye.

"Don't come back to this place," it said. "In a few months, we'll return to Lo. We'll give you plenty of time, but we need to go home. Once we get there, everyone will have to know about your mates and their village. Lo will signal the ship and the Humans will be picked up. If the four of you succeed, you'll be six by then, and perhaps you'll be back at Lo yourselves." It focused on me for a time without speaking, and I could not help thinking that if we weren't careful, we might not live to get back to Lo. I might never see my parents again. Nikanj must have been thinking the same thing.

"Lelka, I have memories to give you," it said. "Let me pass them to you now. I think it's time."

Genetics memories. Viable copies of cells that Nikanj had received from its own ooloi parent or that it had collected itself or accepted from its mates and children. It had duplicated everything it possessed and now it would pass the whole inheritance on to me. It was time. I was a mated adult.

Yet as Nikanj stepped away from Ahajas and Dichaan and reached for me with all four arms, I didn't feel like an adult. I was afraid of this final step, this final touch. It was as though Nikanj were saying, "Here's your birthright, my final gift/duty/pleasure to you." Final.

But Nikanj said nothing at all. When it touched me, I pulled back, resisting. It simply waited until I was calmer. Then it spoke. "You must have this before you go, Lelka." It paused. "And you must pass it on to Aaor as soon as Aaor is mated and stable. Who knows when the two of you will see me again?"

I made myself step into its embrace and at once I felt myself held and penetrated, held absolutely still, but not paralyzed. Nikanj had a gentler touch than I had yet managed. And it still gave pleasure. Even to me. Even now.

Then the world around me seemed to flare brilliant white. I

could no longer see beyond myself. All my senses turned inward as Nikanj used both sensory hands to inject a rush of individual cells, each one a plan by which a whole living entity could be constructed. The cells went straight into my newly mature yashi. The organ seemed to gulp and suckle the way I had once at my mother's breast.

There was immense newness. Life in more varieties than I could possibly have imagined—unique units of life, most never seen on Earth. Generations of memory to be examined, memorized, and either preserved alive in stasis or allowed to live their natural span and die. Those that I could re-create from my own genetic material, I did not have to maintain alive.

The flood of information was incomprehensible to me at first. I received it and stored it with only a few bits of it catching my attention. There would be plenty of time for me to examine the rest. I wouldn't lose any of it, and once I understood it, I wouldn't forget it.

When the flood ended and Nikanj was sure I could stand alone, it let me go.

"Now," it said, "except for the lack of Oankali or construct mates, you're an adult."

I felt confused, stuffed with information, overwhelmed with new sensation, stupefied, unable to do much more than hold myself up. I heard what Nikanj said, but the meanings of the words did not reach me for what seemed to be a long time. I felt it touch me once more with a sensory arm, then draw me to it and walk me over to Tomás, who was making a pack of the Lo cloth hammock and the other things my parents had given me.

Tomás got up at once and took me from Nikanj. He was, I recalled later, careful not to touch Nikanj, but no longer concerned about its nearness. Mated adults behaved that way—at ease with one another because they understood where they belonged and what they should and should not do.

"What did you do to it?" Tomás asked.

"Passed it information it might need on this dangerous trip

with you. It's a little like a drunk Human right now, but it will
be all right in a few moments."

Tomás looked at me doubtfully. "Are you sure? We were
about to leave."

"It will be fine."

I recalled all this later, the way I recalled things I perceived
while I was asleep. Tomás sat me down next to him, finished
putting his pack together and rolling it. Then he took one of
my sensory arms between his hands and said, "If you don't
wake up, we'll leave you here and you can come running after
us when you're sober."

He was amused, but he wasn't joking. He would leave without Aaor and me and let us catch up as best we could. Jesusa
would certainly go along with him.

I groped for him, smelling for him rather than seeing him,
hardly able to focus on him at all. He gave me his hand readily enough, and I locked on to it, focused so narrowly on it that
I began to see and hear him normally through the incredible
confusion of information Nikanj had given me. That information was a weight demanding my attention. It would not begin
to "lighten" until I began to understand it. To understand it all
could take years, but I must at least begin now.

"It's not really like being drunk," I said when I could speak.
"It's more like having billions of strangers screaming from inside you for your individual attention. Incomprehensible . . .
overwhelming . . . no word is big enough. Let me stay close to
you for a while."

"Nikanj said it just gave you information," he protested.

"Yes. And if I began now and continued for the rest of our
lives, I could only explain a small fraction of it aloud to you.
Ooan should have waited until we came back."

"Can you travel?" he asked.

"Yes. Just let me stay close to you."

"I thought that was settled. You'll never get away from me."

5

There was no end to the forest. The trees and smaller plants changed. Some varieties vanished, but the forest continued. It was a heavy coat of green fur on the hills and later on the nearly vertical cliffs of the mountains. There were places where we could not have gotten through without machetes.

There were old trails, ledges along cliff faces that perhaps dated back to a time before the war. Below us, a branch of the river cut through a deep, narrow gorge. Above us the mountains were green and sheer, bordering a blue and white band of sky that broadened ahead of us. The water ran high and fast below us, green and white, breaking over huge rocks. I might survive a fall to it, but it was unlikely that any of the others would.

But my Human mates were in their own country, sure-footed and confident. I had wondered whether they would be able to find their way home. They had traveled this route only once, nearly two years before. But Jesusa in particular was at home as soon as the landscape became more vertical than horizontal. Most often she broke trail for us just because she obviously loved the job and was better at it than any of us could have been. When our trail, narrow ledge that it was, vanished, she was usually the first to spot it above us or below or beginning again some distance away. And if she spotted it, she led the climb toward it. She never waited to see what the rest of us wanted to do—she simply found the best way across. The first time I saw her spread flat against the mountain, finding tiny hand- and footholds in the vegetation and the rock, making her way upward like a spider, I froze in absolute panic.

"She's part lizard," Tomás said, smiling. "It's disgusting. I'm not clumsy myself, I've never even seen her fall."

"She's always done this?" Aaor asked.

"I've seen her go up naked rock," Tomás said.

I looked at Aaor and saw that it, too, had reacted with fear. This trip had begun to do it good. The trip had forced it to use its body and focus attention on something other than its own misery. It had made the safety of the two Humans its main concern. It understood the sacrifice they were making for it, and the sacrifice they had already made.

It was last across the gulf, holding on with both feet and all four arms. "I make a better insect than you do," it told Tomás as it reached the rest of us and safety.

Tomás laughed as much with surprise as with pleasure. I don't think he had ever heard Aaor even try to make a joke before.

There were times when we could descend to the river and walk alongside it or bathe in it. Jesusa and Tomás caught fish occasionally and cooked and ate them while Aaor and I took ourselves as far away as we could and focused on other things.

"Why do you let them do that?" Aaor demanded of me the second time it happened. "They shouldn't be hungry."

"They're not," I agreed. "Jesusa told me they lost most of their supplies coming out of the mountains—accidentally dropped them into those rapids we passed two days ago."

"That was then! They don't have to kill animals and eat them now!" Aaor sounded petulant and miserable. It brushed away my sensory arm when I reached out to it, then changed its mind and grasped the sensory arm in its strength hands.

I extended my sensory hand and reached into its body to understand what was wrong with it. As always, it was like reaching into a slightly different version of myself. It was feeling sick—nauseated, disgusted, oddly Human, yet unable to cope with the Humanity of Jesusa and Tomás.

"When you have Human mates," I told it, "you have to remember to let them be Human. They've killed fish and eaten them all their lives. They know we hate it. They need to do it anyway—for reasons that don't have much to do with nutrition."

Aaor let me soothe it, but still said, "What reasons?"

"Sometimes they need to prove to themselves that they still

own themselves, that they can still care for themselves, that they still have things—customs—that are their own."

"Sounds like an expression of the Human conflict," Aaor said.

"It is," I agreed. "They're proving their independence at a time when they're no longer independent. But if this is the worst thing they do, I'll be grateful."

"Will you sleep with them tonight?"

"No. And they know it."

"They—" It stopped, froze utterly still, and signaled me silently. "There are other Humans nearby!"

"Where?" I demanded, silent and frozen myself, trying to catch the sight or the scent.

"Ahead. Can't you smell them?" It gave me an illusion of scent, faint and strange and dangerous. Even with this prompting, I could not smell the new Humans on my own, but Aaor was completely focused on them.

"Males," it said. "Three, I think. Maybe four. Headed away from us. No females."

"At least they're headed away," I whispered aloud. "Do any of them smell anything like Tomás? I can't tell from what you gave me."

"They all smell very much like Tomás. That's why I can't tell how many there are. Like Tomás, but including a certain odd element. The genetic disorder, I suppose. Can't you smell them?"

"I can now. They're so far away, though, I don't think I would have noticed them on my own. They have a dead animal with them, did you notice?"

Aaor nodded miserably.

"They've been hunting," I said. "Now they're probably heading home. Although I don't smell anything that could be their home. Do you?"

"No," it said. "I've been trying. Maybe they're just looking for a place to camp—a place to cook the animal and eat it."

"Whatever their intentions, we'll have to be careful tomorrow." I focused on it. "You've never been shot, have you?"

"Never. People always aim at *you* for some reason."

I shook my head. "You're picking up Tomás's sense of humor. I don't know what your new mates will think of that." I paused. "Being shot hurts more than I would want to show you. I could probably handle the pain better now, but I wouldn't want to have to. I wouldn't want you to have to."

It moved closer to me and linked into me with its sensory tentacles. "I'm not sure I could survive being shot," it said. "I think part of me might, but not as me."

"You can't know that for sure."

It said nothing, but there was no tenacity to it, no feeling that it could withstand abrupt shock and pain. It thought it would dissolve. It was probably right.

"They've finished eating their fish," I said. "Let's go back."

We detached from one another and it turned wearily to follow me. "Do you know," it said, "that before we left home, Ooan still said it couldn't find the flaw in us, couldn't see why we needed mates so early—needed, not just wanted? And why we focus so on Humans." It paused. "Do you want other mates?"

"Oankali mates," I said. "Not construct."

"Why?"

"I think . . . I feel as though it will balance the two parts of me—Human and Oankali. I don't know what the Oankali will think about that, though."

"If they ever accept us and if you find two that you like, don't let them make their decision from a distance."

I smiled. "What about you? Humans and Oankali?"

It rested one strength arm around my shoulders. It almost never touched me with its sensory arms, though it accepted my own gladly. It behaved as though it were not yet mature. "What about me?" it repeated. "I can't plan anything. It's hard for me to believe from one day to the next that I'm even going to survive." It made a fist with its free strength hand, then relaxed the hand. "Most of the time I feel as though I could just let go like this and dissolve. Sometimes I feel as though I should."

I slept with it that night. I couldn't do as much for it alone, but it couldn't have tolerated Jesusa or Tomás until they had digested their meal. I couldn't imagine it not existing, truly gone, never to be touched again—like never being able to touch my own face again.

Two days later, Jesusa and Tomás told me to give them back the marks of their genetic disorder. We had crawled up the nearly nonexistent trail on the mountain and back down again to the river. We had crossed the trail of the hunters we had scented earlier. There were four of them and they were still ahead of us. And now, when the wind was right, I could scent more Humans. Many more. Aaor's head and body tentacles kept sweeping forward, controlled by the tantalizing scent.

"The more Human you can make yourselves look, the less likely you are to be shot if you're seen," Tomás told us. He was looking at Aaor as he spoke. Then he faced me. "I've seen you both change by accident. Why can't you change deliberately?"

"I can," I said. "But Aaor's control is just not firm enough. It already looks as Human as it can look."

He drew a deep breath. "Then this is as close as it should get. You should change us and camp here."

"We can't even see your town from here," Aaor protested.

"And they can't see you. If you round that next bend, though, part of our settlement will be visible to you. But the way is guarded. You would be shot."

Aaor seemed to sink in on itself. We had made a fireless camp. My mates were on either side of me, linked with me. Aaor was alone. "You should change yourself and go with them," it said. "They'll function better if they are not separated from you. I can survive alone for a few days."

"If we're caught, we'll be separated," Jesusa said. "We'll be shut up in separate places. We'll be questioned. I would probably be married off very quickly." She stopped. "Jodahs, what will happen if someone tries to have sex with me?"

I shook my head. "You'll fight. You won't be able to help fighting. You'll fight so hard, you might win even if the male is much stronger. Or maybe you'll just make him hurt or kill you."

"Then she can't go," Tomás said. "I'll have to do it alone."

"Neither of you should go," I said. "If hunters come out this far, we should wait. We have time."

"That will get you a man," Jesusa said. "Maybe several men. But women don't hunt."

"What do females do?" I asked. "What might bring them out away from the protection of the settlement?"

Jesusa and Tomás looked at one another, and Tomás grinned. "They meet," he said.

"Meet?" I repeated, uncomprehending.

"The elders tell us who we must marry," he said. "But they can't tell us who we must love."

I knew Humans did such things: marry here and mate there and there and there. . . . There was nothing in Human biology to prevent this. In fact, Human biology encouraged male Humans to have liaisons with more than one female. The male's investment of time and energy in fathering children was much smaller than the female's. Still, the concept felt alien to me. To have a mating and somehow put it aside. But then, most construct males never had true mates. They went wherever they found welcome and everyone knew it. There was no permanent bonding, no betrayal, no biological wrongness to contend with.

"Do your people meet this way because they would like to be mated?" I asked.

"Some of them," Tomás said. "Others only feel a temporary attraction."

"It would be good to get a pair for Aaor who already care for one another."

"We thought that, too," Jesusa said. "We meant to go to the village and bring away the people we would have been married to. But they wouldn't be coming out here to be together. They're brother and sister, too. A brother and two sisters, really."

"It would be better, safer to go after people who have already slipped away from your village. Is there a place where such people often meet?"

Tomás sighed. "Change us back tonight. Make us as ugly as we were, just in case. Tomorrow night, we'll show you some of the places where lovers meet. If you go there at all, it will have to be at night."

But the next night we were spotted.

6

We did not know we had been seen. As we rounded the final bend before the mountain people's village, we kept hidden in the trees and undergrowth. All we could see of their village were occasional stonework terraces cut into the sides of forested mountains. Crops grew on the terraces—a great deal of corn, some large melons, more than one species of potato, and other things that I did not recognize at all—foods neither I nor Nikanj had ever collected or stored memories of. These were surprisingly distracting—new things just sitting and waiting to be tasted, remembered. Yashi, between my hearts and protected now by a broad, flat slab of bone that no Human would have recognized as a sternum, did twist—or rather, it contracted like a long-empty Human stomach. Any perception of new living things attracted it and distracted me. I looked at Aaor and saw that it was utterly focused on the village itself, the people.

Its desperation had sharpened and directed its perceptions.

The Humans had built their village well above the river, had stretched it along a broad flattened ridge that extended between two mountains. We could not see it from where we were, but we could see signs of it—a great deal more terracing high up. These terraces could not be reached from where we were, but there was probably a way up nearby. All we could see between the canyon floor and the terraces was a great deal of sheer rock, much of it overgrown with vegetation. It was nothing I would have chosen to climb.

The scent of the Humans was strong now. Aaor, perhaps caught up in it, stumbled and stepped on a dry stick as it regained its balance. The sharp snap of the wood was startling in the quiet night. We all froze. Those stalking us did not freeze—or not quickly enough.

"Humans behind us!" I whispered.

"Are they coming?" Tomás demanded.

"Yes. Several of them."

"The guard," Tomás said. "They will have guns."

"You two get away!" Jesusa said. "We'll have a better chance without you. Wait for us at the cave we passed two days ago. Go!"

The guard meant to catch us against their mountains. We were trapped now, really. If we ran to the river, we would have to go around them or through them, and probably be shot. There was nowhere for us to go except up the sheer cliff. Or down like insects to hide in the thickest vegetation. We could not get away, but we could hide. And if the guard found Jesusa and Tomás, perhaps they would not look for us.

I pulled Aaor down with me, fearing for it more than I feared for any of us. It was probably right in suspecting that it could not survive being shot.

In the darkness, Humans passed on either side of where Aaor and I lay hidden. They knew the terrain, but they could not see very well at night. Jesusa and Tomás led them a short distance away from us. They did this by simply walking down the slope toward the river until they walked into the arms of their captors.

Then there was shouting—Jesusa shouting her name, Tomás demanding that he be let go, that Jesusa be let go, guards shouting that they had caught the intruders.

"Where are the rest of you?" a male voice said. "There were more than two."

"Make a light, Luis," Jesusa said with deliberate disgust.

"Look at us, then tell me when there has been more than one Jesusa and more than one Tomás."

There was silence for a while. Jesusa and Tomás were walked farther from us—perhaps taken where the moonlight would show more of their faces. Their tumors looked exactly as they had when I met them, so I wasn't worried about them not being recognized. But still, they had said they would be separated, imprisoned, questioned.

How long would they be imprisoned? If they were separated, they wouldn't be able to help one another break free. And what might be done to them if they gave answers that their people did not believe? They had, with obvious distaste for lying, created a story of being captured by a small group of resisters and held by separate households so that neither knew the details of the other's captivity. Resisters actually did such things, though most often, their captives were female. Tomás would say he had been made to work for his captors. He had done planting, harvesting, hauling, building, cutting wood, whatever needed to be done. Since he had actually done these things while he was with us, he could give accurate descriptions of them. He would say that his sister was held hostage to ensure his good behavior while his captivity kept her in line. Finally the two had been able to get together and escape their resister captors.

This could have happened. If Jesusa and Tomás could tell it convincingly, perhaps they would not be imprisoned for long.

The two had been recognized now. There were no more hostile cries—only Jesusa's anguished "Hugo, please let me go. Please! I won't run away. I've just run all the way home. Hugo!"

The last word was a scream. He was touching her, this Hugo. She had known they would touch her. She had not known until now how difficult it would be to endure their touch. She could touch other females in comfort. Tomás could touch males. They would have to protect one another as best they could.

"Let her alone!" Tomás said. "You don't know what she's been through." His voice said she had already been released. He was only warning.

"Everyone said you two were dead," one guard told them.

"Some *hoped* they were dead," another voice said softly. "Better them than all of us."

"No one will die because of us," Tomás said.

"We haven't come home to die," Jesusa said. "We're tired. Take us up."

"Does everyone know them?" the softer voice asked. It sounded almost like an ooloi voice. "Does anyone dispute their identity?"

"We could strip them down here," someone said. "Just to be sure."

Tomás said, "Bring your sister down, Hugo. We'll strip her, too."

"My sister stays home where she belongs!"

"And if she didn't, how would you want her treated? With justice and decency? Or should she be stripped by seven men?"

Silence.

"Let's go up," Jesusa said. "Hugo, do you remember the big yellow water jar we used to hide in?"

More silence.

"You know me," she said. "We were ten years old when we broke that jar, and I got caught and you didn't and I never told. You know me."

There was a pause, then the Hugo voice said, "Let's take them up. Someone will probably have some dinner left over."

They were taken away.

Aaor and I followed to see the path they would use and to see as much as we could of the guards.

Of the seven, four were obviously distorted by their genetic disorder. They had large tumors on their heads or arms. They looked different enough to be shot on sight by lowland resisters.

We followed as long as there was forest cover, then watched as they went up a pathway that was mostly rough stone stairs leading up the steep slope to the village.

When we could no longer hear them, Aaor pulled me close to it and signaled silently, "We can't just go wait in the cave. We have to get them out!"

"Give them time," I said. "They'll try to find a pair of Humans for you."

"How can they? They'll be shut up, guarded."

"Most of these guards were young and fertile. And perhaps Jesusa will be given female guards. What are guards but villagers doing a tiresome, temporary duty?"

Aaor tried to relax, but its body was still tense against mine. "Seeing them walk away was like beginning to dissolve. I feel as though part of me has walked away with them."

I said nothing. Part of me *had* walked away with them. Both they and I knew what it would be like to be separated for a while—worse, to be kept apart by other people who would do all they could to stand between us. I would not begin to miss them physically for a few days, but with my uncertainty, my realization that I might not get them back, I had all I could do to control myself. I sat down on the ground, my body trembling.

Aaor sat next to me and tried to calm me, but it could not give what it did not feel in itself. The Humans could have caught us easily then—two ooloi sitting on the ground shuddering helplessly.

We recovered slowly. We were in control of our bodies again when Aaor said silently, "We can't give them more than two days to work—and that might not be long enough for them to do anything."

I could last longer than two days, but Aaor couldn't. "We'll give them the time," I said. "We'll get as close as we can and rest alert for two days."

"Then we'll have to get them out if they can't escape on their own."

"I don't want to do that," I said. "Tomás was talking as much to us as to his people when he said no one would die because of him and Jesusa. But if we try to get them out, we could be forced to kill."

"That's why it's best to go in while we're still in control of ourselves. You know that, Jodahs."

"I know," I whispered aloud.

7

We went up a steep, heavily forested slope, crawling up, clinging like caterpillars. Being six-limbed had never been quite so practical.

We climbed to the level of the terraces, and lay near them, hidden, during the next day. When night came, we explored the terraces and compulsively tried bits of the new foods we found growing there. By then, our skins had grown darker and we were harder for the Humans to see—while we could see everything.

We climbed higher up one of the mountains that formed a corner of the settlement. Just over halfway up, we reached the Human settlement with its houses of stone and wood and thatch. This was a prewar place. It had to be. Parts of it looked ancient. But it did not look like a ruin. All the buildings were well kept and there were terraces everywhere, most of them full of growing things. Away from the village, there was an enclosure containing several large animals of a kind I had not seen before—shaggy, long-necked, small-headed creatures who stood or lay at ease around their pen. Alpacas?

We could smell other, smaller animals caged around the village, and we could smell fertile, young Humans everywhere. Even above us on the mountain, we could smell them. What would they be doing up there?

How many were up there? Three, my nose told me. A female and two males, all young, all fertile, two afflicted with the genetic disorder. Why couldn't it just be those two for Aaor? What would we do with the third one if we went up? Why hadn't Jesusa and Tomás told us about people living in such isolation? Except for their being one too many of them, they were perfect.

"Up?" I said to Aaor.

It nodded. "But there's an extra male. What do we do with him?"

"I don't know yet. Let's see if we can get a look at them before they see us. Separating them might be easier than we think."

We climbed the slope, noticing, but for the most part not using, the long serpentine path the Humans had made. There had been Humans on it that day. Perhaps there would be Humans on it the next day. Perhaps it led to a guard post, and the guard changed daily. Anyone on top would have a fine view of all approaches from the mountains or the canyon below. Perhaps the people at the top stayed longer than a day and were resupplied from below at regular intervals—though there were a few terraces near the top.

We went up quietly, quickly, eating the most nutritious things we could find along the way. When we reached the terraces, we stopped and ate our fill. We would have to be at our best.

On a broad ledge near the top, we found a stone cabin. Higher up was a cistern and a few more terraces. Inside the cabin, two people slept. Where was the third? We didn't dare go in until we knew where everyone was.

I linked with Aaor and signaled silently. "Have you spotted the third?"

"Above," it said. "There is another cabin—or at least another living place. You go up to that one. I want these two." It was utterly focused on the Human pair.

"Aaor?"

It focused on me with a startlingly quick movement. It was as tight as a fist inside.

"Aaor, there are hundreds of other Humans down there. You'll have a life. Be careful who you give it to. I was very lucky with Jesusa and Tomás."

"Go up and keep the third Human from bothering me."

I detached from it and went to find the second cabin. Aaor would not hear anything I had to say now, just as I would not have heard anyone who told me to beware of Jesusa and Tomás. And if the Humans were young enough, they could probably mate successfully with any healthy ooloi. If only Aaor were healthy. It wasn't. It and the Humans it chose would have to heal each other. If they didn't, perhaps none of them would survive.

I found not a cabin higher up on the mountain, but a very small cave near the top. Humans had built a rock wall, enclosing part of it. There were signs that they had enlarged the cave on one side. Finally heavy wooden posts had been set against the stone and from these a wooden door had been hung. The door seemed more a barrier against the weather than against people. Tonight the weather was dry and warm and the door was not secured at all. It swung open when I touched it.

The man inside awakened as I stumbled down into his tiny cave. His body heat made him a blaze of infrared in the darkness. It was easy for me to reach him and stop his hands from finding whatever they were grasping for.

Holding his hands, I lay down alongside him on his short, narrow bed and wedged him against the stone wall. I examined him with several sensory tentacles, studying him, but not controlling him. I stopped his hoarse shouting by looping one sensory arm around his neck, then moving the coil up to cover his mouth. He bit me, but his blunt Human teeth couldn't do any serious harm. My sensory arms existed to protect the sensitive reproductive organs inside. The flesh that covered them was the toughest flesh to be found on my body.

The male I held must have been more at home in his tiny cave than most people would have been. He was tiny himself— half the size of most Human males. Also, he had some skin disease that had made a ruin of his face, his hands, and much of the rest of his body. He was hairless. His skin was as scaly as those of some fish I'd seen. His nose was distorted—flattened from having been broken several times—and that enhanced his fishlike appearance. Strangely he was free of the genetic disorder that Jesusa, Tomás, and so many of the other people of the village had. He was grotesque without it.

I examined him thoroughly, enjoying the newness of him. By the time I had finished, he had stopped struggling and lay quietly in my arms. I took my sensory arm from his mouth, and he did not shout.

"Do you live here because of the way you look?" I asked him.

He cursed me at great length. In spite of his size, he had a deep, hoarse, grating voice.

I said nothing. We had all night.

After a very long time, he said, "All right. Yes, I'm here because of the way I look. Got any more stupid questions?"

"I don't have time to help you grow. But if you like, I can heal your skin condition."

Silence.

"My god," he whispered finally.

"It won't hurt," I said. "And it can be done by morning. If you're afraid to stay here after you're healed, you can come with us when we leave. Then I'll have time to help you grow. If you want to grow."

"People my age don't grow," he said.

I brushed bits of scaly, dead skin from his face. "Oh, yes," I said. "We can help people your age to grow."

After another long pause, he said, "Is the town all right?"

"Yes."

"What will happen to it?"

"Eventually my people will come to it and tell your people they don't have to live in distorted bodies or in isolation or in fear. Your people have been cut off for a long time. They don't realize there's another, larger colony of healthy, fertile Humans living and growing without Oankali."

"I don't believe you!"

"I know. It's true, though. Shall I heal you?"

"Can I . . . see you?"

"At sunrise."

"I could make a fire."

"No."

He shook his head against me. "I should be more afraid than this. My god, I should be pissing on myself. Exactly what the hell are you anyway?"

"Construct. Oankali-Human mixture. Ooloi."

"Ooloi . . . The mixed ones—male and female in one body."

"We aren't male or female."

"So you say." He sighed. "Do you mean to hold me here all night?"

"If I'm to heal you, I'll have to."

"Why are you here? You said your people would come eventually. What are you doing here now?"

"Nothing harmful. Do you want hair?"

"What?"

I waited. He had heard the question. Now let him absorb it. Hair was easy. I could start it as an afterthought.

He put his head against my chest. "I don't understand," he said. "I don't even understand . . . my own feelings." Much later he said, "Of course I want hair. And I want skin, not scales. I want hair, and I want height. I want to be a man!"

My first impulse was to point out that he was a man. His male organs were well developed. But I understood him. "We'll take you with us when we go," I said.

And he was content. After a while, he slept. I never drugged him in the way ooloi usually drugged resisters. Once he had passed his first surprise and fear, he had accepted me much more quickly than Jesusa and Tomás had—but I had been only a subadult when I met them. And adult ooloi—a construct ooloi—ought to be able to handle Humans better. Or perhaps this man—I had not even asked his name, nor he mine—was particularly susceptible to the ooloi substance that I could not help injecting. In his Human way, he had been very hungry, starving, for any touch. How long had it been since anyone was willing to touch him—except perhaps to break his nose again. He would need an ooloi to steer him away from breaking a few noses himself once he was large enough to reach them. He had probably been treated badly. He did not veer from the Human norm in the same way as other people in the village, and Humans were genetically inclined to be intolerant of difference. They could overcome the inclination, but it was a reality of the Human conflict that they often did not. It was significant that this man was so ready to leave his home with someone he had been taught to think of as a devil—someone he hadn't even seen yet.

8

By morning, I had given the cave Human a smooth, new skin and the beginnings of a full head of hair.

"It will take me longer to repair your nose," I told him. "When I have, though, you'll be able to breathe better with your mouth closed."

He took a deep breath through his mouth and stared at me, then looked at himself, then stared at me again. He rubbed a hand over the fuzz on his head, then held the hand in front of him and examined it. I had not allowed him to awaken until I'd gotten up myself, opened the door to the dawn, and found the short, thick gun he had been reaching for the night before. I had emptied it and thrown it off the mountain. Then I awoke the man.

Seeing me alarmed him, but he never once reached toward the hiding place of the gun.

"What's your name?" I asked him.

"Santos." His voice now was a harsh whisper rather than a harsh growl. "Santos Ibarra Ruiz. How did you do this? How is it possible?" He rubbed the fingers of his right hand over his left arm and seemed to delight in the feel of it.

"Did you think you were dreaming last night?" I asked.

"I haven't had time to think."

"Who will come up here today?"

He blinked. "Here? No one."

"Who will visit the cabin below?"

"I don't know. I lose track with them. Are you going down there?"

"Eventually. Have your breakfast if you like."

"What are you called?"

"Jodahs."

He nodded. "I've heard that some of your kind had four arms. I didn't believe it."

"Ooloi have four arms."

He stared for some time at my sensory arms, then asked, "Are you really going to take me away with you and make me grow?"

"Yes."

He smiled, showing several bad teeth. I would fix those, too—have him shed them and grow more.

Later that morning we went down to the stone cabin. The male and female there were sharing their breakfast with Aaor. Santos and I startled them, but they seemed comfortably at home with Aaor. And Aaor looked better than it had since its first metamorphosis. It looked stable and secure in itself. It looked satisfied.

"Will they come with us?" I asked in Oankali.

"They'll come," it answered in Spanish. "I've begun to heal them. I've told them about you."

The two Human stared at me curiously.

"This is Jodahs, my closest sibling," Aaor said. "Without it I would already be dead." It actually said, "my closest brother-sister," because that was the best either of us could do in Spanish. No wonder people like Santos thought we were hermaphroditic.

"These are Javier and Paz," Aaor said. "They are already mates."

They were also close relatives, of course. They looked as much alike as Jesusa and Tomás did, and they looked like Jesusa and Tomás—strong, brown, black-haired, deep-chested people.

Santos and I were given dried fruit, tea, and bread. Javier

and Paz seemed most interested in Santos. He was their relative, too, of course.

"Do you feel well, Santos?" Paz asked.

"What do you care?" Santos demanded.

Paz looked at me. "Why do you want him? Wish him a good day, and he'll spit on you."

"He needs more healing than I can give him here," I said. I turned my head so that he would know I was looking at him. "He'll have less reason to spit when I'm finished with him, so maybe he'll do less spitting. Perhaps then I'll find mates for him."

He watched me while I spoke, then let his eyes slide away from me. He stared, unseeing, I think, at the rough wooden table.

"Will others come up here today?" I asked Paz.

"No," she said. "Today is still our watch. Juana and Santiago will come tomorrow to relieve us."

Santos spoke abruptly, urgently. "Are you really going with them?"

"Of course," Paz said.

"Why? You should be afraid of them. You should be terrified. When we were children they told us the devil had four arms."

"We're not children anymore," Javier said. "Look at my right hand." He held it up, pale brown and smooth. "I have a right hand again. It's been a frozen claw for years, and now—"

"Not enough!"

Javier opened his mouth, his expression suddenly angry. Then, without speaking, he closed his mouth.

"I want to go," Paz said quietly. "I'm tired of telling myself lies about this place and watching my children die." She pushed very long black hair from her face. As she sat at the table, most of her hair hung to the floor behind her. "Santos, if you had seen our last child before it died, you would thank God for the beauty you had even before your healing."

Santos looked away from her, shamefaced but stubborn. "I know all that," he said. "I don't mean to be cruel. I do know. But . . . we have been taught all our lives that the aliens would destroy us if they found us. Why did our belief and our fear slip away so quickly?"

Javier sighed. "I don't know." He looked at Aaor. "They're not very fearsome, are they? And they are . . . very interesting. I don't know why." He looked up. "Santos, do you believe we are building a new people here?"

Santos shook his head. "I've never believed it. I have eyes. But that's no reason for us to consent to go away with people we've been taught were evil."

"Did you consent?" Paz asked.

". . . yes."

"What else is there, then?"

"Why are they here!" He turned to me. "Why are you here?"

"To get Human mates for Aaor," I said. "And now I have to get my own Human mates back. They are—"

"Jesusa and Tomás, we know," Paz said. "Aaor said they were imprisoned below. We can show you where they're probably being held but I don't know how you can get them out."

"Show us," I said.

We went outside where the stone village lay below us, spread like a Human-made map. The buildings seemed tiny in the distance, but they could all be seen. The whole flattened ridge was visible.

"See the round building there," Javier said, pointing.

I didn't see it at first. So many gray buildings with gray-brown thatched roofs, all tiny in the distance. Then it was clear to me—a stone half-cylinder built against a stone wall.

"There are rooms in it and under it," Paz said. "Prisoners are kept there. The elders believe people who travel must be made to spend time alone to be questioned and prove they are who they say they are, and that they have not betrayed the people." She stopped, looked at Javier. "They would say that we've betrayed the people."

"We didn't bring the aliens here," he said. "And why do the people need us to produce more dead children?"

"They won't say that if they catch us."

"What will they do to you?" I asked.

"Kill us," Paz whispered.

Aaor stepped between them, one sensory arm around each. "Jodahs, can we take them out, then come back for Jesusa and Tomás?"

I stared down at the village, at the hundreds of green terraces. "I'm afraid for them. The longer we're separated, the more likely they are to give themselves away. If only they had told us . . . Paz, did people watch the canyon from up here before Jesusa and Tomás left home?"

"No," she said. "We do this now *because* they left. The elders were afraid we would be invaded. We made more guns and ammunition, and we posted new guards. Many new guards."

"This isn't really a good place to watch from," Javier said. "We're too high and the canyon is too heavily forested. People would have to almost make an effort to attract our attention. Light a fire or something."

I nodded. We had made cold camps for days before we reached the village. Yet we had been spotted. New guards. More vigilance. "You have to help us get you away from here," I said. "You know where the guards are. We don't want to hurt them, but we have to get you away and I have to get Jesusa and Tomás out."

"We can help you get away," Paz said. "But we can't help you reach Tomás and Jesusa. You've seen that they're guarded and in the middle of town."

"If they're where you say, I can get almost to them by climbing around the slope. It looks steep, but there's good cover."

"But you can't get Jesusa and Tomás out that way."

I looked at her, liking the way she stood close to Aaor, the way she had put one hand up to hold the sensory arm that encircled her throat. And, though she was a few years older, she was painfully like Jesusa.

I spoke in Oankali to Aaor. "Take your mates tonight and get clear of this place. Wait at the cave down the canyon."

"You didn't desert me," Aaor said obstinately in Spanish.

"I can reach them," I said. "Alone and focused, I can come

up through the terraces and avoid the guards—or surprise them and sting them unconscious. And no door will keep me from Jesusa and Tomás. I can take them down the slope to the canyon. You've seen them climb. Especially Jesusa. I'll carry Tomás on my back if I have to—whether he wants me to or not. So tonight, you take your mates to safety. And take Santos for me. I intend to keep my promise to him."

After a while, Aaor nodded. "I'll come back for you if you don't meet us."

"It might be better for you if you didn't," I said.

"Don't ask the impossible of me," it said, and guided its mates back into the stone cabin.

9

We meant to leave late that night—Aaor with the Humans down their back-and-forth pathway, then down terraces and a neglected, steep, overgrown path to the canyon floor. I meant to go down the other side of the mountain and work my way around as close as possible to the place where Jesusa and Tomás were being held.

It would have worked. The mountain village would be free of us and able to continue in isolation until Nikanj sent a shuttle to gas it and collect the people.

But that afternoon a party of armed males came up the trail to the stone cabin.

We heard them, smelled their sweat and their gunpowder long before we saw them. There was no time for Aaor to change Javier and Paz, give them back the deformities it had taken from them.

"Were their faces distorted?" I asked Aaor.

It nodded. "Small tumors. Very visible."

And nowhere to hide. We could climb up to Santos's cave, but what good would that do? If villagers found no one in the cabin, they would be bound to check the cave. If we began to climb down the other side of the mountain, we could be picked off. There was nothing to do but wait.

"Four of them?" I asked Aaor.

"I smell four."

"We let them in and we sting them."

"I've never stung anyone."

I glanced toward its mates. "Didn't you make at least one of them unconscious last night?"

Its sensory tentacles knotted against his body in embarrassment, and its mates looked at one another and smiled.

"You can sting," I said. "And I hope you can stand being shot now. You might be."

"I feel as though I can stand it. I feel as though I could survive almost anything now."

It was healthy, then. If we could keep its Humans alive, it would stay healthy.

"Is there a signal you should give?" I asked Javier.

"One of us should be outside, keeping watch," he said. "They won't be surprised that we're not, though. On this duty, I think only the elders watch as much as they should. I mean, Jesusa and Tomás left two years ago and there's been no trouble. Until now."

Laxity. Good.

The cabin was small and there was nowhere in it to hide. I sent the three Humans up the crooked pathway to Santos's cave. Vegetation was thick even this near the summit, and once they went around one of the turns, they could not be seen from the stone cabin. They would not be found unless someone went up after them. Aaor and I had to see that no one did. We waited inside the cabin. If we could get the newcomers in, there was less chance of accidentally killing one of them by having him fall down the slope.

I touched Aaor as I heard the men reach our level. "For Jesusa and Tomás's sake," I said silently, "we can't let any of them escape."

Aaor gave back wordless agreement.

"Javier!" called one of the newcomers before he reached the cabin door. "Hey, Javier, where are you?"

The cabin windows were high and small and the walls were thick. It would have been no easy matter to look in and see whether anyone was inside, so we were not surprised when one of the Humans kicked the door open.

Human eyes adjust slowly to sudden dimness. We stood behind the door and waited, hoping at least two of the men would stumble in, half blind.

Only one did. I stung him just before he would have shouted. To his friends he seemed to collapse without reason. Two of them called to him, stepped up to help him. Aaor got one of them. I just missed the other, struck again, and caught him just outside the door.

The fourth was aiming his rifle at me. I dived under it as he fired. The bullet plowed up the ground next to the face of one of his fallen friends.

I held him with my strength hands, took the gun from him with my sensory arms, emptied it, and threw it far out so that it would clear the slope and fall to the canyon floor. Aaor was getting rid of the others in the same way.

The man in my strength arms struggled wildly, shouting and cursing me, but I did not sting him. He was a tall, unusually strong male, gray-haired and angular. He was one of the sterile old Humans—one of the ones the people here called elders. I wanted to see how he responded to our scent when he got over his first fear. And I wanted to find out why he and the three fertile young males had come up. I wanted to know what he knew about Jesusa and Tomás.

I dragged him into the cabin and made him sit beside me on the bed. When he stopped struggling, I let go of him.

His sudden freedom seemed to confuse him. He looked at me, then at Aaor, who was just dragging one of his friends into the cabin. Then he lurched to his feet and tried to run.

I caught him, lifted him, and sat him on the bed again. This time, he stayed.

"So those damned little Judases did betray us," he said. "They'll be shot! If we don't return, they'll be shot!"

I got up and shut the door, then touched Aaor to signal it silently. "Let's let our scent work on them for a while."

It consented to do this, though it saw no reason. It turned one of the males over and stripped his shirt. The male's body and face were distorted by tumors. His mouth was so distorted it seemed unlikely that he could speak normally.

"We have time," Aaor said aloud. "I don't want to leave them this way."

"If you repair them, they won't be able to go home," I reminded it. "Their own people might kill them."

"Then let them come with us!" It lay down next to the male with the distorted mouth and sank a sensory hand and many sensory tentacles into him.

The elder stared, then stood up and stepped toward Aaor. His body language said he was confused, afraid, hostile. But he only watched.

After a while, some of the tumors began to shrink visibly, and the elder stepped back and crossed himself.

"Shall we take them with us, once we've healed them?" I asked him. "Would your people kill them?"

He looked at me. "Where are the people who were in this house?"

"With Santos. We were afraid they might be shot by accident."

"You've healed them?"

"And Santos."

He shook his head. "And what will be the price for all this kindness? Sterility? Long, slow death? That's what your kind gave me."

"We aren't making them sterile."

"So you say!"

"Our people will be here soon. You will have to decide whether to mate with us, join the Human colony on Mars, or

stay here sterile. If these males choose to mate with us or to go
to Mars, why should they be sterilized? If they decide to stay
here, others can sterilize them. It isn't a job I'd want."

"Mars colony? You mean Humans without Oankali are living on Mars? The planet Mars?"

"Yes. Any Humans who want to go. The colony is about
fifty years old now. If you go, we'll give you back your fertility and see that you're able to father healthy children."

"No!"

I shrugged.

"This is our world. Your people can go to Mars."

"You know we won't."

Silence.

He looked again at what Aaor was doing. Several of the
smallest visible tumors had already vanished. His expression,
his body language were oddly false. He was fascinated. He did
not want to be. He wanted to be disgusted. He pretended to be
disgusted.

He was more than fascinated. He was envious. He must
have experienced the touch of an ooloi back before he was released to become a resister. All Humans of his age had been
handled by ooloi. Did he remember and want it again, or was
it only our scent working on him? Oankali ooloi frightened
Humans because they looked so different. Aaor and I were
much less frightening. Perhaps that allowed Humans to respond more freely to our scent. Or perhaps, being part Human
ourselves, we had a more appealing scent.

When I had checked the two Humans on the floor, seen that
they were truly unconscious and likely to stay that way for a
while, I took the elder by the shoulder and led him back to the
bed.

"More comfortable than the floor," I said.

"What will you do?" he asked.

"Just have a look at you—make sure you're as healthy as
you appear to be."

He had been resisting for a century. He had been teaching
children that people like me were devils, monsters, that it was

better to endure a disfiguring, disabling genetic disorder than to go down from the mountains and find the Oankali.

He lay down on the bed, eager rather than afraid, and when I lay down beside him, he reached out and pulled me to him, probably in the same way he reached out for his human mate when he was especially eager for her.

10

By the time it began to get dark, our captives had become our allies. They were Rafael, whose tumors Aaor had healed and whose mouth Aaor had improved, and Ramón, Rafael's brother. Ramón was a hunchback, but he knew now that he didn't have to be. And even though we had had not nearly enough time to change him completely, we had already straightened him a little. There was also Natal, who had been deaf for years. He was no longer deaf.

And there was the elder, Francisco, who was still confused in the way Santos had been. It frightened him that he had accepted us so quickly—but he had accepted us. He did not want to go back down the mountain to his people. He wanted to stay with us. I sent him up to bring Santos, Paz, and Javier back to us. He sighed and went, thinking it was a test of his new loyalty. He was the only one, after all, who had not needed our healing.

Not until he brought them back did I ask him whether he could get Jesusa and Tomás out.

"I could talk to them," he said. "But the guards wouldn't let me take them out. Everyone is too nervous. Two of the guards last night swear they saw four people, not two. That's why we were sent up here. Some people thought Paz and Javier might have seen something, or worse, might be in trouble." He looked at Paz and Javier. They had come in and gone straight to Aaor, who coiled a sensory tentacle around each of their necks and welcomed them as though they had been away for days.

Jesusa and Tomás *had* been away from me for two days. I was not yet desperate for them, but I might be in two more days if I didn't get them out. Knowing that made me uneasy, anxious to get started. I left the too-crowded cabin and went to sit on the bare rock of the ledge outside. It was dusk, and the two brothers, Rafael and Ramón, had gotten into the cabin's food stores and begun to prepare a meal.

Francisco and Santos came out with me and settled on either side of me. We could see the village below through a haze of smoke from cooking fires.

"When will you leave?" Santos asked.

"After dark, before moonrise."

"Are you going to help?" he asked Francisco.

Francisco frowned. "I've been trying to think of what I could do. I think I'll go down and just wait. If Jodahs needs help, if it's caught, perhaps I can give it the time it needs to prove it isn't a dangerous animal."

Santos grinned. "It is a dangerous animal."

Francisco looked at him with distaste.

"You should be looking at Jodahs that way. Its people will come and destroy everything you've spent your life building."

"Go back up to your cave, Santos. Rot there."

"I'll follow Jodahs," Santos said. "I don't mind. In fact, it's a pleasure. But I'm not asleep. These people probably won't kill us, but they'll swallow us whole."

Francisco shook his head. "How's your breathing these days, Santos? How many times have you had that nose of yours broken? And what has it taught you?"

Santos stared at him for a moment, then screeched with laughter.

I looped a sensory arm around Santos's neck, pulled him against me. He didn't try to say anything more. He didn't really seem to be out to do harm. He just enjoyed having the advantage, knowing something a century-old elder didn't know—something I had overlooked, too. He was laughing at both of us. He kept quiet and held still, though, while I fixed his nose. In the short time I had, I couldn't make it look much better. That would mean altering bone as well as cartilage. I did a little of that so he could breathe with his mouth closed if he wanted to. But the main thing I did was repair nerve damage. Santos hadn't just been hit on the nose. He had been thoroughly beaten about the head. His body could "taste" and enjoy the ooloi substance I could not help giving when I penetrated his skin. That had won him over to me. But he could smell almost nothing.

"What are you doing to him?" Francisco asked with no particular concern. His sense of smell was excellent.

"Repairing him a little more," I said. "It keeps him quiet, and I promised him I'd do it. Eventually he'll be almost as tall as you are."

"Seal up his mouth while you're at it," Francisco said. "I'll walk down now."

"Do you still want to come with us?"

"Of course."

I smiled, liking him. It seemed I couldn't help liking the people I seduced. Even Santos. "You'll go to Mars, won't you?"

"Yes." He paused. "Yes, I think so. I might not if you were looking for mates. I wish you were."

"Thank you," I said. "If you change your mind, I can help you find Oankali or construct mates."

"Like you?"

"Your ooloi would be Oankali."

He shook his head. "Mars, then. With my fertility restored."

"Absolutely."

"Where shall I meet you once you've gotten Tomás and Jesusa out?"

"Follow the trail downriver. Come as quickly as you can, but come carefully. If you can't get away, remember that my people will be coming here soon anyway. They won't hurt you, and they will send you to Mars if you still want to go."

"I'd rather leave with you."

"You're welcome to come with us. Just don't get killed trying to do it. You're much older than I am. You're supposed to have learned patience."

He laughed without humor. "I haven't learned it, little ooloi. I probably never will. Watch for me on the river trail."

He left us, and I sat repairing Santos until it was time for me to go. I left him with a fairly good sense of smell.

"Don't make trouble," I told him. "Use that good mind of yours to help these people get away."

"Francisco wouldn't have minded what you're doing to us," he said. "I figured it out, and I don't mind."

"I'll do experiments when my mates' lives are not at stake. Until we're away from this place, Santos, try to be quiet unless you have something useful to say."

I went into the cabin and told Aaor I was leaving.

It left its mates and the meal it had been eating. It had used more energy than I had in healing the Humans. It probably needed food.

Now it settled all four of its arms around me and linked. "I will come back if you don't follow us," it said silently.

"I'll follow. Francisco is going to help me—if necessary."

"I know. I heard. And I still inherit Santos."

"Use his mind and push his body hard. This trip should do that. You should start down now, too."

"All right."

I left it and headed down the mountain, using the path when it was convenient, and ignoring it otherwise. The Humans with Aaor would find it dark and would have to be careful. For me it was well lit with the heat of all the growing plants. I had to climb down past the flattened ridge on which the village had been built. I had to travel along the broad, flat part of the ridge below the level of sight of any guard watching from the village. I had to come up where terraces filled with growing things would conceal me for as long as possible.

11

When I reached the village, I lay on a terrace until the sounds of people talking and moving around had all but ceased. I calculated by hearing and smell where the guards patrolled. I tried to hear Jesusa or Tomás, or her people talking about them, but there was almost nothing. Two males were wondering what they had seen in their wanderings. A female was explaining to a sleepy child that they had been "very, very bad" and were locked up as punishment. And somewhere far from where I lay, Francisco was explaining to someone that five guards on the mountain were enough, and that he wanted to sleep in his own bed, not on a stone floor.

He was not questioned further. No doubt being an elder gave him a few privileges. I wondered how long my influence on him would last, and how he would react to its ending. Best not to find out. I had deliberately not told him about the cave where we were to meet. Willingly or unwillingly, he might lead others to it.

There was a scream suddenly and the sound of a blow. I had lain frozen for some time before I realized it had nothing to do with us. Nearby, a male and female were arguing, cursing each other. The male had hit the female. He did this again several times and she went on screaming. Even Human ears must have been full of the terrible sound.

I crept out of the terraces and into the village.

I was close to Jesusa and Tomás, close to the building I had been shown from the mountain. I could not go straight to it. There were houses in the way and two more high stone steps that raised the level of the ground. The flattened ridge was not as flat as it had seemed. Stone walls had been built here and there to retain the soil and create the level platforms on which the houses had been built. In that way, the houses as well as the crops were terraced.

There were pathways and stairs to make movement easy, but these were patrolled. I avoided them.

Crouching beneath one of these tiers, I caught Jesusa's scent. She was just ahead, just above, and there was a faint scent of Tomás as well.

But there were two others—armed males.

I stood up carefully and peered over the wall of the tier. From where I was, all I could see were more walls—walls of buildings. There were no people outside.

I climbed up slowly, looking everywhere. Someone came out of a doorway abruptly and walked away from me down the path. I flattened my body against a wall of large, smooth stones.

Around me, people slept with slow, even breathing. The angry male, still some distance from me, had stopped beating his mate. I did not stand away from the wall until the person from the doorway—a pregnant female—had crossed the path and taken the stairs down to a lower level.

Farther along the pathway I was confined to, I recognized the round building—a half-cylinder of smooth gray rock. Both Jesusa and Tomás were inside, though I did not think they were together. I walked toward it, all my sensory tentacles in prestrike knots and my sensory arms coiled against me. If I could do this without noise, we could get away, and it might be morning before anyone knew we were gone.

The building had heavy wooden doors.

In time, I could smash them, but only with a great deal of noise. Someone would shoot me long before I'd finished.

I uncoiled one sensory arm and probed the door. Filaments of my sensory hand could penetrate it as easily as they could penetrate flesh. A wooden door set in a wooden frame, held shut by a massive wooden crossbar that rested in a cradle of iron. Very simple. The iron cradle consisted of four flattened, upturned prongs, two fastened to the door with several metal screws and two fastened to the doorframe.

Quickly, carefully, I rotted the wood that held the prong screws on the door. Through my sensory hand, I injected a corrosive, and the wood began at once to disintegrate. I could not have destroyed the door this way, but getting rid of the small sections of wood that held the screws was no trouble. In effect, I digested them.

After a time, the heavy crossbar slid to the floor.

The two men just inside shouted in surprise, then cursed and made several quick, noisy movements. They came together to examine the door and ask each other what could have caused it to fall apart that way.

When I hit the door, they were exactly where I wanted them to be. The door knocked them down before they could raise their rifles. I stung first one, then the other, with a lashing motion of sensory arms. Both collapsed unconscious. It could only have been reflex that caused one of them to fire his gun.

The bullet glanced off one rock wall and spent itself against another.

And suddenly, everywhere, there were voices.

Jesusa was so close. . . . But there was no time.

I stepped out through the doorway, meaning to disappear for a while, try again later.

Outside, there was a forest of long wood-and-metal rifles. People had leaped from sleep onto their pathway, some of them naked, but all of them armed.

I jumped back behind the heavy door and slammed it as people fired into it. I grabbed the crossbar and kicked and jammed it into a prop. It wouldn't hold long against their guns and their bodies, but it would give me a moment.

What to do? They would kill me before I could speak. They would kill me as soon as they reached me. If I went into the area where Jesusa was confined, they might kill her, too.

I reached for the two guards and forced them conscious. I dragged them to their feet, made them stand on either side of me, made them breathe in as much as they could of me.

They struggled a little at first. Then I looped my sensory arms around them and injected my ooloi substance into them. I had to quiet them before the door gave way.

"Save your lives," I said softly. "Don't let your people shoot you. Make them listen!"

At that moment the door gave way.

People poured into the room, ready to shoot. I held the two guards in front of me, held them with only my strength hands visible. The less alien I seemed now, the more likely I was to live for a few more moments.

"Don't shoot us!" the guard under my right hand shouted.

"Don't shoot!" the other echoed. "It isn't hurting us."

"It's an alien," someone shouted.

"Oankali!"

"Four-arms!"

"Kill it!"

"No!" my prisoners screamed together.

"It can sting people to death! Kill it!"

"There's no need to kill me!" I said. I tried consciously to sound the way Nikanj did when it both frightened Humans and got them to cooperate. "I don't want to hurt you, but if you shoot me, I may lose control and kill several of you before I die."

Silence.

"I mean you no harm."

Again the curse, and it was, unmistakably, a curse. "Four-arms!"

And from someone else. "They strike like snakes!"

"I didn't come to strike anyone," I said. "I mean you no harm."

"What do you want here!" one of them demanded.

I hesitated and someone else answered for me.

"Isn't it obvious what the thing wants? The prisoners, that's what! It's come for them!"

"I've come for them," I agreed softly.

People began to look uncertain. I was reaching them—probably more with my scent than with anything I was saying. All I had to do was keep them here a little longer. They might go in and get Jesusa and Tomás for me. The two in my hands would probably do that now if I asked it of them. But I still needed them—for just a while longer.

"If you kill me," I said, "my people will find out about it. And those who shoot me will never live on a planet or know freedom again. Ask your elders. They remember."

People began to look at one another doubtfully. Some of them lowered their guns and stood not knowing what to do. There had always been a fear among Humans that we could read their thoughts. No doubt that was why they had feared letting even one of their people go down into the lowland forest. Most had never understood that it was their bodies we read—inside and out. And if we were alert and competent—more so than I had been with Santos—their bodies kept few secrets.

"Who will speak for you?" I asked the crowd. If they had been Oankali or construct, I would never have asked such a question. I could have made my case to anyone, and the people would have joined person-to-person or through their town organisms, and there would have been a consensus.

But these people were Human. I had to find their leaders.

Two males stepped forward out of the crowd.

"Elders?" I asked.

One of them nodded. The other only stared at me in obvious disgust.

"I mean no harm," I said. "Harm will only be done if you shoot me. Do you accept that?"

"Perhaps," the one who had nodded said.

I shrugged. "Examine your own memories." And I kept quiet and left them to their memories. Meanwhile, without drawing attention to the gesture, I took my hands from the two men in front of me. They didn't move.

"Why do you want Jesusa and Tomás?" demanded the disgusted elder.

"They are my mates."

There was a sudden rush of surprised muttering from the people. I heard disbelief and questioning, threats and cursing, honor and disgust.

"Why should you be surprised?" I asked. "Why did you think I wanted them? Why else would I be willing to risk your killing me?" I paused, but no one spoke. "We care for our mates as deeply as you do for yours," I said.

"It would be better for them to be killed than to be given to you," the disgusted elder said.

"Your people almost destroyed themselves," I said, "and you still haven't had enough killing?"

"Your people want to kill us!" someone said from the crowd.

I spoke into renewed muttering. "My people are coming here, but they won't kill. They didn't kill your elders. They plucked them out of the ashes of their war, healed them, mated with those who were willing, and let the others go. If my people were killers, you wouldn't be here." I paused to let them think, then I continued. "And there wouldn't be a Human colony on the planet Mars where Humans live and breed totally free of us. The Humans there are healthy and thriving. Any Human who wants to join them will be given healing, restored fertility if necessary, and transported."

What happened next was totally irrational, yet somehow, later, I felt that I should have anticipated it.

The disgusted elder's face twisted with anger and revulsion. He cursed me, called on his god to damn me. Then he fired his gun.

One of the two Human guards whom I had held, and then released, jumped between the elder's gun and me.

An instant later, the guard lay dying and the two elders struggled for possession of the disgusted one's rifle.

I saw the murderous elder subdued by his companion and two deformed young people. Then I was on the floor beside the injured man. "Keep them off me," I told the remaining guard. "His heart is damaged. I can save him, but only if they let me alone."

I paid no more attention to what they did. The injured guard needed all my attention. By the definition of most Humans, he was already dead. The large-caliber bullet fired at close range had gone through his heart and come out of his back just missing his spine. I had all I could do to keep him alive while I repaired the heart. The Humans would not murder me. The moment for that had passed.

12

I was hungry when I finished the healing. I was almost weak with hunger. And the scent of Jesusa and Tomás so nearby was tormenting. I could not let the Humans keep them from me much longer.

I began to pay attention to my immediate surroundings again and found myself looking into the eyes of the man I had just healed.

"I was shot," he said. "I remember . . . but it doesn't hurt."

"You're healed," I said. I hugged him. "Thank you for shielding me."

He said nothing. He sat up when I did and looked around at the people who had gathered around us and sat down. We were the center of a ring of elders and aged fertiles—people who looked ancient, but were not nearly as old as the youthful-looking elders. There were no females present.

"Give me something to eat," I told them. "Plant material. No meat."

No one moved or spoke.

I looked at the guard I had just healed. "Get me something, please."

He nodded. No one stopped him from going out, though everyone was armed.

I sat still and waited. Eventually the Humans would begin to talk to me. They were playing a game now, trying to make me uneasy, trying to put me at more of a disadvantage than I was. A small, Human, hierarchical game. They might not let my guard back in. Well, I was uncomfortably hungry, not desperately hungry. And I didn't know their game well enough to play it. At some time they would probably take pleasure in telling me what they intended to do to me. I was in no hurry to hear that. I didn't expect to like it.

I almost slept. My guard came back with a dish of cooked beans and some grain and fruit that I did not recognize. A good meal. I thanked him and sent him away because I was afraid he would speak for me and get into trouble.

Sometime later, Francisco came in. There were three more elders with him. From their looks, they were probably the oldest males in the village. They were gray-haired, and their faces were deeply lined. One of them walked with a severe limp. The other two were gaunt and bent. They had probably been old before the war.

These four sat down facing me, and Francisco spoke quietly. "Are you all right?"

I looked at him, trying to guess what his situation was. Why had he come? It was too late for him to play the part he had promised to play. He was holding himself very tightly, yet trying hard to seem relaxed. I decided not to recognize him—for now.

"My mates are still imprisoned," I said.

"We'll let you see them soon. We want you to know first what we've decided."

I waited.

"You've said your people will be coming here."

"Yes."

"You'll wait here for them." His body inclined toward me, full of repressed tension. It was important to him that I accept what he was saying.

I kept quiet, turned my face away from him so that I could watch him without making him feel watched. There was no triumph in him, no slyness, no sign that he was doing anything more than telling me what his people had decided—and perhaps hoping that I didn't give him away.

"The guards have captured your companion," Francisco said in the same quiet way. "It will be brought here soon."

"Aaor?" I asked. "Is it injured? Is anyone injured?"

"Nothing serious. Your companion was shot in the leg, but it seems to have healed itself. One of our people whom you've tampered with was injured slightly."

"Who? Which one?"

"Santos Ibarra Ruiz."

Of course. I shook my head. Someone in the group of elders groaned. "Is he all right?" I asked.

"Our guards heard him arguing with someone in your companion's party," Francisco said. "When they investigated and took prisoners, Santos bit one of them. He was clubbed. He's all right except for a few bruises and a headache."

Santos had given Aaor away. Who but Santos would? How many lives had he endangered or destroyed?

"What will happen to the Humans we've . . . tampered with?" I asked.

"We haven't decided yet," Francisco said. "Nothing probably."

"They should be hanged," someone muttered. "Supposed to be on watch. . . ."

"They were taken by surprise," Francisco said. "If I hadn't decided to come down and sleep in my own bed, I could have been taken myself."

So that was why he was still free. He had convinced his people that we had arrived after he left. That story might protect him and enable him to help the others. His body expressed his discomfort with the lie, but he told it well.

"Will you keep Aaor here, too?" I asked.

"Yes. It won't be hurt unless it tries to escape. Neither will you. Our people feel that having you here will assure their safety when your people arrive."

I nodded. "Was this your idea?"

The elder with the limp spoke up. "It doesn't matter to you whose idea it was! You'll stay here. And if your people don't come . . . perhaps we'll be able to think of something to do with you."

I turned to face him. "Use me to heal your leg," I said softly. "It must pain you."

"You'll never get your poisonous hands on me."

I would. Of course I would. If they kept Aaor and me here, nothing would stop them for using us to rid them of their many physical problems.

"This wasn't my idea," Francisco said. "My only idea was that you shouldn't be shot. A great many people here would like to shoot you, you know."

"That would be a serious mistake."

"I know." He paused. "Santos was the one who suggested keeping you here."

I did not shout with laughter. Laughter would have made the elders even more intensely suspicious than they were. But within myself, I howled. Santos was making up for his error. He knew exactly what he was doing. He knew his people would use Aaor's and my healing ability and breathe our scents, and finally, when our people arrived, his would meet them without hostility. In that way, I would, as Francisco had said, assure the mountain people's safety. People who did not fight would be in no danger at all, would not even be gassed once the shuttle caught Aaor's and my scents.

"Bring Aaor," I said.

"Aaor is coming." Francisco paused. "If you try anything, if you frighten these people in any way at all, they *will* shoot you. And they won't stop shooting until there's nothing living left of you."

I nodded. There would be a great deal that was living left of me, but it would certainly not survive *as* me. And it might do harm here—as a disease. It was best for us to die on a ship or in one of our towns. Our substance would be safely absorbed into the larger organism. If it were not absorbed, the Oankali organelles in it would find things to do on their own.

Aaor was brought in by young guards. I looked at its legs for traces of a bullet wound, but could see none. The Humans had let it heal itself completely before they brought it in.

It walked over and sat down beside me on the stone floor. It did not touch me.

"They want us to stay here," it said in Spanish.

"I know."

"Shall we?"

"Yes, of course."

It nodded. "I thought so, too." It pulled its mouth into something less than a smile. "You were right about being shot. I don't want to go through it again."

"Where are your mates?"

"At their home not far from here—under guard."

I faced Francisco again. "We agree to stay here until our people come, but Aaor should live with its mates. And I should live with mine."

"You'll be imprisoned here in this tower!" one of the gaunt old elders said. "Both of you! You'll stay here under guard. And you'll have no mates!"

"We'll live in houses as people should," I said softly.

Someone spat the words "Four-arms!" and someone else muttered, "Animals!"

"We'll live with the people you know to be our mates," I continued. "If we don't, we'll become . . . very dangerous to ourselves and to you."

Silence.

My scent and Aaor's probably could not convert these people quickly without direct contact, but our scents could make everyone more likely to believe what we said. We could persuade them to do what they knew they really should do.

"You'll live with your mates," Francisco said above much muttering. "Most of us accept that. But wherever you live, you will be guarded. You must be."

I glanced at Aaor. "All right," I said. "Guard us. There's no need for it, but if it comforts you, we'll put up with it."

"Guards to keep people from accepting your poison!" muttered the lame elder.

"Give me my mates now," I said very softly. People leaned

forward to hear. "I need them and they need me. We keep one another healthy."

"Let it be with them," Aaor supplemented. "Let them comfort one another. They've been apart for days now."

They argued for a while, their hostility slowly decreasing like a wound healing. In the end Francisco himself freed Jesusa and Tomás. They came out of their prison rooms and took me between them, and the elders and old fertiles watched with conflicting emotions of fear, anger, envy, and fascination.

13

We stayed.

We healed the people in spite of our guards. We healed our guards.

Young people came to us first, and went away without their tumors, sensory losses, limps, paralysis. . . . People brought their children to us. Jesusa, Tomás, and I shared a stone house with Aaor, Javier, and Paz. Once we were settled, Jesusa went out and found all the people she remembered as having deformed or disabled children. She badgered them until they began to bring their children to us. The small house was often full of healing children.

And Santos began to grow. I gave him a handsome new nose and he went right on talking too much and risking getting it broken again. But people seemed less inclined to hit him.

The first elder to come to us was female with only one leg. The stump of her amputated leg pained her and she hoped I could stop the pain. I sent her to Aaor because I had more people to heal than I could manage. Over a period of weeks, Aaor grew her a new leg and foot.

After that, everyone came to us. Even the most stubborn elders forgot how much they hated us once we'd touched them. They didn't suddenly begin to love us, but they stopped spitting as we walked by, stopped muttering curses or threats at us, stopped pointing their guns at us to remind us of their power and their fear. They let us alone. That was enough.

Their people, however, did begin to love us and to believe what we told them and to talk to us about Oankali and construct mates.

14

The shuttle, when it arrived, landed down in the canyon. There it could drink from the river and eat something other than the mountain people's crops. No one was gassed. There was no panic on the part of the Humans. It was a measure of the Humans' trust that they let Aaor and me and our mates go down to meet the newcomers. At the last moment, Francisco decided to come with us, but only because, as he had admitted, his long years had not taught him patience.

Seven families had come with the shuttle. Most were from Chkahichdahk, since that was where shuttles lived when they were not in use. They had stopped at Lo, however, to pick up my parents. The first person I spotted in the small crowd was Tino—and I came closer than I should have to grabbing him and hugging him. Too Human a reaction. I hugged Nikanj instead, though Nikanj did not particularly want to be hugged. It tolerated the gesture and used it as an opportunity to sink its sensory tentacles into me and examine me thoroughly. When it had finished, without a word, it reached for Aaor and examined it. It held Aaor longer, then focused on Javier and Paz. They were watching with obvious curiosity but without alarm. They had already passed the stage of extreme avoidance of everyone except Aaor. Now, like Jesusa and Tomás, they were simply careful.

Neither of them had ever seen an Oankali before. They were fascinated, but they were not afraid.

Nikanj flattened its sensory tentacles to that glittering smoothness it could achieve when it was gleefully happy. "Lelka," it said, "if you will introduce us to your mates, we may begin to forgive you for staying here and not letting us know you were all right."

"I'm not sure I'll forgive it," Lilith said. But she was smiling, and for a time, everything else had to wait until Javier and Paz were welcomed into the family and the rest of us rewelcomed and forgiven. I saw Jesusa reach out to my mother for the first time since their break. The two embraced and I felt my own sensory tentacles go smooth with pleasure.

"The mountain Humans decided to keep us," Aaor was explaining to the rest of the family. "Since their only alternative as they saw it was to kill us, we were willing to stay."

"Is this one of them?" Ahajas asked, looking at Francisco.

I introduced him and he, too, met her with curiosity but no fear.

"Would you have killed them?" she asked with odd amusement.

Francisco smiled, showing very white teeth. "Of course not. Jodahs captured me long before it captured most of my people."

Ahajas focused on me. "Captured?"

"No one has captured him," I said. "He wants to go to the Mars colony."

Ahajas went very smooth. "Do you want that?"

"I did." Francisco shook his head. "Maybe I still do."

I looked at him, surprised. He had been one of the hold-outs—very certain. Now that the shuttle was here, he was less ᵉrtain. "Shall we find mates for you?" I asked.

ᴴe looked at me, then did something very Oankali. He ᵈ and walked away. He walked quickly, would have gone ᵗ the steep road and up to the village if Ahajas had not

"Does he have a female mate, Lelka?" she asked me.

I nodded. "Inez. She's an old fertile." She had joined Francisco after bearing nine children. Now she was past the age of childbearing. Francisco had brought her to me once and asked me to check her health. She turned out to be one of the healthiest old fertiles I had ever touched, but I understood that Francisco's real purpose had been to share her with me—and me with her. Yet he had truly wanted to emigrate. Until now.

"Jodahs," Ahajas said, "I think there are mates for him here, now. Bring him back."

I went after Francisco, caught him, took him by the arms. "My Oankali mother says there are people here, now, who might mate with you."

He stood still for a moment, then abruptly tried to wrench free. I held him because his body language told me that he wanted to be held more than he wanted to be let go. He was afraid and confused and ashamed and powerfully drawn to the idea of potential Oankali mates.

After his first effort, he would not shame himself by continuing to struggle against me. I let him go when he truly wanted it. Then I took his right hand loosely and led him back toward Ahajas, who waited with a mated group of strangers—three Oankali. Francisco began to sweat.

"I would give anything at all to have you instead," he told me.

"You already have all I can give you," I said. "If you like these new people, their ooloi can give you much more." I paused. "Do you think Inez will consent to have her fertility restored? Maybe she's tired of having children."

He laughed, momentarily decreasing the level of his tension. "She's been after me to see whether I could get you to make changes in us. She wants to have at least one child with me."

"A construct child?"

"I don't know—although if I'm willing after resisting for a century . . ."

"Take these new people up to see her. Talk to her, and to them."

He stopped me, turned me to face him. "You've done this to me," he said. "I would have gone to Mars."

I said nothing.

"I can't even hate you," he whispered. "My god, if there had been people like you around a hundred years ago, I couldn't have become a resister. I think there would be no resisters." He stared at me a moment longer. "Damn you," he said slowly, sadly. "Goddamn you." He walked past me and went to Ahajas and the waiting Oankali family.

"They are your ooan relatives," Lilith said, and I looked at her with amazement. She had somehow managed to approach me without my noticing.

"You were preoccupied," she said. She wanted very much to touch me and made no effort to hide it. She looked at me hungrily. "You and Aaor are beautiful," she said. "Are you both really all right?"

"We are. We need Oankali mates, but other than that we're fine."

"And that man, Francisco, is he typical of the people here?"

"He's one of the old ones. The first one I met."

"And he loves you."

"As you said once: pheromones."

"At first, no doubt. By now, he loves you."

". . . yes."

"Like João. Like Marina. You have a strange gift, Lelka."

I changed the subject abruptly. "Did you say those people with Francisco were my ooan relatives? Nikanj's relatives?"

"Nikanj's parents."

I turned to look at them, remembering their names. I had heard them all my life. The ooloi was Kahguyaht, large for an ooloi—as big as Lilith, who was large for a Human female. Kahguyaht had not given such large size to Nikanj. Its male mate, Jdahya, was of an ordinary size. The placement of his sensory tentacles gave him an oddly Human look. They hung his head like hair. They were placed on his face in a way would be mistaken for Human eyes, ears, nose. He was the first Oankali Lilith had ever met. She was looking at him now and smiling. "Francisco will like him," she said.

Francisco would like them all if he let himself. He was talking now with Tediin, Kahguyaht's huge female mate—again, bigger than average. She did not look in the slightest Human. He was laughing at something she had said.

"There are people waiting to meet you, Jodahs," Lilith said.

Oh, yes. They were waiting to meet me and examine me and decide whether I should be allowed to go on running around loose. They were already meeting Aaor.

Three ooloi were investigating Aaor. Two waited to meet me. My ooan parents would be busy for a while with Francisco, but these others must be satisfied. I went to them wearily.

15

It wasn't bad being examined by so many. It wasn't uncomfortable. After a time even my ooan family left Francisco to poke and probe us. They took us into the shuttle. Through the shuttle, Oankali and constructs of all sexes could make easy, fast, nonverbal contact with us and with one another. The group had the shuttle fly out of the canyon and up as high as necessary to communicate with the ship. The ship transmitted our messages and those of its own inhabitants to the lowland towns and their messages to us. In that way, the people came together for the second time to share knowledge of construct ooloi who should not exist, and to decide what to do with us.

The shuttle left children and most Humans back in the canyon. Both could have come and participated through their ooloi, but for them the experience would be jarring and disorienting. Everything was too intense, went too fast, was, for the Humans, too alien. Linking into the nervous system of a shuttle, a ship, or a town even through an ooloi was, according to Lilith, one of the worst experiences of her life. Yet she and Tino went up with us, and absorbed what they could of the complex exchange.

The demands of the lowlanders and the people of the ship were surprisingly easy for me to absorb and understand. I could handle the intensity and the complexity. What I wasn't sure I could handle was the result. The whole business was like Lilith's rounded black cloud of hair. Every strand seemed to go its own different way, bending, twisting, spiraling, angling. Yet together they formed a symmetrical, recognizable shape, and all were attached to the same head.

Oankali and construct opinion also took on a recognizable shape from apparent chaos. The head that they were attached to was the generally accepted belief that Aaor and I were potentially dangerous and should either go to the ship or stay where we were. The lowland towns were apologetic, but they still felt unsure and afraid of us. We represented the premature adulthood of a new species. We represented true independence—reproductive independence—for that species, and this frightened both Oankali and constructs. We were, as one signaler remarked, frighteningly competent ooloi. We must be watched and understood before any more of us were made—and before we could be permitted to settle in a lowland town.

Continued exile, then. The mountains. We would not go to Chkahichdahk. The people knew that. We let them know it again, Aaor and I together.

"There will be two more of you," someone signaled from far away. I separated out the signal in my memory and realized that it had come from far to the east and south on the other side of the continent. There, an ooloi in a Mandarin-speaking Jah village was reporting its shameful error, its children going wrong. Both were in metamorphosis now. Both would be ooloi.

"Bring them here as soon as they can travel," I signaled. "They'll need mates quickly. It would be best if they had chosen mates already."

"This is first metamorphosis," the signaler protested.

"And they are construct! Bring them here or they'll die. Put them on a shuttle as soon as you can. For now, let them know that there are mates for them here."

After a time, the signaler agreed.

This produced confusion among the people. One mistake simply focused attention on the ooloi responsible. Two mistakes unconnected, but happening so close together in time after a century of perfection, might indicate something other than ooloi incompetence.

There was much communication about this, but no conclusion. Finally Aaor interrupted.

"This will probably happen again," it said. "An ooloi subadult who doesn't want to go to the ship should be sent here. The Humans who want to stay here should be left here and let alone. They want mates and I think there are Oankali and constructs who are willing to come here to mate with them."

"I believe we will be staying," Kahguyaht signaled. "We've found resisters who might mate with us." It paused. "I don't believe they would even consider us if they hadn't spent these last months living near Jodahs and Aaor."

"Your ooan children," someone signaled.

Kahguyaht signaled very slowly. "Where is the flaw in what I've said?"

No response. I doubted that anyone really believed Kahguyaht was expressing misplaced family pride. It was simply telling the truth.

"Aaor and I want Oankali mates," I signaled. "We want to start children. I think once we've done that and once you've examined our children, you'll know that we're not dangerous."

"You are dangerous," several people signaled. "There's no safe way to begin a new species."

"Then help us. Send us mates and young construct ooloi. Watch us all you like, but don't hinder us."

"Have you planted a town?" someone on Chkahichdahk asked.

I signaled negative. "We didn't know we would be staying here . . . permanently."

"Plant a town," several people signaled. "How can you think of having children with no town to hold them?"

I hesitated, focused on Kahguyaht. It spoke aloud within the shuttle. "Plant a town, Lelka. In less than a hundred years, my mates and I will be dead. You should plant the town that you and your mates and children will leave this world in."

"If I plant a town," I signaled the people, "will Aaor and I be permitted Oankali mates? Will Oankali and construct mates come to the Humans here?"

There was a long period of discussion. Some people were more concerned about us than others. Some, clearly, would have nothing to do with us until we had been stable for several more years, and clearly done no harm. They were in the minority. The majority decided that as long as we stayed where we were, anyone who wanted to join us could do so.

"Plant a town," they told us. "Prepare a place. People will come."

A few of them signaled such eagerness that I knew they would be with us as soon as they could get a shuttle. Humans who wanted mates were rare enough and desirable enough to make people dare to face any danger they thought Aaor and I might present. And Aaor and I were interesting enough in our newness to seduce Oankali who needed ooloi mates. People seeking mates were more vulnerable to seduction than they would be at any other time in their lives. They would come.

16

time later, when the visiting families and the mountain had begun to get together and curiously examine one prepared to plant the new town.

d through the vast genetic memory that Nikanj had

given me. There was a single cell within that great store—a cell that could be "awakened" from its stasis within yashi and stimulated to divide and grow into a kind of seed. This seed could become a town or a shuttle or a great ship like Chkahichdahk. In fact, my seed would begin as a town and eventually leave Earth as a great ship. It would never be a shuttle, though it would be parent to shuttles.

Over the next few days, I found the cell, awakened it, nourished it, and encouraged it to divide. When it had divided several times, I stopped it, separated one cell from the mass, and returned that cell to stasis. This was work that only an adult ooloi could do, and I found that I enjoyed it immensely.

I took the remaining mass—the seed—still within my body to the place that the Humans and the visiting families had agreed was good for people and towns. Several of the visitors and Humans traveled with me by shuttle, since the chosen place was well upriver from the mountain village. There were scattered stone ruins at the new place where the canyon broadened into a large valley. Plenty of land, plenty of water, easy access to many needed minerals. Less easy access to others, according to what the shuttle's senses told us when it had landed and tasted the new place. But whether or not the town had to develop a longer and more complex root system than most towns, everything it needed was within its reach. Including us. Here the town could grow and always have the companionship of some of us. It would need that companionship as much as we did during our metamorphoses. Yet we were planting it too far from the mountain people's crops for it to be tempted to reach them and eat them before it was big enough to feed the people itself. While it was young, it would be particularly voracious. And it would need the space the valley afforded it to grow and mature before it had to deal with mountains.

"This could be a good place to live," one of the elders commented as she left the shuttle and looked around. She was the woman whose leg Aaor had regenerated. She had decided with most of her people to stay on Earth.

"There's room here for many people," Jesusa said, looking at me. She wanted a child even more than I did. It was hard for her to wait for Oankali mates. At least now we knew there were potential mates coming.

I chose a spot near the river. There I prepared the seed to go into the ground. I gave it a thick, nutritious coating, then brought it out of my body through my right sensory hand. I planted it deep in the rich soil of the riverbank. Seconds after I had expelled it, I felt it begin the tiny positioning movements of independent life.

ABOUT THE AUTHOR

OCTAVIA E. BUTLER (1947–2006) was the first black woman to come to international prominence as a science fiction writer. Incorporating powerful, spare language and rich, well-developed characters, her work tackled race, gender, religion, poverty, power, politics, and science in a way that touched readers of all backgrounds. Butler was a towering figure in life and in her art and the world noticed. A critical force, she received numerous awards, including a MacArthur "genius grant," both the Hugo and Nebula awards, the Langston Hughes Medal, and a PEN Lifetime Achievement award.

About herself, Octavia E. Butler once wrote: "I'm a fifty-three-year-old writer who can remember being a ten-year-old writer and who expects someday to be an eighty-year-old writer. I'm 'so comfortably asocial—a hermit in the middle of Seattle— ssimist if I'm not careful, a feminist, a black, a former t, an oil-and-water combination of ambition, laziness, ity, certainty, and drive."